THE MARINER

Also by Tom Golden
THE BADLANDER

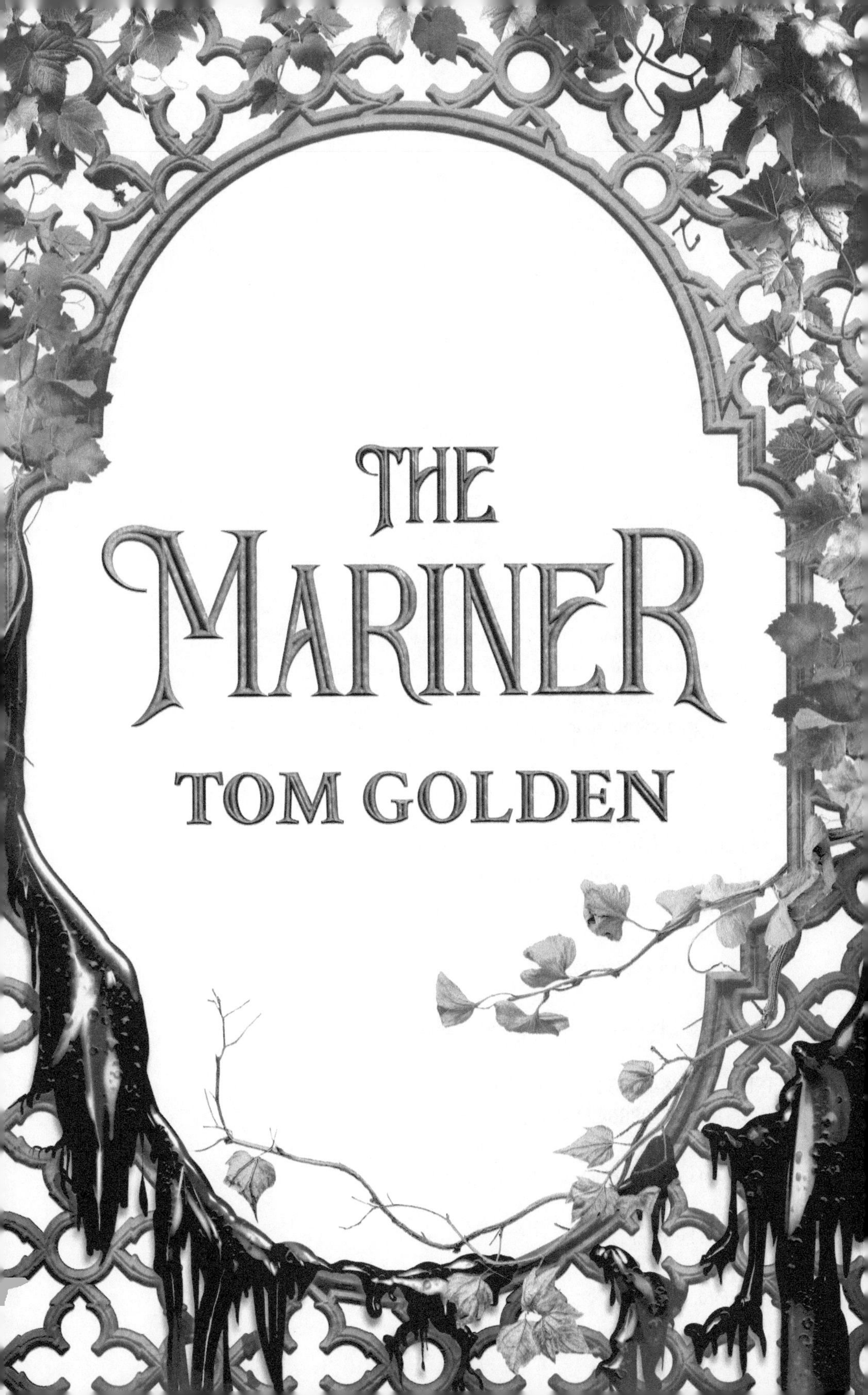

THE MARINER
TOM GOLDEN

First paperback edition 2025

Book design, illustrations, and map by Adam Fyda

ISBN: 979-8-9885421-3-1 (paperback)
ISBN: 979-8-9885421-4-8 (ebook)

Library of Congress Control Number: 2024913772

Published by Thomas Golden

Waterford, Michigan

THE MARINER

TOM GOLDEN

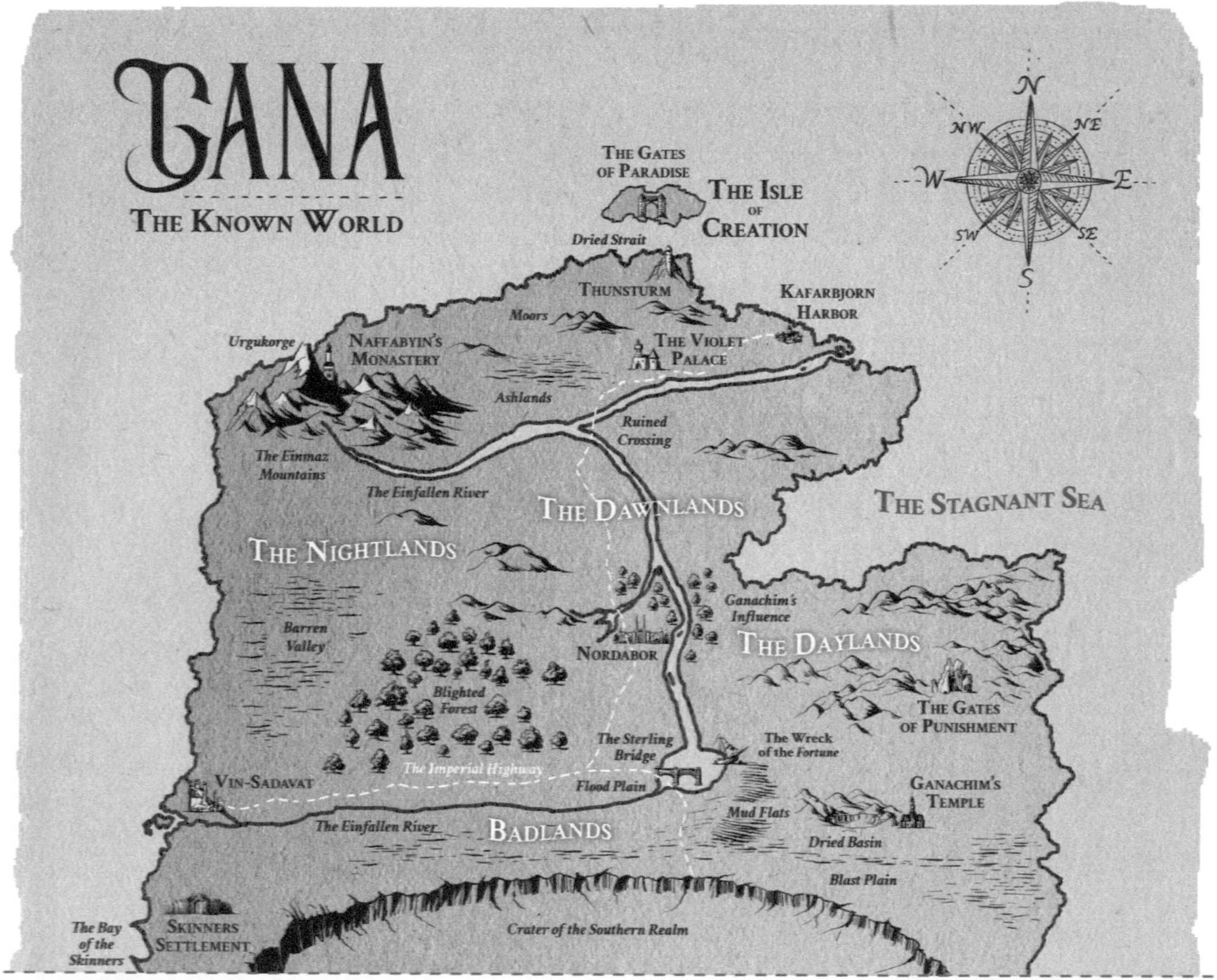

CANA
THE KNOWN WORLD
N
NW
NE
W
E
SW
SE
S
THE GATES
OF PARADISE
THE ISLE
OF
CREATION
Dried Strait
THUNSTURM
KAFARBJORN
HARBOR
Moars
THE VIOLET
PALACE
Urgukorge
NAFFABYIN'S
MONASTERY
Ashlands
Ruined
Crossing
The Einmaz
Mountains
The Einfallen River
THE DAWNLANDS
THE STAGNANT SEA
THE NIGHTLANDS
Ganachim's
Influence
Barren
Valley
Nordabor
THE DAYLANDS
Blighted
Forest
THE GATES
OF PUNISHMENT
The Sterling
Bridge
The Wreck
of the Fortune
The Imperial Highway
Vin-Sadavat
Flood Plain
Ganachim's
Temple
The Einfallen River
BADLANDS
Mud Flats
Dried Basin
Blast Plain
The Bay
of the
Skinners
SKINNERS
SETTLEMENT
Crater of the Southern Realm

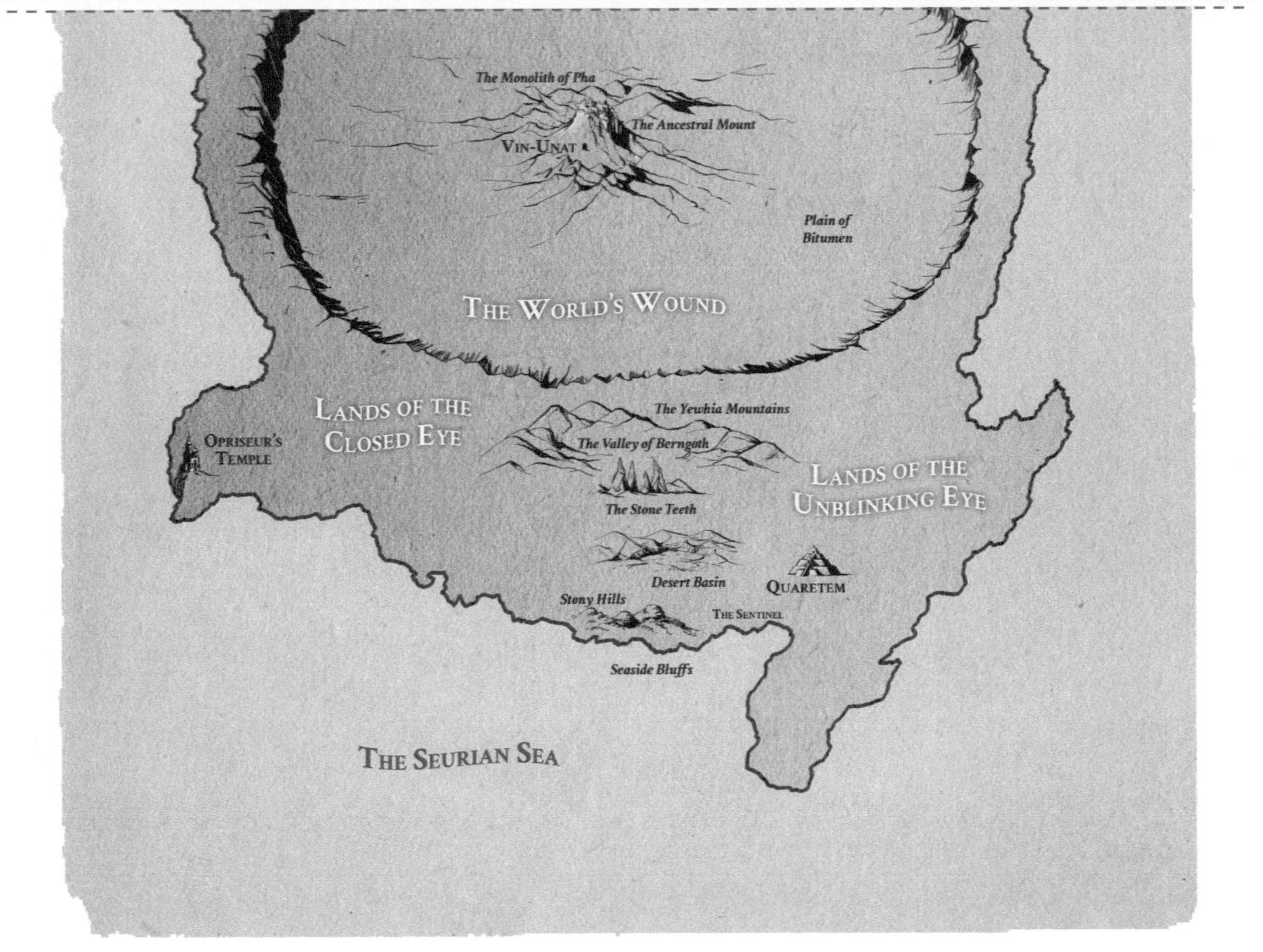

The Monolith of Pha
The Ancestral Mount
Vin-Unat
Plain of Bitumen
THE WORLD'S WOUND
LANDS OF THE CLOSED EYE
The Yewhia Mountains
The Valley of Berngoth
The Stone Teeth
LANDS OF THE UNBLINKING EYE
Opriseur's Temple
Desert Basin
Quaretem
Stony Hills
The Sentinel
Seaside Bluffs
THE SEURIAN SEA

PROLOGUE:
AN OPPORTUNITY

By the light of the perpetual dawn, the last nets were dragged aboard. Within their confines, a meager haul of pale, slight fish wriggled and flopped in a futile bid to return to the water.

Raina Marbuck could remember a time when the nets had been full. Certainly, Baylis had never complained of a poor catch. Now, they were finding that the dark currents of the Einfallen no longer cloaked the treasures they had taken for granted. It had been a gradual decline, but had recently grown undeniable. None of the crew of the *Fortune* spoke of it in certain terms. There was a tacit understanding that acknowledging the problem would somehow compound it.

So, with an uneasiness churning beneath the surface, the fishermen continued to perform their duties, laughing at their crude jokes, smoking their pipes, drinking their liquor, willfully ignoring the growing threat to their livelihood, and to the entire realm. For the shortages they were experiencing mirrored the shortages that had become apparent all around them. The people of Nordabor didn't know hunger yet, not real hunger, but with each passing full-cycle, they were certainly becoming accustomed to a feeling of wanting *more*. Scarcity had become the norm, and yet it seemed that from the Crown on down to the lowliest beggar, none would speak this truth aloud.

This superstitious silence held all tongues in check, or so it had seemed to Marbuck. She was surprised to find, as she prepared to depart the battered old vessel that she called home more often than her actual domicile, that Barrett Winslow, of all people, was willing to speak of the decline.

"Fishwife, c'mere. Your merry old captain wishes to speak with you."

The nickname, which had followed Marbuck from the happier times when she'd only been responsible for selling the fish caught by Baylis and the others, had never bothered her. Expecting nothing of any particular significance, she sidled up next to the captain, who was leaning against the rail near the gangplank. A few of the other fishermen filed past them, bidding farewell to their captain and their first mate until the iron bell of the Vinecrown Keep would announce the commencement of the next full-cycle's work.

"Yes, Captain?" Marbuck said, her thoughts following the others off the boat.

"I wanted to let you know about a little business venture I've got lined up for us," Winslow said, his voice suddenly conspiratorial. "Something that promises a lot more coin than these depleted waters."

The truth of their situation, spoken aloud, made Marbuck's mouth go dry. The fact that Winslow, aboard his own boat, would acknowledge such ill fortune seemed like a bad portent. Marbuck, who hadn't always carried such irrational notions, knew that, during these past three long-cycles, the rest of the crew had rubbed off on her more than she cared to admit.

"We managed a fine haul this full-cycle," she said, not believing a word of it.

Winslow waved a hand dismissively. "No, we didn't. Nor have we for nearing on a long-cycle now, so save your breath with all that. This job won't even involve fishing none. It's a transporting job."

"Transporting what?"

Winslow peered around, wiggling his bushy eyebrows, then laughed wheezily at his own feigned cautiousness. "Transporting the prince on an expedition down south."

"Phir-Ramarian?" Marbuck said, now believing that she had fallen victim to some strange prank.

"Yeah, that's right. The prince is leading a whole contingent of guardsmen and shepherds and such, in search of something *very* important. All at the behest of Phar-Mindorius. Or so Rayburn says."

Fritz Rayburn, the chief purchaser of their hauls, was known to have had dealings with Phar-Mindorius, particularly in providing provisions for the occasional journey beyond the city walls, including Rorik Fontaine's doomed expedition. Ever since that famous company failed to return, sojourns outside of the city, like everything else, had grown scarce. The well-known loss of Fontaine, Phar-Mindorius's esteemed curator, had apparently soured the king on the idea of any further ventures. Despite some vain efforts to follow in his father's footsteps, Rorik's son had never seemed to amount to much, and eventually the promised treasures of old Vingallea that had captured the imaginations of the commoners had been forgotten in the face of their hard reality.

Another major expedition, led by the prince, no less, seemed unlikely. Yet, Rayburn's supposed involvement lent some credibility to what Winslow was saying.

"Okay, I'll bite. What is this important thing? And how far south are we talking?"

"Well, as for what they're seeking, that will take some time to explain. Suffice it to say, I wouldn't agree to nothing until Rayburn made plain what we'd be getting ourselves into. It took some needling, but he told me more than he was permitted to, and, I suspect, less than he knows. It was enough to convince me, though, and I gave him my word that his masters would never know that he let me in on their little secret. As for how far south, well that's what I wanted to talk to you about. We'd be going further than any boat on these waters has gone. I suspect we'll be gone for some time. I know with Elibeth …"

Curiosity had replaced her doubt, but Elibeth had overtaken them both. Leaving her daughter nearly every full-cycle was one thing. At least she still managed to return home after her shift; she could still share a meal with her and see her off to bed. Longer trips occasionally kept her away for a few consecutive full-cycles, and that was already a great strain; to be gone completely, in uncharted waters for an indistinct time, was just not possible.

"I'm sorry, Barrett, I can't."

"Well hold on now, don't decide too rashly. Listen, we are talking a *fortune* here," he said, rapping his knuckles on the rusted railing. "She's going to live up to her namesake. Enough coin that we could hang it up for four, maybe five long-cycles, based on what we're bringing in now. That could buy a lot of time with Elibeth. And anyway, you've already got someone watching her most of the full-cycle anyway. Tell them you'll throw them some extra coin when you get back. You'll certainly be able to afford it."

The amount of pay took Marbuck aback, and she fought with herself before defaulting to her refusal. "I can't just ask Dania to take her for the foreseeable future. Not when your best estimate is apparently 'some time.' She's got kids of her own. And she wouldn't accept payment anyway; she's too kind."

"Well, okay, more for you then."

"That sounds nice, but it's just not feasible. At any rate, Elibeth and I are doing fine. We can get by on what I'm bringing in."

"Raina, please." Winslow's good humor had dimmed, and Marbuck was reminded of the moment she'd opened her door to the sight of him and Gregor Falstaff, red-eyed and wretched. The way they had looked at each other, unsure of how to proceed. She turned away, choosing to stare at the reflection of the cloud-locked sky rippling across the surface of the water.

"Since you joined the crew, I have done everything I could to support you and Elibeth," Winslow continued. "Baylis is never far from my mind, and you know the others feel the same way. But this isn't about charity. I'm not just trying to help you, I need you. There's a reason you're my first mate, and it's not just because Baylis was. As his family, you've always been part of mine too, but if you were a shitty mariner someone else would occupy that seat. Castor might not believe me, but you had better. Without your navigation, we'll run aground, I guarantee it. You have a way of reading the water that the others don't, and you know it.

The Einfallen is tricky, even here, where we've mapped the waters. Down south?" He shrugged.

It was a cheap shot to invoke Baylis, and to play to her pride, but Marbuck did not doubt Winslow's honesty. She knew that she had earned her place through merit. She didn't give a shit what Fenwick Castor might insinuate behind her back.

"You wouldn't be gone more than half a long-cycle, if I had to bet."

Marbuck said nothing. She stared down into the water, the black curls of her hair hanging like curtains on either side of her face. Winslow hadn't mentioned the wages she would lose while the *Fortune* was gone and she was left struggling to find work in the meantime. Not to mention if they really did return rich enough to dock the boat for four or five long-cycles. She would be desperate then, and undoubtedly envious of the wealth she'd walked away from.

Four or five long-cycles, completely free of labor. Or, she could still work, but less. She could use that coin to get Elibeth a proper apprentice-ship when the time came, to set her up for a better future, to offer her security in uncertain times. The promise of this payment opened numerous doors for her. Doors that Baylis's death had shut.

"All we would be doing is transporting them down the Einfallen?" she finally asked. "And they would be serving as our protection?"

"I'm told they're bringing the best royal guardsmen that the Crown has to offer. Everything is expected to go very smoothly. Before you know it, we'll all be right back here counting out our coin."

It was going to be very difficult to tell Elibeth. Her eyes, so much like Baylis's, would betray nothing. At only eleven long-cycles of age, Elibeth was already as fiercely private with her emotions as her father had been. Losing him had only increased her penchant for walling herself off. She would appear to accept Marbuck's departure with the same quietude that she accepted everything, perhaps concealing her real feelings within a joke, just as Baylis would have done. But a mother always knows the true thoughts of her child, and Marbuck dreaded leaving her. Ultimately though, she could not refuse the promise of such a reward, and she hoped that Elibeth would understand.

Marbuck took a deep breath and turned to Winslow. "Okay. I'm in." He smiled broadly, and she held up a finger to check his enthusiasm. "But you're going to have to tell me everything you know."

PART 1:
ON THE BLACK WATER

CHAPTER 1

Marbuck couldn't sleep, but in the blackness of her cell, she dreamed.

Her eyes, denied any actual stimuli, conjured images in the darkness. The faces of those she'd known and those she'd been foolish enough to leave behind. An unseen drip acted as a metronome, seeming to signal the shifting change of the phantoms. The drip was maddening; it sharpened the edge of her thirst. More so, she hated it for disturbing every attempt she made to hold Elibeth's face in her mind's eye. Her daughter would appear before her, fleetingly, before dissipating, replaced instead with the sight of Winslow choking on his own blood. She could still see the bright red bubbles issuing from his lips and clinging to his gray whiskers, could still hear the gurgling rattle of his last gasps.

It had seemed too bright for there to be any danger. To Marbuck, threats like the disfigured monsters that had attacked them belonged to the sort of damp, miserable hole she now occupied. It shouldn't have been possible for them to suddenly emerge from the reedy waters, their hideousness so nakedly clear in the sunlight. Nobody remaining on the *Fortune*, not even the guardsmen, had seemed capable of fathoming what was happening. Though Winslow had learned of the slavers of Vin-Sadavat from Rayburn, and had passed that knowledge on to Marbuck, they had assumed that it was a far-off danger that only the trained soldiers of the

Crown would need to worry about. It was this lack of imagination, this false belief of safety born of their enamored wonder at the shining world around them, which had sown their doom.

Most of them, Winslow included, had appeared to pay the ultimate price for their laxity. Yet, for those who were taken, the horror of the vicious reality they now faced made the quick deaths of their brethren seem merciful.

It was strange to consider that, as long as Marbuck had lived her little life, this place had been festering in the darkness. There could be no doubt that she was now in Vin-Sadavat, for the slavers had hauled her deep into the Nightlands, journeying for many full-cycles. Her views of the city had been short and obscured by her captivity, but the glimpses she'd had were of an immense necropolis. Growing up, her parents had told her tales of Vin-Sadavat, or Buqaardia, as her ancestors, the Aurangzeb, had called it before they'd been conquered by Vingallea. Her parents had spoken reverently of the city, and of Nazradir, the hero of their people, who'd supposedly cast off the yoke of Vingallea and returned Vin-Sadavat to the people of Aurangzeb after the war between the old ones, the ancient gods of legend. Marbuck could only imagine what her parents would have thought had they ever seen what Nazradir's people had become.

These beings, these mutilated cultists, had clearly been practicing their wickedness for generations, and at the center of their savage ways was the worship of their mad god. Of gods, Marbuck understood little. Her knowledge was based on her limited memory of the apocryphal legends of Vingallea, and of what Winslow had told her regarding the expedition's purpose. She knew their leaders had sought hidden gods; here, she was certain, was one of them.

With her fellow captives, she'd been trotted out in front of the being the slavers had called their 'Empress', a strange woman crowned by a silver halo, wearing an eerie, sculpted mask, from behind which her alien eyes had blazed. The experience had been unnerving, and Marbuck was grateful that she hadn't been called upon to speak. One of the guardsmen, Luden, perhaps considering himself their de facto leader, had spoken for them all. He'd declared himself before the Empress, and Marbuck had watched with a mixture of revulsion and a foreign feeling of giddiness, as the Empress had turned her mesmeric attention toward him, and thus secured her first convert. His subsequent mutilation had turned her blood to ice.

Luden had only been the first to fall under her hideous sway. Ere long, they were brought before her again. Despite herself, Marbuck had felt a repulsive excitement to see the Empress again. It was only by holding onto her memory of Elibeth that she escaped unscathed. A second guardsman, Devonshire, submitted then, as did Castor. As horrifying as their conversions had been, the guardsmen were essentially strangers. To see one of her own crewmates defiled had finally purged the strange allure of the Empress from her mind.

Aside from Marbuck, only a final guardsman, whose name she did not know, and her crewmate, Falstaff, remained. Though she hadn't seen him since she'd been returned to her cell, the knowledge that Falstaff lived buoyed her. She knew it was a selfish impulse, for he was now enduring identical torment, but she was grateful that he was there nonetheless, locked somewhere in the same gloomy labyrinth that she was. At least she wasn't entirely alone, sundered from the world she'd known, trapped within a nightmare.

Her surroundings strove to stifle even that barest of comforts. The drip continued, and Falstaff's round, friendly face vanished as thoroughly as Elibeth's had. Winslow's pleading eyes replaced it, staring at her as if she could have done anything to help him. Marbuck hissed out a sigh and rolled fitfully onto her side. A moment later, she sat up, abandoning any attempt to sleep entirely. She rose from the cold, stone floor of her unfurnished cell and, with a guiding hand against the wall, proceeded to the corner she used as her privy. Not even a bucket had been provided.

After relieving herself, more out of habit than any real need to do so, she proceeded back to the corner she'd tried to sleep in. Hunger, as ever-present as her thirst, gnawed at her insides. She'd been given nothing to eat since she'd been taken, and had only been provided with small rations of dirty, metallic water. It was unclear how long she'd been held captive, languishing, as she was, in the blackness, but it'd been long enough that she could feel how thin she'd become, and how weak.

She sat against the wall and hugged her knees to her chest, resting her head on her arms. Her mind began to slip into a blankness that matched her surroundings.

Drip.

She squeezed her eyes shut and there was Elibeth, her lanky arms folded over her chest, eyebrows raised as she listened to Marbuck's pitch. Her disappointment had revealed itself in a short sigh, ostensibly to blow a wayward curl of black hair out of her face. She'd inherited that hair, as well as her dark complexion, from her mother. Baylis had apparently supplied the rest; the expression Elibeth had worn had been so reminiscent of her father that

Marbuck had felt as if she'd been trying to sell *him* on the voyage. Of course, she'd been prepared for that, and the conversation had gone pretty much exactly as she'd expected it to. The trip that followed, of course, had not.

Drip.

Elibeth was gone.

• • •

Long-cycles might have passed as Marbuck sat there, hunched in on herself. Eventually, new sounds slowly wove their way into the grim refrain of her misery. They were introduced so subtly that she hardly noted them, not until the change they heralded became clear. The sound of a horn, distant voices, shouts rising to cries, and all of it building toward a startling crescendo: another horn blast, this one tremendous.

Marbuck lifted her head, now acutely aware that something was happening. Other blasts followed the first, seeming to reverberate down through the very stones around her. She stood quickly, unsure just why, but knowing that something had changed. She had been trapped in a hopeless limbo for what felt like an eternity, cursing herself for throwing away her life and abandoning her daughter in search of easy coin. Now, hearing the growing clamor beyond the walls of her cell, a long-dormant feeling of hope rekindled within her.

Whatever was coming, she would need to be ready. She swept the greasy tangle of her hair out of her face and stretched her limbs and back, the muscles of which had been coiled tightly in perpetual anxiety. Somewhere far above her, an inhuman wail rose and fell. Marbuck licked her dry lips and stared toward the black space she knew the door of her cell occupied. It was entirely possible, she had to admit, that whatever was happening would pass her by, leaving her to starve and rot, forgotten in her prison. She refused to accept this, choosing instead to believe that, perhaps, they had finally come for her.

The leaders of the expedition, finding the *Fortune* wrecked and its crew dead or missing, had surely made for Vin-Sadavat with haste. After all, the intention had been to seek for an old one amongst the ruins of the city anyway. Now they had come, and at any moment, the hateful door that had sealed her into this wretched pit would be pulled open and she'd be free. They would take her, and Falstaff, and any other prisoner still sane enough to seek rescue, and leave this charnel place. She would return to Elibeth and never leave again.

As if her thoughts had conjured them, footsteps could be heard rapidly approaching from the corridor outside. Marbuck's heart hammered against her ribs, creating flashes of white at the edges of her vision. Just as quickly, the steps passed by and receded. No matter. They would come.

This little drama played out three more times; the footfalls of salvation approaching, only to fade again, leaving despair in their wake. By the time the door finally opened, Marbuck's hope had waned. The sight of the two creatures standing in the threshold extinguished it completely. Their scarred faces, lit by the flickering of the torches they carried, promised only that her suffering would continue. Reflexively, Marbuck backed up against the far wall.

"Come on out now, initiate," one of the slavers said. His tone lacked the malicious gaiety that Marbuck had come to expect from her captors. Though she'd be hard-pressed to differentiate between the slavers, who were all similarly disfigured, this one's voice did not seem familiar.

"What's happened?" Marbuck asked, remaining pressed against the wall. The two slavers exchanged a glance and her dream of rescue fluttered weakly.

"It's time to go," the slaver said. "You belong to the Commodore now."

That was something new.

"Who is that?" Marbuck said, stalling, seeking for some avenue to pursue toward her freedom. "What of your Empress?"

The second slaver, who'd remained quiet, turned away, and Marbuck was astonished to hear him stifle a cry.

"You belong to the Commodore now," the first slaver repeated.

Whatever change in leadership, however unexpected, had occurred, Marbuck's basic situation appeared to be the same. As she had from the start, she realized that trying to oppose them would be futile. Though she was no stranger to a fight, taking on two armed men twice her size could only result in her being badly beaten, especially in her weakened state. There was only one path forward; if she was immensely lucky, it might provide a chance to escape.

"Fine, say nothing then," Marbuck said, stepping toward them. She offered her hands and the slaver began to lash them together roughly. "This one's said enough already." She looked pointedly at the second slaver, who sniffled and turned away.

"Usso, control yourself," the first slaver barked. He shoved Marbuck ahead of him into the corridor. "Walk."

The three of them proceeded down the corridor, turning away from the path that Marbuck recognized as the one that led toward the pinnacle of the tower, and the Empress. This new route took them to a curved stairwell, where Marbuck could once again hear the sounds of battle echoing from above. Whatever occurrence had shifted the allegiance of the two slavers, it was apparently still happening.

"Down," the slaver ordered.

Marbuck led the way down the narrow, winding stairs, wishing the slavers had gone before her. A swift kick in the back would have sent them tumbling down the stone steps. She supposed that the same thing must have occurred to them. They were taking no chances with their prisoner.

"So, where is this 'commodore'?" Marbuck asked.

"You'll see soon enough. Now be silent. We are not in the clear yet," the slaver answered. Far above them, the terrible shriek of a shade's birth sounded.

A few moments later, they reached the bottom of the stairwell and proceeded into a hall nearly identical to that which they had left. After taking several turns, the slaver seized Marbuck's shoulder and the three of them stopped. Ahead, Marbuck's eyes detected a hint of light, and she realized that the utter darkness of the tower's interior was being pierced by the dim, but perceptible light of the outside world spilling in through an open doorway.

"Where are the others?" Usso whispered.

"They'll be here."

They continued to wait, and Marbuck wondered if the 'others' included Falstaff. She was about to ask when a baleful moan sounded from beyond the doorway. The two slavers shifted nervously, but, as with the shrieks and wails that she'd heard, the sound had little effect on Marbuck. She knew much of the shades, and had seen firsthand what their unholy eruption from the bodies of the unworthy dead looked like. In another life, she'd sought to be a shepherd, and though her time at the Ivy Citadel had ended when she'd chosen Baylis over her vows, she still retained the divine calm that robbed the shades of their chief menace.

"We can't wait here much longer," the slaver hissed, glancing back down the corridor. Suddenly, he smiled. "Ah, and we won't have to." Two more slavers materialized out of the gloom, carrying smoldering torches and a large chest between them.

"We got it, Karant," one of them huffed as they set the chest down at the slaver's feet.

The slaver, Karant, held a finger to his lips and nodded toward the doorway. "You've done well, Mordwand," he said quietly. "The Commodore will be very pleased."

"He'd better be," Mordwand murmured, mopping his forehead. The slick knot of scar tissue there shined in the torchlight. "The entire city is coming down and he's got us filching Davhal's trinkets."

"I don't think Davhal will mind. Shame."

"Yes, I heard," Mordwand said. "And it's not the most disturbing news to have reached my ears."

The slavers remained silent for a moment, save for Usso, whose wet breaths betrayed his sorrow. Marbuck, ignored by her captors, watched the whole scene with fascination and disgust. To see these beings speak freely with each other, and to hear them mourn, lent them a normalcy that contrasted sharply with their brutal ugliness.

"Where are the other initiates?" Mordwand finally said, nodding toward Marbuck. She did not enjoy being acknowledged.

"Old Stitch brought the newest converts to the ship," Karant explained. "Tordenaar and Gomulte should be fetching the last two refusals."

Marbuck's spirits rose slightly. He had to be referring to Falstaff and the last guardsman, and a ship meant that they were leaving Vin-Sadavat.

"Are we to wait for them?" Mordwand asked.

"Nay, they'll find their way, if they haven't already. The Commodore was chiefly concerned with making sure Davhal's chest was accounted for." Karant reached out a filthy hand and fingered a lock of Marbuck's hair, causing her to flinch away. He chuckled. "And that this one found her way to his ship."

The desire to strike Karant, bound or not, was nearly impossible to suppress. Before it could get the better of her, Marbuck's rising ire was deflated by the objections of the second slaver who'd arrived bearing the chest with Mordwand.

"The Commodore hasn't wasted any time, has he? The Empress's body is still warm, and, by all accounts, the outsiders who assassinated her are still lurking within the city," the slaver said, his pale eyes locked on Karant. "Rather than fulfilling the Commodore's whims, wouldn't we be better served to seek Heilrune and offer our assistance? Word is that he was grievously injured defending the Empress. He will seek vengeance, and he will need help. Shouldn't we offer it?"

There it was. The Empress had been killed by 'outsiders' who'd somehow entered the city, yet Marbuck had been forgotten, or assumed dead. Now those assassins had fled, and Marbuck had been left in the clutches of a rogue slaver who'd claimed her in the aftermath. Her relief at knowing that the otherworldly Empress had been toppled was matched only by her dismay at knowing that no help was coming.

"Nay, forget Heilrune," Karant said. "The Commodore understands something that you, Chrisholm, fail to grasp. The city cannot stand now. Had he all the help he could wish for, Heilrune, injured as he is, would not be able to restore order. It's not just a matter of finding the assassins now. Have you not heard that the lowly have risen in rebellion? Without the Empress, the scales have tipped. And, surely, you hear the shades outside?"

His challenge rebuked, Chrisholm looked at his feet. "Yes, I hear them."

For Marbuck, it was strange to hear the slavers name the shades. She supposed that, despite the very divergent paths the peoples of Vin-Sadavat and Nordabor had taken, they still shared much of their language, including the term 'shade', which had existed since antiquity. It was another bizarre glimpse into the humanity that still existed beneath the twisted visages of the slavers.

"Well, with that being settled, I believe it's time to go. Usso, see what's out there."

"Yes, Karant," Usso said, sounding distinctly unhappy to be given the task. He slunk past the others and peered through the open doorway. After a moment, he returned to them. "There's at least four out there."

"We'll have to run," Karant said. "We have the torches as well." As Karant and Usso set about relighting the torches of Mordwand and Chrisholm, Marbuck wondered at the fact that these people had existed for ages with nothing more sophisticated to fend off a shade with than fire. Of course, they had no way of producing the anointed blades that the shepherds of Nordabor carried; the only weapon that could destroy a shade.

Before she'd abandoned her training at the Ivy Citadel, she'd heard rumor of the source of the holy power behind the blades. Winslow's revelations, reluctantly given to him by Rayburn, had confirmed those suspicions. A hidden god, held captive since the war, provided the sacred blood used to quench the newly forged blades. That same god had, until its recent failings, kept their city alive. When Marbuck really considered it, this strange ritualistic bloodletting that she had been so close to being a part of, she found it difficult to deny the similarities to Vin-Sadavat. Both cities, forsaken in a dying world, had survived thanks solely to a god. Only in the fallen capital, that god had reigned over a realm of slaves, whereas in Nordabor, the god *was* the slave. All things considered, that arrangement seemed to have produced a much better outcome.

"Get the chest, let's move," Karant ordered. Mordwand and Chrisholm, who appeared to be done objecting, hoisted the chest as Karant pushed Marbuck toward the threshold, where a metal door hung open, crookedly dangling from a single hinge. Just outside, several bodies were scattered around a low-burning fire. "Ready to run, my pretty?"

"Yes," she said, refusing to look at him. She hoped that the shades would close in on them quickly. While the slavers quivered in fear, maybe she could slip away.

"Now," Karant said, clutching her arm and forcing her through the door. The party raced down a short ramp and out from under an overhang, reaching a pitted easement alongside a dried channel. Now free of the tower, they ran beneath a ceiling of dark clouds painted in hues of orange and red by the fires of the burning city below. To their right, the shambling form of a shade, flames licking up its back, took notice, its distorted head snapping to face them. It emitted a guttural scream and began to lope after them, oblivious to its own burning body.

Though Marbuck may not have been instantly cowed by the creatures, she was not heedless of them. Without a shepherd's blade, or even a torch, there was nothing she could do now but run alongside Karant, her plots of escape eclipsed by the need to survive. The bellowing of the shade had instantly attracted the others, and the slavers, particularly Mordwand and Chrisholm bearing the chest, would soon be overtaken.

"This way!" Karant shouted, yanking Marbuck to the left and waving the torch above his head. They rushed to the edge of the channel and leapt down into the many long-cycles worth of refuse that had accumulated there. The others scrambled over the ledge behind them, the chest dragging a rut through the debris as Mordwand and Chrisholm stumbled free from the high drift of rubbish. With the chest banging against their knees, they joined Marbuck, Karant, and Usso in racing toward the derelict hulk of a ship which stood mournfully in the channel just ahead. Behind them, the shades tumbled over the lip of the easement, igniting the heaps of garbage.

They reached the dry-rotted hull of the ship and, passing toward the bow, found a broken gap in the desiccated beams of wood. Usso entered first, followed by Marbuck and Karant. A moment later, Mordwand and Chrisholm wedged the chest through and slipped inside.

"What now?" Usso asked, backing away from the breach, wide-eyed.

"We find a way out," Mordwand answered, panting. "And you take a turn with this thing." He thrust the chest toward Usso, who reluctantly took the handle. Chrisholm looked expectantly toward Karant, who shook his head.

"I've got my own responsibility. Let's move." He proceeded through the narrow passageway with the others in tow, keeping his torch low so as to avoid igniting the overhead. Behind them, the first shade reached the breach and began to claw inside. Marbuck looked back and watched as the flames eating away at its blackened flesh began to lick at the dry wood.

"We need to get out, now," she said as they reached the end of the passageway and a fragile-looking ladder. Karant looked at her, his scarred face showing surprise at the unexpected input from his captive. "This ladder won't hold any of us, and certainly not that chest. We need to break through the hull and get out once they're all inside. They're going to set this dried hulk ablaze, and we should help them. Once we're out, we should put the torches to it. Run while they're trapped in the burning wreckage."

Karant gazed back toward the oily bulk of the shade, clawing its way inside. "You heard her, break it down."

Mordwand passed his torch to Karant and stepped forward. From his belt, he unclasped and lifted a broad, inelegant axe. After four mighty blows, he clove a gap in the rotted boards of the hull, just as the first shade shambled toward them, its burning body dragging across the overhead. Karant waved the two torches toward the monster, screaming incoherently. Despite the fact that it was already burning, it instinctively reared back. Mordwand continued to hack away at the hull until the gap was just wide enough to slip through. Usso and Chrisholm went first, the chest catching briefly in the new breach before snapping the dried, jagged beams and sliding free. As Karant held the shade at bay, Mordwand pulled Marbuck through. She could hear the slaver's breath whistling in short bursts, his terror apparent.

Before Karant had even emerged, Usso and Chrisholm had flung their torches toward the gap and fled toward the far end of the channel. The torches struck the hull and fell to the ground, the sparks clinging to, and igniting, the wood. Karant stumbled clumsily through the gap and threw both of the torches he bore back through it, striking the shade as it reached out after him.

"To the gate!" he shouted, racing after Usso and Chrisholm. He snatched Marbuck by the arm and, with Mordwand behind them, they fled from the ship. Marbuck stole a glance backward and saw that, from the first breach they'd entered to the newly hewn one they'd escaped through, the fire had hungrily consumed the ship, surging up the broken mast. No shades remained outside, and the nightmarish howling of those trapped in the flames rent the air.

With the acrid smoke burning in her already taxed lungs, Marbuck staggered to a stop a short distance from the end of the channel, where a tremendous iron gate, covered in the rusted remnants of some ornate design, blocked the way. Set as it was into the massive encircling wall, Marbuck assumed that it must have once allowed entrance into the city for ships coming from the sea. She looked back at the fully-engulfed form of the ship behind them and tried to picture it passing through the gate under a brilliant sun, the reflection of the light on the water dancing across its polished bow.

The slavers hoisted the chest back up onto the easement and began to climb up. Without warning, Karant seized Marbuck around the middle and lifted her. Before she could object, Mordwand had her arms and pulled her all the way up. A moment later, Karant was up beside her, brushing his hands off. "We've nearly made it," he announced as he looked up toward the ramparts at the top of the wall. "I don't see any of the wall wardens."

"Perhaps they've gone to assist Heilrune," Chrisholm suggested.

Karant shrugged and said nothing. To the right of the main gate was a smaller iron door, set into the wall just before them. Karant pulled a long, slightly bent key from a pocket of his leather cuirass, and slid it into a hole in the center of the door. He struggled with it for a moment before the locking mechanism within clicked noisily into place, and he unlatched the door and pushed it open, the hinges squealing in protest.

One by one, the beleaguered party stepped through the threshold and out of Vin-Sadavat. As Marbuck reached the other side, she looked out upon a view of nearly impenetrable darkness. For the first time in her life, she was beholding the Stagnant Sea. The lights of the city reached across the low clouds, stretching meekly above the absolute blackness of the water beneath. For a short distance, the water reflected the flame-lit sky before fading into the perpetual night that continued beyond the coast. The waters had clearly receded; where the sea appeared to have once reached the walls of the city, filling the channel, there was now a craggy outcropping of stone leading down to a ramshackle dock.

There, floating silently on the murky water, was a ship. Though similar in size to the *Fortune*, it more closely resembled the wreck they'd just torched. Lantern lights burned within, illuminating the smooth, rounded sides of the vessel. A single mast reached skyward, nodding gently in the slight movement of the ship.

Karant clapped Marbuck on the shoulder, startling her. "There she is, the pride of the Commodore and your new home: the *Empress's Love.*" He looked back at the walls of the city behind them and sighed. "It is a shame, for this realm to have fallen. I'm sorry you never got to experience the love of the Empress. Yet, soon you'll meet the Commodore, and I'm confident that you'll learn to love your new master, as I'm certain he'll love you." He patted her shoulder again and started down toward the ship.

Marbuck walked on leaden legs, disbelief filling her now that the imminent danger of their flight from the city had passed. There was no sign of Falstaff; he may have been rescued while she was left behind, delivered from her cell into a new horror. Ever her thoughts turned toward her freedom, toward Elibeth, and a new awareness slowly blossomed in her mind. In Vin-Sadavat, she had been trapped beyond all hope. Here, on this ship, she would once again be on the water.

Whatever the Commodore had planned for her, Marbuck would find a way to direct his ship back toward Nordabor.

CHAPTER 2

With the slavers behind her, Marbuck ascended the gangplank. No sooner had her feet reached the damp, warped boards of the deck than two new slavers approached and efficiently slipped free the single line anchoring the ship to the dock and hauled in the plank. Marbuck's eyes lingered on the shoreline; she had now been sundered completely from the world beyond the *Empress's Love*.

"I assume by your presence here that the two of you were able to fetch the other refusals?" Karant asked the new slavers as they wound the rope. One grunted in assent and Karant nodded. "I'll advise the Commodore of our arrival." He lifted one of the lanterns hanging from a brace attached to the deck's railing and walked off toward the stern, leaving Marbuck in the company of the others. She watched him go, the relief at knowing that Falstaff lived striving with her apprehension.

Only a moment later, Karant returned. "The Commodore's calling a muster!" he shouted. The slavers filed into a loose formation behind Marbuck, who felt naked standing before them. They waited in a submissive silence, punctured only by the distant sounds of the imploding city's death throes. Presently, a small group, illuminated by a lantern's bobbing light, approached from the stern. As they arrived, three hunched and cringing slavers broke off and hurriedly joined the formation. Now, only two figures remained standing before Marbuck. One was a small, wiry man, whose long wisps of thin, white hair did nothing to hide the absolute carnage of his face. The other, she was certain, was the Commodore.

With a pompous strut, he paced before his gathered crew, inspecting them with beady, black eyes. Tight rows of perfectly straight, vertical scars lined his entire head, spanning from his bald pate to the bottom of his jaw, where the tight collar of his uniform pressed into his flabby neck. Despite its shabbiness, the uniform would not have been out of place in Nordabor's Hall of Antiquities. It appeared to be the ratty, patched remains of some kind of Vingallean naval attire, complete with tattered epaulets and some tarnished medals pinned to the chest. Undoubtedly, the self-proclaimed Commodore had pilfered it, likely from the very ship he'd claimed as his own.

The cloak clasped about his neck, however, was clearly of his own design. At first glance, Marbuck assumed it to be the pelt of some mangy animal but, as the Commodore slowly walked the deck, seeming to enjoy the subservience of his men, Marbuck came to a nauseating realization. The cloak was actually a hideous patchwork collection of human scalps, the lank tufts of hair hanging together from dried squares of whipstitched skin.

The Commodore ceased his movement and peered at Marbuck, his small mouth pulling into a tight smile. She tried to stare back in defiance, but her gaze slipped away, falling on her own feet. Immediately, she felt disgust with herself for her fear.

"Bring her some water," the Commodore said. He reached out a thick hand and attempted to lift her chin to face him. Indignity extinguished her fear and she smacked his hand away. He jerked back and barked out a short laugh. "Belay that; she seems just fine. I'd have thought that her time in the Empress's accommodations would have left her a little more grateful for the offer of a drink."

Truthfully, the exertions of their flight to the ship had only made her thirst and hunger more severe, and the tantalizing offer of water was enough to make her physically ache. Yet, she would not give this being the pleasure of needing his mercy. She glared at him, willing him to leave her be.

"Have it your way," the Commodore said. He shifted his focus to the gathered slavers and cleared his throat. "Before we begin, I believe we're missing some of our crew. Gomulte, bring out the other newcomers."

One of the two slavers who'd hauled in the plank stumped away toward the bow. Marbuck was surprised to see that, upon closer observation, the brutish slaver was a woman. Though the slavers had revered a being that appeared to be female, Marbuck had seen no evidence that the ruling caste were composed of anything but men.

The Commodore watched them go and then turned his attention to the chest, which Usso and Chrisholm had deposited upon the deck. "I'm very pleased to see this here, Karant. You did excellently."

Karant, who was standing aside, somewhat in front of the others, nodded. Based on the command of the others he'd displayed, and his current position, Marbuck gathered that he was the Commodore's second-in-command.

"Have it brought to my cabin when we're finished here."

"Of course, Commodore."

The Commodore leaned down and examined the iron padlock that fastened the chest shut. "This will have to be removed. I don't want the chest damaged, though. It's a beautiful piece. No doubt a gift from the Empress." He sighed.

"I'll make sure it's removed carefully," Karant said.

"I have no doubt. And here is the rest of my crew."

Gomulte returned, pushing two smaller forms ahead of her. Marbuck's atrophied stomach churned with a mix of sorrow and guilt-inducing joy. Falstaff was shoved beside her, his boyish face now haggard, his left eye swollen shut, his straw-colored hair dark with filth.

"Fishwife," he said, attempting a smile. Marbuck was speechless, and could only clasp his bound hands with her own. Beside them, the only guardsman to refuse the Empress had also been roughly shoved into place. He regarded them with a steadfast solidarity.

"Well, now that we've all arrived, I'll keep this brief. I don't wish to be interrupted," the Commodore said, gesturing toward the rising bulk of the burning city behind them. "The sooner we're underway the better. Most of you have served upon my ship before. Some of you are fresh initiates. Little more than baby uncuts, just beginning what should have been a lifetime of pleasure in the service of the Empress. That life has been stolen from you, and that is a terrible thing. How, or why it happened, I cannot say. This much, I can say: the Empress is gone. I wish, ardently, that this was not the case, but it is. Now, we must move forward. The Empress's realm has fallen. From those bitter ashes we will rise. This is the new purpose that you initiates have been given: to serve me in establishing our new kingdom. Do you now willingly choose to serve me, as you once swore to serve the Empress?"

From the gathered crew, the three slavers who'd arrived with the Commodore stepped forward and knelt before him. In the full light of the lanterns, Marbuck now recognized them. With an intense loathing, she looked at the quailing, disfigured form of Castor. His nose had been lopped off, and though the actual wound had been stitched shut, the open hole in his face wept freely. The two other guardsmen, Luden and Devonshire, knelt beside him. Luden now bore a large slash that passed down the center of his face, splitting his nose and lips, which were healing into an ugly, jagged line. Devonshire sported two similar cuts that crisscrossed his face in a large X, centered between his eyes. The three of them refused to look at Marbuck, Falstaff, or the third guardsman. Luden and Devonshire stared at the deck while Castor looked up at the Commodore with a cowering obedience. To Marbuck, the subservience of all three was appalling. It was a betrayal, and fundamentally different from what she was doing: obeying so long as it kept her alive, biding her time until she could escape. Even without the enchantment of the Empress, these men were willing to swear fealty to the slavers. It was disgusting.

"You must now obey my every command as law. Dissent is death. Pledge yourselves to me."

Castor was the first to speak. "I pledge myself." His injury made him sound congested.

Luden and Devonshire both murmured similar oaths. The Commodore's grimly set face broke into a broad grin. "Alright, on your feet, enough of that. Fresh blood on the crew; it's a wonderful thing. You've certainly made the right choice, and you will be summarily rewarded for it. In time. For now, you will have your first of many shifts at the oars."

The three men had risen, and now Castor looked slightly taken aback.

"Usso, Chrisholm, and Tordenaar will show you to your new labors. I know you won't disappoint me." The three slavers briskly escorted Castor, Luden, and Devonshire toward a nearby hatch. "Karant, take the helm, bring us around to the south."

"Yes, Commodore," Karant said, already moving toward the stern as he spoke.

South was not good. Marbuck knew enough of the geography of the lands beyond Nordabor to know that Vin-Sadavat lay to the southwest. Judging by the dried state of the channel into the city, and the damming of the Einfallen where the *Fortune* had been ambushed, navigating back up the river would be impossible. She somehow had to get the ship headed north along the coast.

Once Karant had disappeared from view, the Commodore turned toward his captives. "Well, what am I going to do with you lot? Do any of you wish to pledge your loyalty?"

Marbuck said nothing, and was not surprised when Falstaff and the guardsman remained silent as well.

"I thought as much. Well, I am not the Empress; I will not keep offering you a blessing, with the only other alternative being execution. I believe in a more nuanced approach. Whenever you're ready to join up proper, I'll welcome you with open arms. Until then, you will be my slaves, and you will serve at my whim. Toil will be all you know. For you, death will not be the punishment, but pain. I will break each of you, and in the end, you will thank me. Now, what am I to call you?"

Once again, they remained silent.

"Oh, please don't be coy. This will be a long voyage if you plan on making every interaction so difficult. So let me make this plain. First off, I will show you civility by giving you my name. You are to refer to me by my rank at all times, but my true name is Bolenz. See? Now you can give me your names. Secondly, if you still refuse, I will have Mordwand scourge you so violently that you will beg for death. He is known as the Prince of the Whip for a reason. And lest you think that I will be merciful enough to allow death to follow, know that I will have Old Stitch here put you back together and nurse you back to health. I will then order Mordwand to punish you again. So, I'll ask for the final time, what am I to call you?"

Mordwand stepped forward, and he now held an iron-tipped whip. Beside him, the thin, white-haired slaver watched. His face was an unreadable blur of nearly smooth, featureless scar tissue, telling of a long life of burned and flayed skin. His watery eyes peered out from contorted slits of tissue, and in them, Marbuck thought she saw a hint of sadness. She assumed that he was Old Stitch, and that he'd witnessed this sort of punishment before, many times. Marbuck did not think that the Commodore, or rather, without his false rank, Bolenz, was bluffing.

"Marbuck," she said. She looked at the other two captives and shrugged.

"Tannahill," the guardsman said.

"Falstaff."

"Now we all know each other. Splendid," Bolenz said, all cheer again. "So, what, aside from manual labor, can any of you offer me?"

The wheels of thought whirred within Marbuck's head. Here was an opportunity to have a hand in the movements of the ship. "I'm a mariner," she said, eliciting a look of surprise from Falstaff. He'd obviously not expected her to answer. "A navigator, actually. I can help you read the water, avoid shoals, find safe harbor, get you wherever you're going without running aground." She failed to mention that she'd only ever navigated a river, and never in the total darkness of the Nightlands.

Bolenz gave her an appraising look. "Well, you continue to intrigue."

Falstaff looked puzzled, but seemed to sense that Marbuck had some intention behind her words. "I served with her on the same crew. She's an excellent navigator."

"Is that so? Well, two fellow seafarers, that's tremendous. I do hope you join the crew in earnest sooner, rather than later. And you?" Bolenz said, looking at Tannahill.

"I am a royal guardsman, in service to the Crown of Vingallea."

Bolenz was unmoved by Tannahill's declaration. "You were. You are a slave in service to me now." With a nasty chuckle he turned to Mordwand. "Remove their bindings; bound hands do little work. At any rate, I'm certain they won't cause any trouble. Take the two men to the brig, they'll begin their shift at the oars soon enough. As for the navigator, I'd like a private audience with her in my cabin."

•　•　•

Compared to the murk outside, the cabin was brilliantly lit. The shining lamps of delicately carven glass, which cast a warmer light than the utilitarian lanterns on deck, only accentuated Bolenz's terrifying appearance. He contrasted sharply with the neat, polished space they now occupied. Whatever he was, Bolenz had clearly worked hard to meticulously restore and maintain the space.

Marbuck had been led into the cabin and sat on a bench before a wooden desk built into the bulkhead. Faded, partly-furled charts were spread across the table. Marbuck stared down at them as Bolenz busied himself at a nearby cabinet. The other slavers had remained outside.

The certainty of what was about to occur turned Marbuck's blood to ice. The specter of rape at the hands of the slavers had always been there. Perhaps their reverence for their Empress had held them in check before. As the inevitable assault drew nearer, Marbuck's focus narrowed. Hunger, thirst, survival, even Elibeth faded into background noise. Whatever happened, she would not allow Bolenz to violate her.

Her eyes wandered across the cabin to a side table near the bed, where, on an empty, greasy plate, a small meat fork rested. She began to slide slowly across the bench, watching Bolenz for any sign that he'd detected her movement. He was humming contentedly.

The floor beneath her suddenly lurched, and she froze. As the ship shuddered into movement, the entire cabin began a rhythmic rocking, causing the dishes in the cabinet to rattle softly. Bolenz turned to face her, bearing two bronze cups and a corked bottle with some dark liquid inside. He raised the hairless skin above his eyes where eyebrows should have been. "Going somewhere?"

Marbuck had reached the end of the bench and was leaning toward the small table in an awkward half-crouch when the ship began to move. She remained there, trying to calculate if she would be able to reach the fork before he was upon her. Bolenz looked from her to the direction she'd been moving in, and his eyes fell upon the fork. A look of amused pity broke across his scarred face.

"A rather shortsighted plan, don't you think?" He stepped toward her and she reared up.

"Don't touch me," she said, looking desperately for something, anything within reach to use as a weapon.

Realization seemed to dawn on Bolenz and, keeping a distance between them, he walked around and sat down on the other side of the table. "I am not as boorish as some of my kinsmen. Even without the fetters of the Empress's order, I would never take a woman who didn't wish to bed me. I've never needed to," he added with a lecherous wink. "With the Empress gone, I'm sure many will fall into base impulses, but you have nothing to worry about on my ship. I'm sorry if any of my crew made you think otherwise."

Marbuck had a difficult time believing that, but also couldn't conceive of any reason Bolenz would bother lying about it. It was possible that, had he intended to rape her, he would have already tried to do so.

"Please. Sit down," Bolenz said, uncorking the bottle and pouring some of the liquid into a cup. He slid it across the table toward her. She made no move, and he shrugged, pulled the cup back and drained it himself. "No, my interest in you is of a wholly different variety," he said, as if answering a question she'd asked. He gestured toward the bench Marbuck had sprung up from. Shaking, adrenaline fading, she lowered herself slowly.

"There, that's better." Bolenz looked at the bottle and frowned. "I suppose all you really want is water, and perhaps a bite to eat. I'll have some of both brought to you once you've been taken to the brig. Some for your fellow slaves as well."

Marbuck assumed that the water would be of the same filthy variety as that provided in Vin-Sadavat, but she yearned for it nonetheless. As for the food, she wondered what could possibly have been cultivated in the dark, and feared that she already knew the answer. Still, her hunger continued to grow, and she could not deny it forever. A clammy sweat broke out on her skin, and exhaustion suddenly swamped her.

"Is it true that you refused the Empress twice?"

The question shook her from her thoughts. "Yes, that's true. So did Falstaff and that guardsman, Tannahill."

Bolenz nodded along. "The three of you present a rare circumstance, you especially. Traditionally, those who refused her blessings would always perish when she grew tired of asking, which rarely took long. But as I said before, I do not share that outlook. Your refusal is enticing to me, a challenge. You are like an unblemished stone, awaiting the sculptor's hand. I look at your flawless face and see the Empress's final gift to me. When the time is right, and when you desire it, and you *will* desire it, I will make the first cut myself."

His voice had grown soft, lilting. Around them, the ship creaked as it picked up speed. The faint sounds of water slapping against the hull could be heard. A lantern flickered briefly.

He did intend to rape her. Not in an immediate, forcible manner, but in the long, insidious erosion of her sanity. He intended to leave her mentally defeated, submitting to his depravity of her own volition. It would never happen. Yet, in his infatuated pursuit, Marbuck saw the possibility of worming her way into Bolenz's thoughts. She could dangle what he wanted before him and bend him to her will until she found the chance to break him.

"That will never happen," she said evenly.

Her defiance had the intended effect. A look of giddy exhilaration flitted across his face.

"We will see," he sighed. "Until then, I will ensure that you remain unharmed, so long as you obey. Mordwand can inflict plenty of pain without touching your face. In addition to your normal duties, which you will be instructed on soon, I believe I can make use of your skills as a navigator. I'm looking to extend my reach into uncharted waters, beyond the Empress's realm. All in due time, of course."

Marbuck tamped down the urge to suggest going north, it would be too soon, too transparent of a suggestion. She simply listened.

"Expansion. I believe it was the way of the past; I know it's the way of our future. For too long we remained stagnant, content to secure our borders, seeking initiates in depleted lands. Expansion and consolidation. All in due time," Bolenz repeated, almost to himself. Abruptly, he stood. "We will speak again before long. For now, get some rest; you'll need it. You'll be manning the oars soon."

CHAPTER 3

With the ship rocking pleasantly beneath him, Bolenz prepared to open the chest. It truly was a handsome piece; the sort of treasure the Empress had held an unlimited supply of in her coffers. At some point, every item of beauty, every bauble and trinket, must have been taken by her as tribute, only for her to gift them back to her most cherished worshippers when they pleased her.

Bolenz had never received a thing.

The fine wood, brass hasps, and tastefully decorative leather straps could be fully appreciated now that the ugly lock had been broken and cast away. Karant, who'd been relieved at the helm now that they were comfortably on course, had worked with a steady hand. He now sat across from Bolenz, occupying the same bench the slave woman had. Unlike her, he had not refused a drink. It had been her loss; the spirits pilfered from the Empress's cellars were yet another treasure Bolenz could now enjoy, and they were splendid.

Though delaying the pleasure was a sort of pleasure itself, he could wait no longer. He flicked open the hasps and lifted the lid, which creaked softly as it opened. Peering inside, his roving eyes were not disappointed. Atop a velvet piling of luxurious fabrics and silken robes in dazzling hues sat a collection of golden coins, shining pearls, leather-bound volumes, and filigreed dishes. All rewards from the Empress, or the seized goods of the initiates Davhal had captured in the wilds.

Lying atop everything was a blade. Bolenz lifted it, admiring the simple but quality craftsmanship of the black leather sheath. He slid the blade free and tested the weight.

"That looks like a mighty fine weapon," Karant said. He obviously expected something for ensuring the chest was brought to the ship and opened cleanly. Though, like his deceased Empress, Bolenz liked to reward his subordinates for their successes, this particular piece would remain with the Commodore.

"It is. I believe I've found myself a new sword." He flicked it through the air in a series of short jabs. If Karant was disappointed, he masked it well. "You may help yourself to anything else."

As Karant rifled through the chest, Bolenz secured his new blade to his belt. His old cutlass, found upon the *Empress's Love*, like every other precious thing he possessed, was set aside with some reverence. It had served him well. He'd carried it ever since he'd come upon the ship, when he'd been a younger man.

Exactly how long ago it had been, Bolenz had no way of really knowing. In the eternal night, time passed unnoticed. The Empress, at least until death had finally come for her, had always remained unchanged. Her followers would grow old and they would die, unless sickness or bloodshed took them first. In the meantime, they did their best to show the Empress their devotion and to hunt for fresh initiates, for new meat. They either served or found others to serve, and only in that way could they grow in eminence. Bolenz had known since his earliest time as an uncut that he did not wish to serve. Others' minds narrowed until they became little more than living meat, animated only by the orders of whatever master currently ruled them. Bolenz's thoughts reached far beyond the Empress's city.

His first patrols into the wastes were like an intoxicating dream. The alien faces of the strangers from the outer lands at first filled him with fear, for it was rare that he beheld any face free of blessings. But he quickly learned that the wanderers were pitiful; either willing to join the Empress for protection or incapable of fighting back.

For a while, this system worked. Bolenz earned the command of his own force, and his capture of new initiates brought him both pleasure and a comfortable position within the inner sanctum. Yet, the Empress's true favor still eluded him. He watched as Heilrune became her most adored champion, a conqueror whose warpath brought numerous tribes of the outsiders to heel.

It was his pursuit for acclaim that had brought Bolenz to new lands, never plundered by the Empress's people. And it was there, within a cavern along the northern coast, that he had found the ship that he would call the *Empress's Love*, in honor of what he sought. She had been lying aground on her beam ends, in a strangely preserved state. The rotten husks he'd passed a thousand times in the city had been nothing like her. Not only was she nearly intact, but the hoard of incredible works within her were unlike anything that existed in the Empress's realm. Bolenz decided rather quickly to put the intricate workings of his mind to the task of restoring her, and ordered work to commence immediately. Though some of his men lost faith and deserted, others remained true. With much labor, the task was finished and the ship, now driven by the strength of his devoted crew, turned toward home.

Yet, the appearance of a beautiful vessel named in her honor did little to sway the Empress. She wanted initiates, followers to fill her city and cry out their adoration until their throats were raw. So, along the coast Bolenz crept, seeking the prize that would finally make her see him. Time passed and still it never came. His hunts returned a pittance, while those who followed the beaten path thrived. It was a bitter truth to accept. As his crew dwindled, he began to see more and more the meaninglessness of his assumed title, the weakening of his power. The other leaders snickered behind his back. White-hot malice grew within him, warping his intentions. He stopped caring about bringing initiates to the Empress, choosing instead to annihilate those few wanderers he found along the coasts. The thrill of scalping them soothed his tortured mind.

And then, just as Bolenz seemed to be losing everything, the Empress and her realm had come crashing down. He was now his own master, freed from his devotions. It was terrible and tragic and perfect.

"Ah, this'll do nicely," Karant said, rising from a crouch before the chest. He now held a black sash shot through with threads of gold and pink. He ran his fingers across the delicate fabric and then tied it roughly about his waist. "Well?"

"It looks fine."

Karant accepted this half-hearted approval and plopped back onto his bench, where his drink was waiting for him. The two sat in companionable silence for some time before Bolenz spoke again, nudging the chest with his foot.

"Davhal was a zealot, or at least played one well. His devotion to the Empress always struck me as rather performative. Whether or not he was a charlatan, the Empress certainly adored him for his very vocal piety. Adulation was ever the key to her grace; while I expanded her reach into new lands, Davhal's fawning won him higher and higher renown. And then this catch. Luck. Simple luck. Well, now Davhal is gone and his spoils have come to me. Fair salvage, I say."

Karant nodded in agreement.

"That's what all of it is, don't you see? Her entire realm; it's salvage for the taking. *My* taking. And I won't be held back by her dogma anymore. I have no issue seeking out those she handled with a gentle touch."

Karant, rattled from his automatic agreement, eyed Bolenz for a moment. "Do you mean the skinners?"

"Why, yes, I do," Bolenz said, enjoying Karant's look of surprise.

"They won't have it, you know. Midga and his ancestors have rejected the Empress and every envoy she ever sent. They'll barter, but they won't serve."

Bolenz shrugged and took a gulp of the exquisite liquor. "Yes, I know and I care not. Her problem was her approach. Midga cannot be swayed by entreaties to return to the true faith. For him and his ilk, harvested flesh is the coin of the realm; they will never cut their own."

"For that alone, I can't believe the Empress allowed them to carry on," Karant said.

"They were too valuable to destroy. Apparently, the initiates they provided were worth the sting to the Empress's ego, and the pittance of skins we traded them. Plus, I believe she always dreamed of them returning to her. They'd been devotees once before, and even when they left, they still honored her. They just refused her knife."

Karant considered this. "So, what is your approach going to be?"

"I plan on offering Midga what he wants, without what he saw as the odious demands of the Empress. There are skins enough in the hold to buy an audience with him, and we've traded with him before; he trusts us. Once he sees our new direction, I believe he will submit. With his men and resources, we might be able to expand. Maybe even establish a fleet …"

"What if he's still not interested?"

"Then we trade the skins for some new initiates and move on."

"To where?"

Bolenz's face spread into a grin. "We now have a mariner who hails from a northern kingdom. She is a navigator, and she knows of lands that've remained beyond our grasp for a long time. When we are ready, she will take us north."

CHAPTER 4

Rough hands shoved Marbuck into the brig and slammed the iron door behind her. Her body, pushed to the limits of thirst and hunger, and now briefly delivered from immediate danger and fear, was racked by a violent shudder. Her knees gave out and, before she could collapse, Falstaff was holding her. He guided her to the floor and they clung to one another, each the other's only comfort in a waking nightmare.

"Did he hurt you?" Falstaff asked.

"No. Not yet."

Falstaff sighed heavily with relief and ran a hand through his hair. He'd been Baylis's closest friend, and, after the accident, he'd held it as his personal duty to look after Marbuck and Elibeth. As someone who generally did not enjoy being 'looked after' Marbuck could have been annoyed, or even insulted. Yet, in the total devastation that followed Baylis's death, it was impossible not to appreciate the kindness and honesty of Falstaff's actions. When Marbuck had been unable to get out of bed, Falstaff had been there for Elibeth. 'Uncle Gregor', as she affectionately called him, had served as the surrogate parent Elibeth had desperately needed when Marbuck had been too lost in her own sorrow to offer any comfort or care. Falstaff had also secured for her Baylis's position on the *Fortune*, though Winslow had needed little convincing. When others, like Castor, had balked at a newcomer taking the position of first mate, Falstaff had advocated fervently for her. His earnest loyalty could be almost embarrassing at times, but it was always endearing.

"Are you okay?" she asked him.

He touched his swollen eye. "Yeah, no worse for wear. Here, one of them brought this by. It's not good, but it's better than nothing." Falstaff offered her a waterskin and she took it, pulled the stopper, and drank greedily. Like the water in Vin-Sadavat, it tasted metallic. Cognizant not to drain the entire skin, she forced herself to stop and then offered it back. Falstaff shook his head.

"I'll take another drag," Tannahill said from the corner of the cramped cabin, where the dim light filtering in through the small, barred window set into the door barely reached him. Caught up in her reunion with Falstaff, she'd forgotten about the guardsman.

"Here you go," she said as she passed it to him. He took a long, slow sip and swished the water around in his mouth before swallowing it. After replacing the stopper, he continued to stare at the waterskin.

"So, what are we going to do?" he asked without looking up. Marbuck and Falstaff looked at each other. "I mean, I assume you two don't intend to submit, or spend the rest of your lives as slaves."

"Absolutely not," Falstaff said.

"Good. We need to get back to shore and try to find the rest of the expedition. I believe Phir-Ramarian led some sort of attack on the city. Captain Mather and the other guardsmen are almost certainly responsible for killing the Empress. If we can get back to them, we can survive. We can still help ensure the expedition is successful."

The success of the expedition was the furthest thing from Marbuck's mind, but the guardsman's idea did have some merit. With little to no resources, even if they did make it to shore, they would not survive without the provisions carried by the rest of the company. And it did seem plausible that the company was responsible for the attack on the city, although they were apparently too preoccupied with killing the city's god to bother with rescuing their imprisoned comrades.

"If the expedition did succeed in toppling the Empress, where would they be going next?" Marbuck asked. "Could we find them?" Her knowledge of their route had been limited to the *Fortune*'s part along the Einfallen. Based on all of the secrecy surrounding the journey, she wondered how much Tannahill knew of the expedition's plans.

"They would be heading north."

"Why?" Falstaff asked. He knew even less than Marbuck, and she felt a sudden guilt for not telling him what she'd known sooner. Of course, she'd been trusted by Winslow to remain silent, and since the attack, she hadn't had much time to speak with anyone. Thinking of the attack brought the memory of Winslow's final moments back with a horrifying clarity, and it took some effort to force it to pass.

"That is the direction in which the thing they seek can be found," Tannahill said carefully. The non-answer seemed to confuse Falstaff.

"That's where the next god is hiding, then?" Marbuck asked Tannahill. He opened his mouth soundlessly, looking very much like a fish out of water. "I think we're beyond the need for secrecy." She turned to Falstaff. "The expedition sought gods. Not their remains, but living old ones, just like the legends describe. For what purpose, beyond destroying them, I don't know, but it's somehow linked to a captive god that's kept Nordabor afloat until recently. Some of this, Winslow told me. He heard it from Rayburn, who was privy to the knowledge of the Crown. Some I've gleaned from my time at the Ivy Citadel. There, it's all out now. Unless you have anything to add?"

Tannahill shook his head, still looking surprised. Falstaff sat with his arms crossed, trapped in deep thought. Finally, he cleared his throat. "So, then the expedition is headed north. And we're headed south."

In spite of everything, Marbuck smiled at Falstaff's plain assessment. His question had been answered, and now that he'd heard the revelations, the confirmation of every old tale, he chose to focus on the basic facts of their situation. The lofty ambitions of their rulers and the implications of their quest meant little to a man who'd never been interested in contemplating anything grander than where the best spot to drop the nets would be.

"Yes, that is essentially the problem," Tannahill said. "We need to get off this ship and head north."

"Or," Marbuck said quietly. "We need to get the ship to take us north."

• • •

In hushed tones, they had discussed Marbuck's plan until sleep finally took them. Unsurprisingly, Falstaff had readily accepted her intentions, giving full-throated support to any plan that might bring them home and reunite her with Elibeth. Tannahill had remained skeptical, but acquiesced when it became clear that it was really the only option they had, short of leaping overboard and trying to swim to shore. In the unlikely event that they actually managed to do that, they would then be lost in the wastes, bereft of any food or water.

Despite her exhaustion, Marbuck slept uneasily. She could feel each heaving movement of the ship taking her further from Elibeth. Her plan was the only one they had, but it was a slow-burning scheme. She had no way of knowing how long it would take to influence Bolenz's decisions, or if it was even truly possible. And despite his assurances, Marbuck dreaded reaching the moment when he finally grew tired of her refusals.

She was hovering in the twilight between the waking world and a shifting tableau of dark dreams when the door of the brig was flung open, slamming into the bulkhead with an explosive bang. All three of the prisoners were startled awake, instinctively scrambling away from the sudden shock. Karant stood in the doorway, and he laughed at their fear.

"It's your turn at the oars; Commodore's orders," he said, his mirth subsiding. "Get up." Behind him, Mordwand stood, his whip at the ready.

Wondering how she would possibly have the strength to man an oar, Marbuck rose on unsteady feet. Falstaff and Tannahill joined her, and the three slaves were led out of the brig and up a ladder through the fore hatch. On deck once again, Marbuck was struck by the eeriness of the ship's passage through the dark water. The steady movement of the air across her face, combined with the constant slapping of the water striking the bow as it cut through the surface, created a sense of great speed. In near-total darkness, it was difficult to gauge how fast they were actually moving. From the bow, a narrow funnel of light illuminated the water before them and swept back and forth across its inky surface. Marbuck couldn't help but admire the ingenuity of the slavers. They'd somehow harnessed the light of a lantern, turning it into a concentrated beam, casting its light far ahead of the ship in search of unseen hazards.

As they proceeded aft, they were approached by Old Stitch, and they shuffled to a stop.

"First shift, eh?" he said pleasantly, as if their forced labor was a rite of passage they'd been eagerly anticipating. "You'll need your strength. I meant to bring some of this by sooner." He held out some brown chunks of dried meat. With a painful lurch, Marbuck's stomach awoke at the sight of the food, and it took some effort to stop herself from taking it. Falstaff and Tannahill remained still beside her.

"I can see that you have some suspicions regarding the source of this meat," Old Stitch said, turning the chunks over in his hand as he spoke.

"Well, I can confirm for you that this is, indeed, human flesh, harvested from initiates too weak to survive. It may seem grotesque to you, being outsiders, but I can assure you that it is quite good. Salted and dried, with a soft texture and a rich flavor. A final gift from the dead. I understand your hesitation, but it has been far too long since you've eaten. You will find no other source of food aboard this ship. You will either eat this or you will die." There was no threat in his voice; he was simply informing them of a basic truth.

Marbuck wanted to say something scathing, to prove her resolve, but she could only stare ahead, willing Old Stitch and his temptations to go away. Once again, Falstaff and Tannahill followed her lead. It seemed that none of them wished to be the first to break.

Old Stitch nodded. "Your shift is going to be very difficult; the food would have helped. I'm sorry for what you're about to endure, and I'll be ready to patch you up after. Please show them some mercy," he said to Mordwand. "Remember, it's their first time."

"You mind your affairs, and I'll mind mine," Mordwand said, shoving Marbuck and the others ahead. She looked back at Old Stitch, the thought of crying out for the foul meat flitting across her mind, but he had already turned away. For what it was worth, she had kept to her convictions. It was yet to be seen what it would cost her.

Their remaining time above deck proved to be brief, as they soon reached another hatch and descended into a dim, humid compartment, where Marbuck was struck by the pungent odor of unwashed bodies. If the bow lantern had impressed her, the machinery of the oars filled her with bewilderment. Having seen, and worked, oars on the *Fortune*, she'd imagined she would be dealing with something similar. Instead, she found a convoluted mess of chains and gears spanning the bulkheads, attached to and surrounding three large capstans that dominated the space. Castor, Luden, and Devonshire each worked one of the contraptions, heaving against a lever that rotated around a base, walking in unison. Tordenaar stalked between them, shouting threats if any one of them started to lag behind. As they pushed, the chains retracted from small ports set in the bulkhead and coiled about the capstan's base. Once it seemed they could go no further, a loud clank simultaneously sounded from each device, and the three men leapt back. The gears in the compartment whirred and the capstans revolved rapidly, spinning the levers in reverse and unfurling the chains back along their paths into the bulkhead ports. The unseen oars, which were apparently built into the hull of the ship, could be felt pulling through the water, driven by the complex apparatus. Once the capstans ceased their spinning, the three men grasped the levers and, panting, set to work coiling the chains once again.

"Marvelous engineering, isn't it? The Commodore's own design," Karant said with genuine admiration. "You'll have plenty of time to enjoy it. Mordwand will be your instructor; I leave you in his hands."

Mordwand wasn't listening. His eyes were fixed on Luden, whose pushing of the lever had turned into a shambling lurch, putting him out of sync with the others. "Tordenaar! Do you not see this layabout?"

"I see him, and I've told him to keep moving."

With an irritated hiss of a sigh, Mordwand shoved Tordenaar aside. "You ought to let your whip do the talking." Luden had just enough time to turn toward his punishment. Mordwand slung the whip across his back and left side with such force that it knocked him flat with a cry. The lever whirred backward and, with a third of the system reversing, the other capstans screeched to a halt, flinging Castor and Devonshire to the floor.

"*On your feet!*" Mordwand screamed at the prostrate form of Luden. He whipped him savagely again, this time across the man's arms as he tried to cover his head. Luden yelped in pain and tried to crawl away, eliciting further blows, each strike of the whip painting his body with a glistening lash mark. He sobbed for mercy as he twisted across the floor, mindlessly seeking any escape from his torment.

The others stood in thrall to the violence before them. With each sickening *thwack* of the whip, Luden's cries grew weaker. Between each strike, Mordwand flicked the whip above his head, spattering blood across the overhead. Marbuck's empty stomach felt like it had turned inside out and she stifled a dry heave. Finally, she could take no more, and she averted her eyes from the carnage.

Castor and Devonshire remained on the floor, and in their wretched faces Marbuck saw plainly their fear and regret. Behind them, Gomulte had crept silently down the ladder and now lingered on the edge of the compartment. With each blow, she hunched her broad shoulders and winced, her deep-set eyes flicking away. As Marbuck watched her, they caught each other's gaze. Gomulte appeared to mouth something, her thick lips moving soundlessly, her scarred face contorting into what looked like sorrow. She then nodded and turned away, proceeding back up the ladder. Marbuck watched her go, feeling as if they'd had some kind of meaningful exchange.

Slowly, she became aware that the scourging had ended. Mordwand stood above Luden's crumpled form, panting. He wiped blood from his face with a cloth and turned to Tordenaar.

"Bring him to Old Stitch."

"I had it under control," Tordenaar said.

"Bring him to Old Stitch," Mordwand repeated, his tone leaving no room for debate.

Tordenaar hoisted Luden up and began to drag him toward the ladder, leaving a bloody smear in their wake. Mordwand turned toward Castor and Devonshire. "Help him get that shit-sack up. Your shift is done."

They scrambled to their feet and began to assist Tordenaar in negotiating Luden's limp form up the ladder.

"Well, I think that served as a proper demonstration of what will occur should any of you slack," Karant said. "Though it has slowed us down. I was hoping for a smoother transition. The Commodore does not like it when we lose momentum."

"My apologies," Mordwand said. "Had Tordenaar given him a small taste of the whip, I wouldn't have had to gorge him on it. And don't you worry about delays; after what these three just witnessed, I'm certain they will be eager to please."

• • •

Working the oars was a torture of physical strain and monotonous hardship, with no end in sight. With each plodding step forward, Marbuck was certain that it would be her last. Only the constant threat of Mordwand's whip kept her moving. The lever continually pushed back against her blistered hands, growing stronger as the chain was coiled. Sweat drenched her, every muscle in her wasted, spent body trembled violently, and she gasped at the swampy air. Her entire existence had narrowed to the lever she clutched.

Finally, after an eternity of pushing, she would hear the mechanism click. Mustering every last shred of strength she possessed, she would fling herself clear of the lever, and, for a brief moment of indescribable relief, she would rest. The capstan would spin, the chains would unfurl, and the oars would propel the ship forward. Then, in an instant, the entire miserable process would be reset, and her suffering would begin anew. Grasping the handle and starting again was the most terrible part, and with each inaugural heave, Marbuck's certainty of pending failure grew. One of them would be unable to continue soon, and would incur Mordwand's wrath. Though her faith in the Void-God had evaporated the instant she'd learned that Baylis had produced a shade, she now found herself praying, not for a deliverance that she knew wouldn't come, but for one of the other two to collapse before she did. It was a horrendous thing to wish for, but she could not help it, and her guilt was extreme.

With phantom lights obscuring her vision, which had dwindled to a dark and fuzzy tunnel, Marbuck realized that her prayers were not going to be answered. Her limbs felt as if they'd turned to lead, and the sounds of their misery had grown distant and muffled. Try as she might, even the knowledge that she was about to be brutally beaten could not keep her on her feet. As the world began to slide out from under her, a booming voice cut through the haze. Someone pushed past her, grabbed the lever, and shoved her away. Stumbling over her own feet, she fell backward into the arms of another, who whirled her around. Bolenz's face filled the narrow cone of her vision.

"Careful, there, I've got you," he said, his voice sounding as if it were coming to her from a great distance. Marbuck's relief at being momentarily released from her misery was so great that she felt a sick gratitude toward Bolenz, who was now supporting her wasted body. "Your labors are finished for now. You and your mates performed admirably. When you decide to join the crew, work like that will certainly elevate you in my esteem."

Marbuck struggled to sift through his words. She knew that what he said was objectionable, but she did not have the capacity to formulate a response. Instead, she allowed him to guide her toward the ladder, where distorted faces materialized out of the fog. Hands lifted her and she emerged from the stagnant compartment into the open airflow of the deck. It revitalized her somewhat, and she was slightly more cognizant of her shambling steps back toward the bow. She managed to fumble down the ladder of the fore hatch on her own, and, as she returned to the brig, she became aware that Falstaff and Tannahill were with her. Once they'd entered their cell, all three of them collapsed to the floor, their ragged breaths filling the space.

Eventually, Marbuck became aware of Old Stitch standing in the doorway. "I warned you," he said. "I'm amazed that you all survived; the resolve you showed was incredible. Still, resolve can only carry you so far. You won't survive the next shift, and it will begin soon enough. You need this. Take it." He tossed a canvas sack into the cell, the contents spilling out across the floor as it landed.

The light of the passageway was nearly snuffed out as Old Stitch shut the door, but Marbuck did not need the full light to know what was lying before her. Scattered around a new waterskin were several hunks of dried human flesh. In the semi-darkness, the three prisoners clawed across the floor toward the bounty. Without discussion, they passed around the waterskin, soothing their parched mouths and ragged throats. Once the water was depleted, they lingered in desperate hesitation. Ultimately, each had already made their decision, and they only waited for some sign that the others would fall with them.

Almost in unison, each of the slaves seized a chunk of meat, and their abhorrent feast began.

Marbuck's mouth exploded with saliva the moment she sank her teeth into the meat. The rational center of her brain had been muted, replaced with an animalistic bliss. Horrifically, the meat tasted incredible, and in no time at all, she'd moved onto a second piece, then a third. As her tremendous hunger finally began to subside, cruel realization settled on her like a mantle. Huddled together, gnawing on every last scrap of meat, they had been reduced to wretched scavengers of the dead, feasting on whatever scraps their masters tossed them.

Having finished, they slumped on the floor, a shameful silence filling the space. Marbuck felt completely annihilated, unable to do anything but curl into a ball as her stomach, suddenly inundated with meat, cramped fiercely. She wanted to scream, and wail, and weep, and rage, but she did nothing. Beneath her, the ship continued its swaying; the oars now manned by the slavers, though she doubted their shifts were so long. Still, they must have found the work odious too.

Numbness stole over her, and her mind, freed from hunger and given a respite from physical strain, began to rise above her humiliation and coalesce around this new thought. Bolenz's crew performed the same backbreaking tasks as his slaves, and, in fact, the newest members of the crew essentially were slaves, and were beaten as such. The scourging of Luden, who'd clearly believed that he'd bought his safety with his blood, must have been a stark reminder to Castor and Devonshire of their true positions on the ship. Surely, the seeds of resistance had been sown as they watched Luden be reduced to a bloody heap. And Gomulte, who appeared to be a seasoned crew member, had seemed repulsed by the wanton violence. In her melancholy, ruined face, there had existed a seed of dissension. Marbuck thought, too, of Chrisholm, who'd disagreed with Bolenz's decisions from the start, and of the sadness in the eyes of Old Stitch.

Perhaps, should manipulating Bolenz into taking them north prove to be untenable, there was another option after all. Cracks existed in the crew, and, should the scales tip against Bolenz, control of the ship might be seized. If a mutiny could be orchestrated, and things played out right, Marbuck could order them northward herself.

CHAPTER 5

Through the countless cycles of her new existence, Marbuck held fast to one thought: she would take the *Empress's Love* north and return to Elibeth. As she languished in the brig, she tried to conceive of ways to urge Bolenz to turn the ship around. Working the oars, she imagined scenarios in which her captors were convinced to follow her, and Bolenz was mercilessly deposed.

Her time at the oars, while still laborious and exhausting, no longer pushed her to the absolute limits of her endurance. With each shift, occurring at random intervals and lasting for ever-changing durations, she became more accustomed to the work. More so, though she hated to admit it to herself, she owed the restoration of her vitality to the meat.

After the first feeding, she'd made no further attempts to refuse the flesh. The best she could manage was to eat less, although that had more to do with the reduced size of the rations and her desire to avoid stomach cramping than any moral holdouts. Falstaff and Tannahill also continued to eat the flesh, and the three of them always ate in utter silence, chewing mechanically, an air of detached humiliation hanging over them. In all of their time together, they never discussed their submission.

They did, however, discuss Marbuck's two plans. Yet, for all their furtive whisperings, they could not conceive of any way to advance either plot. Marbuck hadn't had any other private encounters with Bolenz, and to approach any slaver, even their former crewmates, based on a hunch, was deemed too risky.

As such, they remained in a holding pattern, waiting for some sign to act, all while the *Empress's Love* churned ever on toward some unknown destination. Floating in the darkness, with just the faintest hint of the eastern shoreline visible off the port side, Marbuck could only guess at how long it had been since they'd left Vin-Sadavat. Time meant nothing now; her life consisted only of consuming her rations, trying to escape into sleep, and toil. There was more work to complete than just the turning of the capstans, and Marbuck found those occasional instances when she was set to some other task to be almost pleasurable compared to the drudgery of the oars.

In the quiet shadows of the orlop deck, she found the closest thing to freedom still allowed to her. She'd been assigned to operate the bilge pump, a solitary role removed from Mordwand and the threat of his whip, and she relished this brief taste of privacy. The pump was simple to work, and as she spun the wheel, she began to drift into a blend of memory and fantasy. The rocking of the ship became the rocking of a small fishing dinghy. Baylis and Elibeth were there; he'd been teaching her how to fish. She couldn't have been more than five long-cycles of age, and after concise instructions from Baylis on the art of casting, she had hurled her entire fishing pole into the water with gusto. The shock on his face, and the beaming grin on hers, had made Marbuck laugh until she'd cried. She could almost believe that they were out there now, their little dinghy bobbing on the water, just waiting for her.

"Fishwife," a voice murmured, puncturing her moment of peace. She turned to find Castor lurking behind her. Their hard living had caused him to shed some weight, but he still retained his slouching, doughy shape. Standing nearly a head taller than him, she had a clear view of his pale scalp through the wisps of his thinning hair. He'd taken to wearing a strip of cloth tied across his face, covering his open wound. It had done nothing to reduce the disgust she felt toward him, and had actually elicited sneering laughter from the other slavers, who couldn't understand why he would cover such a blessing from the Empress, one of the last she'd been able to give.

"Yes?" Marbuck said, returning to her work.

"We haven't really had much of an opportunity to talk."

"I had nothing to say to you before all of this. I certainly don't have anything to say to you now." She continued to work the wheel, and, when he hadn't said anything, she began to hope that he'd left.

"I don't understand your hostility," he said, his continued presence disappointing her. "Baylis and I were close friends. All I've ever tried to do is extend that same friendship to you."

A sour anger began to course through Marbuck, and she redoubled her efforts at the wheel.

"I can still help you," he purred.

"Help me? The way you helped yourself by submitting to that monster? Pardon me, but you don't seem to be in a position to help anyone."

"I am a member of this crew," Castor said, his voice taking an authoritative edge. "You are a slave."

Marbuck surprised herself by laughing at this. She released the wheel and turned again to face her erstwhile crewmate. "You fancy yourself my master? Is that it?"

"My old offer still stands. The circumstances have changed, but it still stands." He extended his hand, offering her a large piece of meat. "I can provide for you."

The involuntary rumbling of her stomach failed to cow her. She had endured countless overtures from this ugly little man, one who repeatedly claimed friendship with Baylis but had eagerly sought to replace him. Baylis had barely been shepherded before Castor first offered to take her as a wife, with promises of financial security in exchange for bearing his seed. It had been disgusting and insulting, both to her, and to the memory of her husband. When Marbuck went on to fill Baylis's role on the *Fortune*, Castor had chafed under the authority of a woman he'd hoped would be his prize. Now, as he'd said, their circumstances had changed, yet to him, it was apparently just another chance to try to worm his way between her legs.

Before she could stop herself, she smacked the meat from his hand, causing him to recoil. "*Get the fuck away from me.* You are a filthy, cowardly piece of shit, and you were *always* ugly, but fuck, look at you now." She laughed again, a throaty chuckle she hardly recognized. "You have no power here; you're as much a slave as I am. You sold yourself for *nothing.*"

With unexpected force, Castor lunged against her, pinning her against the bilge wheel. As she raised her arms to fight back, he pressed a dagger against her throat. "Now you listen here, you ungrateful *cunt*. I'm tired of looking. You *will* be mine, like you always should have been. I'd have made you a proper lady; you and your little girl could have been living easy by my hand. You wouldn't be here now, but, because of your own stubbornness, you are. Now, you've got no choice; I'm the only way you'll continue to live on this ship. Now, drop your pants."

This did not frighten Marbuck, for as he'd spoken, a new idea had unfurled itself in her mind, purging even the fear of the dagger.

"What do you think the Commodore would think of his lowliest servant soiling his property? I belong to him now, not you, and he's made it clear that I am the object of his conquest. He wishes to make me submit, to ask for his knife … and more. This," she said, her eyes flicking down toward Castor's dagger, "is apparently beneath him. I can't imagine he would tolerate it from you."

Castor's ragged breaths filled the space. Perspiration, mingling with whatever fluid was leaking from beneath the rag, stood out on his upper lip. He blinked several times and then released her, stepping away quickly as if the touch of her could burn him. She supposed, in a way, it could. Bolenz had promised her that she was untouchable and by invoking the threat of his wrath, it had proven to be true. With no small satisfaction, Marbuck felt the weight of power shift perceptibly in her favor.

"If what you say is true, Fishwife, you'll wish that you'd chosen to be with me," Castor said. "The Commodore might protect you now, but he'll grow tired of your insolence. And when he's done with you, then it will be my turn."

He smiled wickedly, and Marbuck knew that he was perfectly suited to this new existence. He'd been a rotten creature all along, constrained only by the laws of a functioning society. Now, he'd been unmasked.

Before Marbuck could express her loathing, a piercing, inhuman scream echoed from the deck above them. It could have only one source.

Eager for the status quo to be upset in any way that might advance her plots, Marbuck shoved past Castor without a second thought and leapt up the ladder. Her former crewmate, the rejected suitor turned would-be rapist, remained behind, trembling in the dark.

• • •

It did not take her long to locate the source of the commotion. As soon as she passed through the hatch above her, she emerged into a scene of chaos. The ladder had led her into a small compartment adjacent to the oar room, and, as she rose, Tannahill and Devonshire rushed by her, jostling each other for a spot on the ladder leading up to the main deck.

She did not have long to reflect on the lack of fortitude amongst the guardsmen. Through the open door of the oar room, she could see the slithering bulk of a shade rising from the deflated husk of Luden's blood-ied body. He'd never really recovered from his first beating, despite Old Stitch's efforts, and it appeared that he'd just received a second one. Only, this time, there would be no chance of recovery. Mordwand had gone too far, and now he would pay the price for his barbarity. He'd seized a lantern and was swinging it, and his whip, wildly at the shade. The monster paid no mind to the whip, and though it instinctively flinched back from the flame, it seemed to be testing its limits. Mordwand was cornered, and his desperation was obvious. Enthralled, Marbuck remained on the ladder, watching with hateful pleasure as the slaver's doom approached.

From above her, descending footsteps rattled the ladder. She stepped off, making room for the arrival of Bolenz, followed by Karant, Torde-naar, and Usso. As they filled the tight space, she shrank back against the bulkhead.

"Light your torches, now," Bolenz ordered.

"But we could set the whole ship ablaze," Usso said.

Bolenz seized him by the collar. "Then be careful," he growled. He thrust Usso away and turned to the others. "We need to drive it up the ladder and overboard before it wrecks the oars."

Ignored or unnoticed, Marbuck watched as the slavers used a lantern to hastily ignite the torches they'd brought with them. Despite their obvious fear, they worked with a practiced efficiency that she assumed was born from experience; after all, herding the shades with fire was their only method of dealing with them. How often they had to drive them up from below deck, she had no way of knowing, but based on Usso's reaction, it was perhaps a rare event.

Torches lit, they stepped into the threshold just as the shade took an exploratory swipe at Mordwand, who cried out in terror. In addition to the blazing torch he bore, Bolenz had drawn his blade which glinted in the brightness of the fires. Marbuck's eyes locked onto it, and she struggled to comprehend its presence. Without a doubt, she was looking at the work of a shepherd's hand; an anointed blade, a talisman of another life she'd known long ago.

The slavers began to encircle the shade and cautiously wave their torch-es toward it, rescuing Mordwand from what would've certainly been a grue-some death. It soon became clear that Bolenz did not know the power of what he possessed. He held the blade tightly by his side, favoring the torch. He must have assumed that, like all conventional weapons, it would be useless against the shade, accept maybe as a last resort to deflect an attack.

Marbuck watched the delicate dance of the slavers as they sought to expel the shade while trying to keep their flames from igniting the entire compartment, and, before she knew what she was doing, she began to approach Usso, who lingered further back than the others.

"Give me your torch," she demanded.

Usso turned to her, too confused by her sudden presence at his side to say anything. She reached out and snatched the torch from him, and he made no attempt to retain it. The other slavers, preoccupied with the shade, hadn't seemed to notice her yet. Ordered thought had faded away, replaced by a strange certainty that rose from her subconscious. This was the path forward; this was the way back to Elibeth.

She stepped toward the shade, the torch leveled before her the way she'd once been taught to hold a blade. Though she'd forgotten, or disregarded, the rituals of the shepherds, she could still recall the physical training she'd received. It was too late to snuff the shade out in its infancy, but destroying it was still possible. All she needed was the blade.

With a primal cry she lunged forward, bashing the torch against the shade's left shoulder. Screeching, it swung at her, but she had already leapt away and swung the torch again, this time clipping the shade's leg. It was a weak hit, and she scrambled away before the shade could retaliate. She knew that she was being reckless, but Bolenz had to see that she was willing to do more than just prod the shade; she was trying to kill it.

Risking a glance backward, Marbuck saw that Bolenz and the others remained in a loose circle around her, making no move to interfere. The Commodore wore an expression of impressed amusement, and that was good.

With the shade lurching toward her, Marbuck ducked beneath a chain and circled around a capstan, putting it between them. Now focused entirely on her, the shade tried to follow, tangling its protruding mockery of a head in the chains. Flanking it, Marbuck buried her torch into its back, extinguishing the flame deep within the fetid tissue of the shade's torso. The handle of the torch snapped, and Marbuck threw it at the shade as she backed away. She was now weaponless, and though her harassment had stunned the shade, it had not stopped it.

"Your blade!" she shouted at Bolenz. "It's an anointed blade, a weapon of my people that can kill the shades. Give it to me, and I can do it."

It was an incredible gamble; she'd essentially just told him that she could do the impossible. Bolenz, with all eyes locked on him, looked at the sword in his hand, then back at her. The shade began to pull free from the chains.

"Now!" she shouted, her open hand extended toward her captor.

Karant scoffed. "Commodore, she is an uncut, you cannot—"

"Take it. Show me what you can do," Bolenz said, flipping the blade around and offering her the handle. She grabbed it, but he held fast to the hilt. "If she tries anything, maim her, but do not kill her. I will make sure death remains her only hope." He smiled and released his grip.

Marbuck, the blade of a shepherd in her hands once again, turned toward the shade just as it extricated itself. She thought nothing of Bolenz's threats; her attention was focused on the task at hand. With a clumsiness born of fury, the shade shambled toward her. She took a deep, steadying breath, and, as the shade reared up for a killing blow, she flitted to the side and lopped off its right arm in one, decisive strike. The shade flailed backward, putrid blood firing from the wound, and howled. Marbuck wasted no time; she slammed the blade into the exposed right side of the shade, nearly cleaving it in two. The creature, slipping in its own foul ichor, collapsed to the floor and began to dissolve into a horrid puddle.

It was silent, save for the soft hiss of the shade's final dissolution. Then, a noise that Marbuck never would have expected suddenly filled the space: cheers. She looked about her with wonder. Aside from Mordwand, who looked as if he was having trouble comprehending the fact that he was still alive, the slavers were jubilant. They jumped up and down and clapped their hands like gleeful children. Bolenz roared with inarticulate joy, and the others hooted their own pleasure. Marbuck remained riveted to the floor, her thoughts wandering down her arms to the blade still clutched in her hands. At almost the exact moment she began to consider her next move, Bolenz raised a fist and the slavers grew silent.

"Something momentous has happened here," Bolenz said. "A power beyond even that of the Empress, bless her. This uncut from a distant land has shown us that the treasure I reaped from our fallen brother Davhal's horde is more than just a well-crafted sword. It is a magic of the old world, a memory from the time before the Black Water swallowed the ring of blinding fire. With this blade, I can free us from the fear of the shades forever."

The slavers cheered again, and Marbuck became aware that more had gathered in the doorway, drawn by the conflict and the joyful noise that had followed it.

"And I cannot speak too highly of this uncut," Bolenz said, beaming at Marbuck. "Though she has yet to see our truth and pledge herself to our cause, she has fought admirably against a foe that makes even the strongest of us waver. I am not only impressed, I am humbled. Now, if you don't mind." He held his hand out toward her.

Her grip tightened on the hilt. She was now armed with a weapon she knew. Through some divine scheme, or sheer luck, a shepherd's blade had become a slaver's trophy. That weapon had then made its way to her, here, now, in this moment. It was possible that she could kill Bolenz, but what would follow? Would the slavers and their captives, freed from their master, simply kneel to her? It seemed much more likely that she would be overwhelmed and hacked apart by the rest of Bolenz's crew. Undoubtedly, she had made some important gains. Prudence directed her to wait. As much as she wished to lash out, it would cost her everything.

Reluctantly, she turned the blade and offered it to Bolenz. He watched her intently, as if expecting some sort of trick, then took it. Marbuck felt a physical ache of sorrow as the blade, which had briefly seemed like the key to her deliverance, slipped from her fingers. Bolenz held the blade before him, admiring the smears of black blood on the otherwise pristine metal. He hoisted it above his head and the slavers erupted into another round of cheers.

"Come, Marbuck. I wish to host you in my cabin for a private celebration," Bolenz said, sheathing the blade and clapping her on the shoulder. "And don't worry, my original statements still stand. You'll be quite safe with me."

He began to guide her toward the ladder, and the slavers parted before them, still clapping. Behind them, Karant issued an order to clean up the sodden mess left behind by the shade. Marbuck considered warning them about the possibility of growing ill from the foul remains, but she decided she'd rather let the slavers take their chances.

As they reached the ladder and began to ascend, Marbuck looked down. Castor clung to the lower rungs, just below the hatch to the orlop deck. He watched her rise with the Commodore, his face burning with envy.

• • •

Back in Bolenz's private cabin, Marbuck found that she no longer had any qualms about accepting a drink. She'd taken extraordinary risks and emerged not only unscathed, but apparently rewarded. The drink that Bolenz set before her had certainly been earned, and she was nearly certain that it was safe to consume.

She sipped the dark liquor and savored its bite. It tasted of rum, but somehow richer. She wondered if it predated the slavers, as this type of distilling seemed beyond their reach. It was possible that the spirit slowly spreading its calming warmth through her frayed nerves had been bottled while the sun still touched Vin-Sadavat.

"It's good, isn't it?" Bolenz asked. He'd been watching her drink, apparently eager to see her reaction.

"Yes, it's excellent," she said, unable to muster the energy to conceal her enjoyment.

"I thought you'd like it." He sipped his own glass and sighed contentedly. "I'm glad that things are not so contentious between us this time. You seem to have acclimated to life aboard the *Empress's Love* somewhat, no?"

Marbuck looked at him over her glass, uncertain of how to answer.

"Yet, I sense you would still refuse to join my crew?"

"That's correct," she said, careful to keep her tone neutral.

Bolenz sighed again. "That is disappointing. You've already shown me that you possess a fortitude that is rare in this world. I meant it when I said I was impressed. Should you join me, I imagine Karant would very quickly have some stiff competition for my favor. I mean, you faced that shade as if it were just another brigand. Even *I* fear the unworthy dead. Are you certain I cannot sway you?"

Despite everything, Marbuck found herself enjoying the stroking of her ego. Her actions had changed their dynamic completely; Bolenz had started with threats and was now politely requesting that she reconsider her stance.

For a terrifying moment, she did. Her mind scrubbed away his scarred flesh and the memory of his promised atrocities. He'd become reminiscent of Winslow, and she was flattered by his praise and desired his respect. In a perverse way, her bid to earn his trust had ceased to be an act. She saw herself submitting to him and being elevated from a slave to his closest advisor; a partnership of mutual respect in which she would have no problem getting him to order the ship north. He'd almost certainly spare her from the oars, and before she knew it, she'd be back in Nordabor with Elibeth. Yet, the being that returned to Elibeth would not be the same one who left. Would her daughter even recognize the mutilated cannibal who claimed to be her mother?

This thought returned her to herself. She'd lost so much of her humanity already; she would not go further. However desperate she became, she would never take that final step.

"I will not be swayed," she said.

Bolenz seemed to sense that there was some minor defect in her resolve and was content with that knowledge. A small smirk tugged at the corners of his mouth, and he took a sip. Marbuck felt soiled, ruined by the knowledge of what she'd imagined, however briefly. She looked down before she could stop herself, her matted, filthy hair dragging across the tabletop. Realizing that she was losing her advantage, she gulped the rest of her drink and assumed an expression of casual defiance. Bolenz remained maddeningly amused.

"Well, crewmember or not, I may have a new use for you."

"And what might that be?" she asked, conscious of the wobbling scales of her position.

Bolenz finished off his drink and smacked his lips. "Before long, we shall be arriving in an exotic port, a trading post of old. I've done some business there before, secured cargo for the Empress when my own hunts proved less than fruitful." He grimaced slightly, as if the admission of this shortcoming had put a sour taste in his mouth. "The leader of this outpost, Midga, is not like us. He, and the rabble he rules over, are of a less civilized stock. They're known as skinners, and they split from the Empress generations ago, rejecting the true faith and choosing instead a life of heresy. We share common ancestry though, and the Empress always mourned their departure. Bleeding heart that she was, she retained trade with them, instead of annihilating them for their insolence."

Listening to the political history of a people that had long ago succumbed to madness slathered in a religious veneer, struck Marbuck as both fascinating and absurd, and the fact that Bolenz could denigrate the skinners as 'less civilized' was disturbing. Whatever this Midga and his followers did was apparently too much for a man who wore a cloak of human scalps.

"My point is, though Midga has received us cordially enough before, there is reason for caution. Particularly, because I intend to bring him under my banner, and he may be reluctant to show fealty. You ought to understand that." He smiled warmly, but with a shadow of malice.

"And you want me to *navigate* you through the social niceties of this visit?" Marbuck asked.

Bolenz laughed with genuine mirth. "Very clever, but no. I intend to utilize your skills as a mariner once we depart again. At that point,

I'll expect you to guide me to new lands, rife with opportunity. For now, I want you to come along as part of my escort."

"Escort?" she asked, her thoughts lingering on the possibility that, should they survive this strange port, she would have her chance to head north.

"Yes. Your unmarked skin will be an enticing distraction for Midga, and it very well might lead him to join me, just for the pleasure of your company alone."

Marbuck's look of revulsion was immediate, and Bolenz held up a placating hand. "Nothing like that. You still have my word in that regard. But, of course, Midga won't know that." He smiled again. "More so, I want you to come along for my protection."

The mental whiplash of their conversation, combined with her exhaustion and the effects of the drink, had started to take its toll on her. Sluggishly, her mind sought whatever pathway would benefit her the most. She decided that death, should Bolenz's visit go poorly, would not benefit her at all. "Surely, there are plenty aboard who will assist you with this task; you don't need me. I'm no warrior."

"Perhaps not, in the traditional sense, but you demonstrated your skills quite plainly in facing that shade. I want that talent—that *hidden* talent—to accompany me."

Marbuck could feel her mind overheating with the strain of sifting through the possibilities before her. Wrong choices seemed as numerous as the dead-end distributaries that branched off from the Einfallen, their waters growing shallow and stagnant, promising a deadly quagmire for any vessel that blundered into their grip. If she refused to go with Bolenz, she risked her standing with him, and though he would still need her to navigate, he might refuse her suggestions. But, if she joined him in this envoy and survived to win further acclaim, she might command his ear easily. And there was still the possibility of mutiny. If she remained behind on the ship while he and his escort went ashore, perhaps she could engineer her escape. She was locked in indecision, and she ardently wished that she could have a full-cycle to discuss her options with Falstaff.

Before she could make a choice, Bolenz reminded her that it was never her choice to begin with.

"You will be exempt from working the oars until we arrive," he said. "I'll need you fresh and ready for anything. Karant will fetch you when we're ready to go ashore."

Accepting the path she'd been placed on, a new thought occurred to Marbuck. "As part of your guard, perhaps I should carry the anointed blade."

"You are so very bold; it is delightful," Bolenz said. "But, I'm afraid not. You will remain unarmed, at my side, serving as a prize with which I'll impress our host. Should conditions arise in which I need your talents, I will provide you with the blade, but the same rules apply as before. Any betrayal will cost you dearly. Do you understand?"

Marbuck understood plainly. If she was going to make a move, she'd have to be absolutely certain that it would succeed. "Yes, Commodore, I understand."

"Great, that's really great. You may go."

Their business settled, Marbuck rose on wobbly legs and teetered toward the door, the drink affecting her more than she'd suspected. As she stepped outside, she found Gomulte waiting for her on the short flight of steps leading up to the main deck. Wordlessly, the slaver led Marbuck back toward the brig at the bow of the ship.

As they reached the fore hatch, Gomulte unexpectedly planted a thick hand on Marbuck's shoulder and turned her so that they were face to face. Standing so close together, Marbuck was struck by Gomulte's dull, dark eyes, which reminded her of the pitiable, idiot sadness of mistreated livestock.

"He fancies you," she said in a girlish whisper that was totally at odds with her hulking size. "He fancied me once. Don't wait too long." She touched the puckered skin of her face.

Before Marbuck could question this unexpected confidence, Gomulte thrust open the hatch and ordered her down the ladder as if it'd never occurred. As Marbuck was ushered into the brig, she began to wonder if it really had.

Falstaff was at her side the moment the cell door shut behind her. "Are you okay, Fishwife? What happened out there?" he nearly shouted. Remembering that he'd been in the brig since before Luden had gone shade, she realized that he'd probably been driven half-mad listening to the tumult occurring beyond his prison. Tannahill, who'd also risen from the back of the cell when she'd entered, had witnessed the birth of the shade, but his immediate flight had left him with little in the way of news to impart.

"I'm fine," she said, addressing his first question. The second would take more effort, as her thoughts were currently buzzing around in a confused jumble. She hoped that explaining it might make things seem clearer. She waited until the plodding steps of Gomulte could no longer be heard and then took a deep breath.

"I've got a lot to tell you."

CHAPTER 6

Though Bolenz's visits to the bay of the skinners had been infrequent, he'd been there enough that he recognized the crimson glow rising into the sky from their frontier settlement. It emerged from the blank darkness, painting the curvature of the shoreline and stretching across the water, beckoning him. He stood at the bow, feeling every bit the conqueror he wished to be. The prow of the ship cut through the glassy expanse of the water, occasionally sending a soft spray of sea water misting across him. The air rushed by his ears, cold, damp, and invigorating. He breathed deeply of the night air, detecting a faint hint of the fires on shore.

Like the Empress's city, Bolenz knew that the fires were essential to the survival of the skinners. They provided light, heat, the means to cook, and defense against the shades. That was about where the similarities ended. The seat of the Empress's power had been a metropolis, a bustling and vibrant place far removed from the squalid hovels of those who carved out an existence beyond her realm. The fort maintained by the skinners, in comparison, was laughable.

Despite the opportunities that the fall of the Empress had provided, it was still depressing to know that her city, the heart of her realm, had fallen with her. It made sense, though, when he pondered it. After all, the city had been a magnificent extension of the Empress's power, a part of her that was believed to have been born from her dreams. If it'd even had a name beyond being known simply as the Empress's city, it had been long forgotten by Bolenz's time. It was impossible to imagine the city surviving without her. As such, Bolenz had no interest in trying to reestablish any foothold there. His fortunes resided in new lands; he just had to bring Midga and his rabble into the fold first.

Bolenz smoothed his uniform and fiddled with the clasp of the cloak about his neck. Midga must see him as the epitome of authority. When the skinner king learned that the Empress was gone and Bolenz had assumed the mantle of leadership, there must be no questioning of such a claim. Bolenz knew it wasn't strictly true, as the vacuum left by the death of the Empress, whose apparent immortality had negated the need for rules of succession, had probably set into motion countless claims to the throne, many of which were probably more credible than his own. After all, his claim was known only to him and his crew, and his realm was restricted to one ship. That didn't matter, though. All that mattered was that Midga believed him. With bolstered numbers, Bolenz could eventually nurture the deception into truth. Given the chance, he could turn this one ship into a new empire.

The *Empress's Love* began to slow as she entered the bay, experience informing the actions of Bolenz's crew. The ship's draft was too much for the shallow water ahead of them, and the men knew that they'd need to utilize their longboat to reach the shore. Bolenz couldn't help but feel a paternal warmth for his crew, who'd remained loyal despite his flagging fortunes. They had grown proficient in the workings of the ship, mastering the intricacies of the rigged workings and each performing their duties with vigor. He did not need to order them to slow the oars, or to steer to port; they functioned almost as an extension of his own will.

As the *Empress's Love* eased to a stop, he felt a sudden unwillingness to leave his beloved ship. In this tightly contained universe, everything was within his control. Once he set foot on land, he would be contesting with the will of Midga. His insides tightened as Karant approached.

"We're ready to launch the landing party, Commodore."

Bolenz took a deep breath to steady his nerves and smiled. "Excellent."

They proceeded to the port side, where the men had been busy loading the longboat. Rectangular bundles of tightly-packed human skins had been piled into the boat, leaving little room for the landing party, who were now milling about, awaiting departure. Among them, Bolenz spied the downcast face of the mariner from the north. Her thin arms were folded haughtily across her chest, and Bolenz felt a small tickle of excitement at her obstinance. He knew that she wished everyone to see how much she didn't want to be there, and it was in this conspicuous display of contempt that Bolenz detected a faint hint of secret desire. Her submission was just a matter of time, and witnessing his success with Midga would almost certainly hasten her along.

Satisfied with the gathered tribute, Bolenz ordered the boat to be launched. Mordwand and Usso slowly released the twin winches, lowering the boat onto the flat surface of the water. Now that the *Empress's Love* had stopped, the water had become eerily still, and the touch of the longboat sent concentric ripples lapping against the hull of the ship. Karant unfurled a rope ladder over the railing and descended, joined by Mordwand, Chrisholm, and Usso. The two surviving initiates, Castor and Devonshire, who'd proven to be only slightly more capable than their fallen comrade, followed. Bolenz was hesitant to entrust them with such an undertaking, but saw little choice. Already leaving a skeleton crew behind, he wouldn't dare leave his trusted hands outnumbered by those who only obeyed him out of fear. If anything, the presence of two more men would serve to bolster the illusion that he commanded a large force.

"Your turn," Bolenz said to Marbuck, who'd lingered behind. Her eyes, which were as dark as the inky waters that surrounded them, flicked between him and the ladder, and he wondered what she was considering. Without a word, she swung over the railing and descended. As she slipped from view, Bolenz considered for the first time that she might prove to be more of a distraction for him than for Midga.

"Commodore," Old Stitch said, interrupting his thoughts. "Don't you worry; the *Empress's Love* will be in good hands."

Bolenz clapped him on the shoulder, appreciating the perceptive old man for sensing his unease. "I know it. We'll return soon, bearing good news, I'm sure. Until then, I trust her to you." He gave Old Stitch's shoulder an affectionate squeeze and, the informal passing of command over, approached the rail. Before mounting the ladder, he gazed at the shoreline. Now that they were closer, individual fires could be seen dotting the land of the skinners.

It was a magnificent view, and, should his plan succeed, it would all be his.

• • •

The heavily-laden longboat slid gently to a stop, its bow driving into the soft sand of the beach. Almost immediately, the men dropped their oars and disembarked, their boots splashing into the shallow water. They grasped the gunwales and hauled the boat further onto the beachhead. Only then did Bolenz step onto the sand. He would not approach Midga with wet feet.

He turned and offered his hand to Marbuck. She took it, and he helped her step down from the boat. "Stay close to me," he warned. "Remember, we're outsiders, and there are many here who will find your untouched skin enticing, not just Midga. I'll do what I can to protect you. Should the need arise, I expect the same from you." He patted the blade hanging from his belt.

"I understand," she said, her eyes lingering on the sword.

"Unload the skins," Bolenz ordered. The men set to work, hauling the bundles from the longboat and lining them up on the sand. As Bolenz pondered how best to transport them inland, he became aware of several shadowy figures emerging from the tree line. They were clad in loose, drooping garments, and seemed hesitant to fully abandon the cover of the scrawny, desiccated trees.

"Our host has sent a party to receive us," Bolenz announced, alerting the men. "Stay your hand," he added quietly as Mordwand reached for his axe.

It was not unusual for Midga's followers to meet them at their landing point, but it was still slightly unsettling. The skinners were a strange, furtive lot, wary of outsiders and, as far as Bolenz knew, intolerant of anyone beyond their settlement. It was only the precious skins that bought their hospitality. They'd long shared an economy of violence; the skinners sent captured slaves or surplus children, who could only yield their own skins, to the Empress to serve as new initiates, in exchange for what seemed like a plethora of skins, collected from the countless dead of the Empress's city. It was a mutually beneficial relationship which had caused the Empress to lay aside her animosity, and it ensured that her traders remained unharmed.

Except now, she was gone, and the approaching skinners seemed vaguely threatening. Bolenz wondered if they somehow knew already, if his claims had been undermined from the start. Perhaps some other refugee from the Empress's city had reached Midga's ear first. It was paramount that Bolenz be the one to deliver the news of the Empress's fall. Midga had to see him as the heir, the new embodiment of the realm.

"Hail, friends!" Bolenz called to the skinners. "It is I, the Commodore, and I come bearing gifts for your king." With his thoughts tinged by the recent collapse of his own realm's order, it suddenly occurred to him that Midga might have been relieved of his crown at some point. "Midga is still the sovereign in these lands, no?"

One of the skinners stepped forward, the light of the crew's lanterns painting him orange. "Aye, this is King Midga's land," he confirmed, though the mouth of his adopted face barely moved. His eyes twinkled from deep within the flaccid sockets of his skin mask. Bolenz judged not the heretical practices of the skinners; he was, in fact, somewhat fascinated by them. His time among the savages had inspired his own collection of trophies, stitched together into the cloak upon his back, a cloak that men like Davhal had sneered at. It was strange and interesting that beneath their fleshy suits, crafted from the skins that formed the backbone of their society, their own features were as untouched as Marbuck's. The Empress may have chafed at that defiance, which lucrative trade had forced her to accept, but Bolenz found their peculiarities almost endearing, if a bit backwards. They were a provincial lot, but that would only serve his purposes.

"It gladdens me to hear that," Bolenz said. "Our partnership is an old one, and a vital one, for both of our peoples. I look forward to presenting this gift to your king, if you would be so kind as to escort us to an audience with him."

The skinner peered around Bolenz toward the bundles, the static face of his mask betraying nothing of his thoughts. After a moment, he signaled to his brethren, who scurried to the bundles and began collecting them. "We will take you, and your gift, to the king."

"Thank you."

As the final bundles were hefted, Karant sidled up to Bolenz, who was now out of earshot of the skinners. "So far, so good."

"Yes, though I expected little trouble from them. The real challenge comes next," Bolenz said. He looked at Marbuck, meaning to remind her to stay by his side, and saw a look of horrified disgust on her face. It occurred to him that the customs of the skinners were quite foreign to her. "I see you disapprove of our hosts?"

Her head turned haltingly toward him, as if it were on a rusty hinge. "I had believed that you were the very pinnacle of depravity. Perhaps I was wrong."

"Like I said, they're less civilized," Bolenz said quietly, dropping a wink.

Marbuck frowned, her lips pressing into a thin line. Bolenz imagined erasing that frown with his knife, and he smiled.

With the last of the tribute in hand, the skinners began to lead Bolenz and his crew inland. They marched through the increasingly dense remains of whatever undergrowth had once thrived there, creeping up the narrow trunks of the trees. Though Bolenz had participated in this procession before, he still didn't recognize a single landmark. The pathless, death-tangle of the lifeless jungle around him was a complete mystery. He struggled even to keep his footing, while the barefoot skinners, carrying their cumbersome bundles, managed to move lightly through the bracken. They might not have been able to recite the psalms of the Empress, but their physical prowess could not be denied.

Through the pressing darkness of the trees, a new light began to grow. They moved toward it and, before long, they came before a wooden palisade, in which a gate of bones was set. The skinners opened the gate and proceeded inside, with Bolenz and his men in tow. They had entered the fort, and they emerged onto an open concourse, where a central promenade lined with bonfires lit the space brilliantly. All around them were the huts and longhouses of the skinners. The structures were built into earthen bulwarks and covered with low roofs of timber, upon which were stretched broad sheets of human skin. The dried skins were everywhere; wall coverings, flaps for doorways, curtains, even entire flesh tents that housed the lowest members of their society. Fetishes of bone and hair dangled from wooden poles wrapped in skin that jutted crookedly from the ground, towering idols of the flesh they worshipped. It was a place that, on his previous visits, Bolenz had considered inelegant, but imbued with a sort of rustic charm. This time, he was stricken by the realization that this small community, by the mere fact that it remained while the Empress's city had fallen, was now superior. It was a sobering thought.

Marbuck, on the other hand, appeared to have been stricken with a sudden illness. She stared manically at the modest settlement around her, her eyes darting about the place. Her breath came in short bursts, and Bolenz watched with amused pity as she stifled a dry heave. She seemed on the verge of hysterics, and he pulled her close.

"I know, it's positively garish compared to the Empress's city. Unfortunately, this is what we've been reduced to. You've partaken in some of the same customs that these fine folk enjoy, so do not shudder at their eccentricities. Now get ahold of yourself."

She nodded shakily. "I'll be fine."

"You had better be."

They continued to follow their guides, who led them to a long stall, where several women, or subjects dressed in the skins of women, collected the bundles and began to open and inspect them. There had been a minor leak in the cargo hold, and some of the skins had gotten wet. Bolenz hoped that no rot had set in, spoiling his gift and his credibility. The skinners worked slowly, chatting quietly with each other as they sorted through the bundles. A few broke away from the group and slipped off into the shadows. Bolenz was beginning to grow anxious, his apprehension fed by his impatience. He was familiar enough with the fort that, at this point, he could proceed to Midga's residence without the guides. Yet, he knew it was important to follow their customs, and it might seem presumptive to march ahead, so he continued to wait. His men shifted about, reflecting his own restlessness.

Finally, the lead skinner turned back to them. "A fair gift. King Midga has been told of your coming. Now he will be told of your generosity. A feast will be prepared. Come with me."

• • •

Waiting outside the king's longhouse, Bolenz could smell the meat cooking. It set his thoughts ablaze with images of succulent, dripping cuts of perfectly marbled flesh. After subsisting on dried meats for so long, the potential to enjoy a fresh meal alone was enough to justify their journey to the skinners.

Their guide had left them outside of the longhouse and, parting the thick, leathery drapes of human skin, had disappeared into the gloom inside. It hadn't been long before smoke had started to drift from the open slats on the structure's roof, carrying the intoxicating aroma of the coming meal. Bolenz considered it a good omen that Midga had ordered the food prepared so hastily as it spoke of an eagerness to not only meet with his visitor, but to satisfy him.

As if to confirm this theory, the skinner who'd led them to the longhouse poked his head out of the doorway. "The feast is ready. King Midga is happy to welcome you, most honored of guests." He bowed low and held the curtain open. The crew began to file in, with Bolenz leading the way. As they entered, he placed a hand on Marbuck's lower back to guide her alongside him. He felt her tense, but she did not shove his hand away.

Bolenz entered Midga's court with renewed confidence. His intended paramour was on his arm, he was being received with the greatest of honors, and he was the inheritor of a legacy that he was certain would be built into something greater. The anxiety he had felt before now seemed silly; this was his moment, and he would seize it with tenacity.

Together, he and his crew strode from the small, dark foyer into the central room, which stretched nearly the entire length of the structure. A wide fire pit, ringed by a stone hearth, filled the middle of the space. Roasting on a spit above the flames was the reddened form of a skinless human body. Bolenz glanced at Marbuck and, though she looked repelled, he found that there was something else dancing with the reflected flames in her eyes: hunger. Apparently, her stomach cared not for her moral objections.

Just beyond the fire, the dirt floor rose in a small hump, upon which a throne of twisted branches and pale bones reached toward the ceiling. Sitting upon the throne was the skinner king, and he rose as soon as he saw Bolenz.

"Commodore, how wonderful it is to have you as a guest of my court once again," Midga said. Behind the unmoving, pink lips of his skin mask, his voice sounded hale. Bolenz had no idea how old Midga was, but he'd been the king of the skinners for as long as Bolenz had traveled to their land. He was wearing a different, fresher skin than he'd had at their last meeting, that of a blond-haired young man, but he still bore the same circlet of bone, adorned with seven mummified fingers pointing skyward, that constituted his crown. Bolenz recalled how badly Heilrune had wished to add the skinner crown to his collection, and he stifled a smile, knowing that the fallen champion would never get the chance.

"You look well," Bolenz said, choosing not to address Midga by any title. He did not want to disrespect him by using only his name, but to call him 'lord' or 'sire' would be to show submission to his authority.

"You honor me," Midga said, running his hands, which protruded from beneath the flaccid, boneless fingers of the skin he wore, across the belly of the naked suit. "My skin was prepared for just this occasion. The poor boy that it belonged to had been caught trying to copulate with one of my daughters. Their secret skin is for my touch only. His execution was going to be a simple matter until I was advised that your ship had been spotted approaching our shores. When I learned of your generous gift, I decided that the boy would make a fine feast for us." He sighed contentedly. "His secret skin is still warm, its wetness clings to me in a way that the dried skins never could. I can still taste the sweat upon his lips." Midga's tongue slipped through the slightly parted lips and ran across them.

Bolenz could see plainly why the Empress had considered the skinners to be heretics. Their rituals were grotesque, a desecration of the flesh that left their own skin selfishly untouched. He did not understand what'd led them to their strange ways, but he really didn't care either. Their affairs were their own, and as Marbuck had demonstrated with her obvious hunger for the roasting meat, morality was a flimsy business.

"Well, I consider it a great compliment that you esteem our meetings so highly," Bolenz said.

"Of course, you are an old friend. And who is this?" he asked, his blank face turning toward Marbuck.

"This is my slave; she was journeying from the far north when she was taken."

"She does not bear your Empress's blessing."

"No, not yet," Bolenz said, eager to steer the conversation away from the Empress for the time being.

Midga did it for him. "Well, if you wish to barter her before then, I should love to slip inside such a flawless skin." He laughed merrily. "Come, sit, we can speak of trade later. For now, I implore you and your men to enjoy yourselves."

Enjoy themselves, they did. They sat at a long, narrow table that ran the length of the room, joined by dozens of skinners who'd entered the longhouse, talking excitedly. Before long, the roasted boy had been carved up, and served to the eager men. He did not disappoint; the meat was of such a supple richness that Bolenz could scarcely believe it. Skullcaps filled with human milk, pumped from the nursing mothers of the settlement, blood, and brackish water were passed around and helped to wash down the meat. The skinners proved generous hosts, presenting them with various trinkets and baubles. Eventually, Midga called for the concubines, as was expected at such a gathering. After all, Bolenz and his men provided an important service: impregnating the skinner women. The constant inbreeding of their community often produced sickly young, and the seed of the outsiders helped to freshen the bloodlines. Bolenz thought nothing of the numerous children he may have sired. Like with every visit before, he and his men partook without hesitation, as did the female participants. They almost seemed more eager than the men, separating the rear flaps of their skin suits and greedily mounting the exotic foreigners without so much as a word.

As Bolenz fucked one of the women, the loose skin of her suit shifting beneath his grip with every writhing movement she made, he watched

Marbuck. She'd actually managed to refrain from consuming anything, beyond some of the water. Staring at the dirt floor, she remained completely still, seemingly oblivious to the debauchery around her. Bolenz admired her resolve, and found that his growing respect for her made him want to break her even more.

When their work was complete, the concubines departed, and the festivities finally began to wind down. As the men settled into a satisfied drowsiness, Bolenz joined Midga at the hearth.

"As always, your courtesy has been remarkable."

"And why shouldn't it be?" Midga asked. Sitting this close to him, Bolenz caught a glimpse of his actual mouth within the suit. It was slick with blood. "We have long been allies of your Empress. Since my forebears immigrated to this land, our two realms have always enjoyed a loving peace."

Bolenz nodded along. "That long alliance is actually the reason I'm here. I seek to strengthen it in a way that neither of us has seen in our lifetimes."

Midga's false face stared at him. "I'm listening."

This was it, the time to venture forth with his proposition. Bolenz cleared his throat. "I am suggesting reconciliation, a unification of our people."

Leaning back, Midga inhaled a long, slow breath through his nose. The drooping face of the mask pulled slightly inward. "I have made it quite clear that my people and I do not share the same beliefs as you and your kin. I respect the Empress, but I will not worship her, nor will I permit any of my people's secret skin to be sullied in her name," he said, his voice rising.

"You misunderstand me. I'm not asking you to do any of that; I'm only seeking your loyalty in a new venture." Bolenz paused, his heart suddenly thudding against his ribs. "Under my banner."

Midga's head tilted quizzically. "Your banner?"

"Yes."

"Then you have renounced your Empress?"

"Not exactly. She … has fallen," Bolenz said quietly, growing suddenly aware that the ambient murmurs of the crowd had died away.

"What? How?"

"She was assassinated by agents of a foreign land."

With a scoff of disbelief, Midga turned toward the fire.

"Tragic as it was, it has altered the nature of her realm in ways that might interest you. I do not demand the same rituals that she did."

Midga's head whipped back toward him. "You? Oh, I see. You have succeeded her." He sighed. "So, the realm still stands, and under the direction of a new leader. Interesting. Well, I will have to consider your offer, but, for now, I am content with our current partnership." He started to rise.

"Wait," Bolenz said, placing a hand on one of his slick arms. "Our current partnership is, regrettably, no longer tenable. With the Empress, the old ways have been lost as well. Her city fell with her, and much of her order has given way to anarchy. Though her realm, in the traditional sense, is now lost to us, I intend to lead us into *new* lands, ones overflowing with simple folk who will be unable to resist our combined forces. They will be our slaves, our food, and, finally, your skins. Under my direction, we will colonize the world. We could even take the lands still touched by the light, far beyond the Black Water. And, of course, you will still be the master of your own folk, beholden to none but me."

It was now silent in the longhouse. All eyes were on the two of them.

"A generous offer," Midga said. "I am hung up on a single point, though. Why can't our original arrangement stand? Surely your new order has an appetite to match the old? City or no city, you and the loyal legions you still command must desire slaves. After all, I would think that expansion, particularly of the world-conquering type, would require them. Have you not the hunger for new servants that the Empress had? Or are you simply no longer able to hold up her end of the bargain?"

A sour sweat broke out across Bolenz's back. Midga had sniffed out the truth of the matter, and, with his prying questions, Bolenz's hopes dwindled. "Due to our new circumstances, we will not be able to provide you with any more skins, beyond what we just gave you," he admitted. "However, should you join me—"

"Enough," Midga said, raising his hand. "You have come here pretending that all is well and partaken of my generosity, only to try to sell me a fantasy masquerading as an opportunity. All I have heard is that the Empress is dead, her city has been laid to ruin, and you are now a beggar claiming her crown. And you step into my hallowed hall, where I have fed you, and tell me that I will be beholden to *you*? Perhaps you consider me a fool."

"No, I didn't mean—"

"*But most importantly,*" Midga shouted over him, rising to his feet. "Most importantly, you can no longer provide me with skins. My people will have to rely on our own harvest." He raised his arms in a shrug and looked about the room. "It appears that you have nothing to offer. What use are you to me?"

Bolenz's face burned with humiliation, and he struggled to master himself. "I regret that you feel that way. Thank you for your hospitality. My men and I will depart your lands, and leave you to your own devices."

Midga chuckled. "Oh, don't be so hasty. I can actually think of one more use for you. I mourn for the passing of your Empress, ally of old. In fond remembrance, I will commission a beautiful tapestry to commemorate our long history together.

"The skins of her last refugees will serve as the canvas."

CHAPTER 7

For the length of a breath, nobody moved. Then, violence erupted. Having spent the entirety of the feast blocking out everything around her, Marbuck had barely been listening to the two deviants singing each other's praises. Only when the tone had shifted, and a threatening silence had ballooned within the longhouse, had she started to really pay attention. Midga's declaration caught her off guard, and she'd barely processed his words before the skinners attacked.

Marbuck lunged to the ground and rolled beneath the table as their erstwhile hosts set upon them. She was weaponless, hemmed in on all sides by savage ghouls, with escape her only option. She crawled through the dirt beneath the table, squinting through the gloom and kicked-up dust, seeking some exit. Shadows danced as the combatants moved across the light of the fire. Screams shredded the air, and a body slammed onto the table above her, sending hot blood pattering down onto her head through the cracks between the wooden boards. She looked for Bolenz, hoping for a chance to get her hands on the shepherd's blade, but he'd disappeared in the turmoil. So much for his grandiose schemes.

Reaching the end of the table, Marbuck looked around for a way out. Behind her, the percussive pop of a bursting skullcap rose above the din. Cries of panic and the piercing shriek of a shade joined the dreadful chorus of bloodshed. The skinners must have expected an easier fight and a more controlled environment in which to drive any possible shades away. Now, skinner or slaver, they all faced the prospect of a deadly loss of balance. Left unchecked, the shades would soon outnumber them all. If only she could get her hands on the blade.

Abandoning any hope of wading back into the fight and finding it, Marbuck clambered out from beneath the table and ran toward the nearest wall. She dived onto her hands and knees and started to manically dig away at the dirt, pausing only to throw an occasional glance back over her shoulder. Behind her, reckless attempts to drive back the shade with torches had caught part of another wall on fire. The flames licked up the dry wood, racing toward the ceiling of stretched skin. Two more shades could be heard rising from the bodies of the fallen.

Casting aside handfuls of dry earth, Marbuck sought the bottom edge of the wall. She hoped that the structure, which had obviously been built by the skinners, would have a shallow foundation. With a flood of relief, her searching fingers slipped beneath the bottom edge. Ripping more of the dirt away, she felt the coolness of the air outside. Inside the longhouse, the fire was spreading, and the air was growing hotter and smokier. As Marbuck cleared enough of the dirt to worm her way out, the flames reached the skin ceiling, which came down in a rain of sparks, blanketing those inside in burning death.

Coughing, Marbuck scrambled to her feet. With stinging eyes, she looked around, trying to find her bearings. She'd been lucky; the section of the longhouse she'd escaped from had been built upon flat ground. Further along, the structure receded into an earthen mound, one she'd never have been able to dig through. With the fire engulfing the structure, she saw others coming to the same conclusion that she had. Puffs of dirt were being expelled from multiple points along the wall where desperation had forced those inside to dig. The flat sound of weapons bashing against the inside of the wall reminded her of Mordwand smashing their way out of the burning ship in Vin-Sadavat. In another moment, she would not be alone. Whether those who emerged were her attackers or her keepers, she did not wish to receive them.

She slipped into the shadows between two huts and crept hastily along, seeking for a way out of the fort. All around her, strange cries rang out. She assumed they functioned as some sort of warning system, or a way for the skinners to alert each other if they were in need of aid. She spied several figures hustling toward the burning longhouse with sloshing buckets of water. It did not seem likely that there would be enough water in whatever reservoir the skinners used to rescue their king's home. Or their king for that matter. Marbuck sincerely hoped that he'd burned.

"*Fishwife*," a voice hissed from a darkened doorway, causing Marbuck to momentarily seize up with shock and fear. "It's me." Castor stepped into the light, and Marbuck's surprise gave way to wariness.

"Don't touch me," she said as Castor reached out a hand. He yanked it back.

"Of course. I'm sorry for my behavior before; that's not who I am. But we can talk about that later. Right now, I think I can get us out of here. Take this." He held a crude dagger out to her, and, before he could find a reason to turn it on her instead, she took it. "I managed to get out through the front as soon as the fighting started. I took that off one I killed."

Marbuck sensed that this was meant to impress her. It did not.

"I didn't think there was any chance that you were still alive, otherwise I would have—"

"Stop," she said, uninterested in his bullshit chivalry. "What's your plan?"

"Well," he said, pausing to sniff wetly, "the outer fence is just beyond these huts and over that bulwark. I think we can climb over it and slip away while they're all distracted. We can head north. We can go home."

Ignoring the obvious problems with Castor's plan, such as how far they would need to travel through unknown lands with no food or water, the idea of finally being free, totally and completely free, from the slavers was undeniably appealing. Yet, Castor was one of them now, in deed if not in heart. Once they were clear of danger, he would become the danger. More than anything, though, she knew that if she fled into the wilds now, she would be abandoning Falstaff. He and Tannahill remained locked in the brig of the *Empress's Love*. Even if Bolenz never returned to his ship, his remaining crew would carry on his legacy of violence.

"No," Marbuck said as a new plan unspooled itself within her mind. "I'm going back to the ship."

"Are you mad? Why won't you just come with me? Why must you be so difficult? We're finally free!"

"No, we're not. We'd never make it anywhere near Nordabor. Not without a ship."

"Are you suggesting we seize the ship?" He suddenly sounded conspiratorial.

Marbuck regretted sharing her true thoughts with someone whose allegiances had shifted so easily. "I'm going back for Falstaff and Tannahill. You may pursue your own ends; good luck on your journey north."

She turned away, intending to find the gate they'd entered through, and hoping that Castor wouldn't follow. Unfortunately, he trotted after her. "Whatever you're planning, I'm in."

Wishing she'd held her tongue in front of him, she said nothing. The two of them weaved their way between the huts until they reached the main thoroughfare, some distance from the burning longhouse. The building had collapsed, and a tremendous fire now reached skyward, its pillar of smoke seeming to merge with the clouds above. What appeared to be the entire population of the skinners still rushed about the foot of the blaze, leaving the thoroughfare deserted.

Scanning the space, Marbuck was able to recall which direction they'd entered from. As she began to cross the promenade with Castor trailing behind her, she became aware that a throng of people had broken away from the crowd and were coming their way, accompanied by the continuing sounds of battle. Reaching the eaves of a longhouse on the other side of the space, Marbuck and Castor turned to watch.

To her amazement, she saw that Bolenz was still alive. Soaked in blood and now bereft of his cloak, he stood back-to-back in a tight circle with Mordwand, Usso, and Devonshire, the four of them shuffling as quickly as they could toward the gate. Numerous skinners harassed them, trying to penetrate their defense. What truly held them at bay was astounding; Bolenz was driving a shade ahead of them, prodding it with the shepherd's blade and a burning piece of timber, using it as a wedge to push through the encroaching skinners, urging it in whichever direction they were amassing. Marbuck could not help but be impressed with his audacity. Further back, at least three other shades could be seen flailing through the crowd, sowing chaos.

As they neared the spot where Marbuck and Castor were hiding, the attackers began to thin out. Abruptly, Bolenz cast aside the burning timber and charged toward the gate, seizing on the opening. The other three slavers raced after him.

"They're making a break for it, we've got to join them," Castor said.

Mere short-cycles ago he'd been eager to flee on his own, but now that circumstances had shifted yet again, he was eager to rejoin his master. Still, he was right. Whether she could seize the ship now or not, Marbuck knew that her only chance of surviving long enough to see her daughter again was to go with them.

Without consulting Castor, she sprinted after the slavers. Following after them as they veered between two huts, she found herself at the gate just as Devonshire slipped through it. If there had been any guards, the battle must have lured them away. The bone gate hung ajar, and Marbuck shoved past it, plunging into the parched jungle without breaking her stride. The underbrush broke away before her, the dried tangle of vines and bushes blowing apart into dust with the force of her movement. The narrow trees closed in around her and she slowed, if only to keep from colliding into one in the dark. It was impossible to know which way to go, beyond her general sense of direction, so she relied on the sounds of Bolenz and the others crashing through the wood to show her the way. Before long, she staggered through the last of the tangle and onto the beachhead, where the slavers were shoving the longboat back into the water. She realized that she was still clutching the dagger, and she slipped it into the worn leather belt of her ragged tunic, concealing it beneath the loose folds of her shirt, a shirt which had fit her snugly before she'd been starved. To her disappointment, Castor burst through the brush behind her a moment later.

"Wait!" she called, a stitch in her side forcing her to limp crookedly toward the boat.

Bolenz looked up, a brief expression of relief passing over his face. "Marbuck, you never cease to amaze me. Get in." Failing even to acknowledge Castor, he helped Marbuck to the boat and practically threw her in. Rising voices could be heard from the trees behind them, accompanied by more warning cries.

With a heave, Usso and Devonshire slid the boat free of the sand and jumped inside, tumbling over the gunwales. Castor splashed into the water and climbed in after them. Free of the heavy load of the skins, the boat wobbled drunkenly, threatening to dump them all into the cold water. As it steadied, Usso and Devonshire grabbed the oars.

"Row for the ship!" Bolenz ordered. "*Row for the—*"

Something exploded through Usso's chest, showering Marbuck in blood. The slaver made a sound somewhere between a yelp and a wet belch and then slumped over. The long shaft of a spear jutted from his back. The remaining crew stared at him, bewildered. A second spear whizzed by them, passing close enough to Marbuck's head to stir her hair. She dropped onto her belly in the bottom of the boat, just as Mordwand shoved Usso's crumpled form aside and snatched the oar.

"*Go now!*" Bolenz yelled, crouching beside her.

The boat lurched into movement just as another spear sunk into its side. As they pulled away from shore, Marbuck caught a glimpse over the gunwale. The skinners had launched three boats of their own from somewhere further up the shoreline and were now continuing their pursuit. They were closing in, and she could see that a skinner stood in the rear of each crowded boat, holding aloft a spear and taking aim. She ducked back down just as they let them fly in close succession. One splashed harmlessly into the water nearby, another soared overhead. The aim of the third was true, but struck only the bench between Mordwand and Devonshire.

They paddled furiously and the longboat finally started to pull away from their pursuers. Marbuck remained pressed against the bottom, where a small amount of standing water had leaked through the ancient boards. She was now nearly face to face with Usso, who was lying on his side. He was wide-eyed, and his breathing was agonal.

"I'm dying," he whispered, and it was the voice of a terrified child.

Marbuck felt a distant pity for him, seeing the little boy he'd once been buried beneath the scars, but she offered him no comfort.

"Keep going, we're nearly there," Bolenz said.

Marbuck risked a look and found that they'd pulled even further away from the skinners. The *Empress's Love* loomed ahead of them, its lanterns a comforting beacon through the murk. The longboat raced toward the still ship, and just as it appeared that they would plow right into the side of it, Mordwand plunged his oar into the water and the boat began to drag to a stop, spinning to port and coming to rest with a jolt against the side of the ship.

"Drop the ladder!" Bolenz called to the watch above. They must have heard the commotion of their approach, because they were already unfurling the ladder as he spoke.

"Prepare to raise the boat," Bolenz ordered. "Cast down the lines!" From above them, two ropes descended.

Mordwand threw a nervous glance back toward the approaching skinners. "Commodore, there's no time."

"I'm not leaving it, nor will I leave him," Bolenz said, pointing at Usso.

"He's finished; it would be pointless—"

"We've lost enough already. *Do it.*"

There was no further debate. The ropes were hastily lashed to the boat, and it began to rise even as they scampered up the ladder. As the first spears hit the side of the ship, the longboat, with Usso lying inside of it, slammed into the top of the winches and rocked wildly. Bolenz was the last up the ladder, and once he'd reached the deck, Gomulte and Tordenaar, who'd been working the winches, each seized a side of the rope ladder and hoisted it up.

Bolenz looked about at his remaining crew, and Marbuck could almost see the gears of his mind turning rapidly. "Tordenaar, Gomulte, Castor, get to the oars. Devonshire, fetch Old Stitch. Mordwand, get to the helm. *Move!*"

The slavers scattered, leaving Marbuck and Bolenz alone. It had grown eerily quiet, save for the creaking of the longboat dangling from the winches and the gasping breaths of Usso.

"They will try to board. We must be ready," Bolenz said.

Almost in response, a voice called from below. It was Midga.

"I underestimated you, Commodore of Nothing. I imagined that, plied as you were with food and pleasure, you would be taken easily. Now, not only have you insulted me, a pauper demanding my kingdom, but you have burned my home and killed my kin. They fight as we speak, driving off the shades you unleashed."

As he spoke, Bolenz crept to the rail and peered over the edge. Marbuck followed, eager to know the threat they still faced. Standing so close together, it occurred to her that she could drive the pilfered dagger into the back of Bolenz's head and be free of him. The view below stayed her hand. Floating just off their port side, a canoe of pale skin, pulled taut over a wooden frame, bobbed in the water. It was packed with skinners, and Midga stood in the center among them. The dead flesh suit he was encased in had been burned; half of the hair was gone and the exposed scalp was charred. Nearby, the two other skinner canoes floated. Now would not be the time to weaken their defense of the ship. She would not be freed from Bolenz only to be delivered to Midga.

"Worst of all," Midga continued, "you have spoiled the secret skins of so many. They will never provide for us now. They have been ruined, burned beyond all use."

"And you have betrayed my trust and slaughtered my men," Bolenz called down to him. "Faithless is he that would turn on an old ally, a guest of his own home. Whatever happened to you and yours was your own fault. Now I intend to depart. Do not stand in my way, and I'll never return to your lands again."

"It is too late for that. I was ready to provide you with a swift death, now you will be skinned alive. You will watch as I dance within your flesh."

Beneath their feet, the ship shuddered as the machinery of the oars groaned to life. Marbuck became aware that Usso's breathing had stopped.

"Take the ship," Midga ordered.

The canoe angled toward the hull of the *Empress's Love*, with the other two moving off around it. The ship began to pull away, but it was far too slow of a start. Momentarily, the skinners would be close enough to reach out and touch the hull. Marbuck could see them, holding a dagger in each hand, preparing to leap over and try their luck at latching onto the ship. The first one to try bounced off the hull and fell into the water below, his daggers failing to catch in the wood. The second and third skinners to jump made it, and they began using their daggers to scale the side. Undoubtedly, the other canoes were positioning themselves to launch their own assaults on other parts of the ship. Soon, they would be overwhelmed.

From the longboat, Usso emitted a nightmarish wail. Only, it wasn't Usso, it was the shade preparing to erupt from his body. Marbuck was struck with inspiration.

"Give me the blade!" she demanded, knowing her own hidden dagger would take too long to perform the task she had in mind.

Bolenz, who'd drawn the blade in preparation for cutting down the climbers, gave her a skeptical look. With a hissing sigh of exasperation, she pointed at the line connecting one of the winches to the longboat. "Cut the line!" she shouted.

His eyes followed the line to the longboat. Inside of it, Usso's skullcap exploded. As if that was his cue, Bolenz rushed to the line and swung the shepherd's blade. It easily snapped through the rope, and one side of the longboat dropped almost instantly, slamming into the side of the ship directly above Midga's canoe. The skinners reflexively flinched, but the boat remained dangling above them. As it swung, the spasming body within tumbled out and crashed onto the canoe below. The shade burst forth at almost the instant that it landed, sending the skinners who hadn't been crushed beneath it leaping overboard. Beneath the writhing mass, Midga screamed for help. The shade planted one of its newly-formed arms directly onto his head, and, as it pushed itself up, flattened his skull, shooting brains and gore out of the holes of his skin mask. The spastic movements of the growing shade and the frantic leaps of the skinners proved too much for the canoe. It promptly capsized, dumping the thrashing shade into the water, where it quickly sank.

The first skinner scaling the hull had reached the railing, but he'd paused, distracted by the tumult below. It was a fatal error. Bolenz returned to the rail and, in one blow, decapitated him. The headless body slid down, colliding with the second skinner and sending him into the churning water below.

The *Empress's Love* finally began to pick up speed, leaving the skinners of the wrecked canoe flailing in the waters behind them. The other canoes came into view again, and the skinners aboard were now rowing manically after them. Marbuck and Bolenz remained where they were, waiting for any sign of other boarders. Once again, spears soared through the air, clattering onto the deck. At the helm, Mordwand turned to starboard, guiding the ship out of the bay and back into the open water.

"There," Bolenz said, his blade leveled toward the starboard side. A skinner had slipped over the railing and was crouching near the mast. Bolenz raced toward him, howling with fury. The skinner was taken aback, and when he raised his rusted sword to deflect the blow, Bolenz's strike knocked it right out of his hands. He was run through and flipped over the railing with ease, disappearing into the ship's wake.

Suddenly, the deck beneath their feet lurched violently, sending Marbuck to her knees. The sounds of a struggle reached her ears and she looked up toward the helm. Mordwand was wrestling with a skinner, his hands locked on his attacker's wrist, trying to wrench a sword out of the skinner's grip. Behind them, the wheel spun. Bolenz staggered toward the short steps leading up to the helm, and the two men slammed against the wheel, sending it spinning in the opposite direction. The ship lurched again and Marbuck slid across the deck, losing sight of the others.

Struggling to her feet, Marbuck rose just in time to see another skinner coming toward her. She ripped the dagger from her belt and, before the skinner could raise his sword, slashed at him. The knife cut through his skin suit and found the real meat of his belly beneath, eliciting a startled cry. She slashed again, carving a line across his right forearm. He dropped his sword and she continued to slice at his arms, which he held defensively before him. Backing away, he reached the railing just as the ship lurched again, sending him plummeting overboard. Marbuck nearly joined him, her sternum slamming against the railing hard enough to knock the air out of her lungs. She managed to keep her grip on her dagger, and, once she could draw another breath, she concealed it once again.

The *Empress's Love* righted itself, but it still rocked nauseatingly as the oars fought to drag it back through its own circling wake. As the ship struggled to regain its cruising speed, the skinners began to close the distance again. Marbuck headed back toward the helm and found that the skinner attacking Mordwand had been dispatched. Bolenz now manned the wheel, with a wounded Mordwand sitting nearby, clutching his right shoulder.

Devonshire and Old Stitch trotted out of the shadows and approached the helm.

"I apologize for the delay, Commodore. We were waylaid by skinners. Where is Usso?"

"He's gone, though his death provided a little parting gift for Midga." Bolenz smiled grimly and nodded at Marbuck. She felt an unsettling satisfaction in this small show of respect, this acknowledgment that they had shared an important experience and forged a partnership in the heat of battle. "Mordwand's been stabbed, though, please attend to him."

"Of course," Old Stitch said, hurrying to Mordwand's side.

Devonshire lingered near Marbuck. "You okay?" he asked softly.

She looked at him, and the large X carved across his face did not obscure his apologetic expression. In all of her time aboard the *Empress's Love*, she'd barely spoken to the former royal guardsman. In this brief interaction, she immediately knew that he was no Castor; he had not embraced the life of a slaver, but was merely getting by. She saw the potential for another ally.

Thinking all of this, she kept her answer simple. "I'm fine."

•   •   •

There was no further time for talk. His wound dressed, Mordwand insisted that he could hold the wheel steady. Bolenz then ordered fresh arms to take the oars and Devonshire, joined by Falstaff and Tannahill, who were informed of the seriousness of their situation, were set to row. Marbuck had only a brief glimpse of Falstaff as he was led from the brig, and her heart ached for the comfort of her friend's company.

After a relatively smooth transition at the oars, Tordenaar, Gomulte, and Castor rejoined them on deck, and a thorough search of the ship was conducted. No further skinners were found, and as the *Empress's Love* continued at its breakneck pace, their canoes receded into the dark distance, revealed only by their frustrated cries. Bolenz ordered the lanterns extinguished, so as to thwart any attempt by the skinners to track them by the distant glow of their lights, and Mordwand altered their course occasionally, ensuring that they'd lost their pursuers for good.

Finally, after what had to have been several cycles, Bolenz ordered a full stop. The entire remaining crew was summoned to the main deck, where they gathered with a funereal air. Though they'd lost sight of the skinners some time ago, they still cast wary glances into the all-encompassing darkness around them.

Bolenz lit a shrouded lantern, and they all huddled around its faint light. Marbuck had been kept at his side during the entire ordeal, but only now, illuminated by the lantern's glow, could she see how much his bungled ploy had affected him. His pale face, cut through with its purple scars, looked wan and greasy, and dark bags hung from beneath his eyes. When he spoke, his voice was hoarse.

"You all know what's happened. Karant, Chrisholm, and Usso are dead. Their bodies have been denied to us, the final gift of their meat lost. What became of Karant and Chrisholm after death, I do not know, but I hope their bodies burned. At least I know there won't be anyone parading around in Usso's skin."

Murmurs of approval passed through the slavers. All now knew of how Usso's shade had killed Midga, and that knowledge provided just enough satisfaction to stave off their despair. Whether or not they were aware that the idea had originated with Marbuck was less clear, though she sensed a subtle undercurrent of newfound respect directed her way. It was an odd sensation, one that made her feel an unexpected camaraderie toward her captors. She assumed that this was some kind of subconscious survival mechanism on her part, and was loathe to embrace it.

"Which brings me to my next point," Bolenz continued. "Midga may be dead, but that clearly did not end the animus of the skinners. Quite the opposite in fact. There is no hope of bolstering our ranks there. It's a shame that it cost us so much to learn that."

Old Stitch placed a comforting hand on Bolenz's shoulder. "It's not your fault, Commodore."

Bolenz nodded, though the expression on his face was one of doubt. He took a deep breath and continued. "Mordwand is now my second. There will be a short period of mourning and rest, during which all operations will be suspended, save the watch. I will announce our new destination soon, at which point your normal responsibilities will resume. Dismissed."

The slavers began to disperse, and for a brief moment, Marbuck thought that she would be allowed to roam the ship freely. The idea wilted quickly.

"Gomulte," Bolenz said, looking directly at Marbuck, "please bring the *slaves* back to the brig."

A weird indignation shot through Marbuck, a feeling that was entangled with her increasingly complicated understanding of her position on the ship. For a little while, she'd been by Bolenz's side, lured into a sense of comradeship. Now, he was casting her aside as a slave, uncut and unworthy. She began to wonder who was manipulating who. The touch of the hidden knife against her skin brought her back to reality, or at least to that which existed beyond the *Empress's Love*. She could not lose sight of what she was after, or lose herself in its pursuit.

Another thought occurred to her as Bolenz and the others walked away. She could not be caught with the knife. If she was searched, or if Castor told anyone that he'd given it to her, she risked losing it forever. It was a precious thing; one that she knew would have its moment. She needed to stow it somewhere safe, and quickly. Falstaff and Tannahill were already gravitating toward Gomulte, who'd paused to speak with Old Stitch. She knew she had a very narrow window of time in which to operate, and she surveyed the deck around her feverishly, hoping some idea would spring to mind. Then, it did.

Backing away slowly, hoping to melt unseen into the shadows, she moved toward the starboard rail. Blading her body away from Gomulte and the others, she slid the knife free and leaned over the railing as far as her arm would reach. With as much force as she could muster, she pressed the tip of the blade into the outside of the rail and began wiggling it into the wood. It held fast, jutting out horizontally, and Marbuck was confident that it would remain hidden from view as long as nobody leaned over the railing and peered down. The real trick would be remembering the spot where she'd placed it.

Satisfied with her quick thinking, Marbuck turned from the rail to find Gomulte standing before her. Her heart seemed to stop, and a hot sensation of panic shot through her. Before she could even begin to stammer out an explanation, Gomulte pressed one of her thick fingers to her own lips in a shushing gesture. She then nodded, and a little smile creased her bovine face.

"Back to the brig, now," she said, and Marbuck understood.

Trudging back to her prison with Falstaff and Tannahill, a new certainty took hold. Soon, she would no longer need to play for Bolenz's trust, risking her own sanity within the sphere of his influence. His plans had failed, his loyal crew had dwindled. She had won acclaim, and her own network of conspirators was apparently growing. Mutiny was in the air, a growing spark.

Marbuck intended to fan the flames.

PART 2:
MADE TO SUFFER

CHAPTER 8

"It seems like they're getting antsy."

Marbuck looked up. The three prisoners had finished eating their rations, during which they had remained silent, as was their routine. The quiet usually remained for some time, but Falstaff had breached it rather quickly. The smell of the abhorred meat still lingered in their cell, the grease of the meat still coating Marbuck's fingers.

"What makes you say that?" she asked, wiping her hands on her filthy trousers. The perpetual squalor of her existence had driven the memory of clean clothes from her mind as thoroughly as it had erased all thoughts of bathing.

"Well, we still haven't moved," Falstaff explained. "They seem like they're in a rush when they feed us, like they're expecting orders to come at any moment. But we just keep waiting."

There had been five feedings since Bolenz had addressed the crew, and still, there had been no word of any orders. By Marbuck's approximation, over two full-cycles had passed. Discontent amongst the crew was a good thing, but she couldn't capitalize on it while trapped in the brig. It felt like her plot was losing momentum, the goodwill she'd earned wilting as her position left her out of play. Once they'd been returned to their cell, she'd told Falstaff and Tannahill of everything that'd happened. Since then, they'd been unable to do anything with that information but bandy about the same theories and suggestions of what to do next and who to trust. It was maddening. Whatever intrigues were currently occurring aboard the *Empress's Love*, she was not a part of them.

"Apparently, Bolenz remains undecided," she said.

"We ought to make an overture to whoever brings the next batch of rations, depending on who it is," Tannahill said. It was not the first time he'd suggested this course of action.

"It's too risky," Marbuck said. "Gomulte is the only one I would even consider it with, and she hasn't brought any of the rations. If we tried and failed, we would expose our intentions while already powerless."

"Well, what of Devonshire? You said it yourself that he seems like a viable option," Tannahill said. "I knew him well, or at least I did before all of this. He was an honorable man. I agree that if he seems regretful about his actions, he might be swayed to do the right thing."

"Yes, maybe, but he hasn't brought any of the rations, either."

During their long idleness, only Mordwand and Tordenaar had come bearing meat and water, and Marbuck had no reason to doubt their loyalty to Bolenz. In fact, it worried her that none of the others had been tasked with feeding them. Perhaps, Bolenz sensed some dissension in his other crewmembers, and didn't trust them to speak alone with the prisoners. If that was the case, then her mutiny might be strangled in its infancy, the potential allies purged by Bolenz before she ever had the chance to unite them.

"What if Castor should come?" Falstaff asked. "I know he's a shit, but he did give you the knife, and he did want to flee. He's obviously not loyal to Bolenz."

Marbuck sighed. "Would you trust him to hold his tongue? He'd just as soon betray us for the promise of some higher position in Bolenz's imaginary kingdom. He'll go whichever way seems the most promising in the moment. Even if he agreed to help us, he'd just as easily change his mind. As it is, I'm expecting he's already told Bolenz about the knife. I'm surprised I haven't been questioned about it yet." Surprised maybe wasn't the right word. More like unnerved. Her captivity, isolated as she was from Bolenz, made his every action, or inaction, seem all the more sinister.

Their conversation had followed the same circular path that each one before had left so well-trodden, and they lapsed into silence. Fitful sleep would soon follow, and Marbuck curled up in her accustomed spot on the floor, ready to stop thinking for a while.

"What about Old Stitch?" Tannahill said, unexpectedly reigniting the conversation. "What if one of us feigned illness in order to talk to him?"

"He *has* always seemed, I don't know, kinder than the rest," Falstaff added. "He might be sympathetic."

"I doubt it," Marbuck said without rising. Her own hopes of gaining Old Stitch as an ally had long-since departed. "If you'd seen them on deck, you would too. Bolenz treats the old man like his own grandsire."

Tannahill grunted, a sound that signified a begrudging acceptance of her objection. Falstaff said nothing.

Almost from the start of their endeavor, Marbuck had assumed the mantle of leadership. Part of it was her own outspoken nature, but much of it was due to the fact that she had been, almost exclusively, their only source of information. Kept close by Bolenz, it had only seemed natural that she should be the one to craft their escape from his clutches. While Falstaff and Tannahill labored at the oars or languished in the brig, she'd been at their master's elbow. The responsibility wore on her, particularly in these moments of directionless waiting. And she could tell that, at least with Tannahill, there was resentment of her privilege. Perhaps that was by Bolenz's design too.

She clutched her knees and curled into a tighter ball. Every time she began to feel confidence in her plans, her ambitions were checked. It was a bitter reminder that, even though his own designs had been foiled, Bolenz was still a dangerous foe.

Maybe now, more than ever.

• • •

When the order to see Bolenz on the main deck finally arrived, Marbuck was half-crazed with anticipation. With dual certainties, she believed he was going to elevate her to a higher position on the ship, and that he was going to execute her and feast on her flesh. She strove to maintain her composure as Tordenaar led her from the brig, the thin, haunted faces of Falstaff and Tannahill watching her go.

With her heart thumping steadily in her chest, she ascended to the main deck and followed Tordenaar to the helm, where Mordwand and, more troublingly, Castor were waiting.

"What is this?" she asked.

"The Commodore has made a decision," Mordwand answered, his tone unreadable. "He will be joining us shortly."

Marbuck looked at Castor, trying to ascertain what his presence there might portend. He looked fixedly at his feet. Her thoughts flicked to the knife, which hopefully remained where she'd stuck it. If Castor had told Bolenz about giving her the weapon, she was ready. She'd had plenty of time to come up with a story. If Gomulte had said something, though, she would be in a much more precarious position. Her stomach lurching, Marbuck realized how much trust she'd placed in the seemingly dull-minded slaver.

"I see we're ready to proceed," Bolenz said, his voice preceding him. He appeared to form out of the darkness itself, stepping into the dim light of their lone lantern. His defeat, and the deaths of his crewmembers, had obviously continued to weigh on him. Disheveled and stinking of drink, it was clear that he'd spent the time of their idleness getting lost in his cups. He looked over those gathered before him and settled his gaze on Marbuck with a satisfied smile. "And there you are. Thank you for fetching her."

"Yes, Commodore," Tordenaar said.

"For those of you who are not aware, after careful consideration, I have plotted a new course for our future. One that will guarantee the establishment of our own kingdom."

If the others didn't buy this, they made no indication. Marbuck found it hard to believe that any of them, after the loss of their Empress and her city, and the subsequent rout they'd suffered at the hands of the skinners, could possibly be entertaining the notion of kingdom building. There were now less than a dozen of them left, occupying one leaky ship.

"The time has come for you to demonstrate those much-lauded navigation skills, my dear," Bolenz said, still smiling. "I wish for you to lead us north, to the lands you hail from."

Marbuck had nearly forgotten that her original purpose, in his eyes, had been to navigate, and that her own first scheme had been to lead him north. Now, here was that opportunity, served to her easily. And yet, a crucial flaw loomed suddenly large in her mind. The scant view of the shoreline was long gone, forgotten in their desperate flight. In the complete and utter blackness that engulfed them, she had no idea which way north was. Frustration, entangled by suffocating vines of fear, grew within her. She'd finally been given the chance to make her move, to lead Bolenz and his ragged band to certain destruction in a land they knew nothing of, while guaranteeing her own deliverance, and she was being thwarted by such a simple problem.

Between her and Elibeth, there stood a choice. She had to pick a way to go, claim it to be north, and hope that it was. Should she guess wrong, she could lead them further out to sea, or to some unknown shore beyond any knowledge. In the nothingness around them, a wrong choice would lead them to starvation, madness, and death. But choose she must. If Bolenz realized that she was unable to guide them, she would have reached the end of her usefulness. She shuddered to think what new, dark purpose he would concoct for her, his depravity fed by his hopelessness.

She cleared her throat. "May I?" she asked, pointing toward the helm.

"Of course," Bolenz said, sweeping his arm before her in a gesture of invitation.

Marbuck ascended the steps before the helm and gazed out over the bow, squinting into the darkness for any sign of the shore. Aware of the eyes watching her, she assumed an expression of informed consideration as she scanned the entire identically black horizon.

"To starboard," she announced, hoping that some innate sense of direction within her was speaking true. "That will take us north."

"Wonderful," Bolenz said. "There's just one problem, or, an accusation really."

Marbuck's heart leapt up her throat so intensely that it felt as if it might burst out of her mouth.

"You see, when I informed my crew, which I feel compelled to remind you does not include uncut slaves such as yourself, of my intentions moving forward, Castor objected to your role in my plan. Castor, would you care to explain?"

He stepped forward, bearing himself with gravitas. "Commodore, I believe that Marbuck is lying to you. She was a fair navigator; it's true, but only on the shallow river waters of our home. She is out of her depth here and will only lead us to ruin, be it by folly or design. As I told you before, I gave her a knife as a means to survive the skinners. She conceals it still."

The blunt denial of her navigation skills took her by surprise, but the revelation of the knife was expected. As such, she latched onto that. "Do you think me foolish enough to try to hide something like that?" she asked Bolenz, ignoring Castor completely. "Yes, he gave me a knife, but I lost it during the escape. When the skinner attacked Mordwand and the ship was out of control, I was thrown to the deck and I dropped it. I imagine it slid overboard."

"That's a lie," Castor said.

"No, it's not."

"She's either still got it or it's hidden somewhere."

"You're wrong."

Bolenz nodded along, watching the argument. "Would a search of your person or the brig change your version of events?" he interjected, his question silencing Castor.

"No. It's gone," Marbuck said, silently praying that Gomulte had not betrayed her.

"And you understand that the punishment for lying would be extreme?"

"Yes," she said, privately terrified.

"And what of the other claim? Do you possess the skill to guide us, or not?"

She looked at Castor, and his mouth rose in a crooked sneer. Unexpectedly, a red fury exploded within her, and she clenched her fists tightly. It didn't matter that his accusations were entirely true. She would not let him question her prowess anymore, certainly not when it threatened her chances of returning to her daughter.

"What that sniveling little shit has told you is a lie. I alone possess the ability to guide us north. I navigated my prior ship through waters, river or not, far more treacherous than any we've faced out here. Castor slanders me because he is resentful and jealous. He wished to bed me, and I spurned him. Our prior captain recognized my skill and shunned him, as I think you do now. He is a covetous, grasping fool who only swore his allegiance to you so he could cling to his pathetic life for just a little longer. I believe you are smart enough to know that. From the start, I have refused you, yes, but in that refusal you can be certain of my honesty. I have never told you anything but my truest thoughts. I tell you now, he is lying. Not me."

Bolenz looked at her, his face blank. The thoughts moving through his hideous mind were a complete mystery.

"Commodore, she will say anything now to escape your judgment."

"You wished to bed her?" Bolenz asked.

Castor seemed embarrassed and taken aback by the question. "Um, well, yes, I did."

For a moment, Bolenz ran a hand along the stubble of his thick neck, lost in thought. "She insists that you are not really loyal to me."

"Commodore, I swore my allegiance and I stand by that now. You don't need her, nor can you trust her. Let me navigate the ship, I've always been better than her, even if others failed to recognize it. Let me lead us north."

"What if you could have her?" Bolenz asked, ignoring Castor's offer. "What if she could be yours, with my blessing? Would you have her?"

Castor looked as surprised as Marbuck felt. The thought of being chattel, used as a reward for Castor, was as humiliating as it was disgusting. Yet, from everything that Bolenz had said before, she could not believe that he would simply give her to one he so clearly disdained. Castor, however, did not seem to sense anything wrong with this, and he now bounced on his heels like an eager child.

"Yes, absolutely, Commodore."

"I thought as much," Bolenz said. "All I ask in return is a reaffirmation of your loyalty."

"Like I said—"

"I know what you *said*. I want to know if you will reaffirm your loyalty with blood."

At this, Castor wavered. Marbuck watched with horrified fascination as he weighed her fate between his fear of further mutilation and his perverse desire to have her. His eyes met hers, a shared hatred passing between them. Then, with naked lust, his gaze roamed up and down her body.

"Yes, Commodore," he said like a man in a dream. "I will pay the price."

Bolenz grinned wickedly. "Hold him."

Mordwand and Tordenaar grabbed Castor by the arms, and he appeared to suddenly wake from whatever degenerate fantasy he'd been lost in. "Wait, wait!" he cried, trying to pull his arms away.

"Just relax," Mordwand soothed.

"Steady now, steady," Bolenz said, stepping up to them. He looked at Castor's face and pursed his lips. "You couldn't have shown your lack of loyalty more plainly." He stripped the grimy cloth from Castor's face, revealing his disfigurement. "You ought to have borne the final blessing of the Empress proudly. Still, I'm happy you're reaffirming yourself."

Castor nodded shakily, but his arms remained tensely drawn up, held in place by his crewmates.

"This will hurt, but, in the end, it will bind you to me forever," Bolenz said, unsheathing a dagger. He then seized the front of Castor's breeches and pulled them down. Marbuck instinctively looked away, having no desire to see his filthy crotch.

"Hold on, no, please, stop, I didn't—no, stop, *STOP! NO!*"

Castor's shouts grew into a horrendous scream, and Marbuck could not help but look. Bolenz was crouched before him, and Castor was convulsing so violently that Mordwand and Tordenaar could barely hold him still. His wailing reached an ear-splitting crescendo as Bolenz suddenly rose.

Triumphantly, Bolenz raised his fist into the air. Clutched in his blood-ied hand was Castor's manhood. He waggled the wrinkled chunk of tissue about and then cast it to the deck, where it tumbled away into the shadows. Castor continued to scream until his voice cracked with a wet hitch and suddenly ceased. His mouth remained open, his face contorted into a silent mask of agony. Mordwand and Tordenaar released him, and he slumped to his knees, his breeches still pooled around his ankles. Where his genitals had been, an angry crimson gash now stared out from his blood-caked pubic hair. He collapsed into a fetal heap, his entire body trembling, and began to whimper. To Marbuck, that sound was more terrible than every-thing that had come before. It was a hollow sound; the utterance of one who had lost everything and now resided in the blackest pits of despair, from which there was no chance of return.

"Thank you for proving your loyalty," Bolenz said to Castor's crumpled form. "As I promised, she is yours now, to do with as you wish." He turned to Mordwand and Tordenaar. "Take him to Old Stitch."

They collected Castor and carried him away, leaving Marbuck and Bolenz alone on the deck.

"You're right, of course," he said, wiping his bloody dagger on the front of his uniform. He sheathed it, looked at his hands, and licked one finger. He frowned and began to wipe his hands off. "Castor is craven, and, though he nominally owns you, you needn't worry. I don't think he's capable of fulfilling his desires anymore, if they even remain."

"So, you believe me then?" Marbuck asked, watching his bloody hands, trying to keep her composure.

"You could say that. I believe that Castor was a cowardly pretender, and his desire for you amused me as much as his obvious self-interest did. Why, I've known what he was from the moment he set foot on my ship." He raised a warning finger to her, and his good nature was replaced with malice. "But I know what you are too. You had better be able to deliver on your promises. If you are trying to deceive me, you will find only pain. I have given you a long chain, but my patience wanes. A time will come, soon, when you will have to make your choice."

"I know," Marbuck said, wondering what part of her would be the first to go.

"For now, we will get underway, following your guidance. I will escort you to the oars; our reduced crew makes it impossible for me to offer you any more preferential treatment, at least until you join the crew proper. But you needn't worry, your fellow uncuts will be with you. They are proving to be as stubborn as you are, but of course they are under your banner. When you break, they will follow."

Marbuck said nothing, and Bolenz led her to the main hatch. As they walked, she knew that she would not be able to rely on a lucky choice to bring her home. Should they continue to wander fruitlessly, how long would it take for Bolenz to decide that Castor had been telling the truth? Should that come to pass, Bolenz's wrath would be unmatched.

She needed to act.

CHAPTER 9

It had been a punishing stint at the oars, one with no promise of relief. With the smaller crew, it was impossible to man all three capstans without more seasoned slavers being forced to step in. As such, Marbuck began to despair that they would be left to row until their bodies gave out. Tordenaar had been tasked with watching over them, and though he was less menacing than Mordwand, he was not unwilling to brandish his whip. Falstaff received a number of warning lashes, but, thankfully, never fell.

Finally, Tordenaar himself, with Gomulte and Devonshire, took over the oars. Marbuck felt a reckless desire to simply call out her intentions to them, imagining Gomulte and Devonshire quickly joining her in butchering Tordenaar before sweeping across the ship in a wave of revolt. Her total exhaustion joined with her better judgment, staying her hand. Instead, she allowed herself to be led back to the brig by Mordwand, with Falstaff and Tannahill in tow. As they crossed the deck, she saw that their cycles of manning the oars had brought them no closer to any land.

"I wish to see Old Stitch, for my lashes," Falstaff announced.

Mordwand chuckled. "He's a little busy at the moment. Those little scratches will have to wait."

Falstaff furrowed his brow, but said nothing. Marbuck hadn't had the chance to tell the others what'd happened to Castor, and she scarcely had the energy to do so now. Yet, they had to know. She did not have the luxury of waiting until after she'd slept. They all needed to be informed and ready, should the opportunity present itself to court Gomulte or Devonshire.

As she descended back toward the brig, Marbuck realized that the perfect moment might never come.

• • •

Time passed, and Marbuck's fears grew.

Her existence had been monotonous and terrible before but now it was coupled with a constant sense of impending doom. Each time her miserable shift at the oars would end, she would step onto the main deck and find that they were no closer to any shore than they'd been before. Bolenz had essentially vanished, leaving her to dwell obsessively over what he was thinking. The rotating crews of three remained as unchanged as the oppressive horizon, robbing her of any chance to advance her plots. Time might have become meaningless, but she could still feel it narrowing to the moment of her demise.

The first break in the endless sameness came with a visit from Old Stitch. Though Falstaff had been denied an audience with him, he'd decided to pay a visit to the brig of his own accord. He'd checked Falstaff's wounds, determined that they'd mostly healed on their own, provided the slaves with some water and then departed. The short visit had reignited Falstaff and Tannahill's suggestions that Old Stitch might help them, and Marbuck was forced to once again explain why they were wrong. She began to worry that, should he return another time, one of the men might act on their own.

The second change occurred when Castor reappeared, looking not only like a different person, but an entirely different being. Marbuck's memories of the boorish crewmate she'd grown to hate could not be made to fit with the wretched creature that now skulked on Mordwand's heels. He'd grown hideously thin, a fact that was obvious to all since he was apparently no longer permitted to wear clothing. His castration was on full display, a stitched sore weeping into the nest of hair around it. Castor tried to walk with his legs together, shielding his shame from view, but this only elicited snickers from the slavers. He no longer wore a cloth across his face; he'd either been forced to lose it or no longer cared, considering his complete degradation. Though Marbuck had been given to him, he made no attempt to claim his property. In fact, as he shuffled and shivered before his former crew, he remained silent, save for the soft whimpers he emitted when Mordwand gleefully kicked him.

Worse than being subjected to the sight of Castor was the fact that his return had not altered the oar shifts whatsoever. He no longer worked at all; his sole purpose aboard the *Empress's Love* was apparently to serve as a gruesome reminder of what awaited those whose loyalty wavered. For Marbuck and the others, their toil continued unabated.

As she slogged through the endless cycles of suffering, Marbuck slowly became aware of a new, insidious threat: their rations were shrinking. Each portion of dried meat and metallic water was slightly smaller than the last. She surmised that, trapped as they were, wandering the flat blackness of the boundless water, the once-ample stores were now running out. Dwindling provisions would only accelerate Bolenz's ire. Marbuck had no doubt that when the food ran out, so too, would Bolenz's patience with her.

Physically spent, weak with thirst, gnawed by hunger, and certain that she would be summoned before Bolenz at any moment, Marbuck often found herself praying to the Void-God. Waiting for the unconsciousness that passed for sleep to take her, she would beseech the false god of the shepherds to grant her just one chance to ignite her mutiny.

Finally, her prayers were answered.

• • •

"Keep at it! Come on, now, move!"

Tordenaar's whip snapped and pain singed the back of Marbuck's calves. It had been a glancing blow, one meant only to shock her into pushing herself just a little harder. It worked. Marbuck's aversion to the whip had only grown, the fear of its bite hijacking her mind and forcing her battered body into action. She plodded forward, the hated lever of the capstan pressing against the calloused flesh of her palms.

With one final push, she heard the blessed click of the mechanism. She leapt back, eager to savor her brief moment of peace while the gears reset. The lever began its whirring, and a sharp crack rang out. Hope for some sort of catastrophic malfunction in the system gushed through her, and she looked for the source of the sound. As she saw it, her heart dropped.

Tannahill had failed to get out of the way of the spinning lever, and it had struck him in the side of the head. He was now sprawled unceremoniously across the floor, a pool of blood spreading from the broken skin of his scalp. Forgetting the oars, she ran to his side, reaching him just as Falstaff and Tordenaar did.

"*Fuck*," the slaver hissed. "Why didn't the idiot move?"

"I'm sure he tried to," Marbuck said, crouching next to him. He was groaning, and his eyes were open, though they were unfocused and glassy. "Can you hear me?"

"Get out of the way," Tordenaar said, shoving her backward. "He needs Old Stitch."

"I can hear you," Tannahill murmured. "Fucking thing hit me."

Falstaff laughed with relief. "Yeah, it did. You might want to move a bit faster next time."

"Can you stand?" Tordenaar asked urgently, glancing over his shoulder. It occurred to Marbuck that, for the first time since Bolenz had ordered them to set course, the oars had stopped. Tordenaar, who'd been their warden at the time, was probably afraid that he'd be held responsible.

"I think so," Tannahill said, raising his head slightly.

"Alright, up," Tordenaar said, grabbing him and hoisting him to his feet. He swooned slightly and Tordenaar braced him. The slaver then turned to Marbuck and Falstaff. "Someone will be here shortly to set you back on the oars. Don't fucking move until then."

Marbuck, her senses suddenly sharpened by this development, nodded.

Tordenaar guided Tannahill from the cabin and they disappeared down the passageway toward Old Stitch's quarters. Marbuck and Falstaff were now alone, though it would certainly not be for long. What she should do with this brief opportunity, Marbuck wasn't sure. She looked at Falstaff, and he shrugged.

"What's happened?" a voice called from the doorway.

With a burst of giddy elation, Marbuck saw that Devonshire was peering out of the hatch leading down to the orlop deck. She wasted no time and quickly strode toward him. He must have anticipated some sort of attack, because he reflexively shrank back.

"Tannahill got hurt; the lever hit him," she said quickly, kneeling before him. "He was your old partner, a fellow royal guardsman, no?"

Devonshire looked confused. "Yes, of course."

"He has kept his vows; do you wish to reclaim yours?"

"What?"

Marbuck decided it was now or never. "I wish to mutiny. To kill Bolenz and the other slavers. I do not believe that you truly serve him. Help us. You can still return to Nordabor and reclaim your honor."

Devonshire stared back at her, his mouth hanging open, his eyes blinking rapidly as he processed her words. "I will stand with you when the time comes," he said quietly, but with a certainty that was beyond reproach.

Relief flooded through Marbuck, and she clasped his hands. "Soon," she said, and then she rose and stepped back into the oar compartment. Falstaff looked past her at Devonshire and nodded solemnly. Devonshire returned the gesture and descended back to the orlop deck just as the upper hatch was flung open. A moment later, Mordwand came clambering down the ladder, rattling the entire length of it.

"Why have we stopped?" he barked as his boots hit the floor. "Where is Tordenaar?"

"I'm here," Tordenaar called, jogging up to them before Marbuck or Falstaff could answer. "The other uncut was struck by a lever. I took him to Old Stitch."

"And you left these two alone?"

"Would you have rather I sent two uncuts off to wander the ship alone? What does it even matter anyway? There's nowhere for them to go. What can they do?"

Mordwand snorted with derision and looked at the unoccupied capstans. "The Commodore is not happy with the delay."

Tordenaar, who'd been growing indignant, blanched. "We'll get underway at once."

"You certainly will. And *you* can take the uncut's place. Perhaps I'll stick around in case you need any motivation."

"That won't be necessary," Tordenaar said through his teeth.

"See to it that it isn't." Mordwand turned and grasped the ladder. Above him, Castor was just starting to descend. "Get your filthy ass back up there!" Mordwand shouted. Castor scrambled back up as Mordwand ascended.

"Back to your places," Tordenaar said, heading toward his own.

"Is Tannahill okay?" Falstaff asked, and Marbuck realized that she hadn't really considered him once she'd become focused on the opportunity his injury had presented.

"Worry about your own skin, uncut. Now, *move.*"

•　•　•

The rest of her labors passed in a dreamy haze of hope, tempered only by her knowledge that Tannahill, whose support she needed, was injured. She would not be able to rely on him as another fighting body, yet the addition of Devonshire was a fair trade. At the very least, it meant one less supporter of Bolenz.

Thinking of Tannahill in such a detached way left her with a gnawing guilt, especially in light of Falstaff's genuine concern. Still, she could not deny that her desire to escape her bondage overrode all, easily casting down such smaller concerns. She hoped that Tannahill would recover, but still considered it a boon that he'd been injured in the first place. She was now one step closer to Elibeth.

Buoyed by this comforting knowledge, she found that she was able to sleep contentedly for the first time in a long while. It was a dreamless sleep, and the gentle nudging that disturbed it nearly went unnoticed. When Marbuck did finally raise her head, the comforting nothing of her sleep quickly gave way to fear, accompanied by the screaming soreness of her muscles as she tried to scramble away.

"*Shhhh*; it's okay," the bulky form standing above her whispered. It was Gomulte. Marbuck's sleep-fogged mind struggled to grasp her presence there, and she looked to Falstaff, who remained asleep. Gomulte leaned close, and Marbuck could smell her sour breath. "You must come with me," she whispered.

"What's going on?" Marbuck said, her own voice remaining low, conspiratorial.

"I'm going to help you. Come with me."

"What of my friend?" Marbuck asked, suddenly leery of this strange visit.

"I cannot risk taking two of you. We must not be seen."

Marbuck looked at Falstaff again, torn. She did not wish to leave him, but things were moving rapidly now. She had secured Devonshire's support and now might be her only chance to clinch the last piece of her plan. She reached out, intending to gently shake Falstaff awake, so that she might tell him where she was going. Gomulte grasped her wrist.

"There is no time. We must go *now*."

Marbuck's hand hovered above Falstaff, her wariness striving with her desperation. She looked at Gomulte. "Okay. Let's go."

They slipped out of the brig together, and Gomulte carefully shut the door behind them. One of her thick hands folded over Marbuck's, and she led the way across the darkened deck, lighting no lantern, following a path known by memory. They stopped, and, with a soft creak, Gomulte lifted the fore hatch. Dim light rose from within, painting their faces in an amber hue.

"Where are we going?" Marbuck whispered. In the faint light she could see that Gomulte was weaponless. "What about my knife?"

"You won't need it. There is an entire cache of weapons in the storage compartment on the orlop deck."

Marbuck needed to hear her intentions plainly. "And what are we going to do with them?"

"Take the ship. That's what you want, right?" Gomulte said, sounding suddenly unsure of herself. Perspiration stood out on her upper lip.

Marbuck couldn't help but smile. Gomulte was apparently as nervous and unsure of her allies as she was. "Yes, that is what I wish," she reassured.

Gomulte nodded her large head. "We'll grab what we can and go back to the brig. They won't expect an attack to start from there."

It made sense. They would have time to arm themselves, Falstaff included, and to possibly get word to Devonshire. Maybe Tannahill, too, if he was able to fight. With the support of half of the crew, and the element of surprise, they could do it.

As quietly as they could, they descended the ladder, passing the open door of the oar compartment. From within, the sounds of the turning gears and straining men could be heard. Those manning the capstans were too preoccupied with their work to notice the shadowed figures slipping past them, and Marbuck and Gomulte reached the orlop deck without incident. The bilge pump had been neglected, probably on account of the reduced crew, and standing water now rose above Marbuck's ankles as she stepped off the ladder. It was cold, and the smell of brine was overpowering. In the faint light coming from the open hatch above, Marbuck could see some empty casks bobbing in the water. They'd probably been full of provisions at some point, and they served as a stark reminder of the impending starvation.

"This way," Gomulte said, stepping through the flotsam.

It became impossible to see as they left the ladder behind, and Marbuck shuffled through the water, holding onto Gomulte's back. She stopped suddenly, and Marbuck bumped against her.

"It's just through here."

The screeching of a rusted door filled the space, and then they were stepping up into a compartment the water had not yet reached. Marbuck stumbled up the short steps, not expecting them, and Gomulte helped her keep her footing. It was as black as pitch inside, and Marbuck squinted into the nothing around her. The door slammed shut, startling her, and a golden light, brilliant in the blackness, assaulted her eyes with its suddenness. She flinched away, and, as her eyes adjusted to the light, her stomach plummeted.

Bolenz stood before her.

"You've been playing a dangerous game, my dear," he said quietly, setting the lantern he'd lit upon a barrel. "You must have known that you would lose."

Marbuck, stunned into silence, looked at Gomulte. She stepped over to Bolenz, and he caressed her scarred cheek. She giggled, and he seized one of her breasts, yanked her toward him, and kissed her roughly. Once he released her, she stumbled backward, blushing furiously. He turned back to Marbuck with a look of satisfaction. Watching them, her surprise grew into embarrassment. After all of her careful machinations, she'd been easily duped. Rage quickly followed, and she began to tremble with hatred.

"Don't get upset, love. You should have known better than to think that you could hold any sway over my crew, especially Gomulte. She has been mine for a long time. She was eager to test you on my behalf. Unfortunately, you failed."

"Test me?" Marbuck managed to utter.

"Yes, of course. To give you little hints and hopes that, maybe, oh just maybe, you could overthrow me. I told her to tempt you, to offer you an alternative to joining me. That way, if you *had* chosen to swear fealty, I would have known that it was true. Not like your sad little suitor. I knew he was telling the truth, by the way." He held up the knife she'd hidden, waggling it mischievously, and despair wailed in Marbuck's mind. "I simply do not like a pretender. I cannot abide a false vow, and I certainly did not want that from you. I had desperately wished that you would come to me of your own volition. Now I see that you never will. Not without some very intense persuasion."

"I thought you were above all that," Marbuck spat. "I thought you would never take someone who didn't desire it."

"Well, yes, I did say such things. However, you are a wholly different case. And, may I remind you; you intended to incite a mutiny. You are a traitor. Anything short of death will be a mercy. Though you might not see it that way." He smiled, displaying his entire mouth of small, yellow teeth. "Come, let us gather the crew. We have much to show them."

Before Marbuck could react, Gomulte lunged forward and engulfed her in a crushing embrace. "Do not fight," she said in the same simple voice she'd used to lure Marbuck to her end. "Delay will only bring greater pain."

All of the anger, fear, and humiliation within Marbuck coagulated into a despondency so complete that it was as if a gray veil had been drawn over her. She grew still, allowing herself to be escorted to the main deck. There would be no maneuvering out of this; there was no angle from which to bend things toward her will. It was over. As they reached the open air and the first calls rang out to assemble the crew, she stared out at the sea, wishing for death. After striving to escape for so long, it was almost comforting to desire only quiet, peaceful oblivion. Even the risk of becoming a shade seemed preferable to the sunless torment she'd endured and the further terrors that awaited her. If Elibeth could somehow know, she would understand.

Before long, Marbuck stood with Bolenz before the remaining crew of the *Empress's Love*. Only Tannahill was absent; he was either dead or too injured to rise. Devonshire, flanked by Mordwand and Tordenaar, looked ill. Falstaff, on his knees before them, looked as if he might weep. Marbuck could not bear to see him, knowing that her foolishness had engineered whatever suffering he would endure.

"There has been a rot growing within this crew," Bolenz announced gravely. "Left unchecked, it would have threatened everything we are seeking to build. This corruption had sought to supplant me, to destroy the promise of our realm, to snuff out the continuation of civilization, as it was gifted to us by the Empress. I would not let that happen. And now, her plots are unmasked. I present to you all: the would-be mutineer."

He shoved her forward, and Mordwand and Tordenaar jeered. Next to them, Castor shrank back, undoubtedly grateful that he was, for the moment, forgotten. Marbuck wondered if he was still capable of taking any delight in her punishment.

"Now, I know that she was not acting alone," Bolenz continued. "However, it was at her urging that her fellow uncuts continued to resist me. One has slipped into a sleep from which it seems he may not wake. In fact, it was that injury which convinced me to have Gomulte tempt the traitor out into the open. I thought she might be growing desperate. As for you," he said to Falstaff, "I offer complete amnesty. I can understand how she might have misled you. After our current proceedings, you will be given some time to reconsider your loyalties. You will then be given your final opportunity to join me."

Falstaff nodded shakily, and Marbuck wondered if he would end up submitting. He was strong, but one could only endure so much pain.

"Now, it is time to administer justice," Bolenz said, turning to Marbuck. "I will not ask you to submit, for I wouldn't trust such a vow now anyway. Perhaps, after you have been reshaped, you will come to desire it in earnest. Until then, your face will remain the only part of you that is untouched. I still want you to *beg* me for that final blessing. Hold her."

In a nightmarish reflection of what she'd watched them do to Castor, Mordwand and Tordenaar grabbed her by the arms. They forced her to her knees, and Bolenz stepped before her. In his hand was the knife she'd hidden, the knife she'd considered driving into the back of his head. He held it aloft with reverence.

"With the very tool of her treachery, I will teach her to obey."

"Don't touch her!" Falstaff cried.

"Silence, or you will lose your tongue," Bolenz said, and he grabbed a fistful of Marbuck's hair.

Falstaff cried out again, but Marbuck did not hear him. Her eyes were locked on the knife, the rest of the world melting into a meaningless blur. Her hopeless acquiescence disappeared the moment the blade touched her forehead, and she began to thrash violently, screaming incoherently. The slavers held her, and she felt the blade puncture the thin skin just below her hairline. Almost immediately, hot blood began to course down her face, running into her eyes. She didn't feel the knife scrape against her bare skull so much as she heard it, echoing within her cranium. It was the sound of madness, and even her screams could not drown it out.

The sides of her head began to burn, feeling as if they might burst. The knife worked along above her ears, allowing the strained flesh to tear away and peel back. After another excruciating moment in which it felt as if her entire head was being torn from her neck, something ripped free and her head snapped forward, dangling facedown. Even through the thunderous pain, she was aware that the curtain of her hair, which had always hung down, framing her face, was gone. She howled, the agony giving way to misery, saliva and snot mixing with the blood running from her face. The slavers lowered her, letting her slump onto her back, and Bolenz stepped over her.

"Look at you now; you look marvelous," he crowed. He hoisted the bloodied scalp, trailing its mess of long, dirty hair, and placed it upon his own bald head like a crown. The blood, Marbuck's blood, ran in rivulets down the deep, pink scars on his face, staining them crimson. He laughed manically, his eyes dancing with crazed triumph.

Shaking violently, disbelieving the hideous sight before her, Marbuck's hands sought the hair that she knew was still there. Her groping fingers found only tortured, shredded skin and the insane solidity of her bare skull. She wretched, and struggled to roll onto her side before she explosively vomited, which sent pain spiking through her head. She gasped and coughed, her attempts to breathe turning into wet sobs.

With all eyes on him, Bolenz strutted toward Castor. "Care for a feel?" he said, running his hands through his new hair. "Or perhaps a sniff?" He leaned toward Castor, who only cringed away. Bolenz gave him a savage kick and boomed laughter. He then stalked over to Marbuck and seized her by the neck.

"Tell me, do you think yourself ill-used? I knew you were a liar, but I doubted that you were inept," he hissed into her face, close enough that strands of her old hair were brushing against her cheek. "Or was Castor telling the truth about that as well? If we do not sight land soon, I will eat you alive, starting with your hands and feet. You will be dismembered piece by piece, and I *guarantee* that Old Stitch will keep you alive. I will fuck your limbless torso while you pray for death. Only your submission will spare you, and eventually, you *will* submit to me. And you'll mean it."

He thrust her back to the deck, and the torn nerves of her head screamed as her skull struck the wood.

Bolenz straightened up, smoothed his new hair back from his face, and turned to Old Stitch. "She's all yours."

•　•　•

Some small part of Marbuck, the conscious part of her mind which had retreated to the furthest recesses of thought, marveled at the fact that she hadn't lost consciousness. Despite her own wishes, she'd remained awake throughout all of the pain and sickening terror. She'd even staggered to Old Stitch's cabin on her own two feet, with only a guiding hand from the slaver to get her there, as she was blinded by blood. Once inside the stuffy, narrow confines of the healer's lair, she'd collapsed onto a filthy cot. Even then, she'd remained conscious and alert, unable to process what had just happened to her.

It was difficult to say how long she'd been under Old Stitch's care. At some point, as he'd sopped the seemingly endless pouring of blood from her head, she'd finally started to skim the surface of unconsciousness. His methods of healing had brought her back.

Before she'd been able to grasp what was happening, he had strapped her wrists and ankles to the frame of the cot. He'd then shoved a strip of leather into her mouth and instructed her to bite down. What followed, while still painful, had been much worse for the nauseating, alien quality of the sensation. Old Stitch's face, the smooth, tender scar tissue shining with sweat, had loomed over her. He'd held up a narrow iron tool, pressing it against her head, and she'd screamed, seeing the knife again. She'd been mistaken; it was not a knife, but a hand drill, and with it, Old Stitch had proceeded to bore shallow divots into the bare bone of her skull at seemingly random intervals. The spinning of the bit, worked by a squeaking hand crank, evoked the same feelings of madness as the knife had, scraping into the inner sanctum of her mind. Old Stitch had said something about needing to anchor the flesh for new growth, but Marbuck had retained nothing else. At the conclusion of his barbaric treatments, she'd finally slipped into oblivion.

When she'd awoken, it was with a feeling of tremendous disappointment at the realization that she was still alive. As Bolenz had promised, Old Stitch worked dutifully to keep her that way, cleaning and dressing her wound constantly, though it was with brackish water and dirty rags. She'd remained bedridden, too weak from shock and blood loss to even rise. At some point, she'd realized that Tannahill occupied a second cot. At another, she'd realized that he was gone.

Lying there now, detached from any reality but suffering and confusion, Marbuck knew that Bolenz would be coming for her soon. They were never going to find land, guaranteeing further torture, and her submission now would only mean prolonging the misery of her existence. Trapped by infinite despair, she no longer thought of Elibeth.

She thought only of death, her final hope of escape.

CHAPTER 10

As Bolenz sat in his private cabin listening to the bickering of Old Stitch and Mordwand, he realized that it was now impossible to deny his failure. He'd harbored such glorious dreams, and he'd come to believe that his illustrious designs were not only achievable but inevitable. The relentless specter of disaster hounding his voyage had quashed all of that. He'd been forced to bear witness as every shred of his destiny was stripped away, each misfortune accumulating into an undeniable calamity. And now, he couldn't even soothe his battered ego with a drink.

"Commodore?"

Bolenz pulled his eyes away from the now-empty liquor cabinet with some effort. He had not been listening, and Old Stitch was now looking at him expectantly.

"Yes?"

"As I was saying," Old Stitch said with a touch of impatience, "we need a decision. Our current course has brought us nothing. We are facing some serious issues, and if they are not addressed, the consequences could be dire."

"I think it's time we consulted our 'navigator' again," Mordwand said. "Surely she's ready for some further encouragement."

Old Stitch shook his head. "She is anything but. The scalping has left her weak. Begging your pardon, Commodore, but it was too much. I only had the scantest knowledge on how to treat it, and I had to make do with inferior tools. I've seen very few people survive such a thing in the long term. Anything further now would certainly kill her."

Mordwand scoffed, and Bolenz held up a silencing hand. His new second was a simple brute who seemed to revel in violence solely for the sake of it. He did not understand the important nuances of inflicting pain in the right ways and at the right times, and his single-minded lust for bloodshed made Bolenz miss Karant all the more. Old Stitch was right of course. He was wise in the arts of healing and wiser yet in knowing Bolenz's heart. He had indeed let his emotions run away with him, and he'd struck too hard with Marbuck. Still, the ecstasy it had brought him had been indescribable, and her misery had become his sole comfort. It would be difficult to practice restraint with her, but he would need to do just that if he was going to prolong his pleasure. If they were all doomed anyway, he would at least break her before the end.

"I will consult her again, but not now," Bolenz said.

"Consulting her is pointless anyway," Old Stitch said with a sigh. "It's plain now that she has no idea where we are. None of us do."

"Castor claimed to be a better navigator than her," Mordwand said.

Now it was Old Stitch's turn to scoff. "Not that I believe he'd be of any more use to us than she's been, but we'll never know, will we? His punishment appears to have rendered him mute. Again, we're talking about injuries beyond my skill, not that I'm questioning your decisions, Commodore. I just feel that I need to caution you; we cannot afford to lose much more of the crew. Castor's wound has soured, and the corruption is fueling a fever. He will not last long. Too much longer, and his flesh might be too tainted to eat, even if he doesn't produce a shade."

"We'll be fine," Mordwand said flippantly. "Our stores have been restocked by the uncut."

"Hardly. Tannahill did provide some meat, it's true, but not much. He was already thin and his condition before the end only wasted him further. If we hadn't euthanized him when we did, it might have been a complete loss. We're very lucky he didn't produce a shade."

"How long can we draw out what he gave us?" Bolenz asked.

"It's difficult to say. I've put some aside to cure, but all I've got to work with are barrels and sea water. We're not equipped for this sort of thing. It might go rancid while we're trying to preserve it. We might be better suited to just eat what's fresh and continue our current rations, though they might need to be reduced further if they're going to last for any meaningful period."

"Rations can be reduced, certainly for the uncuts," Mordwand said.

"Not if we're relying on them for the majority of our labor," Old Stitch countered. "The threat of pain can only take them so far when they are succumbing to starvation."

"I'm happy to test that theory."

Old Stitch waved his hand dismissively. "It's not just food, but water too. And oil for the lanterns. We are adrift with no way to replenish these things. Soon we will be without any light, all of us too weak to man the oars. When that time comes, we are doomed."

Bolenz looked to the single lantern on the table before them, its sputtering flame casting fitful shadows on the walls that had once been bathed in yellow light. "As usual, you are right, my friend. Our only hope is to find land, and even that promises nothing should we arrive at some unknown shore, bound only by wastes. We will need to reduce the rations, yes, for us all. Furthermore, when it comes to it, we will need to cull the weakest among us, so that their flesh might buy the rest of us some more time. Should it come to it, we three can man the oars. I have not abandoned all hope of reaching land, of escaping this trap that fate has placed us in. Ill-fortune has assailed us, but we must not yield."

Old Stitch and Mordwand murmured their agreement, but Bolenz hardly noticed. His eyes were looking past them, focusing on the hook from where he'd previously hung his cloak. Now, only one scalp dangled there, the only one he needed. The dark hair beckoned to him; he could almost hear the tantalizing whispers of domination. It wasn't *really* survival that motivated him now, for that seemed unlikely. It was his intent to fulfill his promise to Marbuck that kept the blood pumping through him.

Before the end, she would suffer greatly.

• • •

The *Empress's Love* had continued its journey into oblivion, and, one by one, Old Stitch's predictions had come to pass. Their attempts to preserve parts of Tannahill had resulted in the loss of precious meat, and, subsequently, rations of the existing stores had been cut to starvation levels. No longer willing to waste Castor as Mordwand's personal pet, Bolenz had attempted to press him back into service. It'd been too late; wracked by his sickness, he'd collapsed shortly after his shift began. Upon looking him over, Old Stitch had stated plainly that there was nothing he could really do, especially working in the dark. The lanterns had run dry; the final drops of oil, rendered from human fat and brought from the Empress's city, were held in Bolenz's personal lantern, which he guarded jealously, and a single lantern in the oar compartment. With much of the ship locked in darkness, and the remaining crew consumed by a feverish need to keep the ship moving toward some imagined land, many important tasks had fallen into neglect. Bilge water had risen perilously in the orlop deck, mixing with the accumulated filth of the slavers, who'd grown careless in its disposal. Their drinking water, brackish and foul, was already thinned to its limit with sea water; now the remaining casks held the potential of being fouled by their waste.

When the system finally started to collapse, it happened rapidly. As with most of Bolenz's problems, it began with Marbuck.

Old Stitch had reluctantly cleared her to return to her normal duties, and Bolenz had escorted her to the oars himself, once again wearing her hair. The tissue of the scalp had started to shrivel and blacken, emitting a pungent odor that, to Bolenz, smelled like power. He'd delighted in the way she'd cringed away from him and refused to speak. Like Castor, she had been reduced to something meek and obedient, though she remained clothed, with a turban of bandages covering her bare skull. Bolenz could almost believe that she would submit to him, but he dared not ask too soon. She was a duplicitous creature, and he wished to proceed only when he was absolutely certain that she would give him the answer he wanted. That and he wanted to savor stamping out the final cinders of her spirit.

He'd left her to her work, joined by Devonshire and Falstaff, and overseen by Tordenaar. He'd been unwilling to allow Mordwand to oversee her first shift, fearing that he might prove overzealous with his whip, a concern that turned out to be well-founded.

After taking a perfunctory look about the black horizon and seeing the absolute nothing he'd expected to see, Bolenz had retired to his cabin, where Gomulte had been waiting for him. He'd never been particularly fond of her, considering her to be a dull oaf, but she was loyal and willing, and he'd bedded her with violent gusto, wearing Marbuck's scalp the entire time. Lying with her afterward, her thick, sweaty body taking up the majority of his bunk, Bolenz mused on the many ways in which he would violate Marbuck when the time was right.

It was then that he felt the ship slow to a stop.

After waiting a moment to see if the stop was a temporary hiccup, Bolenz rose with an irritated sigh and began to dress. Gomulte stirred and lifted her broad head. Before she could delay him with any idiotic questions, Bolenz was out of the cabin door, lantern in hand, stalking toward the fore hatch. As he threw open the hatch, he spared a brief thought for Gomulte, left in the dark of his cabin. He hoped that she didn't clumsily blunder into any of his treasures.

Descending the ladder, the sounds of commotion reached Bolenz's ears. A sudden anxiety pulsed through him as he registered Mordwand's voice. Bolenz rushed into the oar compartment, just in time to see Mordwand lifting his whip above his head. Beneath him, Marbuck was lying on the floor.

"*Stop!*" Bolenz ordered, but Mordwand didn't seem to hear him. He brought the whip down with a thunderous crack, splitting Marbuck's ragged shirt and painting a crimson line across her left shoulder and back. She yelped, and Bolenz seized Mordwand by the arm and wrenched him backward. He stumbled, then turned toward his assailant with a furious look. It dissolved in an instant when he realized who had grabbed him.

"Commodore, I didn't—she stopped—"

Bolenz drove his free fist into Mordwand's mouth and let him drop to the floor, where he proceeded to scramble away from his master. "I'm sorry," he sputtered, his hands pressed to his bloodied lips.

"Enough," Bolenz said, taking a moment to examine the knuckle he'd split on Mordwand's teeth. He crouched beside Marbuck and lifted her chin to face him. She gazed back at him through wet, listless eyes. "You're okay; he won't hurt you again," he soothed. "I'm here now."

"Commodore, I tried to stop him," Tordenaar said, stepping forward. He'd been cowering uselessly in the corner with Devonshire and Falstaff, the latter of which was slumped against the bulkhead, cradling his head. His cheek had been split open and his left eye was already swollen. "Marbuck just stopped; she refused to man the oar, and she wouldn't answer me. I didn't want to whip her. I know that she's yours, and she's already in rough shape. Mordwand came in before you, and he set upon her. He struck Falstaff when he tried to interfere. He wouldn't listen to me."

"Is this true?" Bolenz asked Mordwand.

"Yes, Commodore," he admitted sheepishly, blood staining his mouth. "She wouldn't obey. She caused the ship to stop."

Bolenz nodded, his rage diffusing into a sort of amused hopelessness. Marbuck's scalp made his own itch, and he scratched beneath the blackening skin absentmindedly. He looked around the compartment, crowded with the gears and chains of the capstans. So much work, so much agonizing over the details of his wondrous designs, so much labor and struggle to make this ship, *his* ship into the vessel it was. A vessel fit for a king, meant to carry him on a journey of conquest. All of it for naught. The ship had indeed stopped, and Bolenz doubted that it would ever move again.

The only thing left to him, his sole consolation in this unjust world, was the woman puddled at his feet. Bolenz now understood, with absolute certainty, that time was short. He could not afford to dither away what little opportunity he had left. Mordwand was proof that the crew, even the loyal crew, would soon be beyond his control. He needed to placate them with a temporary, but generous, offer that could keep them distracted while he went for broke with his darkest desires. After all, Old Stitch appeared to be right again: Marbuck did not seem to have long. Then, when she was spent, submission or not, Bolenz and whatever was left of the crew would be free to spiral into oblivion. The *Empress's Love* would be left to float idly, a tomb suspended in an endless abyss.

"Fear not. I understand your reasoning, and I forgive you," Bolenz said to Mordwand, who was visibly relieved to hear it. "Anyway, I'd like you to gather everyone on deck. I have a new plan."

• • •

In the last light of his lantern, the remaining crew of the *Empress's Love* gathered before Bolenz. They waited for him to speak, and, as he gathered his thoughts, he surveilled them. Most had been loyal to him for a long time. Old Stitch, of course, had been his wisest counsellor. Mordwand, though increasingly susceptible to his own base impulses, had always been a stalwart follower, as had Gomulte, whose simple devotion had never wavered. Faced with the increasing certainty of their doom, the cracks had begun to show in Tordenaar, but he still held to his oaths.

Of his newest recruits, only Devonshire remained. Bolenz doubted that he held any real love for his master, but he'd at least proven himself capable enough to survive, unlike Luden, and loyal enough to simply do what he was told, without exhibiting deceitful, self-serving motivations, like Castor.

Death hadn't taken Castor yet, but it was very close. His fever raged through him, and he'd only managed to make it to the main deck with Old Stitch's help. He shuddered violently as he stood, and Bolenz watched with a mixture of amusement and disgust as he pissed himself, the urine sputtering out of his gash and running down his legs.

"Just get it over with, whatever you're going to do."

It was Marbuck's little champion, Falstaff. In the wake of her humbling, his hostility had only grown. He had not paid for his belligerence yet, but he would. Once Marbuck was finished, he'd collapse under the weight of his grief, and Bolenz would happily use it to break him before he was butchered for meat. Perhaps, Bolenz mused with excitement, he would force Falstaff to watch as he fucked Marbuck's mutilated corpse. The possibilities for his final throes of pleasure were endless.

"My apologies, for keeping you waiting," Bolenz said. He cleared his throat. "I know that you've all started to worry about our situation. It's no secret that our provisions are dwindling, and that our course is uncertain. I have gathered you here for two reasons. Our navigator has, so far, been mistaken in her estimate that we would reach land on our current bearing. It is time for her to reassess our position, and I feel that I can sufficiently motivate her to do so."

Of course, he knew that she had nothing to offer. She stood rigidly, her eyes downcast, her arms folded tightly across her narrow chest. Her mind, hidden just beneath the thin sheet of bone that he'd exposed, contained no secrets to their salvation. His interrogation of her would simply be a show for the crew, a pretext for the abuses that he was about to commit, and one meant to keep the men complacent for as long as possible. His second declaration would also assist with that.

"Additionally, it pleases me to announce that we will have fresh meat again. Castor, though amusing to us all, has outlived his usefulness. Mordwand?"

He did not need to explain further. Mordwand grabbed Castor and walked him to the front of the group, where he shoved him to his bony knees. Standing before him, Bolenz considered how little Castor's wasted frame had to offer. What meat remained might even be tainted by the sickness coursing through the wretch. Still, it was something, and the hungry eyes of his loyal crew did not seem to care about the risks.

"Well, my friend, I release you from your duties, though your remains will continue to serve me. It's a shame that you never got to enjoy the prize that you sacrificed so much for." Bolenz turned to Marbuck. "Maybe a kiss for him before he goes? You could send him off with a wee taste of the feast you denied him."

Marbuck did not move, but Castor still shrank from her, whimpering pitifully.

"I bet you couldn't even stand her touch now. It's funny, I granted you your greatest desire, and it has brought you only misery. I suppose it's just the way of the world," Bolenz said with a sigh. "What appears to be a blessing is often, in the end, a bane."

"Please," Castor murmured.

Bolenz perked up at the utterance. "He speaks!"

"Please," Castor repeated, his voice now high and wavering. "Kill me."

Bolenz nodded solemnly. "I could string you along, but it would only hurt the crew and bring needless suffering to you. I am not cruel. Let all here see that, despite his false oaths, I am merciful. I will grant you your desire once again. And we will eat."

With a flourish, Bolenz drew the blade he'd inherited from Davhal. Then, with one ferocious blow, he lopped Castor's head from his shoulders. The head spun through the air in a high arc and hit the deck with a wet thud; the body it had departed wavered on its knees before it slumped forward, the stump of its neck dumping an impossible amount of blood at Bolenz's feet. He stared at the mess with hungry excitement. The blood seemed to pulse with life. The others began to crowd closer, the copper stench enticing them.

"Wait," Bolenz commanded. "We must be cautious." He raised the blade again, holding it high, preparing to bring it down on the shade that might emerge. He'd used the blade before, during their ill-fated visit with Midga, but that had been bedlam, and he'd only used the weapon to drive the shades away. He had not faced one like this, and he hoped he wouldn't have to. Furthermore, the emergence of the creature would only further spoil their precious meat.

As they waited, all eyes locked on Castor's corpse, Bolenz became aware of a soft glow spreading across the faces of the crew. It was of a greenish hue, and totally different from the firelight that he'd dwelled in nearly all of his life. Once, in his youth, he'd led a raiding party into the east, where a purplish light had started to blot out the darkness. He'd known that to go further would be to step into the full light of the blinding fire, that which scourged the lands beyond the Empress's grasp. Others had ventured into those lands and found great success; the strange light had always driven him away. This light carried that same aura, and Bolenz felt his guts knot with dread.

Almost in unison, the assembled crew looked up toward the source of the glow. With shocked surprise, Bolenz saw that the blade he held aloft was now wreathed in an emerald blur of light, and he dropped it as if it might bite him. The blade clattered to the deck, but nobody paid it any mind. Further above them, the ancient mast, its skeletal frame stretching skyward, had been consumed by the glow, which wavered and shuddered across its surface, painting the entire ship in otherworldly light. Silent, radiant flashes began to illuminate the sky in stark relief. Bolenz could see that the static mantle of clouds which had been the roof of his world was now a slowly undulating mass of twisting vapor.

"What's happening?" Tordenaar whispered.

As if in answer, the cold, stagnant air began to press against them, creating the sensation that the ship was moving at a steady pace. Bolenz's senses struggled to interpret what was happening, and, Castor's body forgotten, he ran to the starboard rail and peered over, expecting to see the water rushing by. It was still, and on its glassy surface, Bolenz saw his own darkened silhouette framed by the eerie light. Above him, the mast creaked ominously.

"Commodore!" Mordwand shouted. He didn't need to say anything further, for, at the same moment, a sickening wail rose. Bolenz turned back to the others in time to see Castor's body begin to violently convulse, the headless shape twisting across the deck. Nearby, the head had started to jitter, the mouth gnashing as it cried, heralding the shade's arrival. Black ichor suddenly spewed from every orifice of the head and the neck of the torso, sending the rest of the crew scrambling away. The twin streams of foul tissue spread quickly across the deck, drawn to one another. At almost the exact midway point between the body and its head, the spreading filth met and began to coalesce into a solid mass.

Stricken by confusion, Bolenz stood still, watching the shade grow. As the humanoid shape began to rise, his mind finally lurched back into motion.

He'd dropped the blade.

He began to circle the forming monster, scanning the deck. After a moment, his eyes settled upon the blade, lying near the deflated body. Now that it was no longer pointing skyward, it had ceased glowing.

Bolenz made it three steps toward the blade before a wall of air slammed into him. He was blown off of his feet and slammed against the deck, his head striking the wooden boards hard enough to send a flash of white through his vision. He tried to roll over, and the air continued to buffet him, ripping Marbuck's scalp from his head and sending it pinwheeling away into the dark. Nearby, the blade skittered past him toward the stern, followed by the tumbling bulk of the shade. Now fear had joined Bolenz's confusion, and he remained low, crawling across the deck with no idea of where he intended to go, the wind ripping across his back. Briefly, he heard screams, but they were quickly drowned out by the sounds of the growing chaos. The *Empress's Love* had begun to rock queasily, the entire sea suddenly churning beneath the ship, whipped into a frenzy by the explosively rising squall.

The rocking quickly escalated into a violent bucking. Beneath Bolenz's groping hands, the very boards of the deck began to bend and groan. Bewildered, he looked toward the sea, where tremendous rolling waves, suddenly visible in a kaleidoscopic array of flashing light, rushed toward the ship. The first of this barrage slammed into the bow, sending a wave of frigid water rushing across the deck. It coursed over Bolenz, and he slid with it, eventually snagging the base of the mast. He clung to it with manic desperation, all thoughts of torturous indulgence blasted from his mind.

The bow rose sharply as the wave buoyed the entire ship and then plunged almost straight down as the ship slid into an enormous trough. Bolenz screamed, but the gale tore his voice away. A violent shudder rippled through the ship as it passed through the bottom of the trough and was wrenched back upward, struggling to climb the next mountainous wave. Bolenz, who'd only ever known the sea as a flat, placid thing, felt his mind breaking at the sight of the monstrous wall of water above him.

The *Empress's Love* slowed in its ascent, and the crest of the wave collapsed upon it. Bolenz gasped just as the water crashed down upon him with a force he never could have imagined. His hands were torn from the mast and he was swept away, clutched in the punishing grip of the wave. A suffocating, icy darkness pressed upon him, accompanied by silence. Certain of his death, his head suddenly split through the all-consuming water and back into the air. Gasping and sputtering, he was shocked to find that he was still on the deck, but was now lying against the starboard rail.

The ship had emerged on the other side of the wave and was now spinning drunkenly down its backside. Bolenz mopped the stinging saltwater from his face and, though he was disoriented, found his bearings. They were sliding into another trough, but the next wave was much smaller. The pull of the air had also grown weaker. Whatever this madness was, perhaps there would be an end to it.

Having only ever piloted a ship across still waters, Bolenz did not understand the danger he was in. Spinning as it was, the *Empress's Love* met the next wave not with its bow, but with its port side. Bolenz watched the wave approach, anticipating that the ship would rise with it. Instead, it broke against the ship in a catastrophic broadside, snapping the mast with a thunderous crack. What had been the seat of Bolenz's domain, his refuge, and his home, was now a helpless plaything. The wave hammered the ship with such a force that it was flipped onto its beam-ends, threatening to dump him overboard and into the maw of the sea. The water coursed over him in a relentless torrent, pounding him against the starboard rail. He struggled to breathe as the water snatched every breath from him, filling his mouth with brine.

When it seemed that he couldn't take anymore, the onslaught finally ceased. Freed from the water, Bolenz took several gulping breaths and wiped his eyes. The ship was still spinning, the starboard side now dragging beneath the choppy waves as they smacked against the hull. The deck was slanted precipitously, with the port side pointing diagonally toward the sky, where the flashing in the clouds had started to taper off, though a strange glow still persisted. The top half of the mast was gone, and it had taken a section of the starboard rail with it, barely missing Bolenz. He gaped at the scene around him, unable to comprehend what'd happened, and in a state of disbelief that he'd survived.

Just as he started to wonder if anyone else had, he heard somebody floundering through the water spilling onto the slanted deck, approaching him from the stern.

"Who—" he started as he turned to greet his fellow survivor. His words were extinguished in an instant, his throat tightening with panic. Lumbering toward him was Castor's shade, now a fully-formed beast. Bolenz took a tremulous step backward, his empty hands held uselessly before him. It had come to this. Everything he'd ever sought had been kept from him. The Empress had dismissed him. His attempts to forge his own way had been thwarted at every turn. The very sea itself had conspired to annihilate his ship. And after everything, he would be denied the final pleasure of destroying his upstart slave. It was his lot, apparently, to meet his end here, at the hands of a coward's shade.

No, he had suffered enough indignation. He would not accept this.

As the shade closed in on him, Bolenz screamed in defiance and lunged toward it. He struck the sinuous body and began to claw at it manically, digging grooves in the greasy tissue, unleashing a lifetime of fury on the creature that had become a totem of his failures. The shade was unaffected by this display, and slashed him in the head with one sharp-fingered hand. The blow sent Bolenz sprawling into the water on the crooked deck. With sudden, searing pain erupting across his head, his anger quickly diffused into hopeless terror. He scuttled backward, pressing a hand to the left side of his head, where his ear and part of his scalp were now hanging in loose, shredded bands.

The shade snatched at him, wrapping one hand around his right leg. Bolenz yanked his leg back as hard as he could, and the shade's grip cinched tightly, snapping his femur in two and sending jagged bone rocketing out of his skin. As one who had inflicted pain many times, Bolenz had believed that he understood it. The sudden breaking of his leg showed him that he'd known nothing.

The shade was determined to teach him more. Its hand, now covered in the blood spewing from Bolenz's wound, slid downward, dragging the ragged flesh of his leg with it, stripping it from the bone, tearing apart the muscle and sinew, and piling it up around his booted foot. Finally, the entire leg tore free, and the shade stumbled backward, its grisly prize swinging from its hand. Bolenz screamed, the agony wracking his entire body, erasing his every thought, reducing his mind to a scoured plain of torment.

Through his haze of suffering, he watched as the shade stepped over him again. Yet, it did not strike. Instead, it screeched and jerked about, flailing its arms and backing away from him. His vision was dimming, but he was able to understand that something had intervened, and the shade was now falling to pieces, crying hideously as it dissolved. In another moment, a different form stood over him, and his eyes struggled to focus on this new face.

"Look at you now; you look marvelous."

It was Marbuck. He'd thought that she was very close to being broken, but now he saw the truth. Her defiance had survived, remaining dormant until fate, unfair as it was, had chosen to smite him in favor of her. In the end, it was him who'd been broken.

He opened his mouth to say something, though he did not know what, but only blood burbled out. He watched as Marbuck lifted the blade, Davhal's blade, the anointed blade of her people. She'd somehow gotten ahold of it. Just another example of his ill-fortune.

She brought the blade down, and Bolenz's pain ended.

CHAPTER 11

The *Empress's Love* continued to rock and spin with the whims of the sea. Though the climax of the bizarre calamity appeared to have passed, the dark water remained tempestuous. Marbuck stood with her feet apart, bracing herself on the slanted deck. Her hands were still wrapped around the hilt of the anointed blade, which remained embedded in Bolenz's head. She'd struck him with such force that the blade had cleaved his skull in two, reaching his open mouth before its momentum was finally halted. His eyes now looked in opposite directions, seeming to peer off over both of Marbuck's shoulders. Blood had pulsed forth from the lethal blow and now mixed with the sea water pooling on the edge of the deck.

She had never killed a person, at least not in such a manner. The skinner she'd fought off during their escape had tumbled overboard; it was unclear if she'd mortally wounded him. She'd dispatched shades, but that was obviously quite different. Still, she was not struck with any overawing feeling of moral complexity. All she felt in that moment was a potent mixture of relief and disbelief.

Bolenz was dead. She had killed him.

A smile slowly broke across her face, growing into a lunatic grin. After everything he'd done, everything he'd taken from her, she had finally had her moment. She had slain him, and she was now free. Of course, that had not changed her chances of survival, which, based on recent events, seemed as unlikely as ever, but at least she had been granted this one thing. Bolenz was dead, and she'd been the one to kill him.

She placed a foot on his belly and yanked the blade back. Bolenz's head came with it until the blade pulled free with a wet, sucking sound. His split head then flopped back onto the deck. Marbuck looked at the blade with something akin to adoration. As she'd tumbled across the deck, beset by a power that had been incomprehensible, she'd seen the blade rattling toward her, as if the Void-God were directing it toward her hand. That was nonsense, of course; a delusional fantasy fed by her desperation. All the same, she had extended her arm and snatched the weapon as it had passed, the blade's edge biting deeply into her right palm, though she'd barely felt it at the time. She'd stared at the sword, dangling from Bolenz's hip, for a long time. Now that it was in her possession, she would never let it go.

She bent down and finessed the scabbard from Bolenz's belt, grimacing at the thick blood coating it. After attempting to wash the majority of the blood off by dunking it in the water, she secured it to her own belt with a feeling of pride. She remained there, watching Bolenz's body rock back and forth with the incoming waves, her competing thoughts rising like a chorus of voices. She was certain that she was doomed, and yet the presence of the blade in her hand convinced her to continue on. Perhaps Bolenz's death was not some consolation prize, but a catalyst for a new hope. Her deep-rooted determination to survive, which she'd believed had been torn away with her scalp, had flared back to life.

She needed to search the ship, to seek out Falstaff and to make sure that the other slavers were either dead or gone. And there were the issues of water and food to address. Though the sea had only existed in stories for most of her life, those tales had carried old truths. She need only smell the briny air to know that the sea water was undrinkable, although the grumblings of the slavers had served as further confirmation as well. That meant she'd need to somehow retrieve whatever casks of drinking water remained. As for food, she'd subsisted on a diet of human flesh for some time. Eyeing Bolenz's body, she certainly felt no qualms about cannibalizing him to survive. In fact, it had a poetic ring to it.

That line of thought ended when Bolenz's body began to jerk and twitch, as Marbuck feared it might. She readied herself, preparing for the coming conflict. As she waited with the blade held before her, she realized that it would be foolish, and pointless, to face his shade. She had no need of his body, which the shade would soon spoil. The slavers might have been able to stomach that corrupted meat, but she would not be able to, no matter how hungry. Death from starvation seemed preferable to death from agonizing sickness.

More importantly, she loved the idea of Bolenz suffering the eternal damnation of shadehood, and this cruel thought actually made her laugh aloud. She sheathed the blade and grabbed ahold of Bolenz's body, hoisting it up by the armpits. Despite missing an entire leg, it was still very heavy, and the increasing spasms did not help. After dragging it a short distance, she reached the point where the rail had been blown away and stopped.

"*Fuck you,*" she hissed. With one final heave, she rolled the body overboard, and it slipped free of the deck. She gave it a hard nudge with one foot and it bobbed away from the ship, rising and falling with the chop. After a moment, it began to thrash about, splashing noisily. Marbuck watched as she walked back to where she'd destroyed Castor's shade. Amongst the murky cloud of the shade's dissolved tissue that hung suspended in the water, was Bolenz's severed leg. It, too, was shaking. She grabbed it, the slippery, flopping thing reminding her horribly of the fish she'd pulled from the Einfallen in a different life, and chucked it overboard.

The shade's scream was mostly muffled by the water, but its eruption was obvious. Marbuck watched as the loose coils of tissue tried to form and coalesce, fighting against the downward pull of the water. The shade did not enjoy the same fleeting buoyancy that the corpse had, and it didn't take long for it to slip beneath the waves for good, dragging the deflated remains of Bolenz with it. As it vanished, Marbuck wondered to what punishing depths it might sink, locked in an eternal prison of soundless, crushing blackness.

She could not imagine a more fitting end to the Commodore.

•　•　•

Once she was certain that her work there was finished, Marbuck ascended the slanting deck and began her search for Falstaff. The deck was slick and, canted as it was, she expected her feet to shoot out from underneath her with each step. The adrenaline that had brought her bounding down to face Castor's shade was dwindling quickly. In its wake, Marbuck began to feel impossibly weak. Her joints felt as if the bones were scraping against each other, and a burning halo of pain encircled the torn flesh of her head. She suspected that the whipping air had stripped away her bandages, but she didn't dare check.

Since she'd been mutilated, Marbuck had refused to touch her head above the level of her eyes, certain that she would go raving mad if she ever felt the smooth solidity of her skull again. Even with her head ensconced in bandages, she'd still refrained from examining the damage. No mirrors existed on the *Empress's Love*, unless Bolenz had used one to admire himself in the privacy of his own cabin, and that helped Marbuck remain ignorant of the extent of her injury. The pain was bad enough; she did not wish to see the truth of what had been done to her.

Despite the screaming protests of her body, she willed herself to continue, tromping toward the fore hatch. All along the visible stretch of the main deck, it was quiet. The horizon beyond the ship was still spinning slowly, lit dimly by the ambient glow of the clouds and the occasional flash of light. Just as Marbuck was beginning to think that everyone else had been swept overboard, the fore hatch swung open, startling her. From within, Falstaff's head emerged, and Marbuck burst into tears at the sight of him.

"You're alive!" she cried, stumbling toward him with her arms outstretched.

"Stay back, Fishwife," he warned, climbing out onto the deck. From behind him, Mordwand rose into view.

"Ah, the other uncut," he said, caressing the whip hanging from his belt. "We'll be able to man the oars after all."

This struck Marbuck as particularly absurd, and she emitted a short, croaking laugh. "Look around you, dumb fuck. This ship is finished."

"Nonsense. We'll get the bilge pump going and right the ship; then we'll go on our merry way. Now, where is the Commodore?" Mordwand said. Behind him, Old Stitch and Devonshire climbed onto the deck.

"I killed him." Marbuck unsheathed the blade.

Mordwand's eyes widened; he hadn't noticed that she was no longer helpless. He licked his thin, scarred lips. "If these tragic tidings are true, then I am now the master of this vessel. We will mourn the Commodore when there is time. For now, I am ordering us to continue, as I'm sure he would have desired. Now, give me that sword."

Marbuck shook her head slowly. "Do you not understand that some sort of cataclysm has happened here? Something beyond your ridiculous fantasies? Bolenz is dead, please let his idiotic delusions die with him."

"I understand that our crew has suffered another great loss. The Commodore is joined in death by Tordenaar and Gomulte, who I believe were swept overboard when they failed to reach the hatch in time. I understand, too, that we've lost their meat. Unless, the Commodore …"

"His shade, and his ruined body, are somewhere beneath the waves," Marbuck said, a fell pride surging through her. Her grip tightened on the blade's hilt, and the encroaching weakness that had been threatening to consume her retreated once again. Knowing that Gomulte, the bitch who'd brought her to ruin, was gone, further fueled her reigniting strength.

"I *also* understand," Mordwand continued, ignoring Marbuck's words, "that it is still just two uncuts and three of the crew. Give me that sword, *now*. I will spare your life, but your murder of the Commodore must carry a punishment." As he spoke, he unclasped his whip, and Marbuck could see that his desire to spill her blood outweighed all other considerations.

"You are nothing but a pale imitation of Bolenz," Marbuck said. "You play at replacing him, but you're a bloodthirsty fool. I would never submit to him and I'm certainly not afraid of you. Not anymore."

And she meant it. She felt only an eager excitement to kill her tormentor, the man who'd stalked the shadows as she struggled with the capstans, the threat of his brutality hanging on her like chains. She thought nothing of being outnumbered; the others had faded into background noise. As such, she did not expect her other long-held plan to suddenly come to fruition.

"You're wrong," Devonshire declared, grabbing Falstaff by the sleeve and hurrying them both away from Mordwand. "She's not outnumbered. I stand with her."

Mordwand was apoplectic. "You miserable little *traitor*!" he shouted.

"Are you really surprised?" Devonshire asked, his voice shaking. "You think I ever really wanted any part of this madness? You think I wanted this done to my face? I only regret that I didn't die with my pride intact. I was a coward to join with you all, and I let those who were stronger than me suffer for it. So, now, I'm doing what I should have done all along."

"You're a deserter," Mordwand said with disgust. "You're only abandoning us now because you think you can save yourself with her."

Devonshire nodded. "Yes, you're right. But I never should have abandoned her in the first place. And I'm going to spend the rest of whatever's left of my life atoning for that."

Marbuck hated Devonshire for allying himself with her oppressors for so long, for promising to join her mutiny and then standing by as she was disfigured. He had been quiet and obsequious, but, ultimately, he was little different than Castor when it came to his trustworthiness. Regardless, she would take his support now.

"You won't have very long," Mordwand growled.

"Enough of this," Old Stitch said. He unclasped his own sheathed sword from his belt and tossed it at Marbuck's feet. Falstaff snagged it before it could slide away. "I do not wish to see any more loss of life, and I can see that Mordwand has lost control." Old Stitch stepped toward Marbuck, leaving Mordwand to stare in complete disbelief. "You appear to be in command now. I submit to you, swear my fealty, and hope for your mercy, as I am an old man who has only ever sought to aid those in need. We'll have to get your head bandaged again soon."

Marbuck was equally in thrall to her disbelief. Mordwand was sputtering with rage, but she wasn't listening. Her deliverance had come, borne by a strange wind. That cataclysm, which had risen from nothing and receded just as quickly, had been a gift, allowing her to kill Bolenz and lead a bloodless mutiny.

Well, bloodless so far. Her new crew needed to eat.

"I accept your pledge," she said to Old Stitch, which elicited a surprised grunt from Falstaff. She then turned to Mordwand. "Drop your whip and your axe," she said, a malicious smirk pulling at the corners of her mouth. "I believe that Bolenz, before the end, had declared that there would be fresh meat, a promise I intend to deliver on, as I'm sure he would have desired. I swear that your death will be painless. That's more than you would have granted me."

Mordwand blanched, and his rage was quickly brought to heel. "You cannot let this happen," he said to Old Stitch, and Marbuck was surprised to hear the profound sadness that had replaced his fury. "You can't do this to me. We are kin; we share a brotherhood forged on the Black Water."

"Know that I love you," Old Stitch said, "just as I loved Bolenz and the Empress. But they are gone, and with them dies the last hope of our people. I'm sorry, Mordwand, but I must now go a different way."

Mordwand stared at him, and tears spilled down his ruined cheeks. He drew his axe and took a deep, shuddering breath. "I have been forsaken, but I will not submit to this uncut cunt. I will paint this deck with her blood."

Here was the first test of Marbuck's new position. "Falstaff, Devonshire. Help me kill Mordwand."

With a clumsy yank, Falstaff pulled Old Stitch's blade free of its scabbard. Beside him, Devonshire deftly pulled his own sword. He'd been eating better than either Marbuck or Falstaff, and he still looked hale and formidable. Marbuck was reminded that he was a trained warrior, and she was grateful for it.

The three of them advanced on Mordwand, and he backed away, baring his teeth like the cornered animal that he was. With a crazed snarl, he cracked his whip at Marbuck, but she leapt aside. Devonshire closed in quickly, and Mordwand, abandoning his whip, brandished his axe with both hands just in time to deflect a blow. Marbuck rushed forward and drove her blade at his exposed side. Mordwand twisted backward, the sword barely grazing his belly, and lost his balance on the slanted deck. He fell onto his back, and Falstaff tried to stab him in the face. Mordwand blocked Falstaff's strike, but the brief distraction cost him. Devonshire plunged his sword into Mordwand's exposed stomach, and he gasped. As Devonshire pulled his sword free, Mordwand tightened into a fetal ball. Devonshire's next strike sank into Mordwand's lower back, eliciting a second gasp. Then, Marbuck and Falstaff were upon him, and no matter how he twisted or writhed, the blows continued, punching into his body, shredding his insides. The entire time, he remained silent, save for sharp, wet intakes and exhales of breath. Finally, as he grew still, a gurgling whimper slipped through his lips. Panting and spattered with blood, Marbuck, Falstaff, and Devonshire backed away from the mess.

Marbuck had been expecting a shade, and was relieved when one did not come. She didn't bother with questioning what cosmic judgment might or might not have occurred at the time of his death. She didn't even compare the intact remains of this twisted, ruthless slaver to her desecrated husband. It did not matter now. What mattered was that Mordwand would be edible.

All the while, Old Stitch had stood idly by. Now, Marbuck turned to him. "You are the last of Bolenz's faithful. I would just as soon do the same to you as I did to him, but for two things. One; I need your healing skills. Two; you have shown Falstaff and me kindness, in your own way. For that, I will spare you."

Old Stitch was looking at the savaged remains of Mordwand as she spoke. When she finished, he shifted his gaze to her. She knew that his watery eyes had beheld untold atrocities, of which this was simply the latest.

"Thank you, Marbuck. And you needn't worry about my loyalties, past or present. As I said to Mordwand, I had nothing but love for Bolenz, and for the Empress before him. Yet, I have ever followed the path that fate has laid before me. It has always been this way, since my mother brought me to the Empress's city when I was but a lad." He smiled sadly, the gesture crinkling his mangled face.

"She had sought to free us from the struggles of the wastes, but died shortly after we arrived. I then began my life as an uncut slave, and it was a difficult transition. I cursed my mother often for my suffering. At that time, the Empress's champion had been a brute called Agan. His only decrees had been to fuck and to eat, and I was a plaything for him and his captains. One of them, Wrevos, usurped him eventually. He pulled out Agan's teeth and fashioned them into a false set to replace his own. Agan was chewed apart with his own teeth right before me, and I simply started to follow Wrevos. I thought I wanted freedom, but then I finally tasted the Empress's blessing. Then, it all made sense. I never wished to rule, only to help my adopted people and to serve dutifully; and I served for a long time. So long that I've forgotten my first name, that which my mother once gave me and the children of the Empress forced me to abandon. I have been called many things, by many masters.

"Eventually, Bolenz's path intertwined with my own, and so that was the way I went. Here now, my fate has branched away again. You and me; our paths are now joined. Yet, I believe they will both be ending soon. So, no, you needn't worry about my loyalty."

Marbuck looked into Old Stitch's face and, in spite of everything, felt pity. The horrors of Vin-Sadavat had been all he'd ever known. He'd suffered a lifetime of horrendous depravity, choosing to forgo their hierarchy of violence to serve as a healer, only to end up here, doomed to death on the endless expanse of the sea.

"I understand," she said, not really knowing how else to acknowledge what he'd told her.

He nodded curtly. "Well, I suppose I'll get to work on Mordwand. We need the meat. Other considerations will have to wait." Old Stitch approached Falstaff and Devonshire, who remained standing over Mordwand's corpse.

'Other considerations'. Yes, Marbuck thought as she looked at the starboard side, which had undoubtedly sunk deeper into the water, they had some pretty serious things to consider.

For now, though, the *Empress's Love* belonged to her.

CHAPTER 12

Using a combination of Mordwand's own axe and a serrated knife retrieved from his boot, Old Stitch set to work on dismantling his former crewmate. It disturbed Marbuck to know that he'd had a second weapon concealed on his person the whole time, but it was also reassuring in a way. Old Stitch could have chosen to feign his surrender and then attacked her with the knife when he was close. He hadn't.

More disturbing than the hidden knife was the indifferent efficiency with which Old Stitch stripped the corpse. She wondered how many former allies he'd done the same thing to, and if she would eventually join their ranks.

"Your head …" Falstaff said beside her.

Reflexively, she reached up, but her hand stopped before it could reach the wound. "How bad does it look?"

He pursed his lips. "Bad."

"The skull itself is becoming necrotic," Old Stitch said, rising from his work. He wiped his bloodied hands on his breeches. "I've tried to keep it covered, but bone isn't meant to be exposed like that. My attempts to promote the regrowth of the tissue don't seem to have worked, either. There isn't anything else I can do, I'm afraid. That blackness will only spread."

"Blackness?" Marbuck asked in a small voice. Old Stitch's words were a death knell, and they rang through her increasingly rotten skull.

"The bone is, uh, well, it's turning black," Falstaff said.

Now Marbuck was certain that she could smell the corruption consuming her head. Her knees suddenly felt weak. "I need to sit down," she said, and she sank to the deck. Almost immediately, Falstaff was by her side.

"Are you alright?" he asked. The question, despite the real concern behind it, irritated Marbuck. Of course she was not alright.

"Yes, I just need a moment," she lied.

"If I could get to my medicine chest, then I could clean and redress the wound," Old Stitch said. "The second deck wasn't flooded yet when we left it; I should be able to reach my cabin."

"You keep working on him," Devonshire said, nodding toward Mordwand's partially butchered body. "I'll fetch your chest."

"It's the smaller one in the cabinet, not the chest at the foot of the cot. You'll have to find it by touch."

"Got it." Devonshire trotted to the fore hatch and descended. As she watched him go, Marbuck realized that the deck had leveled out somewhat, no longer dipping hard to starboard, but only leaning. Unfortunately, it was starting to tilt toward the stern now too, and Marbuck surmised that the lower decks were beginning to fill with water. The ship hadn't just been terminally swamped by the monstrous seas; the force of its battering must have actually damaged the hull.

"We need to get more than just your chest from below decks," Marbuck said as she rose to her feet, shooing away Falstaff's attempts to help her. "We need the last of the dried meat and the water. And something to help us cook or preserve the fresh meat."

"We don't have the means to do either of those things," Old Stitch said. "We have no way to start a fire, not with the lanterns gone. Bolenz's was lost, and the one in the oar compartment must have fallen during the turmoil. We found it broken when we were below. As for preserving the meat, it didn't work with Tannahill. I wouldn't even know where to start now."

Consumed by her own suffering, Marbuck had nearly forgotten about Tannahill. The guardsman, who'd proven to be a steadfast and valiant ally, had succumbed to his head injury and been carved up for food, and Marbuck had not spared him so much as a thought. It was a testament to the depths of her own misery, of course, but it was also an indictment of her single-mindedness. When he'd been of use to her, Tannahill had been vital. Once he was injured, she'd discarded him. Her focus on her own survival, on returning to Elibeth, had made everything else secondary. It was a realization that made her feel like shit, and she tried to convince herself that the same thing wouldn't happen again if Falstaff were injured. He certainly wouldn't forget about her.

"However," Old Stitch continued, "we should be able to retrieve the remaining provisions, with a little luck. There should be one half-full cask of water remaining, and three hunks of meat."

Shaken back to the present by his grim reckoning of what they had left, another miserable thought occurred to Marbuck. They would be forced to eat Mordwand's remains raw, warmed only by his waning body heat. It was vile, and yet her stomach craved it nonetheless.

"You focus on finishing your work," she said to Old Stitch, her mouth beginning to water. "Once Devonshire gets back up here, you can bandage my head. Then we'll worry about getting the provisions."

"What are we going to do then?" Falstaff asked. "Eat until the ship sinks?"

Marbuck had thought about this, and the answer, though dreadful, was obvious. "We'll have to abandon the ship and take our chances in the longboat."

They all looked toward the longboat, which had been left dangling from one end after dumping its deadly payload onto Midga. It was small, leaky, and would serve as their final refuge. Marbuck knew that it was nothing but a stall.

Climbing into the longboat, the four castaways would be stepping into their own grave.

• • •

The salvaging efforts had continued with Marbuck mostly sidelined. It had been frustrating for her to remain sitting on the deck as the others worked, but her weakness had allowed for little else. As Old Stitch, who'd finished with Mordwand's body, wrapped her head tightly in a new stretch of faded, dirty cloth, she'd ran her fingers slowly across the sheathed blade on her lap. It was a comfort to hold it, and she'd imagined that she could draw it swiftly enough if Old Stitch suddenly tried to strangle her with the bandage. He did no such thing, and upon concluding his ministrations, he'd set to work on bundling the different chunks of meat up in anticipation of their imminent departure.

She'd watched as Falstaff and Devonshire emerged from the fore hatch, huffing with the labor of hauling up the final water cask. Falstaff had reported that the entire orlop deck was flooded, and they'd had to swim to retrieve the cask. He'd admitted with a guilty murmur that they'd been unable to locate the last hunks of meat. Marbuck had taken this news in stride, grateful that they'd at least managed to retrieve the drinking water. At a suggestion from Old Stitch, Falstaff and Devonshire had then gone to Bolenz's cabin, in search of any private hoard of rations he might have retained. There'd been no food, but the two men had searched the chest that Bolenz had looted from his fellow slaver. Amongst the useless treasures, Falstaff had found a gilded field glass bearing the coat of arms of Nordabor.

"You take it," he'd said to Marbuck, pressing the field glass into her hands. "If anyone is going to spot a way out of this, it'll be you." She'd gazed at the ornate device, admiring the intricately inlaid depiction of the Vinecrown Keep wreathed by greenery. The heart containing the closed fist and halo of Vingallea was made of an actual carved gemstone. To her, the field glass did not look like something that would have been carried by a mere guardsman, and certainly not an average mariner. It looked like something carried by royalty.

For the first time, a new thought had occurred to Marbuck. Perhaps, the expedition hadn't just failed to free her from Vin-Sadavat. Perhaps, Phir-Ramarian and his men had fallen with the city.

Thoughts of the expedition, something she'd considered infrequently in recent times, were rolling through Marbuck's head as the four survivors hunkered down for their final meal aboard the *Empress's Love*. Old Stitch doled out greasy lumps of raw meat, and Marbuck examined her piece intently. Roughly a cycle ago, it had been a part of a living man whose malice had only been matched by his cruelty. Now, he was dead and she would be consuming him. She sank her teeth into the lukewarm tissue with a sort of spiteful pleasure. The texture was rubbery, but the bloody, juicy quality of the meat satisfied her in a way that the tiny slivers of hard, stale rations had not. Marbuck found that it was now hideously easy for her to eat raw human meat, and she chose not to examine this unlovely truth. Instead, she gazed up into the faintly glowing clouds, wondering that had caused the cataclysm that had saved her.

Falstaff followed her gaze. "What do you think it was?" he asked, as if he'd heard her thoughts.

She tongued a stringy bit of meat from between two molars and spit it aside. "I have no idea. I've never heard of anything like this happening before."

"I have," Falstaff said matter-of-factly. The others looked at him. "Well, tales of the old ones, I guess. Legends, you know, about the Sea-Keeper, and her power to make the waters rage. Or about the war between the gods. That sort of stuff. Do you think it could have been something like that?"

Marbuck considered this. Like many who'd made their living on the waters of the Einfallen, she'd grown up hearing fairy stories of the Sea-Keeper. Her parents had regaled her with the exploits of the old one, who'd once moved the waters of the world, including the distant and forgotten oceans. Considering that the expedition had sought out living old ones, Marbuck now wondered if the Sea-Keeper might have been one of them.

"Yes, that actually makes a lot of sense," she said. "Suppose the expedition found the Sea-Keeper; maybe they stirred her to wrath."

"Or that was a death throe," Devonshire added quietly. He didn't seem to care that Marbuck was aware of the expedition's secret purpose.

"Either way, I imagine that our old comrades had something to do with it," Marbuck said.

Falstaff sighed. "I wish we could know. Really know." It was the closest he'd come to admitting that they were doomed.

"Well, I know nothing of what you speak," Old Stitch said. "The legends of our people only ever concerned the Empress. To speak otherwise was heresy. From her, all the world was born, though much of it was lost in revolt. Perhaps your supposed gods were just her rebel creations."

"It sounds to me like your Empress told her own version of history," Devonshire said.

"Well, it's a moot point," Marbuck said, uninterested in getting into a theological debate about dead gods. "Whatever happened, it makes no difference to us now. What matters now is this," she held up the morsel of tissue she'd been continuing to savor, "and how long it, and our water, will last. Everything else is ancillary."

The others said nothing, the nature of the cataclysm forgotten in the face of their present danger. They finished their food in silence and then passed around a waterskin recovered from the brig. Each took a small gulp, and Marbuck thought that she'd never felt anything as wonderful as the cool water coating her ragged throat.

The ship was now noticeably lower in the water, and the longboat did not have to be lowered far before it reached the agitated surface. It took some finagling of the winch arm to get the boat to settle onto the surface without its downward pointing end simply plunging beneath the waves, but Falstaff and Marbuck managed it. The ladder was unfurled for the last time, and their meager provisions were carefully lowered. Devonshire and Falstaff took to the longboat with ardor, both seeming eager to leave the *Empress's Love* behind. Marbuck descended the ladder with markedly less enthusiasm, foreseeing a hard death in the narrow, rocking boat. Old Stitch came last, and before he stepped off the ladder, he patted a gnarled hand lovingly against the hull of the ship.

They cast off, rowing a short distance away from the sinking ship. With no real destination, there wasn't really any use in going further. The unseen currents that the cataclysm had stirred to life must have felt differently; inexorably, their tiny craft was pulled away from the dying hulk. They sat in the longboat, the very picture of lassitude. They'd survived, scavenged, and escaped, but now there was nothing left to do but nibble and sip their meager rations. Nobody spoke of which direction to go, or how they might find salvation. Nobody spoke at all.

At some point, the *Empress's Love*, had shrunk into the distance. Marbuck watched as the ship's bow slowly tilted upward and the stern disappeared beneath the waves. When the ship was finally dragged into the eternal abyss, it happened quickly and silently.

It was as if it had never been there at all.

CHAPTER 13

For Marbuck, her imprisonment in Vin-Sadavat and her time in the brig of the *Empress's Love* were pleasant dreams compared to the uncountable cycles of suffering aboard the longboat. Impossibly long stretches of time passed wherein not a word was spoken, each of the four survivors lost in their own internal misery. Sitting upright on the hard benches, fitful sleep came and went, the waking time little different from the nightmares of hunger and pain. The constant seepage allowed by the warped boards of the ancient boat ensured that lying down in the bottom was impossible as they would be drenched in frigid water almost immediately. The leak also required them to be vigilant about bailing, which had to be done with cupped hands. As such, their pruned hands were as numb and cold as their soaked feet.

Whatever had caused the upheaval of the sea and the bizarre lights in the sky, it had apparently reached its nadir. The water around them had settled, not into its original flat, glassy plain, but into a gentle, bobbing roll. Above them, the random flashes of light had mostly tapered off, and the ambient glow had faded to almost nothing, leaving them in near-total darkness. Trapped in the longboat, immobilized upon a hard seat in a vast, quiet nothing, the returning dark felt especially oppressive.

Only their rations provided them with any comfort, but it was momentary and actually amplified their agony in the long run. The portions of meat, doled out whenever all four of them agreed it was time to eat, had become punishingly small, teasing their cramping stomachs. Each feeding brought fresh dread as they watched their supply dwindle. The meat had started to take on a sour aftertaste, and they'd tried mightily to weigh their desire to make it last against the need to finish it before it spoiled. This had resulted in a short period of gorging, which in turn, had made their weakened stomachs howl. Marbuck had considered this to be a small blessing; it'd distracted her from the pain emanating sickly from her head and temporarily drove away her thirst.

The shrinking water supply was their chief concern. The cask was now empty; the last of its precious contents were now held in the waterskin. Rations had been reduced to a mere sip, and suspicious, hateful glares were directed at anyone who let the waterskin linger at their lips for more than the briefest of moments. Marbuck sensed that their physical weakness was one of the only factors keeping their growing enmity towards one another in check. Of course, it was difficult not to lash out at anyone near you when you were experiencing such a cruel, cosmic joke. They were dying of thirst, yet water surrounded them, its gentle lapping against the longboat sounding like soft, mocking laughter. It had pushed Marbuck to the limit, and her mad thirst strove to cast off any old notions that she'd held about drinking sea water. Luckily for her, Devonshire had given into temptation first, and the sight of him hanging his rear over the gunwale and firing diarrhea into the sea had reminded her of what she already knew.

His episode had passed, but he remained wracked by nausea. Now he sat, leaning against the gunwale that he'd so recently soiled, staring at Marbuck. Rising from her own miasma of despair, she noticed him watching her.

"Yes?"

He swallowed with some effort. "I'm sorry. For my part in all of this."

Marbuck nodded, expecting that to be the end of it.

"I abandoned my oath to the Crown," he continued. "I swore fealty to that monster, and though I cannot deny that she possessed some kind of strange allure, I also won't refuse all responsibility. The Commodore was only a man, and I followed him just the same. I left you and Falstaff to suffer. Worst of all, I abandoned Tannahill. He alone held true when Luden and I failed. I can only imagine what Captain Mather would think of me now. I deserve this fate. You two don't."

Marbuck was not surprised when Falstaff leaned over and patted Devonshire on the shoulder. "It doesn't matter now. You came through in the end, and the end is all that counts."

Old Stitch watched this exchange and said nothing. He'd made his worldview plain, and Marbuck did not doubt that he would've helped Mordwand butcher her if the numbers had been in the dead slaver's favor. Old Stitch might have been without malice, but he was certainly a creature of opportunity.

As for Marbuck, she was not as quick to forgive as her genial companion. Devonshire, too, had only joined her when victory was all but assured. Yes, he seemed to genuinely loathe himself for his actions, but if the cataclysm hadn't happened, he'd probably be eating her right now. With an icy shudder riding down her spine, Marbuck realized that he might still end up doing so.

"We haven't reached the end yet," she said. "But we'll be there soon if we don't get more food and water."

"There won't be any more water," Old Stitch interjected. "Of course, fresh meat could help with that problem. Before butchering, we could drain the blood and drink it. We could even store some in the cask. It won't sustain us like water would, but it will buy us some time."

For what, Marbuck did not know, but she was willing to drink it all the same. The real issue, that which was obvious but still unspoken, was how they might obtain fresh meat. Old Stitch put their morbid dread and secret desire into words.

"But to do that, we *will* need fresh meat. There's only one possible source; one of us will have to die so that the others might live. I suppose to all of you I'm the obvious choice, but bear in mind, I alone know how to properly butcher a body, so that we might have the most meat. I'm also the only healer."

"You make a compelling case for yourself," Marbuck said. "I imagine we all will, unless there are any volunteers?"

Despite his contrition, Devonshire was apparently not so consumed by regret that he might offer himself up as a sacrifice. He stared at his feet and said nothing. Falstaff's hand had retracted, and he, too, watched his own feet intently.

"Well, we'll have to figure something out," Old Stitch said.

"Yes, eventually. For now, I say we hold off and finish what we have," Marbuck said.

There were no objections, though Old Stitch seemed as if he wished to say something.

Marbuck settled back into herself, and the morose silence returned. It had been difficult for her to deny the opportunity for fresh food and commit to eating the last foul scraps of Mordwand, but Marbuck knew that the alternative almost certainly meant the end of them all.

Unless, of course, they could agree on who would die.

•   •   •

Broken bones were all that remained. Every last strip of edible tissue had been scraped from them, and they'd been snapped apart so that the reeking marrow could be sucked out. That had been, by Marbuck's estimate, something like a full-cycle ago, and she could no longer deny that it was time to restock their ghoulish larder.

Thankfully, she had come up with a solution.

"Hand me the axe," she said to Falstaff without preamble. He'd retained Mordwand's axe, as well as Old Stitch's sword. Old Stitch hadn't asked for it back, and there had been no attempt to return it to the old slaver, just as there had been no attempt to take custody of his dagger. Nobody had any interest in upending the fragile peace forged by their shared need to survive. As such, Falstaff looked at her with concerned surprise, but he did not question her as he passed over the axe. Marbuck took it, and the unexpected weight nearly sent it tumbling from her hands. It was a disturbing reminder of how much strength she had lost.

"What's this?" Old Stitch asked.

"Our answer," she said, leaning over the bench upon which she sat. She wedged the blade of the axe into a small notch on the edge of the bench and tapped against the blunt end of the axe's head with the palm of her hand. It wedged the wood apart and produced a short, splintered piece, which Marbuck snapped off. "None of us are willing to die by choice, so we'll have to leave it up to chance." She repeated the process with the axe and produced a slightly longer splinter. "Four splinters, each a different length. We each take one at random; whoever holds the shortest forfeits their life freely for the rest."

Nobody said a thing as she finished digging out the last two splinters. She leaned the axe against the bench next to her anointed blade and held the four splinters up for all to see. "Are we ready?" she asked.

"If we are to do this, then we must all agree to abide by the results," Old Stitch said. "There can be no quibbling."

To Marbuck, this seemed a forgone conclusion. The possibility of her own death existed, of course, but they had no other choice. To refuse this deadly game was to guarantee their descent into suspicion, madness, and murder. It was why she had conceived of this method in the first place.

"I agree," she confirmed.

Falstaff's eyes were fixed on the splinters. "I agree," he murmured.

"Me too," Devonshire said. He looked miserable and terrified. "How will we draw them?"

Marbuck bounced them in her palm for a moment, thinking, and then wrapped both of her hands around their length, her right fist stacked on top of her left. All but the ends of the splinters had disappeared into her clenched hands. She jostled the splinters about randomly for a moment and then presented them to the others. Four seemingly identical ends protruded from the folds of her right hand. "You each draw one. Mine will be whichever one is left."

Old Stitch eyed her hands, inspecting them for any hint of treachery. "Who goes first?"

She shrugged. "That's between you three."

The men looked at each other, and Old Stitch reached first. The other two did not oppose him. Marbuck released her grip just enough so that he could slide one of the splinters free, the ragged wood dragging across the skin of her palm. He examined his pull blankly, having nothing to compare it to. Falstaff followed, his fingers hovering gingerly over the three remaining pieces. He reached for one, halted, then chose another, pulling it out quickly and squeezing it in his own hand without so much as a glance at it.

"I guess that just leaves me," Devonshire said, leaning toward Marbuck's outstretched hands. He chose one without looking, and, as his splinter slid free, Marbuck's heart began to thump madly against the inside of her chest. Now that her swiftly-formed plan had been executed, she was seized by a fear so powerful that she felt like she might lose consciousness. She took a weak, shaky breath and opened her hand. The others held their splinters out, and they all pressed together to see whose time it was to die. Their eyes scanned the lengths of wood feverishly until the results were clear to all.

Falstaff's splinter was the shortest.

The other three quickly backed away from him, as if his death sentence was contagious. He sat, staring at the splinter in his shaking hand. "It's me," he said. "It's me."

"Well," Old Stitch started, "I suppose we—"

"No," Marbuck interrupted, shaking her throbbing head. She'd thought that she'd be able to accept the results, no matter what. She'd been wrong.

The idea of executing gentle, kind-hearted Falstaff was untenable. She would not abandon him; she would not forget about him as she had Tannahill. He was not just a tool for her survival, to be cast aside when she needed meat to fill her belly. He was her friend, and that mattered far more than following through on her oath to abide by the rules of their deadly game. "No," she repeated, "I don't accept that."

"You must; we all said—"

"I know what we said, and I don't care. I will not let this man die. Absolutely not." Marbuck moved between Old Stitch and Falstaff, her knees grinding angrily after having sat for so long. The longboat rocked with her sudden motion.

"Then you are offering yourself as a replacement?" Old Stitch asked.

Marbuck did not even consider this. After her disfigurement, she'd experienced the complete collapse of her morale. Death had beckoned her, promising an end to her hopeless suffering. But then, the cataclysm had come, shaking off the fetters of her despondency. Since then, her physical agony and the certainty of her doom had only grown, but it didn't matter. She was free, and she'd suddenly become fiercely protective of her life. She had not come so far and endured so much just to have her bones picked clean by one of her former captors.

"No, I'm not," she said. Before he could reply, she snatched her blade and the axe from where they'd been leaning against the bench. She plopped the axe onto Falstaff's lap and gripped the hilt of the blade, which remained sheathed. Falstaff goggled at her, clearly reeling from how quickly the situation had changed.

"Now just wait," Old Stitch said, holding his hands up. "There's no need for any of that."

"I just want to make sure that nobody acts hastily," Marbuck said.

"The only one doing so is you. We had an agreement; all of us. You're jeopardizing everyone's survival by rejecting that now. It's not fair, and it leaves us with nothing, no alternative."

"I don't care."

"Well, what do *you* say?" Old Stitch asked Falstaff. "Does she speak for you? Or will you stand by your word?"

Falstaff gripped the axe purposefully. "I'm sorry, but I can't."

Old Stitch scoffed. "I suppose you won't stand against them now," he said to Devonshire, who'd slunk back to his accustomed spot against the gunwale.

"No, I won't."

Old Stitch threw his hands in the air. "Well, this entire process has been pointless. *He drew the short splinter, and we need to eat.*"

"Yes," Marbuck said, unsheathing her blade slowly, "we do."

Old Stitch watched the blade, and his eyes grew wide. "What are you doing?"

Marbuck suspected that he knew exactly what she was doing. She hadn't intended for it to come to this, but now that things were in motion, it was plain that this was the only choice that made any sense. She and Falstaff would remain united. Devonshire, though he'd joined with the slavers for a time, now stood with her. After all, he'd started as a captive taken from the *Fortune* just as she had. There was only one true slaver remaining. Whatever mercy Old Stitch had shown her, whatever fleeting allegiance he'd sworn, whatever skills he possessed, it didn't matter. If one of them had to die, it would be the slaver.

Her blade cleared its scabbard, and Old Stitch scrambled over the bench he'd sat upon, rocking the boat. "Stop! Who will butcher the meat? Who will treat your wounds? Think about this for a moment!" he said, backing toward the bow.

"I have." Marbuck took another step toward him. Behind her, Falstaff and Devonshire had risen.

"We had a deal, the only deal that made any sense. This is exactly what we wanted to avoid. *Put that sword away*! We can figure something else out!" Old Stitch was now wedged into the bow, as if he wished to shrink into it and vanish. Marbuck stepped over the bench.

"You cannot let her do this!" he shouted at Falstaff and Devonshire. They said nothing, and they didn't need to. Marbuck had sensed their tacit support the moment she'd started to draw her blade.

"*You faithless cheats!*" Old Stitch shrieked. "After all the kindness I've shown you! You're mad if you think she won't turn on you next!" He snorted with derision. "Assuming her wound doesn't take her first. We should be putting her down; she's ill! She'll be dead soon anyway; why not kill her so that we three can survive? Listen to me!" he pleaded.

"So much for the fealty you swore to me," Marbuck said, the confirmation of his mercurial loyalty easing her conscience.

A small, defeated smile pulled at the corners of his lipless mouth. "I never lied to you. I told you that our paths were now intertwined, but only for a little while. I suppose now, my path has come to an end. It was inevitable. But do not delude yourself: yours is finished too. You are dead already, Marbuck. The corruption in your head cannot be stopped. Your comrades might be so cowed by you that they'd never admit it, but they know it as well as I do. *You are dead.* You just haven't accepted it yet."

"Nor will I, until I cease to draw breath," Marbuck said, and, all at once, Old Stitch's hideous face had become the face of Bolenz, Mordwand, Gomulte, all of the monstrous captors who had brought her to this wretched point. "I think you're confusing dead with dying. Let me show you the difference."

Old Stitch fumbled for his dagger, but it was too late. Marbuck closed the small distance between them and drove her blade through his gut. He let out a strange, squeaky cough, and she forced it to the left, opening his belly. He clutched feebly at the bloodied blade as she yanked it free, and his guts spilled noisily at his feet. Old Stitch, already pressed against the bow, slid down onto his bottom. He opened his mouth, burbled out some blood, and began to blink rapidly.

Marbuck stepped back, her breath coming in ragged gulps. Though he'd put up almost no fight, killing him had still sapped her of her rapidly dwindling strength. What little she had left, she mustered in anticipation of the shade that she prayed wouldn't come. They could not afford to lose any of his meat.

Suddenly, Old Stitch jerked upward, trying to rise. He didn't make it very far; he flopped backward instead, kicking at the loose coils of his own intestines, which had fallen into the bloody water at the bottom of the boat. He seized for another moment before taking a final, hitching breath, which culminated in a wet burp. Briefly, his head lolled and then it dropped, his chin coming to rest against his bony chest.

With Falstaff and Devonshire flanking her, Marbuck stared at the body, willing it to remain still. To her dismay, it did not. Just as she'd started to believe that they were in the clear, the telltale shaking of the body began, joined soon thereafter by the sickening wail of the shade's creation.

"Cast it overboard!" Devonshire shouted as he staggered back toward the stern.

"We can't," Marbuck said wearily, leveling her blade. "We need the meat."

"Well, let's hang him overboard then, let the shade drop right into the water," Falstaff said, shuffling past Marbuck to the body. Her fatigued mind had considered fighting the shade to be her only option; now that Falstaff had suggested otherwise, it seemed obvious. She helped him lift the seizing body, and the two of them hoisted it over the gunwale, letting the head hang down almost to the water.

"Don't let him drop!" Falstaff cried as the blood-slick body began to buck beneath them. Marbuck struggled to hold on, taking a knee to the side of the head for her efforts. Before the flailing legs could continue their assault, Devonshire was there, pinning them down.

Finally, the convulsions ceased. Almost immediately, the skullcap exploded directly into the water with a percussive snap, showering them with a fine, briny spray. Old Stitch's scarred face was folded over onto itself as the shade began to slither free from his shattered skull. It disgorged into the sea with a series of foul, muddy plops, and the firm body they'd been holding down began to deflate beneath their hands. The mass of the shade, sinking into the depths before it could fully form, thrashed about, bumping against the side of the longboat. As the last discharge streamed from Old-Stitch's ruined corpse, the splashing of the shade tapered off completely.

Panting, the three remaining survivors, who were now coated in gore and drenched to the bone, slid the deflated skin sack back into the boat. The shade's black ichor still dripped from the open head, and the rest of the remains stank with the sour odor of corruption. Marbuck had believed that, although she'd eaten raw human flesh, she could never bring herself to eat a body spoiled by a shade. Like so many of her previous qualms, this holdout was now easily abandoned. They wasted no time in cutting strips of meat from the strange, loose remains, setting some aside with half-hearted pledges of conservation. Mostly they ate whatever they could get just as quickly as they could get it, jostling against each other like wild animals. Marbuck's first bite was into a stretch of thigh flesh that was oily, chewy, and incredibly repugnant. She fought down her gag reflex and kept going, her ravenous hunger overmastering her disgust. She gulped eagerly at the blood pooling within the open stomach cavity, though it was obviously polluted by the shade's residue.

As Marbuck sucked the last bits of stinking grime from her dirty fingers, she realized that she'd never felt lower in her entire existence. She also knew, without a doubt, that this putrid banquet would only accelerate her fate. Her own sickness would be amplified by the tainted flesh she'd consumed, and her death would be grueling. She wondered if she, too, would produce a shade. If so, she'd undoubtedly be cast into the sea to face the same eternity of torment.

With her stomach already screaming from the influx of rancid meat, Marbuck crawled back onto her bench. Hugging her knees to her chest, she began to weep.

CHAPTER 14

"Mama?"

Marbuck heard the voice of her daughter clearly, but that wasn't possible. There was no way that Elibeth was here with her, though she could not remember why. She was no longer certain where she was; she just knew that it was dark, wet, and unbearably cold. Only the crown of her head was hot, and its intense, throbbing heat seemed to leach the warmth from the rest of her body. She was awake, but she was also asleep. Vaguely, she recalled being violently ill after a period of dizziness that had sent all of creation spinning beneath her. Now, everything was confusion, except for the clear, soft voice of Elibeth, coming to her through the darkness.

"Mama?"

The voice was close, very close. It was in the boat with her. The boat; of course; she was in the longboat. She'd *always* been in the longboat. It was a womb carrying her to her rebirth, a passage of pain that would deliver her beyond the veil of life. And she was not alone in it. Falstaff and Devonshire were there too, locked in their own private death spirals. They probably couldn't hear Elibeth's voice, but then it wasn't *for* them.

"*Mama?*"

"I'm here, sweetheart," Marbuck said, though the voice that spoke was only a projection of her thought. It was better that way, though.

The thought-voice was Marbuck's old voice, not the raspy whisper that she possessed now. Elibeth sounded scared; she needed to hear her mother, not a sick, dying woman.

"Mama, is that really you?" Elibeth asked. Marbuck could now see her; she was standing in the boat, bathed in a bright glow. It was as if the sun had somehow found its way to her through the perpetual night.

"Yes, I'm here; it's okay."

"Something's wrong with Da."

This struck Marbuck as odd. Elibeth knew that Baylis was gone and had been for over three long-cycles. "What do you mean?" she asked.

"He's all soft," Elibeth said, and she began to cry. "And his head is funny."

Though Marbuck didn't understand what was happening, she tried to reach out to her daughter. Her arms would not move. As she sought for the right thing to say, she noticed another form standing behind Elibeth. It stepped into her light, and Marbuck's heart stopped.

It was Baylis.

Or, it had been. What Marbuck now beheld was only the shriveled remains of her husband, the deformed husk that his shade had left behind. By some nightmarish power, the last shreds of Baylis, which Marbuck had watched the shepherds cart away, now stood before her, naked, hideous, and undeniable. His splintered head bobbed on his thin neck, and his face drooped away from the broken skull beneath it. The black juices of a shade wept freely from his eyes, nose, and mouth. He was attempting to smile, and that was more terrible than anything else.

"Hello, Raina," Baylis said, and his voice was a burbling croak. Beside him, Elibeth began to sob silently. He placed a soft, oozing hand upon her shoulder. "When are you coming home?"

Marbuck was petrified by terror and woe, and she could not answer.

"She's already home," a new voice said. "Here, with us."

Marbuck's eyes, unblinking and bulging wildly, panned toward the source of the new voice. Falstaff and Devonshire were gone, and the remaining benches were now occupied by a crew of horrors. Castor was there; his entire body bifurcated by a growing rot spreading from his butchered crotch. From the yawning fissure between his legs, thick cuts of meat were tumbling forth, loosely humanoid forms held together by a web of viscera and bearing the faces of Tannahill, Mordwand, and Old Stitch, each contorted into a silent scream. Beside them lurked the bloated, waterlogged bodies of Gomulte and Tordenaar, as well as the brutalized form of Luden. They stepped aside for Midga, still clad in the burnt skin he'd died in. He tore it away, revealing first the loose skin of Chrisholm, then Karant, then Usso, the head of a spear protruding from his chest.

"Fishwife, c'mere," a wet voice said jovially and then a damp hand was twisting her head back toward Elibeth and Baylis. It was Winslow, and his grinning mouth was full of blood. "Before you know it, we'll all be right back here counting out our coin."

Unable to move or speak, Marbuck could do nothing but watch as this horrific slew of nightmares washed over her. Now, Baylis was seizing Elibeth by the hair, and her cries had grown deafeningly loud. He placed a razor-sharp finger against Elibeth's forehead and began slicing, sending a cascade of bright red blood raining down her face. Marbuck tried to scream, but only succeeded in soiling herself. A moment later, the Baylis-thing was peeling Elibeth's scalp free, and her white skull, smeared with blood, shone brilliantly. The creature masquerading as her husband placed the scalp upon its own head and boomed laughter. Blood ran down its face, mixing with the shade's ichor. The liquid burned deep, straight lines into the face, and now it was no longer Baylis. It was Bolenz.

"You're nearly there," he said, his laughter subsiding. "After all of your refusals, you're nearly there. You could have stood beside me before an endless procession of slaves. Now, you will walk with me in the deep. Take my hand. Submit. SUBMIT. *SUBMIT.*"

The entire phantasmal crew took up the chant. Elibeth's voice rose with them, and she lifted her bloody head. Her face was now a mutilated knot of scar tissue. Marbuck's eyes rolled wildly, manically, seeking for some kind of escape. The dead closed in, their fetid hands grasping at her, seeking to pull her into death. Chanting their hateful refrain, they began to shake her, and she felt sweat erupt across her body. She stared past them, focusing on the blank nothingness of the sky.

Suddenly, there was light.

•　•　•

"Fishwife? *Fishwife! Raina!*"

The terrible chorus had narrowed into a single voice, and now it was only Falstaff shaking her. She swatted weakly at him, still in a confused state of fear. He held her hands back and tried to soothe her. By degrees, her fever vision's hold over her slipped away, and she became somewhat aware of her surroundings again. Bursting into grateful tears, she wrapped her arms around Falstaff.

"You feel a little cooler. I think your fever might have broken." He paused. "For now."

It hadn't been the first wave of high fever that Marbuck had ridden, but it'd certainly been the worst, accompanied as it was by the horrifying dream. She doubted that she could survive another episode like that. Certainly, her sanity wouldn't.

"You scared me," Falstaff said. "The way you were crying out, I thought … well, you know."

Marbuck nodded gratefully. "I know," she rasped. "I need water."

"There's none left, remember?" Devonshire said with a tinge of bitterness. He'd been sitting in his normal spot, watching them. In her delirium, Marbuck had forgotten that her illness had prompted Falstaff to be generous with her water rations, giving her a sip whenever she called out for one. She'd known that she was taking more than her fair share, but she'd been too sick to care. Now that her fever had broken again, guilt gnawed at her. Though they hadn't fared as poorly as she had, both Falstaff and Devonshire had been sickened by Old Stitch's tainted flesh too, and they hadn't taken any extra water.

"I'm sorry," she muttered.

Devonshire grunted and shifted his weight. Falstaff stared at the empty waterskin. A sluggish realization forced itself into Marbuck's thoughts: she could see them. She then looked beyond the narrow confines of their floating prison, and the last of her mental fog was blown away.

The sea, moving still in the aftermath of the cataclysm, had carried them to a place where the ever-present cloud cover had finally broken. What was lying beyond the oppressive smother of the clouds was a sight that Marbuck struggled to comprehend. The sky was dotted with millions of points of white light, which illuminated the darkness, but were not the cause of her amazement. Turning to gaze at the sparkling reflections on the water around them, she had seen something impossible. Far off in the distance, just above the horizon, a strange, jagged line of pure whiteness spread across the sky. It looked like a crack in a piece of fine glass, and from within its brilliance, surging flashes of light could be seen flickering like a faraway beacon. It was undoubtedly the flashes they'd seen before, only now weaker, revealed to them again in the absence of the clouds. Where the shimmering lights of the firmament were breathtakingly beautiful, the crack in the sky was as unnatural as it was off-putting.

"What is it?" she asked, not expecting an answer.

"I dunno, but it's been there since we started to pass out from under the clouds," Falstaff said. "The points of light are stars, I think."

"Yeah, I think you're right," Marbuck said, still looking at the crack. "I remember reading about them in the scriptures at the Ivy Citadel. The Father-God supposedly put them there."

"To navigate by," Falstaff said. "My mum told me that ancient mariners used the stars to find their way."

Marbuck was familiar with these legends, and, seeing stars for the first time, found them easy to believe. If she'd known this secret art when she'd been tasked with directing the *Empress's Love* north, and if the clouds had not held such a stranglehold on the sky above them, maybe things could have gone differently. Of course, she knew that pointless what-ifs were of no use to her, but she couldn't help thinking about them.

"If only we could do that now," Falstaff said.

"Well, I might not know anything about these stars," Devonshire said, "but I'm thinking that way is north." He pointed toward the unnatural crack.

"Why's that?" Falstaff asked.

"It all comes down to the expedition. They were headed north, looking for the last old ones. It can't be a coincidence that they were hunting for these deities and then all this happens. I think we were on the right track when we said that the cataclysm was caused by them. Only, I don't think it was from them killing any one god. I think, maybe, they fucked something up. Whatever happened, it must have been monumental to rouse the sea like that, especially from such a great distance. And I would bet that whatever the expedition did is also to blame for the sky. If we can see that sort of damage from here, imagine what's going on up north."

"What could they have done?" Falstaff wondered.

"I don't know. I don't know what their ultimate intentions were; the leaders of the expedition didn't tell us. Whatever it was, I think they failed."

"Or they succeeded," Marbuck murmured, thinking of the captive god in Nordabor. It was dying, or so Winslow had been told by Rayburn. Certainly she'd seen evidence of Nordabor's decline all around her in the past few long-cycles. If a god's *approaching* death could harm the physical world around them, then what would the *actual* deaths of several of them do? Marbuck did not know enough of the lore surrounding the old ones to even guess at what the effects would be, but she could not imagine that they'd be anything good. It didn't seem to make any sense;

the expedition killing other gods to save Nordabor, especially when the threat to the city's survival was a dying god. Marbuck felt that she was missing something.

Whatever the case, this new consideration brought with it a new fear. While she was a world away, dying in obscurity, Elibeth was left behind in a doomed city, one which was perhaps in even more danger now. Marbuck pictured what the sky-crack must look like that far north, and a squirming dread took root in her stomach. All at once, the horrors of her dream came roaring back with monstrous clarity. When Devonshire spoke again, she hardly heard him.

"It doesn't really matter now, anyway," he said with a sigh. "They're out there. We're here."

"Well, we finally know which way to go," Falstaff said. "We could start rowing."

Devonshire snorted. "We're out of water. It would probably take a long-cycle to row that far. You do the math."

"We could at least try."

"Devonshire is right," Marbuck said. "It would be pointless to even start." She pawed away a tear. The fever dream may have been over, but reality was little better. The finality of their doom was clear, and her despair was absolute. "I'm never going to see Elibeth again."

"Don't say that," Falstaff said quietly.

"She'll never know what happened. She'll be alone, and she'll never understand why."

"You don't know that. We're still here, it's not over yet."

Marbuck shook her head, but Falstaff persisted. "We've made it this far; we just have to find a way to keep going."

"We can't. Not without food or water. We need to …" She trailed off, knowing that there was no plan worth speaking aloud.

"Forgive me," Devonshire said. "I know that I swore to atone for abandoning you to the slavers, but I really hope that you're not implying that another of us needs to die. Because I also know that you two would close ranks against me, and I understand why, but I don't care. I will fight for my life. No matter how little of it is left."

Marbuck was not at all surprised to hear how quickly Devonshire had changed his tune, and she couldn't really blame him. At any rate, she was in no shape to challenge him. At least he hadn't suggested that she should die. Perhaps he didn't think it was necessary to bother; she'd be dead soon enough.

"No, I wasn't implying that; I have no interest in killing anyone else. You can both eat me when I'm dead."

"You're not going to—" Falstaff started.

"I am," Marbuck said. "I am."

The three of them sat in silence, the gentle slapping of the water against the longboat the only sound. Above them, the stars shined with silent splendor.

"I don't want to kill you, either," Falstaff said to Devonshire.

Devonshire smiled weakly. "I'm glad to hear that. I'll follow Marbuck's lead here; you can feel free to eat me if and when death comes naturally."

"There's nothing natural about any of this," Falstaff said. "But the same goes for me."

With their new, morbid contract established, there was nothing left to do but wait.

· · ·

Marbuck was now too dehydrated to sweat, and her unchecked fever had resumed its rise. Her mouth felt acrid and raw, and her tongue had started to swell into a dry, gray lump. Attempts to wet her cracked and withered lips were fruitless. The heat coming off her head was now like a furnace, while the rest of her body was left shivering intensely. Every thought revolved around her thirst, and it took every last shred of her willpower to not start lapping up the standing water at the bottom of the boat. Thankfully, they had cast the final shreds of Old Stitch overboard after his spoiled remains had made them sick. At least that temptation was removed; Marbuck knew that, despite the illness it had inflicted on her, she'd be willing to dip into his poison blood again right now, just to slake her thirst.

Falstaff and Devonshire were not faring much better. They'd grown listless and weak, their labored breaths being the only indication that they were still alive.

The sole comfort left to Marbuck was the view of the stars. They were hauntingly beautiful, and, as long as she didn't look toward the bizarre crack in what she assumed was the north, the view of the sky provided her with a sliver of peace.

Her eyes were slowly roving over each of the unique clusters of stars, sliding toward the point where they would reach the sea and their own wavering reflections, when Marbuck saw it. The eastern horizon had changed. The stars did not reach the sea, but were now blocked by a low, black mass.

She stared at it, squinting, not believing that it was really there. She looked to the south and the west, where the stars still met the horizon, then looked back. Suddenly, she recalled the ornate field glass that Falstaff had given her. She slid it from her ragged belt and leveled it at the eastern horizon. It was undeniable; something was there.

"Land," she said, her uncooperative tongue dragging through her desiccated mouth. The others did not stir. "Land!" she said again, as loudly as she could.

"What?" Falstaff asked, his voice a husky whisper.

"*Land.*" She thrust an outstretched hand toward the east. "*Right there.* Land."

Devonshire lifted his head now. "Impossible."

The three of them stared across the water, struggling to accept that, for the first time in countless cycles, they were looking at something new. Once Marbuck decided that the land was real, she did not want to look away, fearing that it might slip beneath the horizon and be lost forever.

"The oars," she said, the magnetic draw of the land breathing new life into her. She didn't need to say anything else; Falstaff and Devonshire were moving for the oars even as she spoke. Her head swam from weakness and giddy disbelief as she rose from her bench and grabbed the closest oar. She plopped back down near the gunwale and started rowing, her spent body driven purely by manic desire.

Soon the three of them were paddling furiously, heedless of establishing any sort of rhythm, and the boat cut a crooked course through the rolling waves. They paused only to make sure that they were still headed toward the land, and that it was still, in fact, there. As Marbuck heaved the oar, wheezing with each pull, she experienced a disorienting moment in which she thought they were rowing back into the bay of the skinners. Looking at her surroundings again, she was able to dismiss this notion. Now that they were somewhat closer, she was certain that it was not a bay at all, but a strip of relatively flat land that spread out to the north and tapered off toward the south, completely open to the sea.

"Let's aim for that," Falstaff said between gulps of air. He pointed toward the southern stretch, where Marbuck now noticed a shape rising above the rest of the mass. Another look through the field glass revealed a narrow spire of darkness blotting out a straight line of stars. It did not look like a natural formation; it looked man-made.

Her hope, which had lain dormant for so long, suddenly flared back to life. She knew that those occupying the structure might be just another collection of depraved fiends, and she didn't care. She also knew that it might not be occupied at all, and this didn't bother her either. Somehow, after what felt like a lifetime of being lost on the immutable face of the sea, they'd stumbled upon something more than just a barren waste. She could not help but dream of survival now, despite her best attempts to check her excitement.

They continued to row toward the spire for another cycle, aided by the underlying current of the waves. Marbuck's will had to contend with the protests of her body, withered as it was by starvation and idleness. Whenever it seemed that she had nothing left to give, she would look to the shore, checking their progress. Each of these glances revealed that they were getting closer and closer, which bolstered her spirit. She could now see that the spire rose from a large structure built upon a solitary bluff, which loomed over a flat, sandy beach. Further inland, the beach grew into a series of rolling dunes.

As they approached the shore, the booming crash of the surf reached their ears, which fired their spirits for a final push. Marbuck had never heard such a sound before; the currents of the Einfallen had only ever produced a gentle lapping against the shore. The sea, shaken so violently during the cataclysm, had still not fully settled, and here, those lingering waves met the beach in a raucous cacophony. It was a primordial sound, one from a distant epoch, not heard for many, many lifetimes. It was power and life, and Marbuck felt it imbuing her with vitality.

As the longboat skated over the final, breaking waves, Marbuck cried out in a wild scream of triumph. Falstaff and Devonshire joined in with animalistic shouts of their own. Riding a frothing wave, the longboat slid onto the beach, its keel skating across the wet sand. Another wave struck against their stern and lifted them further up the beach. The bow plunged into a hump of sand, and they came to a jarring halt. The wave receded from beneath them, and the longboat remained behind, resting upon the beach.

They had made it to solid ground.

As if they feared that the sea might change its mind, all three of them grabbed their few remaining possessions and scrambled out of the hated longboat as quickly as they could. Tumbling over the gunwale, Marbuck dropped onto the sand and wept with delirious ecstasy, digging her fingers into the damp sand. A wave rushed by beneath her, the cold water dousing her. As it receded, it pulled the sand away from her buried hands. She tried to rise, flopped back into the surf, and tried again. Finally, she staggered away from the boat, joining Falstaff and Devonshire further up the shore, beyond the reach of the sea from which they'd finally escaped.

• • •

Trudging toward the structure, which they'd landed just north of, Marbuck began to shiver violently. Her head was throbbing with heat, and her over-strained and atrophied limbs were cramping. None of this dampened her spirits though; she was still far too exhilarated by the simple act of walking somewhere to pay any heed to her condition. Between her imprisonment aboard the *Empress's Love* and her time trapped in the longboat, she had been immobilized for far too long. To walk where she wished to go, under her own power, was a joy.

The sight of her own two feet propelling her forward was almost more captivating than the sight before her, but not quite, and certainly not as they grew closer to the towering ruin. It was clear from the monumental architecture that the structure had been of some great importance, a seaside temple from the remote past. The lower third of the temple appeared to have been carved directly out of the rock of the cliff face. Above that foundation, megalithic blocks of stone formed the vast bulk of the rounded structure. This outer wall was pockmarked and shot through with large fissures, but remained standing. Beyond a shattered parapet that encircled the flat top, the main tower rose in an elegant spiral, culminating in a curved tongue of stone that dipped downward and pointed back toward the sea. This mysterious spire, its design still clear despite its deterioration, reminded Marbuck of the waves of the sea, which she could still hear breaking upon the beach behind them.

Near the foot of the bluff, they found a series of weathered steps that appeared to lead up toward the temple. Already huffing from their short walk across the beach, the uneven, broken steps presented a serious obstacle. Nevertheless, they started up, winding their way along the eroded side of a sandy slope before proceeding up onto the stonier ground of the cliff. Marbuck's legs trembled from the effort, but she kept moving, her eyes fixed on the temple.

"It looks abandoned," Falstaff observed.

"Yes," Marbuck agreed, pausing to take a gulping breath. "But where else do we have to go? At least it offers some shelter. And who knows? Maybe there *is* someone inside."

"Yeah, maybe," Falstaff said, his hand wandering toward his belt, where Old Stitch's sword and Mordwand's axe dangled.

As they ascended the final steps, Marbuck could see that they led to an entrance; a large, doorless archway, beyond which lay complete darkness. On either side of the opening, immense bas-reliefs stood out in the starlight. They appeared to mirror one another, with both depicting the same scene of divine creation. Born from the outspread arms of a crowned being, a female figure surrounded by waves stretched across the carving. A halo hovered above her head, and in her outstretched hands was an enormous cudgel. Numerous vessels were depicted riding the waves that her tremendous power appeared to be stirring up.

"It's the Sea-Keeper," Falstaff said. "This must have been a temple dedicated to her."

Marbuck studied the ancient carving, which was remarkably intact. Small flecks of paint were even still visibly hanging from some parts. It was certainly a depiction of the old ones, with the Sea-Keeper being the most likely subject, but that wasn't particularly comforting. Marbuck imagined that there were probably numerous monuments to the old ones that predated the collapse of their world scattered across the land, all of them equally empty. The euphoria she'd felt at spotting the tower began to dissolve. If this faraway place was truly deserted, then they'd simply traded dying in the longboat for dying in the empty halls of a forgotten shrine.

"You don't think it's possible that she's here, do you?" Devonshire asked, peering into the open doorway.

"I feel like we would know by now," Falstaff said.

Marbuck was barely listening. A swamping wave of weakness had struck her, and she worried that she might collapse. "Let's get inside," she said. "I need to rest."

Seeing her sudden wooziness, Falstaff and Devonshire helped her across the threshold. The three of them hunkered down close to the doorway, where a short stretch of starlight cut into the blackness. Beyond it, the rest of the temple was hidden from them, save for a few areas of scant light provided by the cracks in the masonry.

As Marbuck rested under the anxious eye of Falstaff, Devonshire attempted to search the temple. Hindered by the darkness, he returned not long after, frustrated and distressed. As far as he could tell, they were utterly alone. No source of water existed, nor was there anything they could possibly eat.

It seemed that, once again, there was nothing left for them to do but lapse into idle suffering.

. . .

Time wore on.

With every waking moment defined by burning thirst, the cycles stretched into infinity. They could not have been in the damp, vaulted chamber for very long, yet Marbuck felt as if they'd languished there for longer than they'd been in the longboat. With the excitements of finding land and reaching the temple now fully dissipated, all of her afflictions previously held at bay had come roaring back. It was dismal, knowing that they'd come so far, yet still failed to change their fate.

Struggling to her feet, Marbuck decided that there was, in fact, one thing she could change. She now had an autonomy that she'd lacked in the cramped confines of the longboat. Here, she was free to walk, and, despite her all-encompassing feebleness, she decided that walking was exactly what she was going to do. Death might be inevitable, but she would not meet it shivering in the dark. She intended to die on her feet, walking as far north as her quivering legs would take her.

Falstaff, of course, would have objected strenuously to this plan, so Marbuck did not share it with him. He would have fussed and argued, or insisted on coming with her. Maybe it was selfish, but she could no longer bear the sight of her friend dying brutally. It was enough to go through it herself but, sitting in the dark, listening to Falstaff's labored breaths was too much. It would break his heart to wake and find her gone, she knew, but so would finding her dead. Better for her to march along this unknown shore and seek for something, anything beyond the ignominious death of an invalid. Perhaps this primitive desire to have a private death was also selfish; after all, she would be denying Falstaff and Devonshire the opportunity to eat her remains. Not that there was much left to eat. The positive side was that she would also be preventing them from being torn to shreds by the shade she might spawn. Truthfully, she was too miserable and delirious to really weigh the morality of her actions. She just needed to go north.

So, with her fever once again running roughshod through her body, Marbuck staggered as quietly as she could toward the doorway. She looked back at the two men she was leaving behind, and her heart ached again for Falstaff. Devonshire, whose morale had collapsed completely when it'd become clear that the derelict temple held no deliverance, was sleeping as well, the deep, languid sleep of one whose body is shutting down. She felt pity for him, but no more than she felt for herself.

She crossed the threshold, stepping back into the starlight, and began to make her way down the steps, the anointed blade bouncing against her hip. Her head throbbed with each plodding step; it felt as if a halo of fire had tightened itself around her skull, its licking flames scouring her mind. The stench of corruption was now inescapable, encircling her head like a miasmic cloud. As she reached the bottom of the steps, her vision wavered and her knees threatened to buckle. She sucked in a few rattling breaths, and, once she felt that she'd composed herself, continued across the sand. The beach stretched away toward the north as far as she could see; a uniform land of rolling dunes on one side, the boundless sea on the other. There was absolutely no sign that any human habitation stood between her and the moment where her battered body would finally give out. She kept going anyway.

She passed the longboat, which had been knocked askew by the pull of the waves, without giving it a second thought. Her vision narrowed into a blurred tunnel, showing only the endless line of beach before her. The pounding surf, though just to her left, had faded into a distant echo, accompanied by faint whispers that seemed to be coming from all around her. She recognized them as the voices of the dead, calling to her, growing louder as she got closer to joining their ranks.

Her face screwed up into a wail, but she made no sound, and her depleted body produced no tears. She stumbled to her knees, and a bitter fury rose in her. She did not want to die; she wanted to be with Elibeth. Her daughter had lost her father to idiotic chance, a dockside fluke born of a frayed rope and a falling barrel. Now she would lose her mother, who'd been lured away by the promise of easy coin. Marbuck cursed herself for being such a fool, for believing that she could buy her way out of her life of drudgery and find some peaceful repose with her daughter. She should have known better; she should have known that nothing that promising could be true. And worst of all, she'd left Elibeth behind to face whatever was happening in the north without her.

Uselessly, Marbuck punched her fists into the sand, gasping with the effort. She crumpled over, but continued to look to the north, toward the daughter she would never see again. Far away, the crack in the sky hovered, a faintly pulsing menace. Her consciousness began to ebb, and, as she started to slip away, she became aware that she was no longer alone on the beach.

Several darkened forms were approaching her.

Marbuck closed her eyes.

PART 3:
LIGHT AND SHADOW

CHAPTER 15

Awareness, true awareness, came back slowly. It began with a dream of sunlight and voices and grew into a knowledge of her own physical form; small movements of her fingers and toes. Gradually, she came to understand that she was not in pain and was, in fact, comfortable, a feeling that had become totally alien to her. She was lying upon soft cushions, a silken sheet draped across her body. She slid her arms and legs across the warm, dry surface, feeling the luxuriant fabric, listening to the gentle whisper of her skin against the bedding. She breathed deeply, her eyes still closed. The shuttered lids were aglow with the light that pressed against them.

Light.

Marbuck's mind stumbled over this realization, and, hesitatingly, she opened her eyes. After so long spent in darkness, the radiance around her was almost too much. She blinked, her eyes blurred and watering, until she could finally examine her strange new surroundings.

She began to wonder if she was dead.

The chamber she found herself in was awash with a golden light that streamed in from a long, narrow window set high on the smooth sandstone wall to her right. The tan walls, shot through with bands of red and purple, were bare, and the room itself was sparsely furnished, but what was there was beautiful. She was lying upon a wide bed with pristine white linens and an elaborately carved headboard depicting exotic birds unlike anything she'd ever seen. Against the opposite wall was an ivory-colored bureau with a built-in vanity, standing upon wrought iron, clawed feet. Her eyes fell on the mirror, which was tilted downward, and her heart fluttered.

Gingerly, she slid from the bed and placed her bare feet onto the tiled floor. She realized for the first time that she was no longer wearing her filthy rags; she'd been washed and dressed in a white silk robe. This didn't disturb or confuse her; she barely took any notice of it at all. Her focus was locked on the mirror, and she walked toward it on legs that were unexpectedly stable, passing a polished wooden door on her left without so much as a glance. Reaching the mirror, she extended a hand she barely recognized. It was clean and thin, the nails neatly trimmed. With a gentle nudge, she tilted the mirror upward.

She studied the face in the mirror for a long time. Logically, she knew it was hers, but she struggled to believe it. Her skin was pale and loose, and her haunted eyes stared back at her from deep sockets, under which hung heavy bags. Her cheeks were sunken, creating the illusion that her teeth were too big for her mouth. Oddly, her teeth felt clean, and her gums looked healthy. She'd been certain that decay had taken over in her mouth, but no sign of it remained. Similarly, but far more astoundingly, the same thing appeared to have occurred with her mutilated scalp. A jagged pink line encircled her head, a lumpish scar denoting where Bolenz had done his work. Above that line, where she'd been expecting to see rotten skull ringed by putrescence, was a pale, hairless stretch of skin. She reached up and touched it lightly. It felt like the thin skin of a newborn.

Marbuck was standing there, dumbfounded, when the door behind her creaked softly open. She wheeled about with a small gasp, pressing her back against the bureau. A man she'd never seen before poked his head into the room and, seeing her, smiled brilliantly, lifting the corners of his great, bushy moustache.

"I thought you might be waking up soon," he said, his voice a jovial drawl. "How are you feeling?"

Marbuck did not answer. She stood riveted to the spot, trying mightily to sort out what was happening to her. She'd lived under the abusive hand of the slavers for so long that this stranger, despite his friendly demeanor, struck her as threatening.

"You still look pretty exhausted—no offense—why don't you have a seat?" the man said, stepping into the chamber. He matched the surroundings, dressed as he was in a tan tunic with a white cape hanging jauntily from one shoulder. Smiling warmly, he seemed oblivious to the fact that she was staring at him like a caged animal. He gestured toward the bed. When she didn't move, he nodded with sympathetic understanding. "I imagine you're pretty confused right now. Well, let me just—"

"Where are my companions?" Marbuck asked.

"They're here, and they're okay. Your fellow convalescents were in rough shape when we found them, but not nearly as bad as you. They told me a little about what happened to you all. Dreadful business. They've been up for a while now; the one, Falstaff, has been very eager to check on you."

The use of Falstaff's name was proof that this man had at least spoken to her friend. Still, Marbuck remained wary. "Where, exactly, is here? And who are you?"

"Here is Quaretem, specifically the Great Ziggurat, and I am Henrick Kemp, a huntsman. I was leading a wide patrol into the lands of the Closed Eye when we found you on the beach. We followed your tracks back to the ruins and found your friends. You're all quite lucky that we were so far west. I wanted to get a better view of that strange mark in the sky, and lo! I stumble upon castaways from a distant land. Very peculiar things have been happening lately, indeed."

A cascade of questions, each jostling to be the first, threatened to overwhelm Marbuck. She caught sight of her reflection in the mirror, and one query rose above the others. "How am I even alive?"

Kemp patted the rise of his belly and hoisted his gray eyebrows, which were as bushy as his moustache. "Well, I have to take some credit there. My ministrations kept you alive long enough to get you here. You'd fallen into the sleep from which there is typically no awakening, so I had my doubts, but the Lady of the Veil set you right nonetheless."

As Marbuck listened, she continued to examine her face. She drew a finger across the circlet of scar tissue. It was very tender.

"Unfortunately, she cannot recover what was lost completely; she can only heal that which remains. Your hair might grow back though, given enough time."

Marbuck could have wept, looking at what she'd become. Yet, an equally powerful feeling of defiant triumph had risen in her. She was alive. She'd been at the absolute brink, and through happenstance, she'd survived. Whatever skills this healer possessed, they were vastly superior to the barbaric methods of Old Stitch. Her body might have been visibly battered, but, aside from some residual wooziness, she felt mostly hale.

Returning north was once again possible.

"Where did you say we were, again?" she asked, turning to Kemp.

"Quaretem," he answered, looking slightly taken aback. Marbuck realized that he'd been expecting some sort of thanks for saving her life, but, for the moment, she was far too distracted by her own interests to care.

"How far is that from Nordabor?"

"Nordabor?"

"Yes."

Kemp pursed his lips. "I'm not familiar with such a place."

"It would be north of here, along the Einfallen. Northeast of Vin-Sadavat."

"I'm sorry," Kemp said, shaking his head slowly, "but I'm not familiar with any of those places, and I've traveled through nearly every stretch of land between here and the World's Wound."

"The what?"

"The World's Wound. You know; the northern crater."

"The *northern* crater?" Marbuck murmured. Suddenly, she felt like sitting down after all. In Nordabor, the first expedition conducted by Rorik Fontaine had established that the fabled southern kingdom of old had been reduced to a horizon-spanning crater, beyond which nothing remained. Now, Kemp was telling her that this was not the case; she was in a location far enough south that the southern end of the expansive crater now lay to the north. Somehow, through a combination of their ceaseless and directionless rowing aboard the *Empress's Love* and the powerful currents in the wake of the cataclysm, they had managed to circumvent the crater and travel further south than any explorer, reaching a land sundered from their own and equally ignorant of their existence. It was a testament to the widespread stagnation of the human race that they could even still understand each other's language after so long apart. More importantly, Marbuck now understood that she was further away from Elibeth than she would have ever guessed was possible.

"I can tell that this comes as a bit of a shock to you," Kemp said. "Your friends had told me that you'd all come from a northern land, but they hadn't specified where, and I don't think it occurred to them to ask how far away Quaretem might be; they were mostly just happy to be alive."

"Yes, thank you," Marbuck said absently. "For rescuing me, I mean."

"Of course. Look, you could still use some rest, I think. The Lady of the Veil works wonders, but when the damage is bad enough, the body needs some time to adjust to its own recovery. I'll return soon. Until then, rest assured that you and your companions will be well taken care of. The Lady's handmaidens will see to any need that you have."

Marbuck's thoughts jumped first to food and water, and then it occurred to her that she felt oddly satiated already. Her thirst and starvation had been so constant, and coupled so deeply with her pain, that their utter banishment was perplexing. As she considered this, Kemp turned to leave, and Marbuck's countless other questions cried out in her mind.

"Wait," Marbuck said. "When can I leave this place?"

"Well, you'll want to make sure you're fully recovered, of course. At that point, I've been instructed to take you and your companions to see Lakna. She's the seneschal of our commune here, and she'll wish to hear all about your journey. I'm sure she'll do anything she can to help you prepare for your voyage home."

"Okay," Marbuck said, feeling suddenly weary. Her body *was* still exhausted, miraculous recovery or not, and the thought of how far she would need to travel to return to Nordabor was not helping. It would be a long and dangerous undertaking. At this thought, her hands reflexively reached for her waist, where the anointed blade had hung. Of course, like her rags, it was gone.

"My things," she asked. "Where are they?"

"Your clothing was pretty ragged and, honestly, rather foul. We disposed of it."

"And what of my blade? Or my field glass?"

"Ah, yes, of course. Well, your weapons and other valuables will be returned to you when you depart. Lakna doesn't permit armed strangers in the Great Ziggurat, which I'm sure you understand. Once she meets you, and you're no longer strangers, I'm sure you'll get them back."

Marbuck did not like this, but she also couldn't argue with the logic. These people had rescued her, taken her in, and healed her. It did not seem outrageous that they might wish to know who they'd offered succor to before they provided her with a weapon.

"Fair enough," she said. "And what—"

"Now, just hold on," Kemp said with a good-natured chuckle. "Save your energy for when you talk to Lakna; you'll have plenty of time for questions then."

Though she considered trying to pry more out of Kemp, she allowed him to depart, as she was beginning to feel the magnetic pull of the plush bed. Slithering back beneath the sheet, Marbuck felt a conflicting churn of emotions; disbelief at this change in her fortunes, joy at her recovery, and guilt for choosing to indulge in restive comfort when she should have been trying to head northward at once. With all of these warring thoughts, Marbuck doubted that she'd be able to fall back asleep.

She was wrong.

CHAPTER 16

The last time that Marbuck, Falstaff, and Devonshire had been together, they'd been ready to eat one another. Their reunion, in the sun-dappled chamber where Marbuck had spent her time recovering, was marked by a sense of unreality. None of them had expected to survive, yet here they now stood, granted a stay of execution at the last possible moment and in a manner they never could have predicted. For each of them, it had been astounding to learn that another stable society existed, one apparently similar to Nordabor, or at least free from the madness of Vin-Sadavat.

Marbuck and Falstaff embraced, laughing and crying, each babbling giddily about their unbelievable fortunes. Devonshire, the perennial outsider, hovered beside them, nodding, smiling, and occasionally trying to throw in his own input. Leaning against the doorway, Kemp watched this scene with contented patience.

"It's really not so bad," Falstaff said, looking at Marbuck's head.

Self-consciously, she'd wrapped a kerchief provided by the dutiful handmaidens around her head. It had slipped back, and Falstaff had seen her scar. She pulled it back into place. "It is what it is. I don't wish to see it."

"At least it was earned in defiance," Devonshire said. Like her own scar, the Lady of the Veil's skills had not erased the large X on his face, which remained as a permanent mark of his shame.

"I'd just as soon have survived unscathed," she said, looking at Falstaff, who, aside from some weight loss, showed no signs of the suffering he'd endured. "But I suppose the important thing is that we survived at all."

"Hear, hear," Kemp said happily. "Truly, your ordeal is a tale that surpasses all of those in recent history. The seneschal is very interested to learn more about it. I've told her the broad strokes, but to hear it from those who lived it is another thing entirely. Shall we?"

As comfortable as her chamber was, Marbuck had been increasingly antsy to see what lay beyond it. She now felt fully restored, and her desire to begin the long trek home was growing stronger with each passing moment.

She turned back to the others and found that they were looking at her expectantly. Their situation had changed, but, apparently, she was still their leader. "Let's go," she said to Kemp.

The three of them followed Kemp into the passage, a wide thoroughfare with floors, ceiling, and walls uniformly lined with white tile. What Marbuck judged to be the outer wall sloped slightly, with more narrow windows built into the upper reaches, lighting the space brilliantly. There was no doubt that, wherever Quaretem was, it was squarely within the Daylands. The sunlight, muted somewhat by the angles of the structure, appeared to be even stronger than that which she'd experienced aboard the *Fortune*, when they'd reached the collapsed bridge that'd blocked the Einfallen.

"These were once the private chambers of the patricians," Kemp explained, waving a hand toward the doors they were walking past. Each appeared to lead to a room identical to the one Marbuck had resided in, and she assumed that Falstaff and Devonshire had received similar accommodations. "A nasty bunch they were, the highest order of the ancient oppressors."

"What happened to them?" Marbuck asked.

"Well, it's said that they were overthrown and cast out when the lands to the north were obliterated. I guess they came from those lands, originally. I'm no expert, though. Lakna knows more of the history, being a native."

"And you're not? A native, I mean."

"No, actually. I was a refugee once, found much like you were. I was taken here and eventually earned a place as a huntsman, so that I might find others."

"So you hunt for people?" Falstaff asked.

"Well, we hunt for anything that might be of use to our commune. If we happen upon those who are lost and forsaken, we do what we can to help."

They rounded a corner and stepped into an immense atrium, where the temperature of the dry air, already quite warm, suddenly became stifling. Adorned with the same white tiles, some of which had fallen away to reveal the sandstone underneath, the space was easily the size of the entire Vinecrown Keep. Marbuck had been inside of Nordabor's seat of power only once, while on an errand to retrieve newly-forged anointed blades during her training to become a shepherd. The Vinecrown Keep had been shrouded in a dour atmosphere, its dim halls filled with the whisperings of the parasitic aristocrats that haunted it. This place was completely different. Winding ramps weaved through an architecture of angles, juxtaposed in an airy, dream-like fashion. Long, glassless windows, tremendous versions of those in the smaller chambers, were built into the walls. Hot, unfiltered sunlight reigned, reflected with astonishing beauty in the long pools of clear, sparkling water that flanked the main causeway. Burbling fountains sent flashing diamonds of spray into the air, which landed with a pleasant pattering sound. To their right, the causeway led to a broad portico of stone columns, around which the pools wrapped. To their left, it reached the outer wall and continued out through a colossal opening large enough for an entire legion to march through. From there, it continued on between twin pools, each filled with gleaming blue water.

Peering through this expansive opening and the enormous windows, Marbuck could see a large swath of the land upon which the Great Ziggurat stood. The causeway ended in a drift of sand just past the edges of the twin pools. Beyond that, sand dunes, wavering in the blistering heat outside of the walls of the ziggurat, were all that was visible. Across from where she stood, the windows revealed a view of the sea. Lost upon those waters for so long, Marbuck had grown to hate and fear them. Now, revealed in the brilliance of the sunlight, the endless stretch of turquoise before her was impossibly splendid.

"Quite a view, eh?" Kemp said, squinting toward the sea.

"Yes, it's breathtaking."

"That's the same water that we were on?" Falstaff asked.

"Oh yes, there's only one sea. The Seurian Sea it's called, and it's supposed to encircle all of Gana. You were lost beneath the Closed Eye," Kemp said, jerking his thumb to the right. "Here, under the gaze of the Unblinking Eye, you can truly appreciate its majesty."

Despite Kemp's use of different terminology, Marbuck was able to understand that Quaretem stood upon the southern shore of a land that she'd believed had been wholly annihilated in antiquity. To the south, the sea swallowed the horizon. To the east, a different kind of sea, one composed of sinuous dunes, stretched away until it became lost in haze. The western end of the atrium did not have any windows, but she didn't need to look that way to know what was there. As for what lay to the north, her view was currently obstructed by her position within the structure. She feared that it would also be a sterile plain of burning sand, one that would stand between her and Elibeth. Of course, sand dunes seemed a paltry complaint compared to the gargantuan crater that would block her way.

Continuing down a series of ramps that led to the main causeway, Marbuck tried not to dwell on the difficulty of the journey that lay ahead of her. After all, nothing could be worse than what she'd already been through.

"This is the Eastern Promenade," Kemp explained as they walked. "The main entrance to the ziggurat. It was constructed so that the light of the Eye, as it opened, would shine directly into the front gate. Of course, that was yesterday and yesterday, before the Eye was split. Now the Unblinking Eye never ceases to shine here."

Marbuck listened to this with genuine interest. Kemp's allusions to an 'eye', whether unblinking or closed, seemed to be the Quaretem equivalent of what, in Nordabor, were known as the Daylands and the Nightlands. As for his use of the word 'yesterday', she gleaned that he was referring to the distant past, before the war between the gods, when the sun was said to have risen and set. She assumed that this terminology was a part of whatever system of time Quaretem had developed, similar to Nordabor's system of cycles.

"The constant light is great for the view, but not so much for the temperature," Kemp said, unbuttoning the top of his tunic and revealing a thicket of gray chest hair, damp with sweat.

"Is that why nobody is here?" Falstaff asked, mopping sweat from his brow.

"You got it. Not many people linger here if they can avoid it; they stick to the side passages, anywhere that's a little more shaded. I enjoy the look of the place, though, particularly the pools. Lakna loves them too. She's the one who actually got them filled again, had a whole team of people figure out how the pumps that pull in the sea water work. I tell you, it's a great honor to be called upon to attend to those pumps. Marvelous engineering. The people who built this place really knew what they were doing."

Marbuck's first thought was of the bilge pump in the stinking orlop deck of the *Empress's Love*. It did not sound like an honor to toil at the controls of some strange machinery; it sounded horrible.

"So, who *were* the builders?" Devonshire asked.

"As I understand it, it was the Quaret people; the founders of the city. They constructed the Great Ziggurat at the height of their splendor."

"And what happened to them?"

"They reside here still. Their ancestors had been conquered and enslaved, forced to toil beneath the very monument they'd built, but when the north was destroyed, they threw off their oppressors and reclaimed what was theirs. The Quaret people have survived here ever since."

With the heat pressing against her, Marbuck found herself wondering *how* they'd survived here. In Nordabor, the captive god had kept life flourishing, while their location in the Dawnlands had kept their climate moderate. Here, the heat was nearly unbearable, and the land outside of the ziggurat appeared to be barren. The only water, as far as she'd seen, was salt water. She'd been provided with no food or drink since she'd awoken, instead sustained only by a strange feeling of satiated fullness. Quaretem was proving to be a curious place.

"Of course, it's not perfect," Kemp continued. "And there are those who would see the old oppressors return, but I won't get into all that. I'm sure Lakna will give you an earful."

Falstaff and Devonshire seemed content to leave that thread unpulled, but Marbuck's curiosity was piqued. Kemp's propensity to deliver information that begged further questions reminded her of what she'd heard of the expedition's badlander guide, Starkad. She'd only ever seen him in passing as he'd walked the deck of the *Fortune*, wreathed in a cloud of pipe smoke, but Winslow had shared many of Rayburn's anecdotes with her. Weathered and grim, Starkad had struck her as a dangerous man. Kemp, on the other hand, was cheerful and gregarious, but he, too, seemed to relish his role as a guide who provided just enough information to leave his audience wanting.

Before Marbuck could ask any further questions, they reached the columned portico, where they were hailed by two men. Clad in ivory robes and carrying halberds, they'd emerged from an arched opening set into the western wall and now stood at attention.

"Lord Henrick," they said in unison.

Kemp waved his hand. "None of that please." He looked at Marbuck and, grinning, shrugged as if they'd previously shared a joke about the absurdity of formal titles.

He led them past the guards and under the archway, which opened into a wide tunnel. After the heat of the atrium, the cool dimness of the space was a welcome relief. They proceeded along a tiled walkway that sloped gently downward, flanked by gently burbling troughs, into which the pools had drained. The light from the atrium followed them, its reflection on the water sending dazzling ripples up the walls of the rounded passage.

The walkway leveled out and, just as the light behind them began to fade, a new light ahead of them heralded the end of the tunnel.

"We are approaching the Oasis Sanctum," Kemp explained, his voice taking on a quieter tone. "It's the formal chamber of Lakna and the rest of the Sanctified, that is, her family. You need not concern yourselves with all of them, but I do wish to prepare you for Roanack. He's Lakna's son and the heir to her throne, but, more importantly, he's the chief warden of the watchmen. They ensure the safety of the commune, and Roanack takes his position quite seriously. Expect his questioning to be a little … pointed."

"I was under the impression that this was just a meeting, not an interrogation," Marbuck said.

"Roanack tends to confuse such things, but his peculiarities are born of his dotage, or so I'm told. You needn't worry; he might snarl beside Lakna, suspicious old crank that he is, but she holds the leash."

"And this old man is Lakna's *son*?" Falstaff asked. "How old is she?"

"Very. Much to Roanack's chagrin," Kemp said with a smile. "Ah! Jalam, always a pleasure."

They'd reached the end of the tunnel, where a young, dark-skinned man leaned against the arched opening, his loose robes doing nothing to hide his muscular physique. He bore a solemn expression, and his beefy arms were folded across his chest.

"Kemp," he said flatly.

"It's 'Lord Henrick' to the likes of you," Kemp said, wagging his finger theatrically and winking at Marbuck. Jalam smiled humorlessly. "The Lady is already inside?" Kemp asked.

"Yes," Jalam answered in the same listless tone. "Everyone is waiting on you."

"Well, I shan't keep them waiting any longer. Come along, now."

As Kemp ushered them past Jalam, Marbuck felt a mixture of excitement and apprehension. Apparently, she was about to meet the healer who had brought her back from the precipice, but she was also going to face any number of questions from the sovereign of this strange land, and her cantankerous son. She had little experience in dealing with nobility, and she would have preferred it to stay that way. Still, this seemed to be the necessary first step in her departure; she could accommodate the whims of her rescuers if it meant securing their assistance with her journey home.

Leaving the tunnel behind, they emerged into a space dominated by a broad set of stone steps. Sunlight filtered in from windows set high in the walls, and, although it was not stifling, it was noticeably warmer as they began to ascend the steps.

"Jalam is the Lady of the Veil's personal guardian. An austere fellow, that's for sure," Kemp said once they were out of earshot. "I think it irks him immensely that Lakna only allows her personal watchmen into the Oasis Sanctum."

"What does the Lady of the Veil need to be guarded against?" Devonshire asked.

"It's mostly just a precaution," Kemp said, not really answering the question. "And here we are."

They'd reached the top of the steps, where two more robed guards were waiting. They hailed Kemp, eliciting another rejection of such frivolous etiquette, and stepped aside at his direction. As they did so, they pulled away a heavy, intricately woven drape, revealing the entrance to the Oasis Sanctum. Kemp gestured for them to enter and, with some trepidation, Marbuck, Falstaff, and Devonshire filed inside. Kemp followed, and the drape fell closed behind them.

The chamber they had entered was a place of stark beauty, a smaller, dimmer version of the impressive Eastern Promenade. Smooth, slanted walls angled toward a high ceiling of white tiles. A tiled walkway bisected a pool of clear water, twinkling with the reflection of the light from the narrow windows far above them. At the other end of the walkway rose a stepped pyramid of cyclopean sandstone blocks. Each step of this terraced dais was occupied. At the lowest step, a dozen or so courtesans mingled, growing silent as the newcomers arrived. On the level above them, a single stone seat was occupied by a shrouded figure whose face was obscured by an opaque veil.

Marbuck knew at once that she was looking at the Lady of the Veil. The healer, who was dressed in black robes, sat rigidly upright, her pale hands folded in her lap. She wore a tall, rounded headdress with a flat top, upon which the black veil was draped, and from which it hung down to below her neckline. For one who was purported to perform such incredible feats of healing, she struck Marbuck as rather ominous, her hidden features calling to mind the mask of the Empress.

On the step above her, the final step before the structure culminated in a spherical fountain, was a wide, golden couch piled high with plush cushions in an assortment of vibrant colors. Marbuck assumed that the ancient woman reclining amongst them could only be Lakna. Her skin, hanging loosely from her hawkish face, had the appearance of old leather. The assortment of bangles and jeweled necklaces dangling from her bony wrists and neck seemed to press upon her withered frame like heavy chains. Atop her head, a large turban adorned with faded feathers from some long-extinct bird threatened to topple her over. Standing beside the couch, looking sour, was an equally-aged man. His shriveled face, crowned by thin wisps of white hair smeared across his bald pate, looked somewhat ridiculous rising from the shining gorget of his polished armor. It reminded Marbuck of the suit of armor Phir-Ramarian had been wearing when the expedition had departed from the *Fortune*; impractical and gaudy.

"Lord Henrick," the old man said, his tone a sarcastic sneer. Kemp did not reject the formality. "You've arrived at last."

"My apologies for the delay, Chief Warden. I simply wished to show the newcomers the splendor of the Great Ziggurat."

"You are a huntsman, not a host. You should—"

Lakna lifted one gnarled hand, and the chief warden ceased speaking at once. "Roanack, please." She looked down from her lofty perch and smiled, an expression that seemed to strip away the long-cycles. It was easy to imagine that she'd been quite beautiful in her youth. "I know that Lord Henrick has graciously welcomed each of you already, but I wish to extend my own courtesy. Welcome to Quaretem. I am Lakna, Seneschal of the City, Matriarch of the Sanctified, and the Oracle of Mighty Setenrah."

Marbuck paid little heed to this litany of titles until she heard the last one. Kemp had failed to mention that there was someone higher than Lakna in Quaretem's pecking order. Of course, her claim to be an 'oracle' to this being, Setenrah, smacked of something more akin to the invocations of the shepherds, who always sought to sway the whims of the Void-God. Either way, Marbuck began to worry about what else Kemp might have omitted from his summarization.

"Lord Henrick has told me of the unusual circumstances that resulted in his finding you," Lakna continued. "Castaway mariners from a distant land; what a tale! I scarcely believe it. It is yet another strange happening, and in a time when odd portents have been rampant. But I don't wish to speak for you. Please, tell me of yourselves and the plight that brought you here, to me."

Marbuck was not at all surprised when Falstaff and Devonshire, who'd surreptitiously crept behind her, did not answer. She cleared her throat, feeling suddenly anxious to speak before so many.

"I am Raina Marbuck," she began. "My companions here are Gregor Falstaff and … Devonshire." She realized with some embarrassment that she did not know his first name.

"Cadon," Devonshire said quietly.

"And Cadon Devonshire," Marbuck said, feeling flushed. Lakna watched her with the patient expression of one who is listening to the rambling tale of a child. But then, to one so old, everybody else *would* seem to be no more than a child, Marbuck supposed. She cleared her throat again.

"We were journeying south with an expedition when we were attacked. Many of our people were killed, and many more, including us, were taken as slaves. The slavers brought us to their city, Vin-Sadavat, in the Nightlands—what you would call the Closed Eye. They worshipped a being they called the Empress; we were forced to stand before her, and she demanded that we pledge ourselves. The Empress—I believe she was an old one, a god, if you know of such things—she had this strange allure, a kind of mesmeric enchantment, and many gave into her. They were mutilated, just like her other followers."

Lakna, listening intently, had leaned forward at the mention of the Empress. Now her dark eyes scanned the scarred visages of Marbuck and Devonshire. The erstwhile guardsman looked at his feet.

"While we were imprisoned there, some sort of insurrection took place," Marbuck continued. "The Empress was killed and the city fell. We were taken by one of the slavers, Bolenz, aboard his ship. We traveled south to another settlement, an offshoot of the slavers. Bolenz's bid to take over there failed and we were forced to flee back into the open water. We ended up getting lost out in the darkness." Marbuck did not wish to get into the specifics of her time aboard the *Empress's Love*, particularly her scalping. She decided to skim over it, hoping that Lakna would not pry. "Then some kind of cataclysmic event happened. I don't know how to explain it, but it drove the sea into massive waves, and it left this strange, well, crack, for lack of a better word, in the northern sky. It also provided us with an opportunity to rid ourselves of Bolenz. We abandoned the sinking ship and took to a longboat, which eventually brought us to the shore where we were found." Once again, Marbuck chose to edit out the horrid details.

Silence followed Marbuck's account. Lakna remained hunched forward, studying the newcomers. At the foot of the pyramid, the courtesans began to whisper rapidly amongst themselves.

"Yes, Lord Henrick told me of the crack in the sky," Lakna finally said. "We cannot see it here, not in the light of the Unblinking Eye, but he described it to me. Very unusual. We did, however, feel the effects of this strange occurrence. The air moved, as if it were being pulled northward, dragging the sands with it. There was much discussion within the commune as to what it could mean. Some said it was a fell omen, but I don't believe so. Those doomsayers do not proclaim the will of Setenrah; that is my responsibility. Setenrah remains undisturbed; therefore, we do not concern ourselves with rumblings from the distant north. Mighty Setenrah protects us. That being said, I am curious about these faraway lands from which you came. You mentioned a Vin-Sadavat?"

"Yes, but that's not where we came from; that was where the slavers took us," Marbuck explained.

"Of course. So, you came from …?"

"Nordabor."

"I do not know this place."

"From what I understand, it's beyond the crater that lies to the north of here, and it's the only scrap of civilization left. Or, at least, I thought it was. Our people didn't know that anything existed south of the crater. We thought that we were it; the last hold of Vingallea."

The whispers of the courtesans grew into urgent murmurs.

"Silence, all of you," Roanack growled.

Lakna shook her head, and the heavy earrings dangling from her stretched earlobes swung gently. "The family is frightened, Roanack; show them some grace. My apologies, um, Raina, was it?"

"Yes," Marbuck answered, wondering what she'd said to cause such consternation among the courtesans. It also occurred to her that they weren't courtesans at all, but the Sanctified, Lakna's own extended family.

"Your home, Nordabor, is a Vingallean hold?"

"Yes," Marbuck answered cautiously. "It was."

"When you mentioned Vin-Sadavat, I found it concerning. Not because of the supposed god that ruled there; Setenrah is the only *true* god. No, my first thought was of Vingallea. I assumed that, perhaps, these 'slavers' you described were Vingalleans. But now, you say that *you* are Vingallean."

"Yes, I suppose." Marbuck had never felt much of an allegiance to the idea of Vingallea. She'd known that her own ancestors, the people of Aurangzeb, had been conquered by them in antiquity, and that the legendary war between the gods had ended their dominance. She'd mostly thought of Nordabor as its own entity, tied to Vingallea through history and the bloodline of its rulers, but essentially separate. She'd been expecting a lot of possible lines of questioning from Lakna, but this had not been one of them.

"Then you are agents of Zeorshut Riengel," Roanack interjected.

The guards who'd been at the entrance to the sanctum suddenly entered and began to march toward Marbuck, Falstaff, and Devonshire with their halberds leveled. Kemp did not move; he stood watching everything unfold with his eyebrows hoisted. Marbuck, who was still too confused to really consider the danger, looked back at Lakna.

"Halt," she ordered, and the guards stopped at once. "Were you commanded to seize these guests? I know my idiot son opened his mouth, but it was with a baseless accusation, not a direct order. Get back to your posts."

The guards turned and hurried back out. Roanack, his face burning scarlet, glowered at Marbuck.

"Again, you have my apologies. Tensions run high during these difficult times. What my son so ineloquently implied, is that you might be agents of the old oppressor, Zeorshut Riengel."

Here was another wrinkle that Kemp had failed to mention. Marbuck was beginning to like this situation less and less.

"You see," Lakna said, "Quaretem was not always the place of freedom that you now find yourself in. Yesterday and yesterday, before the splitting of the Eye, our people were ruled by Vingallea. They were brutal oppressors, enslaving the strong and destroying the weak. When the world was wounded by Setenrah's divine judgment, the oppressors were driven away. Their master, Zeorshut Riengel, has sought to return to power here ever since. He is a sorcerer of great cunning, always trying to foment dissent, constantly endeavoring to worm his way into our sacred stronghold and rot us from the inside. Only the divine vigilance granted by Setenrah has kept us free. So, you must understand, to hear one so brazenly admit that they are Vingallean is quite shocking."

Listening to this, Marbuck began to suspect that Setenrah was more than just a concept. It had been startling to learn, before she'd ever departed on this accursed journey, that the old ones truly existed, and that they still lived, scattered across the world. Now, it was not much of a stretch to assume that Setenrah was one of them, and that he'd fed the Quaret people his version of the war between the gods, placing himself as the supreme being and victor. After all, the Empress appeared to have done the exact same thing in Vin-Sadavat. As for Zeorshut Riengel, if he really *had* been around since before the sun had been frozen in the sky, then his apparent immortality could have only one answer. Whatever the case, Marbuck did not wish to have any part in whatever struggle these two gods were waging over Quaretem.

"Well, I can assure you, Nordabor is not in a position to subjugate anyone, nor do we wish to; my own ancestors were once conquered by Vingallea. There is no greed for conquest among the people of Nordabor. Vingallea is just a memory for us; it exists only in tales now." Marbuck knew this wasn't true. Yes, Nordabor was unable to expand its power, but she knew that if the Crown had the means to do so, they would not hesitate to reclaim Vingallea's former glory. The monarchy was obsessed with their Vingallean heritage, but Marbuck was not about to implicate herself in any kind of Vingallean treachery by admitting that. Falstaff and Devonshire, who knew as well as she did that she was spewing outright lies, did not contradict her.

"Well, that is what an agent of Zeorshut Riengel would say," Roanack said, having regained his composure. "The boldness of your declarations could simply be another layer of subterfuge." This time, Lakna did not silence him.

"Nordabor has had no connection with anyone in the south; we didn't even know it existed."

"Then why was your expedition headed south?" Roanack asked.

Marbuck saw no need to lie about the expedition's purpose. In fact, if they could understand the pitiful state that Nordabor was in, perhaps they would accept that its people posed no threat. "We were seeking for other gods anywhere they might be. Our city has only survived from ancient times because we possess a captive god, one whose latent power has kept nature flourishing when everything beyond our realm became a waste. This god has started to fail, and with it, the natural resources we've depended on are collapsing. What finding these other gods might have accomplished, I don't know; we were captured before the expedition had any success. The point is, Nordabor is a dying city with absolutely no designs to conquer a land that we didn't even know existed."

Once again, silence followed. Lakna picked a piece of fuzz from a cushion and rolled it between two crooked fingers. The Sanctified watched this with intense interest. Kemp rocked back on his heels.

"You have spoken of things beyond my sight, and beyond the lore of our people. Similar to what you claim of your own folk, we did not believe that anything existed beyond the crater. You are compelling, and I am inclined to believe you. As such, you are permitted to join our commune, though I will be keeping a close eye on all three of you."

"You misunderstand me, or you have been misinformed," Marbuck said, glancing reproachfully at Kemp. "We do not wish to stay. We wish to head back to Nordabor as soon as possible. My daughter is there, and I need to return to her."

"Oh, well, of course; if that is what you wish," Lakna said. "Such an undertaking will require ample supplies, though, and a proper guide. Lord Henrick is the best huntsman we have to offer; nobody knows the untamed lands better. He will take you as far as he can, once all is ready. In preparation for your arduous journey, I will make sure that you're outfitted with anything you may need. In the meantime, Lord Henrick will show you to your temporary quarters in the Warren. I do apologize, but chambers within the Great Ziggurat are reserved for the Sanctified, or for those requiring extra care from the Lady of the Veil."

Lakna seemed to consider this the conclusion of their meeting, and the Sanctified began to disperse. It seemed that, in addition to accepting that Marbuck and her companions posed no threat, Lakna apparently had no objections to their departure, and was, in fact, willing to help them. Though Marbuck did not relish the delay, she knew that it was better to be prepared, especially when the voyage before her was so daunting. Yet, something about the entire encounter still disturbed her. As Kemp began to lead them out of the Oasis Sanctum, she turned back to Lakna, who'd begun to confer quietly with Roanack.

"Our possessions," she said. Lakna and Roanack looked at her. "Our things; when will we get them back?"

"There are no weapons permitted in the Warren," Lakna said, her voice gentle. "They'll be returned to you when you depart."

Marbuck did not like this answer, but before she could respond, Lakna and Roanack had resumed their quiet consultation. Feeling that any argument might be pushing her luck, Marbuck turned to depart. As she did so, she caught a glimpse of the Lady of the Veil, who had remained silent and still during the meeting.

Though she could not see them, Marbuck knew that the eyes behind the veil were watching her.

CHAPTER 17

Having delivered his charges to their new quarters in the Warren, Henrick Kemp proceeded back up into the Great Ziggurat. Treading the stone stairways, he left the caves and earthen tunnels of the Warren behind, emerging back into the architectural magnificence of the Quaret people's greatest achievement. The Warren may have offered the citizenry relief from the heat, but Kemp did not care for it. Dim, dank, and crowded, it was everything that the vast, airy chambers of the Great Ziggurat were not. He was grateful to have secured his own private room in the ziggurat, one that offered a view of the dazzling pools, accompanied by the peaceful sound of running water. Of course, the heat beyond his door was extreme, but a little sweat was worth the privilege that his vital role in the city had provided him. The dullness of the Warren was for those who did not serve in such a capacity, those who lived a more menial existence. It was simply not practical to house them all in the ziggurat.

Greeting each person he passed with a boisterous assault of amity, Kemp made his way toward the Oasis Sanctum, where he would receive the next edict of his master. The huntsman, once the heir to an illustrious lineage, whistled as he walked. The life he'd known before, and the sagas of his lost people, rarely disturbed him now. When memories of his igno-minious flight from his ancestral home attempted to caress his mind with bloodied fingers, he would laugh all the merrier, letting the sound knock lose those grasping sorrows. Kemp had embraced his new life, one that had found him in the same way that he'd found many others. Unlike those he'd brought to Quaretem, however, Kemp had fused with this world, happily forsaking the old in order to live in the new. Lakna did not care about her huntsman's past, choosing instead to give him a future. As such, it was a pleasure to serve.

Passing beneath the heavy drape and entering Lakna's chamber, Kemp found his master agitated. Stately as she was, there was no raging bluster, such as would be expected from Roanack, who lingered near her golden couch. No, Lakna merely sat on the edge of the pyramid's lowest tier, dipping her wrinkled feet into the pristine water. Over time, Kemp had become accustomed to her secret moods. Her behavior now was a sure sign of discontent, and her two retainers hovering nearby looked nervous. The rest of the Sanctified, as well as the Lady of the Veil, had been dismissed.

"The newcomers have been shown to their quarters," Kemp announced.

Lakna nodded. "Please, leave us," she said to the retainers. "When I wish to rise, you will be summoned."

With hasty obedience, the retainers scurried out of the chamber. Lakna paid them no mind; she continued to drag her feet through the water, watching the small ripples that her movements created. Kemp shifted from one foot to the other, waiting to be either sent away or directed toward his next task. He hoped that she had something in mind; he preferred to remain busy.

"By the grace of mighty Setenrah, we have inherited this damaged world," she finally said. "He has entrusted me, in particular, with maintaining this city of peace. It is a terrible burden." She lifted a ring-laden hand to her eyes, as if she were momentarily overcome.

"Of course, Your Grace," Kemp agreed.

"Always the greatest threat has come from within. From those who've heard the honeyed words of Zeorshut Riengel, who've been fooled by the lies of the old oppressor. Ceaselessly he threatens our order. You know this as well as I do."

Kemp did. Periodic purges carried out by Roanack's trusted watchmen always revealed the enemy's agents. Often, these traitors were longtime troublemakers; rabble-rousers who stirred up problems everywhere they went. Sometimes, they were those you would least expect, upstanding citizens or, in rare cases, members of the Sanctified. Guided by Setenrah's divine communications, Lakna could always direct Roanack to those who'd been corrupted, even if they hadn't revealed their cankerous intentions yet. In their trials, the arrestees would always claim their innocence, but the evidence was beyond reproach. Executions would follow, and Zeorshut Riengel's machinations would be checked once again.

"But now, you have unwittingly brought me a new threat."

A jolt of alarm shot through Kemp; he'd never done anything to earn Lakna's ire before. She must have sensed his sudden distress, and she smiled kindly. "I do not fault you for it; who could have guessed that these newcomers would be anything beyond the hapless wanderers we usually take in? Now, I've listened to the testimony of this Marbuck woman. If it is a new stratagem of the oppressor, then it is a bold one. I think it more likely that she is telling the truth. A proposition that is, perhaps, more dangerous."

"How so?" Kemp asked, striving to conceal how much the brief moment of fear had shaken him.

"It means that Vingallea remains. Not just in the form of one who seeks to infiltrate, but in an entire city, a final stronghold of their ancient might. Somehow, they have remained ignorant of us here. Do you think that will last if these refugees are permitted to return there bearing tales of the wondrous place that saved them? Marbuck said that their city is failing and seeking southward for anything that might save them. What do you think that their rulers will do when they learn of what we have here? The conqueror's blood will reawaken in the veins of whatever warlord holds dominion there, and they will set their eyes on the prosperous lands to the south. A ravenous horde will descend upon us, and we will be reduced to slaves once again. They may even reunite with Zeorshut Riengel. It will be within Setenrah's power to deliver us, but we cannot depend on his intervention. He may just as easily find a new seneschal, new Sanctified, among their ranks. I speak his divine word, but I am not privy to his every thought. He is mercurial, and should our appeasement lapse, I fear he may abandon us."

"Surely you don't mean that," Kemp said, surprised by her open disparagement of Setenrah. He knew the importance of satisfying their god's appetites more than anyone, but he found it difficult to believe that Setenrah would simply discard them if their ability to meet his needs was interrupted.

"I do, and I'd rather not find out if I'm right. Those three are not to leave this place, do you understand?"

"Yes, Your Grace."

"Their departure is to be delayed by any means necessary, but care must be taken to quell any suspicion that may arise. You have earned their trust, Lord Henrick. I want you to continue to keep a close watch on them, and to use your influence to keep them calm and compliant."

"Why don't you let *me* put your mind at ease?" Roanack objected. "Allow me to take care of them. I'll make sure that they never leave."

"Tempting, but I will not waste three perfectly suitable tributes and risk resorting to a lottery. It makes the people uneasy, and uneasiness is a cradle to revolt. I detest taking any of our own; they are never willing participants, no matter how much the Lady floods their minds with her soothings. No, I want those three, and Lord Henrick can keep them content."

"Mother, his work lies in hooking these folk, not entertaining them, and certainly not monitoring them. Leave that to me."

"Your methods have their merits, Roanack, but I do not want these three rounded up and placed in a cell, even as a precaution. You know that Setenrah is displeased by any tribute with a troubled mind or an injured body. He wants them to be pristine and docile, led willingly into his arms. If you arrest these three, they will be frightened, they will fight, and they will be marred. He will know."

"Yes, Mother," Roanack said mechanically.

"Their scars alone worry me, but I think they'll be well enough that he won't object."

"Yes," Kemp said, "the Lady of the Veil certainly outdid herself with them."

"Yes ... well, Lord Henrick, I'm placing my trust in you," Lakna said. "I expect that you will prove to be as dependable as ever. You did not rise above your station for nothing, after all. Should you succeed in this task, you will please me immensely. More importantly, you will find favor with Setenrah should he be satisfied with our offering."

Discussing the particulars of their arrangement, and his own role in it, was distasteful to Kemp. It also served as a stark reminder of what his own fate might have been had he not proven to be so useful. Still, duty was duty, and as unseemly as the process could be, there was no doubting the importance of it. "Consider it done," Kemp said.

"Thank you. Setenrah has not come to collect his tax for some time, so I believe he will be here before too long. They must be held until then. The payment of all three will surely exceed his desires, and receiving three at once will hopefully keep him satiated for a longer time.

"Regardless, Setenrah will see to it that they never return north."

CHAPTER 18

From the moment Kemp had closed the round, wooden door of their new living quarters on his way out, Marbuck had felt trapped. Once the three of them were alone, Falstaff and Devonshire had quickly unloosed their tongues, reigniting the excited discussion of their new circumstances. As they spoke of their immense luck, Marbuck checked to see if the door had been locked from the outside. It hadn't, which was a relief, but her disquiet remained.

"It's hard to believe, really," Falstaff said, oblivious to Marbuck's examination of the door. "I mean, we were dead. I really thought I was already dead at one point. And now, here we are, in a place not that different from home. I never would have imagined such a thing."

"It feels like a dream. I keep expecting to wake up in the longboat," Devonshire said, looking around in disbelief. Even the cramped hovel they'd been deposited in seemed a wonder to him. Marbuck wished that she could share his enthusiasm. Waking up in the sunlit ziggurat had been astounding; being moved into the Warren felt punitive.

From halls of ancient splendor, they had descended into a place not unlike the passages of Vin-Sadavat. It was a correlation that Marbuck had not enjoyed making, and it had been far too easy to picture slavers emerging from the darkness. They'd passed through a dirt-floored tunnel and entered a cavern system lit not by fires, but by shafts cut through the rock above them. Sunlight streamed in through these narrow ports and was amplified by a series of mirrors affixed to the walls and floor. This natural illumination had helped to dispel some of Marbuck's rising anxiety, but the scene it had revealed was still a far cry from what Lakna and her Sanctified enjoyed above.

Hundreds of people had been bustling through the central chamber, moving toward whatever task they performed in their microcosmic civilization. They'd been uniformly thin, nearly malnourished even, but had moved with vigor and spoken in hale voices. It'd appeared to be a hive of contentment, and the residents had paid them little mind as Kemp led them across the space. To Marbuck, it'd almost seemed like they'd been actively ignoring the newcomers.

Kemp had explained that the Warren was where the majority of the populace lived and worked, safe from the oppressive heat, sustained by their modest attempts at farming, and fulfilled by the important role that each played in maintaining Quaretem's great society.

"What do they farm?" Falstaff had asked as he'd peered with interest at a woven basket from which a shriveled old woman had been scooping out a handful of a dull brown substance.

"Mushrooms, mostly; nothing else can really grow down here. The Sanctified have access to the ziggurat gardens, which yield a little more variety, and a small selection of livestock that's been maintained for a long time, but for the average folk it's mushrooms and salt water. The same water pumped in for the pools, actually; it cycles into a well down here."

"How can anyone possibly live on that?" Marbuck had asked.

"Well, that's where the Lady of the Veil comes in. She is Setenrah's gift to us; has been, for a long time."

Marbuck had started to realize that Quaretem's understanding of time was not very sophisticated. Everything seemed to have happened a 'long time' ago; how they measured anything in the present was unknown, but it seemed to rely on guesswork and, perhaps, ingrained routine. More importantly, she'd started to gather that the Lady of the Veil was more than just a skilled healer, and she'd asked Kemp to elaborate.

"You'll experience one of her healing rituals soon enough," Kemp had answered. "Then you'll understand."

As they'd continued through the Warren, Kemp had actually managed to answer a question that'd been steadily growing in Marbuck's mind.

"Up that way, you'll find the Pit. It's a section of the cavern that suddenly drops off into a chasm. When the waste is collected, it's brought there and dumped. It's also where we drive the shades."

As with the slavers, it'd been interesting to learn that time and distance had not altered this antique term. And, just as the slavers had, the Quaret people had also discovered that the only way to drive off a shade was with fire. Kemp had explained their methods, noting that they were actually seldom used. The Lady of the Veil's abilities had rendered death a more predictable event, and, as such, most people died of old age at the Pit's edge. The unsupervised birth of a shade was an exceedingly rare occurrence.

"There must be thousands of them down there," Marbuck had said, thinking of how many long-cycles must have passed since the practice had begun.

"Not at all. Setenrah empties the Pit when he comes here; he takes the shades away."

"Setenrah comes here? And he takes the shades?"

"Yes. I've never seen it happen, but yes. Only Lakna, Roanack, and the Lady of the Veil are permitted to receive Setenrah."

That statement was exactly the sort of mysterious bunk that'd fueled Marbuck's suspicions. What, exactly, she suspected was unclear. But now, as she listened to Falstaff and Devonshire prattle on about how magnificent Quaretem was, Marbuck was certain that something about the place was off, and, prepared or not, she was ready to leave.

"It's a shame that we couldn't stay up top, though," Falstaff said.

"I don't want to *stay* here at all," Marbuck blurted out. The other two looked at her, noticing her irritation for the first time. "I need to get back to Elibeth. I couldn't even begin to guess at how long we've been gone now; I can't afford to sit around idly while more time slips away."

"Fishwife—"

"Lakna was expecting us to join them here; who knows how long it'll take for her to organize supplies for us? It didn't seem like our departure was a priority. I mean, why move us to these living quarters if we're going to be leaving soon?"

"Raina, listen, I—"

"So now we're stuck here waiting, with no way of knowing what's happening in Nordabor. The cataclysm that hit us down here was powerful enough to break the sky in the north. That crack could be right above Elibeth; right above everyone we know and love."

"*Raina!*"

The torrent of thoughts that had been spilling out of Marbuck's mouth ceased at once. She couldn't recall a single time that Falstaff had shouted at her, and she was unnerved by his sudden anger.

"I know that you're worried about Elibeth," he said, his tone soft again. "I am too. But the fact of the matter is we can't leave now. We've got nothing. If we just march out into that desert, we're not going to make it very far, and you know that."

"Fine, you're right," Marbuck said, feeling an itch of irritation at his sound reasoning. "So we should just go to Lakna now and tell her that we need to leave immediately. We won't be rude about it; I know these people have done a lot for us. We'll just pressure her a little, to speed things up."

"'Done a lot for us'? They saved our lives, Raina. If Kemp hadn't found us, and if the Lady of the Veil hadn't healed us, we would be dead. I hate to disagree with you, but I don't want to do *anything* that might offend Lakna or anyone else here. And more so, we need to rest."

"Rest?" Marbuck asked. "All we've done since we got here is *rest*."

"And after what we've been through, we've needed it. I'm sorry, but I'm not ready to embark on something like the journey north just yet. The Lady might have healed my body, but she can't heal my mind. I am *weary*. Until very recently, we lived every moment in agony and fear. This place has offered a respite from that, and I'm not ready to leave."

"Do not lecture me about what we went through," Marbuck said, snatching the kerchief from her head. "You emerged from it unscathed. You weren't the object of Bolenz's perverted obsession. I endured all of that for *one reason*: to make it home to Elibeth. I don't care what this place offers; Elibeth is not here. We need to go home."

"*My home is gone!*" Falstaff suddenly bellowed. "My home was the *Fortune*, not Nordabor. I have no wife, no child; my *family*, my *loved ones* were that crew, and they're all *dead*. You're not the only person who has suffered, Raina. I've stood beside you through all of this; I've done everything I can to support you, and, believe me, I want you to reunite with Elibeth more than anything, but your focus on your own intentions is *exhausting*. We will leave, soon, when everything is ready. But for now, we need to recuperate from the trauma we've *all* endured."

Marbuck listened to this with a creeping numbness. Shame and rage warred within her, resulting in a sour stalemate that left her speechless. Everything that Falstaff had said was correct and also hateful nonsense. She opened her mouth, a bile of confused indignation churning inside of her. Finally, she turned to Devonshire, who'd slunk as far away from them as the small space would allow.

"And you? Where do you stand?"

"Well," he started slowly, "I'm inclined to agree with Falstaff."

Marbuck threw her hands up. "Living up to your vows again, I see."

Devonshire frowned. "It wasn't only you that I wronged, and I'm not sworn to obey your every decree. Falstaff was as much a victim of my choices as you were, and I'm free to agree with him as I please. I sympathize with you, but I don't have anybody waiting for me in Nordabor either. I'd just as soon stay here and start anew. You said it yourself, with that crack in the sky we don't even know what we'd be returning to; it might be better to take Lakna up on her offer."

"And what about your other vows?" Marbuck asked, dimly aware that her anger had pulverized her better judgment. "I would have thought you'd be eager to return to Nordabor and repent for your failures to the Crown. Didn't you say something once about betraying your fellow guardsmen?"

"Yes, I did." Devonshire admitted. "Thank you for reminding me of my disgrace once again. Now that I really think about it, I believe I would be executed as a traitor should I ever return to Nordabor. And I would deserve it. And if I were to return clothed in lies, I might live, but under the constant burden of my shame. Here, I'm nobody; I'm just a man. No oaths, no duties, just a man with a clean slate. I think I might prefer that. Good luck on your journey, I'm certain you'll be leaving very soon."

He brushed past Marbuck, yanked the door open, and stalked out. The door banged against the inner wall and, shuddering slightly, swung closed again. Marbuck and Falstaff stood in the thick silence left in Devonshire's wake, each waiting to see if a fragile peace or another explosive volley would follow.

"I'm still with you, Raina," Falstaff finally muttered. "When you leave, I'll be at your side. I just hope we don't leave until we're really, truly ready. Otherwise, we'll never make it back. I'm going to go check on him."

Marbuck said nothing as Falstaff followed after Devonshire. The door latched yet again, and she was alone. Falstaff had struck a conciliatory note, exiting with an air of gracious forgiveness. This just made her angrier, and her rage was matched only by her embarrassment and self-disgust. Under the roil of her fury, a current of reason spoke plainly. She'd been unreasonable, cruel, and selfish. From the inception of their nightmarish detour, she'd focused only on what *she'd* wanted, on *her* plans, *her* suffering, thinking of little else. Even now, she found that acknowledging it did little to change it. Devonshire's issues seemed a trifling matter compared to Elibeth. Falstaff was simply dragging his feet. And yet, they were absolutely right about her. This duality, the awareness of her selfishness and her casual acceptance of it, collided with her conscience, and she felt terrible.

She remained standing there, her eyes fixed on the closed door, for some time. Eventually, her mind still grappling with everything that'd happened, she turned away and plodded over to the narrow, rumpled cots that occupied the space. The argument had depleted her, and the strange feeling of fullness that had sustained her was now beginning to fade.

There were four cots, and each one was situated within a divot carved into the stone wall. She picked one at random and slid into the tight space, taking care not to scrape her head on the jagged top of the small enclosure. Once she was lying down, the space had the feel of a coffin that was open on the left side. It was not comfortable.

She stared up at the low ceiling above her; it was not even an arm's length away from her face. In the ragged stone, sixteen short, vertical lines had been carved in groups of three, their whiteness showing clearly against the darker rock. She puzzled over them, tracing each one with her finger, wondering who might have carved them. Of one thing, she was fairly certain: whoever they were, they'd been keeping track of something. To Marbuck, it looked like an attempt to record the passage of time, based on whatever timekeeping system they understood. But if that was the case, then why had the tally ended at sixteen?

And what had become of the tally maker once the count had stopped?

CHAPTER 19

Each time Marbuck scooted into her sleeping alcove, the hope for an imminent departure grew more remote. And each time she found herself staring at those cryptic white lines, she would lift a splinter of rock that she'd found and add one to her own tally.

Four white lines had joined the original sixteen.

A certain rhythm to life in Quaretem had started to emerge, a system of waking, working, and sleeping that was not unlike Nordabor. Marbuck was under no obligation to perform any of the labors that sent the citizens of the Warren buzzing about, and she watched these activities with a disdainful curiosity, free to roam about as she pleased. The Quaret people cheerfully ignored her, offering only the most basic acknowledgment of her should she physically obstruct their eager scurrying from one task to another. These jobs were varied, and included collecting and removing waste, shoring up parts of the tunnel systems that were believed to be sagging, harvesting the dark, ruddy mushrooms that apparently comprised their entire diet, and collecting buckets of brackish water from their well.

Marbuck's hunger and thirst had fully bloomed, and she'd sampled both the mushrooms and the water after Falstaff had brought her some in an apparent peace offering. They'd hardly grunted at one another, but that hadn't stopped Marbuck from devouring the modest meal. It had tasted like old dirt, and the water had only made her thirst burn more intensely, as she'd known it would. Her fear of a return to the physical agony of the longboat was only stymied by the proof of survival that surrounded her. The people appeared to thrive, despite their meager foodstuffs, and Marbuck assumed that whatever the Lady of the Veil did to supplement them would also apply to her. Still, she realized with a tinge of guilty horror that her depleted body was actually craving the dried meat of the slavers.

Adding to her discontent was the behavior of Falstaff and Devonshire. The two men, particularly Devonshire, had taken to their new surroundings and had even volunteered to help with the menial labor. Both had hardly spoken to her since their row, and in their pursuits they had developed a slightly chummy relationship with several of the Quaret who dwelt near their hovel. The natives had received them coolly, but Falstaff's affability and Devonshire's eagerness to earn a place among them countered much of the initial standoffishness. Desiring no part in their commune, Marbuck had held back, which had only fueled her growing certainty that the Quaret people were beginning to actively dislike her for her apparent aloofness. If her lingering amongst them dragged on any longer, Marbuck was certain that she would need to assimilate somewhat, if only to remain in their good graces and secure the assistance she'd been promised.

There had been no meaningful updates on that front. She'd had no further contact with Lakna and could not reach her. The tunnel back into the Great Ziggurat was blocked by watchmen, who'd cordially but forcibly informed her that none were free to go there without a summons from the Sanctified. Apparently, the fear of an assassination attempt orchestrated by Zeorshut Riengel kept Lakna and her family sequestered from their people.

In their absence, a hierarchy of the obsequious had evolved in the Warren. Certain people had managed to gain favor with the Sanctified, serving as their proxies amidst the rabble. They organized the labor and managed the distribution of food and water, but even they were beholden to the watchmen, who ceaselessly walked the tunnels, halls, and corridors of the Warren, bronze sabers dangling from their belts. Clearly, the ban on weaponry did not extend to Lakna's chosen. The Quaret clearly wished to avoid all contact with these ominous protectors, and Marbuck didn't care for them either. In her own wanderings, she'd watched as two of them had approached a man who'd been tinkering with a support beam. They'd started questioning him, speaking in gruff, hurried murmurs. The man had started to protest and they'd seized him at once, dragging him away.

The other workers had fixedly ignored the event and resumed their work as soon as the man's cries could no longer be heard. What whispers Marbuck had managed to overhear had hinted that the man must have been an agent of Zeorshut Riengel, perhaps seeking to sabotage the tunnel he'd played at maintaining. There had also been entreaties to Setenrah for his continued protection.

The episode had disturbed Marbuck. The Warren did not feel safe, for multiple reasons. She'd redoubled her efforts to depart and had been rewarded with nothing but obstacles, though Kemp had presented each one with his typical gaiety and an assurance that all efforts were being made to get her venture underway. She'd appealed to him for another direct audience with Lakna, and he'd regretfully informed her that the seneschal was resting; being at such an advanced age, she occasionally fell into extended bouts of lassitude, from which she always emerged reinvigorated. When asked on another occasion if she could assist in the gathering of provisions herself, Kemp commended her for her desire to help, but denied her request, citing the need to keep the storerooms secured against any attempts by agents of Zeorshut Riengel to destroy their precious supplies. Though *he* trusted her, rules were rules. During Kemp's latest visit, she'd suggested taking only what she could obtain in the Warren. Kemp had told her that without the Lady of the Veil's interventions, it would not be enough to sustain her.

At this, the volatile mix of frustration and curiosity that'd been brewing within her had erupted. She'd demanded to leave at once, to speak with Lakna, to know all there was to know about the Lady of the Veil. Kemp had weathered her tirade with a polite smile, but something within his eyes had betrayed a deep worry.

"Once you experience her ritual, you'll understand, and you'll feel a great amount of relief, I promise you that," Kemp had said. "It so happens that her handmaidens have announced the commencement of a ritual in a short time. I came here now to inform you of that, actually. I'd planned on taking you and your companions."

Having appeased Marbuck, Kemp had taken his leave, promising to return after the second feeding. Despite her better judgment, Marbuck felt a sulky desire to go without Falstaff and Devonshire. They didn't seem at all concerned about who the Lady actually was, or how she performed her apparent miracles. Marbuck hadn't shared any more of her concerns with them, believing that they would simply consider her questions an affront to the generosity of their host. Similarly, she had not told them about the tally marks. Still, they were her companions and Falstaff was her closest friend, no matter what argument had occurred. She resolved to attend the ritual with them, and now awaited their return with anxious anticipation.

Falstaff arrived first, entering the hovel with a smile that withered at the sight of Marbuck. "Raina," he said with awkward formality.

"Kemp's been by."

"Oh?"

"Yes. He intends to take us to one of the Lady of the Veil's rituals."

Falstaff's face brightened. "I'd heard about that. Word came from the handmaidens while I was helping with the gathering. I'd assumed we'd be going; I'm excited."

Apparently, Falstaff was more curious than she'd given him credit for. Of course, his curiosity was like that of a happy child. Marbuck was not quite so sanguine.

"It will be interesting, certainly. Listen, I—"

"You don't need to say anything," Falstaff said. "We were both out of line. Let's just leave it that."

It wasn't really an apology; but then, whatever she was about to say probably wouldn't have been one either. Ultimately, he was right, and had been about several things. Of course, she'd been right about a few things too. She decided not to point out how long the preparations for their departure were taking, not wishing to reignite any conflict and knowing that he'd be with her whenever they finally did leave.

After a short period of caution, they fell back into the natural patterns of their old friendship. They discussed the Warren, and the different tasks Falstaff had joined in with, speaking in their normal, comfortable banter. For Marbuck, it was an immense relief to be speaking freely with Falstaff again. Though their estrangement had been fairly short-lived, it had been a huge source of her gloom. Now, as they spoke, she could actually feel her spirits rising rapidly.

That crescendo was halted when Devonshire entered the hovel.

He eyed them, and from the look on his face, he clearly understood that they'd reconciled. Marbuck imagined that he might not be so interested in settling their quarrel. After all, she'd been particularly nasty to him, and he'd already made his intention to stay quite clear. She wondered if he would change his mind, and decided that, really, it didn't matter. They could make the trek without him. She'd make it alone if she had to.

"I assume you two have heard about the ritual?" he asked.

"Yes, Kemp came by. He's going to take us there," Marbuck said. She certainly wouldn't apologize to a man who'd betrayed his countrymen and held her captive until it was no longer advantageous for him to do so, but she had no issue being civil.

"Okay, that works for me," he said casually. Apparently, he was willing to follow her lead. Perhaps he'd recognized that she and Falstaff would once again present a united front, and he'd decided that any additional bickering could only alienate him further. Whatever the reason, he made no attempt to reopen the wounds of their last encounter.

Falstaff took the reins of the conversation then, talking at length with Devonshire about the jobs he'd tackled and the people he'd spoken with. Marbuck was happy to step aside and let them chat. She'd repaired things with Falstaff, and that was the important thing; having only a polite coexistence with Devonshire was perfectly fine with her.

As they spoke, she watched the door, waiting for Kemp's return.

• • •

"Right this way, my friends."

Kemp pulled aside a ratty, frayed drape, revealing a broad, sloping tunnel packed with natives. From the moment they'd left the hovel, Marbuck had seen numerous people all headed in the same direction. Citing his extensive knowledge of the Warren, Kemp had led them down a claustrophobic path that was little more than a gap between the cavern walls, promising that they would circumvent the crowds. In this, he had been correct. They now stood on a lip of rock overlooking the throng beneath them. Every eye was directed toward the end of the tunnel, where a plain, stone altar stood beneath a vaulted ceiling.

"This is the Tabernacle. It's here that the people gather to experience the ritual, and it's through there," Kemp said, pointing at a black curtain that hung over an opening in the wall behind the altar, "that the Lady of the Veil resides. She'll be joining us soon."

The curtain, which was adorned with various glass beads and metallic baubles, swayed slightly in some small current of air passing out of the darkness behind it. Marbuck watched this gentle movement, nearly hypnotized by the calm slowness of it. The low roar of the crowd dissolved into a background hum. Her stomach growled.

With a sudden flourish, the curtain was pushed aside. The crowd grew silent as four handmaidens streamed into the chamber and took up spots alongside the altar. Marbuck squinted at them, trying to tell if any of them had cared for her, but their identical robes and headdresses of white feathers made it impossible to tell them apart. Jalam came next, slipping through the curtain and peering suspiciously at the crowd, as if he expected a sudden attack. Like the watchmen, he, too, possessed a bronze saber. It remained at his belt, but he kept a tight grip on the hilt. Marbuck followed his watchful gaze and wondered if anyone in the crowd secretly belonged to Zeorshut Riengel. If Quaretem really did rely on the Lady of the Veil to survive, then she would be an obvious target for anyone looking to cripple the commune. It was no wonder that Jalam looked antsy.

After surveying the people for a moment, he turned and hoisted the curtain up. The Lady of the Veil then entered, moving with impossible grace, seeming to almost glide toward her rough altar. Behind her, Jalam let the curtain drop and stepped off to the side, where he stood with an air of formal readiness. As the Lady reached the altar, one of the handmaidens stepped forward.

"That's Katiek. She's the arch-maiden; the Lady's principal servant," Kemp whispered.

Marbuck looked more closely at Katiek as she took a place at the front of the crowd. For being the leader of the handmaidens, she appeared to be rather young, and Marbuck did not recognize her as one of those who'd cared for her. With an aura of meekness, Katiek looked at the gathered natives, her large, worried eyes peering out from beneath her headdress. Suddenly, she flung her arms up over her head, and her thin lips broke into a broad, giddy smile.

"The Lady of the Veil welcomes you all!" she shouted, her voice surprisingly resonant. "Blessed are the Quaret, beloved still by the One Who Remembers. She is prepared to give unto you of herself. She has gathered her strength. Let all those present drink it in. Deliverance for now, until deliverance forever."

"Deliverance for now, until deliverance forever," the crowd droned back at her.

Marbuck found it odd that Katiek hadn't mentioned Setenrah during her invocation. She leaned over to Kemp. "Deliverance from what?" she asked. Kemp merely placed a finger to his lips and nodded toward the altar, where the ritual was continuing.

Her pronouncement complete, Katiek had returned to the altar, where she and the other handmaidens now stood with bowed heads. During Katiek's address, the Lady of the Veil had remained at the head of the altar, statuesque and still. Presently, she lifted her hands above her head, palms up, and her veiled face tilted slowly toward the ceiling. As she watched, Marbuck realized that she was holding her breath.

For one brief moment, the air shimmered around the Lady, a rippling distortion that rose from her upturned palms. As Marbuck, who'd been expecting the Lady to speak, tried to understand this strange occurrence, the ripple suddenly rocketed outward in an expanding wave, washing over those closest to the altar and continuing to spread unimpeded. Instinctively, Marbuck tried to shrink away from this phenomenon, backing into Kemp, who caught her and held her steady. Before she could try to wrench herself out of his grip, the wave enveloped her.

Immediately, an intoxicating euphoria bloomed within her, surging out from her core and into her limbs, which erupted in gooseflesh. Her fingers, toes, and scalp tingled, and her hunger and thirst were replaced with a sensation of complete satisfaction. She felt the wave exit her body as it continued on its trajectory, taking some of the ecstasy with it, but leaving behind a profound, robust haleness. Marbuck gulped in a deep, rich breath that filled the deepest recesses of her lungs. She had never, at any point in her life, felt better than she did now. For the first time, she understood how she'd been brought back from the absolute brink. In that moment of overwhelming serenity, the power wielded by the Lady of the Veil seemed capable of rebuking death itself.

"Well, how do you feel?" Kemp asked. He was beaming, and Marbuck wasn't certain, but she thought that she might be as well. All around them, the Tabernacle was filled with the sounds of bliss. People laughed, cheered, wept with joy.

"I … well … incredible," she managed, eliciting a laugh from Kemp.

"I thought as much. And you, my friends?"

"I feel like I've just eaten the greatest feast I've ever had," Falstaff said, peering down at his stomach with a puzzled expression. He looked up with a grin. "And like I'm ten long-cycles younger."

"I think I might be drunk," Devonshire said, wavering on his feet.

"That'll pass, and without the nasty aftereffects."

"So, what exactly just happened to us?" Marbuck asked.

"You've been restored. By Setenrah's blessing, the Lady was given to the Quaret to sustain them in ways that their piddling foodstuffs and brackish water never could. Without her, we would perish. She heals the sick, mends the injured, strengthens the infirm, satisfies hunger, and slakes thirst. She is a wonder, of that there is no doubt."

"She's remarkable," Falstaff said, watching her, mesmerized.

Marbuck had also found her eyes drawn back to the Lady, and she was once again reminded of the Empress, though her lingering elation barred her from dwelling on any darker connotations. Instead, it was a simpler connection that she made: the wave of restoration produced by the Lady of the Veil was as impossible and otherworldly as the Empress's enchanting gaze had been. The explanation for this seemed obvious: the Lady of the Veil was one of the hidden old ones; she was a god. With Setenrah and Zeorshut Riengel being suspected of possessing the same divinity, it seemed that Quaretem was some sort of nexus for these beings. It was peculiar, and had Marbuck not been so jubilant, this realization might have disturbed her more. For now, she was content to savor her restoration.

Having concluded her ritual, the Lady of the Veil had leaned on the altar, letting her head, crowned with its high headdress, hang. Once they recovered their senses, Jalam, Katiek, and the other handmaidens gathered about the Lady, taking her by the arms and helping her back toward her private quarters. Marbuck was surprised to see her looking so feeble. It seemed that the expulsion of so much healing energy had left her depleted.

As her retinue led her away, the Lady leaned toward Katiek, who nodded at whatever her master was saying to her. The arch-maiden then looked up toward the ledge that Marbuck and the others occupied and her eyes locked with Marbuck's for a brief moment. Then, she turned back to the lady and said something, just as they slipped beneath the drape and vanished. Marbuck wondered what that look meant, and a remote disquiet formed the first, small fissure on the surface of her newfound contentment.

With the ritual complete and the Lady gone, the natives began to file out of the Tabernacle. Apparently in no hurry to join with the shuffling crowd, Kemp advised them to wait, and they remained on the ledge above the shrinking crowd.

"It has not gone unnoticed that you two have been joining in with the labor," Kemp said to Falstaff and Devonshire. "Lakna is impressed."

A queasy feeling of exclusion moved in Marbuck's belly, accompanied by a new conviction to join in with them as soon as possible. She could not risk falling out of Lakna's good graces, not when her ability to mount a successful journey home was entirely dependent on the seneschal's whims.

"You and your people have done so much for us; I just thought I'd repay the favor as much as I can before we leave," Falstaff said.

"And I wish to stay," Devonshire added, somewhat sheepishly.

At this, Kemp started slightly, and the words seemed to linger in the air, encircling his head. "You want to stay?"

"Yes. I'm hoping to earn a place here. I have no desire to return to Nordabor; there's nothing there for me now."

Kemp nodded slowly as he listened, his gray eyebrows knitting tightly together. "That's admirable, and a notion that I certainly understand. I'll talk to Lakna, see if her offer still stands."

"I would appreciate it," Devonshire said. He did not look at Marbuck. If he had, he might have observed an expression of disinterest. She'd already accepted his decision and was far too preoccupied with her own situation to give his choices any more thought.

As the stream of natives dwindled into a trickle, Kemp decided that it was time to lead them back through the narrow passage. They emerged a few short-cycles later, joining with the last of the dispersing crowd. Kemp bid them farewell, repeating his intention to speak to Lakna on Devonshire's behalf. He strutted off down the tunnel, and Marbuck, Falstaff, and Devonshire headed back toward their hovel, each quietly enjoying the buzzing high of the ritual's aftermath.

Unexpectedly, a hand grasped Marbuck's wrist. Her first thought was of the watchmen, and she whirled about to see Katiek standing before her.

"My apologies. I did not mean to startle you," she said. Her voice was no longer booming, but soft and squeaky. "The Lady asked me to speak with you." Her eyes flicked toward the natives moving slowly by them. "She asked me to do it discreetly."

Ahead of them, Falstaff had noticed that Marbuck was lagging behind. He nudged Devonshire and the two of them turned back.

Katiek licked her thin lips. "The Lady wishes to meet with you. Just you. After she's had some time to recuperate from the ritual, I will summon you. Do not seek her out before then, and do not speak of this to anyone. I must go."

Just as Falstaff and Devonshire reached them, Katiek turned around and trotted away, the feathers of her headdress shaking with her hasty movement.

"What was that about?" Falstaff asked.

Marbuck's newfound peace had been cloven in two, and she didn't know what to say.

CHAPTER 20

Though Kemp had experienced the ritual many times, it usually never failed to set his cup running over with bliss. Something was different this time. On top of the restoration he'd just experienced, he should have been pleased with himself as, so far, he'd fulfilled Lakna's wishes with aplomb. The ritual would certainly keep the three northerners in docile comfort until Setenrah came to collect them, and his success seemed assured. Even Marbuck's incessant nagging had been silenced.

Yet, sharing the experience with them might have been a mistake. Roanack had been right; he was not accustomed to playing host to those harvested for the tax. Normally, he would deliver them to Lakna, enjoy some rest within the Great Ziggurat, catch a ritual, and return to the wild wastes to resume his hunt. The other huntsmen who'd discovered the northerners with him had already set out again; his special task had held him here, forcing him to face the simple humanity of those he'd presumed to deliver into Setenrah's clutches. What their divine protector did with them after that, he did not know, but he was certain that it was not good. Why else would Lakna do everything in her power to avoid sending her own people?

And now, thanks to the time he'd spent keeping an eye on them, he was aware that Falstaff was an honest, if simple, man; one who was eager to repay kindness and earn his keep. He and Devonshire both had been working diligently to assist in any way that they could. It kept them busy, but it also made many of the natives uneasy. Like Kemp, they did not wish to bond with those they were condemning.

Worse yet, in Devonshire he now saw a reflection of himself. The scarred man was certainly running from something, and he clearly hoped to find some salvation in Quaretem. It was a pity that he'd never be given the opportunity. Kemp knew that if he wasted his breath trying to convince Lakna to spare Devonshire it would only cause her to doubt his suitability to the task at hand. She would never permit Devonshire to live, not if there was even a remote possibility that word could reach the kingdom, this Nordabor, from which he hailed. All it would take was one errant remark finding its way to Zeorshut Riengel, and the might of the old oppressors could be set upon them once again. Kemp may have felt some empathy for Devonshire, but he did not want to be responsible for Quaretem's potential ruin.

It was frustrating to have grown to like the two men. With Marbuck, he did not have that problem. Her sour, suspicious nature had increasingly worn on him. However, since she'd first mentioned her motivation for returning north, things that Kemp had intended to keep buried forever had begun to stir. The more she'd spoken of it, the more her words had threatened to dredge up these carrion memories. He did not wish to hear about her daughter anymore, and he hoped fervently that the happiness delivered by the ritual would keep her quiet on that front. At any rate, he intended to distance himself from the three northerners, trusting that Setenrah would come for them soon. He'd worked hard to secure his place in Quaretem, and though he'd always known there was a nasty truth that underpinned his life in Lakna's commune, it was something he'd successfully avoided examining. This experience had certainly tested that ability, and he was ready for it to be over.

Kemp did not speak any of these thoughts aloud as Roanack escorted him to Lakna's balcony. He'd gone to the Oasis Sanctum with the intent to report to her, only to find the chief warden in her stead. His first thought had been that she was resting; Roanack had instead informed him that she was looking for signs of Setenrah's pending arrival. Now the two men were making their way to the balcony, and Kemp found himself in the awkward position of being alone with Roanack, a man who he'd rarely spoken to outside of the shadow of his mother. As such, an uncomfortable silence lay thickly between them.

Just as Kemp was beginning to believe that Roanack might actually prefer the silence, he broke it.

"I understand that you've just attended a ritual with the northerners."

"I did what Lakna asked of me," Kemp said, immediately leery of Roanack's questioning. The chief warden had never made any attempt to conceal his scorn for the immigrant who'd risen to prominence, earning the trust of Lakna and escaping the fate shared by all other outsiders. Kemp suspected that if Roanack could find a sufficient reason to eliminate him, he would do so with alacrity.

Roanack nodded. "Of course."

"Word travels quickly."

"My watchmen report all unusual occurrences to me."

"Well, I understand that they're not privy to all that we've discussed, so their ignorance as to what constitutes an 'unusual occurrence' can be forgiven," Kemp said with a crooked grin. "Regardless, I was under the impression that *I alone* had been charged with watching the northerners. You wouldn't be contradicting Lakna's orders, would you? Or were your men watching me? If so, I'm flattered, but a little confused."

"Mind your tone with me," Roanack said, raising a warning finger into Kemp's face.

"My apologies, Chief Warden, I only meant—"

"I don't care what you *meant*. I'll never understand why my mother cares for you; why she saw it fit to elevate you beyond your station. Your skills as a huntsman do not justify being subjected to your brand of folksy nonsense. Your bravado is grating, your good cheer an affectation. You are a parasite, a tax that somehow escaped collection. Do not presume to speak to me with disrespect again. My mother will not always be there to shield you." He smiled thinly. "Now, come along."

Though Kemp held little regard for Roanack, this interaction had served as a reminder that the old man was not to be taken lightly. Humbled, Kemp said nothing and trotted after Roanack, cursing himself for being so flippant. The ritual's lingering effects had left him feeling confident and untouchable, and he'd momentarily forgotten his place. Now, with his ego freshly bruised, the thoughts exhumed by Marbuck scratched at the back of his mind again, smelling blood. For a brief moment, Kemp's ears rang with a single, piercing shriek. He cleared his throat, shook his head, and hissed out a sigh. By forcing himself to focus on the bright pool that paralleled the walkway upon which he was walking, he managed to settle his thoughts. He was not there, in the past; he was here, and here, he had a job to do.

The two men arrived at Lakna's balcony. Passing through an open archway flanked by two watchmen, they stepped out onto a wide, oval shaped balcony ringed by an ornate, iron railing and shaded by an overhanging lip that jutted out from the structure above them. Far below, the boundless desert dominated the northern horizon, its dunes eventually meeting the sky in a distant blue haze.

Despite being in the shadows, the balcony was still oppressively hot, and Kemp could feel his light tunic clinging to the sweat on his back. Lakna, her eye pressed against an ebony telescope inlaid with delicate jade etchings, didn't seem to mind the heat. She panned the telescope slowly along the horizon, seeking for any sign of mighty Setenrah. Kemp wondered why, being his oracle, she could not sense his approach. Maybe he didn't wish her to; the thoughts of a god were unknowable.

Kemp and Roanack stood in the heat, waiting for Lakna to acknowledge them. Finally, Roanack's impatience overrode his subservience. "I assume there's no sign of his coming?"

"No," Lakna said without turning.

"Mother, you've been at this for too long," Roanack said. "Leave it to my spotters; their watch is ceaseless and they can be trusted to report to us the moment there's any sign. Their scopes work just as well as yours. Please come inside; I'm sure this heat is too much for you."

Lakna turned from the telescope, and Kemp could see that her brow was dry. "At my age, the heat is a comfort. The light is straining my eyes, though."

Roanack made a show of rushing to his mother's side and taking her by the arm. He began to guide her away from the rail and she shrugged him off. "Lord Henrick," she said, brightening as she noticed Kemp's presence.

"Yes, he was looking for you. I believe he has something to report," Roanack said. "From the ritual he attended with the northerners."

Lakna, like the rest of the Sanctified, had never attended a mass ritual in the Warren, choosing instead to have the Lady of the Veil attend to her needs in the privacy of the Oasis Sanctum. Kemp sensed that she enjoyed hearing about the rabble's experiences, if only to contrast them with her own.

"You truly are keeping a close watch on those three," she said. "Their labors have kept them occupied, and the ritual should keep them happy. I'm glad that you made certain they attended."

Roanack pursed his lips but remained silent.

"I imagine it left them satisfied?" Lakna asked.

"Yes, Your Grace," Kemp answered. "I have no doubt that they'll be in the right state of mind when Setenrah arrives."

Lakna looked to the horizon again. "I do hope so. The effects will not last forever."

Roanack's eyes bounced between his mother and the huntsman. "Yes, well, I'm sure Setenrah will speak his will to you soon. Should you wish to deal with the northerners more—"

"They are for Setenrah," Lakna said, her voice cutting through Roanack's with ease. "I will not waste three perfectly suitable tributes. Do not try to sway me again."

"Yes, Mother, of course." Roanack pursed his lips again.

"Lord Henrick, I am pleased with your diligence. My request has kept you here longer than you are perhaps accustomed to. I do hope the call of the open lands has not been too persistent. I'm sure you're eager to resume your work beneath the Eyes."

"My work is wherever I'm needed. I enjoy my explorations, but I wish to help the commune however I can."

"You are a good man," Lakna said, and, with a bony grip, she squeezed his arm affectionately. "Your duty will be finished soon. Setenrah will have them and you will be free to acquire more as you please. Thank you for doing this."

"Of course, Your Grace."

Her words had been kind, but in the darkest part of Kemp's secret heart, he knew they rang hollow.

Rather than dwell on this sad truth, Kemp went on to explain to Lakna everything that had occurred at the ritual and during his most recent discussions with the northerners, though he omitted Devonshire's desire to stay. Similarly, though he believed that they had no immediate connection whatsoever to Zeorshut Riengel, he didn't say so. Lakna had previously expressed the same opinion, but Kemp still worried that reiterating it now might make it seem like he was defending those she'd already decided were an enemy. It was a decision that he knew was colored by his guilt for sympathizing with the northerners. He reminded himself that they didn't need to be in direct league with the oppressor to constitute a threat, and that he was doing the right thing.

When he'd finished his report, Lakna reinforced this conviction by once again thanking him profusely for his efforts, efforts that not only helped her but protected all of Quaretem. As he departed, leaving her to her telescope and her quietly stewing son, Kemp felt some measure of reassurance. He was grateful for Lakna, not just for delivering him from the snapping shadow of his past, but for soothing his anxious mind. Though his self-loathing skulked within him still, she had managed to at least restore his faith in what he did. It was a sort of restoration that was not so different from that offered by the Lady of the Veil, nourishing in its own vital way. She had reminded him that without his actions, without the role he played in the commune's survival, the Quaret people would risk annihilation.

And, tragic as it was, he knew that the hapless vagabonds from the north had their own role to play too.

CHAPTER 21

Despite Katiek's admonishment, Marbuck had told Falstaff and Devonshire of her pending meeting with the Lady of the Veil the moment they'd returned to their hovel. The clandestine nature of her encounter with the arch-maiden had dimmed the effects of the ritual, and she now felt shaky and wired. The two men shared her curiosity, if not her dread.

"I envy you, actually," Falstaff said. "After experiencing what she's capable of, I would love to meet her."

Aware of how recently they had patched things up, Marbuck had to restrain herself from responding caustically. "Yes, I'm certain it will be interesting, but don't you find it the least bit alarming? Why the secrecy? What could she possibly want from me?"

"Maybe she plans on offering some special ritual before our departure, and she's just being cautious, what with Zeorshut Riengel's minions on the prowl. I guess you'll find out when you go."

Marbuck chewed on this for a moment, her hands planted on her hips.

"You two realize what she is, right?" Devonshire asked. "I mean, they've already said that Setenrah is a god. I think it's pretty plain that she is too. What else could do what she just did?"

"I was thinking the exact same thing," Marbuck agreed.

"She keeps the people here alive, and she's no dying slave. What they've got here is just a better version of what we had in Nordabor."

"You really don't need to make your case any further. I get it; Quaretem is perfectly splendid and you're staying. I'm not so certain that everything here is exactly what it seems, though," Marbuck said, walking toward her cot. "Here, look at this."

Falstaff and Devonshire shuffled over and peered into the alcove.

"Look at these tally marks. Someone was keeping track of their time here, and, at some point, they stopped. Why? Who occupied this room before we did? Where did they go?"

The two men exchanged a glance of shared skepticism, and Marbuck felt a strong urge to throttle them.

"Those could have been left for any number of reasons," Falstaff said. "They could be a thousand long-cycles old; this place is ancient. Look, I think you're jumping at shadows, Fishwife, and I get why, but this is different. The Lady of the Veil is not Gomulte. By all appearances, she is a god, not some slaver trying to trick you."

"The Empress was a god too," Marbuck said. "I don't think godhood exempts the Lady from acting with malice."

"Why would Kemp rescue us, and the Lady heal us, if this was all just some ruse meant to hurt us?" Devonshire asked.

"That was before they knew where we came from. You saw how we were questioned after Vingallea came up; we were nearly attacked."

"Yes, and then Lakna invited us to join them! It was a misunderstanding, and she knows now that we have nothing to do with Zeorshut Riengel."

"I don't know," Marbuck sighed. "I just don't like this."

"Well, then maybe a private meeting with the Lady is exactly what you need," Falstaff said. "She might be able to put your mind at ease."

"At any rate, I don't think it's a trap," Devonshire added. "We're defenseless; the watchmen could seize us at any time. They wouldn't need to lure you anywhere. I think we're fine."

Once again, Marbuck restrained herself. She wanted to remind Devonshire that it was easy for him to say as he had not been the object of the last trap. He'd been the one who'd promised to stand with her, but once Gomulte had betrayed her to Bolenz, he'd simply watched as she was mutilated. Though she understood his reasoning, it was a difficult thing to forgive. She chose instead to ignore the speaker and instead consider the content of his words, as well as those spoken by Falstaff. On the surface, their ideas were completely rational, their reasoning sound. Yet, that sane, measured consideration seemed to be missing something, some monumental contamination at the heart of Quaretem, hidden just beneath the patina of tranquility. Whatever it was, Marbuck supposed, she would not know until she met with the Lady of the Veil.

"I guess what you're saying makes sense," Marbuck said, cloaking her true thoughts. "I'll meet with the Lady, as requested."

The men seemed satisfied that, for now, she'd set aside her misgivings. As for Marbuck, meeting with the Lady seemed to be her only option. After all, she was sure that Katiek would summon her before the supposed preparations for her departure were finished.

Assuming, of course, that they ever were.

• • •

As she waited, Marbuck worked.

Following through on her earlier decision to join in with the labor, she'd thrown herself into whatever jobs she could find. Her previous aversion to any sort of assimilation had left the natives even more standoffish than when she'd first arrived in the Warren, but Falstaff's budding chumminess with several of them had provided her with an inroad. She'd started to tag along with him, and the natives simply accepted her presence, though they did not embrace her. The work was almost always menial, dirty, and exhausting, but it kept her distracted and, she hoped, would eventually ingratiate her to the locals. If lending a hand pleased Lakna then she would continue to do so, with the hope that Lakna would be more inclined to expedite her promised assistance. It all felt like a political game, and Marbuck detested it.

For his part, Falstaff worked blithely, never griping about the jobs and never voicing any concern that Lakna might be withholding her assistance for some unknown purpose. Marbuck suspected that the return to routine labor was pleasurable for him; he'd loved serving on the *Fortune* and had never sought to journey across the world. He'd certainly never dreamed of becoming embroiled in danger and calamity, and despite his support of Marbuck and his concern for Elibeth, he seemed to be in no rush to embark on another difficult voyage. For him, Quaretem truly was a blissful respite.

Privately bitter at having to partake in the drudgery, Marbuck found it difficult not to resent Falstaff's apparent contentment. She focused on the labor instead, and there was no work more effective at making her forget the particulars of her predicament than that done at the Pit. Dumping the waste was only a part of it, granted it was a truly wretched part. The collection and hauling of the waste, which was slopped out of dented metal pails left outside of the door of each hovel and dumped into a foul-smelling barrel, was a miserable operation. But it was when those barrels were tipped over the edge of the Pit and their stinking contents spilled into the blackness below that the paramount function of the chasm was revealed. At the distant bottom were the numerous shades that'd been dumped into the darkness. Marbuck found it impossible to dwell on her own troubles when she could hear their tormented mewling and moans, accompanied by the scrabbling of their claws over the filth-coated rocks beyond the reach of the light. Languishing there, they endured periodic rains of waste while they awaited Setenrah's arrival. Marbuck could only guess at what happened to them after that. She doubted that their ultimate fate would be any less tragic.

It had also been at the Pit that she'd witnessed Quaretem's equivalent of a shepherding. A frail, withered husk of a man had been guided to the edge by four younger men. They'd helped the elderly man, who'd seemed to be no more substantial than a wisp of smoke, to the ground. He'd been lying on his back, with the top of his head resting on the very edge. The younger men had murmured softly, holding his hands and comforting him. Marbuck had been stricken by his appearance; the Lady of the Veil must have kept him alive far beyond his natural lifespan. She'd wondered if he'd chosen to die, or if he'd finally reached a point where even the Lady could no longer prop up his failing body.

Whatever the case, it'd been clear that he was in his final spiral. A moment later, he'd been gone, and the younger men had backed away. With expressions of profound sadness, they'd watched as a shade exploded from the dead man's head and, slithering into the open air, tumbled away into the darkness below. Once they'd decided that it was safe to do so, the young men had tipped the shriveled body over the edge and departed. The waste dumping had resumed shortly after. No shepherds; no ceremony; just a practical removal of the dead. As someone disillusioned with the Void-God, Marbuck could appreciate that.

Aside from the death of the old man, Marbuck had only seen the workers stop for one other reason: watchmen. From time to time, their patrols would bring them to the Pit, where they would look at the filthy workers with derision. Their very presence was enough to put the workers on edge, and on one occasion, they'd hauled away a man who Marbuck had later learned was accused of espionage and sabotage. According to one of the workers she'd been eavesdropping on, Zeorshut Riengel had designs on the Pit; plans that included unleashing the shades trapped within upon the Quaret.

After any arrest, an execution usually followed. Marbuck had learned that here, too, the Pit was utilized. She'd been helping Falstaff tip over a sloshing barrel of waste when, suddenly, the faint stream of light that filtered in from above the Pit had expanded into a brilliant beam. She'd squinted up into the light just in time to witness a screaming shape fall from above and plummet into the Pit. The cry had ceased the moment its source had struck the bottom.

"What just happened?" Marbuck had asked. The light had already narrowed back into its original dimness by the time she'd spoken.

"The natives call it the Deceiver's Door, and it startled the shit out of me the first time I saw it open. Sorry, I should have warned you about it. It's how the agents of Zeorshut Riengel are executed; they're just dropped right through the hatch. I guess it connects above to the dungeon in the Great Ziggurat. The lucky ones die right away; the shades finish off the unlucky ones." Falstaff's face had blanched. "And the unluckiest ones join the shades."

It was a system that was as efficient as it was brutal, and on that occasion, the executed man had been one of the lucky ones. Marbuck had not witnessed any further executions, and she sincerely hoped that she would not have to.

Despite routinely working herself to the point of exhaustion, she could not fully extinguish the shadow that hung over her; a sense of dread so palpable that she felt like she was facing her own execution. The relentless physical action could not totally mask the true inactivity of her existence. In actuality, she was waiting; waiting to hear from Lakna; waiting to be contacted by Katiek; waiting for whatever it was that disturbed her so much about Quaretem to reveal itself. She was trapped in an endless procession of nothing, behind which lurked something that she didn't yet understand, but that she knew was treacherous.

And so it was that Marbuck's collection of tally marks had continued to grow. It was with a nascent despondency that she found herself alone in the hovel, lying in her cot after a particularly grueling shift. As she scratched out her seventeenth tally, there was a gentle knock at the door. With some effort, she swung her legs off the cot and rose. She padded over to the door and cracked it open. Katiek, now bereft of her exotic headdress and looking quite plain, was waiting on the other side.

"The Lady of the Veil is ready for you."

CHAPTER 22

The tunnels of the Warren were mostly deserted, particularly the smaller passages that Katiek led Marbuck through. These offshoots, which departed and rejoined the main thoroughfare at random intervals, seemed to contain only residential hovels, the occupants of which were either off working or sleeping inside. Consistent with Katiek's earlier warning to keep the meeting confidential, they skulked unseen along the edge of a chamber wherein four watchmen were speaking with a small group of laborers. Marbuck's apprehension grew. If the secrecy was necessary to protect the Lady from Zeorshut Riengel's many eyes and ears, then why avoid the watchmen? For a moment, Marbuck was back in the orlop deck, the stinking, frigid water biting at her ankles as she followed Gomulte's hulking form. She could see the lantern ignite, the hideous face of Bolenz, triumphant. Then, Katiek was leading her through the Tabernacle and the nightmare was gone. As they approached the curtain behind the altar, Marbuck silently prayed that she was not repeating her mistake.

Katiek parted the curtain and held it aloft for Marbuck to enter first. As she stepped into the dim space beyond the doorway, her heart thudded, her throat tightened, and a flush rose in her face, reaching her scalp and setting her scar tingling. The curtain dropped behind her and her eyes fought to adjust to the gloom.

"She's just ahead," Katiek said softly.

Knowing that her voice would waver, Marbuck opted to nod her understanding. They continued down the narrow hall until it bent sharply and ended before a simple wooden door, beside which Jalam waited. Soft light emanating from a single window set in the door illuminated his face. He did not look happy about Marbuck's arrival.

"Were you seen?"

"Probably, though not by anyone who would understand or care," Katiek answered.

Jalam frowned, apparently unsatisfied with this answer.

"We avoided the watchmen, and I saw nobody that I suspect of being an informant," Katiek reiterated.

"Did you speak of this to your companions? Or anyone else?" Jalam asked Marbuck.

"No," she lied.

Jalam eyed her, weighing her simple answer. "I must search you."

Marbuck, who'd been deprived of her autonomy in countless ways since being torn from the deck of the *Fortune*, felt her indignation stir. "No," she repeated. "You won't. I have nothing, and I am here at your master's behest. I'd just as soon return to my cot; I'm quite tired."

"Wait," Jalam said as she turned to go. He looked at Katiek, who shrugged. "Fine. You may pass. But I will be right here, and I will not hesitate to enter if I'm needed."

"You won't be," Marbuck said.

Jalam hesitated for a moment longer, than turned the latch and held the door open. Marbuck looked at Katiek, and she gestured toward the open door. With a deep breath, Marbuck stepped into the sunlit room beyond.

The door shut gently behind her, but she didn't notice. As soon as she entered the chamber, lit by a single fat beam of sunlight pouring in from a hole bored in the ceiling, her gaze was drawn to the being who occupied it. Seated at a bare wooden table was the Lady of the Veil, clad in her black robes, her face hidden even in the privacy of her own chamber. She extended one graceful hand and held it out toward the chair opposite her.

"Please, sit."

It was the first time that Marbuck had heard her voice, and in those two softly spoken words she detected some intangible quality that betrayed the Lady's otherworldly origin. With stiff legs, Marbuck walked to the table and lowered herself onto the rickety wooden chair offered to her.

All the while, she could feel the Lady's eyes watching her from behind the blankness of her veil.

Marbuck settled into the chair, the legs of which wobbled beneath her. Feeling awkward, she plucked a piece of lint from the sleeve of her tunic and then folded her hands in her lap. The Lady remained perfectly still.

"I'm sorry that I could not fix you completely," the Lady said.

Marbuck, who'd imagined a dozen ways that their meeting might start, had not expected it to be with an apology.

"In another life I could have," the Lady continued. "Sadly, my light has dimmed since then."

Whatever the Lady of the Veil's intentions, and whatever the result of their discussion, Marbuck realized that she owed her life to the Lady's ministrations, and she'd never had the opportunity to express her gratitude.

"Thank you," she murmured. "You saved my life; I don't begrudge you a scar."

"May I see it?"

With shaking hands, Marbuck removed her kerchief.

After briefly assessing her work, the Lady of the Veil's head moved in a faint nod. Marbuck took this as the cue to put the kerchief back in place.

"I must apologize again for the manner in which we're meeting. After everything you've been through, I imagine that it's put you a little on edge."

Marbuck considered adopting an air of indifference, but something in the Lady's tone made her will buckle. "Yes, well ... it has," Marbuck admitted.

"You needn't worry. I simply wish to talk."

"About what?"

"I was fascinated by your account of your travels. In all my time in Quaretem, you are the first person to bring news of life beyond the World's Wound. I have toiled for so long under the belief that there was no hope beyond that which I could bring to the Quaret. If what you speak of is true, then you have disabused me of that notion."

Marbuck said nothing, lost in the power of her voice. It reminded her of still water, beneath which churned a powerful current. To hear her speak was to listen to an echo of distant eons, a sound that rang in the air of the forgotten past.

"I know what you are," Marbuck suddenly blurted.

The Lady remained completely still. When she spoke, her voice was low. "I thought that you might, having met others of my race. Tell me again about her."

"Well, um, like I said before, they—her followers—they called her the Empress—"

"I'm sorry, you misunderstand me. I don't mean her, though I have my theories about that. No, I meant the god of your city ... the captive god."

"Oh," Marbuck said. "I know little about it, save for the fact that whatever power it still possesses has been enough to keep nature flourishing within our realm, and that, for whatever reason, it's starting to fail."

"Interesting ... you speak of 'it' as a commodity," the Lady of the Veil said, and there was no malice in her voice, only a profound sadness. Realizing the insensitivity of her word choice, Marbuck's face burned scarlet. "Perhaps that is what the last of us have become. A crutch for the dying race of man or a beast to be flushed out of the wilds, such as those others you spoke of."

"I didn't—"

"Of course, there is a third path," the Lady said, ignoring Marbuck's words. "That which this 'Empress' apparently followed. I know much of that path and where it leads. To hear that it can end in such a way as it did for her is a comfort, though also a reason to mourn again. I had believed that Tariono's folly had led to her death long ago; I did not realize that she had lived to be so consumed by corruption."

"Tariono? You knew this god?"

"Yes, of course. Well, based on what you said of her power to allure, I believe it was Tariono that you encountered. She was the God of Beauty once."

"And what about you?" Marbuck asked. "What are you the god of?"

The Lady said nothing for a moment, her form as rigid as ever. "I have wished to speak with you ever since I heard you describe your city's captive god, but prudence has stayed my hand. I needed to be certain that you could be trusted, and I needed to discern what Lakna's intentions were. Already I have divulged much, for I never speak freely of what I am to anyone but Katiek and Jalam, and the arch-maidens and guardians who preceded them."

"Why couldn't you trust me? I'm no danger to anyone here; all I want is to leave, to return to my daughter," Marbuck said. Her curiosity was burning; she felt that she was wading ever closer to the truth. "You think that I'm an agent of Zeorshut Riengel?"

"You have been told many lies about this place."

Marbuck felt her chest tighten with a combination of dread and bitter vindication.

Slowly, the Lady lifted her hands to her veil. With a delicate touch, she pinched the ends of the fabric and began to lift it, revealing the ancient face beneath. It was that of a young woman with soft, round features, framed by light brown curls. She was not particularly beautiful, but she exuded a sort of kindly sweetness that belied her power and age. Only her eyes told the truth; they were the color of alabaster, and in them Marbuck saw the depths of time.

As the veil rose higher, Marbuck saw that the Lady was not actually wearing a headdress; the veil had simply been draped over and was hanging from the halo that hovered above her head. It appeared to be made of interwoven bands of white satin, and it glowed with a warm, inner radiance.

Marbuck sat back. For the first time, she was entirely overcome with the strangeness of it all. Sitting before her was a being that had existed for longer than she could fathom and who'd witnessed things she could only guess at. And unlike the Empress, she did not appear to be disturbed, and was not a terrifying despot living in a monstrous fantasy of her own making. This being, as undeniably alien as she was, somehow looked like a normal woman. Through the ceaseless walk of time, she'd managed to hold on to her sanity. Her knowledge of bygone ages that were otherwise shrouded in mystery was undoubtedly expansive. Though Marbuck was no scholar, she was still astounded by the magnitude of their meeting.

"You asked me what my domain is," the Lady said. "I am Reie, God of Mending, and I have striven for a long time to keep the people of Quaretem alive. By my hand is illness vanquished, rent flesh reformed, and death forestalled. My power, weakened as it is, satiates hunger and slakes thirst. Every healer who has ever walked forth since the time of the Great Culling owes their craft to my teachings of old. Tell me, do you know the history of which I speak?"

Marbuck shook her head.

"Do you know anything of the history of my kind?"

"Very little," Marbuck admitted.

"If you're to understand what's happening here, and what it is I want from you, then I must start at the beginning."

"You want something from me?"

"Yes. But first, you must understand."

"Okay."

Reie nodded, and her halo moved in perfect unison with her head. "Formless we were, in the beginning, my siblings and I. We erupted into existence at the behest of our creator, the creator of all the cosmos,

Alminnian. He carved us out of his own being after the Great Culling. Before us, before Alminnian had eradicated mankind in order to restart it, humans worshipped the firstborns, Ganachim, God of the Earth, Opriseur, God of the Sea, and Naffabyin, God of the Wind. They were the primordial gods, and they held sway over a simpler species.

"Of the firstborns, always Ganachim was the favorite of mankind. Opriseur's thoughts were as deep and unknowable as the waters she called home."

Marbuck remembered her parents telling her tales of the Sea-Keeper, and the seaside temple dedicated to her in which she'd sought refuge. Apparently, Opriseur had been the god's true name, and Reie had known her. It was astonishing.

"Some, usually those in pursuit of power, sought Naffabyin. He always thought little of mankind and treated his worshippers with amusement until he grew tired of them. Then his mocking delight would turn to anger and finally to annihilation. Only Ganachim ever held a love for mankind that matched her father's, and this, in spite of all they did to destroy the works of her hand.

"Because as mankind grew, so, too, did their ambitions, and they turned to wicked ways. They befouled the natural world they'd been gifted and turned on one another, descending into violence. Hoping to guide them, Alminnian created Nuroh, God of Knowledge. He instructed mankind on everything and anything they wished to know, but the gift of knowledge only fueled their avarice and lust for power. So the Great Culling was enacted, and the slate was wiped clean. Alminnian decided to birth a new pantheon to join with the old, a collection of numerous gods meant to guide and inspire every facet of human existence. I was a part of that creation. Unfortunately, so were my brothers Ulesreto, God of Judgment, and Aedesda, God of Punishment.

"Together, they were tasked with handling those humans who still turned away from Alminnian's pure vision for mankind. Upon each human's death, Ulesreto would pass judgment; the worthy went to Alminnian's Paradise; the unworthy would be hauled away by Aedesda to his realm, where they would suffer eternally as a shade. This system worked for some time, but then the two brothers grew tired of their positions and abandoned them."

Marbuck listened in stunned silence. Here was a clear explanation for why the shades existed, free of apocryphal trappings. This was the reason why fervent prayers to the Void-God were now the only recourse to avoid that miserable fate. The shepherds beseeched the shadow of the Father-God, hoping that it would now play the part that these two gods once had.

"They each sought to topple Alminnian and usurp his position at the pinnacle of creation. They allied themselves with Vingallea, which was as ambitious as they were, and launched a rebellion."

"I've heard of this," Marbuck said slowly. Some of the names and concepts rang a bell, but Reie's version of Vingallea's involvement contradicted what little history Marbuck remembered. She recalled being taught that Vingallea had been a noble, misled people, not an active instigator of rebellion. She found herself inclined to believe the god who'd actually been there. "The war between the gods. Our people know enough of the past to know that it's the reason why our world is broken."

"Broken indeed; the war was disastrous. From what I can surmise, the brothers ultimately failed, though it was at a tremendous cost. Alminnian was killed and his world was decimated. The sun ceased its movement in the sky, life withered to waste. The majority of his power was destroyed with him. I can still feel the moment his strength was torn from me, and I knew that he was gone. It was a catastrophe, and until you came along, I believed that there were only two survivors."

"Aside from yourself?" Marbuck asked. "Setenrah and Zeorshut Riengel?"

"You are partially correct. After the war, I was left unmoored. The bustling academies dedicated to my teachings were gone. Everywhere I tried to establish some foothold of preservation fell to ruin as millions perished in the aftermath of the war. Bereft of their gods, what was left of humanity devoured itself. I wandered, hidden, while everything that Alminnian had built and his children had fostered collapsed. And then I came to Quaretem.

"Hugging the coast, it was far enough away that it mostly avoided the fate that befell the southern kingdom of Vingallea, which was annihilated during the war. The World's Wound is all that's left of the cradle of Vingallean society. When I arrived in Quaretem, the Great Ziggurat remained almost untouched by the ravages of the war, though the shockwave from the destruction of the southern kingdom had flattened most of the other buildings in the city. It was a testament to the prowess of the original Quaret architects, I suppose. I found that the natives, who'd long toiled under their Vingallean masters, had taken advantage of the chaotic aftermath of the war and overthrown their oppressors. Being sequestered in the Warren, the Quaret had been unaffected by the shockwave, whereas the Vingalleans above ground were thrown into disarray."

"Lakna said that Zeorshut Riengel was their master, and that it was Setenrah who created the World's Wound," Marbuck said.

"Again, partially correct. Setenrah possesses great power, but there's no way that he could commit destruction at that level. His strength is of a decidedly different nature, one better suited for the role he plays now," Reie said, doing nothing to hide the scorn in her voice. "You see, in Quaretem I found a good people, and in me they found salvation. With my power, limited as it is now, I was still able to help them survive. By the time I'd reached them, they'd nearly exhausted every last resource they'd possessed and were contemplating turning to more desperate measures."

Marbuck, who was quite familiar with the methods implied by that euphemism, said nothing.

"But tragedy was avoided, and our little commune thrived. And then Setenrah found us. He, too, had been left wandering after the war. He had served as a high captain to Aedesda, and when the rebel cause faltered, he was left to his own devices. He is no mighty protector; Lakna's pontificating is a pack of lies. He is the God of Pestilence, and he holds sway here by the threat of extermination alone."

"Pestilence?" Marbuck asked. "Why would such a god exist?"

"Before the rebellion, Alminnian's pantheon was a system of perfect balance. The world needed a check to the otherwise unstoppable growth of life. In the beginning, he was a servant of Ganachim, a lesser spirit meant to assist her with the culling of old life in order for her to bloom new growth. His responsibility was never meant to be one of malice, but it became one. As such, he aligned himself with Aedesda, inflicting disease upon humankind for his own pleasure. Aedesda had even promised that he would let Setenrah take over the punishment of man once he ascended Alminnian's throne.

"Having lost that opportunity, Setenrah saw our commune as a second chance to indulge his desires. He has no interest in ruling a kingdom, only in satisfying his sick whims. He could destroy us all, but instead he allows us to survive, so that he might periodically pluck individuals from our midst and take them back to whatever hole he resides in. Rather than wipe us out, he pleases himself with the complete degradation of one victim, a system he designed and, by his own account, enjoys immensely. He has been doing this for generations now, and very few know the truth. What Quaretem was before his arrival exists only in my memory now."

With a furrowed brow, Marbuck considered everything she'd learned so far. Her suspicions had been right; Quaretem, in its own way, was as defiled as Vin-Sadavat had been. But the Empress had not faced any other divine opposition. "How can Setenrah threaten anyone here if you're capable of curing any ailment? It seems to me like your power would trump his."

"Unfortunately, no. I suspect that if he were to fully exercise his abilities, I would not have the strength to rebuke him. I might stop him for a time, but in the end, many would die. Worse yet, they would suffer terribly. And if his diseases *were* to fail, he could resort to unleashing his legion of the unworthy dead. He has collected every shade produced here since he assumed control, taking them north with him when he departs. I know that he cannot control them, but I believe he holds them captive. He's been quite clear that he would let them overrun us should I defy him. I do not wish to test this, and so I've remained subservient. It has been the only way to ensure the survival of the Quaret."

Marbuck pictured generations of shades moving in a tremendous horde. The havoc they would wreak would be unspeakable, the people powerless to stop them. "Aren't there any others who would stand with you? You said that few know the truth. Does Lakna? Does she know that she speaks lies?"

"Yes, every seneschal has known the truth. Once Setenrah cemented his rule by demonstrating what would happen to those who defied him, he established the Sanctified from those most willing to obey him in exchange for his mercy. They actually believe that he's capable of sparing them from becoming a shade upon death, a falsehood that Setenrah happily encourages. The Sanctified were left to rule in his stead, tasked with ensuring that his supply of victims never dwindles. All knowledge of Setenrah's true nature was suppressed; to even speak of it was forbidden. As such, it was forgotten by most. Beyond Lakna, I'm certain that Roanack, being her heir, knows the truth. How many more know, I'm not sure."

"So the natives don't know what Setenrah really is," Marbuck said slowly, gathering her thoughts. "They think he protects them from Zeorshut Riengel. So, what is *he* then? Another god?"

"Zeorshut Riengel doesn't exist," Reie said quietly. "Or, rather, he doesn't exist anymore. He was a man once; a Vingallean aristocrat who'd served as the colonial governor of Quaretem at the time of the war. Now he is a name only, a phantasm meant to instill fear, a fabrication used to control."

"I don't understand," Marbuck said, but as soon as she spoke, her thoughts turned to the watchmen. Wherever they went, their dogged persecution of the supposed 'agents' of their enemy created a wave of disquiet, coupled with timid subservience.

"When the Quaret overthrew their Vingallean oppressors, Zeorshut Riengel was killed. The Quaret had loathed him; they'd said he was a brutal oppressor whose sole desire was to squeeze every last bit of profit from his slaves. As was common with his ilk, he considered the Quaret to be less than human, and he treated them accordingly. He cast a long shadow over those who survived his reign and the generations of offspring that followed. In time, that memory became distorted, a process I could do little to impede. Not with the Sanctified actively driving it.

"Setenrah, desiring to keep his supply of victims as docile and unwitting as possible, twisted the understanding of our arrangement until the Quaret came to see him as their protector, shielding them from the return of a cruel master." Reie smiled humorlessly. "I believe that he enjoys the irony nearly as much as he enjoys the cruelty."

"So, Lakna can basically do whatever she wants under the guise of protecting the people?"

"Oh yes. And she relishes that power, despite her protestations to the contrary. She uses the specter of Zeorshut Riengel as a means to prop up her unjust arrests and executions, to stamp out anyone who questions the order of things. Believing themselves to be free, the people are held in thrall to the terror of the law. And all the while, she claims to channel the will of Setenrah. She is no seer. She's as afraid of him as anyone, perhaps more so because of the privileged position she stands to lose should she fail him."

"Is that true of all of the Sanctified? The entire family is totally complicit in this?"

Reie shrugged, and it was strange to see such a human mannerism come from her oddly still frame. "Much like Setenrah's real nature, I'm not sure who knows the full truth regarding Zeorshut Riengel, aside from Lakna and Roanack. Lakna prefers to keep certain knowledge compartmentalized. I think that many might know or suspect that things are not what they appear to be, but none have been willing to risk upsetting the balance. Sadly, that includes me. Only Katiek and Jalam share this knowledge, and I have sworn them to secrecy. They understand the necessity, vile as it is."

A small, disturbing thought wormed its way to the surface of Marbuck's mind, and once it had revealed itself, the certainty of it seized her completely. "Kemp—the huntsmen. Tell me, why do they seek out refugees?"

Reie took a deep breath and exhaled it slowly. "For Setenrah."

Marbuck leapt to her feet, sending her chair clattering to the floor. She'd increasingly suspected that Lakna was preventing her departure, preventing her from returning to Elibeth. To hear it confirmed still infuriated her. The reason why frightened her more. She now knew exactly what had become of the tally maker, and that her own count would end just as abruptly. "All of this, the healing, the bullshit reception, this little history lesson, it's all just to—"

"I understand why you're upset," Reie said, unfazed by Marbuck's anger.

"You do? That makes me feel *much* better. How many others did you empathize with as you nursed them back to health before sending them to slaughter?"

"You must understand, I've only ever done what I had to do. Defiance would mean the complete extermination of the Quaret."

"And their lives are worth more than mine? Or Falstaff's? Or the countless others you've done this to?"

"Many outsiders have been sacrificed, yes," Reie said, and her voice was heavy with shame and sadness. "We've had no choice. Setenrah requires his victims to go to him freely; hale, happy, and eager. The Quaret might understand the need for Setenrah's tax, but they still don't want to be chosen for it. They understand inherently that to be taken is to die. Even with my power, I can only soothe their minds so much. Though it certainly isn't because of any altruistic desire, Lakna does everything she can to avoid taking from the native population. It creates unrest, discontent, uprisings that can result in contentious crackdowns. All things that threaten our survival, for if Setenrah fails to get what he wants, we are finished. Outsiders don't know anything, and they please him the most. It is hideous, but it has always been for the greater good. Each singular life buys time for an entire people to live."

"Fuck you and fuck these people. They've let us live alongside them, knowing all along that we're just fodder for their protection. They're no better than Lakna, and neither are you."

"You mustn't blame them; they don't really understand. They live in immense fear, tempered only by their faith in Setenrah's protection. I doubt that even the watchmen or the huntsmen know the full truth. But if you wish to hate me for my part in this, then go ahead. I hate myself for it. It has been a terrible thing to be a part of, but I have seen no other option. Not until you came along, anyway."

This statement dampened Marbuck's rage somewhat, if only because it rekindled her curiosity. She glared at the god sitting humbly before her and, with some effort, mastered herself. "What do you want from me?"

"Lakna has held the false threat of Vingallea's return over Quaretem for a long time, as have her predecessors. Now, in you, she sees that threat as a reality for the first time. I have no doubt that she intends to deliver you and your companions to Setenrah. But Lakna sees only what affects her. In your report of the north, I see much more. Please, sit."

Reie gestured toward the overturned chair. Marbuck looked at it. She considered kicking it away and storming out, but she didn't. If everything Reie said was true, she was never going to leave this place. Not unless it was in the clutches of Setenrah.

She righted the chair and sat back down.

"The answer for us both lies in the past," Reie said. "Prior to launching their coup, Aedesda and Ulesreto courted the gods who they thought might be sympathetic to their cause. It turned out, of course, that they had whispered into many receptive ears. Alminnian had grown increasingly preoccupied with the spirits of those humans deemed worthy enough to join him in Paradise, and there were many who'd felt that he was neglecting his first creation, our world, Gana. And all the while Vingallea continued to run roughshod over the rest of humanity, sowing misery and subjugation. But, at the time, there were few among Alminnian's most loyal supporters who seriously considered these gripes to be the first stirrings of a rebellion. That changed when Casapax was murdered by Tariono."

"The Empress?" Marbuck said.

"Yes. As I said before, her tale is one of folly. Tariono was one of the first to openly join with the brothers, though her reveal was not planned. She believed that she could reach ever greater heights of beauty, and thus receive greater adoration, if she took the reins of creation from Alminnian. Casapax learned of her involvement with the brothers and what they were planning. She was the God of Inspiration and Tariono's twin sister. Beautiful in her own right, she'd influenced some of mankind's greatest works, though man always worshipped beauty more."

Marbuck listened intently, her anger nearly forgotten. Every sentence carried revelation. She wondered if the death of Casapax was one of the reasons why mankind had grown so stagnant. Without divine inspiration, the patterns established countless long-cycles ago had continued to slouch on endlessly, unchanging. Language hadn't evolved; almost nothing new had been invented; the skills needed to accomplish great works had escaped them. Whether it was Nordabor clinging to the last vestiges of Vingallea, or the slavers repeating the same violence for generations, or the Quaret perpetually laboring at the behest of a master, it was all the same. Mankind was a shade haunting a world that had died long ago.

"When Casapax threatened to go to Alminnian," Reie continued, "Tariono murdered her. Her death, the first case of deicide to ever occur, was felt by us all. With the first blow struck and no chance of working their plot surreptitiously anymore, the brothers openly declared themselves, with Tariono their only known supporter. Not realizing the extent of the rot they had instigated, Nuroh called a war council.

"Many who joined us that day would later reveal themselves to be in league with the brothers. They listened patiently, playing the part of loyal subjects. They reported every word back to the brothers, and there were many words spoken. Nuroh had plans for everyone. He claimed to speak for Alminnian, who, despite the growing rebellion, couldn't be bothered to leave Paradise and join our gathering. Without our creator, the most important attendees were the firstborns. Upon their shoulders, the war effort fell. In one way, this was disastrous. Naffabyin had already sworn allegiance to the brothers, and his betrayal cut us deeply. On the other hand, Opriseur was ready and willing to serve; her dedication to Alminnian was nearly unmatched. Only Ganachim held more love for our father."

Reie paused, her head bowed. She was staring at her hands, which were folded neatly on the table, but what her ancient eyes were really seeing was beyond Marbuck's grasp. When she spoke again, it appeared to take a great effort.

"After the council, I begged her not to fight. I told her to wait, to let the brothers' infighting consume them, to let the competing egos and desires tear their rebellion apart. She wouldn't listen. I kept trying, but eventually it was too late. Ganachim told me that Ulesreto had mobilized the Vingallean legions and was marching a mighty host north to the Isle of Creation, and that the final conflict was now inevitable. She told me that Alminnian had called upon all who remained loyal to go north and fight." Reie swallowed. "And I refused the summons to war."

Much of this history was beyond Marbuck, including the full extent of Vingallea's involvement. She was certain that the scholars in Nordabor's Hall of Antiquities would pay any price for this knowledge, but it rolled over her like a wave, leaving behind only the anguish in Reie's voice.

"Ganachim left without me for the last time. She was disgusted, called me craven. She wasn't wrong. Perhaps if I'd gone with her everything would have been different. Maybe Alminnian would have lived. My power was small compared to that of the titans who fought on that distant battlefield, but who knows? At any rate, Ganachim never made it there. Aedesda ambushed her on the road north. Setenrah was with him.

"It is a chief pleasure of his to remind me of this pain, and he spares no opportunity to gloat over it each time I'm trotted out before him.

He claims to have killed her himself, to have watched her lifeless body sink into the muck of the Einfallen. I never felt her loss, like with Casapax, but at that point, death and pain had become a constant hum in all of our minds, so it's hard to say. I never saw any reason to believe she'd survived."

For Marbuck, the final piece had slid into place. "Until now," she said.

A faint smile touched Reie's lips. "Yes, until now."

"You think that the captive god in Nordabor is Ganachim?"

"Why wouldn't I? It's not difficult to imagine that the men of Nordabor discovered her somewhere on the shores of the Einfallen. She would have been severely weakened not only by the assassination attempt, but by the loss of Alminnian. They would have known what she was, and being Vingallean, they would have had no qualms about using her to save themselves. From everything you've said about how Nordabor has survived, it sounds like her latent energy at work. It makes sense."

"Yes, it does," Marbuck agreed.

"And if Setenrah had been certain of her death, then why did he remain behind? I've spoken to him enough to glean that he was not at the final battle. Aedesda went north and, as far as I can gather, died with the rest. So why didn't Setenrah? I think maybe Ganachim escaped their initial attack, and Setenrah was tasked with finding her and finishing her off. I bet he never found her, and he simply assumed that she must be dead."

Reie was speaking quickly now, her rekindled hope burning hot. Marbuck found it infectious, but only because it presented her with an avenue of escape.

"So, that's what you're after? Ganachim?" Marbuck asked.

"If I could only reach her, I could heal whatever is ailing her before it's too late. Then, if I could free her from her servitude, she could return here with me. Our powers combined would turn Quaretem into a haven, and without Aedesda to aid him, Setenrah would be too weak to oppose us. He could even be destroyed, and we would finally be free. Even his shades would be useless; Ganachim *is* life, her mere presence can destroy the shades, an ability that Ulesreto always resented and Aedesda always loathed." Reie smiled again. "More than a few times she disagreed with Ulesreto's judgments and denied Aedesda his prize."

Marbuck needed no further proof of Ganachim's identity; it was, after all, the captive god's blood that provided the anointed blades with their power against the shades. She decided not to tell Reie about this ritualistic bloodletting of her fellow god.

"You want me to take you to her," Marbuck said, and she strove to conceal the slyness leaking into her voice.

"That is the bargain I sought to strike. I will help you and your companions escape this place if you escort me to Nordabor and help me free Ganachim. You say that you know little about her, but I suspect that you know more than you are letting on."

Marbuck had to bite the inside of her cheek to keep from grinning. Reie thought that she knew more than she actually did, and she would happily indulge that belief if it greased the rails of her escape.

"I have a connection with the Crown that can get you to Ganachim," Marbuck lied. "A merchant courtier who is very close with the king. He can get us in. I can help you free her."

There was a kernel of truth in this; she had known Rayburn, who had worked in close conjunction with the Crown, but only in passing. Winslow had been the one to deal with Rayburn directly; she was barely an acquaintance. And, at any rate, Rayburn had been with the expedition. It was doubtful that he would even be in Nordabor, much less alive.

Ultimately, her contacts were irrelevant. Even if she could speak with Phar-Mindorius, she was certain that he would never permit them to see Ganachim, if she was even still alive. And there was definitely no way that he was going to release the only thing preventing Nordabor's collapse, not without a fight. Should he learn what Reie was, he would probably have her seized, too. Then Reie would be reunited with Ganachim in chains. It occurred to Marbuck that she could actually save Nordabor by orchestrating this. She could trick Reie into being taken by Phar-Mindorius, and he would undoubtedly force her to heal Ganachim just enough to function. Nordabor would survive, and she would be a hero. This possibility held about as much appeal as actually freeing Ganachim, an endeavor that would doom Nordabor and possibly save Quaretem, and one that she had no intention of pursuing. She did not care, really, about either city. They were both corrupt holdovers from a dead time, ruled by the final remnants of the old order, desperate to hold onto the last strands of power. Whatever happened to Reie once they arrived in Nordabor didn't matter to her. All she cared about now was getting back to Elibeth. Everything after that was secondary. She may have been deceiving Reie, but turnabout was fair play; the entire commune had been lying to her, perfectly content to buy their peace with her blood. She would tell Reie whatever the god wanted to hear if it helped her achieve her ends.

"Excellent," Reie said, and she breathed a small sigh of relief. "I had hoped to secure your assistance. With that in mind, much has already been prepared for our escape. Jalam will be coming with us, and he'll make sure that any supplies we might need are prepared. With my presence, you won't have to worry about food and water, at least.

"Katiek will remain behind to organize the securing of the Warren. Our absence will not go unnoticed for long, and Lakna will be furious. Katiek has been fostering discontent, though discreetly enough to avoid the attentions of the watchmen. When the time is right, she will reveal the truth about Setenrah and Zeorshut Riengel and instigate a revolt. She will ensure that the entrances to the Warren are blocked and that those watchmen inside are overtaken. That should buy the people some time. I will make sure that that time lasts as long as possible by performing a ritual as close to our departure as I can. It will be tricky, for the ritual weakens me greatly. Hopefully whatever I give them will be enough to sustain them until I return. The rations should help too, but we'll still need to make the journey as quickly as possible. That is where I'll need your help as well. I'm essentially a prisoner here. I have not left this place in ages, and my knowledge of the geography of our world might not reflect what's out there now. Certainly, once we're north of the World's Wound, I will need your guidance to reach Nordabor."

"That won't be an issue," Marbuck said, thinking that it might be. Suddenly, she was struck with a visceral memory. She'd made a similar claim before, to Bolenz, and it hadn't gone well. Recalling that terrible misstep reminded her of the potential that this, all of this, was a fabrication meant to ensnare her. Looking into Reie's earnest, hopeful face, she decided that only one of them was currently dealing in deception.

"Good," Reie said, and she abruptly rose, pulling her veil back over her face. "Katiek will contact you again when we are ready to act. She will have more information for you then. In the meantime, you may tell your companions of our plan, but only if you are certain that they can be trusted to remain silent until the time is right."

"I understand," Marbuck said, rising from her chair.

Reie, once again in the guise of the Lady of the Veil, walked Marbuck to the door. There, she placed a hand on her shoulder. It was delicate, but it carried a supernatural weight that made Marbuck's heart skip a beat.

"You will see your daughter again."

Marbuck smiled weakly. "Thank you."

As she left the Tabernacle, she felt the first small stirrings of guilt.

CHAPTER 23

The dull cavern hallways of the Warren were the same, but everything had changed. The sunlight streaming in through the high shafts seemed too bright, the darkness pooling in the corners like that of a grave. The natives that Marbuck passed avoided her gaze in the same vague way, but now she could almost see the secret knowledge of her preordained fate etched upon their faces. Knowing their duplicity, her budding guilt had quickly withered. Part of her wanted to lash out, to snatch each one and beat them until they gasped out the truth in a final confession. It wouldn't have done any good; hearing her doom again would do nothing to alter it. There was only one path that would lead her out. Unfortunately, it required her to bide her time going through the motions of normalcy, lest any suspicions arise. It was a tall order. It was hard enough to wear a smile while shoveling shit; doing so while knowing that she might be snatched at any moment was nearly impossible.

As with so many of the things she'd endured, Marbuck was grateful that Falstaff was there with her, though he did not appear to share her gratitude. As soon as she'd returned to the hovel, she'd told him of the meeting with Reie. He had not taken the news well. She'd had to wake him up from a deep slumber, and he'd listened to the recounting with a bleary, defeated expression.

Now, another period of work had begun, and his disposition had not improved. As they'd slogged through their labors together, he'd remained uncharacteristically sullen. The only comfort for him was in knowing that Reie, who'd so enchanted him as the Lady of the Veil, was innocent in his eyes. Marbuck was still loath to pardon her completely; compliance due to the circumstances was still compliance. And Reie couldn't cry ignorance like the natives. Her reasons for knuckling under to Setenrah might make sense, but Marbuck still resented her for the role she'd taken in the long-running butchery. After all, Marbuck knew that she'd only been spared because she was particularly useful.

It didn't matter, at least not to her, that that usefulness was built on a foundation of lies. Falstaff, on the other hand, was almost as disturbed by Marbuck's deception as he was by that of the entire population of Quaretem, a population he was still strangely attached to.

"So what's going to happen once we reach Nordabor and you tell Reie that she's now on her own; that there was never any chance of you getting her to the captive god?" he'd asked. "You're luring her away from these people, leaving them entirely defenseless, based on a promise you can't keep."

"I wouldn't keep it even if I could," Marbuck had spat, struggling to contain her impatience with Falstaff. "And forgive me if my conscience isn't weeping for these people. They certainly haven't lined up to help us. And Reie is only willing to help us based on my access to Ganachim. She'd never even have approached me otherwise. This is the only way."

Rather than being incensed by her belligerence, Falstaff had been sagacious. "Reie and the natives are only doing what's necessary to survive. We've been doing the exact same thing. Have you forgotten that it was you who first betrayed the bounds of our agreement on the longboat? I lost; it was me who was supposed to be killed, but we turned on Old Stitch instead. Slaver or not, we proved faithless when it came to our own survival. Now, how can you hold these people to a different standard? How can you expect them to jeopardize their own survival for an outsider? You expect them to risk sacrificing themselves, or those they love, for a stranger? Think of what you would do in their place, or if Elibeth was in their place. Especially if it was all you'd ever known."

Falstaff's argument had cowed Marbuck, though it had not convinced her. She'd mumbled something about figuring out how to come clean to Reie at some point, but without any real conviction. She suspected that Falstaff knew that her intentions remained the same, and that was a large reason for his current melancholy.

Similarly, Falstaff was disturbed by her exclusion of Devonshire. He hadn't been in the hovel when she'd returned, and she'd considered that a blessing. Reie had told her only to confide in her companions if she trusted them, and Marbuck had quickly realized that Devonshire did not fall into that category. He was far too enamored with Quaretem and had made plain his desire to stay, as well as his disdain for returning to Nordabor. With his history of shifting allegiances, it was not difficult to imagine that the opportunistic ex-guardsman might betray them to Lakna in some misguided attempt to secure a position amongst the Sanctified. Marbuck had shared these reservations with Falstaff, and he'd initially balked, though he'd eventually admitted that her argument had some merit. Not wanting to leave Devonshire to die should her suspicions be unwarranted, they had agreed to tell him, but only when the plan was already in motion. Marbuck did not want to give him any opportunity to betray them.

Despite this joint decision, Marbuck had still worried that Falstaff might be unable to restrain himself from telling Devonshire. Her concerns had so far proven to be unnecessary. Devonshire's continuing attempts to ingratiate himself to the natives had kept him occupied elsewhere in the Warren, and they hadn't crossed paths with him yet. Apparently, his desire to earn a place in the commune did not extend to dumping the waste; he hadn't been known to darken the doorway of the Pit, and this had caused her to gravitate toward the task, knowing that Falstaff would come with her.

Wheeling another load to the edge, Marbuck wondered how long she'd be able to stall their inevitable meeting. At some point soon, the three of them would be sharing the hovel again, and the air would be thick with secrets. If she knew Falstaff, and she did, he would find it unbearable to deny his natural inclination toward honesty.

She looked across the top of the barrel at her old friend. The signs of their ordeal had nearly been erased by the healing of Reie, and though he remained thinner, his face had regained its round, childlike aspect. His naïve capacity for kindness could be charming, until it wasn't. Devonshire and his fickle loyalty constituted a real threat, yet Falstaff would have blithely informed him of their plan, based simply on the fact that he considered him a companion, a friend even. Marbuck had no such feelings toward Devonshire and his self-serving declarations of fealty. Perhaps her assessment was harsh, and her prejudice the offspring of paranoia, but with escape so close, she did not want to take any risks.

"Ready to tip it?" Falstaff asked, planting his hands on the sides of the barrel.

"Yeah," Marbuck said. With a grunt of exertion, she pressed her shoulder to the barrel and heaved. It toppled over and the foul contents sloshed out and poured into the darkness below.

Falstaff wiped his hands on the legs of his pants. "I'll grab a couple shovels."

Scraping the last clinging bits of gunk from the ribs of the barrel was not a pleasant task, and Marbuck bore a scowl of disgust as Falstaff trotted toward the far end of the Pit, where a motley assemblage of rusted tools was kept.

"Not up to any mischief, are you?"

Marbuck nearly cried out at the sound of the voice behind her. Her heart had rocketed up her throat at the same speed that her bowels had nearly dropped out of her. Striving with all her might to appear casual, she turned to see Kemp standing before her. As usual, he was smiling, and Marbuck was absolutely certain that he knew. Somehow, her plot had been revealed and he'd come for her. Just as Bolenz had lured her into a trap by pulling the strings of what she'd believed to be her own guile, now this man held her under his thumb. She swallowed, trying to force open her throat, which her fear had pinched shut. Opening her mouth to speak, she prayed that her voice wouldn't waver. Before she could find out if it would, Kemp spoke again.

"You've certainly got tongues wagging. Your sudden interest in lending a hand has made quite the impression as of late; I don't think there's a single task down here that you haven't tackled, and apparently you do not shy away from the less savory ones. Why, it's enough to make me think you've changed your mind about leaving." Kemp waggled his eyebrows roguishly. "Why the change of heart?"

Alarms screamed in Marbuck's head, and she could feel her scar burning with the intensity of her flush. "Well, I've been here for a while. I don't enjoy being idle, and helping those who helped me just makes sense." She was slightly relieved to hear that her voice sounded normal.

Kemp nodded. "Following the lead of your compatriots, eh? Well, it's a welcome change. Unexpected, but welcome. The cynic in me might have guessed that you were only working to make a good impression with Lakna. I'm glad to hear that it's for more noble reasons."

It was impossible to gauge what Kemp was getting at. He might have known everything, he might have known nothing. Marbuck smiled vacantly. "That wouldn't hurt either."

"What wouldn't?"

"Making a good impression. Perhaps Lakna might be inclined to speed up my departure. I do wish to return to my daughter soon. I've been away for far too long, and I would not have Elibeth believe that I've abandoned her. I *need* to get back." The truth of this simple statement turned her fear to hatred. Since their first meeting, Kemp had been stringing her along, pretending to care while all the while planning for her death. She found herself wondering if the huntsman who ensnared desperate wanderers with the false hope of salvation had any family of his own. It suddenly seemed important to pluck at that thread, to try to wring even a drop of shame out of the jovial killer. "Tell me, do you have any children?"

Kemp's smile faltered. An expression that Marbuck had never seen before took up a fleeting residence on his normally jolly face. It passed as quickly as it had come, and an artificial smile followed. Marbuck took a small step backward. She became aware of the Pit's yawning presence behind her, could hear the distant moaning of the shades.

"I'm afraid not," he said, his voice oddly flat.

"Well, if you did, you would understand my anxiety to leave. You would not fault me for doing things to earn Lakna's favor, not when she alone holds my fate in her hands."

"Oh yes, of course," Kemp said. "Lakna knows of your efforts, though there is nothing you could do that would make her care more or less about your plight. It is a simple issue of logistics, not anything personal. That being said, I do believe that preparations are nearly complete. You'll be leaving very soon."

Marbuck nearly barked out a bitter laugh. Even now, Kemp still dangled her hope before her. If he really was aware of her plan, he was every bit as sadistic as Bolenz had been. She allowed herself to believe that maybe he didn't know; maybe he was still operating under the impression that she was ignorant and compliant. Either way, she had to play along.

"That's great news," she said, and the words tasted acidic.

"Ah, and here's Falstaff, working as diligently as ever," Kemp said with all of his normal gusto.

Falstaff was walking slowly toward them, the two shovels he'd retrieved held stiffly at his side. Marbuck knew that, like her, he was rattled by Kemp's presence; she just hoped that he'd be able to conceal it.

"Any word on our departure?" he asked as he reached them. Marbuck was impressed; he'd spoken with a level of nonchalance that she would not have thought possible.

"I was just telling Marbuck that the final preparations are nearly complete. You'll be leaving very soon." Kemp paused, and something like pathos seemed to come over him. "To be honest, I'll be sad to see you go. You're a good fit here."

Falstaff looked nonplussed. As for Marbuck, she didn't know what to make of Kemp's words. Genuine compassion seemed out of the question, yet such false sentiment seemed needless, unless he simply enjoyed toying with his prey. A prospect that wasn't impossible, considering his line of work.

"Well, I'll get out of your hair." Kemp's eyes flicked to Marbuck's covered head and he actually looked somewhat embarrassed. "Your—well, you get it. I'll let you know when everything's ready."

Kemp left them to their work, and as they slowly began the task of scraping the barrel clean, they spoke in hushed tones.

"What do you make of that?" Falstaff asked. "Do you think he suspects anything?"

"I have no idea," Marbuck said. "But either way, I get the feeling that we're running out of time."

•　•　•

Her words turned out to be prophetic.

Several cycles later, Marbuck and Falstaff began to make their way back to the hovel, with Marbuck dreading the inevitable encounter with Devonshire. She'd managed to stall their return while also tackling a very necessary task by taking a detour to the well, where cold, cavern pools allowed her to wash the grime of the Pit from her body. She'd dressed in one of the identical tunics provided, leaving her filthy one behind for whoever would be tackling the laundry next, and rejoined Falstaff, who'd also bathed. There'd been nothing else to do then but return to their quarters. In truth, her labors had left her with a profound exhaustion that seemed to be emanating from her very bones, and she was eager to rest. Hopefully, Falstaff felt the same. Perhaps they could bypass any interaction with Devonshire if they just went straight to sleep. Of course, they couldn't avoid him forever. At some point, Falstaff would be unable to exclude him any longer.

Marbuck was pondering this, lost in thought as she plodded through the sparsely occupied tunnel, when she saw Katiek approaching her. The arch-maiden looked equal parts relieved and frantic.

"Oh blessings, I've found you," she squeaked, grabbing both of them by the arm and dragging them toward a shallow alcove in the closest wall. Her eyes darted across the tunnel; the few lingering natives walking ahead of them hadn't looked back. More importantly, there were no watchmen present. "He's coming."

Once again, Marbuck felt the crawling tendrils of fear grasping her insides like a vise. "Setenrah?" she asked, her voice a whisper. She already knew the answer.

Katiek nodded. "Whenever he's close, the Lady can sense his coming, even before the spotters can see him, for he is like her. And he's *very* close now. We need to go."

Strangely, Marbuck's first reaction to this news was to be grateful that she'd had the chance to bathe. Falstaff's concerns ran a bit deeper.

"What about Devonshire? Where is he?"

"I do not know," Katiek said. "Jalam and I were sent to find the three of you. Now that I've got you two, there's no time to search further. I must get you out of here. Hopefully Jalam will find your companion."

"He won't have any idea what's going on," Falstaff said, glancing sharply at Marbuck.

"Jalam will have to do his best to explain it to him quickly," Katiek said. "Now follow me."

Falstaff sputtered, but before his argument in favor of searching for Devonshire could fully form, Katiek was already striding away. He looked at Marbuck with a pained expression, and she shrugged. She would not abandon her chance to escape to search blindly for Devonshire. She trotted after Katiek, and a moment later, Falstaff reluctantly followed.

Together, they crept through the Warren, and it soon became clear that they were headed toward the Tabernacle. Marbuck's exhaustion had been blotted out, replaced by a sort of hyper vigilance. Her head swiveled; violence was expected around every turn. Each step increased her certainty that they would be intercepted by a contingent of watchmen.

Somehow, they weren't. They reached the Tabernacle without incident, and Katiek led them toward the black curtain. As she passed through its dark folds, Marbuck felt some of the weight on her shoulders slip away. They had made it to Reie's private chambers undetected.

She allowed herself a sliver of hope.

CHAPTER 24

"Thanks again for arranging this."

Devonshire was the very picture of humble gratitude, and Kemp was certain that the scarred man meant every word. It certainly didn't make things any easier.

"Of course. I don't see any reason why Lakna's offer wouldn't still be on the table. Still, an in-person entreaty will certainly help."

Devonshire nodded eagerly. "I wonder if she'd be willing to consider allowing me to work as a watchman. I've served in a similar role before."

"Perhaps," Kemp said. He was barely listening. The sourness in his stomach had increased into a full-blown churning. What he was doing was far beyond his purview, but Lakna had been clear. The northerners were to be brought to her at all costs.

The spotters had detected Setenrah's approach in the usual way. Orders had gone out to clear the Eastern Promenade. Those permitted to live in the Great Ziggurat had returned to their quarters, as had the spotters, who, like everyone else, were not allowed to receive their god. Only Lakna, Roanack, and the Lady of the Veil enjoyed that privilege, and they'd prepared for his arrival accordingly. Lakna had issued the command to bring Marbuck, Falstaff, and Devonshire to the Eastern Promenade. Kemp had been relieved. Finally, the trio who'd constituted such a threat to their people would be gone, he'd be free to return to his hunt, and things would settle down again. But then the report had come in: the northerners were not in their quarters, and they could not be located. Immediately, concerns of a conspiracy took hold, and Lakna had been apoplectic. She'd mobilized every watchman and huntsman within the Ziggurat and set them on the task of finding the northerners. With Kemp she'd been rather direct; as the one who'd been primarily charged with their keeping, he especially bore the responsibility of finding them.

The menace in her words had been clear, and they had thrust Kemp into an unfamiliar situation. His task had always been a simple one; one that he'd completed with exceptional prowess. The burden of this additional role was something he hadn't asked for and something he now cursed. It had threatened the security of his way of life and forced him to examine some ugly truths in a far more intimate way.

And now it would bring him face to face with Setenrah.

In her desperation, Lakna had made it clear that whosoever found the northerners was to come straight to her, no matter the timing. Setenrah must not be denied, even if it meant violating the policy of keeping his presence discreet. Subsequently, as soon as Kemp had found Devonshire, who'd been scraping some fungus from a damp cavern wall in a rather obscure passage, he'd cooked up the false story of getting him an audience with Lakna, and they'd set off at once. Wrapped up in his own concerns, Devonshire did not seem to notice the extra watchmen moving hastily through the Warren. Kemp knew that finding the others would fall on them; he needed to bring his catch to Lakna immediately. Mostly he hoped that the watchmen would succeed, but a very small part of him felt differently. It was yet another unfamiliar sensation.

Kemp and his unwitting prisoner emerged from the Warren and into the blinding brightness of the Great Ziggurat. It was deserted. Devonshire continued to babble a few steps behind him, seemingly oblivious to the fact that they were nearly jogging now. Kemp wanted to get him to Lakna and return to the hunt as quickly as possible. For some unaccountable reason, he hoped to avoid encountering Setenrah. The god may be their protector, but his presence felt ominous. Perhaps it was because Kemp knew that he was originally meant to be in Devonshire's place. He did not want to be put back there.

They reached the Eastern Promenade, where the heat struck them like an invisible, oppressive hand. Trotting down one of the walkways, Kemp could see Lakna, Roanack, and the Lady of the Veil waiting on the causeway below, looking toward the vast opening in the eastern wall.

"Wait here for a moment, please," Kemp said to Devonshire as they arrived at a small bridge that crossed one of the resplendent pools running alongside the causeway. Devonshire did as he was asked, and Kemp crossed the bridge and approached Lakna, Roanack, and the Lady alone. Lakna regarded him with a mixture of relief and irritation, seeing Devonshire, but only Devonshire, waiting behind him.

"Where are the others?" she asked, and Kemp watched a single bead of sweat break free from her desiccated forehead. It pooled in between the deep creases there and was quickly erased by the pounding heat.

"I don't know," he admitted. "As soon as I found Devonshire I came straight here. Everyone else is still searching, I'll go join them."

"Mother," Roanack said, and he looked miserable in his formal armor. His waxy face was drenched in sweat.

Lakna let out a long, angry sigh. "Well, one is better than nothing, I suppose. There might still—"

"*Mother*," Roanack said again. "He's here."

Lakna followed Roanack's gaze then quickly turned to Kemp. "Get him over here," she nearly whispered. "Do not say anything unless you are addressed. Do not mention the other two; he will only be expecting one anyway. We'll deal with them after."

Kemp was nodding, but his eyes were locked on the thin, black shape that had suddenly come into view at the end of the causeway where the stone gave way to sand and the pools ended.

"*Go*," Lakna hissed.

Kemp shuddered back into motion and returned to Devonshire. He found it difficult to reestablish his normal demeanor, and Devonshire noticed.

"What's wrong?" he asked. "Bad news?"

Devonshire was so ignorant of what was happening that his pedestrian concern was almost confusing. Kemp blinked and licked his lips. "No, not at all. C'mon, she's ready for you. There's someone she wants you to meet."

A look of puzzlement settled onto Devonshire's face, but he followed all the same. As they gathered with the others on the causeway, Setenrah arrived.

The god passed through the tremendous threshold and into the Ziggurat, moving with a strange, gliding swiftness. As he grew closer, his unnatural height became more apparent. Beholding him, Kemp felt his knees weaken. He had not expected their holy benefactor to be so abhorrent. He was skeletal, his entire mass seeming to float within the folds of the black robe that enveloped him. The robe itself looked to be made of no material Kemp had ever seen. It was slick and oily, sweating tar-like drops that fell sizzling to the hot stones of the floor below. The robe didn't seem to drag along the floor so much as it squirmed in a quivering wave, bearing him along. From the waist up his form emerged from the robe: a bony chest, a long neck, and a narrow, hairless head. His damp skin, apparently impervious to the relentless burning of the Unblinking Eye, was the color of raw milk.

The true proof of Setenrah's otherworldliness hovered above his head; an undulating halo that was actually a noxious cloud of insects. These pernicious beings were rare, seen only in the Warren and only occasionally. It was believed that the wave of healing energy emitted by the Lady also helped them to survive. Seeing an entire swarm of them; bloated flies, wriggling maggots, coiling centipedes, all writhing about each other, intertwined in a fetid mass of movement, was nearly too much. Kemp felt his mouth go dry, save for a rising trickle of bile at the back of his throat. Zeorshut Riengel must have been a monster beyond comparison if this creature was their divine shield.

The scuttling bulk of Setenrah's lower half came to rest before them, and he appraised them with beady eyes, glimmering from deep within wrinkled sockets. It looked to Kemp like he'd begun to decompose, that his shriveled eyes had rolled back into his skull. Horribly, his thin blue lips curled into a smirk as his gaze fell on Devonshire. Kemp could not tear his eyes away from the god long enough to see what Devonshire's reaction to this might be, but he could imagine.

"Mighty and Benevolent Setenrah!" Lakna declared, and Roanack helped to lower her into a kneeling position. He struggled to follow after her, and Kemp suddenly remembered that he was an active participant in this spectacle. He dropped quickly enough to bang his knees painfully against the floor. Beside him, Devonshire did the same, emitting a small, panicked gasp. Slowly, the Lady of the Veil joined them.

"Subduer of the Mighty!" Lakna continued from her position of subservience. "Pitlord Who Delivers Us from the Unworthy Dead! Begetter of All! Inhabiter of the Throne of the Infinite! Oh, Lofty Master, Highest Being of Eternity, we adore you!"

The last of her declaration echoed around them and out into the desert sands. Silence followed, and Kemp stared at his hands planted on the floor, swept up by a feeling of unreality.

"You honor me, as always," Setenrah said, his voice sending a chill down Kemp's sweat-caked back. It seemed to him to be the voice of time itself; a husky whisper that somehow filled the space. "You may rise."

Reluctantly, Kemp stood. Beside him, Roanack struggled to his feet and assisted his geriatric mother to hers. The Lady had already risen and did not offer to help them. Kemp looked at Devonshire. He was standing, but barely. He swayed on his feet as if he was about to swoon. Kemp placed a bracing hand on the man's back.

Setenrah leaned down toward Lakna, his thin frame bending nearly in half. From beneath his oily cloak, a gaunt arm extended. With hideously elongated fingers he took Lakna by the chin, tilting her face up toward his. "I can still see the young woman you were when you replaced your father as my seneschal. You have been one of my favorite servants; unfailingly loyal. And now I see that you have once again fulfilled your end of our ancient bargain." He turned his long head toward Devonshire.

"Of course, Great One," Lakna said. It must have been strange, Kemp thought, for one so accustomed to wielding power to be in the place of the supplicant. He could relate.

"And who is this?" Setenrah said, releasing Lakna's chin and gesturing his spindly hand toward Kemp. "He bears the garments of your regime; surely he is not meant for me?"

Knowing that, at one point, he *had* been intended for Setenrah filled Kemp with a terrible sense of frailty. The life that he'd forged for himself was based entirely on Lakna's decision to use him, and beyond that, on Setenrah's whim.

"Oh, no, this is my most valued huntsman, Lord Henrick Kemp. He brought this one here for us," Lakna said, pointing to Devonshire, "and I implored that he stay, so that he might bask in your glory."

This explanation must have satisfied Setenrah, for he smiled and leaned in close to Kemp. His impossibly large face was now close enough that Kemp could see the network of blue veins running beneath his skin. The god's breath was charnel.

"It is a rarefied honor, indeed. Lakna must have grand intentions for you. Perhaps an heir?" He turned back to Lakna. "Anything less would be violating the normal terms of our arrangement."

"Yes, Great One. Lord Henrick is of unimpeachable character. His future here will be one of great importance."

Setenrah nodded. If Lakna's eloquently worded and entirely vague answer displeased him, he did not say so. He instead swiveled toward the Lady of the Veil. "Hello, Reie."

Kemp had never heard the Lady referred to as such. She remained completely still, making no indication that the name meant anything to her.

Setenrah smiled broadly, and his teeth looked like the broken gravestones of Kemp's homeland.

"I do miss the sound of your voice; I hope to hear it again soon. These one-sided conversations can be so very tiresome. You and I are all that's left. We need each other; these ephemeral bags of flesh, speeding toward death from the moment they spill from the womb, they cannot grasp even a shadow of what we know. Talk to me."

The Lady of the Veil said nothing.

"You will not defy me forever. Nothing is beyond my grasp. I could make you speak. I could make you *scream*," Setenrah said. He leaned in so that his corpse-lips were brushing against her veil. "Just like I made *her* scream."

Before she could respond in any way, Setenrah reared up and away from her. "Well, I suppose I could just have a chat with Zeorshut Riengel instead, but I suspect he'd have just as little to say." He looked at Lakna and chuckled, a sound like the rattling of old bones. Lakna smiled tightly. Suddenly, Setenrah descended upon Devonshire, who quailed beneath his gaze. "Now let me take a look at you."

"He has been held to your specifications," Lakna said.

Setenrah breathed deeply. "Yes, I can see that. You've done well. I can feel his haleness, marred now by confusion and newfound terror. It has bloomed explosively, shattering the tranquility that he felt before." He paused, examining Devonshire, who was bewildered to the point of stupefaction. "This scar is interesting ..."

"He came to us like that. The Lady did all she could to repair it," Lakna said.

"I see," Setenrah murmured, and Kemp began to fear that he might be taken as a replacement for the damaged goods that the god refused. Setenrah reached out and pressed a finger to Devonshire's forehead. "We'll just need to cover that nasty blemish up."

"Please—"

Before Devonshire could finish, his face erupted with pox; swollen, pus-filled blisters that spread out rapidly from the point where Setenrah had touched him. Reflexively, Kemp leapt backward, desperate to pull himself away from the flourishing contagion. The swollen boils distorted Devonshire's face into a ruddy mess of blood and milky fluid while new pox burst forth on his arms. He gasped for breath, his bloodshot eyes dancing madly as his overwrought brain struggled to understand what was happening to him. His entire body began to jitter and a dark stain spread across his pants. A moment later his knees buckled, and he collapsed into a twitching heap. His swollen, split lips flapped with each ragged breath he sucked in. He was in agony, his body hijacked by marauding disease, but he was alive. And that was somehow worse.

Kemp stared at the ruined form of Devonshire. The absolute certainty that he would suffer the same fate if Setenrah so much as noticed him was the only bulwark against his rising vomit. He felt something in his mind unbuckling; a hidden chamber containing every suppressed doubt he'd ever harbored about Lakna and Quaretem suddenly venting. The wayward vagabonds he'd collected from the wastes had been given to this monster. He had delivered them into untold misery. But of course, he'd always known that they were going to die. The greater good had demanded it. Really, Zeorshut Riengel was to blame for their circumstances; he was the reason they were forced to pay this hideous cost. This thought did not make Kemp feel blameless, but it did soften the edges of his guilt. They sharpened again as a new question formed in his mind.

Setenrah made a soft humming sound of contentment and stretched back up to his full height. "Exquisite. I hope the Pit is no less satisfying." He passed brusquely by them, carried again by his bizarre living robe. Kemp knew where he was headed; to the dungeons and the Deceiver's Door. The watchmen would have cleared the Pit of any possible onlookers by now. Setenrah would soon be raising the shades from their subterranean prison and through the hatch, so that he might take them away with him. It was an act that had seemed miraculous and benevolent before. Now, it just made him wonder who exactly the door had been named after.

As soon as he was completely certain that Setenrah was gone, he turned to Lakna. She seemed to be expecting some sort of comment, and her eyebrows were raised in anticipation.

"This—he is—that's our—"

"Yes," Lakna said, cutting through his stammering. "That is Setenrah, to who we owe everything. Unpleasant, I know. You were never meant to see him, but now that you have, I expect you will use your best discretion in keeping what's occurred here private."

Kemp looked down at Devonshire, who was mewling weakly. "I didn't know …"

Lakna snorted. "You knew enough, my friend. I wouldn't think that a peek behind the curtain would rattle you."

"Of course not," Kemp lied, struggling to achieve something akin to his normal demeanor. He glanced at the Lady of the Veil, who still hadn't moved. Suddenly, his atrophied conscience exhumed itself from the crypt of willful ignorance he'd built around it. The importance of preserving appearances with Lakna dimmed before the need to know the truth. "What did Setenrah mean when he said that Zeorshut Riengel would have little to say? Why would he even be speaking to him? And why did he laugh about it?"

"Lord Henrick, you are an intelligent man."

"Mother," Roanack said.

"You have earned yourself a position here that would be the envy of any person, and I think that you're more than entitled to an explanation."

"Mother, what are you doing?"

"*Silence*," Lakna ordered. She smiled kindly at Kemp. "I do not wish for you to leave this momentous occasion with any worries, with any doubts or questions. Things in our commune operate in the way they do because of the systems that we have, systems that have been in place since yesterday and yesterday. You have seen Setenrah; you have observed his horrid truth. I did not intend for it to happen, but now that it has, I am grateful. It offers an opportunity for us, one that I should have pursued in the first place. I wish for you to remain as unflinchingly faithful as you've always been. Since our first meeting, I have held a special affinity for you, the haunted man who would become my ward. I would have never imagined that an outsider could do what you've done, but here you are: a Quaret as much as anyone here. Now, I wish for you to join *us*, to become one of the Sanctified. We can work out the particulars later, a marriage with one of my granddaughters will have to be arranged, certainly, but now is not the time for details. Now is the time to clear the air of any last mystery. No more secrets, Lord Henrick. Do you understand?"

"Yes," Kemp said, though he wasn't entirely certain that he did.

Lakna cleared her throat with a phlegmy rattle. "Zeorshut Riengel died long ago."

Roanack made a small noise of dismay, but Lakna ignored him. "He is no threat to our people. He is a tool to keep an unruly, uncivilized, and unpredictable population in line, so that the peaceful continuity of life in

Quaretem might continue forever. So that the bloodline of the Sanctified, *my* bloodline, might survive forever. By Setenrah's mercy we live; all that he requires is the occasional tax. That is why you are so important. Without the work you do, we are forced to lose our own to the tax. If we lose too many of our own, we risk losing the faith of the people, and then we risk losing everything that has been granted to us. So, we collect the outsiders, we distract the people, and we root out any potential troublemakers. And that now includes those who might bring word of our prosperity back to their kingdom in the north, those who would bring the *real* Vingallean oppressors back. There, now you know everything." She smiled again, and it was the gentle expression of a doting parent. "I spared you from that," she said, pointing at Devonshire, "because I knew you were different. And now I'm certain that you'll understand."

Kemp's face betrayed nothing because there was nothing to betray. His thoughts were a static haze born of overwhelming revelation. The framework of his being, what he believed himself to be, had been toppled to its foundations and quickly rebuilt, the same pieces hammered into an ugly new shape. This information, this accident of happenstance, had opened strange new doors for him. Behind those previously unimagined doors there apparently waited the pleasures of a charmed life. There also lurked things that squirmed. Things that had teeth.

Not since Henrick Kemp had fled the implosion of his old life had he been faced with such an absolute alteration of his world. It had nearly destroyed him then. Now it offered him a chance to choose a life more befitting of his lineage, a life that the random cruelty of the world had previously denied him. The perception of himself that had been left behind with the cries of the dying might be reclaimed.

"I do," Kemp said slowly. "I do understand. And thank you, Your Grace, for everything."

Lakna nodded, smiling still, and her eyes were wet. "Welcome to the family."

It didn't take long for Setenrah to return. When he did, it was with a train of new followers. Entombed within tendrils of coiling blackness, offshoots of Setenrah's robe-flesh, seventeen shades dragged along behind him. They thrashed in vain, gnashing their wet mouths, wailing with equal parts fury and anguish. It was a sight that Kemp could not have conjured in his strangest nightmares. Without a word, Setenrah glided past them toward the exit, extending another tendril to scoop up Devonshire, who managed only a short, terrified hoot. His eyes locked with Kemp's, and Kemp looked away. It was the last he would ever see of Devonshire.

Once Setenrah had faded into a small, black form wavering in the superheated air, Lakna let out an audible sigh of relief. She turned to Kemp and placed a gnarled hand on his arm.

"We have narrowly avoided disaster. Now, Lord Henrick, if you would be so kind, please find the other two. The time for subterfuge has passed, and the tidy outcome I had sought is not to be. We will settle with them now, and Setenrah can have their shades."

Kemp nodded. "I know what I must do."

CHAPTER 25

Their flight from the Warren had led back to Reie's chamber, and while it provided a temporary reprieve from the watchmen, it appeared to be a dead end. Marbuck was also surprised to find that Reie, the mastermind behind their escape, was absent. As Katiek strode toward a cabinet standing at the back of the room, Marbuck questioned this.

"The Lady is required to receive Setenrah," Katiek explained. "It would be particularly suspicious if she were not present for his arrival. We'll have the advantage of their confusion, and, eventually, their wrath, only beginning once they realize that they can't find you. If the Lady failed to join Lakna now, the hammer of the watchmen would fall much sooner." Katiek scooted the cabinet aside, revealing an extremely narrow crevice in the wall behind it. "I can lead you no further. Preparations must be made for the coming revolt, and the siege that is sure to follow. This path will lead you to the lower chambers of the ziggurat, where the pumps are located. The chambers are partially flooded, and few aside from those working the pumps should be present. That's not to say that there won't be any watchmen, so remain vigilant. Follow the backflow chute; it will lead to the exit, and to the shadowed cliffs at the seashore. Wait at the Sentinel. It's a stone monument depicting a giant head; I'm certain you will see it. The Lady and Jalam will follow shortly after, when Setenrah has gone. With any luck, Jalam has already found your companion and they'll both join you even before the Lady arrives."

Marbuck and Falstaff listened to these instructions intently, apt pupils memorizing the most important lecture they might ever hear. When it was clear that Katiek would not need to address any follow up questions, she ushered them through the crevice and pulled the cabinet back into place, leaving them in total darkness.

"Farewell for now," she said from the other side. "We will see each other once more, at the time of final deliverance."

Marbuck disagreed, certain that she'd never see Katiek again. For what it was worth, she was at least grateful for the help the arch-maiden had provided. "Yes," she said. "And thank you."

"Go," Katiek replied.

The pathway that followed was almost impassably tight. Forced to shimmy through the space, her body constantly scraping against the rough cavern walls, Marbuck found herself longing for the open halls of the Warren. As she scooted along, random juttings of rock collided with her elbows, knees, and even her head, sending a white flash through the current blindness of her vision. Having to crouch awkwardly at several places, her already tired joints felt like they'd been lubricated with splintered glass.

Eventually, the pathway tightened to the point that they were forced to wriggle through on their bellies. In the oppressive darkness, it was suffocating. To Marbuck, it felt as if the full expanse of the Void itself coiled around her, pressing ever tighter until her body should burst apart and flatten. Based on Falstaff's ragged breaths behind her, he was faring little better. She began to fear that, being larger than her, he would end up wedged into a space from which he could not free himself. Thankfully, such a moment never came. The space grew large enough that they could crawl again, and a faint glow accompanied by the sound of running water heralded the end of the path.

They arrived before a square of stone, outlined by a golden light that shone in from the space beyond their hole. At the bottom of the stone, Marbuck could just make out a pair of rusted hinges.

"It looks like a door," she whispered to Falstaff.

"Well, open it," he whispered back with more than a hint of panicked urgency.

She worked her fingers into the slim gap that allowed in the light and found that the stone itself was rather thin. She pulled it back slowly on its spring hinges, and the corroded metal squeaked as the door folded back into the tunnel. Scooting onto the flattened door, she peered out into the chamber beyond. It was darker than she'd expected. The dim light filtering in through some faraway window and reflected across numerous mirrors had only seemed bright in comparison to the absolute darkness behind them. A combination of copper pipes, green with age, and stone troughs ran alongside a narrow, tiled pathway. The sound of burbling water filled the space. Most importantly, it appeared to be deserted.

Without any further hesitation, Marbuck shimmied out of the opening, ungracefully twisting herself around to land on her feet as best as she could. She then helped Falstaff out, and as his weight left the stone door, the springed hinges lifted it back up. Once shut, it was indistinguishable from the stone masonry around it. How, exactly, Reie had gone about developing this route was unclear, but what was clear, was that she had been harboring some hope of escape for a long time. How many lifetimes had passed since Reie had overseen this pathway's creation, all while she awaited some final component to engineer the overthrow of Setenrah? Marbuck could only guess. She didn't really care about the ultimate success of Reie's designs, but she was thankful that they had so neatly aligned with her own. At least insofar as they'd provided her with an escape route.

"Is that the backflow chute?" Falstaff asked, looking at the largest of the stone troughs. It was half-filled with clear water, which ran steadily to the left, following the slight, downward angle of the trough.

"I don't know," Marbuck said, examining the system around the trough. It was impossible to know if the water was coming or going. "Only one way to find out."

They crept along the walkway, and Marbuck was grateful for the muffling sounds of the water around them. It allowed them to slip, unseen, past a chamber occupied by roughly two dozen natives. They were working zealously, turning levered wheels and operating groaning metalworks. The resemblance to the miserable capstans of the *Empress's Love* was undeniable. The chief difference, and the saddest one, was that she'd known she was a slave. Here, the natives actually considered such labor to be an honor. They'd been fooled into believing that they were free, the receivers of a privileged position, and all just so that their master could enjoy a tinkling fountain.

They left the natives behind, and, as they went, the piping became more complicated. It was now a convoluted mess of bending and connecting lengths of metal speckled with briny deposits seeping from weakened seams. The walkway turned into a series of stone steps descending downward, leading them into a vast, flooded chamber. There, the steps continued down beneath the surface of the water and disappeared into the shadowed depths below. Shimmering reflections of the water's surface danced across a number of stone columns that stretched away into the darkness far above them. To their right, the trough fed into a large, corroded pipe, which dropped steeply into the flooded chamber before continuing horizontally toward the far end of the space, visible not far below the water's surface.

"Well, what now?" Marbuck asked.

"We swim," Falstaff said.

"To where? We don't even know if this is the right way, or what's out there to swim to. I know this much though: Katiek needs to reassess her definition of 'partially flooded'. It looks like this whole *place* is flooded. I don't want to paddle out there and end up with nowhere to go."

"We'll just swim back here if there's no other way."

"Look at this maze. We'd be just as likely to end up—"

"*Shh.*" Falstaff pressed a finger to his lips and pulled Marbuck down into a crouch. "Voices," he whispered.

Over the thrum of the pipes, Marbuck could just make out the sound of multiple people speaking. It sounded as if they were coming closer. Her eyes scanned the murk around them, seeking for somewhere to hide. They fell on the mouth of the pipe into which the trough ran. She tugged Falstaff's sleeve and pointed toward it. His face twisted into something between skepticism and fear, but she ignored it and mounted the few steps back up to the end of the trough. Falstaff followed, as she knew he would.

The voices were growing clearer as Marbuck swung over the lip of the trough. She attempted to lower herself in slowly and immediately slipped, plunging clumsily into the lukewarm water. She'd been expecting to creep into the shadowed mouth of the pipe, where she could lurk until the threat passed; now she found the current much stronger than she'd anticipated and the interior of the trough too slick to gain any traction. She managed to push her head back up above the surface just in time to watch the black mouth of the pipe consume her. Before she could do anything more than gulp a single breath, she was falling.

For a moment, she was weightless; just one part of a plummeting sheet of water surrounded by darkness. Then, the bottom of the pipe rose up to meet her. Carried as she was within the flow of the water, her landing was cushioned, but not so much that she didn't still bash her tailbone against the metal bottom of the pipe. Sputtering, she managed to right herself, but she was still unable to stop. Her fingers slid uselessly against the slick interior of the pipe, and her feet were too busy keeping her upright to do anything else. Sluggishly, her mind accepted her current situation. There was no going back now; she just had to hope that the next drop-off wouldn't kill her, or that she wouldn't end up in a section of the pipe that was filled to the top. As it was, chilly water struck her face at regular intervals. The seams in the submerged pipe were leaking. If even one of them burst, she'd certainly drown.

On she went, the current quickening as the pipe took on a more downward trajectory. The leaking from the seams stopped, which Marbuck considered an encouraging sign. Soon, several feeder pipes joined with her route, adding to the noisome torrent. It became increasingly difficult to keep her head above water, and she pumped her arms and legs vigorously to stay abreast of the breaking flows of the additional streams. Just as the water seemed to be reaching a terminal velocity, a crescent of light appeared ahead of her. It grew exponentially until Marbuck was suddenly bursting forth from the end of the pipe, wheeling head over feet in a roaring tumult of water. Kicking her legs, she breached the surface, coughing and spitting. She mopped the water from her face and looked around.

The pipe had disgorged her into a large pool, into which several similar pipes were spilling their contents. Sunlight shone brilliantly from the opposite end of the large, open space. The water of the pool was gently, but steadily pulling in that direction. It appeared that, although she'd bumbled her way there, she'd still managed to reach the exit. Unfortunately, she'd arrived there alone.

No sooner had this thought occurred to her than Falstaff tumbled from the end of the pipe. She swam toward him, fighting the implacable current, and reached him just as he popped up from beneath the surface. He blinked away the water and, seeing her, grinned.

"You're daft, Fishwife."

"That wasn't my intention, believe me." Marbuck paused to take a deep breath. "It seemed to work, though. See for yourself."

Falstaff examined their surroundings for a moment as they treaded water, drifting toward the light. "Let's get up there," he said, gesturing toward a concrete lip at the edge of the pool.

They swam to the edge, Marbuck nearly floundering by the time they reached it. Falstaff hauled himself up first, and then extended a hand to Marbuck. He hauled her up, and she flopped over the edge, sodden and dripping. Panting, they both leaned against the short wall they'd just climbed over. They were now on a pathway that ran alongside the pool. From this new position, Marbuck could see that the far end of the pool spilled over a broader concrete slope and ran toward a long, low opening, spanned by a metal grate. It appeared to be the last obstacle between them and the world outside of the Great Ziggurat. Ahead of them, the pathway dropped off in a series of tall steps that would hopefully lead them right to the exit. Eager to reach it, Marbuck hauled herself to her feet. She froze as she realized that they were not alone.

A native woman had stepped out of an alcove across from them. Sweaty and begrimed, she'd obviously been toiling at the pumps. She stared at them with naked fear and surprise.

"You're not supposed to be down here," she managed.

Soaking wet, exhausted, and seized by anxiety now that her escape was dangling before her, Marbuck could not summon even a whiff of guile. A fell blankness descended over her, and she started toward the native, unsure of what exactly she intended to do, but certain that the nervous woman would not be given the chance to tell anyone what she'd seen. Nothing would thwart her escape now, not after everything she'd endured.

"We were asked to help out down here," Falstaff offered. This explanation, coming from a foreigner who the native must have known had been earmarked for Setenrah, and who'd just climbed out of the drainage pool, was not convincing. She took a step backward, her eyes flicking between the woman approaching her and the larger man telling her lies.

All of Marbuck's rage, which had accumulated on her soul in the same way that the ugly halo of scar tissue had formed on her flesh, narrowed into a deadly focus. In the dull, timid face of the woman before her she saw the idiot whims of fate that had put her there. She saw Baylis's ruined carcass, Winslow's glib assurances of success; she felt the sting of Mordwand's lash, and the searing bite of Bolenz's knife; she heard the lies of Kemp and Lakna, spouted again and again. It seemed that all of existence had risen against her, stacking every sort of cruel opposition imaginable in her way. And now, at this final moment, it had mustered a weak-minded slave who would undoubtedly tell her masters about the escaped sacrifices she'd seen. Reie seemed to trust these people, believing that, in the end, they would be loyal and true. Marbuck did not share this sentiment; she believed their self-preserving servility to be too firmly ingrained.

"*Raina, stop.*" Falstaff had her by the arm, and he whirled her around to face him. "Whatever you're thinking of doing, stop." His voice was low and severe. It did not allow room for debate. "This woman's no threat. Let's go."

Marbuck was prepared to berate him for his naivety, but the words died on her lips. A girl no older than Elibeth had emerged from the alcove behind the woman and clung onto her arm. Marbuck looked at the two of them, and in an instant her blind rage flooded away, leaving behind a barren plain of longing and despair. In seeking to return to her daughter, she'd nearly made an orphan of another. She knew that she'd be returning to Elibeth scarred, physically and mentally, but she could not go that far, she could not succeed by subjecting others to the fate she was fighting so hard to avoid.

"Go," she said, overcome with an intense feeling of shame. "Leave us. Forget what you've seen."

The woman nodded shakily, took her daughter by the hand, and disappeared back into the alcove. Marbuck started toward the steps, unable to look at Falstaff. Long-cycles of friendship had taught them enough about each other that no other words were necessary. Marbuck knew that she'd nearly crossed a line; Falstaff knew that she knew. To his credit, he did not address it further. He merely squeezed her shoulder once as he plodded along beside her.

The two of them climbed down the steps and reached the grate, through which they could see their goal nestled between opposing walls of red rock that rose steeply on either side of the narrow vale before them. At the bottom of a craggy slope, down which the water flowed in a roughly cut channel, was a towering stone edifice. The base of the structure spanned the water, creating a bridge across it and a final spout from which the water cascaded noisily, striking the sparkling mirror of the sea and sending wide bands of ripples gliding across the otherwise placid surface. The view was spectacular, marred only by what Marbuck assumed was the pipe that fed all of Lakna's fountains. Coated in brine and encrusted with the shells of long-dead barnacles, the cyclopean pipeline stretched from the sea to some upper intake built into the bowels of the ziggurat. To Marbuck, the metallic behemoth looked like a bloated, decaying worm.

"That must be the Sentinel," Falstaff said, pointing to the stone edifice. "Katiek said we couldn't miss it."

Marbuck nodded in agreement, still feeling too rattled to speak.

It did not take them long to find a sizable gap in the ancient, rusted grate. They squeezed through and began to pick their way down the slope. The sunlight pressed down upon them like a tremendous fist. At first, it was welcome, drying them within a short-cycle. Very quickly, though, it became unbearable. Thankfully, as they continued down, they slipped into the shadow cast by the eastern cliff face, the jagged pinnacle of which blocked the otherwise unfettered power of the sun. The temperature dropped to a tolerable level, and, now that Marbuck was no longer subjected to the sun's blinding glare, she looked back at the Great Ziggurat.

Gazing out from within the ziggurat, she'd known that it was massive. Now, beholding its scale from below, the stepped pyramid seemed less like a man-made structure and more like a natural formation, something the Father-God might have lifted up from the bedrock at the very founding of creation. It dwarfed the cliffs, which were really just the ragged ends of a plateau on which the ziggurat had been built. Lofty as they were, the cliffs only rose to the height of what must have been the ziggurat's base on the other three sides.

Not only was this desert colossus the largest structure she'd ever seen, it was also a sight of incredible beauty. Though scarred by the wars of the distant past and the steady depredations of time, its majesty remained undimmed. Each step boasted what looked like intricate carvings, but had to be bas-reliefs of gargantuan proportions. They depicted all manner of exotic creatures roaming a primordial jungle, frozen in stone. Haloed figures representing the gods were present, as well as other forms that Marbuck imagined were the renowned figures of Quaretem's history. They lined every level, eternally acting out momentous events long forgotten.

Though much smaller in comparison, the Sentinel was no less impressive. Reaching the base of it and rounding the structure, Marbuck marveled at the sheer size and detail of the face depicted. It was a square-jawed man, noble and handsome, with a sharp nose, full lips and a circlet upon his head. With a steadfast gaze, his stone eyes gazed out over the sea.

Marbuck and Falstaff passed beneath his watchful stare as they crossed the bridge and descended a few short steps to a small spit of beach at the base of the structure. The Sentinel now stood between them and the ziggurat, and Marbuck felt a fleeting sense of protection. They hunkered down in a sandy pit beneath the Sentinel's chin with nothing left to do but wait. The pleasant sound of the water spilling from the last drop-off beneath the bridge filled the air, and a fine mist rising from the waterfall cooled them further. After a short time, Falstaff looked ready to nod off.

As for Marbuck, the peaceful waiting increasingly felt like a precursor to disaster. The guilt she'd felt for her actions with the natives was slowly morphing into a certainty that she shouldn't have let them go. She should have opted for something in between murder and carelessly releasing them, but her thoughts had been too muddled by the whole affair to come up with anything but absolutes.

She rested her head against the cool stone behind her. With fear slowly eclipsing her hope, she followed the Sentinel's gaze out to sea.

• • •

Despite Marbuck's trepidation, the steady sound of the falling water, the warm air, and her own exhaustion conspired to lull her to sleep. She battled the temptation; Falstaff, on the other hand, had given up the fight. He had slumped over some time ago, and was now snoring gently. Marbuck had decided not to disturb him, so, with heavy lids, she kept watch. Periodically, she peered around the base of the Sentinel, certain that she would see watchmen approaching. Though it had been the plan all along, it still surprised her when one of these quick checks revealed Reie and Jalam scrambling down the craggy slope. With a small pang, she noted that Devonshire was not with them.

"Wake up," she said, nudging Falstaff. "They're here."

He lifted his head slowly; it appeared to weigh more than the stone one behind them. "Who? Reie?" he asked blearily.

"Yes. Jalam too."

"Is Devonshire with them?" Falstaff sounded suddenly alert, and he began to pull himself to his feet.

"No."

Falstaff stopped, one knee still planted in the sand. His brow furrowed as he worked through this new information with great effort. "Okay," he finally said, nodding to himself.

Marbuck offered her hand and helped him up, just as Reie and Jalam were crossing the bridge. The fugitive god had eschewed her black robes, opting instead for a simple white tunic beneath a leather jerkin. More notably, she had discarded her veil, the uncanny halo above her head now floating freely. She looked calm, almost buoyant. Beside her, Jalam looked as sour as ever, and his hands hovered near the bronze saber hanging from his belt. Spotting Marbuck and Falstaff, they descended the last steps and joined them beneath the Sentinel.

"Katiek guided you well, I see," Reie said.

"Yes, my—um—your—uh," Falstaff stammered. He was staring at her, and Marbuck remembered that he'd never seen her without her covering.

Though Falstaff had been exposed to a god before, having seen the Empress and her halo, this was obviously quite different. The Empress had been a terrible sight; Reie's divinity, coupled with her oddly casual and humanlike demeanor, appeared to have robbed Falstaff of the ability to speak coherently.

The god smiled kindly. "You may call me Reie."

"Okay, yes. Reie," Falstaff repeated, his face reddening.

"Where's Devonshire?" Marbuck asked, seeing that Falstaff was too flustered to ask the question. She expected that she already knew the answer. It did not surprise her when Reie's smile evaporated.

"Kemp got to him first," Jalam said. "I am sorry."

"So, he's been taken by Setenrah?"

"Yes, I'm afraid so," Reie confirmed.

This seemed to return Falstaff to his senses. "Can we rescue him?"

"Setenrah has already left, taking your friend and a train of shades with him," Reie said. "Though I do not know where he's headed, I do know that it's north of here. And he goes *directly* north. To chase after him now, we would have to go back through the ziggurat and pursue him into the desert. It would tax even my power to prevent you three from succumbing to heat-death in the wastes. Setenrah may be able to shroud his prisoner within his own form, but I have no such ability to shade you from the sun. Furthermore, even if we were able to reach him, it would be foolish to risk a direct confrontation with him now; I am certain that we would fail. There is too much at stake to go after one man. Unfortunately, I fear that your friend's fate is sealed."

Marbuck certainly pitied Devonshire, but she would not mourn for him. The guardsman had changed sides several times in his effort to survive, and now he'd finally chosen wrong. In truth, she found having the possibility of a rescue attempt removed from the table to be something of a relief. Beside her, Falstaff cleared his throat and looked out over the sea. He accepted this flight of his final hope with a heavy sigh.

"It's a shame that we could not get to him sooner," Reie said. "But it was good fortune that Katiek reached the two of you when she did. It did not take long for Lakna to mobilize all of the forces at her command in search of you. Before Setenrah arrived, she was at least keeping up an appearance of calm control. Now that he's departed, the search has only grown more frenzied. When it becomes clear that I've left, it will turn violent."

"Katiek will handle it," Jalam said. "She knows the Warren; she'll hold them off."

"I have faith in her, but she can't keep the watchmen out forever," Reie said. "Nor can she and the others live off the power that I gave them forever. I wasn't able to do a full ritual; things unfolded too quickly. We will need to move with the utmost haste. First, we will go west until the light fades. Then, free of the sun's heat, we will go north. We'll have to pass directly through the World's Wound, for we cannot take the time to circumvent such a vast obstacle."

As daunting as that sounded, Marbuck was hung up on a more immediate issue. "How will we go west without going back through the ziggurat? We can't scale these cliffs, and I doubt that any of us—well, any of us humans—could swim for so long, even with your bolstering."

Reie's smile returned. "The Sentinel is an impressive feat of art and engineering. Much of what I once taught to the leaders of Quaretem, those who came before the seneschals of Setenrah, is still remembered. They know the history of Gana in their own distorted way, but they do not know the significance of the Sentinel. If they did, they might have felt compelled to topple it. After all, it was only reverence for a deeper past that stayed the hands of the first Quaret to escape bondage. It is very fortunate for us that it still stands."

For one in such a hurry, Reie seemed to be savoring the reveal of her plan. Marbuck imagined that, after multiple lifetimes of near-muteness, her sudden liberation had made her garrulous.

"It was carved to depict Phar-Daenavian, the Vingallean king who conquered Quaretem," Reie continued. "From his line came Phan-Ellara, and it was in emulation of her ancestor that her own lust for dominion grew. Her aspirations eventually brought her to the rebel brothers and set Vingallea on the path to ruin. But before that, she had this carving commissioned, in veneration of the ancestor who'd inspired her conquests.

"Like so many of Vingallea's works, though, it was simply their own mark placed on something that already existed. The Sentinel predated even Phar-Daenavian's arrival. It had been built by the same Quaret who'd engineered the Great Ziggurat, and it depicted their greatest chief, Mumazamba. Phan-Ellara had her artists simply carve away at the original face and alter it to her liking." Reie reached up and touched the bottom of the lower jaw that jutted out above them. "Their work was slipshod, at best. Their hasty renovations created a void within the structure, a gap between the old structure and the new additions. And this is where I've hidden the means of our escape. I had it constructed during the onset of Setenrah's ascendancy, fearing that our carefully balanced society might tip into mindless slaughter should Setenrah ever tire of our arrangement. With this, I would have a final recourse to take who I could and escape. Now, the time has finally come to use it, and thankfully, while it's not—"

Reie froze, and her eyes looked beyond her audience. Marbuck turned to follow her rigid gaze, and then silently cursed her protracted explanation.

A detachment of watchmen had reached the bridge.

There was nowhere to hide. Instinctively, the escapees closed ranks, and Jalam moved to the forefront, drawing his saber. Weaponless, Marbuck felt naked. She knew that, if it came to it, she would plunge into the sea and swim until her body gave out. Nothing could compel her to return to the confines of the ziggurat.

Having their prey cornered, the watchmen moved unhurriedly, filing across the bridge in neat order. Marbuck counted twelve of them. They were followed by Roanack, in full regalia, and, to her utmost disgust, Kemp. He was outfitted with what she had to assume were the implements of the hunt. Baldrics with numerous pouches crisscrossed the metal cuirass he now wore, a club and a hatchet dangled from his belt, and a canvas sack was slung across his back. Undoubtedly, he'd been prepared to pursue them for however long it would take. The pursuit had been woefully brief, and the duplicitous huntsman was clearly pleased with himself. An amiable smile was plastered on his face, and Marbuck wanted to wipe it off with the heel of her boot.

The watchmen filed onto the sand and parted for Roanack and Kemp. What Marbuck had first taken to be smug confidence in their movement was now revealed to be something else entirely. They clung nervously to their sabers, their eyes locked on Reie. It occurred to Marbuck that, like Falstaff, they'd never seen her without her covering and probably didn't even realize that the strange, haloed being before them was the Lady of the Veil. Roanack, too, looked nervous, but his apprehension was coupled with indignation.

"Why are you uncovered?" he asked without preamble, seemingly more upset by her appearance than her presence on the beach. Beside him, Kemp kept on smiling.

"I no longer answer to you," Reie said.

Roanack scoffed. "You are quite mistaken. I don't know what you think you will accomplish throwing in your lot with these upstarts, but if you're planning to abandon your responsibilities here then I'm very disappointed in you, as is my mother. You would condemn us all to death, and for what?"

"I care not for your approval, or your chiding tone. You and your mother are less than children in my eyes. Your lives are a momentary blip of time to me. You're nothing but the latest puppets to dance on Setenrah's strings. I act for the people of Quaretem."

The watchmen exchanged confused looks with one another. Roanack pursed his lips, certainly aware that Reie could spill secrets that might loosen the loyalty of his men. He cleared his throat. "You speak nonsense. Worse yet, you seem to have been taken in by the lies of these foreign agents. 'The people of Quaretem'? Why, it was one of these very people who reported encountering your new friends by the retention pool."

Marbuck's heart dropped at the same moment that her ire rose. She shot Falstaff a reproachful look and he shrugged sadly. His modest contrition was enough to diffuse her; despite the native's actions, Marbuck knew that she wouldn't change anything. If she'd actually killed that innocent, misguided woman, she'd never have been able to live with herself. The native hadn't been an enemy combatant faced in the heat of battle, or a vicious captor who needed to be toppled. Killing her would have been murder, ugly and unadorned. She could not return to Elibeth as a murderer.

"She said that they nearly attacked her, *and* her daughter," Roanack said, adopting a maudlin tone. "Thankfully, I was informed of this quickly enough to mount an offensive. I just never imagined that you would be with them."

"If this woman felt compelled to report to the watchmen, it was simply because she's too indoctrinated by lies to know any better," Reie said, and Marbuck sensed that she was the target of this explanation. "She cannot be faulted for this. She doesn't even understand that she's a slave."

At that word, the watchmen stiffened and a chorus of angry rebuttals rose.

"There are no slaves in Quaretem, not anymore!" Roanack shouted, and the rabble settled down at his words. "These *Vingalleans* would have us all fettered again, and you are helping them! But it is hopeless for you; you're hemmed in here, and should you be foolish enough to even attempt to scale these cliffs, contingents of watchmen are waiting above to intercept you. There is nowhere left to run. Now, come with me."

The four of them did not move, and Marbuck could hear Jalam breathing in sibilant bursts. His muscled form was entirely taut, and she knew that he was prepared to unleash violence in an instant. Across from them, the line of watchmen braced themselves, awaiting Roanack's command.

"Have it your way," Roanack said. "Seize—"

There was a sharp crack, and the chief warden's head snapped forward. For a moment he stood there, his head lolling on his thin neck, hanging over the gorget of his armor. A bright red bloom stood out amidst his thin hair. Then, all at once, he collapsed in a heap. Standing in the space he'd just occupied was Kemp, his bloodied club held aloft. Nobody moved as confusion reigned. In one fluid motion Kemp slid the canvas sack from his shoulder and lobbed it toward the escapees. It landed in the sand at Jalam's feet with a soft thud.

"Weapons!" Kemp shouted.

As if that had been their cue, the watchmen finally shuddered into motion. Those closest to Kemp turned on him, while the flanks seemed torn between seizing him, tending to their leader, and dealing with the escapees.

"Stop now or—" The panicked ultimatum of the watchman closest to Kemp was never finished. Kemp had taken his hatchet in his other hand, and he chopped the man's right knee apart in one swing, sending him cartwheeling to the ground with a piercing cry.

Now Marbuck was finally moving, and she yanked open the sack. To her astonishment, it contained the field glass, Mordwand's axe, and the anointed blade. She quickly pocketed the field glass, tossed the axe to Falstaff, and unsheathed the blade. It shone brilliantly in the daylight, and Marbuck felt something akin to delight. With the blade—*her* blade—back in her hands she could not be stopped. She vowed in that moment to never be weaponless again.

Kemp had retreated onto the narrow bridge, and with the club in one hand and the hatchet in the other, he held off the tightly clustered advance of several watchmen trying to mount the steps. Two men were trying to hoist Roanack to his feet while the remainder, seeing that their adversaries were now armed, faltered. Beside her, Jalam lunged forward, bellowing a war cry. Caught in the ecstatic frenzy of the unexpected advantage, Marbuck sprang after him. The first watchman Jalam encountered lifted his weapon to block the incoming strike and failed spectacularly. Jalam's saber came down in a tremendous blow, buckling the man's arm and snapping his sword in two. He fell to one knee and Jalam kicked him in the face, sending him sprawling.

Unmanned by the sudden viciousness of Jalam's attack, the remaining watchmen backed away, adopting a defensive position. Roanack was left slumped on the sand; the two watchmen who'd been with him joined their companions and formed a wall of six men. Beyond them, three more were still trying to reach Kemp. A fourth man was lying at the foot of the steps, his helmet cloven in two, a crimson bloom soaking into the sand around him.

Jalam wasted no time in continuing his assault. Apparently heedless of the danger, he charged into the six men, busting their ranks. As four of them heaped on top him, the last two circled the pile, seemingly unsure of what to do. Marbuck raced toward the back of one of them. From the corner of her eye, she could see Falstaff approaching the other.

The tip of her blade, driven before her, struck the man in the back. His armor buckled with the force of the attack, but did not break. Marbuck's blade glanced off the dented metal and the man staggered forward. She swung her sword at the watchman's neck for a killing blow, but he regained his footing and turned about in time to parry the attack. With a flick of his wrist, he locked his saber's hilt onto her blade and attempted to wrench it from her grasp. She held on, but was yanked in toward the man. They were now close enough that she could see the stubble on his ruddy cheeks, and she caught a whiff of his sour breath just as he slammed his helmeted head into her face.

The world went white and suddenly she was on the ground, her blade gone. Above her, through a stunned haze and the blood in her eyes, she saw the watchman closing in. Without thinking, she whipped a handful of sand into his face. He snarled and staggered back, and Marbuck scrambled to her feet, bumping into her blade in the process. She scooped it up as she ran backward, putting distance between her and her attacker. Mopping the blood from her eyes, she reassessed their small battlefield.

The air was filled with a hot, coppery stench, and the sand was caked with blood. Agonal moans rose from the shattered bodies scattered across the beach. Jalam was lost amidst a heap of twisted limbs. Falstaff had managed to catch the other watchman by surprise; he was curled up on the sand clutching his side. Falstaff hovered over him, clearly reluctant to finish what he'd started.

The watchman that Marbuck had been fighting with was also taking in his surroundings, squinting and blinking away the sand. He didn't notice that Kemp had stepped over the three additional bodies piled up at the foot of the steps and was now approaching him. He finally turned at the sound of Kemp's huffing breaths, but before he could raise his saber above his waist, Kemp cracked him in the jaw with his club. The man spun almost gracefully from the force of the blow before collapsing at Kemp's feet. The fight was finished.

As her capacity for rational thought returned, Marbuck found herself fixated on Kemp. The man who had brought her to this darkly farcical place, who'd rescued her only to serve her up to his god, had rescued her again, but for what reason? Across the carnage, he actually smiled at her. It was not his typical sly grin but was something almost sheepish, apologetic even.

Before she could fully consider the implications of Kemp's actions, Reie brushed by her, her arms outstretched toward the spot where Jalam had fallen. Marbuck could feel the thrumming force of the power that she was expelling, and the air wavered around her. The heap of bodies shuddered and Jalam emerged from within, glistening with blood and flecked with sand. He clambered free of the other bodies and staggered toward Reie. By the time he reached her, he was walking as if he'd suffered no injury at all.

Reie turned toward Marbuck, and a small burst of the same invigorating energy that she'd felt during the ritual washed over her. Instinctively, she touched her forehead and the bridge of her nose. Though they were still wet with blood, they were free of any wound.

"There," Reie said, pointing toward the man with the cloven helmet. "Watch him. I've kept the others alive, but the damage was too severe and too sudden for him."

Marbuck realized what was happening. Reie had used a sliver of her power to keep Roanack and the watchmen alive, though she wasn't certain whether it was a show of mercy or simply to avoid dealing with any shades. Either way, she'd managed to save them all, save for the one unlucky fellow whose body, thankfully, remained still.

Once it was clear that they were safe, Marbuck turned to Reie. "We should finish them off all at once and go before any shades are born. We can still hide our escape."

"I would not have taken you for an executioner," Reie said reproachfully. "These men may be misguided, or in Roanack's case, wicked, but they are still Quaret. I do not wish to see any Quaret die; I seek to free them all. I will do all I can to spare them from death, especially a violent one. I do not believe in violence."

"And yet it persists," Kemp interjected, still wearing a contrite smile. The others now turned their attention to him. "But I admire your virtue. The Lady of the Veil, I presume? Veil-less, now, of course."

Reie nodded. Beside her, Jalam seemed to be awaiting further instruction. Marbuck privately chafed at Reie's rebuke; it was easy to abstain from violence when your hulking guard could perpetrate it for you.

Kemp sighed. "I didn't wish to kill anyone. I struck that boy a little too hard, is all. As for the others, killing them would make no difference anyway. Roanack wasn't bluffing; this vale is surrounded. There are plenty of watchmen left up above to snatch you, and, either way, they'd figure out what happened here."

"What, exactly, *did* happen here?" Marbuck asked him.

"Well, my first thought was that you might have escaped from the ziggurat, and I'd been preparing to search for you when I heard that you'd been spotted. I tagged along with Roanack, much to his chagrin. I managed to pilfer your confiscated weapons before we set out thinking they'd make a nice peace offering. They came in handy rather quickly, I think."

Marbuck eyed him, trying to understand this matter-of-fact recounting of his betrayal. "Why did you do this? What is it that you want?"

In an instant, the last vestiges of Kemp's smile slid away. The face beneath the genial mask was haunted. "I came to Quaretem as a refugee. Through pluck and loyalty, I distinguished myself enough to secure a place here, but it was a place earned with blood. I knew what I was doing, to the extent that I knew outsiders would die so that the people who'd rescued me could live. As long as I clung onto that ideal, that I was working in service to the greater good, I could do anything that Lakna asked of me. Whatever it took to protect us all from Zeorshut Riengel. But then I met the supposed source of that protection, and I learned, by pure happenstance, that he protects us from nothing. It's all a lie." Kemp took a hitching breath and cleared his throat. "I led people to unimaginable torment based on a lie. Not to save anyone, but to please Setenrah's desires. And worse yet, to sustain Lakna's privilege. I don't know if she's actually managed to delude herself with all of her sanctimonious talk, but it makes no difference. She perpetuates a lie to protect herself. And I fed people to that monster for her. I'm finished with all of that. If you're all leaving, I wish to come with you."

He bowed his head in penitence, awaiting their judgment. It was difficult for Marbuck to reconcile her perception of Kemp with the pitiful man standing before her. "Why should we trust you?" she asked.

Kemp made a sound somewhere between a laugh and a sob. "What angle could I possibly be playing? I just killed a watchman and clubbed the seneschal's heir in the head. I don't think I'll be welcomed back here." He took a step toward Marbuck. "I've made a lot of terrible mistakes. I thought that, here, I might wash them away. I only buried them under new atrocities. That ends now. I will get you back to your daughter."

Marbuck did not know what to say. She'd nursed her hatred for Kemp until he'd turned into a totem of all those who'd deceived and abused her. His unexpected change of heart could not easily erase so much enmity. Thankfully, Reie answered for her.

"I know your story well, Henrick. You have fallen into the same pattern of deception that many before you have succumbed to. In my experience, it is rare that one can see the pattern, much less leave it behind. Whatever you've been, you are welcome to change. You may join us, though I must warn you that you have much to learn regarding our true purpose."

Marbuck did not object to Reie's decision, but she certainly didn't embrace it either. For the first time since her ordeal had started, Marbuck found that she was not the leader. She was happy to relinquish the position, so long as Reie's choices aligned with her own intentions. Once they deviated, Marbuck would happily abandon Reie and her dreams of freeing Ganachim. It would be difficult when the time came for that, but she would figure it out.

With solemn gratitude, Kemp thanked Reie. Falstaff, Marbuck was certain, would accept Kemp the same way he'd accepted Devonshire. Only Jalam seemed to share her displeasure; he'd been entirely unmoved by Kemp's confession, but, faithful as he was, he said nothing.

"I assume that you're intending to go north, back to your city beyond the crater. I can guide you as far as the World's Wound; nobody knows the lands between here and there better. And you needn't worry about any huntsmen following us. I know how they track, and I know how to throw them off," Kemp said, some of his normal bravado leaking back into his voice. "But there's still the issue of the patrols above us."

"Your guidance will be very welcome," Reie said, stepping back beneath the Sentinel's chin. "And we have nothing to fear from those patrols." She reached up and pressed a hand against one of the square blocks that made up the monument's bottom jaw. It gave slightly at her touch, then, like the hidden door in the ziggurat, it dropped open on rusted hinges. As it opened downward, a large bowl-like shape slid out of the space beyond and thudded into the sand. It appeared to be comprised of thin branches wound tightly around each other, overwrapped with dried animal skins. Remembering the skinners, Marbuck *hoped* that they were animal skins.

"You two are mariners, no?" Reie asked Marbuck and Falstaff, with a hint of amusement. "Do you not recognize a boat?"

• • •

The five of them launched the wobbly coracle, piling inside once they'd waded far enough into the water. Marbuck was surprised that they managed to stay upright, and outright shocked that the ancient skins stretched across the coracle's frame had remained watertight. Reie's escape craft, constructed untold long-cycles ago, had been well-preserved in the dark, dry void within the Sentinel.

Inside the coracle, two rudimentary paddles had been stowed. Like the frame, they were made from tree branches, something that Marbuck considered a testament to their great age. Based on what she'd seen, it didn't appear that there had been trees in Quaretem for a long time.

Jalam and Kemp, undoubtedly eager to ingratiate himself, took to the paddles. The coracle gained some momentum and began to pull away from the beach, leaving the moaning, semi-conscious Roanack and his watchmen behind. The Sentinel seemed to watch them go, only slipping from view once they'd paddled far enough to the west. On their right, the sea cliffs rose to a dizzying height. Beyond them, the sunbaked tip of the Great Ziggurat dominated the skyline.

The sunlight, doubled in intensity by its reflection on the placid water, was punishing, but Marbuck didn't care. Occasional bursts of Reie's ministrations kept her mostly comfortable, as did the intermittent stretches of shadow cast by overhangings of rock. She looked at Falstaff who was too enraptured by Reie to pay her any mind. Marbuck couldn't help but smile at her friend's obvious fawning. But the real source of her happiness was that, for the first time since the *Fortune* had been attacked and she'd been abducted, she was truly, completely free.

And she was going home to Elibeth.

PART 4:

THROUGH THE PAST

CHAPTER 26

Shadows stretched up the walls of his modest chamber, but Fritz Rayburn focused on the light. His fire crackled, the flames dancing merrily. Warmth came with the light, and Rayburn savored it, scooting his worn armchair as close to the hearth as he could. The darkness of the room behind his high-backed chair would begin to press in on him if he let it. The thrice-locked door provided some comfort against the anxieties that had taken root in his mind, but the light of the fire soothed him much more. That, and his pathological glances at the chamber's single window; a small square of clouded glass through which the meager light of the perpetual dawn filtered in. The need to remind himself that he was ensconced within the walls of Nordabor, surrounded by a lifetime's worth of old logbooks, ledgers, and charts was a constant itch. They were artifacts of a simpler time; the pedestrian life he'd led working as a merchant provisioner. Since his return, he'd been answering for the entire absent expedition, a task far beyond his depth, and one that was terribly reminiscent of the self-blame he'd felt after Rorik's disappearance. Still, he was grateful to be back in his home, even if the safety it provided was mostly an illusion now. After what he'd endured in the badlands beyond the city, he appreciated whatever fortified stability Nordabor had to offer.

Unfortunately, as if he'd trailed in the pervasive chaos of the wastes behind him, things in Nordabor had started to slip. It was more than just the slow failure of the natural world around them. The death spiral of their captive god had certainly been the opening act of their collapse, but it had been their misbegotten attempt to halt that death that had accelerated their fate. The power of the Crown, and the king's court, had started to buckle. The ripples had spread, and Rayburn could feel the approaching end as clearly as if it were exhaling softly on the back of his neck. Soon, it would be panting in heavy, slobbering breaths. Then it would be sinking its teeth into his throat.

They called it the Erosion.

It had started with an ominous hum that had risen to a petrifying roar. The air itself had moved then, tearing through the city, ripping down the numerous stalls and tents of the Mercantile Causeway and flattening the shabby, prosaic structures of the slums. Before the chaos had suddenly ceased, the Vinecrown Keep itself was said to have shuddered to its very foundations. In the end, it had managed to emerge from the phenomenon relatively intact, having lost only one of its four turrets. Likewise, the other structures of the old kingdom had survived mostly unscathed, a fact that the shepherds had been quick to attribute to the mercy of the Void-God.

That mercy had been in short supply. The shepherds had been kept very busy dispatching the numerous shades that had been born from those killed in the slums, crushed in the rubble of their own hovels. Nordabor had certainly teetered then, but the wonder of the sky above them had been enough to occupy the people. Whatever had moved the air had pried loose the impenetrable ceiling of clouds that had hovered over Nordabor ever since the sun had stopped its movement in the sky. The purple majesty of the dawn, with the glimmering sun hanging low on the eastern horizon, was visible for the first time in any of their lives.

More striking, however, was the presence of the tremendous line of light reaching across the sky in splintered angles and jagged offshoots. The firmament itself had taken on the appearance of a cracked window pane. This startling view had been read as an omen by Phar-Mindorius. The king had chosen to consider it a clear portent that the lost expedition, and his missing son, had ultimately succeeded. Rayburn, who'd helped to lead the first aborted rescue mission sent after Phir-Ramarian, harbored severe doubts. Those only grew as the newly exposed sky was blotted out by the reeking smoke of the burning fields, choked as they were with the numerous bodies of those killed during the phenomenon. Soon, only the flickering glow of the crack could be seen through the billowing death clouds.

A subsequent search party, which Rayburn had been blessedly spared from, had been sent to confirm Phir-Ramarian's victory. Instead, it had discovered the Erosion. The scouts reported that beyond the northern lands of Faedalia, nothing now remained. At the stunted horizon line, the crack dissolved into a shimmering distortion of saturated colors that dominated the sky, flashing in impossible configurations. The anomaly puckered downward until it ceased, giving way to a profound darkness. All around it, the land had simply fallen away into a blackness beyond comprehension. It was as if some invisible cosmic hand was tearing away their reality, blotting out existence and dragging it into an infinite nothing. The Erosion was slow, but it was undeniably spreading, the inexorable consumption slowly moving south.

It wasn't clear what had caused it, but its steady approach from the north, where the Gates of Paradise had been believed to be, seemed to imply that the expedition might have made it further than Rayburn had thought possible, and that whatever they had attempted there had gone catastrophically wrong. Many who were privy to the expedition's purpose, once-secret information that was now spreading like a disease, were of the same mind. The fact that the expedition had perished as a result was considered a given.

This had struck a terrible blow to the king's hopes, but it had not extinguished them completely, to the detriment of all. Rayburn now felt that each passing cycle only brought him closer to a gibbet.

He leaned forward, slurping some tepid broth from a can. It wasn't much, but it was something. Having been a provisioner, he still had access to a private store of tinned goods. It helped to alleviate the pains of the severe rationing that'd recently been imposed upon the populace. It was just one of the latest troubles that had befallen their plagued city. And all because the expedition had tinkered with something far beyond their understanding.

It still seemed impossible that any of them could have made it to the Gates of Paradise. To Rayburn, even the prospect of them escaping from the sadistic slavers of Vin-Sadavat had seemed preposterous. After all, he held no illusions about his own survival which had been nothing but a miraculous fluke.

He'd been fortunate enough to have a horse, just one of the three the expedition had taken along. It'd been Lord Fontaine's horse, and in a moment of generosity, he'd allowed Rayburn to ride it in his stead, an act that had saved Rayburn's life.

When the slavers had come, he'd awoken to the sounds of their rampage. By sheer luck, they had not targeted his tent first. He'd snatched up his pack and emerged into a scene of increasing bedlam. The horse, hitched to a stake by his tent, had been anxiously pawing at the ground, as eager to flee the fires and shouting as he'd been. Rayburn had released the line, careful to keep the animal from fleeing heedlessly, and leapt onto the saddle. With survival his only thought, he'd driven the horse onward.

On those rare occasions when Rayburn did manage to sleep, he saw Eldred Moore. The high shepherd's face was twisted by terror and desperation, just as it'd been when Rayburn had ridden over him, the horse trampling him under foot and leaving him for dead. In the dreams, Moore, waving his thin arms uselessly, would beseech him with the same frantic pleas. Rayburn always ignored them, just as he had in the waking world. The dreams were an unchangeable reenactment of what he'd done, and they forced him to relive his callous abandonment of the old man. It was Rayburn's greatest shame, and a part of his survival that he'd never divulged to anyone.

The rest of his escape and return had been lauded by many as an undertaking of heroic endurance, though, in truth, Rayburn knew that it was no less pathetic and craven. His reckless driving of the horse had gotten him away from the immediate danger of the attack, but the rugged terrain of the dead woodland had proved to be too much for the frightened animal. Galloping wildly, the horse had plunged a hoof into an uneven pit and snapped its leg. With a wild scream, the animal had suddenly toppled forward, flinging Rayburn from the saddle. For a brief moment, he'd been airborne, then he'd hit the ground and tumbled into a knot of brittle, desiccated underbrush. Sprawled there, stunned, with his pack twisted beneath him, Rayburn had found himself thinking about how he'd had no idea that horses could scream. The animal had come to rest not far from him, its back broken. It'd been trying to get back on its feet, its simple mind unable to comprehend its hobbling. Rayburn had remained still, uncertain of his own condition, and watched the animal. The smell of blood had been everywhere. He remembered hoping that it wasn't his.

By the time he'd finally risen, the horse had died. He'd been shocked to find that being thrown from the saddle had left him with nothing worse than superficial scratches. The sounds of the massacre had faded away, and he'd started walking back to the camp to check for any survivors he might've been able to help. Well, that was the story he told, anyway. In truth, he'd continued fleeing on foot. His general sense of direction had governed his footsteps, and he'd headed toward what he'd believed to be the east, desperate to return to the light.

Eventually, the sky had started to show signs of the static dawn, and Rayburn had nearly wept with gratitude. He'd continued along, skulking through the shadows, determined to avoid contact with any living thing. Eventually, he'd reached his goal: the remnants of the Imperial Highway. He'd known that it would lead him back to Nordabor, so, wary of attack, he'd headed north, paralleling the road.

Rayburn, more than anyone, understood the science of rationing. Even still, his victuals had been nearly depleted by the time he'd spotted the rising spires of the Vinecrown Keep in the distance. Worse yet, he'd been getting by on little more than a sip from his canteen before each march. How long those marches had actually lasted wasn't clear. His conception of time had slipped, devolving into time spent walking and time spent sleeping. The constant hunger, thirst, and toil had been a punishing experience, and in that regard, his return *had* been a trial of extreme endurance. But the burning shame that had haunted his every step home, and now lurked on the edges of his consciousness at all times, made his physical suffering somehow feel artificial.

The titled nobility had not seemed to sense any issue with his tale. His arrival, apparently as the sole survivor of the expedition meant to redeem the failures of the last vanished expedition, had created quite a stir amongst them. The aristocrats of the court were astounded by his story, and, despite his best efforts to avoid talking about it, Rayburn often found himself pressed into indulging their desires to hear more about his exploits.

Phar-Mindorius, however, had treated him with a cool cordialness. The king was certainly not overjoyed by Rayburn's dire account of what had befallen the expedition. His prodding, skeptical questions left Rayburn with the sense that Phar-Mindorius could smell the rot in his tale. Rather than coddle him as a valiant survivor, the king had made his expectations quite clear: Rayburn may have returned, but if he didn't make use of his own escape by bringing aid to the others, then his second lease on life would prove to be short-lived.

Ultimately, Rayburn had failed in that endeavor, and now the reports from the north had sealed his fate. There was nothing left to do but sip his broth and await his death, however it might come.

In that manner, he found himself passing yet another time normally allotted for sleep, losing track of the cycles completely until a series of staccato knocks sounded against his door. They startled him from his mournful reveries, and he lurched to his feet, dread nearly strangling him. With leaden legs he proceeded to the door. There, he hesitated, his hand hovering above the first of the bolts. Another round of knocks sent him cringing backward. Once they ceased, he steeled himself with a deep, shuddering breath and unfastened the door, opening it just wide enough to peer out. Through the crack, he saw the scowling face of Under-Captain Sarena Nedelkoff. With a sigh of relief, he opened the door wider and ushered her in.

"Sorry if I woke you," she said as she shuffled by him. She didn't sound very sorry; she sounded distracted, and she threw a final glance back through the doorway just as Rayburn swung the door shut.

"You didn't," he said, sliding the bolts back into place.

"You look like shit," Nedelkoff said. Rayburn had grown accustomed to the royal guardsman's blunt statements. She meant no offense; it was simply an observation made by a pragmatic mind. And she wasn't wrong.

Rayburn slumped back into his chair and extended an offering hand toward a nearby stool. "I assume this isn't a social call?" he asked, smiling weakly.

Nedelkoff perched on the stool like she was expecting to have to leap off it at any moment. "It never is."

"Well, how might I be of service to the Crown? Has Phar-Mindorius decided to empty the city of every last guardsman to continue his fruitless search? Am I to prepare provisions for the entire citizenry, pressed into search parties? I've told him that there's not enough. Supplies have been exhausted; crop yields are paltry, the fishery is depleted, livestock numbers have fallen to the bare minimum needed to maintain the bloodlines. There is nothing I can do, short of hiking out there myself. And we both know how that turned out last time."

Nedelkoff's face softened. "There was nothing you, or I, or anyone else could have done about that. You did as the king asked; you led us back to Vin-Sadavat. Whatever happened to the expedition there, whatever caused the city to implode, it was over before we got there. You know as well as I do that we didn't have the means to keep searching, not after we lost half our scouts. We brought Phar-Mindorius some hope, if nothing else."

"Yes, and that was part of the problem," Rayburn grumbled, his thoughts lingering on the scouts. Those who'd returned had reported that they'd been ambushed by wayward slavers fleeing the burning city. Men had lost their lives searching for the expedition, and Phar-Mindorius had only seen their loss as an impetus to order further searches, spearheaded first by Nedelkoff, and then, after she'd failed to produce his son, by Captain Vitus, the chief officer of the Royal Guard. With Phir-Ramarian's death all but confirmed, the king was still wasting their dwindling resources on a search that everyone knew was already over. Nobody had the fortitude to contradict Phar-Mindorius, and he wouldn't have heard it anyway. The city, already bending under the weight of unrest, was now patrolled by a mere skeleton crew of guardsmen. Rayburn was just thankful that Nedelkoff was currently stationed in Nordabor, otherwise, some less-sympathetic representative of the Crown might be demanding his assistance.

"I don't disagree," Nedelkoff said. "Hope was a good thing in the beginning, for us all. Now, not so much."

"Now it's just delusion, and we've all enabled it. After you saw the Erosion there should have been—"

"Believe me, I understand. Phar-Mindorius is the only one who doesn't. I doubt that even High Shepherd Badgett and his fellow mystagogues believe the false visions they're spewing. But they hold his ear nonetheless."

Rayburn shook his head. "I expect they believe every word of it, and that's far worse."

They lapsed into a dreary silence, thoughts of Badgett hanging thickly between them. The high shepherd had risen to prominence in the wake of the phenomenon, the fear and confusion birthing a new level of fanaticism amongst certain shepherds. His subsequent ascension to Phar-Mindorius's inner circle had been meteoric. Rayburn had heard rumors that Badgett's sudden influence served as an endless source of frustration for Vitus, who was now forced to balance his bootlicking with his desire for rational leadership. Rayburn had heard darker whisperings as well; that Badgett's most devoted apostles, who shouted praise to the Void-God incessantly before the altars of the Ivy Citadel, had willingly blinded themselves, so as to better see the Void. Badgett, on the other hand, must have had no trouble seeing it as he'd done no such thing.

Rayburn loosed a sigh of resignation. "So, what does the Crown want from me now?"

"I'm actually not here in an official capacity."

This struck Rayburn as rather odd; *everything* Nedelkoff did was in an official capacity.

"I'm here to warn you," Nedelkoff continued. "I've received word that your arrest will be ordered very soon. Apparently, Phar-Mindorius wants you clapped in irons for failing to provide the provisions that the Crown demands. He considers it treason; abandonment of the prince."

Rayburn scoffed with indignation and disbelief. Though he'd sensed that such a fate was approaching, its sudden arrival had still shocked him. His surprise was rapidly swallowed by dismay. "What—how can I—?" he sputtered.

"I can get you out."

"Out? Of Nordabor? And go where?" Rayburn had listened well to Nedelkoff's descriptions of the Erosion. She and her scouts had been the ones who'd discovered it. She'd seen the maddening distortions, heard the grinding rumble as entire slabs of reality tumbled into nothingness. She knew what was coming, and that nowhere would be spared.

"Someplace where you'll at least have the chance to run. The people don't really understand yet; they're no more aware of the true danger of the Erosion than they are of the existence of the slave-god, and that secret has been leaking more and more ever since the expedition got underway. What they do understand is that their prince and his important expedition have been lost, a terrifying and deadly phenomenon has torn through their city, and, in the wake of all of that, their sovereign has started to display some very erratic behavior. They're staring down uncertainty, extreme shortages, and violent crackdowns on any dissension. Many see these things as their cue to depart."

"Even if someone wanted to, hasn't Phar-Mindorius ordered the gates shut? I thought only the search parties were allowed to leave the city," Rayburn said. In the king's infinite wisdom, he'd restricted movement out of the city under the guise of protecting the citizenry from any marauding badlanders or slavers, citing the 'uncertain times' the people of Nordabor faced. To Rayburn, it seemed more like a way to prevent mass flight from the city. If the king lost his people, he would be a king no longer.

"And the shepherds," Nedelkoff added. "Those zealots still go to the burning fields, squawking all the while about how everything is unfolding according to the Void-God's will. They have their own routes out of the city. There are more ways out than just the main gates, for those with the right authority. And not all of the guardsmen left are as blindly loyal as the high command and the shepherds. A network has developed, for those who disagree with the king's handling of our current state of affairs. I can get you to them."

Rayburn had never been a particularly cunning man, so it was difficult for him to detect guile in others. Still, he appraised Nedelkoff with something bordering on skepticism. In all of the time he'd known her, traveling the wastes and coordinating supplies for the further search efforts, he'd never doubted her loyalty to the Crown. But he'd never doubted her intelligence either. Or her integrity. She could see that they were on a sinking ship, and she'd had the common decency to try to save him. Rayburn decided that he had no difficulty trusting her.

"Okay," he said, being careful to tamp down on the nascent hope that her gesture had awoken in him. "When do we go?"

Nedelkoff scanned the room around them. "Gather anything you absolutely need and nothing else. We need to go now."

CHAPTER 27

Under an azure sky, five figures plodded along the snaking crest of a dune, their silent footfalls disturbing sand that hadn't been touched in an eon. The previously unforgiving sun had sunk to the very edge of the eastern horizon, its softened rays now shining almost horizontally, kissing the sand with a golden light. Above them, the brightest stars were now visible, dotting the permanent dawn. It was a silent land, one balanced between chilling darkness and burning radiance, and it was exactly where Marbuck wanted to be.

Returning to the Dawnlands had been a homecoming of sorts. After so much time spent in the extremes, being back in the temperate dimness she'd known all her life made her feel closer to Nordabor than she knew she actually was. They still had a long way to go, but at least every step was now taking her in the right direction. And as taxing as the trek was, it was still preferable to her time spent in stagnant captivity, or in the wobbling coracle for that matter.

The initial excitement of their journey west had faded first into tedium, then into a vague sense of dislocation. It'd seemed to emanate from her own gut, and it had made her uneasy. Her situation had changed so rapidly that, when her new reality had finally settled in her mind, it'd all seemed so strange and fragile. She'd gone from being a prisoner to bracing herself in the makeshift boat of a god, who'd happened to be there with her, accompanied by one of her former captors. Kemp's presence in the coracle had reminded her of Old Stitch in the longboat, and that connection had only conjured memories that had further poisoned her disposition.

Thankfully, their proximity to the cliffs had assured her that she was not adrift in a boundless sea, Reie's power had made starvation and thirst impossible, and Kemp, odious as Marbuck found him, was no slaver.

The sun's light had also served as a reminder that her situation was different, although the relentless glare had taken on a hateful aspect all its own. She had greeted the darkening sky as an old friend.

Not long after they'd reached the Dawnlands, the cliffs had fallen away into squat bluffs, and, easing the coracle in between two juttings of rock, they'd found a spot low enough to climb ashore. Jalam had been the last to disembark from the coracle, his eyes bouncing across the handful of stars glinting above them. Reie had smiled at his childlike wonder, guiding him by the arm as they walked along the craggy shoreline. Heading north, the party had left the coracle floating in the water. It had served its long-await-ed purpose, and none of them had any intention of returning to it.

By Marbuck's estimate, another full-cycle had passed while they'd picked their way through the stony hills. Kemp had taken some time to get his bearings, but, after minimal backtracking, he'd grown confident in his route, and in his belief that they'd lost any possible pursuers. Eventually, they'd reached a point where the bluffs had tapered off, giving way to the sea of sand that apparently constituted most of the southern end of the continent.

Their journey through this cool, twilight desert had been blissfully uneventful. They moved in a loose single file, with Kemp trudging ahead of them. Jalam followed, the expanse of dawn sky forgotten, his watchful attention focused solely on Kemp. Reie ambled along behind them. If she had any reservations whatsoever about Kemp's joining them, she hadn't said so. In the coracle, she'd even explained to him the details of what they intended to do. He'd nodded along gamely, asking few questions. The two had known each other for a long time, without either really knowing any-thing real about the other. Kemp, who'd recently had his understanding of his life in Quaretem turned upside down, accepted Reie's revelations, and her true identity, with a sort of penitent fealty. Marbuck wasn't entirely sure what to make of it.

Falstaff, as she'd expected would be the case, had accepted Kemp with-out hesitation. She almost envied his trusting nature. It allowed him to float through life, buoyed by his own positivity. Her own ever-present leeriness was as exhausting as it was dispiriting.

"Marbuck," Kemp called unexpectedly from ahead of her. She looked up to see that he'd stopped, with Reie and Jalam gathered beside him. "Might I borrow your glass?"

"Sure," she said, slipping the gilded field glass out of her tunic pocket. With some reluctance, she handed it to him.

"Thank you," he said. He squinted to the north, where the crack in the sky could be faintly seen through the gloaming, and lifted the glass to his eye. "Quite a piece," he murmured as he scanned the horizon. "Nearly as powerful as the telescopes of the Great Ziggurat, and not even a third of the size."

Marbuck peered past him, trying to discern what he might be looking at. After another moment, he lowered the field glass and handed it back to her.

"We're on the right track," he announced. "We're about halfway across the desert basin. This stretch is the desert's narrowest point, hemmed in by the bluffs we came from to the south and the Stone Teeth to the north."

"The Stone Teeth?" Falstaff asked.

"They're the southern end of a mountain range that runs along the northern border of the desert. They're fairly steep, but the mountains beyond them are not particularly difficult to hike through; I've been north of them."

"I believe you're referring to the Yewhia Mountains," Reie said. "They are an old range, one of the first that Alminnian raised up from the dirt. Even before the fall, they'd eroded considerably. Kemp is right; they should not pose much of an issue."

"Once we cross these Stone Teeth, then we'll reach the crater?" Marbuck asked.

"Well, not exactly," Kemp said with an evasive smile. It was every bit the look that he'd worn in Quaretem, and Marbuck hated it.

"Elaborate," she said flatly.

"Well, beyond the Stone Teeth, the terrain changes considerably. The mountains drop away into a broad, marshy valley that we're going to have to pass through. On the far side of that valley, the northern stretch of the mountains butt up against the rim of the World's Wound."

"Can we go around this valley?" Marbuck asked. "If the mountains encircle it, why don't we just stick to the higher ground?"

"For the same reason that we can't go around the World's Wound," Kemp said, looking at Reie, who nodded her understanding. "We don't have time for a lengthy detour. But worry not; I know the way through the morass."

"Oh? Had a lot of experience hunting down there, have you?" Marbuck sneered.

Kemp smiled sadly. "No. The valley was my home before I came to Quaretem."

"You hail from Berngoth, then?" Reie asked with genuine interest, ignoring Marbuck's enmity.

"Yes, and when I left there, I took a small boat south," Kemp said, sidestepping any further elaboration on his old home. "A little metal thing I called the *Tinpot*. Now, I know we're all sick to death of riding in a boat, but we'll need one to navigate the swamps that surround Berngoth. I left the *Tinpot* cached at the edge of the marsh."

"So, your former home, Berngoth, is this place safe?" Falstaff asked.

"As safe as anywhere else, I suppose," Kemp said, and he flashed his manufactured smile. "We'll be fine."

"I can't speak for what became of Berngoth after the war, but in the old times it was a beautiful place," Reie said, a distant look in her alabaster eyes. "It was a land of cool, clear lakes and hanging willows, surrounded by the low mountains, draped in their verdant raiment. Ganachim truly outdid herself in dressing those old peaks. Even after Vingallea arrived and established their principality there, the valley remained a haven. Of course, this was when Vingallea was still in its early ascent, focused on the wonders of human creation and guided by benevolent gods. Over time, as Vingallea's thirst for conquest grew, Berngoth forgot its pastoral beginnings. Generations of plundered wealth had given rise to powerful families who enjoyed roles of preeminence in the Vingallean courts. Zeorshut Riengel, the *real* Zeorshut Riengel, actually came from Berngoth. The hold became known for supplying the Vingallean armies with well-bred war mastiffs. The kennels of the Berngoth aristocracy were legendary; I can't recall a single Vingallean monarch who did not utilize them for their hunts. I had thought, being so close to the World's Wound, that everything in Berngoth would have been laid to waste, and all life extinguished. It appears that I was mistaken."

"Well, I don't know about all that," Kemp said, "but I know some folks managed to survive in those swamplands. More importantly, I know how to get us through them."

Reie smiled, but it did not reach her eyes, which remained glazed with foggy reminiscence. "Okay, Henrick, lead us to your *Tinpot*."

• • •

Marbuck had by now heard so many half-truths and veiled insinuations that she took it as a given that Kemp knew more than he was letting on. She also understood plainly that there was no point in trying to wrench an answer out of him. Whatever he was leading them toward, it was north, and north was good. Perhaps it was due to a lack of imagination, but there just didn't seem to be any possible risk of being led into a trap, or any motivation for Kemp to do so, unless he was running a particularly intricate and needlessly complicated scheme. So Marbuck chalked it up to some idiosyncrasy on Kemp's part, born of whatever shameful past he carried with him. Whatever it was, Marbuck didn't care. Kemp's issues were his own, and he was free to nurse them privately as much as he wished, as long as he kept leading them north.

And that he did, only stopping occasionally to check their course with the field glass. Marbuck nearly let him hold onto it, if only so that there was one less reason for him to speak to her, but she was seized by a strange sort of possessiveness. The field glass, like the anointed blade, had become hers, and she would not part with it easily. Soon, it didn't matter. The Stone Teeth rose on the horizon, and whatever landmark Kemp was relying on to find their specific route through the cliffs was now clear to him.

When they reached the boulder-strewn slopes of the mountains, they stopped for the first time since they'd left Quaretem. Marbuck's understanding of time had completely evaporated; aside from some nodding off in the coracle, she had not slept since before her last shift at the Pit. She and Falstaff had escaped the Great Ziggurat, joined with Reie and the others, fled in the coracle, made landfall, and marched across the entire swath of desert without any actual sleep. Reie's restorations made such a feat possible, but the seemingly endless procession of time, coupled with the lack of real food and water, made her feel punchy. Her physical body may have been propped up by the god's power, but her mind felt stretched. Reie seemed to sense the mortal limitations of her companions, being the one to call the halt.

They ate dried mushrooms and drank brackish water, and paired with Reie's bolstering, it was a feast that set Marbuck's taste buds tingling. Afterwards, Reie, who looked somewhat fatigued herself from the exertion of keeping the others alive, stood watch while they slept. Marbuck doubted if she'd let them sleep more than a couple of cycles before waking them, but, like the food, it was enough. The march resumed with gusto, and for

Marbuck, whose eagerness to reach Nordabor exceeded even Reie's, that was just fine.

Kemp led them through a series of switchbacks running along the face of the ragged cliffs. The eroded rectangles of yellow stone reaching skyward really did resemble the teeth of some colossal maw. The low rays of the golden sun touched the tops of them, framing them spectacularly against an ashy wall of cloud that hung immobile over the lands beyond them. Kemp observed that, when he'd been there last, the sky beyond the Stone Teeth had been clear. The same force that had cracked the northern sky had apparently sucked a static bulk of clouds up from the south and its sudden cessation had left them anchored over the valley. Marbuck didn't mind; the clouds blocked out her view of the unnatural crack, and having a dim cloud ceiling above her head would be a comforting reminder of home.

After scrambling up a final slope of loose scree, they arrived at the base of one of the tremendous teeth. Moving alongside it, they came to the point where it butted up against the next tooth. There, Kemp led them to a small gap between the rocks; a fissure in the stone that would allow them to shimmy through to the other side. One by one, they filed in.

As Marbuck waited at the end of the line, she scratched absentmindedly at her scarred head and looked over the desert they'd just crossed. She was mildly surprised by just how high they actually were; from their vantage she could see the entirety of the sands stretched out in waves before her. A faint hint of the seaside bluffs could be seen at the furthest rim of the horizon. Seven dark shapes on the side of a particularly large dune caught her attention. Fearing huntsmen, she trained her field glass on them. They were only wandering shades, wayward horrors that posed no threat from such a distance. She examined them as they moved haltingly toward the crest of the dune, their pointless labors stirring a sense of pity within her. Some dormant part of her that remembered the lessons of the Ivy Citadel felt a calling to free the shades from their eternal fetters.

"Ready, Fishwife?" Falstaff asked.

Her gaze lingered on the wretched creatures for just another tick. "Yes," she said, pocketing the field glass and turning toward him. "Lead the way."

They squeezed into the gap, which was scarcely wider than the passage they'd taken out of the Warren. In short time, the dawn light shrank away behind them. The darkness would have been complete were it not for the faint glow of Reie's halo bobbing ahead of them. In the tightness of the crevice the sounds of their breathing and their shuffling steps were amplified, filling the narrow space. Marbuck moved mechanically, her thoughts drifting far away.

She could see Elibeth, not as she'd appeared in the terrible nightmare aboard the longboat, but as Marbuck had seen her last, when she'd left her in Dania's care for what was supposed to be a relatively short journey. Elibeth had been smiling with delight at the antics of Dania's four younger children, who revered the wise young woman of eleven long-cycles who stayed with them so often. Elibeth had bid farewell to her mother in the distracted way children do when they are eager to run off and play. Marbuck, failing to foresee the disaster looming ahead of her, had planted a single kiss on the squirming girl, hugged her once, and left, her thoughts on the coin she would soon be collecting.

Elibeth would be older now, how much older Marbuck couldn't be certain. She hoped that Elibeth's prolonged presence hadn't burdened Dania too much; she certainly had her hands full with her own children, and her husband, Hamish, brought in very little coin working for a tannery. Marbuck had promised Dania a tidy sum for watching Elibeth; she now felt that she owed the woman a fortune for taking her daughter in for so long, a fortune she, of course, did not have. During all of her suffering, consumed as she'd been by the basic need to survive, it hadn't occurred to her that, should she actually manage to make it back, she would be returning empty-handed. Whether or not the expedition had succeeded, the situation in the north had undoubtedly changed. It seemed unlikely that she would ever collect the riches that had lured her into this venture in the first place. Now that she really considered it, the thought stung. The added unfairness left her feeling malignantly bitter.

Gradually, natural light bloomed at the end of the crevice which helped return Marbuck to the present, and she shrugged off the vivid recollection of Elibeth with some effort. She slipped out of the fissure and found herself facing a landscape of low, barren plateaus, each fringed with the dried shells of long-dead tree trunks. It was difficult to tell if any of these cliffs rivaled the height of the teeth, which now rose behind them, but Marbuck doubted it. They certainly weren't as steep.

What they lacked in height, they made up for in vexation. Kemp's path, which did not resemble an actual pathway at all, took them across the crumbling sides of the plateaus and into the sunken dells that existed between the rising humps of the ancient mountains. These were choked full of petrified trunks, as well as generations of dried undergrowth, which burst into stifling clouds of dust as they tromped through them. It did not take long for them to be smeared in sooty grime from head to toe. Marbuck's eyes stung and her body ached from continuously clambering over small obstacles. Occasional boosts from Reie numbed the discomfort and kept her moving, but they did nothing to soothe her irritation at their surroundings.

Kemp paused to consider their route only a handful of times, and, to his credit, they did not backtrack, or at least Marbuck couldn't tell if they did. By the time the mountains started to drop away in earnest, she guessed that something like three full-cycles had passed, but it was impossible to say for sure. The constant disorientation was beginning to make her feel unmoored from reality. How Reie, who'd lived this way for an eternity, could remain sane was beyond Marbuck.

The end of their toil in the mountains came suddenly. They were skirting the edge of a bluff, trying to keep above the tangle, when, rounding the side of the embankment, they were met with their first unobstructed view of the valley below. A murky swath of gray and green spread out before them, a sprawl of crooked trees rising from a vast bog. Eerily still wisps of vapor clung to the ragged tops of the trees, seeming to almost mingle with the low-hanging clouds above. A few shafts of light penetrated the clouds, the dawn sun reaching down into the swamp and setting the vapor aglow. Through some fluke of nature, the meager sunlight and the water had allowed life to sustain a tenuous hold there. Some of the trees, though withered, still retained some languid foliage. At the furthest reach of their view, the northern stretch of the Yewhia Mountains was just visible through the gloom.

"It's remarkable," Reie said, stopping to take in the view. "I can almost see how it was before the war. The mountains to the north must have shielded the valley from the worst effects of the destruction that created the World's Wound. I imagine the heat of that event boiled away most of the lakes, but it looks like enough of the water remained, displaced and befouled, yes, but enough nonetheless to preserve just a little of Ganachim's designs. If we succeed, she could restore it all."

The god's eyes blazed. She was no longer there with them, she was lost in the impossible depths of her endless life, striving to push away the failures of her past in order to conjure a future in which her wildest hopes would come to pass. In that sense, she struck Marbuck as remarkably human. Marbuck thought it unlikely that the grim valley of Berngoth would ever again match Reie's memory of it, but she didn't say so. As long as Reie had faith, she would buttress Marbuck's own intentions.

"We will live to see it done," Falstaff said, placing a hand upon the god's shoulder. To Marbuck, his earnest vow was equal parts annoying and embarrassing.

Reie, however, did not see the absurdity in a supreme deity being comforted by a mere mortal. "Thank you," she said, smiling warmly. The expression nearly erased the strange otherworldliness that she exuded. Once again, she seemed very human.

"Well, step one is to reach the *Tinpot*," Kemp said. "And we're nearly there."

"Go on then," Jalam said. His tone was cordial, but Marbuck sensed that he had grown impatient with Kemp's winding route.

"Of course, my friend," Kemp said, cheerfully ignoring any hint of hostility. "Right this way."

•   •   •

The travelers descended toward the edge of the swamp, plodding over ground that was increasingly soft. Kemp led them across strands comprised of fallen brush, avoiding the worst of the muck. The still air became clammy, pressing upon Marbuck with an oppressive humidity. To her surprise, tiny insects flitted around them. Reie beheld these pests, which she called midges, with delight as they were yet another indicator that at least some of the natural life that Ganachim had designed so long ago still remained. Marbuck found the midges bothersome, and she swatted them aside with increasing spite.

Finally, after following along a mossy hummock that bordered a wide swath of cloudy water, Kemp announced that they'd arrived. Stepping up to the edge of the hummock, Marbuck saw that the eroded bank rose above a muddy cove, wherein a large pile of detritus had collected. Within the tangled branches and dead leaves, she could just make out the shape of a small boat.

"She's no beauty, that's for sure. Just a leftover metalwork of the old times, not a finely crafted work of art like your coracle," Kemp said, winking at Reie. "But she'll get the job done, believe me. We've just got to uncover her."

He climbed down into the cove, using the exposed roots of a tree to lower himself onto the mud. After a few sinking steps, he was at the boat's side, stripping the camouflage off it. Laying the brush on top of the mud, he created a makeshift bridge for the others to cross. They joined him below, and, in a few short-cycles, the *Tinpot* was uncovered.

Its design could only be described as utilitarian. The body of the vessel was a series of tarnished plates of dull gray metal, riveted together into a rectangular shape that tapered toward the point of the bow. Patchwork plating showed where numerous repairs had been performed by inferior hands. The bare deck was large enough to accommodate the five of them without being too cramped, but offered nothing in regards to comfort. The only features were a small platform in the middle, bearing an empty divot where a mast might have once been attached, and the pilothouse, a box of dented metal that rose from the deck near the stern. It was hardly large enough for a single person to stand inside of, and whatever wheel it had once housed was long gone. Two long metal poles were stowed along the starboard side; Marbuck guessed that they would be used to push the boat along the stagnant, shallow waterways of the swamp. Similar methods had been used to prod the *Fortune* away from hidden shoals when the current of the Einfallen made hasty course corrections necessary.

Kemp climbed over the boat's low rail and planted his feet on the deck, looking over the puny vessel with something like trepidation. The look passed quickly and he grinned at the others, his arms extended in a gesture of welcoming. "May I present to you … the *Tinpot*." He extended his hand to Reie and she took it. He hoisted her up and helped her over the rail.

"Welcome aboard."

CHAPTER 28

Kemp had never expected to be back aboard the *Tinpot*, but then his life had taken many unexpected turns. In a simpler time, he had never conceived of exploring the world beyond the cloistered peace of Berngoth. He'd certainly never dreamed of a place like Quaretem, populated with living legends from the dimly remembered past. But once he'd been there, returning to Berngoth had been the furthest thing from his mind.

Marbuck had changed all that. The sour woman who he'd discovered in the unlikeliest place had blown his world apart. He didn't resent her for it, nor did he feel gratitude toward her. Implacably focused on her own intentions, he doubted that she even considered the broader ramifications of her arrival. Her appearance had been like a physical manifestation of destiny, unstoppably dragging everyone in Quaretem into an unknown future. Through her singular desire to return to her daughter, she'd set things in motion that could fundamentally change reality. If what Reie sought came to pass, it would mean an end to everything Kemp had known and the beginning of a new world. It was difficult to comprehend.

In a narrower sense, for Kemp, it meant an end to his willful ignorance, his life of privilege, and his obedience to Lakna. He could help to end her self-serving reign and, more importantly, Setenrah's butchery.

Paramount to all of that, though, was the completion of the one task that had been the catalyst to everything that had followed: reuniting Marbuck with her daughter.

It was funny; Kemp did not actually care for Marbuck. She struck him as pugnacious and selfish, quick to anger and even quicker to bend others to her purpose. He actually pitied Falstaff, who seemed incapable of disagreeing with her, and was easily browbeaten when even a whiff of dissent was detected. Yet, despite Marbuck's many flaws, she was fiercely obsessed with being there for her child. It was no great mystery to Kemp why this single redeeming trait was of such importance to him. His soul was a fractured mess of shortcomings, and he'd discovered that quintessential piece to be missing when he'd needed it most.

Redemption was impossible; what was done was done, he knew that. But when their route had become clear, and he'd seen which way they had to go, he'd considered it further proof of what fate intended to do with him. For the others, it was simply the most direct route. He didn't plan on telling them how much more it meant to him unless it was absolutely necessary. It was his private shame, and his private burden to set things right. From his home he had fled in disgrace; now he would return to correct what he could. It was another step on the path that Marbuck's arrival had laid before him.

That path was now leading them deeper into the shadowed bogs of Kemp's ancestral home. After a bit of a struggle, they'd managed to push the *Tinpot* free of its muddy berth, and now Marbuck and Falstaff were manning the poles, guiding the boat at Kemp's direction. It had been Reie's idea for the two seasoned mariners to push them along. She'd vetoed Jalam's suggestion that he and Kemp do so, based on the assumption that Marbuck and Falstaff were more familiar with that sort of work and Kemp would need to be free to focus on their route. At the realization that she would be taking orders from Kemp, Marbuck had looked as if she'd been asked to eat a plate of shit.

Nevertheless, Reie's system seemed to be working well, though it'd left Jalam aimlessly pacing the deck. Deprived of any immediate purpose, he didn't seem to know what to do with himself. Kemp might have found it amusing were he not so preoccupied with his own recollections. As he ordered adjustments to their course, allowing ingrained memory to guide him, he surveyed the land he'd once been heir to.

As a young man, it had seemed boundless, a wild realm teeming with untold mysteries. He'd grown up listening to the tales of the old glory of

Berngoth, and he'd often imagined the swamps echoing with the baying of the hounds of the hunt, long-dead even in the time of his grandsires. It'd surprised him to learn from Reie that Berngoth had once been a part of Vingallea; he'd never learned of them or their domination of the world until he'd come to Quaretem. For him, and his people, Berngoth had been the total sum of civilization. Though the world had changed long ago, they remained, surviving by their own mettle and the bounty of the swamps.

Under the tutelage of his father, he'd learned the crafts of that sub-sistence; how to navigate the treacherous pathways of the bogs, how to detect, avoid, and defend himself against the dangers, and how to trap the various animals that prowled the dusky undergrowth. Trapping was the predominant focus of their people, for it was the key to their survival. The swamps offered plenty, but only if one knew how to claim it. Kemp's father had known that; his lessons in trapping had taken precedence over everything, even teaching the art of governance. To him, trapping was the foundation to every other facet of their lives. In hindsight, that focus might have been a mistake.

When his father had died and Kemp had inherited the dukedom, the title held by the rulers of Berngoth since antiquity, and one that now made more sense given his new understanding of Berngoth's subservience to Vingallea, he'd been ill-prepared for the challenges of leadership. He'd longed to spend his time wandering distant glades, not settling petty dis-putes between squabbling crofters. At least being tied down at Tarn Manor had allowed him more time with Taiyonna and Blythe.

Kemp felt a wave of dread bloom in his chest and roll through him, making him shudder. Their names had been shunted to the deepest vault of his mind since before he'd even been granted lordship in Quaretem. Their sudden re-emergence in his thoughts now made him feel fragile. Despite the pain it caused him, he strove to embrace that feeling.

He was going to have to face a lot more than just their names before he was done.

• • •

As the *Tinpot* made its way toward Berngoth's central ward, where Tarn Manor and the other remaining estates had constituted the bulk of his people's settlement, it became increasingly difficult for Kemp to mask his growing fear. Thankfully, the others were too preoccupied to notice.

Marbuck and Falstaff were busy with the poles while Jalam kept a self-appointed watch on their gloomy surroundings. Only Reie seemed to have sensed his distress, or it might have just been his imagination. Demonstrating her ability to remain unnaturally still, she stood by the railing, watching the gnarled trees gliding past them. Except for when she was watching him. Even without her veil, she was completely unreadable, and Kemp did his best to ignore her.

Rounding a bend, they came upon the first sign of human habitation that they'd seen since leaving the Sentinel. It was the crumbling remains of an ancient canal wall, and Kemp remembered it well.

Marbuck braced her pole against one of the wall's moss-covered stones and nudged them away from it. As the *Tinpot* slid alongside the wall, two sets of skeletal remains came into view, the heaped collections of bone and ragged, mildewed clothing visible amongst the weeds sprouting from the top of the cracked wall.

"Know anything about this?" Marbuck asked, turning to Kemp.

"I thought you said this place was safe," Falstaff said at almost the same time.

"I said it was as safe as anywhere else," Kemp said, ignoring Marbuck's question entirely. "In my experience, nowhere in this wide world is particularly safe, and, safe or not, we must pass this way."

"Where, exactly, is this way taking us?" Jalam asked, his eyes lingering on the carcasses as the boat slowly passed them by.

"North, of course."

"And what of your people's settlement?" Reie asked quietly. Her even tone was maddening, and Kemp felt as if she had opened his head and examined every squirming secret inside. "Are we going there?"

"Our route passes it." Kemp smiled. "There's nothing to worry about. We'll cruise on by and be out of these swamps before you know it." He was stalling, still uncertain of what his plan was, beyond knowing that he would somehow, someway, confront Obed and answer the questions that had haunted him for so long.

Blessedly, no further questions followed. The wall slid away behind them and—

—the four men mounted the wall, which constituted the most solid strip of ground they could have asked for.

"This spot will work brilliantly," Kemp said, examining their surroundings. He turned to Retlow. "The boars will ford the water here. Let's set up the snares."

His valet nodded and set to work unpacking their equipment. Kemp sighed contentedly, pleased to be out in the quiet expanse of the swamps, temporarily free from the pressures of his position.

"Do you want us to set up here, too?" Baumann asked. He and Fitzroy had already begun to drop their packs, apparently assuming that they already knew his answer. The two courtiers had been trapping with their duke for a long time and it did not surprise Kemp that they believed they could anticipate his wants. This time, he surprised them.

"No, this spot is good, but I'd rather not saturate it. My father always stressed the importance of variety. Too many boars die in this spot, they stop coming to this spot. If we rotate our trapping grounds, they will never empty."

Impressed by his own wisdom, Kemp began to assemble the snare. Retlow knelt beside him, wedging the first stake into a crack in the wall. Focused on their simple but rewarding work, they paid little mind to Baumann and Fitzroy. It was by the providence of a random fluke that their lives were spared.

One of the snare's counterweights was split, and the sand inside had run out. Kemp turned to his companions to see if they'd brought an extra one. As he unexpectedly turned, he surprised the men again, but not as much as they surprised him. Fitzroy stood above him, his gutting knife held aloft, his other hand reaching out for Kemp. Instinctively, Kemp rose to his feet, and Fitzroy faltered. From the corner of Kemp's eye, Baumann lunged toward him, his own knife raised.

By now, Retlow had noticed that something was wrong, and he tackled Baumann before his attack could connect. Kemp lifted his hatchet from his belt, just as Fitzroy regained his composure.

"What are you—?" Kemp started, but Fitzroy was coming at him with his knife held high, his teeth bared. It was a clumsy attack, one born of a plan that'd gone awry, and Kemp could have made short work of him had he not been equally handicapped by his utter confusion. All he could manage was to step out of the way of the swinging knife. The thought that he might need to kill Fitzroy, a man who'd been a trusted servant and friend for as long as he could remember, simply had not formulated yet. Still, some things were second nature to him, and, as such, he reflexively booted the man in the ass, sending him sprawling over the edge of the wall and splashing into the water below.

In the meantime, Retlow had managed to wrest the knife from Baumann's grasp and was now pressing it to his neck. Baumann was breathing rapidly, his bulging eyes locked on Kemp, who was still struggling to understand what was happening.

"What is the meaning of this?" Retlow cried, his own confusion apparent.

Baumann answered with an animalistic growl, bucking beneath Retlow's grip. The knife slipped away from his neck and he twisted around trying to scramble out from beneath his captor.

"Stop!" Retlow ordered, still unwilling to hurt his erstwhile companion. Baumann kicked him in the face, sending him tumbling backward. The knife clattered to the stones and Baumann leapt for it. Before he could reach it, Kemp planted his boot on the knife's blade. Some primal part of his mind, one that was free of the trappings of his conflicting emotions, shuddered to life, and he brought his hatchet down on Baumann's head.

Kemp had never killed anyone before. In a purely physical sense, it was strangely identical to killing any other animal. The sound of the hatchet splitting through Baumann's skull, the color and consistency of the blood, even the final rattling breaths; a dying boar would have been no different. But this dead animal was Baumann. It just didn't make sense.

He did not have long to consider it. Fitzroy had climbed back up the wall. He was panting, sopping wet, and still in possession of his knife. Kemp could tell that he was wavering, the sight of Baumann's corpse unmanning him. It didn't matter as the decision was made for him. Retlow, blood streaming from his broken nose, had also shed any lingering doubt about their situation. He plunged his own gutting knife into Fitzroy's belly, then again into his chest, before the man could commit to fighting or fleeing. Fitzroy crumpled into a wet heap, and Retlow kicked his knife away.

Kemp approached Fitzroy slowly, caught in a swamping wave of unreality. "Why did you do this?" he asked. His own voice sounded muffled.

Fitzroy's eyes rolled in his head, and he mumbled something, blood burbling out of his mouth. In a moment, he was gone.

It was quiet again, but everything had changed. Retlow was saying something about getting away from the bodies, about the risk of shades being born. They had no fire to drive them away, and no reason to stay with the bodies. Kemp was hardly listening. The horrific implications of the attack were solidifying in his mind. Baumann and Fitzroy had been working together; they'd launched a coordinated attempt to take his life, to assassinate him. There might be others involved, and he might not be the only target. Taiyonna, Blythe, and Obed were all back at Tarn Manor. He had to get to them, he had to—

—follow just a bit further along this stretch and the trees would thin out. It was a route Kemp had traveled countless times, and he knew that the roofs of Berngoth's estates would soon be visible. His heart had started thumping wildly, and he took a long, slow breath to steady himself.

The *Tinpot* continued along its course, alternately gliding easily on the water's surface and lurching as Marbuck and Falstaff forced it through muddy shallows. As Kemp had known would be the case, the water soon broadened, leaving the largest of the partially submerged trees behind. On their port side, the highest cupolas and turrets rose into view over the reeds.

"We're reaching the lagoon now," Kemp said in his best approximation of cheery nonchalance. "My people's settlement will be on our left shortly. I think we ought to stop there; I might be able to resupply."

"We don't need supplies," Marbuck said.

"Perhaps not, with the Lady's bolstering, but it might be nice to slake our thirst with fresh water, and to eat something beyond mushroom rations. I believe we deserve a little comfort beyond basic survival."

An unmistakable expression of longing descended over Falstaff's features, and he looked at Marbuck like a pleading child. She rebuked him with a sharp glance, then turned back to Kemp. "We don't have time for idle comforts, or for you to gab with old friends. We have what we need."

"As the provider of 'what we need', I feel that I should have a say in this," Reie said. "If Henrick wishes to stop, we will stop. Fresher provisions might fuel us more than you think, and they would give me a rest. Even just giving you each the bare minimum to keep you standing is starting to tax me. My power is not without its limits."

"Well, I suppose it's settled then," Kemp said before anyone else could chime in. "I'll tell you when to beach her."

Marbuck scowled, but said nothing. Jalam looked similarly unhappy, but that didn't matter. If Reie had told him to drown himself, he would have been underwater before she'd finished speaking.

They rounded the final bend and entered the lagoon proper. On their left, the old estates of Berngoth dotted the shoreline, choked with brown weeds and obscured by moss-laden willows. In some distant epoch, they had been stately manors; gleaming white edifices with large windows and pillared porches, crowned by gabled roofs. In Kemp's memory, they had still boasted much of that splendor. Having been away for so long, he now saw the slanting, moldering structures for what they really were. In the warped planks and broken windows he saw a people playacting at the illustriousness of their past. Compared to the polished splendor of the Great Ziggurat, the crooked belfries and sunken roofs of Berngoth were embarrassing. This place had been his once, but to be the ruler of such a decrepit wreck now seemed utterly meaningless. And yet, it had cost him everything.

Evidence of that tragedy was most abundant in the burnt shell of Tarn Manor. The gutted remains of his family home still stood, the blackened beams of the roof reaching skyward. The sight of it brought tears to Kemp's eyes. He could still feel the heat of the flames; smell the acrid scent that had accompanied the total destruction of his life. The yawning expanse of time shrank away and he was there again, racing—

—up the hill upon which his home rose. Dragging the Tinpot *ashore had been exhausting, even with Retlow helping him, but it was not the reason his heart was hammering. He slowed down, trying to keep his movements calm and normal, not seeking to draw attention to himself. Darkened windows could conceal many watching eyes, and Kemp had no idea how deeply the rot had set in.*

With Retlow a couple steps behind, sniffing and wiping away the rivulet of blood seeping from his nose, Kemp rounded the porch and reached the front doors. Everything looked completely normal, which was somehow more threatening. Behind those doors, he could find the comfort of his family and loyal retinue, and he could set to work rooting out any further conspirators. Or, he could find that he was not the only target, and the murderous plot had already claimed his family. Existing in both realities simultaneously was torturous, so, without delay, Kemp pushed the double doors open.

Two sentries were waiting in the foyer, and they both bowed deeply. Their presence, though routine, startled him. They straightened, seemingly oblivious to any disturbance in their duke. They made no indication that they'd noticed Retlow's bloodied nose. It could have been due to prudence, or because they'd been expecting some level of violence. As Kemp strode by them, the hairs on the back of his neck rose in anticipation of a blow that did not arrive.

He and Retlow entered the main hall, where the taxidermied trophies of a bygone age leered down at them. The hall was deserted, save for Obed, who was standing at the window behind the throne of antlers, yet another memento from the time of the old hunts. He was looking out at the lagoon, the dawn light streaming through the window, one of the only ones that still boasted intact glass, framing his lean form. As Kemp approached him, skirting along the edge of the long hearth in the center of the space, he breathed a small sigh of relief. At the very least, his brother was still alive.

Obed turned at his arrival, and he raised his eyebrows at Retlow's bloody nose.

"Where are Taiyonna and Blythe?" Kemp asked before Obed could utter a word.

He looked confused, then worried. "They're upstairs, in the solar."

Kemp felt a tremendous weight lift from his heart, and he clapped Retlow on the shoulder.

"What's happened?" Obed asked. "Where are Fitzroy and Baumann?"

"They tried to kill us," Kemp said, hardly believing the words as he said them.

"They failed," Retlow added.

"That's preposterous! If this is your idea of a joke—"

"I wish that it were, brother," Kemp said. "They attacked us while we were setting up the snares by the old canal wall. And I'm worried that they weren't acting alone, that someone might be planning to target Taiyonna and Blythe. Or you."

Obed raised his eyebrows again.

"We need to gather anyone whose loyalty is unimpeachable and formulate a plan. If there is indeed a conspiracy, it needs to be flushed out immediately."

Obed nodded smartly. "Absolutely, Henrick. I'll summon the retinue. For now, why don't you head up to the solar and be with your family? You've been through quite a shock by the looks of it. Retlow, you come with—"

"GET THE FUCK OFF ME!" a voice shrieked from the gallery above. The three men turned their attention upwards, and Taiyonna came into view, a sentry snatching at the back of her dressing gown. She clutched the railing as the man seized her about the waist. "He's trying to kill you! Obed's trying to kill—"

The sentry wrapped a gloved hand over her mouth and wrenched her away from the rail. Kemp stood riveted to the floor, flabbergasted. Boiling beneath his shock was a profound rage. "Release her!" he bellowed, but the sentry dragged her back toward the solar, a second man arriving to assist with the flailing prisoner.

"They won't answer to you anymore," Obed said quietly, and then the devastating weight of Taiyonna's words burst through Kemp's anger, and a boundless sorrow born of betrayal took its place.

"You?" Kemp managed to ask, his voice a husky croak.

"It was supposed to be a very smooth transition. After your tragic accident, I would have inherited the dukedom. Your wife and child would have been sequestered in mourning. Sequestered, because your nosy bitch overheard my instructions to those two idiots who couldn't even perform a simple

task. At least my men caught her eavesdropping before she could get to you. She might require a little extra time to process her grief. I'm thinking at least until my coronation. By then I imagine that Taiyonna will have overcome her loss and, if she desires to secure a place for her and her daughter, she will be willing to become a duke's wife once again. I'll gladly have her, and Blythe will be treated fairly, I promise you." Obed paused, lost in thought for a moment. "Yes, minor hiccups aside, my plan is still quite salvageable. It will just require a few tweaks. I'm not worried; the people will swallow whatever I tell them."

"The people are loyal to Duke Henrick," Retlow said, and he'd drawn his knife. Kemp, hardly able to process the terrible truths unfurling before him, fumbled his hatchet and his club from his belt.

"You are not the people," Obed said. "They have long craved my leadership, not the feckless whims of a layabout who spends more time pursuing his own fancies than tending to the needs of his people. Why, I'm already their leader in all but name. The will of the people should not be denied because of some antiquated nonsense about birth order."

"I see through your sanctimonious words," Retlow fired back. "You forget that I served your father, and that I've known you since your mother traded her life for yours. I had thought you'd grown out of your petulant sense of entitlement. I—"

"Enough!" Obed cried. "I've spent too much of my life listening to your preaching."

"And you still need to hear more, apparently."

Kemp simply watched their exchange, his churning emotions overcoming him. Through the cacophony, one thought arose: His wife and daughter were being held upstairs and he needed to get to them. He started to walk away.

"Where do you think—"

—we should land her?"

Kemp blinked, realizing that Falstaff had asked him a question.

"Where should we land?" he asked again.

"Oh, uh, there, right there," Kemp said, pointing at a short spit of sand interrupting the uniformity of the scrubby bank.

Marbuck and Falstaff guided the *Tinpot* to the place. As they made their final approach, the metal hull began to scrape against the silty bottom with a gentle hiss. The boat came to a stop a moment later, its bow pointed slightly upward as it rested on the sand. With a few grunting heaves, Marbuck and Falstaff poled it slightly further onto the shore.

"That'll do," Kemp said. If he'd beached the *Tinpot* in the same way back then, rather than dragging it fully ashore as was his habit, what had followed might have played out differently. It was just another mistake that he'd built his misery on.

"Shall we?" Reie asked.

"We?"

"I'm coming with you. It wouldn't be safe to go alone."

Kemp weighed his options. He could argue against it and risk causing further consternation about his errand, or he could just let her come. He had a distinct feeling that she'd be joining him regardless of what he said.

"Well, alright, let's go."

"Where she goes, I go," Jalam said.

"Of course."

What Kemp had intended as a very intimate experience was quickly becoming a crowded affair. Thankfully, he did not have to worry about Marbuck volunteering to join him. Sweaty and flushed, she remained leaning against her pole, Falstaff at her side.

"We'll watch the boat while you're away," she announced with more than a hint of derision. Kemp wondered briefly if she'd leave without them, but that was nonsense. It would be suicide to depart without Reie, and Falstaff, obedient as he may be, would surely draw the line there.

Kemp, Reie, and Jalam swung over the rail and plopped into the sodden sand below. After a few arduous steps, they made it to firmer ground. Above them, the charred hulk of Tarn Manor brooded.

"This way," Kemp said, guiding them up the slope and away from the shell.

"Where are your people?" Reie asked. "This place looks deserted."

She wasn't wrong; Berngoth had never been bustling, but the current emptiness was eerie. "I'm not sure, but I would venture a guess that we can find someone at the Lodge. It's up this way."

They reached a cracked and pitted boulevard, lined with a dreary procession of sagging mansions. One of them, on the northern stretch of the boulevard, was the Lodge. It had been Obed's private residence before his coup; with Tarn Manor ruined, it was the logical place for his usurping brother to still reside.

As they walked, their footsteps sounded muffled in the heavy, damp air. Kemp was surprised that he found the mugginess so uncomfortable. He supposed that he'd grown quite accustomed to the dry heat of Quaretem, or perhaps the newly-arrived cloud ceiling had intensified the clammy dankness. Either way, he felt like he was moving sluggishly, the air itself dragging against him, stifling his momentum. Behind him, Reie loosed a melancholy sigh.

"What's wrong?" Jalam asked.

"I can see this place as it was. I remember the carriages carrying the nobles, the handsome steeds. The hounds following their masters, tails wagging. I remember the smell of the blooming willows and the touch of the breeze coming across the lake. The last time I was here, Ganachim was with me, and her splendor was everywhere. Now look at it."

On their left, a waterlogged cemetery now dominated their view. Broken crypts leaned drunkenly, their treasures looted long ago, the chaff of their defiled occupants scattered across the soggy ground. All across the field, coffins jutted crookedly from the mire, forced into the open air by the saturation of the earth that had once held them. It was a view that Kemp had been expecting. Lost in the labyrinth of his own recollections, he hadn't been thinking about how much deeper Reie's memories went. For a moment, all of the follies that he'd spent a lifetime lamenting felt infinitely childish, dwarfed as they were by the abyssal sadness of the elder being beside him.

His little sorrows might be insignificant to a god, but he'd tended them nonetheless. There would be time enough to examine his mortal shortcomings when his work was finished. Beyond the cemetery, the Lodge awaited. With grim determination he—

—mounted the steps of the grand staircase. Behind him, Obed was ordering him to stop. Kemp wasn't looking, instead focused on the gallery above, his thoughts boring through the closed door to the solar. He thought he heard Blythe cry out, and his footsteps quickened. Retlow must have lunged for Obed, because his brother suddenly shrieked for the guards.

Sentries streamed into the main hall, men that Kemp had considered his. They converged on Retlow and rushed up the staircase behind Kemp. He was almost at the landing when the first blow knocked his feet out from under him. He landed heavily, tumbling down a few steps before he was able to twist around and face his attacker. The sentry held a short sword above his head, one of the rusted remnants of the old days that the guards had always carried and rarely used. He was poised to bring it down on the man he'd sworn to serve. Before he could, Kemp booted him in the chest, sending him flying into the men ascending behind him. Pain erupted in Kemp's right leg, the sentry's initial attack having left a long gash across his calf. If the blade had been sharper, it might have taken his leg off.

He hoisted himself to his feet in time to meet his next three attackers. He still held his club and his hatchet, an implement of the hunt far better maintained than the ceremonial swords of the sentries. Its keen edge had tasted blood often. In Kemp's blooming wrath, it would soon taste more.

Kemp buried his hatchet into the first man's collarbone, then swung his club into the chin of the second. The third man tried to stab Kemp in the gut, but he forced the body of the sentry stuck to his hatchet in between them. The weight of the dying man shifted before him and suddenly he was falling. The tangled combatants toppled down the steps, taking more sentries with them. A flash of white in Kemp's vision announced that he'd reached the bottom, slamming the back of his head against the floor in the process. A horrific wail filled the main hall, and, dazed as he was, Kemp thought it was Blythe crying out again.

The panicked screams around him cleared his mind. He scrambled to his feet, yanking his hatchet free. The sentries around him had momentarily forgotten about trying to kill him. A shade was slithering free from the body of a sentry felled by Retlow, who had put the hearth between himself and the growing monster. Kemp's valet was drenched in blood; he was clutching a sword recovered from one of his attackers, his teeth bared in a feral grimace.

One of the dead men at Kemp's feet began to shudder violently and the sentries scattered. Some rushed to the hearth, snatching burning branches from the pit it surrounded. Their instinct to expel the shades eclipsed their new master's orders. Kemp took advantage of the distraction, scanning the chaos for Obed. He spotted his brother, crouching behind the throne of antlers.

For a moment, Kemp forgot about his wife and child. He forgot about his own safety and the risk to everyone that the shades posed. His world narrowed to his cowering, traitorous brother. He stalked toward him, but the bulk of the fully formed shade slid between them. Deftly, Kemp returned his weapons to his belt and plucked two burning branches from the fire. He swung them wildly at the creature, which emitted a squealing hiss and squirmed out of his way. He spotted Obed again, just as he began to scamper away from his hiding spot. Without a second thought, Kemp launched the makeshift torches after him.

The first struck the throne of antlers and, spraying sparks, clattered onto the seat, where the fire hungrily erupted across the dry wood. The second sailed over Obed's ducked head and crashed through the window. Unhurt, he spared a glance for the burning throne, then slipped through a side door and disappeared into the hallway beyond. Consumed by the hunt, Kemp raced after him, limping on his wounded leg.

Obed ducked through the scullery and burst through the servant's door there, escaping into the yard. The door bounced back on its frame and shut as Kemp reached it. He threw himself against—

—the door was ajar.

Kemp hovered on the threshold, his hand partially extended. He licked his lips and, looking back toward Reie and Jalam, forced a smile. Fueled by his own false bravado, he nudged the door open fully and stepped inside.

Immediately, he was hit with the sour stench of filth. Behind him, Jalam coughed.

"I don't think we're going to find any fresh victuals in here," he wheezed. Beside him, Reie's lips were pressed into a thin line, but she seemed otherwise unaffected. She nodded Kemp on, and he sensed that she somehow knew this detour had nothing to do with food and water.

The three of them crept into the shadowed foyer of the decaying manor. A mildewed runner under their feet silenced their footfalls. To their right, a grand staircase rose to nothing, the upper level having sloughed off the structure, collapsing in a rotten heap around the base of the staircase. Narrow beams of dim light filtered in through the countless cracks and holes in the sagging roof.

Kemp had played in the Lodge as a boy, when his aunt had occupied it. When Obed had taken up residency there, it had continued to be a place of escape. If Tarn Manor had been the seat of governance, then the Lodge had been his family's retreat. They'd stood almost within view of each other, but the distinction in function had been clear. He knew the mansion as well as he'd known Tarn, and it did not surprise him when he heard voices coming from the parlor, the best-preserved room in the place. If Obed was anywhere, it would be there.

Once again, the door was ajar. This time, Kemp did not hesitate. Gripping his hatchet, he shouldered the door open. At once, six cadaverous faces turned toward him, their shock and fear apparent. He did not recognize any of them. The foul odor was nearly overpowering now, emanating from the squalid occupants of the room. Behind him, Jalam gagged and spat. Reie touched his arm gently, and, looking at the huddled wretches before him, Kemp lowered his weapon.

He'd found what he'd been looking for.

CHAPTER 29

The version of Obed that populated Kemp's darkest memories was a shifting phantom. It was born of his childhood affections, mingled with recollections of the brother he'd grown into adulthood with, a man he'd loved and trusted. It was also soiled by the knowledge of what that man had done. Despite these fluctuations, the look of the man was always the same. Obed in his prime; a tall, lanky man with a hard, angular face, framed by curtains of black hair. A neat goatee, a high-collared formal shirt. Obed had loved the history of their people and treasured their family's lineage, doing everything he could to emulate the look of the long-dead subjects of the surviving portraits hanging in their halls.

What remained of Obed now was nestled in a heap of dirty blankets, surrounded by his last emaciated attendants. When Kemp had left, his brother had been a hale young man. Now, he was a withered husk, aged beyond his time by whatever ravages had befallen him during Kemp's absence. His goatee had become a coarse, yellowed beard clinging to sunken cheeks. The formal clothes of his youth had been abandoned in favor of a loose-fitting sark, within which his wasted frame swam, his narrow chest rising and falling with each labored breath. His hairline had receded and his fingernails had grown into dirty claws. Beneath darkened lids, his eyes moved fretfully.

Despite all of his degradation, Kemp could still see the man who'd haunted his dreams. Somehow, pity stirred within him. "Do you know who I am?" he asked, but Obed did not answer.

"No," a sunken-mouthed crone said after a moment. She was crouched beside Obed, and she rose with obvious effort, pointing a gnarled finger at Reie. "What sorcery is this creature before us?" The light of Reie's halo shone in her rheumy eyes.

"Worry not about her," Kemp said. "Your rightful duke addresses you."

The crone cackled. "My 'rightful duke' is lying right there, gasping out his last."

"No, he is only a usurper. I am Duke Henrick."

"Ah," the crone said quietly. Behind her, the other attendants murmured. "Of course. It has been a long time, forgive me. Nobody thought you'd ever return, not after what you did."

"Obed's accusations were lies."

"Of course," she repeated. "Yet none looked for your return."

"Well, it seems you have not fared so well under Obed's leadership."

The crone faltered. "Well, no, not now. We did for a time, though. Duke Obed opened the land for us all; we trapped and hunted to our heart's content."

Kemp smile humorlessly. "He never did pay any mind when our lessons turned to trapping. He allowed the lands to be depleted, didn't he? His *generosity* became your starvation."

"Aye, it did. He was a fool in the end."

"Are you here all that's left?"

"Aye," she said again. "Some left in search of better lands. Many starved. Others turned to a rather distasteful form of scavenging. The shades took the rest."

Kemp tensed. Berngoth's fetid air had felt oppressive, its streets and homes eerily deserted. Now, the silence that permeated the place seemed pregnant with malice. Obed and his last followers had completely lost control, and untold numbers of shades could be roaming freely anywhere. Kemp looked back at Reie; her expression mirrored his feelings. They could not risk staying much longer.

"Face me, brother," Kemp said, pushing past the crone and kneeling beside Obed. The other attendants shrank away, powerless to intervene in whatever came next. "Wake up and look at me! I wish to talk with you!"

Obed's lids rose and his eyes found Kemp's. Some small jolt of vitality seemed to have passed through him, and Kemp sensed that Reie had given him just enough of her power to wake him up. He smacked his lips and took a shuddering breath, his eyes searching the face before him.

"Henrick?" he croaked with dawning disbelief.

The many versions of this confrontation that had festered in Kemp's imagination during his long exile now jockeyed for supremacy in his mind. "Yes," he nearly whispered. His fantasy had become reality, and it was all he could manage to say.

"Often have I seen your face. All the more as we fell into ruin. Every time I close my eyes, you are there. And now, my eyes are open, and here you are. Are you real?"

"I'm afraid so, brother. I've come back to settle things."

Obed lifted his gangly arms in a gesture of welcoming. "There is nothing I can do to stop you."

Kemp paused, the weight of the question he meant to ask pressing down on him so heavily that he could scarcely breathe. Worse yet, he thought he already knew the answer. "Did they survive the fire?"

Obed shook his head very slowly, and a single tear streaked his grimy face. "I'm sorry. I'm—

—who they want!" Obed shouted into his face, blood spraying from his mouth. "Only I can restore Berngoth to its old glory! You're nothing but an idiot brute!"

Kemp slammed his fist into Obed's mouth again, knocking a tooth out in a messy gush of blood. His blind fury had driven the pain of his injured leg from his mind, and he'd charged across the yard after his craven brother. He'd tackled Obed and, forgoing his weapons in favor of a prolonged beating, commenced to raining blows onto his head as he straddled him.

Obed's eyes rolled back for a moment, and he laughed crazily. "My point exactly."

"How could you do this to me?" Kemp demanded, seizing Obed by the collar. "My brother! How could—"

He fell silent as he noticed the orange glow flickering across Obed's face. His brother's broken mouth spread into a crimson grin. "You ought to have been more careful. It appears that the fire you started has spread."

Kemp had allowed his world to narrow until it was comprised of nothing but Obed beneath him; now it rapidly expanded, revealing his terrible mistake. He whirled around to face Tarn Manor, his home, where Taiyonna and Blythe had become captives, crying for him to rescue them. The mansion was now an inferno. A smattering of sentries stood outside of it, the flames casting their long shadows across the yard. Nobody was trying to put out the fire; the dry-rotted wood burned too quickly, too fiercely. The licking flames were punctuated by shrieks coming from within. Human or shade, it wasn't clear; trapped in searing agony they sounded the same.

"You let them burn," Obed crowed. "You let them burn just to beat me."

"No," Kemp said, disbelieving. "They must have gotten out, they had to—

As if in rebuttal, the upper floor, where the solar was, collapsed in a seething cloud of flames and smoke. A hot gust of air buffeted Kemp, and he nearly collapsed beside Obed. He staggered a few steps toward the blaze, his hopes strangled by the hideous reality before him. Dimly, he became aware of a gathering crowd. The people—his people—had come to witness his ruin.

"Look at your duke!" Obed cried out behind him. Kemp turned to see that his brother had managed to get back up, and he was now addressing the crowd. "Overweening pride. Self-indulgence. He's never cared for any of you, only for chasing his own desires. He's neglected you all. You scrape by while he dithers away his time, sporting, feasting, and ignoring you. Ignoring his own family. And in his shunning, he has allowed perverse jealousies to bloom in his heart. He has accused me of taking Taiyonna from him, of siring Blythe. And in this fit of madness, he has tried to murder me. He has set fire to his own home, the pride of our ancestors, so that he might snuff out his own wife and child."

Horrified gasps passed through the crowd. Kemp felt as if he was trapped within an unspooling nightmare. Nothing that was happening could be real.

"He would not believe them, so he locked them inside and condemned them to the flames. I couldn't save them," Obed said. His feigned sorrow was a warped reflection of Kemp's actual anguish, and the impossibility of the situation washed over him again.

"I barely saved myself," Obed continued, gesturing toward his bloodied face. "But now his sins have been laid bare. You can all see him for what he really is. We cannot allow this atrocity to stand. I can lead us, just as I've always tried my best to do, if only we bring this murderer to justice and end his reign. What say you?"

The murmurs of the crowd grew from shock and sorrow to anger and hatred. Kemp watched as the people chose to believe what they wanted to believe. His denials, his desire to explain the truth, they died on his lips. In one regard, Obed had been right, and that was enough to damn him now. He had been aloof and disinterested in the affairs of his people. Obed had always been there to answer their needs; they trusted him, they liked him. It was easy for them to believe his words, to believe that Kemp had done all he was accused of, because doing so would eliminate him. It would give the people a path toward the future they wanted. The past was burning down; Obed's ascension was now complete.

The crowd began to move in toward him. The sentries by the burning wreck advanced as well, their shadows bobbing over the weedy ground. Retlow was gone. Obed stood triumphant, his arms held aloft, the people his to command. Kemp looked toward what remained of his home. He considered racing toward the fire, clambering inside in a final bid to rescue his wife and daughter. In the end, he decided that he could only rescue himself.

Spying a gap in the closing noose, he broke for the lagoon, where the Tinpot *remained as his only chance to escape. He—*

—stood up, taken aback by Obed's penitence. He'd been expecting to finish the fight that his brother had started, not to hear the confessions of a confused invalid. Obed was now babbling profusely, weeping through a tangled mess of apologies. Once again, Kemp was surprised to find that he felt pity for the miserable creature that Obed had become.

In a way, he supposed it was a creature of his own making. After all, he had been complicit in their father's treatment of Obed. He had never been abused, but he'd always been shunted aside, disregarded as a spare. Where their father had spent ample time tutoring him, he'd only ever expressed a cursory interest in Obed. Perhaps their father had blamed Obed for the death of their mother. Though he'd never said as much, Kemp, who barely remembered his mother, had always suspected that to be the case.

Kemp knew that, although he'd loved his brother, he'd blithely ignored his pain, having convinced himself that Obed was happy being in a position of servility. He had been free to enjoy the benefits of the dukedom while his docile brother had handled the boring, trivial, and irksome problems of the people. It should have come as no surprise that a cankerous resentment had grown in Obed. He had been master of Berngoth in all but name.

Yet the failure of Berngoth now proved that he'd been less fit to rule than he'd imagined. And that insidious belief in his own superiority had cost Taiyonna and Blythe their lives. Kemp knew that he carried much of the blame for that, but not all of it.

"Stop," he said, looking down at Obed. His sobs had been wracking his frail body, and even his attendants had backed away, apparently disturbed by the mental collapse of their dying leader. "That's enough, stop."

At Kemp's command, Obed's cries tapered off into hitching breaths. After a moment, he sniffled wetly and looked up.

"Mercy?"

"You want *mercy*?" Kemp asked, his old rage rekindling. "You tasked underlings with my murder. You slandered my name and seized my birthright. You caused my—my family—my beautiful child, the woman I loved—*I would have never lost them if you hadn't betrayed me*! I have spent every moment of my life since then running from what I've done, what you *caused* me to do. And not just to them, as you well know. You turned me into what I am. You made me lose everything. My choices have condemned me, yes, but *you* forced me to make them. So, you ask for mercy? No, I have no mercy for you, pitiful as you've become. I bring only justice."

Kemp lifted his weapons from his belt, and Obed closed his eyes. The attendants must have known it was over. Led by the crone, they scurried away from their duke, slipping through one of the narrow, broken windows that flanked the room's sooty fireplace and disappearing into the gloom outside. Kemp paid them no mind. He stood over his brother, his heartbeat thudding in his ears, ears that still echoed with the screams that had come from within the flames. Obed's lips moved soundlessly, and his eyes remained closed. Kemp considered saying something else, but no words seemed capable of conveying his pain. There was only one thing left to do now.

Suddenly, a hand grasped his arm and turned him. Reie was at his side.

"You speak of bringing this man to justice. It seems that he is already imprisoned within the failing machinery of his mind. I know not all that has passed between the two of you, but I know *you*, Henrick. Whatever you did, there is goodness in you. Otherwise, you would not have joined me. I believe that I understand the drive that caused you to forsake Lakna, to embark on this journey. And I gather why you needed to stop here along the way. The shame of failing to act, the burden of deserting those you love; these are things that I know. There are stains upon my soul as well. So, you can do what you came here to do, or I can heal this man and his followers, to join us or to go their own way. I leave this decision to you, and I will support you whatever you choose."

Kemp stared at her, lost in the divine mystery of her gaze. For a moment, everything else faded into the background; Obed and Jalam were gone, as was the parlor itself. Kemp stood upon the plains of time, facing an unfathomable being whose existence was beyond his capacity to comprehend, whose expansive lifetime of experiences, good and bad, far exceeded his own. But, somehow, it now walked with him, and offered its acceptance with no strings attached. It was strangely freeing and terrifying at the same time. He wanted to make the right choice.

Reie's hand lifted away and Kemp was back in the parlor, his nostrils filled with the feculent stench of his brother's ruin. He looked down at Obed, who seemed to be slipping back into unconsciousness. The small boost that Reie had given him had already started to ebb. Kemp took a long, slow breath and closed his eyes.

He could see Taiyonna, her emerald eyes, the spill of her flaxen hair, impossibly straight and smooth. The beauty of her lips parting in a smile. The small birthmark on her neck; a magnetic target for his kisses. He could see Blythe, the dusting of freckles across the bridge of her nose, her red curls bouncing as she ran. He could hear her squealing laughter. They were so close, and then a terrified scream from outside shattered the illusion. He opened his eyes and they were gone.

"Something's happening," Jalam said, drawing his saber and stepping close to them. As if in confirmation, another panicked cry sounded. "We need to go *now*."

Before Kemp could say anything, the crone suddenly reappeared at the window.

"Help me!" she begged, her dirty hands clutching the window frame, the loose skin of her thin arms waggling. "*Help—*"

The bulk of a shade blotted out the light behind her and, in one swift motion, tore her away. She loosed a ragged scream that ceased abruptly, and then the shade was pressing into the frame, groping inside with its long fingers.

"Come on!" Jalam cried, and he actually grabbed Reie by the sleeve and yanked her toward the door.

Kemp remained rooted to the spot where he stood, his thoughts still stuck on the decision he'd been contemplating. The frame splintered as the shade forced its way through, spilling onto the floor with a heavy thud. As the shade began to rise, Kemp realized that it was too late. After everything he'd done to arrive at this spot, fate had taken the final choice out of his hands.

Reie had pulled free from Jalam and now grabbed Kemp. "Come, Henrick," she said, her voice insanely calm. He obeyed, staggering backward just as the shade stretched to its full height. It was a hoary beast, its flesh hardened into a cracked carapace, draped with moss and slime.

As Kemp turned to flee, he took one last look at Obed. His eyes were closed; he was totally unaware of what was happening. He—

—was grinning. His plan, however messily, had succeeded. The rabble, whipped into a bloodthirsty frenzy, might not have seen it, but Kemp did. His final glimpse of Obed was of his grinning face.

There was no longer any time to look. Kemp raced toward the shore, his pursuers closing in on him. One emerged from the glare of the fire to his left, approaching swiftly. It was plain that this attacker would easily intercept him.

"Duke Henrick!" the man shouted, and Kemp realized that it was Retlow. Hope bloomed momentarily, and withered just as quickly.

"My family?"

"I'm sorry, I couldn't reach them," Retlow said, breathing hard. "We have to go."

The brief waxing and waning of this new hope was somehow worse than the raw pain of the initial loss. It rent Kemp's heart into shreds, and it took everything he had in him to follow Retlow to the Tinpot. The two men slammed into the hull of the boat and heaved it forward with all their might. It slid across the wet grass and into the water, its bow spinning outward.

"Get in!" Retlow ordered as the first sentries reached them. Kemp flung himself over the side of the boat, the deck rocking beneath him as he tumbled onto it. He scrambled to his feet and seized one of the poles. Retlow had stepped into the water, where he'd stricken down one of the sentries and was fending off the second. Others would reach them in a moment.

"Come on!" Kemp shouted.

Retlow ran through the second man and pushed him away. As he waded in up to his waist, two more attackers splashed into the water behind him. The momentum of the Tinpot had carried it some distance, and Kemp halted it with the pole. "Come on!" he cried again.

Retlow engaged the two newcomers, thrashing wildly. In the flurry of foaming water, another fell. The other sentry lunged back toward shore, unmanned by the ferocity of Retlow's defense. Retlow turned and swam toward the Tinpot, where Kemp had extended the pole. He reached up and—

—the cemetery was now on their right. Dozens of shades were emerging from the field of broken crypts, drawn by the commotion. They slithered out of the sinking tombs and burst free from mossy hillocks where they'd been lingering in near-dormancy. Their eyeless heads bent toward the fleeing trio, and then they were moving again, loping after their prey. From back near the Lodge, the screams of Obed's last followers echoed through the damp air.

The route back to the *Tinpot* was fairly direct, but still Kemp led the way, with Reie behind him and Jalam serving as a rearguard. He was lagging behind, his head swiveling, his saber held at the ready. To Kemp, his watchful vigilance seemed unnecessary. Faced with the impending wave of shades, hasty retreat was the only option.

They ran past the final stretch of the cemetery's corroded wrought iron fence and the blackened shell of Tarn Manor came back into view. For the second time, Kemp found himself fleeing his ancestral home, with the *Tinpot* offering his only hope of survival. It was surreal.

Behind them, the shades reached the fence. Some climbed over it, tearing their oily flesh on the decorative spikes that ran along the top in the process. Older, hardier shades, more akin to the one that had dispatched the crone, burst right through the rusted metal. All the while, they emitted a dreadful screeching. Kemp wished he could plant his hands over his ears, but he concentrated on running instead.

Rounding the front of the charred ruin, Kemp spotted the *Tinpot*. On the deck, Marbuck and Falstaff were standing, looking their way. Undoubtedly, they had heard the cacophony of the shades.

"*Shove off!*" Kemp screamed, waving his arms frantically.

At once, Marbuck and Falstaff sprang into motion, driving their poles into the silty bottom. The boat first lurched away from the beach, then pulled free of the bottom, gliding easily across the murky surface of the lagoon. Marbuck and Falstaff labored at the poles, attempting to halt the boat's movement before they drifted too far.

Reaching the shore, Kemp wasted no time with wading, instead leaping as far as he could and plunging headlong into the water, the chill of it hitting him like a punch to the gut. His dive was not graceful, and he floundered more than he swam, but he still managed to reach the *Tinpot*, where Falstaff helped pull him aboard. Panting, he turned around to help Reie, who'd jumped in after him. Though the soft glow of her halo remained undimmed, the rest of her condition struck Kemp as very human. Her curls were plastered to her cheeks, which were flushed from exertion and the cold water, and she was shivering. Her tunic, soaked as it was, clung to the curves of her body. Despite everything Kemp had been through, he felt a small tickle of amusement; Falstaff seemed incapable of looking at her, and his face was burning crimson.

The feeling didn't last long.

"Jalam," Reie said, wiping the water from her face.

Kemp's attention snapped back to the shoreline. He had been right behind them; now he was limping down the hill, a shade—

—exploded out of the shallow water, striking against the hull of the Tinpot. *The boat rocked violently and Kemp was sent sprawling, the pole clattering to the deck next to him. He clambered back to the rail, looking for Retlow. The newborn shade was whipping about, rising and falling as it formed.*

Through the misty plume it had sent up, Kemp spotted Retlow. He was tread-ing water, sputtering as each turbulent swell churned up by the shade's wild movements rolled over him. Kemp knew that he didn't dare call out; the sound would draw the shade to him. Instead, he fixed Kemp with a pleading look. Kemp was certain that if he could just maneuver the boat around the shade and back toward the shore, then he could reach Retlow. But on the shore, the sentries had now gathered, the newest arrivals bearing torches. The shade was solidifying, and a second was rumbling to life in the shallows nearby.

Kemp turned away from Retlow and poled the Tinpot *forward with all his might.*

"Henrick!" his loyal valet screamed, and his voice was condemnation. It was followed swiftly with the noise of the shade leaping upon him, and the guttural cries of a violent death.

Kemp did not look back until long after he had slipped into the labyrinth of the deep woods, the Tinpot *guided expertly between the sunken trees. With the bedlam that Obed's coup had unleashed, none had been able to follow him. If they were to try to track him later, none would succeed. He had escaped.*

In the silence of the lands he'd thought himself master of, Kemp fell upon his knees and wept bitterly, hysterically. He screamed until he was hoarse, pounding his fists against his own head and ripping out fistfuls of his hair. Finally he slumped into a near-catatonic state, his eyes staring fixedly into nothing. His brother had betrayed him; his people had rejected him. Taiy-onna was dead. Blythe was dead. Retlow was dead. Every person who he'd loved, and who'd loved him, was gone. And it was his fault. He'd abandoned them all, blinded by pride and in service of his own survival. His ruination was utterly complete.

After a long time, he rose. With no direction in mind, he—

—ordered the *Tinpot* brought back toward the shore. He could not risk beaching it completely, but he could get them closer. As the mariners guided them back in, Reie started toward the rail, looking as if she intend-ed to jump. Kemp pulled her back.

"I'll get him, you worry about healing his limp," he said, and then he was jumping back into the water. The chill was less of a shock this time, and being closer, it was a shorter swim. Kemp was stumbling onto the shore just as Jalam was approaching the water, his limp fading, but not gone. A hulking shade was now directly behind him, its arms extended.

Without hesitation, Kemp pulled his club free and flung it at the crea-ture. It sailed over Jalam and struck the shade in the head, causing it to flinch backward, its long arms seizing back reflexively. Kemp grabbed Jalam and half-carried, half-dragged him the rest of the way.

"Swim!" Kemp ordered as the two men splashed noisily into the water.

"I can't," Jalam said, and Kemp realized that, growing up near the water, and later having access to the Great Ziggurat's pools, he'd assumed that everyone could swim.

"Just do your best," Kemp said, and a moment later they were shambling awkwardly through the deeper water, the shade crashing in after them.

Just as they reached the point where they would have to swim, Kemp spotted the poles thrust out before them. He grabbed onto one and helped guide Jalam to the other. Holding on, they were pulled toward the *Tinpot*, and then hands were grabbing them and hauling them aboard. The roar of countless shades charging into the water behind them was almost deafening.

"*Go! Go! Go!*" Kemp shouted, seizing one of the poles from the deck. Falstaff grabbed the other and they set to work with mad intensity.

A single, slime-coated hand rose from the water and grasped the stern rail. The first shade had reached them. As it tried to hoist itself up, the entire boat tipped upward at the bow, dumping Kemp onto his back.

"Get it off!" he screamed.

Marbuck slid down the tilted deck until she reached the stern, where she planted her boots on the rail, the shade's hand between her feet. She drew her blade and slammed it down. To Kemp's astonishment, her attack severed the hand easily, and, in a gout of black blood, the arm receded. The bow dropped with a tremendous splash, and the boat wobbled drunkenly for a moment. Then, Kemp and Falstaff were back at the poles.

Soon, they'd reached a depth where the submerged shades could not reach them, and a speed that left them behind. As Kemp had so long ago, he guided the *Tinpot* into the old growth. This time, he looked back. The pain was still there, but it was different, and that was enough.

●　●　●

"So, I can't help but notice that you didn't come back with any fresh supplies."

Marbuck stood before Kemp, her hands planted defiantly on her hips. He felt irritation flare, but he was too spent to really engage with her. Reie had given what she could, but even she had felt the strain of their escape.

The five travelers had decided to rest, and they were in the process of settling on the deck of the *Tinpot*, which floated peacefully in an open stretch of water.

"Well, no, unfortunately I did not," Kemp said, swatting some midges away. "My people's community collapsed during my absence."

"I'm sorry to hear that," Marbuck said without a hint of sympathy. "Will there be any more unexpected detours to your old stomping grounds?"

"Fishwife," Falstaff said, trying to nudge her away.

Marbuck ignored him. "Any other mystery visits that might get us all killed?"

"This journey belongs to us all," Reie said to Marbuck, and her voice had taken on an imperious edge. "We all know what you seek, and we wish to see your hopes fulfilled, but that does not mean that you and your purpose dictate every decision that we make. Henrick felt it necessary to stop here, whatever the reason. Nobody was harmed; it is done. I'm certain that there will be no further delays, but not on account of your demands."

Marbuck stared at the god, her jaw clenched, flush seeping up her face. Reie turned to Kemp. "What say you, Henrick?"

"Uh, yes—no more delays."

Reie held her hands up to Marbuck, her eyebrows raised.

"Fair enough," Marbuck said through her teeth.

"And while we're on the subject of mysteries, I'm curious about that sword of yours. How is it that it was able to hurt the shade?"

A look of unease descended over Marbuck. "It's a relic of my people," she said vaguely. "There are others like it. It's how we fight off the shades, how we destroy them."

"Destroy them?" Kemp said. As long as he'd lived, he'd never heard of a shade being seriously injured, much less destroyed.

"Yes," Marbuck confirmed.

"Interesting," Reie said. A distant expression settled on her face, and they lapsed into silence. Marbuck shifted on her feet. Suddenly, Reie came back to them with a tight smile. "It will prove to be quite useful, I'm sure. Henrick, a moment?"

"Of course," Kemp said, feeling like he was missing something.

The two of them proceeded to the relative privacy of the stern, behind the pilothouse.

"I cannot claim to know of everything that transpired in your past, but I have learned much during our stop. I sense that you wish to keep the details private?" Reie said quietly.

Kemp nodded. "Yes."

"It is your history, and your tale to tell. I will speak nothing of it. And you needn't worry about Jalam; he will remain silent if I bid him to do so. Plus, I think he's too grateful and embarrassed by your rescue of him to say anything." Reie smiled again, and this time it was warm. It made Kemp smile, too.

"Bear this in mind, Henrick," she continued. "We cannot change our past, but we can always change our future."

Reie touched his arm lightly and walked away to join Jalam near the bow. Temporarily alone, or as alone as he could be on the small boat, Kemp leaned against the rail and gazed out at the shadowed boughs of the hanging willows that surrounded them. He took a deep breath.

It was not redemption that he felt, but more a small sense of closure. In that moment, he chose to believe Reie. His future *could* take a new direction, and already had.

Now it was time to help Reie change the future for them all.

CHAPTER 30

When the *Tinpot* slid to a stop for the last time, Marbuck was happy to leave it behind. She hadn't enjoyed taking orders from Kemp, or being subject to his whims. His unplanned stop had nearly cost them dearly; had Reie been lost, all hope of making it back to Nordabor would have been lost with her. Worse yet, Reie flippantly dismissed how close they'd come to disaster, and had even jumped to Kemp's defense. Whatever experience they'd shared, it was apparently none of her business, despite the fact that they'd been gambling with her life, too. Even Jalam, who'd never seemed to like Kemp, remained silent about what had occurred. It was vexing.

In any case, it was over, and Marbuck had been assured that there would be no further distractions. She didn't put much weight into that promise, but she didn't have any other options either. For better or for worse, she was stuck with Reie. At least until she got to Elibeth. But that was a thorny problem for another time. Similarly, she remained steadfast in her decision to keep the origins of her anointed blade a secret. She was on shaky ground with Reie already; she did not want to risk raising the god's ire by revealing just how complacent she'd been in the bloodletting of Ganachim.

Ultimately, the journey through Berngoth had culminated in an unpleasant feeling of separation from the others, including Falstaff, who clearly disapproved of her behavior. As such, leaving the *Tinpot* and the miserable bog behind would be a welcome change; a chance to reset their dynamic, not to mention an escape from the stifling humidity, laborious poling, and ever-present midges.

The waters had been growing increasingly shallow for some time, forcing them to muscle the vessel over numerous shoals. Now, they'd finally reached a point where the fen had fully given way to a tract of spongy turf, sloping up and out of the dwindling woodland. It was clear that it was time to abandon the *Tinpot*. Kemp was the last one to disembark, and he looked reverently at the boat before joining the others on a nearby hummock.

"From here on out, my knowledge of the land dims a bit," he announced as he reached them. "Rarely did I ever come this far north in my hunts, and I always approached from the east or west. Still, it shouldn't be too difficult to get us through the last gasp of the mountains."

"Yes, the northern arm of the Yewhia range was the most eroded, from what I can recall," Reie said. "Shielding Berngoth from the brunt of the devastation could have only worn them down further."

"And just beyond lies the World's Wound," Kemp said. "I've only ever seen it once before; a damned eerie sight. Once we get there, a route through will be anyone's guess, but I'll do my best to find us a path."

"Thank you, Henrick," Reie said, and she extended one hand before them. "After you."

The travelers began to trudge across the soft, wet ground, leaving the last of the trees behind. Gradually, the land sloped upward, becoming increasingly firm as the valley ended in a series of barren downs, punctuated by weathered hilltops. Marbuck thought that the term 'mountain' had been applied quite liberally here. Spied from afar when they'd first entered the valley, the northern stretch of the Yewhia Mountains had looked like a more substantial challenge. Now, wandering within the ranks of the ancient, rolling hills, she found that they barely constituted a brisk hike. It would have been almost pleasant if it hadn't left her free to consider what lay ahead.

The problem of climbing down into, and crossing, the horizon-spanning crater had been temporarily set aside in the face of more immediate concerns. Now they were nearly there, and their plan to cross it consisted of nothing more than cautious optimism that such a feat was even possible. It did not leave Marbuck feeling particularly confident.

As usual, Falstaff did not seem overly concerned. He and Marbuck had once again fallen behind, bringing up the rear of their small, staggered procession, and he was quietly humming to himself, gazing at their surroundings. Marbuck was distracting herself by attempting to recognize the tune, some frivolous ballad popular with the bards who haunted the dockside taverns of Nordabor, when Falstaff suddenly spoke.

"It's beautiful here, in a desolate sort of way, you know?"

"If you say so."

"Sights we were never meant to see, yet here we are."

"Here we are," Marbuck said, echoing the words if not the sentiment.

Falstaff easily detected her bitterness. "I know we got thrown into all this, and there's been a lot of misery, but there have been moments of goodness too. Incredible things way beyond what we could have imagined. Certainly beyond anything I ever imagined." He looked up ahead at Reie, and Marbuck's scar itched. She said nothing.

"You're going to have quite the tale for Elibeth when we get back," Falstaff continued.

"I'll try to skim over the parts where I was tortured," she said, and the vitriol in her voice surprised even her.

"I'm—I'm sorry, Raina," Falstaff said, and his contrition was so sincere that Marbuck felt instant shame.

"No, I'm sorry. I shouldn't have lashed out at you. I just—I don't know. It's like a constant pain, not being with her. A wound that won't heal, that *can't* be healed until I reach her and make sure she's okay. I never should have left. Everything we've been through? For me, it's all been to get back, that's it. I don't see anything in it but obstacles in my way."

Falstaff nodded. "I get it, as much as anyone who isn't a parent can, I suppose. And you didn't do anything wrong, shipping out with us. You just wanted to provide for her, to help her. Doing whatever you can to help those you care about is completely understandable." He looked toward Reie again.

"Is this the part where you lecture me about lying to her?" Marbuck said quietly. The others were far enough away that she was confident that her voice wouldn't reach them, but she wasn't taking any chances.

"You will go your own way, there's nothing I can say to change that. But once we get you to Elibeth, I plan on staying with Reie and seeing this through."

"And how do you intend to do that?"

"I'm going to follow through on your supposed plan and talk to Rayburn. Winslow was chummy with him, I'm sure he'll let me bend his ear."

"*I'm* sure that he's dead. He was with the expedition. Whatever they did up there was catastrophic enough to break the sky. I can't imagine that anyone came back from something like that."

"Well, maybe your lack of imagination is the problem."

Marbuck sighed. "Even if he was alive, and even if he did manage to get you an audience with Phar-Mindorius, the king would never let Ganachim go. He'd just try to imprison Reie. With both of them, he might actually be able to save Nordabor."

"Well, I've got to try. We're going to save a lot more than Nordabor if we can free Ganachim."

"I suppose you mean Quaretem."

"Those people are victims in all of this as much as we are. They are Setenrah's slaves, whether they think they're free or not. And if we don't succeed, if we don't come back and liberate them, they will all perish. Mothers and children included. When you're reunited with your own child, when your nightmare is over, will you really be able to walk away with no regard for those just like you? You would be okay condemning them all to death, because of—of what? A grudge? They were doing the only thing they knew how to do to survive."

"I thought you weren't going to lecture me."

Falstaff scoffed and shook his head. "Fine, I'm done."

"Look, whatever happens to them happens. I can't worry about that right now. My focus is on getting Elibeth and getting as far away from all of this as possible."

"Where will you go? How will you survive?"

"We'll find a way."

"Reie is the only way."

Marbuck smiled humorlessly. "What was that about lacking imagination?"

"Forget it," Falstaff said, and he quickened his pace, leaving her behind.

She felt a fierce satisfaction, but it dissolved quickly. She was tired of being at odds with Falstaff, and there was no victory in driving that particular wedge further. The worst part was that in moments of quiet reflection, when she was free to wander the corridors of her own mind, she saw a frank and ugly truth. She knew that everything he'd said was correct. She would have said anything to secure Reie's help, but her refusal to even try to keep her word was looking increasingly callous and spiteful. Reie had been part of Setenrah's arrangement, but she was not its architect, she was its thrall. Marbuck knew that she could help to topple that corrupt system, or, after she'd achieved her ends, she could simply walk away.

Marbuck looked ahead toward Falstaff, who was drawing nearer to Reie and Jalam, and silently cursed him for his uncompromising goodness.

It had taken root in her subconscious. The right thing to do and what she wanted to do were diametrically opposed, and she knew it.

She wondered, when the time came, which she would choose.

• • •

As they walked on, they passed the first evidence of the calamity that had created the World's Wound. The ground was now totally sterile, stripped of any lingering vegetation. In its stead, countless fragments of glass crunched beneath their feet. It littered every stretch of flat earth, and was gathered in thick drifts in the eaves of every outcropping of the worn hills. Reie surmised that it was a result of the extremely high temperatures generated by the explosion, and explained that for a long time after the blast, everything around the crater had been blanketed in a toxic, super-heated death cloud. Marbuck tried to picture a roiling plume of smoke and fire filling the entire sky and consuming the surrounding hills, and found that she couldn't do it.

She was unprepared for the utter annihilation displayed by the crater itself.

The gentle rise of the hills ended suddenly in a wall of pushed up and buckled stones, pointing crookedly skyward. The pressure ridge stretched east and west as far as they could see.

"We're here," Kemp said. "I'll see if I can scout out a path."

He commenced to scrambling up the rugged wall, leaving the others to watch from below.

"This is the crater's rim," Reie said. "The furthest reach of whatever power shattered Gana."

"Do you have any idea what it was that did this?" Falstaff asked.

"I cannot know for certain, but I suspect that only Alminnian would have been capable of such power. Based on the scale of the destruction, I am certain that Vingallea's southern kingdom was his target, especially now that I know that Nordabor and the rest of the north were spared."

"That fits with the assumptions made by our explorers when they first discovered the crater," Marbuck said.

"Why would Alminnian have targeted just the southern kingdom?" Falstaff asked. "Why not all of Vingallea?"

"If he'd wished to destroy all of Vingallea, then he would have been forced to destroy everything. By the time of the war, Vingallea had extended its reach into all lands. While I don't doubt that Alminnian could have done so, I doubt he would have wanted to. From what I understood of his stance, distant and aloof as he was, he wished for a peaceful return to his normal system. He might have targeted only the southern kingdom as a symbolic act. It was Vingallea's original homeland, after all. He might have thought that doing so would force Vingallea to capitulate. I can't say for sure though; his thoughts on the war were only ever communicated to us by Nuroh."

Falstaff nodded gamely, though Marbuck was certain that some of the specifics were lost on him.

A few short-cycles later and Kemp had reached the top. He slipped in and out of view as he examined the tumbled wreck of stones that comprised the apex of the wall. Finally, he deftly navigated his way back down and, reaching them, announced that he had found a viable path into the crater.

"That simple, eh?" Marbuck said.

"It is a massive space, don't get me wrong, but it's the sheer size of it that actually helps. Steep as it is, it's all made up of large, scalable rocks, just like this," Kemp said, patting the jumbled wall behind him. "At least as far down as I could see. Plus, it looks like it starts to level out the lower you get. I think it's definitely climbable."

"Excellent," Reie said.

"Bear in mind, we're not all experts like you," Marbuck said. Fear had started to spread its black wings in her mind; she'd never climbed anything greater than the mountain passes they'd previously come through.

"If Henrick says that it is climbable, then it is climbable," Jalam said. He nodded to Kemp, who'd hoisted his eyebrows up a degree. "Show us the way."

"Of course," Kemp said, a small smile turning up the ends of his moustache.

The two men proceeded up, and Marbuck watched them go. "I guess everyone loves our resident huntsman now," she observed sardonically.

"It has been hard-won for him," Reie said. "And if you can let go of your anger, he might win you over, too."

Before Marbuck could respond, Reie followed after the men.

"She's right, you know," Falstaff said, passing by Marbuck. This time, she chose not to respond, knowing that whatever she had to say would be foul.

Instead, she fell in behind Falstaff and began to follow the winding way up that Kemp had plotted out. With little difficulty, she crested the top of the pressure ridge and beheld the World's Wound for the first time.

Her eyes dutifully reported what they were seeing, but her mind refused to believe them. The entire horizon now consisted of the crater, its rim running off into haze in both directions and its far side lost over the breadth of its bottom. Had it not been for the uniformity of the tremendous bowl-like expanse, she would have thought it a canyon of impossible size. The fact that a living being had carved it out of the earth in a single cataclysmic blast made her feel infinitely small. Of course, that being was supposed to have created everything, a much more substantial feat, but one completed during the primordial beginning, predating even Reie. This was, relatively, far more recent, and stood as concrete evidence of the great powers that had been wielded in the cosmic struggle that had doomed their world.

"Like I said," Kemp murmured. "Damned eerie."

Marbuck looked at him, then at the others; they all seemed to be affected by the view in the same way that she was. Reie, especially, seemed hypnotized by the crater. Its creation had occurred during her long lifetime and, looking at it, her thoughts seemed to be lost in the foggy depths of time.

Turning her own gaze back toward the crater, Marbuck noticed that the cloud ceiling above them started to break toward the north. The crack in the sky was faintly visible. Long ago, the earth itself had been broken; now the sky had been, too. She shuddered, seized by a sudden and distinct certainty that time was running out.

Without speaking, the travelers began their descent.

CHAPTER 31

Their journey down the heaped boulders and loose scree of the crater's wall started with vertigo-inducing terror and morphed into backbreaking tedium. Hunched over, they picked their way from one stable outcropping to another, with Kemp carefully scouting ahead and doubling back to guide them. Backtracking was common, with many routes terminating suddenly in sheer drop-offs.

Exhaustion and body aches drove Marbuck's fear away. Spending most of her time focusing on the footing directly beneath her, she did not look out at the enormity of the open nothingness around her. That was good, as the few times she was forced to notice it, she felt like the empty air was somehow pulling at her, threatening to peel her off the wall. It was in these moments that she was grateful that Reie was doing little to stave off their weariness, saving her power for a time when it might be truly needed.

Such a time arrived in the form of a shifting handhold. Falstaff was just below Marbuck, bracing himself as he waited for Reie to finish passing through an unnervingly vertical stretch. It forced the climbers to wedge their fingers into a narrow gap between two stones and scoot down until their legs were dangling. Then, they had to let go and trust that they could keep their balance when they landed on a thin lip of stone below. Kemp and Jalam had already cleared the obstacle, and they were able to steady Reie as she dropped.

Falstaff looked up at Marbuck. "Remember what I said about moments of goodness? This isn't one of them." He flashed a shaky smile and crouched into the space. With a deep breath to steel himself, he fit his hands into the gap and began to shuffle downward. Marbuck watched him with a simmering dread, fearing both for his safety and for her own. After all, she was next.

When he'd lowered himself as far as he could, Falstaff froze.

"You've got to let go," Kemp said. "We'll catch you."

"I know," Falstaff said, but he remained still, one cheek pressed against the red rock.

"You're closer than you think," Jalam said.

Falstaff started to turn his head to look, and both men implored him not to.

Marbuck watched this unfold with her heart thudding against the inside of her ribs. Her mouth was dry, her hands were clammy, and she was beginning to lose touch with all sense of time again. It had been too long since she'd last slept, and it suddenly seemed reckless to be making the descent without getting any natural rest first, especially not while Reie was being stingy with her ministrations. All at once, her exhaustion no longer felt like a welcome distraction, but a dangerous liability.

When the rock she was leaning against moved, her wavering focus snapped back, igniting animal panic. As the rock tilted away from her, she wheeled her arms and fell backward, sliding briefly before catching a solid foothold. The rock continued its forward pitch until its vast weight finally carried it away.

"*Watch out!*" Marbuck screamed.

The thunderous crack of the massive stone crashing into the rocks below filled the air. As it tumbled, it tore loose other rocks and sent them tumbling down in a crushing cascade. Each echoing boom mingled with the new sounds of the descent, nearly drowning out the hysterical screams coming from just below Marbuck. She scrambled to the space previously occupied by the rock and peered down.

Falstaff was the source of the screaming. He still dangled from the wall, but now he was kicking against it, his crushed hands pinned in the cleft that had been pushed shut by the weight of the falling rock. Below, the left half of the ledge occupied by the other three was gone, and they were now huddled together on what remained. Relief mingled with guilt; they were all still alive, but they weren't through it yet. Marbuck's carelessness had placed Falstaff in extreme peril and total agony.

"We'll get you free!" she cried, scooting down as far as she could and groping for the edge of the rock. Her fingers found it, as well as Falstaff's shattered hands; he yelped as she bumped against them. She began to pull up on the rock with futile desperation, oblivious to her own body weight draped across it.

Below, Jalam had wedged himself into a tight crevice in the wall and wormed his way up. Kemp, standing with one foot braced against the wall and the other on Jalam's shoulder, could almost reach where Falstaff's hands were trapped in the vise of stone. He lifted his hatchet, and Falstaff's eyes widened as he saw it.

"No—please, please, please," he sputtered.

"We have to save his hands!" Reie called from below. "I can't heal them if they're lost completely."

Marbuck's useless tugging at the rock increased as she imagined Falstaff's arms ending in stumps. Tears blurred her vision as she pictured them; she could actually see the pink knots of scar tissue woven by Reie. Her own words haunted her. She'd derided Falstaff for emerging unscathed from their ordeal aboard the *Empress's Love*. Now, he faced an injury that would not only disfigure him, but one that would leave him permanently maimed. Her grief was extreme, and she screamed with rage as she pulled. The rock did not budge.

"Marbuck! Marbuck! *Look at me!*" Kemp was shouting. His words finally cut through her mania, and she looked at him.

"We need leverage, and you need to back up. You're on the rock."

Marbuck looked down and, realizing her error, clambered back. Kemp wedged the blade of his hatchet into the slim gap around Falstaff's hands and reached for where his club used to hang. His hand patted at nothing and realization dawned on his face.

"Grab me a stone," he said to Marbuck.

Looking around, she spotted a stone the size of her fist. She grabbed it and passed it down to Kemp, heedless of the danger of hanging over the edge. He turned it in his hand, seeking the grip most suitable for his need. Once found, he began to pound the stone against the head of the hatchet, driving it further into the gap. He then tapped the handle to the left, twisting the hatchet until the handle pointed straight out from the gap.

"Here we go," he said, tossing the stone away. "I'm going to lift the rock. Falstaff, you're going to fall as soon as your own weight pulls your hands free. Do you understand?"

Falstaff nodded shakily, but said nothing.

"Reie, be ready to catch him however you can."

"I'm ready."

"Let's go, I can't hold here much longer," Jalam said through gritted teeth.

Kemp grabbed the handle and drove it upward. His face purpled with the strain, and his breath came in hissing bursts. Beneath him, Jalam struggled to hold him aloft as his boot dug into his shoulder. Marbuck watched helplessly, wishing there was something she could do.

With a final burst of strength, Kemp muscled the hatchet just as far as it needed to go. The handle snapped with a loud crack, but Falstaff slipped free. With a gasp of surprise and pain, he fell, landing on top of Reie. The two of them collapsed into a heap, and for one horrifying moment it seemed as if they would both fall from the ledge, but they remained. Kemp reeled back, thrown off balance by the sudden break of the hatchet's handle. He wobbled precipitously before righting himself. He then wasted no time in scrambling down from Jalam's shoulders. As soon as he'd reached the ledge, he helped pull Jalam free of the crevice. Together, the two of them gathered around Falstaff and Reie.

Concern for her own safety had dissipated completely, and Marbuck swung over the edge. Grabbing the broken end of the handle still jutting from the gap, she lowered herself until she was dangling in the same spot that Falstaff had been.

"I'm coming down," she yelled.

"I've got you," Kemp said.

She let go, her stomach lurching briefly, and then her boots were on solid ground and Kemp's hands were on her back, steadying her. The lip of stone had barely enough space for them, and they huddled tightly around Reie, who was cradling Falstaff. The god's eyes were squeezed shut in concentration, and Falstaff was looking at his mangled hands with unabashed amazement. A soft, golden light enveloped them, and the bloody, torn skin encasing the pulverized bone seemed to ripple. The twisted and flattened fingers appeared to inflate and straighten themselves. Reie took a small, gasping breath; the light flared and then went out. Nobody spoke as Falstaff slowly moved his fingers. Aside from the smears of blood, there was no indication that they'd ever been injured.

Falstaff realized that he was still lying against Reie, and he scrambled to his feet. "You healed me completely," he said with a small laugh. "Incredible. Thank you."

"You can thank me by helping me up," she said, the weariness in her voice apparent.

"Of course," Falstaff said hurriedly, and he and Jalam helped her to her feet. Falstaff then hugged Jalam, whose eyes widened in surprise. "And thank you, my friend. And you, of course." Falstaff reached out and pulled an equally-surprised Kemp into the embrace. "You saved not just my hands, but my life. I am indebted to you both."

Marbuck breathed a shuddering sigh. As soon as Falstaff broke away from the others, she clasped his restored hands. "I'm sorry. I accidentally dislodged that rock. I was careless." Falstaff was shaking his head, but Marbuck went on anyway. "You could have been killed. Any one of you could have."

"It's fine, Fishwife. It was an accident, I'm fine."

"Do not mourn for tragedies that might have been," Reie said. "Everyone here has made mistakes. We must not bind ourselves to them—or keep them shackled on each other."

Marbuck was too relieved to resent the thinly-veiled lesson. In truth, she didn't really need it. She could have picked it apart, insisting that her accident was totally different from Kemp's duplicity, but she didn't care to. Her mistake had humbled her, and Kemp's actions had managed to blunt her deep-seated loathing of him. Villainous as his part in Quaretem had been, here, on the side of the World's Wound, he'd acted heroically. Marbuck was surprised to find that he'd risen in her esteem, though she'd never give him the satisfaction of knowing it. She did not wish to see his smug grin.

"Well, there was one tragedy," Kemp said, looking up at his broken hatchet.

"Take my axe," Falstaff said, reaching for it. "You're better suited for—"

"No, no. Keep it. I've still got a knife."

They each insisted for a time before Falstaff finally relented. Reie had watched the exchange with a tired smile, and now, seeing that the matter had been settled, she cleared her throat.

"Why don't we find a spot to rest?"

• • •

It'd taken longer to find a stable place to rest than any of them had wished, but eventually, they'd settled on a relatively flat outcropping just large enough to accommodate them all. After a long and dreamless slumber so deep that it'd felt like courting death, Marbuck had been shaken awake by Falstaff. He'd given her a single morsel of desiccated mushroom, and together, the travelers had consumed the last of their scant provisions. With renewed vigor, and reduced hostility, they'd continued their descent.

Falstaff's close call remained in the forefront of Marbuck's mind, thoroughly reigniting her fear of the climb. As they'd continued, though, it'd become clear that the worst was behind them. The sheer sides had gradually dropped away, turning into a rough slope comprised of pulverized chunks of stone. By Marbuck's estimate, roughly two full-cycles of climbing downward had passed before they'd found themselves walking on almost level ground. A dull slog across a final stretch of uneven terrain had finally brought them to the bottom of the crater.

The view from the top had been overwhelming in its enormity; the view at the bottom was uncanny in its surreal emptiness. The detritus of the ancient blast that had made up the walls of the crater was no longer present. Stretching out before them was a vast, silent plain of rough bitumen, painted intermittently by the dawn light breaking through the clouds. Featureless, it stretched away into forever. To Marbuck, it was as if the western sea that had once held her in its clutches had been turned to stone, and now held her again.

"Shouldn't be too hard to keep our bearings now," Kemp said, his voice sounding dull and flat in the still air. "Eventually, we'll reach the northern side. Then we get to climb *up* for a change." He smiled, though it didn't reach his eyes.

Jalam tapped a boot on the hard surface beneath them. "How is this so uniform? It is like a giant road."

"I imagine that the blast scoured this land down to its very foundations, melting whatever remained into this," Reie said. "I expect that it's all we'll be seeing until we reach the northern wall."

Marbuck started to formulate a guess of how long it was going to take for them to do that, but stopped. It was better that she didn't think too much about it.

Having no reason to tarry, they started across. The air seemed to grow staler as they went, carrying a faint smell of tar. Occasionally, Marbuck would glance back toward the southern wall. It never seemed to be any further away. The best thing that could be said about the walk was that it was not taxing. It was, however, maddeningly boring. Free from having to expend all of their mental energies on plotting out and navigating their way through hostile environments, they fell to talking about themselves to pass the time, swapping anecdotes about their pasts.

Unsurprisingly, Kemp was gregarious, though his stories carried more than a whiff of embellishment. He regaled them with tales of his exploits in the tangled morass of Berngoth, hunting boars larger than any man and capable of thwarting any trap. One boar, theatrically named Gore-Tusk, was said to have killed a dozen men before Kemp tracked it to its lair and ended its bloody reign with nothing but the gutting knife he still carried. Absurd, yes, but his easy willingness to share his stories succeeded in loosing the tongues of his companions.

Falstaff emerged as a natural storyteller, though he was too modest to inflate his role in anything. He was rarely the focus of his stories, instead focusing on humorous episodes involving his time aboard the *Fortune*. In these, Marbuck found herself drawn in, offering her own viewpoint and recollections. She actually found herself laughing heartily as they compared their versions of an incident wherein Baylis had sewn a dead fish into Castor's cot, allowing the increasingly foul stench to torture him. It'd only been when the smell had started to permeate the entire boat that the trick had been revealed. Castor had been apoplectic, Falstaff recalled. Marbuck was pleased to find that she could talk about Castor without conjuring images of his miserable end.

Even the normally taciturn Jalam spoke, telling of his youth in the Warren, and of exploring the furthest depths of the caverns with Katiek. A ghost of a smile touched his lips then, and Marbuck wondered if he and Katiek shared more than just a desire to serve the Lady of the Veil.

Reie said nothing, but listened with the air of a doting parent enjoying the happiness of a child. The little moments that made up their short lives must have seemed incredibly banal to her, but she seemed to appreciate them nonetheless. Marbuck wondered if, laboring under the burden of so much time, Reie ever envied the brevity of human life. Marbuck certainly wasn't jealous of Reie's longevity; her own short life had brought enough strife.

Eventually, the wells of memory ran dry and the travelers lapsed into silence. And still, the walk continued. Between the long stretches on their feet, the blankness of sleep offered brief respites. Marbuck did not even try to keep track of these stops. In the heart of the World's Wound, time had no meaning.

A dark shape on the horizon finally broke the monotony.

"Are you all seeing this?" Falstaff asked, squinting into the distance.

"Looks like I was wrong," Reie said. "There *is* something else out here."

"What do you suppose it is?"

Reie shrugged. "I have no idea."

Even through her field glass, Marbuck saw nothing more than an angled line of darkness standing up from the dark gray ground.

There was nothing to do but keep walking until they were closer. The shape became their new focus, guesses at what it might be the dominant topic in their conversations. Periodic checks of the field glass revealed little, until they'd finally gotten close enough to glean what it was they were seeing. Reie was the first to understand.

"Ahh," she said, lowering the field glass and offering it back to Marbuck. "I believe I've solved our mystery."

The others listened intently, their eyes moving between Reie and the shape that had hung teasingly before them for what'd felt like ages.

"At the height of Vingallea's splendor, great statues were raised along the main road into the old capital, called the Way of the Ascendant. The Vingalleans revered it; it was the route taken by the very first settlers to depart with the intent of expanding their dominion. In those elder days, it had been called the Old Planter's Track, as it'd been a simple dirt path that cut through their fields of grain. Eventually, the settlers became conquerors, and their armies trampled the fields into waste. It was no matter, though; they didn't need the crops when they could collect tribute from the lands they'd seized. The paved road came next, and then the statues. They depicted the kings and queens of Vingallea, and they were mighty works. Wrought with techniques that lacked the finesse of the Quaret, but imposing in their own brutal way. That appears to be a part of one of them."

Marbuck looked again through the field glass. It took her a moment, but she descried the shape of a bent arm jutting forth from the bitumen. It held a broken scepter, the pieces of which were lying against a partially buried head. She guessed that, were it standing, the megalithic statue would have dwarfed the Sentinel.

"How do you suppose it survived the blast?" Kemp asked.

"I don't know. The Way of the Ascendant ran north to south, directly from the city center. We should be firmly west of it. Perhaps the blast flung it out this way."

"Can we get a closer look?" Falstaff asked.

"It'll get closer as we go, but if you're looking to go right up to it, I think that'll take us too far off track," Kemp said.

Ultimately, the decision was unanimous. Fascinating as the wreck was, the distance to reach it was deceptive, and they could ill afford a long delay. The travelers continued on their way, and by degrees, the statue grew closer before sliding off to their right and receding into the unbroken emptiness. At the same time, the field of bitumen began to slowly rise, and they perceived that the horizon seemed closer and steeper. The flat sameness of the land gave way to a tortured mess of fissures, ridges of buckled stone, and immense slag heaps. After only a short time of struggling across this new terrain, Marbuck found herself longing for the plain they'd left behind. Still, the rising elevation kindled a hope for an end to the crater, and over each successive ridge the travelers looked eagerly for the rise of the northern wall.

Cresting an outcropping of basalt columns, they found something else entirely.

Stretching away before them was a tremendous bowl-shaped divot in the land, almost a second crater within the bounds of the first. Yet, this space was not a flattened blankness. The land stretched downward in the same agonized heaps as those they'd just ascended, but here it was littered with dozens of the titanic statues, their broken limbs reaching crookedly skyward, their shattered heads staring blankly into a landscape that matched their own ruination. Away to the northeast, painted orange in the permanent dawn's light, was a rising butte of stone, the top of which appeared to have been carved into a rectangular keep. Encircling this singular mesa was a multitude of shattered structures, their foundations flooded by a broad moat of black tar.

Beholding this strange land, the travelers stood in silent awe of it. Finally, Reie spoke.

"I cannot believe that it still stands."

"What is it?" Marbuck asked quietly, seized by a sudden notion that malevolent ears were listening.

"It is the remains of Vin-Unat, the first Vingallean city and the capital of the southern kingdom. It is in this place that Vingallea, as a nation, was born. That," Reie said, gesturing toward the butte, "is the Ancestral Mount. Upon its apex, the first Vingallean king was crowned. He took for himself the name Phar-Artomaw, and it was under his banner that the disparate tribes of Vingallea were united after the Great Culling. He, too, commissioned the royal fortress upon the top of the Ancestral Mount. It is called the Monolith of Pha, and it is carved into the very bedrock. I suppose that's how it survived as well as it did. That and the detonation must have occurred directly above here, flattening the city but sparing it from the worst of the wave of destruction that spread out in every direction."

"If this place was fortified enough to withstand something like that, and was so revered, then why did they ever relocate the main capital to Vin-Sadavat?" Marbuck asked, recalling the tales her parents had told her of old Buqaardia's fall. "That was Phan-Ellara's doing, right?"

"Yes. Phar-Artomaw had been the first to sow the seeds of Vingallea's ambition, telling his followers that they would spread across all of Gana, but Phan-Ellara was the culmination of that desire. She was the apex of a long line of despots whose thirst for domination only grew with each successor. I believe that after her conquest of Aurangzeb she took their capital as her own because she reveled in the humiliation of her newest subjects, who had fought valiantly against her. Ostensibly, though, she established the new capital in order to consolidate her power and launch a new era for the empire. It seems she also delighted in the beauty of the place, though she quickly ordered Vingallean architects to alter the original works. This, of course, was after she had the old sultan's head put on a pike. He was called Prishnah the Pardoner, for he'd been known for his great clemency. Phan-Ellara did not subscribe to such beliefs; after she'd had him executed, she ordered that every possible claimant to his throne was to be castrated and have their eyes put out. Any satrap who was willing to swear fealty to her was allowed to retain their little cut of power. Resistance to her ascension was pretty thoroughly snuffed out before it could really even begin."

Even in the stories of her parents, always told in private lest their words should reach the ears of anyone who might object to the romanticizing of pre-Vingallean history, Phan-Ellara was not depicted as such a sadist. The folk tales more commonly taught to children in Nordabor contained not a word that might besmirch their greatest queen. Undoubtedly, the scholars in the Hall of Antiquities would have been shocked to learn the horrid truth of their history, the undercurrent of brutality that ran beneath the heroic deeds recorded in their moldering tomes. Marbuck, however, had no trouble accepting Reie's account. After all, she'd lived during Phan-Ellara's reign, and she could attest to the fact that Vingallean history was littered with countless examples of cruelty and oppression. It was no wonder that the mere specter of Vingallea's return was enough to bind the Quaret to Setenrah.

As they all mulled over the lurid details of Vingallea's past, Falstaff's words defending the Quaret came back to Marbuck, and she realized that he was looking at her deliberately. She pursed her lips and avoided his gaze.

"So, if this was the epicenter of the blast," Kemp said, scratching at the beard growth that had been steadily joining his mustache, "that must put us at about halfway to—"

"He's here," Reie said abruptly, her voice shrill, her eyes wide.

"He—who?"

"*Setenrah.*"

A claustrophobic horror descended on Marbuck; the inevitable execution that had haunted her in the narrow tunnels of the Warren had suddenly arrived. Her head swiveled wildly, seeking the threat. Beside her, Jalam drew his saber in one fluid motion while Falstaff fumbled his axe from his belt. Kemp reflexively groped for both of his missing weapons, then yanked free his knife.

Reie's gaze was now locked on the Ancestral Mount. "There. I can sense him. Faintly, but he's there. I can only hope that he does not sense me."

All eyes turned toward the ruined fortress that crowned the plateau.

"This must be where he goes when he returns north," Kemp said. "Which means …"

Marbuck was already ahead of him, scanning the vista with her field glass. Understanding burst into her mind with black radiance. "The shades. They're all here."

What she'd initially taken to be a gently undulating moat made up of some kind of dark slurry was actually thousands of shades, pressed together into a heaving mass and contained within a tar-like webbing. She lowered the field glass in disbelief. Reie plucked it from her hand and examined the shades below.

"This is where he's been taking them; every shade he's ever collected from Quaretem and who knows how many more that he's stumbled upon in his wanderings. That ichor holding them, it is his own foul discharge. It seems that he is attempting to recreate Punishment here, pretending to have the mastery over suffering that the war's failure denied him. It is a clumsy aping of Aedesda's realm of old, but it is terrible nonetheless. This is the legion that he could drag to Quaretem and unleash upon us." Reie looked at Marbuck. "Long I served Setenrah. This is why."

Marbuck didn't know what to say. Thanks to her time with the shepherds, she had shed the mindless fear that the shades so easily awakened in others, but, seeing so many now, that fear had been exhumed.

"If Setenrah is up there, then so is Devonshire," Falstaff said. "We could rescue him."

"There is no rescue for him," Kemp said quietly. "I'm sorry, my friend."

"Well, we've got to at least try," Falstaff said, turning to Reie.

"Simply put, it would be suicide," she said. "Even for me. We cannot harm the shades, aside from Marbuck with her blade, and she could not possibly take them all. And that is without even taking Setenrah into consideration. If your friend is still alive, then he is suffering greatly, and for that I, too, am sorry. But without Ganachim, there is nothing we can do. We must go on our way. When we free Ganachim, and she is restored, we will cleanse this place."

Falstaff knew better than to try to appeal to Marbuck on Devonshire's behalf. Instead, he looked at Jalam, who patted him on the shoulder and shook his head. "We cannot free him, but we can still free many more. Deliverance forever."

Falstaff took a deep, shuddering breath and nodded. "Deliverance forever."

Kemp cleared his throat. "Well, as I was saying, we're about halfway now, I would guess. If you're worried about detection, we should probably keep to the outer edge that we're on, follow it until we're north of the city. It will take us out of the way, but it's better than being noticed."

There were no objections to this plan, so, skirting the western ridge of Setenrah's domain, the travelers resumed their journey.

CHAPTER 32

The northern wall of the crater rose from the arid flatness, growing incrementally over untold cycles until it encompassed the entire horizon. Above its red walls, the final wisps of cloud had tapered off, showing a pale blue sky dotted with the brightest stars. Obscured by the bulwark of the wall, only one jagged line of the crack was visible. It seemed to stretch above them, and they craned their necks to look at it. Cold white light flickered within, punctuated by brief glimpses of a darkness beyond comprehension. All around the unnatural scar, the firmament itself seemed to pucker and ripple. Looking at it made Marbuck feel dizzy, and she was grateful that her view of the entire crack was blocked.

They had not slept at any point since leaving Vin-Unat behind, all of them eager to put as much distance as they could between themselves and the charnel city. By the time they reached the foot of the northern wall and stopped to rest, they were all nearing a state of delirium, their minds stretched, buoyed only by Reie's mending. The burden of their survival had clearly taken a toll on the god; she was drawn and wan, her halo faded to an ashy gray. As her human companions plunged into sleep, she assumed the watch, slumping against a rock and staring vacantly into nothingness. Her kind did not require sleep, but exhaustion had clearly dulled her senses. Marbuck was too tired to care.

She might have slept for a thousand long-cycles. When she finally awoke, everything around her looked the same. If it hadn't been for the different position of the sun, she might have worried that they'd accidentally returned to the southern wall. The climb up certainly looked to be every bit as daunting as the climb down had been, even with renewed vigor. Still, there was a convivial atmosphere amongst the travelers, especially Reie, who had recovered completely. However dangerous the climb was going to be, it would take them out of the World's Wound.

Methodically, they began to make their way up the wall. Memories of Falstaff's injury returned to Marbuck with gruesome vividness, and each handhold seemed tenuous at best. As usual, Kemp went first, plotting out the course that the others were to follow. After a grueling stretch spent creeping along barely passable outcroppings, Marbuck found herself unable to resist the urge to look down. It was less frightening than it was dispiriting; they had not made it very far from the ground.

On and on the climb continued. Kemp would lead them to a point where they would stop, crouched beneath a jutting boulder, or holding on while they teetered over the abyss. Sometimes, he would be gone for a few cycles, returning red-faced and worn. Often, he would have to start over, finding that his proposed route led to an impassable obstacle. Marbuck allowed her mind to go dormant, shifting down into a lower state of existence as Kemp directed her every movement. The climb became a process of extreme tedium, occasionally interrupted by small moments of terror that brought her back to herself.

When Kemp's jovial voice boomed down from above, announcing that he'd reached the top, the true, undeniable top, and the exit from the crater, Marbuck did not believe him. There had been several false alarms already. They'd scaled a number of areas that had looked like the end of the escarpment, only to find that they'd concealed further heights of jumbled stone. Despite her best efforts, her doubt was tempered by the feverish conviction with which Kemp led them up to the point he had reached.

Being careful not to lose her focus on her handholds, Marbuck followed the others up a crevice that ran between two smooth walls of stone. Above her, Kemp hoisted himself up onto the top of the wall to the right and disappeared from view. Reie came after, and Kemp's arm came back into view, pulling her up and away. A joyful laugh sounded from above. Jalam joined them next, and he actually cheered. Now, Marbuck could not stop the flood of hope that had burst her doubt asunder. With reckless abandon, she and Falstaff scrambled hastily after the others. Falstaff was hoisted up, then Marbuck was lifting her head above the edge and Kemp and Jalam were pulling her up.

Dusty badlands stretched away before her. They had crossed the World's Wound.

• • •

Their jubilation wilted quickly as the full ugliness of the broken sky was now revealed. Flashing and convulsing, it hung over the northern horizon like a pulsating lesion, painting the surrounding air with smears of shifting color. The five of them stood beneath the madness, watching its fluctuations. None could discern what it meant, or what it was, beyond a vague assumption that it had been caused by the expedition's meddling.

During their lengthy trek, Falstaff had freely shared everything he knew, or surmised, about the original purposes of their expedition, and what he guessed might have become of it. Reie had seemed content to ignore the crack when it had been a distant anomaly, the bizarre side effect of a broken world being further shredded by the folly of the last Vingalleans. Her focus had rested solely on Ganachim. Faced with the unsettling distortion now, and knowing that they were approaching it, Reie suddenly seemed far more concerned. Marbuck wondered if it was simply fear for Ganachim, or herself, or perhaps something more profound. After all, if it *had* been caused by the expedition destroying the hidden gods they'd been seeking, that meant the end for more of Reie's kin. It was hard to fathom what that might mean to an eternal being, and Reie offered nothing of her thoughts on the subject, save for her urgent desire to reach Ganachim before it was too late. It was a single-mindedness that Marbuck could understand.

"Well, I think it's time for me to officially pass the role of guide over to you two," Kemp said, pulling his gaze from the sky and addressing Marbuck and Falstaff.

"Yes, I suppose," Marbuck said. "But we never even came close to the crater. We stayed behind with the boat while the expedition went south. I don't know which way to go aside from continuing north."

"Me neither," Falstaff added.

"Your boat—you were traveling on the Einfallen, yes?" Reie asked.

"Yeah, until a collapsed bridge blocked the way right where the river started to bend west. That's where we were waiting when the slavers first attacked us."

Reie nodded, thinking.

"Well, we seem to be closer to the lands of the Closed Eye than when we started," Kemp said. "I think we strayed further west than we intended. Your city—Nordabor—is it lighter there? Do we need to go eastwards?"

Marbuck examined the dusky light around her. The distorted northern sky complicated her assessment, but she could still tell that the sunlight in Nordabor was brighter. "Yeah, I think we do," she said. Falstaff nodded his agreement.

"If we head to the northeast, we should eventually reach the Einfallen, where it runs westward toward the sea," Reie said. "Or, it did when I last walked these lands. You said it was blocked?"

"Yeah, it had broken its banks and flooded the whole area around the bridge."

"I see. Well, even if it's dried completely, we should still be able to follow the riverbed to where it was flooded, and then follow the river north to Nordabor."

"If we know that the city lies northeast of here, then why don't we just cross the river and keep heading on that bearing?" Kemp asked.

Reie was shaking her head, her halo moving in perfect unison. "We'd be risking getting lost in the wilderness. We might know the general direction we're headed, and that's been fine up until now, but now we need precision. Otherwise, we could pass the city entirely, or get bogged down in some impassable terrain. Following the river might add some time, but it is our only sure way of making it to Nordabor."

"Fair enough," Kemp said.

"Some guides you are," Jalam said to Marbuck and Falstaff with a good-natured chuckle. "It sounds like the *river* will be our only guide."

"More or less," Marbuck agreed with a small laugh of her own. It was surprising, and refreshing, to hear humor coming from the somber guardian. She realized with a sudden squirm of discomfort that, at some point, her hostility toward her foreign companions had fully given way to something akin to friendship.

"She will be providing guidance of a different sort," Reie said, looking at Marbuck with a smile. "You will get us to your contact in the city, and to your king. You will get me to Ganachim."

"We'll see it done," Falstaff said, saving Marbuck from having to form a response. Though she was worried that Falstaff was hitching himself to disaster by committing to helping Reie, she was grateful that *somebody* would be fulfilling the bargain that she intended to abandon. Perhaps her desertion would not be such an issue with Falstaff remaining in her stead. Still, the fact that she was willing to let her friend march into doom so that she could avoid it did not sit well with her, and she realized that her eagerness to return to Nordabor was now striving with a growing dread.

Elibeth, she reminded herself, it all came down to Elibeth. If she could just get to her, then she could figure out the rest.

• • •

After a short rest, the travelers resumed their march.

Like the southern rim of the crater, the northern side was littered with countless fragments of glass and boulders of various sizes; the remnants of the tremendous spume of superheated mass that had rained down on the area at the time of the crater's formation. They moved hurriedly, eager to put the World's Wound behind them.

Beyond the blast plain, they entered the badlands proper. Walking upon hard-packed dirt and dull stone, they picked their way through winding canyons and ravines dotted with brittle scrub. To Marbuck's eyes, the withered vegetation looked positively verdant compared to the bituminous nothing of the crater. Eventually, these patches of brush were joined by tight clusters of withered trees, each situated on the edge of a barren gulch. After crossing a number of these gulches, Jalam voiced his concern that they may have unwittingly passed the Einfallen. After a brief debate, they continued on their way, the general consensus being that, even if it were dry, the bed of the Einfallen would be much wider than anything they'd encountered so far.

That assumption proved to be correct. Emerging from a dusty thicket, they beheld the mighty Einfallen, or what remained of it. Within a broad trough of dried mud, a turbid stream ran toward the west. At the sight of the water, foul as it seemed, a deep, undeniable thirst exploded into Marbuck's mind. She ran across the cracked surface of the dried bed and fell to her knees in the slime that remained beside the sluggish stream. Doubling over, she gulped down the cold water, which tasted metallic and sour. She cared not; it was real water, and no amount of Reie's power could fully erase her body's need for it. When she was finally satiated, she sat up, only to find that Falstaff, Kemp, and Jalam had joined her. Reie, anticipating that the water might make them ill, preemptively enveloped them in a wave of healing energy, doing nothing to hide her amusement at their animalistic behavior.

Once they'd filled their long-empty water vessels, they proceeded east, with the diminished Einfallen burbling mournfully beside them. Being close to the river, the terrain remained fairly flat, and they walked without difficulty. Following the gentle curves of the riverbed, they encountered the scattered ruins of numerous settlements that had once thrived at the water's edge. The exposed pilings of docks that had long since rotted away jutted out of the dried muck. Slumped huts and broken foundations were strewn across the hills that rose beyond the riverbank. A half-sunken stockade surrounded a broken tower, the parapet of which had crashed to the ground at some point. Reie surmised that it had once been a border keep of Aurangzeb, manned by men who'd watched vigilantly for signs of aggression from the south. Now, like all of the wastes surrounding it, it was vacant.

The emptiness of the land, though not dissimilar from the other places they'd passed through, now struck Marbuck as sinister. Even with each step taking them further into the light of the sun, the crumbled structures and dead woods around them seemed to conceal untold threats. This was not an irrational fear; indeed Marbuck knew exactly why she was wary. They were nearing the point in which the slavers had first taken her, setting in motion everything that had followed. She wondered if any of the Empress's scattered cultists still wandered these lands, seeking fresh meat for whatever depraved rituals they continued to carry out in their dead god's name. It seemed unlikely, what with the apparent collapse of Vin-Sadavat, but not impossible. As such, she remained watchful.

Ultimately, the only signs of any recent habitation they encountered were the remains of a small fire and some gnawed bones. It was unclear if these were left behind by badlanders or slaver refugees, but whoever they'd been, they were gone. Marbuck's anxiety, however, remained.

It was amplified when the colossal slabs of the fallen bridge first came into view. They'd firmly entered the Daylands and the air had grown hot, though it was still tame compared to the blistering heat of Quaretem. Dancing in the shimmering air, two tremendous sloping pylons stood on either side of a jumbled stretch of collapsed roadway. All around the wreck, a wide marshland stretched, shining brilliantly beneath the sun. After being dragged into the darkness as a slave to Bolenz and barely slipping out of Setenrah's noose; after crossing oceans, deserts, and the broken center of their world; after surviving horrendous torture, cataclysm, and deception, she had reached the point where it had all started. The fallen bridge, the twinkling expanse of the flood plain; everything was just as she'd left it. She couldn't begin to guess how much time had passed, and yet it remained unchanged; her memory peeled from her mind and restored to existence before her very eyes. Only now, the distortion in the north shone faintly in the hazy blue sky. Things weren't really the same, no. The sky had been scarred, and so had she.

"Do you think there's anyone there?" Falstaff asked her. Whether he meant slavers or anyone from the expedition was unclear, but, either way, he seemed to be as rattled as she was.

"If there is, we'll see them from a long way off. We'll be fine," she said, sounding far more confident than she felt.

They continued toward the wreck, bending south to follow the edge of the marsh. Marbuck's initial observations hadn't been entirely accurate; the flood plain had receded somewhat after all, shrinking the distance between its edge and the remains of the bridge. It meant a shorter walk, and a closer view of the ruins. Eventually, they crossed a cracked stretch of broken cobblestones and brown weeds; an ancient road, running straight into the marsh to the north and away into the badlands to the south. Reie explained that they had reached part of the Imperial Highway, which had once stretched from the furthest holds of Vingallea in the distant north to Quaretem, where the road had long been lost beneath the sands. In between, the highway and its offshoots, which had been built upon existing roadways, had connected to every major Vingallean hold. It had been the artery of imperial might, commerce, and communication. The collapsed bridge, called the Sterling Bridge, had been a major connection, uniting Vin-Unat and the rest of the southern kingdom with Vin-Sadavat and the empire's expanding northern sphere. Marbuck recognized the bridge's name; she'd heard it before from members of the expedition when they'd first arrived.

"Why didn't we just take this road north, then?" Kemp asked.

"In many places, it is worn away entirely," Reie said. "After all, it once passed through Berngoth, and yet I would venture a guess that you never saw it."

Kemp shook his head.

"It is lost completely beneath the swamps. I imagine it's lost in many other places as well. I wished to follow a more lasting landmark, so I put my faith in the permanence of Alminnian's creation over that of mankind."

Marbuck decided not to point out that the creation had outlived its creator, as had mankind. There was no reason to antagonize Reie, and, at any rate, traveling on an open road seemed riskier than keeping to the wilds. If the Imperial Highway led to Vin-Sadavat, then slavers who'd abandoned the city might have chosen to haunt the roadway around it instead.

The true gut punch of their return to the Sterling Bridge occurred when they'd rounded the edge of the marsh and proceeded north, along its eastern edge. There, the land was devoid of even weeds. A hard, flat plain of red rock stretched away to their right before giving way to rising canyon walls; a baked scab of dried mud lay beneath them and to their left. Disturbing this dull canvas was a trail of countless footprints and wheel tracks punched through the muck, which had dried into a record of a bygone passing.

"This must be the expedition's path," Falstaff said.

"There are prints going in both directions," Kemp observed.

Marbuck followed them with her eye. The relatively straight path led toward the water and the ruins of the bridge. Something else was there, too. Marbuck peered through her field glass, certain of what she'd find. Rising crookedly from a heap of stones was the skeletal wreck of the *Fortune*. It, too, was where she'd left it, though it appeared as if it had been stripped down to its frame. She'd known that she would eventually see it, but actually doing so still sent a shiver jittering down her back. Suddenly she was on the deck of the *Fortune* again, watching as Winslow choked on his own blood. She could hear the screams of her crewmates, feel the rough hands of the slavers snatching her. Something touched her shoulder and she started. It was Falstaff.

"It's hard to look at it, huh?" he said. The others had wandered ahead, allowing them a moment of privacy to share their grief, but he still spoke quietly.

Marbuck swallowed, suddenly feeling like she might be sick. "Yes," she managed.

"I sometimes wonder if this might all be some passing fancy, a dream or something. Everything that's happened, and now we're back here. It's hard to fathom."

"Yes," Marbuck said again.

Falstaff smiled at her and gave her shoulder a soft squeeze. "I told you once that the *Fortune* had been my only home, my only family, and that it was gone. That's still true, but I see now that I'm a part of a *new* family, one that promises to change this world, to *save* it. I'm worried about what awaits us in Nordabor, but I know that whatever it is, we will get you to Elibeth. And I believe that we can save Ganachim, too. I hope that you stay with us, Raina, that you remain a part of this family. I wouldn't know what to do without you."

Marbuck could have been angry with Falstaff for bludgeoning her with yet another pitch to help Reie, but she wasn't. In fact, she was surprised to find that his words pierced her, summoning an upswell of heartache that flooded her eyes with hot tears. She pawed them away and stared fixedly at the *Fortune*. Ever since Baylis's death, she'd felt that she and Elibeth had existed apart. There had been people who'd been there for her; Falstaff and Winslow; Dania and Hamish, but they were not family, not really. Losing Baylis had gutted her completely, erasing everything she'd thought her life had been, and she'd folded in on herself, taking Elibeth with her. The idea of walking away from all of that pain and isolation, of taking Elibeth into the warmth of a new family, was appealing, but it was also an extraordinary risk. Reie's plot hinged on a lot of maybes, clouded by one stark certainty: failure would mean death.

Marbuck sniffed and wiped her eyes again. She was determined not to let the weight of this moment bind her to any new oaths that she might later regret. Falstaff sensed that it would be unwise to push her. He squeezed her shoulder again and turned to catch up with the others.

After a moment, Marbuck joined them.

PART 5:

THE UNBROKEN CHAIN

CHAPTER 33

The shadowed woodlands echoed with the sound of the world's ending. It came routinely now; a deep, resonant twang; a snapping, grinding reverberation. More than mere noise, it was a physical presence, or rather, the cessation of one. Marbuck felt it thrumming malevolently within the gaping nothingness eating away at the sky. Each unnatural peal seemed to pucker reality toward it, creating a faint shimmering blur in everything that she saw, as if it was somehow distorting her very eyes. She could feel her skin tingling and her teeth moving minutely in her gums as it pulled at her very being.

And then it would taper off and everything would return to normal. They would laugh nervously and try to shake off what they'd just experienced, but a residue of fear remained. Though it was only a strange sensation, and not a crippling force, Marbuck was certain that it was getting worse. Whatever it was that was happening in the north, it felt like a promise of doom.

Their natural surroundings seemed to know it as well. A sense of anticipation hung in the air, as if the trees themselves were holding their breath. The Einfallen's dark waters, lower than they'd been when she'd left, cruised by silently. Walking across the forest floor, littered as it was with countless pine needles, the sound of their footfalls was extinguished completely. For the most part, they did not speak, though there'd been no conscious decision to remain silent. A hush had fallen over the forest, an enchantment that had taken hold in the absence of Ganachim's waning power.

Though Marbuck was reticent to point it out to Reie, it was clear to her that the area sustained by Ganachim's presence had shrunk considerably. They had only recently entered woodlands that still thrived; much of what had been green and full during the trip south had withered. This did not seem like a good sign. Falstaff, too, said nothing about it, though Marbuck chalked that up to his endless optimism more than any sense of discretion.

The others were able to shrug off their anxieties by focusing on the pleasure of walking through living lands. Unlike the dreary bogs of Berngoth, or the failing woodlands they'd just traversed, the conifers around them were robust, thick with needles and emitting a rich, sweet smell. The smaller bushes and shrubs were lush and vividly green. Jalam, running his fingers across them, beheld each vibrant leaf like it was a revelation. Every time a creature scurried across their path, Kemp looked as if he wished to plunge into the woods after it. The relative abundance of fauna had clearly reignited his passion for the hunt. Reie seemed to be affected more than any of them, but she looked at their surroundings with an expression of melancholy longing. Marbuck supposed that she was seeing Ganachim in every living thing. Though her features spoke of wistfulness, her words were hopeful. She stated several times that the proliferation of life was a sure sign that their journey was almost over. Whether it was or not, Marbuck couldn't be sure. She recognized no specific landmarks, and resigned herself to looking for the rising spires of the Vinecrown Keep around every bend of the river.

"It's starting again," Jalam said, looking skyward.

A crackling rumble rose from the north, echoing through the woods around them. Beneath their feet, the ground began to tremble. The trees actually swayed from the force of it, the rigid wood creaking in protest after an epoch of stillness. The travelers reflexively pressed together, watching the uncanny movement. Marbuck blinked repeatedly, trying to will away the faint shimmer that hung over everything. The noise seemed to bounce across the vault of the sky, coming from all directions at once, before fading into a low groan. Then it ceased, and all was quiet and still again.

"Well, at least it's not midges," Kemp said with a jittery smile.

Marbuck barked a short laugh; he wasn't wrong about the nuisance the midges had posed, but it was more so his strident need to bring levity to every situation that amused her.

"They're getting stronger and happening more often," Reie observed, saying aloud what Marbuck had already been thinking. "We need to keep moving. I fear that time is short."

There was no disagreement, and they resumed walking, quickening their pace. Though none of them really knew what was happening, the urgency of their mission was clear. The ragged hole in the sky clearly posed a danger, even if the actual nature of it was beyond their understanding. A sinister whisper caressed the back of Marbuck's mind. Perhaps they were already too late. Nordabor was gone, consumed by the emptiness that was gobbling up the sky. They would reach the spot where the city had stood, only to find a scoured land devoid of so much as a gravestone to mark her daughter's end.

She tried to tamp down on this thought, to suffocate it in the furthest depths of her mind. Still, its tendrils squirmed free, oozing cold panic. She started to feel light-headed, and her breath came in quick, little gulps.

Falstaff touched her arm. "Fishwife, are you—"

"*Shh*!" Kemp suddenly hissed, throwing a finger to his lips and thrusting his other arm out to stop them. "*Voices*," he whispered, gesturing for them to get down.

The five of them scrambled to their bellies, and Marbuck's imagined fears crystallized into instant alarm. A kaleidoscope of different terrors turned in her thoughts, and it took everything she had not to let them engulf her. Most of all, it was her anger that pierced through the shroud of fear. She had not passed through so many fires just to quail at the shadow of smoke. She would not allow herself to falter now, not when she was so close. Her breathing steadied just as Kemp crawled ahead, urging them all to stay put.

They'd hunkered down in a small hollow, and Kemp now scooted to the upper edge of the side they'd been approaching. After briefly surveying what lay ahead, he shuffled back to them in a low crouch.

"There's a camp," he reported. "It's set up in a clearing just beyond here."

"A camp?" Marbuck asked.

"Yes."

"Maybe it's another expedition," Falstaff said to Marbuck.

"I don't know what your previous expedition was like, but this camp looks pretty disorganized," Kemp said. "Maybe two dozen makeshift tents, a few wagons. People just milling around."

"Badlanders?" Falstaff suggested.

Marbuck shrugged. "Whoever they are, they're standing between us and Nordabor. We have no reason to engage with them; let's just sneak around."

"Did they look like they were in need of help?" Reie asked Kemp.

"They looked fairly ragged, but I don't think they were desperate, no."

"It doesn't matter," Marbuck said. "Again, we have no reason to approach them. In fact, if it *is* another expedition, then you're in danger. Remember, our expedition was hunting gods. They might try to kill you, or they might see you as another prize for the king. You should conceal that, just in case." She gestured toward Reie's halo.

A look of resignation passed over Reie's face, and she pulled a folded black cloth from an inner pouch of her jerkin. "I had hoped that this wouldn't be necessary, but I believe your prudence is justified." She unfolded the cloth and pulled it over her halo, disappearing once again behind her dark veil.

"At any rate," Marbuck continued, "my connection to the Crown is in Nordabor, not here. If we're going to get you an audience with the king, best we do it on our own terms. Let's keep moving."

The others looked at each other, but nobody offered a rebuttal.

"Okay, I'll lead the way around," Kemp said. "Stay low."

As she crept along behind Kemp, Marbuck breathed a sigh of relief. The last thing she needed now was for Reie to become entangled with this group, for ill or otherwise. If it were, in fact, another expedition, then its leaders might have their own motives, and Marbuck would be trapped, subject to their whims. That could mean a hasty return to Nordabor, but it could also mean impressment into the ranks of a new company marching further into the wilds. She had no interest in getting wrapped up in another doomed exploit dreamed up by Phar-Mindorius, and she would not abide captivity again. And even if they did allow her to go, it wasn't like she could leave Reie now; she had no way of really knowing how much further she had to travel and Reie was her only means of survival. Without the god's artificial bolstering, her famished body would probably collapse quickly. She could gamble her life on chugging river water and gnawing on whatever lichens she could find, but she doubted that it would be enough for a body that had been denied real sustenance for so long. For better or for worse, she needed to follow the original plan, and that meant keeping Reie close until the very end.

They moved slowly, keeping to the dense tree cover on the outskirts of the clearing. Skulking along the camp's eastern edge, Marbuck was able to catch glimpses of the shabby settlement through the branches. Tents of patchwork canvas hung languidly over hewn tree limbs and smoldering firepits dotted the space. Small groups of people huddled around them; she could hear them now; murmuring, indistinct voices punctuated by the occasional laugh or shout. From what she could see, it did not look like the camp of an organized campaign. If it *was* another expedition, it was a clear indicator of how desperate the situation in Nordabor had become.

A singular rumble came from the north, but petered out before reaching its normal level of intensity. A knot in Marbuck's chest tightened and loosened accordingly. Her back was beginning to ache from retaining the crouched position that stealth demanded. They'd nearly circumvented the camp.

Kemp's head snapped to the right and he froze. "Look—"

"Show your hands!" a voice commanded from the trees. Suddenly, six men materialized out of the thickets around them. They were clad in the colors of the forest and plain leather armor. Each bore a crossbow, leveled directly at Marbuck and her companions. "Hands! *Now!*"

"Listen to them," Reie said, lifting her hands and rising slowly to her feet.

The others followed her example.

"They've got weapons," one of the men said.

"I see them," the first man answered. He stepped forward, lowering his crossbow a degree. "You'd be a fool to travel these lands without one. Who are you? State your business here."

Kemp was looking at the man's crossbow, not with fear but with naked curiosity. Marbuck realized that he and Jalam would have no familiarity with such a weapon. She hoped that they didn't do anything stupid as a result.

"We are travelers en route to Nordabor," Reie said.

The man examined her veiled face. "Why?"

"We seek an audience with the king."

The man blinked once. "Why?" he said again.

Reie had grown unnaturally still; the Lady of the Veil had returned. "Our business is our own. Let us pass."

"Hassa, go alert Avehav. Tell him we're bringing in some outsiders who he'll wish to talk to. Tell him what they've said."

"Yes, sir," one of the men said, and he ran toward the camp. Marbuck watched him go, certain that these men, based on their weapons and demeanor, were guardsmen.

"You are free to keep your secrets from me," the leader of the men said. "But you're walking through territory claimed by Naroga Avehav. If you wish to continue, you will tell him your purpose. Now, walk." He gestured with his crossbow for them to proceed toward the camp.

With an air of haughtiness, Reie complied, and the others fell in behind her. The guardsmen escorted them, their crossbows at the ready.

"I pride myself on my woodcraft," Kemp said convivially. "But you boys managed to get the jump on me. Impressive." The guardsmen said nothing. "What are those contraptions you're carrying?" he asked to another round of silence. "I'd love to take a closer look at one."

"Keep talking and you will," one of the men growled.

Kemp chuckled. "Hang in there, kid. I'm sure your threats will carry more weight when your chin boasts more than three whiskers."

Being young among older veterans was clearly a sore subject for the man. He lunged at Kemp, whose hands were immediately snaking around the crossbow. Before he could snatch it away, the leader was between them.

"Back up!" he shouted, clubbing Kemp between the shoulders with the butt of his crossbow. Kemp faltered, dropping to one knee. The leader then snatched the young guardsman by the collar. "Control yourself, you twit," he hissed, shoving the man away. He turned to Reie. "Get your man up."

Reie touched Kemp's back, and his grimace of pain faded almost instantly. "Please don't try anything again," she whispered to him.

Kemp nodded. "You've got it." He stood up and faced the leader with a smile. "Sorry, but you can't really blame me for trying."

The leader grunted, gesturing for them to move.

A moment later they emerged into the clearing, where several people had assembled to wait for them. They were a ragtag bunch, but their arms and bearing spoke of being guardsmen as well. Further back, a larger group of curious, but cautious, onlookers had gathered around the nearest tents.

"It sounds like they gave you a little trouble, Winfield," one of the men said, stepping forward. He was short and slight, with the dark features of Aurangzeb.

"There was a little squabble, nothing more," the leader, Winfield, answered. The young guardsman's boyish face burned scarlet.

"Well, I'm glad that nobody was hurt. My apologies, travelers headed to Nordabor. You must forgive my men; their many long-cycles of service have left them with ingrained habits that can be a bit heavy-handed. With strangers, caution is always necessary, but so is courtesy. I am Naroga Avehav, and these are my lands. I am prepared to grant you passage through them, but first you must quench my curiosity and suffer my wariness. These are strange times, and my relations with the Crown are … strained. So, tell me, why do you wish to speak with the king?”

Reie remained silent and still for nearly a short-cycle, and the air was thick with tension. Finally, she spoke. “The king has something that I need.”

“Is that so?” Avehav said, stroking his beard. It was meticulously groomed, an odd luxury for someone living in the wilds, and one that struck Marbuck as being fueled by pure vanity. “And what might that be?”

“That is my business.”

Avehav laughed lightly. “And, should you reach the city, how do you expect to gain an audience with Phar-Mindorius?”

“I am accompanied by a mariner who has a direct connection to the king, via a merchant courtier who is held in his esteem,” Reie said.

“Oh?” Avehav said, his voice dripping with condescension. “And that would be …?”

“Me,” Marbuck said reluctantly.

Avehav looked at her, really seeing her for the first time. What he beheld was a gaunt, weathered woman with a kerchief tied around her head. He did not seem to be terribly impressed.

“You’re very odd, you and your companions. When I ordered the guards to watch my lands, I expected them to encounter badlanders, shades, the king’s enforcers, maybe even others who might wish to join us, but I never expected to find a band of peculiar folk wishing to travel *to* Nordabor.”

Marbuck’s patience was rapidly ebbing. “You speak of ‘your’ lands. Under whose authority do you claim them? Is this not the realm of Nordabor? Are we simply being waylaid by a preening bandit who enjoys playing liege lord as much as he enjoys his own voice?”

Avehav’s pompous demeanor slipped a few notches. “I claim these lands under no authority but my own, for they have become forfeit. Nordabor is now a hermit kingdom, reduced to the city alone. The gates are sealed; the people are held as prisoners, forced to pretend that the end is not coming, all so that their king might continue to playact the role of a wise monarch leading an everlasting realm. I spoke out against the king, tried to awaken the people to what he was doing. I escaped into exile before they could drag me to execution. The people in this camp, we are all those who’ve managed to escape—guardsmen, merchants, farmers. We all wish to be free from oppression, and to escape the Erosion.”

"Erosion?" Reie asked.

Avehav gestured toward the hole in the northern sky. "That. Phar-Mindorius and the loyalists of his court still deny it, but the Erosion is growing closer, tearing apart the world as it comes; erasing it. The lands north of the city have already disappeared. Many believe it's connected with the expedition that went missing. That is another part of Phar-Mindorius's madness; he is convinced that his son is still out there somewhere. So, go ahead, you are free to leave. See where your mariner gets you. I reckon it will be into the dungeons of the Vinecrown Keep, where the shepherds will question you about the expedition. Those peddlers of the occult are as delusional as their king, and their methods are not gentle."

Marbuck listened with a feeling of profound despair. She'd felt as if the phenomenon, the Erosion, had been growing stronger. Apparently, it was, and in a manner that was difficult to comprehend. She'd also suspected that the expedition was to blame, and it appeared that was probably the case. Whatever they had done had not only annihilated them, but had also set in motion the end of everything. If Avehav was right, and the dread filling the pit of her belly told her that he was, then Nordabor would soon be destroyed. Elibeth was there, a slave to Phar-Mindorius's despotic fantasies, and to try to reach her would be to walk right into a cage. And then what? If the Erosion was steadily increasing, then nowhere would be safe. Everything would vanish into nothingness, the Void that the shepherds so revered. Marbuck felt like she might collapse. She looked at the others; their faces mirrored her own feelings. Behind the veil, Reie's thoughts were unknowable.

"You speak of many troubling things," Reie said, her voice quiet.

"I speak only the truth. Nordabor is lost to us; soon it will be lost forever. And then these lands will be next. We will be moving on, claiming new lands until there's nowhere left to go." Avehav smiled sadly. "You may join us, if you wish."

"We cannot. I have faith that my friend will get me to the king," Reie said, looking at Marbuck. "He will listen to reason. This can be fixed. If we are free to go, then go we shall."

Marbuck squirmed, seeing that her plan had reached its inevitable conclusion prematurely. Elibeth remained just beyond her grasp. Her only supposed contact, Rayburn, had been lost with the expedition. Approaching Nordabor would result in their imprisonment, and Reie's disguise would not last long under scrutiny. She needed to warn her away now, but to do so would be to lose any chance of finding Elibeth in the city. It would also lay bare her duplicity. Her mind whirred, seeking a solution. She was dimly aware that Avehav was granting their leave, and that Reie, Kemp, and Jalam were moving. Falstaff was staring at her pointedly. She opened her mouth, not knowing what she planned to say, and then it happened.

"Mama?"

CHAPTER 34

It was the voice of memory, love, and loss, and Marbuck could not believe that it was real. She'd heard it before, in the longboat, when she'd been locked in the haunted dreams born of her death spiral. Surely, her mind had cracked, and the phantom voice had slipped free again.

"Mama!" It was insistent, and so close.

Marbuck turned slowly, her eyes scanning the crowd by the tents. Someone had split from the group and was now racing toward her. It was Elibeth.

She did not speak; she couldn't. All Marbuck could manage was an animalistic wail of longing and relief. Everything else was forgotten as she staggered forward to meet her daughter. She fell to her knees and Elibeth slammed into her, locking her arms around her in a desperate embrace. They wept together then, and Marbuck tried to apologize for her absence, tried to explain everything that'd happened, but she could only make inarticulate sounds.

"You're alive," Elibeth finally managed to say.

Marbuck pulled back then and examined her daughter, suddenly afraid that she was mistaken. It was Elibeth, certainly, but she'd grown lankier, and her face had leaned out.

"You're a woman now," Marbuck observed. "What's happened?"

Elibeth laughed. "Not quite, Mama."

"How long have I been gone?"

Elibeth thought for a moment, thrown off by the question. "Ever since the Erosion started timekeeping has slipped, but maybe like two long-cycles now?" She really looked at her mother. "What happened to you?"

Marbuck's hand reached reflexively toward her kerchief. Before she could say anything, Reie was standing above them.

"Unexpected fortune has brought you back to your daughter," she said warmly. Behind her, Falstaff, Jalam, and Kemp were beaming. The huntsman was actually crying.

Elibeth looked up at the strange, veiled figure, and then noticed Falstaff standing behind her. "Uncle Gregor!" she exclaimed.

Now Falstaff was crying, too. "Hey, kid."

The entire crowd of people had encircled their reunion, and Marbuck realized that Dania, Hamish, and their four children were there. She rose shakily, totally overwhelmed and eager to express her gratitude to the family who'd taken her daughter in. Reie blocked her way.

"One blissful reunion will hopefully beget another. Your daughter is safe with these refugees, but time remains short. Take your moment with Elibeth, and, when you're ready, we will continue on. She will be waiting for you when we return."

The words rolled over Marbuck, and she struggled to compose a response. She'd just found her daughter after long-cycles of misery and anguish, and now she was being told to take only a 'moment' before resuming her service to Reie. For all of her human-like trappings, this careless disdain for the weight of what was occurring showed Reie for what she really was. As a god, immortal and aloof, the connection between one human being and their child was nothing, not when compared to the god's own designs. In a spasm of indignation, Marbuck forgot about the needs of the Quaret, or the looming danger to the world at large. Her old rancor for Reie and her deceptions burst free from its dormancy.

"You think that I'm going to leave my daughter now? Having *just* reunited with her?" Marbuck shook her head fiercely. "No. Our little partnership is done. I have what I sought; I'm staying with Elibeth."

"And what of our bargain?" Reie asked, surprise leaking into her voice. "You would prove faithless when you are needed the most?"

"The bargain was a *lie!*" Marbuck shouted. Her rage had emboldened her, and the liberation granted by the sudden confession was intoxicating. "You held the key to my freedom, to my daughter, and then you told me exactly what you wanted! Of course I promised to deliver it to you! I have no way to reach the king, certainly not now. If you want to free Ganachim then you'll have to tear down the entire city yourself. I have nothing to offer you. I'm surprised that one who is so practiced in deception would not expect it from others. Or had you forgotten that I was nothing more than chum to you at the start? Meant to be strung along with lies until your master could collect me. Only for my *usefulness* did you offer a bargain."

Marbuck wished that she could see the hurt she'd inflicted on Reie's face, but the impassive veil revealed nothing. All around them, confused murmurs passed through the crowd. Avehav, who'd previously been holding court, had faded into the background, and now looked completely lost.

"Mama, what's going—"

"It's okay," Falstaff said, cutting between Marbuck and Reie. "I can speak to the merchant. I know him, too. I can still help you."

"Oh, enough already!" Marbuck said, fuming at her besotted friend's servility. "Rayburn was with the expedition; he's dead and you know it. You've known it all along."

"You have known from the start that she was deceiving me," Reie said quietly. It was not a question, but an accusation. Falstaff blanched.

Immediately, Marbuck was seized by remorse. Falstaff had never been anything but a true and steadfast friend, and she had just dragged him down with her out of spite.

"He's innocent," she blurted. "This was my plan alone. What little he knew of my lies he disapproved of. He's spent the entire journey trying to convince me to actually follow through with the bullshit scheme I'd concocted. He thought it could actually be done. Don't fault him in any of this."

"It *can* be done," Falstaff said to Reie, gingerly placing a hand on her shoulder. "It might not be how we'd planned, but I promise you we will find a way. We don't need Raina." He turned to Marbuck and Elibeth. "I'm happy that you two are together again, more than you can know. But my journey doesn't end here."

"Nor does mine," Kemp said, stepping forward. "I swore I'd reunite you with your daughter, and, well, here you are." He smiled. "I didn't expect to part like this, but, then, nothing between us has been easy. Either way, I wish you nothing but good fortune."

Jalam stood with them as well, but he had no kind words for Marbuck. He appraised her with a venomous glare.

The sundering of their long companionship was happening very suddenly, and Marbuck found that a slimy guilt was taking the place of her righteous anger. She could feel many eyes watching her intently, most of all those of her wondering daughter. Marbuck had returned from presumed death, only to be immediately exposed as a treacherous deserter.

"You are right," Reie said to her. "I am guilty of everything you've accused me of. I suppose we used each other from the start. I sought to atone for my mistakes, and in doing so, I had thought that we'd forged something greater than our beginning. I am sorry to discover that was never the case with you. Still, I hope for the best for you and your daughter."

She turned swiftly and began to walk away. The others followed after her. Falstaff gave a last reproachful look before joining them.

Marbuck sought for something profound to say, no longer wishing to inflict pain, but instead wanting to make them understand. Long had she warred with herself, weighing Elibeth against everything else. Now, she had finally reached Elibeth, and the joy of their reunion had been poisoned. It was infuriating that she felt this way, that her actions toward Reie could overshadow her happiness now. She owed nothing to anyone, least of all her former captors. Self-loathing and the stubborn assertion that she'd done nothing wrong clashed within her as she watched her erstwhile companions leave.

"I'm not actually dead, you know," a voice called from the crowd.

All eyes turned toward its source, and a plump, bald man in disheveled robes stepped out meekly from the throng of people. It took Marbuck a moment before astonished recognition blazed into her mind. It was Fritz Rayburn.

Falstaff laughed as he realized who was standing before them. "Well, would you look at that!" he exclaimed.

"I- I'm not sure what I have to do with any of you, but it seems you've been laboring under the impression that I'm dead … and—well—I'm not," Rayburn said. "From what I can gather, you need me to reach Phar-Mindorius on your behalf? So you can … free Ganachim?"

The crowd's murmurs increased, and Marbuck wondered how much these people knew of the captive god.

Suddenly, Avehav found his voice. "Quiet! Quiet everyone!" The guardsmen repeated the order until the rabble sank into silence. "It seems there is much to discuss here, for these travelers have brought unlooked-for portents of great interest to us all. I think, perhaps, this situation might be better understood if those involved could speak to each other in a more private venue." He turned to Reie and the others. "Come, my friends, let us stoke a fire."

•   •   •

They'd returned to the woods beyond the outskirts of the camp, where a perimeter of guardsmen led by Winfield insured their privacy. Apparently, Avehav did not mind indulging the guardsmen's ingrained habits when it was in service to his commands. A fire had been started in a hastily constructed ring of stones, and Marbuck sat beside it with Elibeth in her arms. Avehav had insisted that, as one of the travelers, Marbuck join them, and she'd been too exhausted to resist, provided that Elibeth was permitted to come along.

Reie, Falstaff, Kemp, Jalam, and Rayburn rounded out the impromptu meeting. There had been a series of awkward introductions, during which Marbuck's exposed deception had hung about like a rank odor. Rayburn seemed to be oblivious to it, more concerned with the fact that he didn't actually remember Marbuck or Falstaff, and he apologized profusely for not recognizing members of Winslow's crew. Marbuck wasn't surprised; they'd been mere acquaintances, and her appearance had admittedly changed.

Once the formalities had been taken care of, they'd moved on to weightier matters. There had been much to discuss. Avehav and Rayburn had provided more information regarding what was happening in Nordabor, explaining that the lower classes, first driven to desperation by shortages, the lockdown of the city, and crackdowns on any dissent, had nearly risen in revolt when the Erosion's approach had finally become clear. Knowledge of the true extent of the danger had been mostly suppressed, but the mere presence of a gigantic hole in the sky that seemed to be getting larger had apparently been enough to cause an uproar, despite assurances from the Crown that all was well. Information about the expedition's purpose and a captive dying god had been spreading too; long-held rumors and whispered tales had been exposed by those in the court who'd become disillusioned with the king, of which Avehav was one. Loyalists, spearheaded by the shepherds and the most slavish of the royal guardsmen, had helped to quash any budding rebellion in a brutal fashion. Avehav, who'd been quietly organizing an underground network of dissidents to help others flee the doomed city, was forced to flee himself. Dania and her family, with Elibeth in tow, had been amongst those he'd helped escape. For his part in Elibeth's survival, Marbuck was grateful to Avehav, who, without his audience, had shed most of his pretentiousness.

In addition to his flight from Nordabor, Rayburn had recounted his return from the outskirts of Vin-Sadavat, where the expedition had suffered a second slaver attack, from which he'd narrowly escaped.

Falstaff, with a few additional comments from Marbuck, had told of everything that had befallen them since the first slaver attack on the *Fortune*, and how they'd come to find themselves in Quaretem. Marbuck had not been keen to dive into such a heavy tale so quickly with Elibeth, and she was grateful that Falstaff had the good sense to leave out the foul details of their time with the slavers. There would be a time to share more of that with Elibeth, but it wasn't now. What little they had conveyed had still been enough to fascinate her, and she'd listened raptly.

From there, Reie had taken up the threads of the story, explaining Setenrah's grip on the people of Quaretem, and her belief that Ganachim could free them. Still leery of Avehav and Rayburn, she'd neglected to mention that she was a god, only referring to herself as a healer and a follower of the old ways. She'd segued into Marbuck's claim that Rayburn could get them to the king, and thus to Ganachim, carefully avoiding any whiff of condemnation. Rayburn had listened to this plan with keen interest and a sort of flattered surprise at the idea that he might be of such vital importance. Now he sat back and sighed heavily, taking in everything he'd heard.

"Tell me," Reie said, her voice bearing a slight tremor. "We've spoken much of what's befallen your city, and of our own plans, yet one thing has only been alluded to. Does Ganachim still live?"

"As far as I know, yes, though the situation appears to be dire," Rayburn said. "Of course, her end has seemed imminent for some time; ever since I first learned of Ganachim, her death has been looming. It's difficult to know, with her kind. I will say this though, the slow decline that we've all been trying to ignore has become a total collapse. Don't let these lingering woodlands fool you, Nordabor will be indistinguishable from the badlands soon. The living lands are shrinking rapidly, and Nordabor's resources have already failed. The shepherds have even ceased making their anointed blades; they fear the bloodletting would finish her." He shrugged. "More leaked secrets. Even their mysterious order has been exposed. Strange times."

"Anointed blades," Reie said, disgust and understanding coloring her voice.

Marbuck saw no reason to hold back now. "Yes, they're the weapons of the shepherds, used to destroy shades. They're quenched in Ganachim's blood, which gives them their unique properties. This is one of them." She tapped her blade.

"I see," Reie said coolly. She turned a degree toward Rayburn. "So do you believe that freeing her is possible?"

"Yes, I suppose."

"Then you will help us?"

Rayburn cleared his throat. "Well, under normal circumstances I would be able to arrange a meeting with Phar-Mindorius, but we couldn't be any further from normal circumstances. As it is, I've been absent from the city for many full-cycles. I was going to be arrested for failing to help the prince. If I were to come back now, I'd only be arranging a meeting with an executioner."

"Surely the king would hear you out if he knew what we offered," Reie said. "I would think that he would see healing Ganachim as the solution to all of his problems. Truthfully, she might be. She was the mightiest of the firstborns. Beyond freeing my people from Setenrah, she may be able to save your people. Restored, her power to create life might be enough to stave off what you call the Erosion."

Rayburn was shaking his head. "You know much of the old ones, I gather. Lord Fontaine would have loved to pick your brain." He chuckled softly at his own musing. "But you do not know Phar-Mindorius. He would never risk losing his control over Ganachim. She's the foundation of his power. I suspect that he would see her perish before he would see her freed. And it matters not; though she still clings to life, there can be no improvement. You might be a learned healer in the lands you hail from, but we're talking about a *god*. I doubt any work of man can reverse what's happening to her."

Reie listened to this patiently, saying nothing to contradict him.

"I mean, that's what the expedition was all about. They sought another way out of our doom because they knew that healing her wasn't possible; she's finished. Sooner or later, she's finished."

"We gathered that the expedition was hunting other gods," Falstaff said. "You say it was to avoid our doom. What were they actually after?"

"They knew that the other living gods held the pieces of a broken sword: the Scale of Judgment. They hoped to get these pieces and reforge the sword. It was a key, I guess. They were planning on using it to open the Gates of Paradise. The expedition was supposed to save us all. They'd actually managed to get three shards from one of the gods, Veathyadell, as I recall. I suppose they must have gotten them all, considering the Erosion. I imagine the gates didn't function as predicted."

"Fascinating," Reie murmured. Marbuck guessed that she was fitting this information into her own assumptions about what had happened to her kin after the war.

"Yes, indeed. Unfortunately that botched plan was our last hope. I'm sorry, but I really don't think there's any chance of healing Ganachim."

"I can heal her," Reie said.

Rayburn looked at Avehav, who shrugged. "How can you be so certain?"

Reie reached for her veil, eliciting a small noise of protest from Jalam. She ignored it, and with a flourish, she pulled the veil away. Rayburn and Avehav bore nearly identical expressions of surprise, their eyes locked on Reie's halo. Elibeth clung to Marbuck, rigid with fear and amazement.

"You said that no work of man can heal her. I am Reie, God of Mending. *I* can heal her."

"You- you're a god," Rayburn stammered.

"Yes, that's correct."

"Her power kept us alive through our entire journey north," Falstaff said. "She sustains every person in Quaretem. She can save Ganachim."

"And I believe that Ganachim can save us all," Reie said.

"This is unbelievable," Avehav said.

Marbuck was used to being in the presence of a god, and she waited with tired impatience for their wonder to fade. Only for Elibeth did she reserve any understanding. "It's okay," she whispered to her wide-eyed daughter. Elibeth nodded shakily, not looking away from Reie.

"Well, I suppose this changes things," Rayburn said dazedly.

"I should think it would," Reie agreed.

Rayburn blinked several times. "Perhaps we were never meant to find salvation beyond the gates. Maybe we were meant to forge it ourselves, here. If Ganachim can be saved, if *we all* can be saved, we have to do whatever we can to make it so. Phar-Mindorius will be unyielding, I promise you, even faced with the divine. I expect that he will fight. Either way, I will help you."

"As will I," Avehav said. "If freeing this god can stop the Erosion, if it can help us depose Phar-Mindorius and build something new, you have my full support. Whatever resources I can provide are yours."

Marbuck was annoyed by their zealous embracing of Reie's quest. Even if they could free Ganachim, there was no guarantee that she would be able to deliver on anything that Reie said, least of all stopping the Erosion. But more so, she was annoyed by the shame she felt. These two men, having just learned of what Reie sought to do, were willing to risk their lives to help her. Faced with the same choice, Marbuck had opted to go her own way. She realized that Elibeth was looking at her, and she avoided her gaze.

"I am humbled by your bravery," Reie said, and she clearly meant it. Marbuck frowned, her guilt and irritation growing.

"Well, I think I speak for us all when I say we're happy to have you aboard," Kemp said. "So, now what? What's our plan?"

"It seems to me that your original plan is all we really have," Rayburn said.

"The hopeless one?" Kemp asked.

Rayburn shrugged. "Knowing that Ganachim actually *can* be healed if we reach her makes the risk worth taking. We do face the same issues, though. Not to mention, should Phar-Mindorius learn what you are, he might wish to imprison you, too. He could try to force you to heal Ganachim just enough to save her, but little enough that he can still keep her enslaved."

Marbuck nodded, having considered the same thing.

"I still believe that the king will see reason," Reie said.

"And if he doesn't?" Kemp asked. "Our new friends are not making me confident that he will. We need a contingency plan."

"Perhaps we operate two plans at once," Jalam said. He turned to Reie. "I do not want you to walk right into this king's palm, for I do not think that he will receive you as anything but a prize. I believe we should have someone else pose as a healer, introduced by Rayburn. They can gauge the king's reaction, and should he prove to be unexpectedly agreeable, then you can always step in. Otherwise, I suggest that you be brought into the city in secret, to attempt a separate rescue while the king is distracted."

The others sat in silent contemplation of this idea. Finally, Rayburn spoke. "It seems almost certain that the fake healer and myself will end up imprisoned—or worse."

"We would not leave you behind," Reie said. "With Ganachim healed, we would be able to free you easily. But, should this distraction work, where would we even begin to look for her?"

"She is held somewhere in the Vinecrown Keep," Rayburn said. "I know that much."

"That's a start, but how do we even get into the city to begin with? You might be able to deliver yourself to the guards, but if I'm to remain hidden, I will need to infiltrate the city somehow."

Rayburn scratched his chin, and then, eyes lighting up, he looked at Avehav. The other man squinted with thought, then the same idea appeared to bloom in his mind and he nodded his approval. Rayburn turned back to Reie. "You won't be arrested at the gates because you'll already be under arrest."

"We have a contact still operating within the city," Avehav explained. "An under-captain called Sarena Nedelkoff. She smuggles people out of the city. We'll have her smuggle you *in*. As her 'prisoner' she can walk you right to the dungeons of the Vinecrown Keep; as fine a place as any to start your search."

Reie's lips curled into a small smile. "Brilliant."

"I wish to stay by your side, as always, but I will volunteer to accompany Rayburn in your stead if it means protecting you," Jalam said.

"No offense, my friend," Kemp said, "but if someone is going to schmooze this king, it won't be you. You're a little too … dour. I humbly volunteer my own expertise for the role of the mysterious healer from a distant land." He affected a little bow.

"Indeed, I think you might be the perfect man for such a job," Jalam said with the slightest hint of a smile. "All the better, for now I may remain at your side, my lady."

"If you'll have me, I'll go with you, too," Falstaff said to Reie.

"Of course, thank you both. And thank you, Henrick."

Kemp nodded. Marbuck wished to be elsewhere.

"I believe I can further aid your cause," Avehav said. "As soon I'm certain that you've made it into the city, I can lead a small contingent of men to the main gates. We'll launch an attack that will pull away the already-strained resources of Phar-Mindorius. With any luck, the keep itself will be left nearly empty."

"I am indebted to you," Reie said.

"You will owe me nothing if your plan succeeds. Any risk is worth taking if it might save the people of Nordabor from a delusional tyrant."

They were lofty words, Marbuck thought, coming from someone who'd recently occupied a comfortable position within that tyrant's court. Having ditched his nobility, Avehav now fancied himself a revolutionary fighter. Marbuck wondered if he'd enjoyed formal training in swordplay as a perk of his privilege, and if experiencing real danger would make him crumble. This cynical line of thought ended abruptly, though, when Marbuck realized that Avehav's willingness to abandon his position actually lent *more* credence to his words. A nasty little voice in the back of her mind reminded her that not everyone was as self-serving as she was. She did her best to ignore it.

"So, what's our next move?" Kemp asked.

"I'll send out a courier immediately to notify Nedelkoff," Avehav said. "We'll arrange a meeting place and time, as best as we can estimate one. Once we meet with her, I'll explain the plan. I doubt that she'll raise any objections. Then we go. Until then, rest. I'll make a tent available to you, as well as food and drink. I'll let you know when it's time."

What had started with an air of mistrust had quickly grown into a camaraderie born of conspiracy. As the gathering rose to part, Marbuck realized that she alone had been shunted aside. Falstaff spoke rapidly to Elibeth in his congenial way while the others regarded her in a friendly, if somewhat detached manner as they returned to the camp. Nobody said a word to Marbuck, though, save Avehav, who dismissed her in a stilted manner.

She'd reunited with Elibeth and successfully excised herself from Reie's plans. Somehow, it did not feel like a victory.

CHAPTER 35

While the others were shown to their new accommodations, Marbuck followed Elibeth to the tent she'd been occupying. It was built of a lashed-together wooden frame, overlaid with scraps of canvas, blankets, and frayed rugs. Inside, it was homier than Marbuck had expected, with rudimentary designations for different sleeping areas splitting off from a central space where a round rug covered the ground and a few cushions served as chairs.

Dania, Hamish, and their children were waiting there to greet them. Marbuck wept openly, overcome with gratitude. She embraced Dania while the children jumped merrily about them. Hamish watched happily from the side until she pulled him, too, into the hug. She began to apologize for failing to return with a single coin, but Dania quickly waved her words away. They spoke briefly, their conversation consisting of little more than Marbuck saying repeatedly how thankful she was. Under the auspices of gathering some food from the camp's modest store, a motley collection of foodstuffs comprised of whatever the refugees could take with them, Dania and Hamish left the tent, shooing their children ahead of them. They had granted Marbuck and Elibeth their first moment of privacy. It was surreal.

"I don't remember their names. The kids, I mean," Marbuck said, her eyes lingering on the closed flap they'd just left through.

"Arnar's the oldest. Then the two girls; Isola and Petra. The youngest is Ernaby."

"How's it been with them?"

"It's been great. They've treated me like one of their own."

Marbuck smiled, her eyes welling up again. "That's good."

They stood silently for a moment, mother and daughter simply looking at each other.

"I still can't believe you're alive," Elibeth said.

Marbuck made a sound caught between a laugh and a sob. "I can't either."

"All of that stuff they were talking about, everywhere you've been; it's incredible. Traveling with an *old one*, I can't even wrap my head around it. I'm just so glad you're back."

They embraced again, holding each other tightly, saying nothing. Marbuck would have been content to stay that way forever, but Elibeth eventually pulled away. Her eyes traveled up to Marbuck's kerchief. She said nothing, but she didn't need to.

"There's a lot more to the story," Marbuck said. "I did some terrible things to get back to you. Endured terrible things." Before, she'd wished to stave off this conversation, now she suddenly felt compelled to tell Elibeth everything. She reached up and pulled off her kerchief. Elibeth did not flinch. "The man who held me captive—the monster who took me—he- he did this." She took a deep, shuddering breath. "He scalped me ... I killed him." Tears ran hotly down her cheeks. It seemed that she would never run out of them.

"Whatever you did, you did it because you had to," Elibeth said, gripping her hands tightly. "You came back for me, and that's all that matters."

Marbuck nodded shakily. She'd been fixated on returning to her child; now she was being comforted by a level-headed young woman. Elibeth had changed, and she'd missed it. More than ever before, she could see Baylis in her.

Elibeth reached up and lightly touched the tortured scar that encircled Marbuck's head. A faint fuzz of short, wispy hair now clung to the tissue of her scalp. Elibeth ran her hand across it. "You are my mother. *This* doesn't matter. You're still you. And you came back." Now she was crying again. "*You came back.*"

They hugged each other tightly, still enveloped in grateful disbelief. For Marbuck, the feeling was now joined by vindication; everything she'd done had been worth it in the end. The newfound justification curdled quickly.

"Those people—the old one, Reie—she helped you and Uncle Gregor," Elibeth said, pulling away. "She saved your life."

"Yes." It was complicated, but beneath the layers of deception, that was the truth.

"And now she's trying to save the other one, the captive one. Then that one will stop the Erosion?"

"So she believes," Marbuck said tightly.

Elibeth nodded to herself. "And you were supposed to help her?" The question landed like a hammer.

"I told her what she wished to hear, in order to secure my freedom. So that I could come back to you."

Elibeth nodded again. "I understand. I hope that they succeed, though. It sounds like it would end all of this. I don't really know what else could."

"I don't either," Marbuck admitted. Silence stretched between them.

"Well, I don't think you need that," Elibeth said without preamble, pointing at the kerchief clutched in Marbuck's fist. "You're beautiful."

Marbuck smiled, though her thoughts lingered on Reie. "Thank you." She shoved the kerchief into her pocket. She didn't know if she was ready to discard it, but she wanted Elibeth to think that she was strong, especially in light of her desertion of Reie.

Elibeth returned the smile, and it was all Baylis. Marbuck felt like an impostor.

• • •

Dania and her family returned in a tumult of laughter and voices, bursting into the tent and beckoning Marbuck and Elibeth to join them outside. Dania, whose eyes had flicked across Marbuck's scar without so much as a pause, set to work at a roaring fire, where several pots had been set upon a metal grate. Hamish busied himself with trying to rein in the children, who, in the manner of all children, asked Marbuck bluntly about her 'funny-looking head'. She didn't mind; she was simply relieved to be with old friends who had absolutely no connection to Reie or her plans.

The food, a random assortment of whatever Dania could get ahold of, was the best food Marbuck had ever eaten. There was stringy beef, brittle hardtack, shriveled turnips, and spotty potatoes. It didn't matter; it wasn't human flesh or dried mushrooms. Marbuck tried mightily to eat slowly, knowing that her atrophied stomach would riot at the influx of real food. She failed, gobbling everything in sight. By the meal's end, her guts were a mess. She knew that Reie could easily alleviate her symptoms, but her pride would not permit her to ask.

Eventually, the festive atmosphere of their reunion waned, and their beds began to call to them. The children fought it at first, especially Ernaby, but each succumbed in turn. Hamish followed shortly after. Marbuck rose to see Elibeth off to bed, as she had before, and was somewhat hurt to find that, in her absence, Elibeth had grown accustomed to going to bed by herself. Still, they hugged and kissed before Elibeth slipped into one of the tent's darkened corners, the strange sense of unreality still buzzing between them. Then, only Marbuck and Dania remained by the fire, which had dwindled into a gently-crackling glow.

"Another one?" Dania asked, uncorking a bottle.

Marbuck's stomach was in knots, but the novelty of drinking wine again after so long could not be resisted. She nodded, and Dania refilled her dented metal cup. She took a sip and her head swam pleasantly, which helped her to ignore the pain of her bucking stomach.

"For what it's worth, I think it makes you look like a warrior," Dania said, gesturing toward Marbuck's head.

"Oh, thanks," she said, taking another sip to mask her discomfort. She'd decided to follow through on ditching the kerchief, and it was proving to be difficult.

"Listen, Warrior, I'm ecstatic that you're back, believe me," Dania said, leaning forward, "but don't you take Elibeth away from me. She's as much a part of this family as any of my little ones. I suppose you'll just have to stay with us if you want to see her." She grinned broadly.

Marbuck turned the cup in her hands. "I guess I will. Thank you for taking her in, and for taking me in now, I suppose."

"Of course!" Dania said, and she squeezed Marbuck's arm. "You're part of the family now, too."

"Where will we go?" Marbuck asked after a short pause.

Dania breathed deeply through her nose. "Avehav says that we'll need to pull up stakes soon, and I believe him." Their meal had been interrupted by the rumbling from the north, and naked terror had briefly shot across Dania's face before she'd caught it. For the sake of her children, no doubt, she could not permit her fear to show, but it was there. "I suppose we'll go wherever he goes. As long as all of us refugees stay together, there shouldn't be any dispute over food. At least not until it starts to run low. But who knows? Maybe we'll run out of ground first." She'd meant it in jest, but the humor had withered on her tongue. "I'm scared, Raina."

"I am, too."

"Is there anything to what your companions were saying?" Dania asked.

"I don't know," Marbuck said, not wanting to think about them.

Dania downed the rest of her cup and smacked her lips. "Well, there's obviously a lot to unpack there, not to mention everything you've been through. When you're ready to talk, I'm ready to listen."

Marbuck was about to thank her for the thousandth time when she noticed Kemp approaching them. She no longer wanted her wine.

"Oh, here's one of them now," Dania observed.

"Hello, ladies," Kemp said as he reached them. "Sorry to interrupt your merrymaking. Might I borrow you for a moment?" He offered his hand to Marbuck.

Ignoring it, she rose, igniting a spasm in her belly and wooziness in her head. The drink had affected her more than she'd thought. "Sure," she said with forced lightness. The two of them walked some distance away, reaching the privacy offered by the trees.

"What is it that you want?" Marbuck asked, eager to be done with him.

Kemp smiled, as he always did. "Do you recall our first meeting? Not, obviously, when I found you on the beach, but after you'd been healed by Reie?"

"Yes." She did not need yet another reminder that she owed her life to Reie, or Kemp for that matter.

"You didn't really trust me at the beginning, and for good reason it turned out. I don't know if I've ever truly apologized to you."

"Is that what you're doing now?"

"That's what I was doing by helping you get back to Elibeth. But it wouldn't hurt for me to put it into words. I'm sorry I lied to you. I'm sorry that, because of me, you were nearly lost to Setenrah. I'm sorry that Devonshire was."

If he'd meant to move her by invoking Devonshire, he'd miscalculated. Marbuck eyed him, wondering what his angle was. "Thank you," she said stiffly.

"Getting you back to Elibeth wasn't just about apologizing, though. It was about doing something right to try to atone for my wrongs. We didn't stop in Berngoth for supplies. I led us there because I left my wife and daughter to die there. Berngoth had been my realm, and I'd failed as a leader. My brother launched a coup to seize power, and I tried to kill him. I was reckless in my pursuit of him, and I accidentally set fire to my own home. Taiyonna, my wife, and Blythe, my daughter, they were trapped inside. I could have tried to save them, but I chose to save myself." Kemp took a deep breath and forced a smile that held infinite sadness. "I wasn't done yet, though. I also abandoned my last loyal comrade to secure my escape."

"Why are you telling me this?" Marbuck asked, rigid with horrified disbelief.

"At first, my pain and guilt were larger than you can fathom," Kemp said, ignoring the question. "I was lost in it, swallowed completely. Every moment I saw them. When I could manage to sleep, they were alive again. Then I'd awaken, and the reality of their deaths would crash down on me. I had lived my entire life in the comfortable belief that everything would always be pleasant, that death only came with old age, that we had *so much time* ahead of us. Then, the curtain was yanked back and the hideous truth was laid bare, and I faltered. The weight of my failure hangs on me always; fetters you cannot see and that I cannot shed. I tried to bury it by serving Lakna. Piling more bodies on top of it didn't work. Then you came along, and you had that strength, that boundless devotion that I had lacked. So I committed myself to reuniting you with your child. It is a great relief to me that that reunion has finally come to pass."

"I'm glad," Marbuck said, not really sure of how else to respond.

"It's still not enough, though," Kemp continued. "I know it never will be. All I can do is just keep striving to make things right. So now I'm going to do everything I can to reunite these two gods, for Reie has the same drive that you had. Ganachim, the Quaret, they are her family, and her love for them runs to depths beyond our grasping. You got your reunion, now she deserves to get hers. None of us would be here without Reie, whatever the original circumstances of our meeting. You are a part of this, and, if I were you, I would feel compelled to see it through."

"Well, you are *not* me. I can't pretend to understand your grief, or how it compels you, and I pity you for what you've been through, but our path together has reached its end." As soon as the words left her mouth, Marbuck was reminded of Old Stitch and his talk of intertwining paths. She pushed the thought away. "Reie doesn't even need me. Why do you care?"

"Because, despite your ceaseless attempts to dissuade me, I've actually come to admire you. Believe it or not, I consider you my friend. I'd started to think that you were fonder of our little group than you let on, that our companionship meant something. It seemed to me that we were in it together, not just to reach Elibeth, but to save Quaretem. I mean, it looks like we could be saving a lot more than that now, and I think you know it.

Falstaff, bless him, he's too worried about upsetting Reie to come see you, and she's too proud to say a word, but I'll tell it to you straight. We want you to come with us, even Jalam, angry as he is. Like I said, you are a part of this. It seems an ill omen to go on without you. And mark me; if you run away now, you'll regret it."

"I'm not running away from anything."

Kemp pursed his lips and nodded. "Just think about it, that's all I'm saying."

"There's nothing to think about."

"Right. Well—I'll be off then."

She said nothing, and he left her standing by the trees. She watched him go until her gaze slid to the tent where Elibeth slept. From the north, the Erosion rumbled.

CHAPTER 36

By Marbuck's estimate, roughly three full-cycles had passed since they'd first arrived in the camp. She'd spent the time since with Elibeth, walking along the Einfallen, speaking of things old and new. They did not address the fact that the river was rapidly dwindling. Even since her arrival, the waters had receded until they were little more than a stagnant creek, resembling the southern branch beyond the collapsed bridge. Marbuck dismissed the idea of a dam upriver; it seemed much more likely that the river's source had simply disappeared into the Erosion. It was incredibly strange to watch the broad, dark waters which had played such a large part in her life drain away. She wondered what Falstaff thought of it.

The refugees, increasingly numb to the constant slew of disaster, seemed to pay it no mind. They continued about their business, turning to several casks of water that had apparently been stored in preparation for such a possibility. Maybe they were putting all of their faith in Avehav's ability to save them, or maybe they were simply in denial. Either way, Marbuck had to respect their stalwartness, and Avehav's foresight. With Rayburn's assistance, he'd arranged for the very last of the merchant's hoarded provisions to be smuggled out of the city, as well as the assortment of foods supplied by individual refugees, ensuring that nobody went hungry.

To Marbuck, any food had been a banquet. Each meal had been enjoyed in the company of Elibeth, Dania, Hamish, and the children. It was pleasant, but Marbuck could not deny the feeling of foreboding that tainted every moment. The Erosion would not allow its presence to be forgotten, and Marbuck found herself ruminating on what awaited her former companions. When word came that they were leaving, she found herself inexorably drawn toward the crowd that had gathered before them.

It seemed that the entire encampment had gathered to see off the strange travelers. Reie, her veil in place, stood alongside Jalam, Kemp, and Falstaff. Like Marbuck, they had eaten heartily, and they now carried a small selection of provisions with them. They were joined by Rayburn and nine of the former guardsmen, including Winfield. Presiding over the entire affair was Avehav.

It was common knowledge that they sought to free Ganachim, though Avehav had been keen to keep the exact details of their plot a secret. He held no fear that the Crown had infiltrated his camp, but long practice at operating in secret had taught him discretion. When it came to the importance of their quest, however, he'd spared no words. Now, as they prepared to depart for their arranged meeting with Nedelkoff, Avehav's full powers of performance were on display.

"We set forth now on nothing less than our final hope. From lands beyond all knowledge, these wanderers have come, bearing the means for our emancipation. I can attest to their power, and their ability to restore the old one. By doing so, Phar-Mindorius's reign will end. The long history of domination by the polluted bloodline of the ancient invaders will be toppled."

The crowd cried out in excitement, and Avehav paused to enjoy it. Marbuck, with Elibeth, stood among them, but did not join in. Looking at the faces around her, she saw many others who appeared to be descendants of the people of Aurangzeb. There were others who seemed to be of Faedalian origin, and a smattering of light-skinned Vingalleans. All present appeared to be united in support of Avehav's words, even if their knowledge of the history within them was sketchy. Marbuck found his speech to be disconcertingly political. She wondered if he imagined himself as an appropriate replacement for the king. If so, harnessing the rage of the slums was certainly a canny strategy. Too bad it didn't matter; soon there would be nothing left to rule over.

"However, what we seek transcends the question of governance," Avehav said gravely. "Our people are held before a yawning abyss. It grows with each passing moment. This old one, restored and released, can halt that end."

The crowd cheered again, and Marbuck hoped that he was right. Reie had said that Ganachim *might* be able to stop the Erosion; her ability to do so had quickly morphed into an immutable fact. At least the Erosion figured into Avehav's calculations at all.

"I am forced to leave you now, in order to do all I can to aid these travelers in their quest. It's not an easy decision to make, but it must be done for the sake of all. I leave you in capable hands, though. Hassa will lead in my stead." Avehav gestured toward one of the guardsmen standing nearby; Marbuck recognized him as one of the group who'd initially captured them. "A unit of guardsmen remains under his command to protect you until we return. And we will return."

A third cheer sounded. His display of oratory might concluded, Avehav turned to join the others. He must have assumed that he would have the final word, because he bore an expression of mild surprise when Reie stepped forward.

"Avehav speaks much of ending Phar-Mindorius's reign, and from what I understand, doing so would be a noble act. He has also spoken of our hope that Ganachim can stop the Erosion. I wish to tell you all that, even if Nordabor is spared, it should still be abandoned."

Reie paused as confused murmurs spread through the crowd. Avehav looked as if he'd eaten something sour.

"Ganachim and I are going to return south, to my people, who suffer under a tyrant far greater than the last vestiges of Vingallea. I speak of a god called Setenrah. Only Ganachim can destroy him and wipe away those who rule in his name. Then my people, the Quaret, they will be truly free. Free from slavery, fear, oppression. Released from beneath the boot of those who cling to the past, and those who would use it as a pretext to commit atrocities. I invite each and every one of you to come with us. I will extend the same invitation to all those liberated from Nordabor."

The crowd gaped at her, now silent. Marbuck couldn't help but smile; she could almost see the gears of Avehav's mind turning feverishly as he tried to figure out where he might fit into this new order.

"You may doubt me, and that is understandable," Reie said. "Let me alleviate those doubts." She tore the veil away without hesitation, and the entire crowd gasped as one.

Avehav sensed an opening and eagerly stepped in. "You see! You see the power we have behind us! She is an old one—a god! She will deliver us! Wherever we go, we will be free! These lands matter not; what matters is that *we will be free!*"

The crowd exploded into a joyful cacophony. Before them, Reie was serene. It was a testament to her inherent goodwill that she was willing to bring every citizen of Nordabor, Vingallean or not, back to Quaretem with her. She would probably even accept Phar-Mindorius, if the old king was willing to part with his crown. This offer of salvation was important enough to her that she'd been willing to openly declare herself. Ignorance and superstition might have caused things to play out differently. It was fortunate, then, that Avehav was there to mold the reaction of his followers. There were certainly benefits to having a demagogue around.

Marbuck watched all of this with intense interest. When the cries of the crowd faded, and the small procession started for the north, she was momentarily startled to find that she wasn't with them. It struck her then; a terrible sense of being sundered from her fate and from ones that she had come to love. For so long, she'd been an integral part of them. Now she was just another face lost in the crowd. She'd thought that their departure would roll the guilt and doubt that she'd been feeling from her shoulders. It had, only to sink it into the deepest pit of her stomach.

Suddenly, Elibeth's hand was squeezing hers. She looked at her daughter and was amazed yet again to find that she was hardly taller than her now.

"Just promise you'll come back again."

Marbuck blinked. "What?"

"I can see how you're looking at them. I know you gave her your word, and that you did it for me. Well, this is bigger than you and me now. If you want to help them, go. I'll be okay with Dania, and she'll understand. Just promise me you'll come back again."

"Elibeth, honey, no; I'm not going anywhere." She pulled her into a hug.

"I know you'll come back," Elibeth said, ignoring her denial. "You did before; you crossed the entire world to reach me. This is just a little trip to Nordabor. I know you want to go, that you want to help her. I want you to do it. I want you to help her save us all."

Marbuck said nothing as she held her daughter. Her eyes were following her companions. She knew what the right thing to do was. She supposed she'd always known. Faced with the end of everything, she could not just sit back and hope that they succeeded. If she wanted to ensure that her daughter had a world to continue growing up in, she had to go with them. But it was more than that. She knew that she really did owe everything to Reie, and in truth, she *did* want to help her. Not out of obligation, but because she wished to be there for her friend. Never had she expected to feel kinship with the god, yet here she was.

"Mama, they're leaving," Elibeth said. "I'll be here when you get back."

Marbuck's eyes flicked between them; her daughter and the new family she had found. She grasped Elibeth's shoulders. "I promise that I'll come back."

Elibeth kissed her cheek. "I know you will. Now go." Her voice was Baylis's, and Marbuck felt like her heart was going to burst. She hugged Elibeth a final time before tearing herself away and weaving through the last of the dispersing crowd. Breaking into a run, she headed toward the gap in the trees through which the party had disappeared only a moment before. She looked back just once to see Elibeth still there, watching her go. She mopped her eyes with the back of a hand, smiled, and waved. Marbuck's own tears were instantaneous, and she nearly turned back. Instead, she returned the wave and plunged into the trees.

The party had not made it much further; Marbuck saw them just ahead of her. She wasted no time, shouting for them to wait. The guardsmen whirled about, their hands at their weapons. Seeing the source of the shouting, they relaxed.

"Reie," Marbuck said, breathing hard. The guardsmen parted, revealing Reie and the others. Falstaff's face lit up as he saw Marbuck, any umbrage he might have felt apparently forgotten. Only Kemp's smile was bigger, lifting his moustache almost to his eyes.

Reie, however, appraised her coolly. "Yes?"

"I'm coming with you."

"That isn't necessary. We don't need you," Reie said, and she began to turn away.

"No, I suppose you don't, but I made a deal. I may not have meant it then, but I mean it now."

"Go be with your daughter."

"Look, I'm sorry," Marbuck nearly shouted. "I used you, and even when I had the chance to follow through with my word, I turned my back on you. I was wrong. I was selfish, and I was wrong. I can see now that there's no running from this. It's not hyperbole to say that you and your plan are the last chance for all of humanity. And I believe you—I *actually* believe you—when you talk of a new world for everyone. I want to be a part of that; I want that for Elibeth. You got me back to her. Now please, let me help you get back to Ganachim."

Reie's face was as unreadable as if it were still hidden beneath her veil. "And what of Elibeth?"

"She told me to go; she understands what's at stake. She'll be okay."

"Welcome back!" Kemp said before Reie could respond. He brushed past her and threw an arm around Marbuck's shoulders. "Things just weren't the same without your cheery face."

"Fishwife," Falstaff said, coming to her side. His eyes were glistening. She couldn't help but smile at his pure joy.

"Well, shall we continue on?" Kemp asked the group at large, though the question was obviously aimed at Reie. All eyes turned to her.

"You see the way now," Jalam said unexpectedly. "To be honest, I doubted that you would. I am happy that I was wrong, and I freely grant you my forgiveness. I wish for you to walk with us on our journey of liberation. Deliverance forever."

Marbuck was shocked by, and grateful for, Jalam's input. She looked at Reie, whose eyebrows were hoisted, and wondered where her judgment would fall.

"Well put," Reie said to Jalam, and her face broke into a warm smile. "You could instruct me on my own teachings." She looked at Marbuck. "I have allowed my hurt to blind me. Your actions were far more justified than I was willing to admit, especially considering that you were right about me. Had I been in your place, I would have done the same thing. It pleases me that you are here now, and that our bond has risen above the manner of our meeting. I am prepared to abandon any grievance that lies between us."

"As am I," Marbuck said. They had reached the point of understanding; they were no longer the woman who'd been marked for death and the god who'd served the executioner. The pall that had hung over them from the start was finally dissolving, and Marbuck was glad for it.

"Well that settles that," Kemp said, giving Marbuck a hearty shake before releasing her from his grasp. "Shall we?"

Rayburn, who'd been watching their exchange intently, was startled back himself. "Oh, yes, of course," he said, dabbing at his forehead with a cloth.

"Alright, men, let's move," Avehav said to the guardsmen, if only to insert himself into the conversation.

Marbuck fell in beside Falstaff as they began to walk, slipping back into the same rhythm that she'd grown so accustomed to. It was comforting to know that, this time, Elibeth was safe. Or, as safe as anyone could be with the end of everything rapidly approaching. Marbuck felt like she'd lifted a veil of her own, one woven of fear and doubt, and one that had obscured her vision of the larger events unfolding. She thought of Katiek and the rest of the Quaret, and wondered if Setenrah had learned of Reie's absence yet. She thought of the huddled prisoners, trapped within the walls of Nordabor, and of Ganachim, deteriorating somewhere in isolated torment. It was all just like her own story, only writ large. Across the entire expanse of their fallen world there was pain, longing, suffering, hope, love; everything she had experienced and endured. Hers was not a singular existence, but a small part of a reality spun into being by a god that had long since died. The Erosion was the bitter inheritance shared by all, as was the cruelty of the misbegotten creations that danced across their creator's grave. Marbuck now felt a new weight settle upon her, not one born of a single-minded desire stained by dread, but one formed by the dream of mending everything that had been ruined. She allowed herself to believe that Reie and Ganachim would, in fact, bring the deliverance that Jalam spoke of.

And if they did, Elibeth would not just be safe now, but forever.

• • •

Once again traveling through the unvarying woodland, it was easy for Marbuck to imagine that they'd never come upon the camp at all. Only her knowledge of Elibeth and the presence of their new comrades dispelled the illusion.

It was strange to be joined by so many others. Winfield and his guardsmen were a fairly insular group, but Rayburn and Avehav more than compensated for their aloofness. Oozing nervous energy, Rayburn was prone to babbling. It was clear that he did not want to be at the mercy of Phar-Mindorius, and Marbuck considered him all the braver for committing to do so anyway. Avehav, as glib as ever, walked the line, speaking to everyone in turn. Inevitably, he cornered Marbuck, pulling her away from Falstaff.

"It's exciting to be joined by a fellow descendant of Aurangzeb, particularly one who has been within the walls of the old capital. You know, I have always dreamed of reclaiming that place." His voice dropped slightly. "Not for the Crown, but for our people. I wish to scour away the stain of Vin-Sadavat and restore Buqaardia."

"There's nothing left to restore," Marbuck said matter-of-factly.

Avehav was not be dissuaded. "Well, I understand that it's been left to ruin, but based on what Reie says of Ganachim, I believe it can be done."

Marbuck doubted that, having regained her strength and freedom, Ganachim would be interested in pursuing a former aristocrat's pet project, but she did not say so. Instead, she grunted noncommittally.

"It would be poetic," Avehav continued, oblivious to her doubt. "The final descendant, heir to a lost kingdom, reclaiming his rightful place with the aid of the god he'd helped to free. I would not expect you to know this, of course, as my family always kept it a secret in order to protect us from persecution, but I can trace my lineage back to the last sultan."

This claim had apparently captured Reie's attention; she'd fallen back to listen, though Avehav remained unaware. Catching Marbuck's eye, she shook her head. Remembering what she'd said about the grisly fate of Prishnah the Pardoner and his heirs, Marbuck knew that Avehav was either lying or mistaken. She imagined it to be the latter, but she lacked the desire to correct him. If his delusions of grandeur were what motivated him to help, she saw no need to dispel them.

"Yes, it's said that he escaped Phan-Ellara's purge and took refuge in the eastern desert. There, he swore that his line would retake Buqaardia and restore Aurangzeb. By infiltrating the court, his descendants sought to make that happen. And now, here is our chance."

"Poetic, indeed," Marbuck said, thinking it much more likely that Avehav's ancestor was probably one of the faithless satraps who'd secured a spot in the court by swearing fealty to Vingallea. At some point, his family had probably rewritten their history in order to make it more palatable, a notion that was certainly not unheard of in Vingallea.

"What strange providence placed you in our path, I cannot say, but it is a boon to have one of such illustrious lineage aiding us," Reie said.

Avehav hadn't known that she was listening, and his surprise quickly evolved into a satisfied smile, though one that he strove to mask with humility.

"However," Reie said, "I do not want you to harbor any misconceptions about what we are doing here. I am grateful beyond measure for your help, so I want to be clear with my intentions. Like Nordabor, Buqaardia is finished. Your people will be free, but they will never reign over anything again. The old systems failed, not just those of mankind but those of the gods as well. In Quaretem, a new age will begin, one free of the trappings that brought us here. I think it important that we be transparent with each other. Freedom, you spoke of, not the restoration of Aurangzeb. So is it freedom for the people that you truly seek, or something else?"

Avehav must have known that he'd arrived at a crossroad. His smile had withered, and his brow had furrowed. He opened his mouth, closed it, and opened it again.

"You need not decide now. Whatever your ultimate aims may be, for the time being, our common goal assures your loyalty. I know a thing or two about such arrangements." Reie looked at Marbuck, who flushed, though the words had not been said with malice. "But know this: a time will come when you will have to make your choice, and I will not abide any grasping treachery. Nor will Ganachim."

Avehav had blanched. "Of course," he managed.

"I'm glad we understand each other," Reie said pleasantly.

She left them then, trotting lightly to catch back up to Jalam. Marbuck watched as Avehav struggled to resurrect the bravado that Reie had just stricken down. Failing to do so, he settled for a curt nod and dropped away, leaving Marbuck alone.

He did not speak to her again.

• • •

The meeting place provided Marbuck with her first view of the Vinecrown Keep since leaving it behind so long ago. They'd crossed what remained of the Einfallen, which had been barely enough to wet their ankles, and come to a small clearing, where the spires of the city could be clearly seen. Rising above the trees, the greatest example of Nordabor's power and stability had changed. Framed by the jagged edges of the Erosion reaching across the sky, the Vinecrown Keep was now a battered, haunted thing. The clouds may have been swept away, but the dawn's light was lost in the pulsating darkness looming over everything. One of the four turrets was gone, leaving behind a jagged hole in the top of the structure, into which part of the roof had collapsed. Rayburn had spoken of mass burnings of the dead after the cataclysm, and evidence of those fires blackened the three remaining turrets. It seemed insane that anybody would choose to remain in such a place, but of course, madness was said to hold sway in the court of Phar-Mindorius.

"I'm having a difficult time believing what I'm seeing," Falstaff said beside her. They were waiting for Nedelkoff, and there was nothing to do but marvel at the nightmarish view.

"That about sums up this entire odyssey," she said.

Falstaff chuckled. "You're not wrong. I'm glad you're here."

"I know; you've told me several times."

"And I'll probably tell you a few more times before we're through."

He nudged his shoulder against hers and they stood in companionable silence. After a moment, Marbuck realized that Falstaff had shifted his gaze to Reie.

"She's going to change everything," he said.

Marbuck had long resented Falstaff for his eager discipleship, which had often bled into infatuation, but now that bitterness was gone. She was surprised to find that she actually agreed with him.

Before she could say so, a shrill whistle sounded from a nearby thicket. Winfield responded with a whistle of his own. After a brief pause, a woman emerged from the shrubbery, plucked an errant leaf from her sleeve, and unnecessarily smoothed back her hair, which appeared to be permanently encased in a severe braid. There could be no doubt that it was Nedelkoff. She wore the uniform of a royal guardsman, and a scowl to match.

Rayburn rushed forward and clasped her hand. "It's good to see you again."

She nodded professionally, scanning the crowd. Her eyes settled on Reie and her eyebrows rose minutely.

"Under-Captain," Avehav said, striding toward her. "I'm pleased to find that you're still able to answer my summons. I don't wish to cast aside pleasantries, but we have much to discuss, and our time is short."

Nedelkoff was still looking at Reie. "Indeed, it is. I suspect this operation is going to be a bit … different. Let's talk."

CHAPTER 37

Within the vacant chamber of the absent vizier, the grinding peal of the advancing Erosion was somewhat muted. Phar-Mindorius, the last king of Vingallea, sat not upon his throne, but on the high-backed wooden chair that his divine advisor had once occupied. He had long discarded all hope that the vizier might miraculously return, but he still nursed a dull, unspoken belief that some residue of the enigmatic being's wisdom lingered, which he might somehow absorb. Unfortunately, not a whiff of guidance remained.

Over and over, Phar-Mindorius turned the Skullcap Crown of Phan-Ellara in his hands. He ran his fingers over the bone, feeling the slight deviations of the cranial sutures. It was strange to consider that the mind of Vingallea's greatest monarch had once been held within it. The crown now felt unbearably heavy whenever he wore it, as if its renowned source was somehow rejecting him. He removed it whenever he was free from his official duties, which was now more often than not. Safe in his sheltered privacy, he studied the relic he no longer felt worthy of, ruminating on things that might have been.

It was terribly unfair that his life should be so accursed.

"What have I done to be abandoned like this? How did I wrong you? Please, don't leave me on my own," he rasped to the silent room. Nothing answered but the quiet hum of destruction.

Phar-Mindorius sighed. Even his voice reeked of weakness now. Under the endless, pressing burden of maintaining the peace and stability of the realm, he had been stripped of his vitality. Where his predecessors had enjoyed informal titles that boasted of their prowess, those who remained in the court had taken to calling him the 'Whispering King', though never to his face. Despite his other infirmities, his ears still heard their derisive gossip just fine. They spoke of a weakened, doddering man who didn't even have the strength to raise his voice in command. They were not wrong. He was, in fact, reduced to whispering his orders to his servants.

Of course, they weren't really his orders anymore anyway, if they ever had been. His hidden vizier had been his puppeteer before, he saw that now. In his desperate need, he'd allowed the vacuum left by the vizier's disappearance to be filled by two men: Captain Eleazar Vitus and High Shepherd Anton Badgett. They were regents, in practice if not official capacity. Their assistance was far from flawless, though, and they bickered ceaselessly. Their views almost always conflicted, save for one thing: they were still loyal to their enfeebled sovereign.

In a way, Phar-Mindorius found it fitting that he should be physically collapsing. It was as if he were inextricably bound to the well-being of Nordabor, and by default, the slave-god that had sustained it. Ganachim's life was the spring that fed Nordabor, and, like him, it had nearly run dry. It was astounding that she still lived at all; it was now possible that the Erosion might consume them before they were forced to consume themselves.

According to the latest reports of the scouts, the Erosion had been steadily accelerating, and its arrival was nigh at hand, the hole chewing on the edge of space now little more than a full-cycle's ride from the city. Half of the scouts sent to monitor it hadn't bothered returning but had simply fled south. Vitus, who'd seen it himself and was quite grateful to be back in the city, was of the opinion that it was a threat, and he evasively hinted at believing, at least in part, the tale spun by the God Eater. Phar-Mindorius, in all but his darkest moments, rejected that narrative outright. Most of his court followed suit, blind loyalty and a fixation with power eclipsing their fears. As for the remaining citizenry, ignorance of the true danger had kept them mostly docile. Phar-Mindorius knew that it wouldn't last, not with the Einfallen drying up. When they learned the full truth, they would trample each other in a mindless bid to escape, dissolving the very last of Vingallea in the process. He couldn't allow that to happen, not while he could still fix everything.

For, while the Erosion was the greatest source of Phar-Mindorius's despair, it was also, paradoxically, his only source of hope. This feeling grew from the beliefs held by Badgett and his subordinate shepherds. They saw the Erosion as the culmination of their faith, as the second coming of the world's creator, first reborn as the Void-God, now released from cosmic exile. Phar-Mindorius could certainly understand why; it was easy to equate the emptiness coming for them with the deliverance that the shepherds prayed for over every dying person.

Recently, the shepherds had taken these prayers even further, loudly chanting them as they openly worshipped the broken sky. Some, including Badgett, claimed to have entered a trance-like state in which they could hear the voice of their deity and bear witness to his mighty works.

It was during one of these events that Badgett had supposedly received the vision that Phar-Mindorius obsessively clung to. His own faith had always strayed more toward a belief in the divinity of his own revered bloodline, though he'd always paid proper lip service to the Void-God. Now, he desperately wanted to believe.

According to Badgett, the expedition had succeeded. Phir-Ramarian had recovered every shard of the Scale of Judgment, and in the hands of the heir of Vingallea, it had been reforged. He had opened the Gates of Paradise, and Paradise was the Void. Instead of waiting for every citizen of Nordabor to march north, the Void was coming to them, to deliver them to eternal bliss. Phir-Ramarian, the Scale of Judgment held aloft like a conqueror's standard, was riding before it, the herald of the Void-God. It was a breathtaking vision.

In a rare moment of boldness, Vitus had cautioned Phar-Mindorius not to put too much stock into what could be nothing more than a delusion born of fanaticism. Phar-Mindorius had rebuked him harshly. Enamored as he was by his own prestige, and fearing to lose it, Vitus had not mentioned his doubts again. In truth, Badgett's vision wasn't exactly the fulfillment of destiny that Phar-Mindorius had been picturing, but it still meant saving his realm and the legacy of Vingallea. Most importantly, it meant that his son was still alive. For that reason alone, he *had* to believe.

Badgett had said nothing regarding the rest of the expedition, and Phar-Mindorius found that he didn't really care. He could live with the loss of them all, even Cyprian. His remorse for shunning his nephew was forgotten in the face of the momentous events unfolding before him. Phir-Ramarian was all that mattered now; he was the hinge on which it all turned.

Phar-Mindorius thought often of one of the last times he'd spoken with his son. He had been in his chamber, preparing for the expedition's imminent departure, his loyal scribe Pike helping him into his formal armor. The rest of the royal procession had already been assembled; a retinue of courtly retainers and guardsmen waiting below. Phar-Mindorius had dismissed Pike, and then it had just been the two of them; father and son; king and heir. He hadn't needed to impart the importance of the expedition on Phir-Ramarian, but he had anyway.

"We are the last links of an unbroken chain that stretches back to the beginning of life itself," he'd said, planting a hand on his son's broad shoulder. "Though its distant links recede far into the past, its strength remains undiminished. We cannot allow it to be broken now."

Phir-Ramarian had nodded solemnly. "We will not be the last, Father. The chain of our blood will stretch on into eternity. Vingallea's glory will continue forever, and we will be remembered as the ones who restored it; the ones who brought our people to Paradise."

Tears had threatened to spill from Phar-Mindorius's eyes then, and he'd beheld his son as something more than a man. He'd become the embodiment of their people, the savior upon which the weight of history had fallen.

Now that he was gone, his ultimate fate shrouded and only tantalizingly hinted at by prophecy, Phar-Mindorius could only see his son as the boy he'd once been. His memory was awash with images from a happier time; his son's first shambling steps; his little voice reciting his letters; the way he'd splashed giddily during his baths, sloshing nearly every drop from the stone basin he'd been washed in; riding together through the verdant woodlands. Looking back, Phar-Mindorius was stricken with how blissful those simple times now seemed. Of course, it had all come crashing down when his desire for a second child had taken Nelsinore from him. Perpetual gloom had descended upon his life then, and he'd taken refuge in his role as the king. Affairs of the state had taken precedence, tutors had taken Phir-Ramarian, and entropy had started to take Ganachim. Consumed by his desire to sustain the realm, Phar-Mindorius had lost himself and much of his relationship with his son. At some point, it had become difficult for him to separate the boy he'd raised from the title clamped to his name. Now, dejected and alone, Phar-Mindorius wished that he'd forgone all the talk of continuity and simply told his son that he loved him instead.

Perhaps he would still get a chance to do so.

Phar-Mindorius lurched to his feet and gingerly made his way down the steps of the absent vizier's platform. A moment later, he emerged back into his bedchamber. He knew that Vitus, who'd rarely delegated the task of guarding the king since returning from leading the search parties, would be waiting just outside, but he didn't want to talk to him. He was in no mood to speak with someone who would only agree out of obligation and fear of reprisal. Ganachim was always an option; she wouldn't say anything one way or another. He still spoke to her often, though he'd been spending more and more time in the vizier's seat. She, of course, offered nothing, where perhaps some divine touch might be felt in the hidden chamber of the vizier. Furthermore, her decay was like a mirror of his own, and seeing it did nothing to comfort him.

That was where Badgett excelled. Phar-Mindorius intended to see him now, wishing to have his nerves soothed by gentle words. With any luck, Badgett had experienced another reassuring vision.

He shuffled to the chamber's door and, opening it, found Vitus just where he'd expected him to be. The captain's demeanor, however, was quite unexpected. He turned toward the king with a jittery nervousness, his pouchy face flushed. The razor burn encircling his neck had turned an angry shade of purple.

"What's happened?" Phar-Mindorius asked, expecting a multitude of catastrophes.

Strangely, Vitus's mouth twitched with a suppressed smile. "Your Majesty, the guardsmen manning the main gates have apprehended two travelers approaching the city from the south. They walked right up to the gate and offered no resistance. The guardsmen report that one of them is Fritz Rayburn."

A short burst of rage rattled Phar-Mindorius's thin frame. Rayburn had been entrusted with keeping the expedition provisioned. Instead, he'd unexpectedly shone up in Nordabor spewing tales of tragedy. Then, called upon to support his prince, the craven merchant had refused. Before he could be held accountable, he'd fled the city, like so many others who'd chosen desertion over service to their king. Phar-Mindorius hated the apostates, and had done everything in his power to prevent the spread of their dissension. He knew that leaks still existed, though, and Rayburn was a prime example.

"Excellent. See to it that he's made an example of," Phar-Mindorius said, wincing against the pain of his throat. It hadn't occurred to him to question why Rayburn had returned at all.

"Of course, my lord," Vitus said briskly, "but there's more. Rayburn was trying to bring the other man to see you. He supposedly hails from a distant land beyond the crater."

"There is no land beyond the crater."

"Yes, I know, Your Majesty, but that's not all. He says that he is a healer. He says that he can save the old one. He called it 'Ganachim.'"

Phar-Mindorius had become as rigid as stone, gazing vacantly into nothing. Vitus stared at him expectantly.

Finally, the king turned to his captain. "Bring them to me."

CHAPTER 38

The air in the tunnel was heavy with the reek of burned human flesh. They crept along slowly, mindful not to slip in the foul accumulation of gore and polluted water that coated the stone floor. Nedelkoff led the way, holding aloft a single lantern. Reie, with her halo once again covered, Jalam, Falstaff, and Marbuck followed behind.

Marbuck had known that such tunnels existed, though she'd never entered one. From her own stint at the Ivy Citadel she'd learned that the shepherds utilized such spaces to cart out the desecrated dead, particularly when the deceased had been a person of high standing whose ruined body might create a spectacle were it to be paraded through the streets. The shepherds used the main gates just as often, though, particularly when they were returning to the city after concluding their unpleasant business. The conventional wisdom was that, seeing the befouled, stinking shepherds, the rabble might consider their own fate and be inspired to be more diligent in their prayers.

According to Nedelkoff, the use of the tunnels had generally increased since the gates had been ordered shut. Via her own observations and the reports of fellow dissidents, she'd located a number of them. The one she'd led them to was in disrepair and still used rather infrequently. That was good as encountering shepherds would not spoil their plot outright, but it would complicate things. Remaining undetected was worth enduring the stench.

That stench had been the first indicator that they'd reached the burning fields. It had hung in the stagnant air, a harbinger of the gruesome vista that awaited them. It seemed to cling to the surrounding foliage, which had been coated with a greasy residue and flecked with ash. Emerging from the last of the trees, they'd come upon the field itself. It had spread out before the blackened walls of the city, a rolling tract of smoldering carcasses and noxious pools. Many of the torched bodies had been dumped in tumbled heaps, a testament to the great loss of life that had ushered in the Erosion's birth. Marbuck had seen the fields before, but that had been before such a large influx of the dead.

Seeing Nordabor again, surrounded as it was by a vast moat of ruined corpses, she'd been stricken by what a terrible sight the supposed last bastion of civilization really was. Stripped of its noble façade, it was little different from every other brutal outpost that had managed to survive in their barren world. It was a grimy holdover from an ancient time, as stained by violence as Vin-Sadavat, as steeped in oppression as Quaretem. Only the enslavement of Ganachim had kept them from devolving into something that probably would have rivaled the depravity of the skinners. More than anything, the sight of the city had reminded Marbuck of the Monolith of Pha, encircled by its legion of shades. She'd known in that moment that Reie was absolutely right about Nordabor; it held nothing but the last clinging vapors of Vingallea. All of the esteemed lineages and illustrious lies were meaningless when weighed against the Erosion.

The imminent arrival of the Erosion was now a certainty. Nedelkoff had personally seen the shuddering edge of the remaining world, where the land had been cleaved away and fallen into nothingness. The latest reports had put the Erosion at only a full-cycle's ride from Nordabor. Prior to hearing from Avehav's courier, Nedelkoff had been preparing for her own permanent departure. She'd spoken about the spreading collapse of their reality in a detached, mechanical manner. Marbuck supposed that it was her way of processing something that was incomprehensible, which was what Marbuck had been striving to do ever since she'd first seen the crack in the sky.

However one might reckon with it, a simple truth was now clear: time was running out. They needed to get in, free Ganachim, and get as far away from Nordabor as possible.

With the city in sight, the group had separated to pursue their plot. Their parting had been brief, but heavy with import. Kemp had been all smiles, of course, but Marbuck had suspected that he'd been striving to mask his fear. Rayburn's fear, on the other hand, had been quite evident. Expecting to be quickly apprehended, they'd tromped off toward the main gates with nothing but the clothes on their backs and not a weapon between them, save Kemp's knife, expertly hidden on the huntsman's person. Marbuck hoped that it would be enough.

Avehav, Winfield, and the rest of the guardsmen had kept to the tree line, making their way toward the same gate. Avehav intended to launch the attack after the passage of two cycles, as best as he could estimate. Everyone had known that it would be impossible to execute a plan based on precision timing; each of them understood that they would have to play their part and hope that everything came together more or less at the right moment.

Marbuck and the others had set off then, picking their way across the burning fields. The slowly wafting smoke had obscured them, allowing them to creep, unseen, to the city walls. Along the way, they'd passed near three shepherds who'd been extinguishing a sufficiently burned body. The shepherds had been quickly enveloped in smoke and lost, having given no indication that they'd spotted the strangers moving across the field.

Nedelkoff led them first to the wall, pitted and cracked when viewed up close. Then, after briefly skirting along the wall, they'd arrived at the tunnel's entrance. Brushing aside a mess of tangled bramble, Nedelkoff had revealed a rusted iron door inlaid with rotten bands of wood. It had been left slightly ajar, propped open by a lantern. She'd snatched the lantern and led them into the tunnel beyond. Marbuck had expected the stench of the fires to abate, but the smell had fully permeated the tunnel, their clothing, and probably their nostrils. It wasn't until Nedelkoff announced that they'd reached the end of the tunnel that the smell finally diminished.

"Up these steps, there's another door," Nedelkoff explained, hanging her lantern on a hook. "We'll be coming out near the Healer's Ward. It's pretty well deserted so we should be able to pass through unseen."

Reie's interest had been piqued by the reference to healing. "Deserted? I would think there would be a high demand for healers during such turbulent times."

"There are few left who practice such arts, and fewer still who actually make it before the healers. The shepherds either stand by with the dying or the death is too rapid for any intervention. The ward is essentially empty now. There's no healing in this place."

Marbuck thought of Baylis's death, and how there'd been no chance for him to be healed. Death came swiftly, or it came with plodding inevitability. She'd never put much stock into the antiquated lore of the healers. They'd only ever seemed to minister to the needs of the elite, prolonging death with their quackery, but never stopping it; a far cry from the forgotten god who'd been the source of their craft. It made sense that, facing the imminent end of everything, their talents for useless stalling had been abandoned.

"So, all memory of my teachings has been lost," Reie said softly.

Nedelkoff looked at the covered form of Reie's halo, seeming to assess the high strangeness of the being before her. "Aye, it has. Many things have been lost." She cleared her throat. "Okay, line up. I need to collect your weapons. Then I'll bind your wrists."

• • •

Leading her small train of prisoners, Nedelkoff strode with the confidence of one who unquestionably belonged. Marbuck, on the other hand, was shocked by how out of place she felt in her own city.

Her time away had certainly changed her perception of Vingallea's last hold, but it was much more than that. What had been a bustling, stable place, albeit one that had started to teeter, was now a derelict shell. Marbuck had been picturing them slipping out of the door and blending into whatever people were milling about the Healer's Ward. Instead, they'd entered a trash-strewn alley that was entirely deserted. The Healer's Ward itself was a squat, gray structure from which a single tower arose, crowned by a narrow, sloped roof. Most of the clay tiles that had comprised that roof were gone, and a singular, jagged crack ran down the entire tower. There were no healers present; they saw only a single man, stinking of drink and sprawled across the pitted steps leading to the ward's front doors. He twitched as they passed, and Marbuck wondered if Reie had briefly ministered to him.

Leaving the Healer's Ward behind, Marbuck was given a tour of Nordabor's devastation. Many structures had been flattened completely, and the few people they encountered scurried out of sight quickly. Only loudly chanting shepherds and roving bands of city guardsmen walked freely. They were young and boisterous, lazily saluting Nedelkoff and jeering at her prisoners as they passed. Guardsmen had always been defined by their military discipline, but the dregs who swelled their ranks now reminded Marbuck more of slavers. They swaggered about, inflated by their newfound power, thirsty to wield it. Many nervous eyes peered through the cracks of shuttered windows. Anything resembling normal commerce had been abandoned; it seemed that the citizenry was living in a state of captive waiting, fearful of wanton persecution and ignorant of their true proximity to doom. They made Marbuck think of fish captured in a net; blank, desperate, faces.

Continuing toward the Vinecrown Keep, Nedelkoff led them by Angler's Row. It was an old street, lined by townhomes that had long ago been divided into tenement houses. Running from the Mercantile Causeway, which had been decimated by the cataclysm, to the quays and dockyards that Marbuck knew so well, it was where her home was, or rather, had been. She supposed that the musty flat was still there, her few, worthless possessions waiting just where she'd left them. She felt a brief tug at her heart. Her home hadn't been much, but it had been a happy place, for a time. She'd given birth to Elibeth there, a nest in which she and Baylis's love had grown. It had also been haunted by his absence. All things considered, it was not difficult to pass it by. She had left it for the last time long ago so there was no need to return to it now. Elibeth wasn't there, and there was no time for useless dredging of the past.

Wherever they went, it was eerily silent, save for the rumbling from the north. It had become nearly constant, punctuated by crescendos of twanging, snapping booms. In just the time since they'd entered the city, the Erosion's impact had become more pronounced. An unreal shimmer buzzed in the air, giving everything a strange sense of thinness. Marbuck could feel that shimmer passing through her, as if her entire body was being loosened by the uncanny vibrations. It felt like she might come apart completely, lost in a swirl of disconnected particles. Panic was nipping at her heels, and she pressed her wrists into her bindings as hard as she could to stave it off. The pain was still real, and it seemed to solidify her.

Nedelkoff had not skimped on their bindings. She'd tied their wrists tightly with rough stretches of rope, and then linked the four of them together with a longer line, which she held taut as she marched them through the empty streets. She was girded by weapons; from her belt dangled Marbuck's blade, Falstaff's axe, and Jalam's saber, alongside her own sword. As she walked, the instruments of bloodshed clinked against each other. Weaponless and bound, Marbuck really *did* feel like a prisoner, and that was nearly as unpleasant as the effects of the Erosion.

Finally, they reached the wall that encircled the castle grounds, where two royal guardsmen flanked an arched gateway leading inside. Like their city counterparts, these men were young, with one of them sporting an acne-speckled face. They, however, did not seem to be enjoying themselves, looking as if they were eagerly awaiting permission to abandon their post and run. Recognizing Nedelkoff as a direct superior who might release them, they proved to be deferential.

"Under-Captain," they said in unison, snapping off salutes.

Nedelkoff returned the gesture hastily. "Open the gate," she commanded.

They did as they were told, and Nedelkoff yanked the rope. "C'mon, you lot," she growled, starting forward.

"Quite the haul," one of the guardsmen observed with a nervous chuckle.

Nedelkoff stopped and turned back. "Are you speaking to me?"

The guardsman's face turned bright red in an instant. "Sir—I just—"

"Do not *ever* address a superior with familiarity. I am not your tavern pal, with which you can swap stories. You are relieved of duty. Both of you. Perhaps next time you will mind your business and hold your tongue."

The guardsmen stood with identical expressions of shock and humiliation. Then something like relief dawned on the one who'd been the target of Nedelkoff's ire. "We're dismissed?"

"Yes."

"What of our post?" the pockmarked guardsman said, utterly confused. "There's no relief to take over. There'll be—"

"I will not tell you again."

"Of course," the first guardsman said. "Thank you, sir." He snatched the sleeve of his counterpart and pulled him away.

"They would have stood here until the ground vanished beneath them," Nedelkoff said as she watched them go. "There was no relief coming. Phar-Mindorius might not know it yet, but his Royal Guard's chain of command is disintegrating as we speak. Soon, only Vitus will remain."

"Vitus?" Reie asked.

"The chief officer of the Royal Guard. He's a career bootlicker and a poor replacement for Captain Mather." She paused, realizing the need for further explanation. "He was lost with the expedition; a good man and a fine leader. Anyway, Vitus knows what the Erosion is—he took over the search parties after my team discovered it—but he's too spineless to tell the king anything but what he wants to hear. Vitus will either die with him or be the last to desert him. Well, except for maybe Badgett. He's the supreme high shepherd, and he's either delusional or deranged. Either way, Phar-Mindorius listens to him over anyone, even Vitus."

If Marbuck had retained any hope that Phar-Mindorius would willingly free Ganachim, it would have evaporated now. He'd apparently surrounded himself with sycophants and lunatics; he was not going to bow to the reason of strangers.

"With any luck, we won't be bothered by either of them," Nedelkoff said. "Come on."

She led them through the castle grounds, past dry, cracked fountains, withered hedgerows, and crooked statuary, surrounded by weeds. Rounding the side of the keep, they eschewed the front doors in favor of a smaller entrance set into the eastern side of the building. There, the light of the perpetual dawn, overshadowed as it was by the Erosion blotting out the sky, managed to faintly touch the last, brittle vines clinging to the keep.

"This is the guardsmen's postern. It's how we get prisoners into the dungeon without troubling the esteemed nobles of the court, and it's how I'll get you there now. After all, we wouldn't want to upset any titled dandies." Nedelkoff smiled fiercely, and then produced an iron key from a ring on her belt. A moment later and the door was unlocked and swung open to reveal a series of stone steps leading down into darkness. She snagged a lantern from a hook on the wall, lit it, and descended.

Bound together, Marbuck and the others followed.

CHAPTER 39

Captain Vitus was waiting for them in the foyer.

"Fritz Rayburn," he said good-naturedly. "I'd thought we'd seen the last of you."

Rayburn attempted his best approximation of a casual smile. "Captain Vitus, you must know that I have only ever been an obedient servant to the Crown. If my actions troubled anyone, then I beg your pardon. I knew that my plan would be frowned upon by the king, but I had to go through with it. I was *certain* that I could secure help for us elsewhere. And here it is." He gestured toward Kemp, who bowed slightly.

Vitus examined the foreigner with skepticism. "Enthralling, but you waste your explanations on me."

"Of course," Rayburn said. He felt a sudden and urgent need to urinate.

"I must commend your work here," Vitus said, turning to the two guardsmen who'd escorted Rayburn and Kemp from the main gates. "You were right to have this brought to my attention. These two were searched, correct?"

Rayburn's heart stuttered; the guardsmen *had* searched them, but they had not located Kemp's knife, concealed within the high collar of a tightly-laced boot. It was all they had should their reception prove to be less than cordial. Now, he was certain that they were going to be searched again, and that Kemp's knife would be discovered.

"Yes, sir," one of the guardsmen said. "They had nothing on them."

"Good. You may return to your post now."

Rayburn realized that he'd been holding his breath, and he cautiously released it.

"Yes, sir," the guardsmen said, saluting. As they turned to go, one of them halted reluctantly. "Sir, I apologize, but there's one more thing. The gate to the castle grounds was unmanned when we passed through it." The guardsman winced as if he were expecting Vitus to explode at him. The captain merely nodded, his lips pursed.

"Thank you for notifying me. It will be addressed."

"Thank you, sir." The guardsman joined his partner and, together, they marched off, leaving only Rayburn, Kemp, and Vitus in the foyer.

Rayburn had never seen it so empty. It seemed that, deprived of their sinecures, the nobility no longer saw a reason to congregate there. He wondered how many had gathered their households and arranged for safe passage from the city, choosing to take their chances in the wastes. Not one of them had joined Avehav. They would certainly be in for a rude awakening, especially going it alone; the world beyond their comfortable chambers was an unforgiving place, even without the Erosion.

"Well, shall we?" Vitus said, one hand resting on the hilt of his sword.

"Of course," Rayburn said again, and the three of them proceeded toward the grand staircase and the throne room.

"Your keep is a bit gloomy," Kemp observed. "Quite different from what I'm used to."

Rayburn shot him a glance, fearing that his inane chatter might cause them trouble. Kemp only grinned and winked. As they entered the throne room, he whistled low. Rayburn wasn't sure if he was reacting to the tremendous size of the space, or its dilapidated state.

The throne room of the Vinecrown Keep had never really been a lively place, at least not in Rayburn's lifetime, but it had always carried a sense of regal majesty. Boasting broad fireplaces, rare Vingallean relics, and walls lined with elaborate tapestries, it had been the prime example of the continued strength and stability of their realm. Then, the Erosion had burst into existence, the violence of its formation tearing away one of the keep's spires and rattling the entire structure. Part of the gabled roof had gone with the collapsing spire, and the hole in the ceiling now showed a pale sky shot through with tendrils of distorted darkness. Several of the tapestries had fallen in crumpled heaps, and not a single servant remained to hang them back up. The fireplaces were as cold as the grave.

Even the massive skeleton of Aedesda, discovered long ago by Ror-ik Fontaine, had not been spared. One of the wires holding it aloft had snapped, and the skeleton now hung crookedly, its halo askew, lending a sense of drunkenness to the God of Punishment's remains. It would have been comical were it not so piteous.

It was this macabre display that had captured Kemp's attention. Gazing fixedly at it, he hadn't seemed to notice the old king occupying the marble throne in front of it. Rayburn did, though, and seeing Phar-Mindorius again turned his blood to ice. The old monarch who could end his life with a single word was practically swimming in his mildewed robes. Stress had driven the last vestiges of the original black from his beard, leaving only a matted plume of yellowed white. The Skullcap Crown of Phan-Ellara sat as crookedly on his head as the halo above the dead trophy behind him. His eyes alone shone with authority, as if the younger man who'd held sway over a prosperous land was now locked within a husk that mirrored his dying realm. The authority was not alone, though; it walked hand in hand with madness.

Vitus stepped forward, clearing his throat. "Announcing! Phar-Min-dorius, Lord of the City of Nordabor and High King and Savior of the Collected Realms of Vingallea!"

His announcement rang through the empty hall. The sad adherence to meaningless titles and pageantry only highlighted the destitute state of Phar-Mindorius's court.

Having completed the task of the now-absent herald, Vitus gave a curt little bow and stepped over to stand beside the throne. Rayburn found himself wondering what had become of the king's herald. He decided that he didn't really want to know.

"Phar-Mindorius wishes to extend a gracious welcome to his guests," Vitus said. "One, he recognizes as a foreign dignitary. The other, as a prior subject. Phar-Mindorius would like for you to explain yourself, Rayburn."

Rayburn looked at Phar-Mindorius whose expression had not changed. He swallowed and stepped forward. "Your Majesty, I offer my utmost apologies for my absence. I know the trying times that we inhabit, and I know the great weight that you labor beneath. I never intended to abandon my oaths to the Crown. I simply wished to avoid burdening your mind with further troubles. Had I failed, you would have forgotten me completely, writing me off as a deserter. Had you known of my task, and I failed, it would have been another tragedy that I did not wish for you to suffer. I only ever sought to serve your best interests, and in finding this healer, I believe I have."

Rayburn had rehearsed these lies countless times, knowing that speaking them aloud would be incredibly difficult. He hoped that his discomfort came across as pure nerves, and not the result of his inability to lie convincingly.

With a wave of his hand, Phar-Mindorius summoned Vitus to his side. The Whispering King rasped something into Vitus's ear, and the captain nodded his understanding. He turned to Rayburn.

"Phar-Mindorius is not an ignorant rube; he knows deceit well. He is reserving his judgment until he hears from this supposed healer. Give an account of yourself, stranger."

Kemp stepped forward casually, hands on his belt, chest forward. His demeanor was everything that Rayburn's was not.

"Your Majesty," he drawled, nodding to Phar-Mindorius. "I am Henrick Kemp, of Quaretem. I've heard much from my friend here of your wisdom and glory. I must say, he sold you short. Verily, you are a king worthy of your crown. And your people! A hardy, steadfast lot, for sure, and one deserving of a better fate than that which is approaching. Rayburn told me of your god. He told me that she's the key to your kingdom, and that she's dying. I can change that; I can heal—"

Phar-Mindorius lifted an imperious hand and Kemp stopped his pitch. Vitus leaned in for his next lines, and Phar-Mindorius supplied them.

"How is it that you come from beyond the crater?" Vitus asked. "And how can you possibly heal a god? What knowledge could you even have of them?"

"Quaretem was spared from the destruction of the old war, just as Nordabor was. And in Quaretem, certain old ways have survived. I learned of them from one greater than myself."

Vitus waited for a further explanation, and, seeing that one wasn't coming, leaned toward Phar-Mindorius. The king waved him away and, grimacing, sat up straighter.

"I have heard such things before," Phar-Mindorius rasped. His voice sounded like someone slowly tearing strips of parchment. "A foreigner who emerges from nowhere, speaking glibly of esoteric things. I put my hopes in such a stranger once before. Whether he was right or wrong, I cannot say. I have my hopes, but only time will tell. Either way, I do not know what to make of you. I do not believe that Fritz found you on some journey, yet I sense some truth to your tale. I am of two minds. If you speak truly; if she *can* be restored …"

"Sire," Vitus said, before Rayburn or Kemp could answer. "It seems to me that we have nothing to lose. It would be most prudent to allow this man—"

"*Cease this at once!*" a reedy voice cried. Rayburn turned to see Badgett, flanked by eight shepherds, striding into the room from the foyer. His black, curly hair, shot through with gray, bounced on his shoulders as he strutted toward them. "Why was I not notified of this meeting? Why did I hear of it only through the gossip of the guardsmen, overheard by my own shepherds? What is the *meaning* of this?"

Vitus looked as if someone had shat on his supper. "My apologies, High Shepherd Badgett. I sent for you; my summons must not have reached you."

"Unlikely. Rather, I think that you intended for me to be absent, so that you might fill our king's head with alarmist nonsense."

"That's absurd," Vitus said. Rayburn suspected that it was not. He also suspected that Badgett's arrival would not help them.

"Sire, forgive me for my delay," Badgett purred, cozying up to the throne. "Had I known, I would have come immediately. Such wild claims must be thoroughly vetted. False hopes should not be nurtured."

Phar-Mindorius's countenance had clouded over, the sharpness of his eyes receding into the wrinkled prison of his face. Rayburn realized that, however briefly, the king had been allowing himself to hope. Badgett had snuffed it out.

"High Shepherd, it gladdens me that you are here," Phar-Mindorius whispered. "I admit, I was caught up in possibility. It was rash not to await your arrival, so as to heed your counsel."

Rayburn could hardly believe what he was hearing. He'd known that Phar-Mindorius had become increasingly reliant on Badgett, but he'd never expected to hear the king explaining himself to one of his subjects. Truly, Phar-Mindorius was held in thrall to the high shepherd's supposed visions.

"It is not my counsel, but the Void-God's. Ever does he seek to guide the faithful," Badgett said. He turned to Kemp. "*You* are the healer?"

"That's right."

"And you can—what? Utilize some secret method to bring a *god* back from the brink of death?"

"I can."

"No."

"No?" Kemp asked, his friendly smile faltering.

Badgett turned back to Phar-Mindorius. "Sire, these two are charlatans. Pay no heed to their false promises, their wicked deceptions. Their words might glitter, but they are poison. They are saboteurs, seeking to accelerate the end of your reign."

"If what they say is true, then they might *save* your reign," Vitus interjected.

"If what they say is true, then they would be damning us all!" Badgett shouted. "They would see your son turned away at the gates, the promised absolution *spoiled*. Phir-Ramarian is the Void-God's will incarnate. Would you flinch now, at the final moment of your trial? Would you cast away everything that your bloodline has sought for in a moment of doubt and weakness? We're speaking of universal *ascendance*! I have seen it! You are the steady hand; Phir-Ramarian is the sword! Together, you will bring Vingallea into eternal glory within the Void-God's embrace! He is almost here!"

As if in confirmation, a thunderous peal rattled the entire keep. The stone floor beneath them seemed to buck, and Rayburn struggled to remain standing. The kaleidoscopic lights shivering along the edges of the Erosion flared, flooding the hole in the ceiling with an otherworldly glow. The remaining roof groaned ominously, and pieces of timber clattered down around them. Aedesda's skull grinned wickedly as the skeleton rattled about on its wires, seeming to dance gaily to the music of the world's end.

With a series of snapping reverberations, the episode ended.

"He is eager now; the smell of us fills his nostrils. His pace quickens." Badgett stared reverently at the patch of exposed sky. "We will be within him soon, and our perfection will fill eternity."

"Yes, High Shepherd," Phar-Mindorius said, and tears spilled down his wrinkled cheeks. He squeezed his eyes shut and tilted his face skyward. "Oh, please, Lost Father of the Void, please bring my son back to me. Guide him before your immeasurable might." The gathered shepherds joined him in a litany of murmured prayers.

Rayburn, panting with terror and disbelief, could only gawp. He'd always thought that Badgett, who'd once been a relatively obscure member of his order, was simply an opportunist who had weaseled his way to power. Now, he understood that Badgett was something far more dangerous. He was an eloquent lunatic with a total belief in his own delusions and a masterful ability to convince others of their veracity. In short, they were fucked.

He looked toward Vitus, who seemed to be the only one left in Phar-Mindorius's court who was capable of rational thought. The captain was aghast, watching his king dissolve into weeping invocations.

"I hate to interrupt," Kemp said loudly. "But your man here is dead wrong. You need to let us heal Ganachim or we're all finished—not delivered, or saved, or forgiven—finished. You, me, your kingdom—there will be nothing left. Take us to Ganachim."

Everyone was silent now, their eyes on Kemp. Rayburn felt himself trembling and strove to stifle it. His mind skipped across his countless fears; he wondered if Nedelkoff had managed to lead the others to Ganachim, and where Avehav and his men were. Their plan, rather loose from the start, seemed to be unraveling. It occurred to him that, should Phar-Mindorius unexpectedly relent, he had no way of notifying Nedelkoff. Nor did he know how the king would react to the revelation that Kemp was not the healer, but another god was. In his fragile state, a new deception might cause him to change his mind. Rayburn felt his chest tighten. Everything was pressing in on him at once.

Phar-Mindorius seemed to swell with hatred, his malice animating him in a way that stripped away the long-cycles. He rose to his full height, the very picture of imperial authority. Rayburn thought that, in that moment, Kemp must have appeared to Phar-Mindorius as the embodiment of every foreign threat that had ever hounded him throughout his hapless reign, every outsider who had ever disturbed the continuity of his realm. He was the unknown wastes that had opened up to swallow Rorik Fontaine without a trace; he was Duncan Starkad, promising a way out; he was any other badlander, pawing at the gates; he was the slavers, ravaging the expedition; he was the hidden gods, withholding the only means to survive; he was peace denied and serenity revoked.

"You dare to issue commands before my throne?" Phar-Mindorius boomed, his voice rising to its previous timbre. "You are speaking to the High King of Vingallea. Those of my bloodline have been the masters of mankind since the beginning of time; Vingallea colonized the world. I know not, and care not, for the customs observed in your savage land, wherever it is. For all lands, living or dead, belong to Vingallea. You are in the court of your king, and you will not speak out of turn again. Captain Vitus, seize him."

Vitus, who'd seemed to be lagging a few steps behind in the conversation, was snapped back to the present by an order he could understand. He began to draw his sword.

"Wait!" Rayburn shouted, unsure of what he was doing. All he knew was that deception had not worked. Perhaps the truth would. "Your Majesty, there is another old one with us. She is called Reie, God of Mending."

"What are you doing?" Kemp hissed.

"She can heal any wound or illness, and she wishes to restore Ganachim," Rayburn said, ignoring him. "She believes that Ganachim can stop the Erosion. It would mean saving us all, but it would also mean the end of Nordabor. She intends not just to heal Ganachim but to free her. They will go south together, to liberate her own people. She wants us all to join her in Quaretem. Even you are welcome, if you're willing to abdicate, for she says there will be no kings in this new place. Please, there is still time to leave the sorrows of Nordabor behind. She can free you from it all. There's no other way; this is how it's got to end."

Rayburn had never imagined that he would ever address his sovereign with anything but deference. It had taken everything he had to do it, and he now felt utterly spent. With the exhaustion came a strange sensation of pride. He had never been a bold man; only now, at the end, had he proven his quality. Whatever awaited him, he could at least face it knowing that he'd done everything he could.

It was if time had stopped. Phar-Mindorius remained standing; Vitus's sword remained half-drawn. Badgett stood watching his king, his mouth moving soundlessly. Rayburn could tell that he was trying to conjure the right words to bend this new information to his beliefs. This would decide everything. Phar-Mindorius could prove his wisdom. He could set his crown aside and, together, they could go to Ganachim.

"Lies," Phar-Mindorius muttered.

It was never more than a dream. Phar-Mindorius could not separate himself from his power any more than Rayburn could separate himself from his own skin.

"Lies," Phar-Mindorius said again.

"Yes," Badgett agreed in an excited whisper, his face vulturine.

Vitus let his sword drop back into its sheath. "Sire—"

"*LIES!*" Phar-Mindorius shrieked. "My son rides for us as we speak, and you want me to abandon my lineage, release the god my ancestors salvaged, and swear fealty to another one? And you promise *freedom*? There is no freedom in a collar. I will not pledge *my* kingdom to the gods. Vingallea did not belong to Ulesreto—I certainly won't give it to any other false claimant. Vingallea belongs to *me*. The gods destroyed this world; I will bring my people out of it. Only the Void-God remains to us, as wronged by the lesser gods as we were. The Void-God will release us from this corpse-world. But you will not live to see it. Seize them."

Rayburn's pride evaporated, replaced instead by total panic.

This time, Vitus hesitated. Phar-Mindorius did not notice, though, for at that moment, a sweating, red-faced guardsman burst into the throne room.

"Invaders have breached the main gates!"

A fluttering joy rose through Rayburn's despair. Not only had Avehav launched his attack, but his meager force had actually made it inside the city. Stretched as thin as the guardsmen were, they'd apparently failed to hold the gates.

Phar-Mindorius visibly sagged at this report, crumpling back into his seat. "Invaders?"

Vitus's eyes flicked toward Rayburn and Kemp. Gears seemed to be turning in his mind. "Sire, with your leave, I will take the castle garrison and quell whatever is happening at the gates."

"Yes, Captain, of course," Phar-Mindorius whispered absently.

Clearly relieved to have extricated himself from a situation he found distasteful, Vitus departed with the other guardsman. Rayburn had mistaken the news of the attack for something good; now he realized that all it had done was provide Vitus with an excuse to avoid responsibility for their fate without disobeying his king. He was as shrewd as he was gutless.

Badgett turned to his shepherds. "You four, gather your acolytes and make haste for the gate. We cannot allow shades to overrun us now, not when we're so close."

The appointed shepherds hurried away without question, and Badgett turned his attention back to Rayburn and Kemp. He was clearly pleased to have Vitus out of his way.

"Are you behind this attack?" Badgett asked.

"Perhaps," Kemp said with a sly grin.

"Duplicitous to the last. Sire, correct me if I'm wrong, but you were ordering these men seized? It may be beyond the normal scope of my duties, but might I fulfill that order?"

Phar-Mindorius stared vacantly through him. "Yes ... seize them."

"As you wish. Go ahead, men."

Rayburn squeezed his eyes shut as the shepherds closed in.

Chapter 40

"Invaders! *Invaders*! To the gates!"

The call to arms echoed through the lower passages of the Vinecrown Keep. From within a damp, disused cellar, Marbuck listened to the last fading shouts and footsteps of guardsmen hurrying toward the attack.

"It would appear that Avehav has come through," Jalam said.

"Indeed," Reie agreed.

The five of them were pressed together in the tight space, waiting for the sounds of alarm to abate before continuing on their way to the dungeons. Nedelkoff had pulled them inside when the first cries were heard and remained closest to the exit, peering through the small gap between the door and its warped frame.

"I think the whole garrison is going," she said.

"For ten men?" Marbuck asked.

"Avehav might be 'leading' them, but I would bet that Winfield is calling the shots. He's adept at this sort of combat; he'll have striven to fool the guardsmen at the gates into thinking they're being assaulted by far more than ten men. If he's managed to get inside, he'll be sowing chaos wherever he goes. Lighting fires; striking quickly and retreating; constantly moving."

"How long do you think he can he keep that up?" Falstaff asked.

"Hopefully long enough," Nedelkoff said. She looked through the gap again. "I think it's clear. I'm going to cut your bindings, but keep them looped around your wrists; we need to at least maintain the illusion that you're prisoners. To the same end, I'm also going to keep your weapons for now."

Marbuck did not love this, but she understood it. For now, it was enough just to be freed from her bindings.

Once Nedelkoff had released them, they slipped back into the passage. Moving in the same order as before, they made their way through a series of hallways and stairwells that all looked identically dreary. For Marbuck, it was hard not to be reminded of Vin-Sadavat. There, too, she'd been led as a prisoner through black halls while the city collapsed into bedlam. The chaos hadn't exploded in Nordabor, not yet, but it was near. The most recent fluctuation of the Erosion had shaken the entire keep. They'd frozen as the stones around them groaned and dirt and dust sifted down from the ceiling. Marbuck had expected to be crushed by the collapse of the castle at any moment. The event had passed, and they'd survived, but she knew the next time might go differently.

"It's just through here," Nedelkoff said as they reached an iron gate. She retrieved another key from her belt, fiddled with the lock for a moment, and then swung the gate open. It screeched horridly on its ancient hinges. The noise attracted a greasy-looking guardsman who wandered out of a nearby alcove. Marbuck took him to be the jailer.

"Get a move on," Nedelkoff ordered for the benefit of her new audience. Her prisoners filed inside and she closed the gate with an equally awful sound. Throwing a furtive glance over her shoulder, she pantomimed locking it.

"What's all this?" the jailer asked. He was sallow-skinned, unshaven, and imbued with a general filthiness. It seemed that, having spent so much time in the dungeons, he'd become little different from those he guarded.

"Why, it's a parade in your honor, Clusk!" Nedelkoff said. "What the fuck does it look like? They're prisoners, you simpleton."

Clusk's ugly face pinched with irritation, but he knew his place. "Of course, Under-Captain, my mistake. Are these the invaders?" he asked cautiously.

"Yes, some of them," Nedelkoff said. "Why aren't you out there hunting down the rest?"

"Somebody had to stay behind."

"And it's just you here? The other jailers were summoned to the gates?"

"Yes," Clusk said, with just a hint of suspicion in his voice. "Captain Vitus ordered the entire garrison to mobilize. Well, aside from me. Like I said, somebody had to stay behind and watch the prisoners. I'd have thought that you of all people would know the captain's orders." Clusk looked at the prisoners again, and it was clear that he knew something was off.

"No shepherds, either?" Nedelkoff asked.

"No, uh-uh."

There was no longer any need for secrecy.

Calmly, Nedelkoff turned to her prisoners and began to hand each of them a weapon from her belt. As they took them, their bindings fell away. Clusk watched this unfold with fascination, utterly nonplussed. When Nedelkoff had finished, she turned to him.

"You have been a jailer for nearly your entire tenure with the Royal Guard, correct?"

Clusk nodded slowly.

"So, I would imagine that you are privy to information that might not be readily known to those who do not concern themselves with the housing of prisoners, such as myself."

"What's going on?"

"Pay attention, Clusk. I don't wish to hurt you."

"Okay." He nodded again.

"Do you know such things or not?"

"What things?"

Nedelkoff sighed with exasperation. "Where is the captive god held?"

Clusk snorted. "What? You think I know anything about that? I didn't even know the damn thing existed until after the—"

Nedelkoff closed the distance between them in an instant and seized him by the collar. "Do not lie to me. *Where is it*?"

"I don't know anything about it! Honest! I house drunks and upstarts and kooks! Not *gods*! You'd have to ask a shepherd; they wouldn't trust a lowly jailer with that kind of knowledge," he said with a tinge of resentment. "Shit, you know they've practically taken over down here anyway, coming and going as they please, *questioning* the prisoners. I just feed the poor bastards and make sure they stay put. Nothing more."

Apparently satisfied with his answer, Nedelkoff released him, shoving him away. Fussily, he smoothed the grimy collar of his uniform.

"He's lying, he must be," Reie said.

"I don't think he is," Marbuck said. "The shepherds have always known of Ganachim, not the guardsmen. Unless, I suppose, they were a part of

Phar-Mindorius's inner circle." She looked at Clusk. "I'm going to go ahead and assume that our new friend here is not. So, if Ganachim's not being held here, then only a shepherd will know where she is."

"Too bad we didn't catch one down here," Falstaff said.

"So, we'll just have to find one."

"Good luck with that," Clusk sneered. "They're all in a tizzy. First, that traitor merchant turns up with some foreigner; now, an attack. But I suppose you know more about all of that than I do." He looked at Nedelkoff with contempt. "A traitorous under-captain; if Captain Mather could see—"

Nedelkoff cuffed him in the head and, before he could react, ripped his sword free from its scabbard and held it to his throat. Clusk looked at the blade with disbelief.

"Get in that cell," Nedelkoff said, gesturing with her head toward the nearest cage.

"Okay, okay," Clusk said shakily. He slowly slid away from Nedelkoff and backed into the open cell. She slammed the gate shut and thrust her hand between the bars.

"Your keys?"

Clusk looked at his own belt, partially obscured by his gut, and retrieved his keys, which he promptly handed to her. "I don't know what you're after here, but Phar-Mindorius will have you hanged for this."

Nedelkoff shrugged and turned to the others. "We ought to search the dungeon, just in case. Perhaps there's a hidden passage that only the shepherds use."

"I agree, but we can't just leave this man here," Reie said. "It would be a death sentence."

Nedelkoff seemed to consider this. "Somebody stay put with him while we search, make sure he keeps quiet. When we go, I'll leave his keys just out of reach." She looked at Clusk. "I'm sure that you'll figure out a way to reach them eventually, and by the time you nab them and let yourself out, we'll be gone. I'll even leave your sword here for you. Sound fair?"

Clusk's jaw worked, perhaps containing an indignant outburst. "Yes," he said tightly.

It was quickly decided that Jalam would remain behind to watch Clusk. The others split up and began their search, each heading down a different corridor.

Marbuck, who was immensely pleased to have her blade back, proceeded further into the dank chill of the dungeon. It stank like piss and human filth, and the deeper she went, the more prisoners she encountered. Kept far away from any casual visitor, these miserable individuals were undoubtedly those subjected to the interrogations of the shepherds. Their faces were haggard and drawn, staring blankly at Marbuck as she passed. Devoid of hope, she knew them well; they were a mirror of her own suffering at the hands of sadistic captors. An overwhelming desire to free them rose in her. She knew that Reie would agree, and that she would tend to them as well. But first, the search had to be finished.

It seemed like a waste of time. The dungeon was built uniformly, and absolutely nothing hinted at a secret passage. Reaching a dead end, Marbuck started back. Falstaff's silhouette stepped into the far-off mouth of the passage ahead of her.

"Find anything?" he called.

"No! This is pointless; Ganachim's not here!" she shouted back. She took maybe three more steps before she was startled by a prisoner suddenly pressing against the bars of a cell on her right and reaching for her.

"Ganachim?" he croaked.

"Don't touch me," she shot back instinctively.

"You're seeking Ganachim?" the prisoner asked.

Marbuck stared at his dark, emaciated face. "Yes. What do you know of her?"

"Free me and I can take you to her."

"Don't listen to the God Eater!" another prisoner jeered from somewhere in the darkness.

"I can take you to her," he repeated, ignoring the other man.

Marbuck found this claim unlikely, but, having nothing to lose, forged ahead. "You know where she is?"

"I do."

"How? Who are you?"

"I know because I was a shepherd once. My name is Leon Galt."

CHAPTER 41

"So, that's it?"

"That's it."

"We never stood a chance. Even if everything had gone right, we would have opened the gates, only to find a howling abyss."

"The Void."

"Yes, I suppose it was. Does that restore your faith at all?"

"Not really."

"Paradise must have ceased to exist when the Father-God died. It must have been some kind of extension of him, tied to his power. Nobody considered that. Not even the old ones."

"Aye."

"And so there's no hope."

"Not anymore."

Lady Fontaine had reached out to him then. He'd taken her hand, already weak with the ebbing of her life. Not long after, she'd let go of him and slumped over. Galt had watched as her breathing had grown from ragged to agonal. She'd snored wetly and then she'd been gone. Thankfully, her body had remained still. He'd sat with her for a long time before he'd finally risen.

Looking back, Galt was unable to pinpoint what exactly had driven him to get up. After all, he had lost everything. Solgard was dead; Ulesreto had murdered her right in front of him. Lady Fontaine and Mather were gone; they'd both succumbed to the injuries they'd received during their final bid to stop Ulesreto and Nuroh. Galt had been left utterly alone, the last survivor of the entire misbegotten expedition. Their purpose had been revealed to be a hopeless fantasy that had only accelerated the end of everything. His faith had been extinguished; his body had been broken.

And yet, he'd risen. Some foundational part of his being had insisted on continuing to live, despite the overwhelming evidence that it was futile.

Being careful not to put too much weight on his twisted knee, he'd shambled back to Ulesreto's body, lying at the foot of the Gates of Paradise. In his last act, the usurper god had managed to close the gates, shutting off the howling destruction of the Void, or more accurately, delaying it. Galt had looked around, assessing the insanity around him. Ethereal, violet light had danced and twitched before his eyes; quivering flashes of geometric patterns flickered everywhere. Impossibly straight lines of darkness had flashed in and out of existence. The surrounding cliffs had been whittled down to rounded nubs, and the skeletal behemoth of the Father-God had been broken and flattened. Permanent cracks in reality had spread out from a hole in the sky, where the firmament itself had been torn away. Similar fissures had branched out from the gates, the gaps providing a view down into black eternity. Observing it all with a dull, detached acceptance, a plan had begun to formulate in Galt's mind.

He'd bent down slowly, groaning from the effort, and scooped up the Scale of Judgment from where it had fallen. Though its ambient glow had faded, he'd found that it was hot to the touch. The heated blade had turned out to be perfectly suited for the task he'd had in mind.

Holding aloft the sword that had been the cause of so much suffering, Galt's battered body had been animated by bitter satisfaction. He'd slammed the blade down across Ulesreto's back, further cracking the splintered remains of his armor. Wedging the blade into the widened crack, he'd split the armor apart, exposing the skin of the god's back. Muscled and bronzed, it had been striped numerous times by the rushing cloud of detritus that had penetrated his armor. Galt had reflected on two things then: the justice of Ulesreto being butchered by his own aptly named sword, and his overwhelming hunger.

The hot blade had cut easily through Ulesreto's flesh. Having removed a strip of tissue, dripping with black blood, Galt had hesitated for only a moment. Then, he'd eaten. The meat had been oily and chewy, strangely reminiscent of fish. To his starved mind, the taste had not even registered.

He'd eaten greedily then, clumsily slicing off ragged pieces and gobbling them down until his face was caked in a mixture of Ulesreto's blood and that which had been oozing from his own pulverized nose and blistered burns. There had been no attempt to pace himself, and his atrophied stomach had been overwhelmed. He'd eventually puked up most of what he'd eaten, and the agony of vomiting with a broken rib was what had finally slowed him down. It hadn't stopped him though; he'd simply resumed eating with a steadier pace, managing to keep down every bite he'd consumed.

Having stripped everything he could from the back of the carcass with the broad strokes of the Scale of Judgment, he'd decided that a more delicate touch was needed. He'd plucked free his dagger, which he'd recently deposited into the side of Ulesreto's head, and set to work carving off every last strip of edible meat from the god's mutilated back. At some point, he'd slept. Upon awakening, he'd resumed his ghoulish work, moving on to the rest of Ulesreto's body. When he'd finally finished, he'd had a full belly and a sizable pile of raw meat. Without consciously choosing to do so, he'd collected provisions for his journey home.

He'd had no great desire to return to Nordabor. Reporting their failure to Phar-Mindorius had not occurred to him, nor had returning to the ranks of the shepherds at the Ivy Citadel. Nordabor had become his destination by default; it was the only place where he might continue to live. For whatever reason, blighted as his life had become, he'd been unwilling to relinquish it.

Wincing with pain, he'd shuffled out of his tunic and tied the sleeves together. He'd felt the coldness of the air with the same sense of disconnection with which he'd experienced everything else. From Ulesreto's heaped remains, he'd removed the pauldron that had not been damaged by Mather during their battle. He'd placed it on the front of his tunic and, using it like a bowl, he'd piled the meat inside. Hoisting the tied sleeves, he'd slung the whole makeshift pack across his chest. It had been sloppy, heavy, and had only held half of the meat he'd accumulated, but it was all he'd been able to manage. He'd figured that it would be better to carry a manageable amount, knowing that the meat would begin to spoil soon anyway.

After eating a final helping from the pile that he was leaving behind, Galt had set off. Using the Scale of Judgment as a makeshift cane, he'd shuffled across the fractured landscape, pausing only to cast one last glance at the bodies of Mather and Lady Fontaine. He'd left them where they'd fallen, seeing no reason to do otherwise.

With no higher thought, he'd plodded across what was left of the Isle of Creation, passing the broken remains of the world's creator. The sloping path out of the charnel valley had been eroded down to a gentle rise. Galt had stumbled his way to the top and stopped to rest. As he'd caught his breath, he'd surveyed the landscape beyond the isle, which had changed appreciably.

The flat glassiness of the Stagnant Sea had been transformed into a chopping roil, awash in the light of the flashing disruptions of reality. The dried strait had been erased, filled in by the sloshing expanse of water. Galt had not despaired but rather sat and picked a piece of meat from between his dirty teeth. Examining the chunk he'd pulled free, he'd briefly considered the strangeness of eating an immortal deity. Then, he'd flicked the piece away and, with a grunt of effort, rose to his feet to resume his journey.

The path down to the beach had been slightly steeper, but Galt had managed. The last of the deadfall had been stripped away, leaving the way clear. At the bottom, he'd passed Opriseur's mangled remains. The god's body had been battered and twisted, apparently as a result of being dragged across the shoreline and slammed into a shelf of rock. Bent at an unnatural angle, the body had been tightly wedged into a crevice, with only a leg and an arm protruding. A smear of black gore had shown where the body, compressed further and further into the thin gap, had burst apart. Reduced to slurry, it had whipped out of the gaps in the stone and continued its flight toward the Void.

Galt had passed that violent spectacle without pause. It wasn't until he came upon a piece of petrified wood lying on the water's edge that he'd stopped. How far it had traveled before coming to rest in that spot, and from what deep recess of the earth it had been pulled, Galt had no way of knowing, but he'd considered it a fortuitous event. He'd lifted the wood up and tested his weight on it, finding it to be sturdy and nearly the perfect height for a crutch. He'd then regarded the Scale of Judgment, which, for all of its cosmic importance, had made a shitty cane.

His next actions had been purely instinctual. Without a second thought, he'd limped toward the nearest flickering gap, a perfectly symmetrical seam, winking in and out of existence. Getting close to it, the hairs on the back of his neck had stood up, and the violet, golden glow of it had instilled a sort of primal fear in him. Before he could falter, he'd thrust the Scale of Judgment into the gap. Silently, it had tumbled away into nothingness. Galt had scrambled back then, unable to abide being close to the gap any longer. Once he'd gotten far enough away, a feeling of relief had washed over him. Whatever else happened, nobody would ever open the Gates of Paradise again.

Having disposed of the sword, Galt had turned his attention toward the crossing of the strait. Swimming had seemed out of the question, considering the state he'd been in, and yet he'd plodded into the water anyway, with no clear plan of what exactly he was going to do. Ultimately, the water had never risen higher than his knees; though the sea had been moved by the pull of the Void, the majority of it must have receded when that pull stopped. Not enough to drain the strait completely, but enough to make it passable.

Galt's new crutch had sunk into the sandy bottom with each halting step, and the salt water had stung the countless cuts and scrapes on his legs. Eventually, the coldness of the water had actually soothed his pain. On he'd gone, making no attempt to reckon the passage of time, until at last he'd reached the mainland. It, too, had changed.

Though the fractures in reality had lessened by then, evidence of the Void's destruction had still been readily apparent. All across the cape of Thunsturm, the sand had been stripped away, exposing the bedrock and erasing the last of the ancient fortifications left over from the war. The cyclopean lighthouse had vanished, having apparently been razed to its foundation. Similarly, the colossal siege engines had been plucked from the sand like so many playthings. To Galt's enervated mind, it had meant nothing but a clearer path forward.

As he'd left the shore behind and ascended toward the moors, the first snapping reverberation had echoed from the Isle of Creation. It had startled him, and he'd redoubled his pace, as best as he'd been able to.

Through a stripped and barren land, Galt had trekked onward. His mind had remained blank, devoid of thoughts regarding Solgard or the expedition. Reaching Nordabor had ceased to be his intent; he'd kept going only to get as far away from the fragile, broken world to the north as possible. He'd walked; he'd eaten; he'd slept. At some point, he'd ditched the pauldron-sling, putting back on his tunic and shoving the last, slimy meat into his pockets. He'd eaten it until it'd started to turn rancid. Finally, when he'd been unable to stomach the last scraps, he'd discarded them and continued on. His thirst, no longer culled by the blood held within the meat, had quickly become intolerable. All the while, the broken sky behind him had periodically emitted its booming death rattle.

Then, though he'd scarcely believed it could be possible, he'd come upon the rutted track that constituted the northern arm of the Imperial Highway and, just beyond it, the Einfallen. He'd shambled toward it as quickly as he'd been able to and plunged into the icy water, nearly drowning himself as he gulped straight from the river. The water fortified him in a way that the blood of the usurper had not.

After drinking until he'd felt ill, he'd flopped back onto the northern shore, not trusting his own strength to swim across. Panting, he'd examined the lifesaving obstacle before him, his sluggish thoughts beginning to coalesce around the need for a canteen of some sort; his had been lost during the final conflict. Focused as he'd been on this conundrum, he'd still failed to formulate any solution. Time had continued to pass, wherein he'd done nothing but drink from the river and languish on its shore, paralyzed by his inability to craft an answer. He'd drifted in and out of sleep for full-cycles, growing weaker from starvation all the while. This had further convinced him that he would never be able to swim across. The issue of the canteen had vexed him; he'd known that, should he even make it across, he would be leaving the water behind, guaranteeing his death from thirst. All the while, the ominous grinding in the north had reminded him that he must move on.

Consumed by this quandary, he'd failed to notice the arrival of several people on the southern bank, until one of them called out to him. At first, he'd thought they were nothing more than a hallucination; phantoms of the expedition. Solgard, joined by Moore and Daeg; Mather and Lowther; even the odious Lord Fontaine; all there to welcome him into the ranks of the dead. He could vaguely remember reaching out to them, suddenly aware of the extent of his delirious exhaustion. They'd forded the river and revealed themselves to be no illusion born of a failing mind, but a search party, headed by Captain Vitus.

Somehow, against all odds, Galt had been rescued.

The journey back to Nordabor had been made in the greatest haste; Vitus had been eager to report his discovery to the king. Galt, in a halting and jumbled manner, had given an account of everything that had befallen the expedition. Much of it had seemed to be beyond Vitus's understanding, but the captain had done his best to follow along, even as the tale had reached its unbelievable climax. He'd also provided Galt with a description of what was happening in the north. He and his scouts had been monitoring what they'd called the Erosion, and Galt had not been at all surprised to learn that the damage caused by the Void was spreading. Most importantly, though, Vitus had seen to it that Galt was given ample food and water, clean clothing, basic treatment for his injuries, and an opportunity to rest.

Such hospitality would not last.

His return to Nordabor had been like a dream, one that had flirted with unease before giving itself entirely to nightmare. To actually come back to the place they'd spoken of returning to so often had been surreal. He'd never expected to set foot in Nordabor again; to do so had been like returning from the dead. Despite his miraculous survival, there had been no celebration of his homecoming, not that he'd desired one. Instead, he'd been quickly and quietly escorted through the city, allowing him just enough time to observe the further decline of the place. A brief glimpse of the Ivy Citadel had stirred nothing in him. Observing the dour atmosphere, Galt had wondered if the disturbance in the north was solely to blame, or if Ganachim had, in fact, perished.

Vitus had wasted no time, bringing him directly to Phar-Mindorius. The haggard old king had received him with careful courtesy. Anton Badgett had been standing beside him, wearing the robes of a high shepherd. Badgett had been a middling nobody in their order, and his unexpected presence at the king's side had been surprising, but not an immediate cause for concern.

Galt had assumed that his account of the expedition's doom would crush Phar-Mindorius; he had not, however, expected to be furiously rebuked. Phar-Mindorius had sat through the entirety of Galt's narrative with a passive expression painted on his face. Galt, speaking in a mechanical, detached way, had eventually opted to stare at the floor as he'd delivered his terrible news. Doing so, he had not noticed the simmering rage building within the king which had finally exploded when Galt had described dropping the Scale of Judgment through the seam.

Phar-Mindorius, hoarsely shouting, had accused him of being a faithless deserter who'd concocted the entire tale in order to paper over his own treachery, going so far as to say that he'd sabotaged the expedition and knew of their actual whereabouts. Urged on by Badgett, he'd refused to accept that the Scale of Judgment was gone, or that the Gates of Paradise had opened upon anything but the means to their salvation. He'd denied that Starkad had been Ulesreto all along, or that Nuroh had been involved in any way. Most of all, he'd rejected the notion that Phir-Ramarian had submitted to Tariono, and that he'd been subsequently murdered by Lord Fontaine. Galt, growing frustrated with the flat denial of everything he'd endured, had implored the king to listen to reason, even telling him to check for the absence of the hilt, which had been stolen by Nuroh. Badgett had intervened then, insisting that Phir-Ramarian must have actually taken it with him, without the king's knowledge. Galt had been baffled by this insane rejection of the truth, and by the king's apparent faith in Badgett. He'd said as much, and Phar-Mindorius had responded by ordering him imprisoned. In the king's mind, Phir-Ramarian lived, and no amount of evidence could change that. Galt knew that Phar-Mindorius would cling to this delusion until the Void consumed them all.

And so he'd been thrown into a hole. Vitus, for all of his friendliness on the journey back, had accepted his king's orders without question and left Galt to rot. Worse yet, Galt had been turned over to Badgett and his followers. Disgusted by Galt's abandonment of their beliefs, the shepherd interrogators had been brutal. Men he'd known, men he'd served with, had beaten him with religious fervor. The torture had not been creative, but simple and relentlessly severe. He'd been bashed by the flat of their blades, punched and kicked, stomped upon, and thrown to the ground. Often, the shepherds hadn't even bothered to ask him anything, simply beating him because they'd been told that it was what the Void-God wanted. Other times, Badgett had hovered by the entrance to his cell, demanding that he confess to being a murderous deserter, and that he admit that Phir-Ra-marian was not only alive but the living conduit of the Void-God. Galt had refused, and the beatings had continued. In disbelief of his story, they'd taken to mockingly calling him the 'God Eater', shoving excrement into his mouth and demanding to know if it tasted divine.

He'd escaped the wrath of the old ones and the collapse of reality, only to have his own people subject him to ruthless torment and abject humiliation. And still, somehow, Galt wished to live. And now, standing before his squalid cell, unlooked-for and unexpected, was his chance to do just that. This strange woman, her head ringed by a ragged scar, had come seeking Ganachim. Galt had never been able to discern whether or not the god was still alive, but he knew where she'd be if she was, and he offered his services in exchange for his freedom.

"You were a shepherd?" the woman asked. Her voice was painted with equal parts skepticism and a desire to believe.

"Yes," Galt confirmed. "I've been to the grotto where she's held; I've taken part in the bloodletting rituals."

The woman seemed to consider this for a moment. "I've got something over here!" she shouted down the hallway. She turned back to Galt. "You better not be full of shit. How'd a shepherd end up in here anyway?"

"I told Phar-Mindorius the truth," Galt said. "About the expedition."

"What do you know of the expedition?"

"I'm the only one who survived it."

The woman raised her eyebrows. "Is that so? Well, you're not the *only* survivor. I was on the expedition; I was a part of the *Fortune's* crew, so was Falstaff here," she said, indicating the man who'd just trotted to her side. "Fritz Rayburn survived, too."

Now it was Galt's turn to raise an eyebrow. "Really? How—well, never mind. We'll have plenty to discuss later. Perhaps, for now, you'd be so kind as to release me."

Two others arrived; a royal guardsman and a figure shrouded by a strange headdress.

"He says he was a shepherd who survived the expedition and got locked down here for talking about what happened. He claims to know where Ganachim is," the scarred woman reported.

"It's the only lead we have, and we have nothing to lose," the shrouded figure said in a soft voice. "Release him."

The guardsman produced a key and unlocked the gate. "You survived the expedition? What happened? How did you get here?" she asked as Galt limped out, eliciting a chorus of cries for freedom from the other prisoners.

"One of your compatriots found me by the Einfallen—Vitus. The rest is a long story."

The guardsman nodded her understanding. "I see."

Looking at the strange quartet of rescuers standing before him, Galt's curiosity was stirred. He decided that it was his turn to ask questions. "Who are you people? Why do you seek Ganachim?"

The others turned toward the shrouded woman. "We are travelers from a distant land," she announced. "We have come for Ganachim so that I might mend her injuries and free her from her enslavement."

Galt decided not to mention the possibility that she was already dead, lest they choose to return him to his cell. Instead, he asked her what made her think that such a thing was even possible.

"Let me show you," she said, lifting her shroud.

CHAPTER 42

As one who had been both master and servant, Kemp had seen many examples of groveling. During his tenure as duke, he'd listened disinterestedly to the appeals of his people, often arbitrating disputes based on whatever decision would let him return to his own business the fastest. As Lakna's huntsman, though, he'd witnessed true beseechment. The hapless Quaret who'd been branded as agents of Zeorshut Riengel had begged for their lives in any number of ways. Their attempts had rarely been successful, but their actions had imprinted on Kemp's memory nonetheless. Now, knowing that he was outnumbered, and that he needed to drag the diversion out for as long as possible, he opted for a new strategy; one built on the remembered pleas of the condemned.

As the shepherds advanced, Kemp suddenly threw himself to the ground. "*Please, stop*! *I'm begging you, please!*" he wailed, holding his trembling hands above his head.

As a distractionary technique, it could not have worked better. The shepherds stopped short, taken aback by the burly foreigner who'd gone from ordering their king around with an air of bravado to collapsing into hysterics in an instant. Even Rayburn stared down at Kemp with surprise, as fooled by the ploy as the shepherds were. Kemp, lowering his face to the floor to exaggerate his supplication, had to suppress a smile; he was now playing the part of the penitent with gusto.

At least until he could get to his knife.

"What is this?" Badgett said.

Kemp lifted his head, his eyes swimming, his lips pulled into a moue. The leader of the shepherds was glaring down at him.

"I'm sorry, Your Majesty," Kemp said, directing his words toward Phar-Mindorius. The king was still sinking into his throne, his cloudy eyes looking through the events occurring before him. "None of it's true; the god, the healing, coming from the south; we made it all up!"

"What?" Rayburn said, totally lost.

"So your claims were nothing but a blasphemous fantasy?" Badgett asked.

Kemp nodded eagerly. "We were just trying to bluff our way into the keep." Anticipating the next question, his mind whirred.

"Why?"

"To steal."

"To steal?" Badgett said, apparently unimpressed with this answer. "To steal *what*?"

"I'm sorry!" Kemp wailed, scuttling backward like a wounded animal. As he did so, he twisted his right side away from the shepherds, shielding his right hand from view. "I can't say."

"You can't say? Can you?" Badgett said, turning to Rayburn.

The poor merchant was completely flummoxed. "Honestly—no—I don't know."

"Everything this false healer has uttered is stained with lies," Badgett declared to Phar-Mindorius, who nodded along. "Even now, during this pitiful display of contrition, he deceives. To what end, I cannot say, save the halting of our reclamation. These agitators, and their comrades at the gates, clearly seek to defile your ascent, to spoil our awakening. There is great mischief at work here, and I *do* believe that one of the Void-God's old, bastard offspring is behind it. Worry not, sire, for I will parse out the truth. Men, seize them!"

Phar-Mindorius, who was still nodding, said nothing.

Obediently, the four shepherds resumed their approach. Two of them reached Kemp and ordered him to his feet. As he rose gingerly, sniffing and keening, the impatient men reached out to grab him.

Badgett had held everyone's attention with his bloviating for just long enough. In one fluid motion, Kemp punched his knife through the bottom of the closest man's jaw. He grunted wetly, his hands shooting up toward the knife just as Kemp ripped it free. At the same moment that he started to crumple, bright blood cascading down his front, his shocked partner leapt backward. Kemp flicked his knife toward him twice, but the man remained just out of reach as he continued to retreat.

Seeing the commotion, the other two shepherds stopped just short of reaching Rayburn, who scurried over to Kemp's side. The fat little man was breathing so hard that Kemp feared he might keel over before anyone even laid a finger on him.

"Take this," Kemp said, snatching up the dead shepherd's blade and thrusting it toward Rayburn.

"I—I don't know—that is to say—"

"*Take it.*" He shoved the hilt of the blade into Rayburn's hands and, pulling him by the sleeve, backed away from the body.

The three remaining shepherds circled around Badgett, who remained standing before the throne, his face a mask of furious disbelief. Behind him, Phar-Mindorius was sitting with such complete stillness that he seemed to have been replaced with a lifelike effigy.

"Vandercolt, Ellsworth, take the king and go," Badgett said with forced calmness.

"Take me?" Phar-Mindorius said huskily as two of the shepherds approached him. He allowed them to take him by the arms and assist him to his feet.

"Yes, sire," Badgett said, his eyes never leaving Kemp. "It is clear to me now that I have judged these two correctly."

"I will admit, that tactic was probably a bit unscrupulous," Kemp said, wiping his knife clean on his pant leg. "But, what can you do?"

"Dishonorable heathens," Badgett spat. "At the bidding of their master, they would tear down everything that your illustrious bloodline has been building toward. The machinations of the old ones killed the Father-God and nearly ruined Vingallea. Now, they seek to thwart the Void-God's glorious rebirth and topple us once and for all. No. This cannot come to pass."

"You speak truly, High Shepherd," Phar-Mindorius said, stepping down from his throne. "Thank you for your wisdom."

Badgett nodded importantly. "Take the king to the grotto," he said to his men. "Ensure that he is not disturbed while he awaits the Void-God's arrival. And while you are there, guarantee that Ganachim does not complicate the Void-God's designs. The time of assimilation is nigh; her power, what little remains of it, is no longer needed. Make sure that nobody, god or otherwise, can interfere."

"Yes, High Shepherd," the men said in unison.

As they began to guide Phar-Mindorius toward a doorway set into the far wall, Kemp moved to cut them off, eliciting a panicked squeak from Rayburn. Badgett and his last remaining shepherd quickly stepped between, blocking Kemp's pursuit. He paused, his knife buzzing in his hand, his eyes watching the king slip away. He could not let them reach Ganachim before Reie did. Steeling himself for bloodshed, he started forward again, just as the body of the dead shepherd began to twitch, and a crackling moan came from its blood-choked throat. He backed away then, putting the spawning shade between him and Badgett. Phar-Mindorius slipped out of sight.

"What do we do now?" Rayburn asked, coming to his side.

"We fight. Other than that, we just have to hope that Reie gets to Ganachim first," Kemp said quietly, his words hidden from Badgett by the yowling racket of the shade's birth. "With any luck, we distracted the king and his minions long enough, and Avehav's diversion thinned out the rest of their defenses."

"Do you think she'll succeed?"

Kemp smiled. "Sure, why not? But just in case, you're going to go after the king."

"I am?" Rayburn asked.

Before them, the shade exploded into being. Badgett and the other shepherd, who'd been standing over the writhing body while simultaneously watching Kemp and Rayburn, fell on it at once, hacking it into sizzling pieces.

"Go now," Kemp said. "They can't be moving too fast hauling that dotard along. Do anything you can to delay them."

"I can't—"

"You *must*. I'll hold these two off. When I'm finished with them, I'll catch up."

Rayburn pursed his lips, appearing to hold back his objections with some effort. He didn't seem to be convinced that he could do anything to stop Phar-Mindorius, or that Kemp could handle both Badgett and his servant. In truth, Kemp wasn't either, but he decided to keep that to himself.

Rayburn took a shuddering breath and offered the shepherd's blade to Kemp. "Do you want—"

"No, you'll need a weapon. I've got my knife. *Now go.*"

He gave the smaller man a little shove and the momentum carried him into a sprint that Kemp would not have thought him capable of. Rayburn circled widely around the mess of the shade, where Badgett was babbling some ridiculous litany, every other word of which was affirmed by his slavish subordinate. His head snapped up as he spotted Rayburn.

"Stop him!" Badgett commanded.

The other shepherd broke into a run, but Kemp was already moving to block him. He heard the sound of Kemp's footfalls overtaking him and turned to fight. He'd been prepared to deflect a strike from Kemp's knife, his blade held close to his body. Kemp had anticipated this. As such, he'd already shoved the knife into his belt, instead opting to leap to the side of the man, where he snatched the end of his trailing cloak and wrenched it up and over the shepherd's head with both hands. The tip of the shepherd's blade punctured the cloak as Kemp pulled it down over him, pinning his arms and sword against his chest. The shepherd bent over and tried to twist back and away, but, by then, Kemp had his knife in hand again. Twisting the cloak about his left arm to cinch it tightly, he proceeded to plunge his knife into the back of the shepherd's head in three quick jabs. The man dropped heavily, and Kemp quickly pulled his arm free of the cloak and whirled about, checking his surroundings. Rayburn was gone, having vanished through the doorway. Badgett had been running toward him, but he slid to a stop as soon as Kemp spotted him. Keeping his eyes on Badgett, Kemp stooped to pull the shepherd's sword free of the tangled cloak. He tested the weapon's weight and smiled.

"These are certainly well-crafted. And Ganachim's blood is the secret, eh?"

Badgett's eyes widened, but he said nothing.

"Well, at any rate, I'm not going to let you go after Rayburn, and I suppose you aren't going to let me go after your king. So, I guess it's just the two of us." He raised the blade and the knife, holding them as he'd once held his club and his hatchet. "Until it's not."

The two men circled each other slowly, the rumbling of the Erosion the only sound.

"Obscene," Badgett finally said. "You fight like a filthy badlander."

"It beats being dead, I suppose."

"You murdered two of my most fervent adherents."

"I don't know if 'murder' is the right word, but I *did* kill them. I'll allow you that much."

Badgett glanced at the dead shepherd, lying in an unceremonious heap, the cloak, now sticky with blood, still pulled over his head. "At least he died with his righteous dignity intact."

"Unlike your friend over there, huh?" Kemp said, nodding toward the foul slick of the destroyed shade.

"There are secret heretics everywhere, even amongst the upper echelon of our order. Thankfully, I delivered him, before his shade could further interrupt our proceedings here. But, I'll admit, I was surprised. Alas, only the Void-God can shine a light into the darkest corners of a man's soul, and only he can pass judgment now. I expect that you'll be swiftly condemned when he looks into *your* profane soul."

"Perhaps," Kemp said. "But first you'll have to kill me."

He began to stride directly toward Badgett then, his weapons leveled, a smile still creasing his face. Trickery would not work now; Badgett had seen how he'd fought and would likely be expecting anything. Kemp decided that he would have to resort to brute force and intimidation and noted with pleasure that the high shepherd backed up a few steps. Hopefully, Badgett would prove to be more bark than bite.

Favoring the weapon he knew, Kemp kept his knife in his right hand. He was now close enough to see the creases around Badgett's eyes, and still he made no move. Badgett, to his credit, had managed to stand his ground after those first reflexive steps back. Kemp knew that he couldn't play this game forever; should Rayburn find the king and his escort, he would not be able to put up much of a fight. He would need help.

It was time to act.

Kemp thrust his sword forward, and Badgett, with a sharp cry, deflected the blow. Pivoting, Kemp drove his knife toward Badgett's gut, but he was already twisting away. Kemp tried to snag the end of the high shepherd's cloak on the edge of his sword, being perfectly content to repeat that stratagem, given the chance, but Badgett moved too quickly, leaving Kemp to drive his sword up into thin air. Then Badgett was upon him.

He had just enough time to leap clear of a killing blow. Badgett slammed his blade into the floor, directly where Kemp had just been standing. Landing awkwardly on his knees and elbows, Kemp lurched back onto his feet, turning to find that Badgett was almost on top of him. He managed to block a vicious chop that made his blade ring in his hands, but the force knocked him off kilter and he stumbled backward and fell onto his bottom. Badgett reared up for another blow and Kemp blocked it again. As he did so, he stabbed blindly with his knife, which skidded across Badgett's forearm. He squealed and pulled back, giving Kemp a chance to scoot away and regain his feet.

Badgett quickly realized that he wasn't badly hurt, and started to close in again. Kemp was breathing hard, surprised by the high shepherd's ferocity. He'd considered Badgett to be nothing more than a blustering fanatic, but his easy dispatching of the shade should have been taken as a warning. He was treating Kemp like one of them now, aiming to destroy him with the same relentlessness. For the first time, Kemp began to worry that he was outmatched.

He didn't have long to think. Badgett plunged his blade forward and Kemp parried with his own. Once again, Kemp's knife sought the high shepherd's belly, but Badgett spun away to Kemp's left. Ramming his left elbow backward, Kemp connected with Badgett's head. He staggered and Kemp whirled around, bringing his knife down with the intent of plunging it into Badgett's back. It hit his cloak and sank into nothing. Badgett had dropped to his knees and was now driving his blade straight up into Kemp's side.

"No—"

A sharp, hot pain filled Kemp's chest and he gasped. From some vast distance, he heard the sound of his sword clattering to the floor. Then Badgett's hand was shoving him backward and the blade was pulling out of him. The pain did not leave with it, and it was suddenly difficult to breathe. He stumbled back from the force of Badgett's push and fell ungracefully against the raised platform of the marble throne.

"It looks as if the Void-God will get his chance to examine your soul after all," Badgett crowed. He bent down and picked up the blade Kemp had dropped. "An anointed blade would never suffer the besmirchment of a heathen's hands. It's no wonder that it failed you."

Kemp wasn't really listening. In his dealings as a huntsman, death had been a constant. He'd led many unwittingly to its door, and he'd known that he would arrive there himself at some point. Yet, despite this understanding, he found that the whole experience was quite a bit more painful and frightening than he'd ever imagined. And to think, he'd foisted this, and far worser fates, on so many. His old guilt thrummed along with the flexing agony that clutched his insides with every breath. The truth was that he *deserved* this. Still, he wasn't going to give Badgett any satisfaction. If he had to die, he was going to take the unctuous little shit with him.

He bared his teeth in a rictus grin, the coppery taste of blood filling his mouth, and began to drag himself along the edge of the platform and away from Badgett. He was surprised to find that he was still holding his knife. Now, if he could just catch his breath and get up, he could fight.

"What's the matter?" Badgett asked with feigned concern. "Are there no more lies ready to spring off that forked tongue of yours? Have you nothing else to say before I deliver you?"

There was actually a lot that Kemp wished to say, but his weak, whistling breaths didn't seem to be providing him with any air. He tried to rise, but faltered and fell back. By now, he'd circled around to the back of the throne, and Badgett had followed at a safe distance, savoring every moment of his demise.

A snapping boom sounded from the sky without warning, accompanied by a cacophony of twangs and tearing sounds. The entire keep seemed to wobble with the force of the Erosion's fluctuation, and the air around them was suddenly alight with flashing, geometric shapes. Seams in reality were stretching apart, exposing the black nothingness that was seething just below their thinning world.

"Behold the glorious calamity!" Badgett cried with giddy laughter. "He will bring us to his bosom and cradle us in his love forever! The unworthy dead will be expunged from the records of eternity and all those who are blessed will be plucked from the nothingness of the Void, just as he is being reborn of it! In his light we will rejoice! In his magnanimity we will find perpetual comfort!"

Kemp didn't see anything remotely comforting in the bizarre, flickering lines around him, beyond knowing that Badgett could see them too, and they were not just the hallucinations of a dying mind. Their intensity flared, and the keep filled with variegated light. Kemp could feel the stones of the floor rattling apart beneath him, and he watched as a large chunk of the roof adjacent to the existing hole came crashing down, the sound of it small compared to the continuous roar around them.

Badgett actually jumped up and down with unrestrained joy, his gangly movements mirroring those of the mounted skeleton, jittering on its wires above and between them. One of the two remaining hooks on which a wire had been fastened popped loose from the wall, causing the whole thing to lurch forward and drop slightly. The last remaining hook shuddered with the extra weight, the stone wall crumbling around it. Kemp fixated on this, and his thoughts turned.

The Erosion's latest episode began to subside, and Badgett held his free hand aloft, as if he were reaching out to touch the receding madness. His eyes were closed and his mouth was hanging open.

Kemp sucked in a wet breath as best he could. "Do you need to change your skivvies?" he croaked.

Badgett's mouth snapped shut as his eyes snapped open. "You waste your last breath on vulgarities?"

"I have a few breaths yet to spare, you ugly son of a bitch."

He could actually see the moment that Badgett decided that he was done playing. The high shepherd's sour expression broke into one of triumph, and he stalked toward Kemp.

As he always had, Kemp smiled.

With the last of his waning strength, he lifted his knife and took aim. Badgett bladed his stance and held up his sword in a defensive posture, preparing to easily dodge or deflect this last attack. Kemp, his dying mind filling with phantoms of the past, held his shallow breath and launched the knife—

—after him. The first struck the throne of antlers and, spraying sparks, clattered onto the seat, where the fire hungrily erupted across the dry wood. The second sailed—

—far wide of Badgett, who barked a short laugh, not realizing that he'd never been the target. With a hollow clang, the knife struck the final hook holding the dead god's bones aloft, knocking it free of the last tenuous hold of the wall. At the sound, Badgett looked up.

All at once, the colossal skeleton plummeted, crashing onto the floor of the throne room and flattening Badgett beneath a jumble of broken bones and tangled wires. The ebony halo rolled free from the wreck and, losing momentum, spun down until it came to rest on its side.

Enveloped in a cloud of settling dust, Kemp threw his head back and loosed a wheezy laugh. He'd had one more little trick to pull after all. It was just too bad that he wouldn't live long enough to tell anyone about it. He didn't bother trying to get up again, opting instead to lean back against the throne's platform. It was a real shame, considering that Reie could have easily restored him. But she wasn't there; she was off rescuing Ganachim, hopefully.

It was strange. The long road of his life had brought him to this distant land, where he'd helped to reunite a woman, one he'd originally intended to deliver into death, with her child. He'd witnessed the unraveling of the world, and he'd sought to stop it. He'd been fatally wounded by a complete stranger, all while trying to free a god he'd never met, in order to help another god. His ending was about as far removed from his beginning as he could possibly imagine. It was as if his life had actually been three lives, each entirely distinct from the others. He'd had his time as duke, enjoying the love of his wife and daughter; his time as Lakna's servant, a butcher for Setenrah; and his time as a follower of Reie, which he hoped had made up for the failings of the other two lives.

But it was just as Reie had said. Nothing he'd done had changed his past; it was as immutable as it was tragic. But, he hoped, his actions had at least changed the future, even if he wouldn't be around to enjoy it. Maybe that was the cost of redemption.

Beneath the heap of bones, Badgett's crushed body began to stir. Kemp laughed again, delighting in the irony. A moment later, the wailing started. Then, the body's skullcap burst and the newborn shade slithered into its skeletal prison. It bucked wildly, further cracking the splintered ribs. It would not be contained for long.

Kemp didn't care, he would be departing shortly. He'd never really adhered to any notion of the afterlife, but, in his final moments, he thought of Taiyonna and Blythe.

Perhaps he would be seeing them soon.

CHAPTER 43

A tide of liberated prisoners streamed out of the dungeons, charging wildly down whatever passages they guessed might lead out of the keep. As Marbuck had imagined would be the case, Reie had been all for freeing them. She'd directed Nedelkoff to release them, and a few short-cycles later, the task had been done. Lame and ill, they'd shambled out of their cages, staring at the revealed god with awe. With a burst of her power, she'd restored them and told them that they were free to leave. She hadn't asked for their help, and not one of them had offered any. Reie didn't seem to mind; she'd clearly freed them because it was the right thing to do, not because she'd expected any assistance from them. Personally, Marbuck felt that they could have shown a little more gratitude, but, at the very least, she was glad that they'd be providing yet another chaotic distraction.

Only one prisoner remained behind with them, and he'd taken some convincing.

When Reie had removed her veil, the imprisoned ex-shepherd had not reacted in the way that Marbuck had been expecting.

"You're one of them," Galt had said, limping backward until he'd been pressed against the bars of his cell. "A god."

"Yes," Reie had said plainly.

"These *things* orchestrated the death of every other person on the expedition," Galt had said, speaking to Marbuck and the others. "You can count me out."

Marbuck had found this to be a troubling, and interesting, statement, but in her own experience, the gods had proven to be no different from humans when it came to morality. Reie was certainly nothing like Setenrah or the Empress.

"Whichever of my kin you encountered, and whatever they did to you, I had no part in it," Reie had said. "There will be ample time for airing your grievances later. For now, if you want your freedom, you must trust me. I am willing to trust *you*, for I need your help."

Galt had started to argue, but Reie had responded by hitting him with a concentrated blast of her energy. Stunned into silence by his total physical restoration, Reie had taken the opportunity to hastily introduce herself and her companions and to explain their intentions in the briefest sense. She'd concluded by telling him that, if he wished to live, he had no choice but to trust her. Examining his mended injuries, Galt had agreed, but his mistrust had remained. He'd told her to abstain from taking him unawares with any more sorcery and to stay away from him. Reie, as placid as ever, had not seemed to be disturbed by his recalcitrance but agreed to do whatever he asked just as soon as they reached Ganachim.

The last fleeing prisoners slipped from view just as their party returned to the entrance of the dungeon. Jalam was waiting beside the only cage that remained locked, the slightest hint of a smile on his lips.

"Why am I not surprised?" he said.

"About releasing the prisoners?" Reie asked.

"Yes. Your goodwill knows no bounds, my lady. Who is this joining us?"

"He is called Galt, and he knows where Ganachim is."

Jalam nodded, and as was his wont, asked no further questions.

"Please, won't you free me just as you've freed the rest? I've done you no wrong," Clusk whined from within his cell.

"Here you go," Nedelkoff said, and she dropped the jailer's keys onto the floor outside of his cell. "Just like I said I would. Good luck."

They departed then, leaving Clusk to call after them in tones of desperate anger. Reie expressed some reluctance in leaving him like that, but Nedelkoff assured her that as soon as Clusk got himself under control he'd figure out a way to reach the keys. Meanwhile, they'd be reaching Ganachim.

Assuming, of course, that Galt actually knew where she was.

The surly prisoner now led the way, moving swiftly through the shadowy corridors. Reie's halo, which she'd left defiantly uncovered now that their ruse was finished, provided some extra light, but Galt appeared not to need it, walking with the surety of memory. He also seemed to be relishing having his wasted body restored, moving along with spry agility. As they went, Marbuck became increasingly certain that he was either leading them directly to Ganachim or straight into some kind of trap. Briefly, she thought of Gomulte.

That bitter reminiscence was interrupted when another tremendous detonation rattled the keep around them. They froze where they stood, bracing against one another, waiting helplessly to see if this would be the one that finally brought the end. It seemed to go on forever, and the violent quaking was accompanied by shuddering patterns of emptiness, glowing with a strange light, that flickered in and out of view. Marbuck had seen the beginning of these seams, but now they seemed to be coming apart right before her eyes. She felt like her mind was about to join them, and her knees began to buckle. A rough hand seized her by the arm and braced her, and she turned to see Galt. He didn't seem to be fazed at all by the disintegration of reality around them.

"Don't look at them," he shouted over the din.

She closed her eyes and waited. It helped. She found that she was less afraid of being driven insane and able to focus much more on the relatively pedestrian fear of being buried alive.

The episode finally began to abate, but not before a stretch of the passageway behind them caved in, filling the corridor with loose stones, dirt, and debris.

"We need to keep moving," Nedelkoff shouted.

Galt did not need to be told twice and proceeded without even checking to see if anyone was following him. Marbuck, who'd been distracted by the collapse, only started to follow when Falstaff pulled her along.

They proceeded down a spiral stairway, which now sported a sizable crack running through the stone of its central pillar, and along yet another dark corridor. Galt paused, considering, and then led them around a corner. He trotted halfway down the next hallway and stopped before an unremarkable wooden door. Marbuck and the others piled up behind him.

"This is it?" Reie asked.

"This is it," Galt said. "Ganachim is held in the grotto just beyond this door."

"It's unguarded."

"The keep is a maze, and this door is as plain and unadorned as hundreds of others just like it. Anonymity has always been its security."

There was no handle, and Jalam moved to push the door open. It didn't budge. He gave it a few more test pushes and turned to Reie. "It appears they've adopted an extra security measure. It's barred from the other side."

Falstaff stepped forward, holding up Mordwand's axe. "Allow me."

"Hey! *Hey!*"

Every head turned toward the sound of the voice to see Rayburn waddling down the corridor from the opposite direction. He was panting, red-faced, and holding an anointed blade.

"What's happened?" Nedelkoff said, grabbing ahold of him as he reached them.

He gulped some air, his head bobbing up and down with the effort. "Phar-Mindorius and two shepherds … they're going to Ganachim now … they're going to kill her."

"She's still alive, after all," Galt mused.

Rayburn looked at him, and some dim recognition floated in his eyes.

"*Kill* her?" Reie said. "Get us through this door."

Falstaff stepped up and, with a grunt of effort, sank the axe into the soft wood of the ancient door.

"I tried to follow them … but I lost them," Rayburn said watching Falstaff with some puzzlement.

"No worries," Nedelkoff said, thumping him on the back. "Ganachim's through this door. If they got here first, we'll stop them."

"How did you …" Rayburn trailed off, looking at Galt. Galt looked back at him, and then held his hand out for the blade. Rayburn, still trying to discern who Galt was, handed it to him without question. Galt examined it with a rueful expression.

Marbuck pushed in front of Rayburn. "Where is Kemp?"

Rayburn's broad face sank. "He stayed behind to hold off Badgett … he said he'd catch up."

The axe thumped into the door again, and the wood split. Marbuck barely heard it; to her infinite surprise, she was deeply shaken by Kemp's absence.

"We have to go back for him," she said.

A third blow broke the door asunder.

"We must reach Ganachim first," Reie said, her voice suddenly ragged with fear. "We'll find Henrick after."

"He would understand," Jalam said, and Marbuck believed him. Kemp, after all, had proven his devotion to Reie's cause time and time again.

Falstaff tore away the last boards, and they began to scramble through the opening.

"Mind the steps!" Galt shouted as they piled through. "They're slick."

"*Stop!*" Reie shrieked as soon as she entered. It was a piercing sound, one full of heart-rending pain. Once Marbuck got a clear view of the grotto below, lit by a large fire burning within a metal basin, she could see why.

In the center of the cavern, suspended from chains, was Ganachim. Reduced to a monstrous ghoul, she was unlike anything Marbuck had been expecting. Gray, fungal skin was flaking off her bones, exposing what looked like a combination of spoiled meat and rotten wood. Her head hung limply, framed by a few loose strands of filthy hair and crowned by what remained of her halo; a deteriorating crescent of cankerous mold. Her arms were nearly thin enough to slip free of the rusted manacles holding her aloft, and her legs dangled into a fetid pool, surrounded by a slime-coated riverbed that led away into darkness. Two shepherds, blades drawn, were rapidly approaching her.

Phar-Mindorius, his crown in his hands, stood nearby. At Reie's cry, his head snapped toward her, and he jammed his crown back on. "You're too late," he cried in a cracked voice.

"*STOP!*" Reie screamed again, but before she could even start to descend the steps, the shepherds lunged forward and began plunging their blades into Ganachim's belly.

With an inarticulate cry of anguish and rage, Reie flung her hands out, and the light of her halo flared. The air before her rippled in a swirling eddy, rushing from her outstretched arms and enveloping the unmoving form of Ganachim. The shepherds were momentarily taken aback, but then redoubled their efforts, stabbing her again and again.

Without orders or forethought, Marbuck ran down the steps, intent on stopping the shepherds. Hitting a patch of slime, her foot slid out from beneath her. Somehow, she managed to right herself, and made it to the bottom intact. Falstaff, Jalam, and Nedelkoff arrived just behind her, and the two shepherds, seeing their approach, turned to face them.

"You're outnumbered," Marbuck said. "Drop your blades."

"I cannot allow you to stop the Void-God's arrival," Phar-Mindorius said stepping toward the standoff. "My son is almost here. He rides before deliverance."

"That is *not* deliverance," Jalam said. He gestured toward Reie, who, teeth bared and hands outstretched, was still pouring her power out into Ganachim. "*She* is."

"I will not allow another scheming old one to destroy Vingallea. My—"

A deafening, splintering sound tore through the grotto, accompanied by an otherworldly bloom of light. A shockwave buffeted Marbuck, knocking her to the ground, which vibrated wildly. Quivering fractals filled the air, joined by successive, tooth-rattling booms. With a thunderous crack, the back wall of the grotto peeled away, and groaning hideously, slid off into black nothing. The air puckered toward this new hole, pulling steadily at everything. What remained of the cavern continued to rattle violently, raining stones down. The stagnant pool at Ganachim's feet drained away, the water spuming off into thin air. Marbuck stared at the hungry maw of the Void with pure terror. A spastic shudder of flaring light filled the cavern, and Marbuck buried her head in her arms.

Finally, the throe of the Erosion subsided into a low hum and a steady pull of air. Marbuck looked around cautiously, certain that the ground beneath her was going to drop away at any moment, or that the keep, its foundation being erased beneath it, would collapse. Everyone else was similarly dazed and beginning to rise. From within the new hole torn in reality, flashes of violet light painted the remaining walls of the grotto.

With a plummeting stomach, Marbuck realized that Ganachim was gone. Where she'd been, a lone chain dangled from what remained of the ceiling.

CHAPTER 44

Phar-Mindorius looked into the Void, and his doubt warred with his hope.

Crown askew, he struggled to rise. Nearby, his two remaining shepherds, Vandercolt and Ellsworth, regained their feet, and seeing him, rushed to his side. As they hoisted him up, Phar-Mindorius looked toward the empty space that the slave-god had occupied for ages. She was gone, and in her absence, the end had arrived. How odd that, to save his realm, he'd had to guarantee the destruction of the crutch that had held it up for so long. In the end, the Void had swallowed the slave-god, guaranteeing his success. Assuming, of course, that Badgett's prophecies had been true.

Otherwise, Phar-Mindorius knew, his folly would be unmatched.

The invaders who'd sought to topple him were also getting to their feet, and at the top of the steps was the old one who'd apparently orchestrated it all. Whatever she'd been doing to Ganachim had clearly taken its toll on her. Her halo had turned a waxy gray, and she remained on her knees, seemingly unable to rise. Beside her, Phar-Mindorius noted with displeasure, were the treacherous merchant and, somehow, the God Eater. Apparently, the plot to overthrow him had run even deeper than he'd expected.

"It's finished," Ellsworth declared. "Nothing now stands between Vingallea and its ascendance to the creator's side."

Phar-Mindorius nodded, wondering how, exactly, that ascendance would occur, and how his reunion with Phir-Ramarian would unfold.

"Shall we purge this holy place of the false god?" Ellsworth asked.

"Its presence may still hinder the arrival," Vandercolt added.

These two were nothing if not loyal to Badgett's vision. Their own certainty helped to drive Phar-Mindorius's doubts back into the shadows of his beleaguered mind. "Yes," he said, nodding again. "Yes, purge them all. Clear the way for my son."

"Phir-Ramarian is *dead*," the God Eater said.

"Silence, traitor," Phar-Mindorius barked. He turned to his shepherds. "Remove his tongue before you kill him, so that I might personally smite the author of so many lies."

"Yes, Your Majesty."

A new idea occurred to Phar-Mindorius; an addition that would leave his own personal mark on the Skullcap Crown, so that the generations of monarchs that followed him would forever bear his trophy. "And bring me the old one's halo."

"Not going to happen. You're still outnumbered," a bald, scarred woman said, brandishing her sword. Beside her stood two men and a turncoat guardsman, yet another conspirator. "Nothing has changed that. If you try to touch Reie, we will kill you."

"Have at it, we're all dead anyway," the God Eater grumbled.

"You've failed," Phar-Mindorius said, ignoring the God Eater. "To pursue this old one's agenda now is just stubborn foolishness. Recant now, and I will offer you—"

A primal bellow sounded from the Void, and, startled, Phar-Mindorius turned toward it. His eyes widened as he observed dark tendrils creeping up and over the broken edge of the ground. Like seeking fingers, they worked their way across the ground until they found random juttings of stone to wrap around. With a shiver of fear, Phar-Mindorius realized that they were vines.

They snapped taut, pulling forth from the chasm a colossal human figure, great and terrible. It was muscular and curvaceous, draped in broad leaves. Its brown skin glowed with power; its eyes shone with a primordial light, the green and gold of the first life to spring from the soil beneath an ancient sun. A splendid wreath of blooming flowers hung above its head, shedding petals of a thousand hues onto its broad shoulders. The vines, emerging from its mantle of foliage, guided it gently to the ground, setting it before Phar-Mindorius, where it towered over him.

There had been truth to the claims of the invaders after all; the god, the one the scarred woman had called Reie, had restored Ganachim. The slave-god had been freed.

Ganachim took a step toward Phar-Mindorius, and he scrambled backward. "Restrain her," he rasped. "*Restrain her.*"

Ellsworth was the first to move, though whether he was trying to fulfill his king's order or not was unclear. It didn't matter. Ganachim seized him in one hand, hoisted him up, and dashed his head against the stony ground, spilling the pink and gray paste of his brains in a shower of blood at Phar-Mindorius's feet. She then tossed his ruined body into the chasm and took another step forward.

By then, Vandercolt had bolted away.

"Stop, you coward!" Phar-Mindorius called after him. "Restrain her! Obey your king!"

The shepherd did not look back, scampering past the invaders, who, equally awestruck, made no move to stop him. He raced up the steps, and, halfway up, slipped, his feet flying out from beneath him. He landed on his neck with a disturbing crunch, tumbled down a few steps, and came to a stop in an awkward sprawl.

Phar-Mindorius could not believe that the creature he had long considered his own property, the catatonic wreck that he'd confided in countless times, was the same being as the robust behemoth closing in on him. His mind felt watery; the thoughts produced by his own senses seemed insubstantial. In a rush of terrible clarity, he finally allowed himself to understand that everything he'd believed in had been obliterated; every dream he'd ever harbored had been dispelled. His people had deserted him; even Vitus and Badgett were absent at the end. Vingallea was going to die with him.

Phir-Ramarian wasn't coming. There was only the Void, unleashed by his own misguided actions.

"No, this isn't real," he whimpered, still backing away.

Ganachim opened her mouth, as if testing it. "It is," she said, and her voice was harmonious, beautiful, and extremely frightening. Phar-Mindorius clapped his hands over his ears.

On the steps, Vandercolt's body began to shake. The God Eater stepped forward, a blade held before him, but it wasn't necessary. Without turning away from Phar-Mindorius, Ganachim sent a vine snaking toward the body. The skullcap exploded apart and, as the shade slithered free, the vine ensnared it, glowing brightly. It tightened around the newborn shade until, with a shriek, the shade burst apart into a flurry of dust. As the vine receded back into Ganachim's foliage, nobody spoke, shocked into silence by the display of raw power.

"Long have I suffered here in this foul pit, while an endless parade of increasingly deluded fools lorded over me," Ganachim said. "But you were the worst. You and your incessant, petulant *mewling*. I heard every word. I lingered on death's edge for so long, trapped in a darkness occupied only by pain and the grating sound of *your voice*." She looked at Reie, who remained slumped over. "Until now."

She snatched Phar-Mindorius with sudden and implacable force, and he felt urine jet down his legs. She brought him up to her face, where her previously rheumy eyes bore into him.

"*Stop her!*" Phar-Mindorius cried raggedly. "I command you all, as subjects of the Crown, to obey me! Help me, *please!*"

Nobody moved.

"Ganachim, please," Phar-Mindorius begged, tears spilling from his eyes and coursing down his wrinkled face, "I was never anything but kind to you. I only ever sought to care for you, to *nurture* you. We sustained the realm *together*."

Her face tightened into a scowl and the massive hand holding Phar-Mindorius tightened, compressing his chest and forcing his breath out in a wheezing squeak. The Skullcap Crown of Phan-Ellara slipped from his head and, with a dull clank, bounced away into the shadows.

"Wait."

It was Reie. She had struggled to her feet, supported by Rayburn.

"I have not come to perpetuate the horrors of the past," she said, pausing to take a labored breath. "What these people have done to you is unforgivable, but there was a time when you loved mankind, and I know that those feelings dwell within you still. What *I* did to you was unforgivable, and I hope that some of your love for me remains as well. I came here for you, Ganachim, not to atone, for I expect no forgiveness, but to begin anew. We can forget the past. We can build a future together. Please. I wish to build it on mercy."

"Mercy?" Ganachim asked.

"Yes. For me. For mankind. Even for him."

Ganachim seemed to consider this, her grip loosening just enough that Phar-Mindorius could breathe. Finally, she nodded to herself.

"Mercy," Ganachim said again. "You know my nature. I yearn for peace; for the renewal you speak of. We have much to navigate, but I feel this future could, indeed, come to pass. For you. For mankind. But not for him."

Before Phar-Mindorius could truly understand what was happening, he was sailing through the air. A brief glimpse showed him Ganachim, her arm outstretched, and the others watching him go. Then, he was falling beneath the crust of the world and descending toward the Void.

He tried to scream, but his howling was quickly silenced by the whipping ferocity of the air rushing about his falling body. Following the trajectory of Ganachim's throw, he moved almost diagonally at first, allowing him a fleeting glimpse of a tiny island of solidity floating ahead of him. As he dipped below it, he briefly recognized it for what it was: the Gates of Paradise, hovering on a tiny patch of intact land; the nexus of reality's collapse. His greatest desire now mocked him with its malignant, impossible presence. At the foot of the white marble arch was the skeletal carcass of Ulesreto.

Phar-Mindorius was finally convinced of his own catastrophic failure.

Above him, reality was quickly receding into a lip of lighted texture in a vast nothingness. Bizarre, impossible colors raced by him as his velocity increased. Phar-Mindorius felt himself being pulled by the abyssal emptiness, stretched into infinity. He tried to scream again, his overwrought mind having no other recourse, and his voice was stripped away in a metallic reverberation that sent the colors around him swirling with lunatic menace.

Finally, with no poignant last words, or solemn remembrance of his legacy, but only a panicked, incoherent yelp, his entire body dissolved into a stream of rapidly dissipating particles, erasing every shred of what had once been Phar-Mindorius.

The chain had been broken. The line of the kings of Vingallea had ended.

CHAPTER 45

Against all odds, the God of the Earth had been restored, and Marbuck's awe was matched only by her fear. Ganachim spoke of mercy for mankind, but Phar-Mindorius, as her primary captor, had not been spared. That was understandable, but Marbuck worried that her ire might extend to other Vingalleans. She glanced nervously at the anointed blade in her hand, one that had been forged by Ganachim's suffering. Pledges of peace or not, there was no real telling when Ganachim's wrath would be truly quenched.

As such, Marbuck began to have serious doubts about their plan when Ganachim turned to face her and the others, having finished her observance of Phar-Mindorius's demise. She bore a fell expression, one that was equal parts ferocious satisfaction and loathing.

"I will not condemn you for that," Reie said, still leaning heavily on Rayburn. Galt stood nearby, but didn't seem interested in lending a hand. "What you have endured—I cannot imagine."

Ganachim said nothing.

"I am sorry," Reie continued, her voice hitching. "For refusing to answer the call to war. For abandoning our father; for abandoning *you*. You were right about me. And all this time, I thought you'd been killed. And then I learned of your imprisonment, and I came as quickly as I could. These humans helped me get to you; they are righteous and true of heart."

Ganachim's emerald eyes scanned across Marbuck and the others.

"I know that there is so much more that needs to be explained, but it must wait. We need to leave this place at once."

"Yes, I know," Ganachim said. "I have heard my captor's lamentations. I know what is happening. I do not fear it."

"There are many others who do," Reie said. "And there are yet other malignancies at work still in this world. Setenrah lives."

Whatever feelings of hatred Ganachim had felt for Phar-Mindorius must have been dwarfed by her enmity for Setenrah. At the sound of his name, her face twisted into a mask of furious contempt, and the vines emerging from her back began to writhe. Marbuck took an involuntary step backward.

"I know that he was with Aedesda when you were ambushed. He has told me as much, gloated over it, actually. He told me he killed you. I should have never left you to go north alone. I should have been there." Reie sank in Rayburn's arms and pressed her hands over her face.

A fissure of pity seemed to split Ganachim's rage, and she approached Reie, causing the others to scatter out of her way. Vines slithered ahead of her, rising up the steps and encircling Reie gently. Rayburn backed away, allowing the vines to lift Reie and bring her before Ganachim.

"You are not a coward," Ganachim said. "I was blinded by pride, and indignation, and unquestioning adherence to our father's flawed vision. I refused to see any validity to the grievances of the rebels, and I cast you aside for believing in the inevitable collapse of their schemes. I thought there was only one way forward, and I was wrong. Look where it led me. I am grateful that you went your own way, for you are here now."

The gods embraced each other then, their foreheads pressed together, weeping with joy at their reunion. Falstaff was crying, too, watching them. Jalam looked immensely satisfied; Nedelkoff still looked stunned. On the steps above, Galt stared into space indifferently, but Rayburn actually clapped with delight. With a tug of sorrow, Marbuck thought of Kemp; he wasn't there to witness the culmination of everything they'd fought for.

Despite her leeriness to interrupt, Marbuck was about to suggest that they find Kemp and get out of there when a rising groan from the emptiness beside them reminded everyone of their pressing need to depart. The gods pulled away from each other with obvious reluctance, and then Reie spoke with sudden composure.

"We need to leave. Now. But first we must get to Henrick," she said, as if she'd been channeling Marbuck's thoughts.

"He was in the throne room when I left him," Rayburn said.

"Can you lead us there?" Jalam asked.

Rayburn frowned. "I took so many turns and—"

"I can," Galt interjected with a sigh.

"I will take us there," Ganachim said. "In a more direct manner. Point me toward it."

There was some confusion as to her intentions, but the rumbling increased and the shimmering distortions began to return, so Galt wasted no time. Hastily, he made a best guess, based on his sense of direction, of where the throne room would be in comparison to the grotto. Ganachim nodded curtly and turned toward the section of the cavern's ceiling that Galt had indicated. She then urged everyone to get behind her.

"It will be a pleasure to topple this prison," Ganachim said, and she stretched her arms out above her head. The foliage spanning her shoulders shuddered and thick, roping vines raced up her arms and fired outward, driving into the ceiling. She began to sway and chant, the words spilling from her rapidly. An aura of green light surrounded her, and with an explosive cry, she channeled her power into the outstretched vines. They began to burrow into the rock, cracking it apart and churning within, pulverizing the stone as they bore a way through. The noise of the destruction nearly matched that of the Erosion's next volley, which was growing with each passing moment.

Marbuck, watching this display with amazement, did not notice the vines encircling her until they tightened. Confusion was her immediate response, followed quickly by a wave of terror.

"Do not be afraid," Ganachim's voice boomed, cutting through Marbuck's panic. "I will carry you out."

All around Marbuck, the others had been lifted in a similar manner, and based on their expressions, they'd been similarly frightened. All except for Reie, who was watching Ganachim with an almost bleary-eyed expression of relief. Her restoration of Ganachim had clearly taken everything she had; the emotional exhaustion that had come with it must have been even greater.

Having tunneled some distance into the cavern's ceiling, Ganachim began to ascend, using the canopy of vines she'd created to lift herself into the air. Marbuck's boots left the ground with a dizzying feeling of disbelief. She was not concerned about falling, or being crushed; she was simply astonished by the unbelievable circumstances she now found herself in.

On they went, carried by Ganachim as she bored her way through the bowels of the Vinecrown Keep. They passed the severed arteries of numerous corridors, revealing glimpses of the empty tunnels collapsing around them. Looking backward, Marbuck saw that the ground they'd just occupied had dropped away into the Void. She hoped fervently that they could reach Kemp before the entire keep did the same.

Finally, they burst forth into a larger area, and Nedelkoff shouted for Ganachim to stop. She did, and Marbuck lurched forward as the vine bearing her came to a sudden halt. As she was lowered to the ground, Nedelkoff addressed them.

"We've reached the scullery. The throne room is just through that passage," she said, pointing toward a threshold to their right. "Looks like your estimate was pretty close, herder," she added, addressing Galt.

"I'm not a shepherd," he said flatly. "Not anymore."

Ganachim didn't seem to notice this exchange, which Marbuck considered fortunate; learning that one of her former torturers was in her midst might reignite her fury. Instead, she was focused on making her way toward the throne room. Reie remained cradled in her vines, and she was saying something to Ganachim that Marbuck couldn't hear.

By then, the Erosion's latest tremor was already fading. It had either been some kind of aftershock of the one that had torn the grotto asunder, or a precursor to something much larger. Whatever the case, Marbuck didn't want to stick around to find out.

Ganachim forced her way through the doorway, destroying it as she went. If she had not left a verdant bloom in her wake that held back the collapse of the passage, the others would have been left behind, trapped inside the scullery. Marbuck passed beneath this protective netting of foliage with caution and wonder. A moment later, she emerged into the wreckage of the throne room, where a massive hole in the roof revealed a quivering gyre of distortion that now dominated the sky completely. Trying mightily to ignore it, Marbuck joined the others in searching for Kemp.

It did not take long to find him.

His body was slumped against the back of the throne's platform. He had not produced a shade, and, although it might have just been her imagination, Marbuck was not at all surprised to see that a smile creased his bloody face.

"Is there any chance that he …?" Jalam said.

"You've got to be able to …" Falstaff said at the same time.

Reie shook her head.

Marbuck examined Kemp's features, recalling every way he'd ever made her feel. There had been hatred once, but it had certainly given way to kinship. Like her, he'd been a refugee making his way in a world populated by forces far beyond his control. His path had been a dark and winding one, but it had eventually led into the light. She was grateful that he'd helped her get there as well.

"I think I've found Badgett," Rayburn said from behind them. Marbuck turned to see him looking at a heap of what she'd initially dismissed as rubble. Now she saw that it was actually comprised of massive bones, and crushed beneath them was a bloody, deflated body.

"I think I've found him, too," Galt said with a note of bitter humor in his voice.

A shade was wandering aimlessly on the opposite side of the throne room. Before anyone could comment further, the next fluctuation of the Erosion arrived with a deafening twang. Almost immediately, a warping wave rode up from beneath them, shaking the walls of the keep. As it passed through her, Marbuck felt her very being loosen, as if she might disintegrate completely. In its wake, she felt extremely nauseous and disoriented.

"Go now!" Reie screamed.

"I can stop this madness," Ganachim said.

"No, it is too late for this place! We cannot risk it now. We are needed elsewhere."

Ganachim stared at the smaller god for just a moment. Without a word, she stalked toward the opposite end of the hall, and the others followed. Marbuck, casting one last glance at Kemp, raced after them.

Approaching the exit, the shade saw them coming. Before it could do anything more than look at them, Ganachim obliterated it with the same casual ease with which she'd destroyed the shade in the grotto. They exited the throne room then, descending a broad staircase. Behind them, Marbuck heard the remaining roof collapse with a roaring groan. Rushing down the steps and through a foyer, Ganachim blew the front doors out of their way, and they emerged into the open air.

They raced across the castle grounds, snaking their way around the splitting seams of their reality. As they reached the outer wall, the Vinecrown Keep buckled. The three remaining turrets began to sink downward in unison, the pressure of their fall causing the stones beneath them to explode outward. The entire structure began to fold in on itself, but before it could collapse completely, the foundation finally gave way, and the whole keep dropped at once, swallowed by the Void.

Marbuck did not have long to marvel at this incredible sight.

Their flight continued, moving from the vanished keep to the bedlam of the city proper. All around them, the divisions of their society had been swiftly abandoned. Peasant, guardsman, noble, merchant, shepherd; it didn't matter now; imminent death had made them all equals. The people fled in every direction, their collected screams mingling with the reverberating booms of the Erosion. Marbuck watched as a noble, bearing armloads of looted treasure, scurried by them. Preoccupied with his meaningless plunder, he failed to notice Ganachim looming over the crowd.

"We must save as many of them as we can," Reie shouted over the din. Seeing Ganachim's frown, Reie touched her arm. "They knew not what sustained them."

Once again, Ganachim considered Reie, and once again, she obliged her. After a quick discussion, Reie's plan was enacted.

"*SOUTH!*" Ganachim bellowed with a volume unmatched by any human voice. "*SALVATION LIES IN THE SOUTH! GO NOW! SPREAD THE WORD! SOUTH!*"

Her presence, suddenly noticed by the fleeing people, seemed to frighten them nearly as much as the Erosion did, yet they heeded her words. The tide of the crowd shifted, driven before Ganachim. All along their route, the call to go south spread, and more and more people joined them until Marbuck found herself pressed in on all sides by a wall of humanity. The people, eager to be delivered from the nightmare engulfing their lives, did not question the fact that Ganachim was not leading them toward the main gates. She eschewed the gates completely, choosing instead to level a large portion of the city's southern wall.

Like blood from a mortal wound, the people of Nordabor streamed out of the massive gap in the wall, leaving behind the corpse of their emptied city.

PART 6:

ECHOES OF THE OLD WAR

CHAPTER 46

The exodus finally stopped when they reached the refugee camp. The worst of the Erosion had been left behind, but its inexorable approach left little doubt in Marbuck's mind that they would be moving again before too long.

The relatively small clearing was entirely inundated with the sprawling mass of people. They stood dazedly, stunned individuals and clustered families clutching whatever they had managed to take with them. Swept up in the converging crowd, seeking any way to escape Nordabor, they'd moved with an animalistic instinct. Now that their flight had temporarily ended, they were coming to terms with their strange new reality.

Breaking away from Reie and Ganachim, who were speaking to each other quietly at the center of the pressing throng of people, Marbuck tried to seek out Elibeth. Snaking her way through the crowd, she overheard snippets of confusion, fear, and agitation. The discordant chorus rose until Ganachim ordered them all to be silent. The crowd complied with a suddenness that could only be commanded by the divine. Every eye was directed toward the restored god; even Marbuck had been startled from her search. Ganachim stood with her arms folded, vines coiling above her, forming a sort of litter upon which Reie was raised above the crowd. She still looked ashen-faced and worn, but her features bore the undeniable presence of happiness.

"People of Nordabor," she said. "I know that you are frightened. I know that you have been visited by disaster, speeding upon the heels of woe. I am here to tell you that the time of your suffering is at an end. Phar-Mindorius has fallen. The old order is finished, a new life begins now."

The crowd remained eerily silent.

"I am Reie, God of Mending. I came to Nordabor to free the engine of your survival. Some of you may know what that means, and many others might not. I am speaking of Ganachim, God of the Earth." Reie gestured toward the towering god holding her aloft. "Some of you were complacent in her enslavement; know that it matters not. A creature, doomed to die, can be expected to take certain measures to ensure its survival. There will be no ill will harbored toward you. As I said, a new life awaits you now. One without the burdens of the past; without kings or commands; all of you will be forgiven, equal, and free to pursue whatever you wish, as long as it brings no harm."

Now scattered murmurs passed through the crowd. Marbuck wondered if a people conditioned to obey for fear of the consequences could ever believe, much less embrace, such concepts.

"I wish to be clear," Reie continued. "Ganachim and I will not be your masters, and you are not beholden to obey us now. No oaths need be sworn. Any who wish to depart to seek their own way may do so. Any who wish to be a part of our future may accompany us south, where we will deliver my own people and establish our free realm for perpetuity. Together, I believe we can even stave off the Erosion."

The uneasy chatter of the crowd increased.

"Though you ask for no oaths, I give you mine now."

Heads swiveled, seeking the source of this declaration. The crowd parted and Marbuck saw Avehav, bloodied and ragged. He did not kneel, but stood before the gods with an air of humble deference. She was surprised to see that he'd survived the assault, and that he was willing to abandon his own intentions to follow Reie and Ganachim. She was not, however, surprised by his theatrical entrance.

"My men and I were some of the last to leave Nordabor. I watched from beyond the burning fields as the city—the entire city—vanished. And do you know what I felt? Hope." Avehav laughed with a nervous giddiness, and to Marbuck it seemed like a rare glimpse of the real man beneath the political posturing. "We are *free*! Nordabor was our home, yes, but it was also our prison. We labored beneath the legacy of our

Vingallean forefathers and their mistakes for far too long. I always imagined that I would somehow clean the slate by restoring my own ancestors, but I see now that our freedom, our *true* freedom, resides in abandoning the broken past entirely. I believe in the promise you offer, and I am humbled by your power. I freely abdicate any claims to royalty; Buqaardian; Vingallean; it doesn't matter. I forsake them all to join in this new future. I forsake them for freedom."

Avehav broke into tears then, stumbling forward and collapsing before the gods. Perhaps he'd simply calculated that a quick and early show of submission would grease his path to power and security, but perhaps not. Even Marbuck, who admittedly held a deep reserve of cynicism, found his words to be moving. Ultimately, it didn't really seem to matter. If everything was going to be equal, political maneuvering would quickly become extinct.

"Please, rise," Reie said kindly. "I am grateful for your assistance, and for your faith."

Sniffling, Avehav stood. He actually seemed to be slightly embarrassed, and Marbuck decided that the emotional outburst had most likely been genuine; public weeping probably clashed with his carefully curated image.

"We must resume our journey south soon, and all those joining us will need their strength," Reie said, glancing at Ganachim. "Avehav spoke of our power, yet you have all borne witness to but a small part of it. That changes now."

The crowd stirred at this vaguely threatening statement, but their disquiet did not last. An emerald aura enveloped Ganachim, and the earth around her exploded into life, spreading outward in an expanding wave of verdant growth. Weaving throughout the crowd, foliage bearing all manner of organic foodstuffs sprang up from the parched ground. Lush branches bearing exotic fruits and vegetables in a rainbow of different vibrant colors surrounded them, and the people gasped in relief and delight. At the same time, Reie sent a wave of her healing energy into the crowd. To Marbuck, it lacked the intensity of what she'd delivered at the ritual, but that was understandable considering her weakened state. To the people of Nordabor, who'd never experienced such a thing, it must have bordered on euphoric, especially when coupled with the copious amounts of fresh food that had just miraculously emerged before them.

There were no further speeches; it seemed that none were necessary.

• • •

Despite the grinding rumbles from the north, the cautious atmosphere had settled into one of relative comfort. The people filling the space and the surrounding tree line had started to coalesce into different groupings, each gathered about a roaring bonfire, enjoying the bounty provided to them. Taking advantage of this natural inclination, Avehav had directed his men to move throughout the crowd and assist in organizing these loose formations into permanent groups, in order to make the pending journey south go as smoothly as possible. Winfield and Hassa had taken the reins on this endeavor, while Avehav joined the other architects of Ganachim's rescue beside a great fire.

The eponymous god had not joined them. Despite her willingness to provide for the people, Ganachim had remained brusque and standoffish, which Marbuck could fully understand. Rather than interact with the people, Ganachim had wandered to the furthest outskirts of the glade. Reie had stayed with her, and the two gods were now speaking privately about matters that Marbuck could only guess at. She, too, had refrained from joining her comrades by the fire as finding Elibeth had taken precedence.

Momentarily distracted by Ganachim's titanic presence moving through the shadows of the trees, Marbuck failed to notice that Elibeth had found her first.

"Mama!"

Marbuck whipped around at the sound of her voice, and Elibeth plowed into her, hugging her tightly.

"You did it!" she said, her voice muffled as she buried her face in her mother's shoulder.

"Yes," Marbuck said with an odd little laugh, one born of a slowly dissolving disbelief. "We actually did."

Over Elibeth's head, she saw Dania, Hamish, and their brood approaching. She beamed at them, and they smiled back.

"You'll have to tell me everything," Elibeth said eagerly, breaking their embrace.

"I will," Marbuck said. Dania and Hamish reached them, and Marbuck hugged them both tightly. "Thank you, for everything."

"Of course," Hamish said.

Dania's eyes were wet, and she laughed merrily. "Elibeth is welcome any time you need to run off and rescue an old one. She's family. *You* are family."

It was a reunion that was perhaps even more joyous than the first, which had been tainted by her deceptions and indecision. Now, she was back, and riding a heady wave of victory. It seemed that nothing could dampen her spirits; fear of the Erosion's inevitability and Setenrah's malice were shunted aside. Even Kemp's death was momentarily purged from her mind. For the first time in a long time, Marbuck was experiencing unbridled happiness.

As they enjoyed each other's company, plucking fresh berries from a vine and drinking the sweet nectar of exotic gourds, Falstaff ambled over to join them. Elibeth greeted him with gusto, and he was absorbed into the easy flow of the conversation. Eventually, Marbuck sensed that he was distracted, and she followed his gaze to Reie. Marbuck hoisted an eyebrow and watched him until he noticed her with a start.

"Are you ever going to tell her how you feel?" Marbuck asked.

A crimson glow spread across Falstaff's face, and he shook his head. "Oh no, definitely not. She's a god, Fishwife. I've always understood that nothing was going to happen. And, anyway, her heart clearly belongs to another." He smiled, nodding toward the gods. Reie was now resting her head against Ganachim, running a hand through her leaves.

How love worked between the gods, with their interwoven existence and complicated hierarchy of power and familial relationships, was a mystery to Marbuck. Looking at them now, though, it was easy to imagine that the bond they shared was something more than just a cosmic kinship. It made Marbuck all the happier that they'd been reunited.

Falstaff cleared his throat. "Well, I know the others wanted you to join us by the fire, if you're ready."

Marbuck looked apologetically at Dania.

"Oh, go, go," she urged, shooing Marbuck away.

"Can I come, Mama?" Elibeth asked.

"Yes, of course," Marbuck said, surprised that she'd even felt it necessary to ask. "I'm done leaving you behind. From now on, where I go, you go."

Elibeth squeezed her arm and smiled. Together, they followed Falstaff to the fire and settled in beside the comforting flames to a chorus of greetings. The light of the fire was almost enough to blot out the unnatural glow of the sky, which remained as a whispered promise of the approaching lunacy that would soon erase the glade entirely. Marbuck took comfort in knowing that they would be long gone before it arrived.

Looking around the group, Marbuck saw Nedelkoff, Rayburn, and Avehav exchanging accounts of their actions. Galt, apparently having nowhere else to go, had remained loosely associated with them, sitting off to one side, absentmindedly gnawing on a piece of corn as he stared into the flames. Jalam, sitting quietly, looked uncharacteristically wistful. Marbuck wondered if he was thinking about Kemp; after all, she'd felt Kemp's absence the moment she'd sat down, like the reopening of a barely-clotted wound.

"Oh, by the way, I'm happy to report that our friend Clusk made it out," Nedelkoff announced with a smirk. "I saw him with a few other guardsmen."

"Good," Falstaff said. "I wonder how he managed to escape."

"Well, at first, he was none too pleased to see me, but he actually perked up when I asked him just that. I think he was rather proud of himself. He said he took his jacket off and used it to snag the keys."

"Speaking of being jacketless," Rayburn interjected while the others took a moment to consider Clusk's ingenuity, "I saw Captain Vitus in the crowd. He'd ditched his jacket and insignias entirely. Apparently, he didn't wish to be associated with the old order."

"And to think, until very recently, he and his men were doing everything they could to kill us," Avehav said. "I suppose it won't always be easy to follow Reie's teachings."

"No, but to understand that and still wish to follow her is an admirable thing," Jalam said.

"At any rate," Rayburn said, "Vitus was just following orders. Weak-willed as he might be, I don't think he ever meant to do any real harm. He clearly disagreed with Phar-Mindorius and Badgett, even if he was too subservient to do anything about it." He sighed heavily, turning to Marbuck, Falstaff, and Jalam. "I suppose if he had, Kemp might still be with us. I didn't know him well, but I could tell he was a good man. He certainly taught me a thing or two about courage, something I'm ashamed to admit I've often lacked. It was an honor to stand beside him. I wish it could have gone differently. I'm sorry."

"It's not your fault," Marbuck said. "But thank you."

They lapsed into silence then, the weight of their loss tempering the mirth of victory.

"They're coming," Galt said around a mouthful of food.

Marbuck turned to see that Reie and Ganachim were approaching, pausing only to politely acknowledge the awestruck people parting before them. As they reached the fire, Reie greeted them not as a conquering god, but as an old friend. Ganachim, still unaccustomed to such companionship, behaved more like Galt, lingering on the edge of the conversation.

There followed a great recounting of tales. Each of them shared how they'd come to be there, and the stories, fragments of which were already known to some of them present, often intersected with each other, creating a narrative that flowed smoothly from person to person. Marbuck, at first reticent to recount her own travails again, found herself increasingly comfortable speaking to the others. Her destiny had become entwined with theirs, and she realized that her story was but a part of the whole. Even Galt spoke eventually, explaining in a flat and monotone voice the ultimate fate of the doomed expedition, a tale rife with disaster and ending in ruin. Reie and Ganachim listened to the denouement of their brethren with quiet solemnity. Old allies and rebels alike had been destroyed. Whatever their machinations, whatever they'd become, they had all been children of Alminnian in the beginning. Marbuck thought that it must have been like losing a part of yourself. It was as fascinating as it was horrifying.

The talking continued for many cycles, and at some point, Marbuck realized that a silent crowd had encircled them. Word of their deeds was spreading out into the populace, and Marbuck wondered if she was experiencing the birth of a new stable of legends. It was certainly a strange feeling.

Finally, when it seemed as if their words had run dry at last, Reie announced that all those present should try to sleep, as natural rest would be a scarcity upon the road. Marbuck knew how much it had taxed Reie to keep their small party alive on the northbound trek, and she wondered how Reie would manage to fuel a tireless march for so many. Of course, this time, food and drink would be abundant, and that would surely lessen the load.

As Marbuck pondered this, watching the crowd slowly disperse, Ganachim crouched above her. She had to remind herself that there was no reason to be afraid.

"The unknowable hand of fate brought you to Reie," Ganachim said, holding Marbuck in her supernatural gaze. "But it was your actions that brought you both here. Whatever your original purpose, I thank you. If not for you, I would have perished with my prison. And then, everything would have been lost."

Without waiting for a response, Ganachim rose and strode away, following Reie. Marbuck sat, dumbfounded. A being present at the founding of reality had just thanked her for essentially preserving their entire continued existence. It was difficult to fathom.

Elibeth put it in simple terms. "See," she said, nodding sagely, "you did the right thing."

CHAPTER 47

The journey south could not have been more different from the journey north. What had been a small band of desperate venturers, often anxious and divided, was now a multitude marching steadily toward a better future, even if one of their original group was now sadly absent. Mistrust had given way to companionship; fear had been replaced with hope. Their long shot plan had actually come to fruition, and now, instead of approaching the Erosion, every step put a little more distance between them and its expanding destruction. Aside from the long crack in the sky, almost all evidence of the Void's spread had been left behind. Marbuck knew that it would catch up eventually, but it was still satisfying to no longer hear its approach.

Perhaps the greatest difference was the lack of their previously constant persecutors, hunger and thirst. Before, they'd been artificially erased by Reie's power, but now they were truly gone. Everywhere the refugees went, abundant life flourished around them, providing ample foodstuffs, and although Ganachim could not restore the barren Einfallen, the juices and nectars she provided thoroughly quenched any thirst.

With this growth also came a complete alteration of the landscape around them. The monotonous palette of browns and grays had been taken over by a riotous display of life's brightest colors. Everything around them had exploded into vibrancy, making the supposed flourishing of life that had come with Ganachim's enslavement look paltry in comparison. Marbuck never tired of seeing the brilliant range of colors surrounding her; the vivid green leaves; the pink and violet flowers in their myriad forms; the dark blues and crimson reds of the exotic fruits. Above them, lush trees now formed a tangled canopy. Beneath their feet, spongy moss and soft grass cushioned their steps. To Marbuck, it seemed a paradise surely greater than any that had existed beyond the accursed gates.

Aside from Galt, who remained pensive and forlorn, everyone else seemed to agree. A sense of optimistic gaiety held sway over all, and there was little to no discussion concerning the eventual arrival of the Erosion or the pending confrontation with Setenrah. Marbuck didn't mind; after everything they'd been through, she was happy to temporarily indulge in some serenity.

On they traveled in this manner, following Ganachim and Reie in a long, loose procession. They moved along the riverbed, resting sporadically, but never traveling for so long that any real exhaustion overtook them. The equipment of the original refugee camp was brought with them, but the ramshackle tents and ratty blankets were increasingly abandoned in favor of the natural lodgings produced by Ganachim; hammocks of bracken and boughs, comfortable nests for the people to safely bed down in. The watch, too, was essentially abandoned. No sign of a shade was seen, and Marbuck doubted that any would approach such an obvious source of danger. Furthermore, Marbuck suspected that Ganachim was somehow aware of everything that her power touched; any potential enemy, shade or otherwise, would not make it very far into the tangled undergrowth that girded her zone of influence.

Avehav's guardsmen kept busy in other ways. Embracing his new, self-appointed role as the arbiter of order, Avehav directed his men to ensure that the people remained loosely organized. It certainly lent a flavor of normalcy that many found comforting to the proceedings, but it was mostly Ganachim's influence that truly held them together. To stray beyond the range of her power was to catch a depressing glimpse of the wasted world beyond.

Marbuck had no problem staying with her group; a loose assemblage of those most involved in the rescue. She spent her time simply enjoying the company of Elibeth and Falstaff, and visiting with Dania and Hamish, chatting amicably as the children chased each other through the beams of the dawn sun that passed through the foliage and painted the forest floor. Rayburn and Nedelkoff remained close as well, never straying too far in their wanderings. Marbuck enjoyed listening as Falstaff and Rayburn swapped old stories of Winslow's antics. Often, Jalam would join them, too. With Reie spending most of her time with Ganachim, he found himself somewhat devoid of purpose. He did not seem bothered by this, only somewhat confused as to how to spend his time now that he was no longer required to be constantly vigilant. Marbuck couldn't help but be amused by his efforts to referee the raucous games of the children.

Even their arrival at the ruins of the Sterling Bridge and the cessation of the forest failed to dampen Marbuck's spirits. For one, the wreck of the *Fortune* remained out of sight, and she did not look for it. Of greater comfort though, were the new ways in which Ganachim's power manifested. Rather than harness the existing trees, as she had in the forest, she turned the entire stretch of monotonous, drying mud flats and parched outcroppings of rock into a rolling meadow of exquisite beauty, punctuated by rapidly growing saplings to shield them from the increasingly powerful sun.

For the first time, their new path diverted from the old. Instead of following the curve of what had been the Einfallen, they continued directly to the south, only veering slightly to the west in order to join with the remains of the Imperial Highway. By doing so, they skirted closer to the eastern edge of the Dawnlands and avoided the increasing heat and light of the Daylands. The air remained temperate and the light a gentle comfort as they moved through a region that Marbuck had never seen before.

The ugliness that those lands had undoubtedly bore prior to Ganachim's arrival was now difficult to imagine, replaced instead by a sea of waving grass and naturally blooming orchards. The Imperial Highway was effectively erased as they went, the emerging verdure bursting up through the ancient cobblestones, quickly swallowing them in the undergrowth. Even the ruins that dotted the landscape had been transformed into showcases of Ganachim's power, wrapped as they were in a thick mantle of flowering vines, shining brilliantly against the azure sky.

It was only when the pressure ridge at the crater's edge rose into view that Marbuck felt the first stirrings of dread. Its presence heralded a return to peril. The memory of crossing the crater was not so distant in Marbuck's mind, and though she expected that Ganachim's presence would somehow make the descent easier, the danger could not be eliminated entirely. Nor was the horrible spectacle of Setenrah's legion of shades forgotten. Reie had spoken of Ganachim 'cleansing' the ruins of Vin-Unat, and Marbuck had no reason to believe that they were not going to head directly there to do just that. She'd witnessed how easily Ganachim could destroy the shades, but that had been one at a time, not thousands of them at once. Of even greater concern was the fact that they were held in thrall to a god; Reie had sensed Setenrah lurking within the fastness of the Monolith of Pha, and he would undoubtedly resist any opposition with everything he had. Before they could liberate Quaretem from Lakna, or even worry about staving off the Erosion, Ganachim would have to face one of her own kind, one who had beaten her before. Should she fail, their newborn hope would be thoroughly snuffed out.

Perhaps in consideration of this pending trial, a somewhat lengthier period of rest was spent at the crater's edge. Marbuck passed this time in the same pleasant manner that she'd grown accustomed to, except now with an undercurrent of anxious anticipation. Now that a better future dangled tantalizingly before her, it all seemed incredibly fragile. Compulsively, she reminded herself that Ganachim would not be outnumbered by belligerent gods this time, that Reie would be there to help her topple Setenrah, and that the element of surprise would be theirs. This mantra helped her tamp down on her rising fears. Elibeth helped as well, and Marbuck strove to emulate her optimism and sense of unfettered wonder. Her amazement at the dizzying height of the crater's wall made Marbuck's heart swell with love; her penchant for standing far too close to the edge, however, triggered maternal panic. Elibeth, like all adolescents, shrugged off this mortal peril without a second thought. It was simultaneously wonderful and exhausting.

It came to pass that Marbuck's fear of the descent, at least, was unwarranted. She'd suspected that Ganachim might ease the climb, but what the god actually did was far more impressive. While the people rested, Ganachim descended ahead of them. With her seemingly inexhaustible power, she created a tremendous latticework of dense foliage, forming a wide trough which gradually sloped downward along the wall of the crater in a series of long switchbacks. There would be no climbing at all, replaced instead with a relatively easy walk.

When all was ready, the people broke camp and, in a massive procession, filed onto the ramp. Feeling the slight swaying of the countless vines and branches beneath her, Marbuck couldn't help but feel some trepidation. Knowing that Ganachim's work would be tested by the weight of so many people did not help. Yet, as they continued, her apprehension dissolved. The ramp held them without issue, the rising sides of the trough eliminated the possibility of accidentally falling, and the vertigo-inducing view was mostly obscured by a screen of foliage. In truth, it was impossible to worry as she watched Elibeth bounce happily along on the springy surface.

Life during the descent was little different from the rest of their journey, save for being on an incline. They walked, they ate, they rested, and they enjoyed each other's company. Reie and Ganachim continued to be somewhat distant, and Marbuck began to wonder what they were discussing during their intervals of privacy. The history they shared was obviously greater than Marbuck could imagine. Even excluding the enormous length of time they'd spent separated, their lifespans had been unfathomably long, stretching back into the dimmest depths of the past. There must have been a lot to cover. Adding into consideration any talk of their plans for the future, both immediate and distant, and their words had to be incapable of running dry. As was often the case, thinking about their great age made Marbuck feel very insignificant. If all went as planned, the two gods would still be wandering sunlit glades together long after Marbuck's bones had turned to dust. She wondered if Reie would remember her.

Emerging at the bottom of the crater, Marbuck found that Ganachim's power was even enough to transform the bleak wasteland of the World's Wound. The petrified bitumen burst asunder, giving way to the same beautiful vegetation that she'd already been reveling in. What had been a miserable slog across a hardpan desert on their previous trek now promised to be every bit as painless as the rest of their southbound journey.

At least until they reached Setenrah.

· · ·

The approaching conflict was finally addressed the very next time they established a camp. By then, the northern wall of the crater had been left behind, and the bitter landscape surrounding them had been turned into a large, comfortable grove. All around, folk were bedding down in the soft thickets. As Marbuck prepared to do the same, Jalam summoned her for an impromptu meeting with Reie, Ganachim, and the other leaders. He advised her that the council was convening at the southern edge of the encampment, and then hurried off to collect the others.

Marbuck, accompanied by Elibeth, was actually one of the last to arrive. The two of them settled in beside Falstaff, who was seated with the others in a rough circle. A fire had been kindled in the center of the gathering, built out of habit more than any need. Once Jalam arrived, Reie cleared her throat. Marbuck wondered if she actually needed to do so, or if she was just imitating human behavior.

"We are nearing Vin-Unat," Reie said solemnly. Beside her, Ganachim's large, scowling face was turned toward the south. "We fully expect to find Setenrah there, and it is our intention to confront him."

This did not surprise Marbuck, and it seemed that the others were of a similar mind as nobody said a word.

"For those of you who were with me on the journey north, you know what it is that we face," Reie continued. "I imagine by now that the rest of you have heard of the shades held there. Words do not suffice. It will be a danger unlike any we have encountered before."

"Why go there at all, then?" Rayburn asked suddenly. "Why not just go around it and wait for the Erosion to take care of Setenrah and his shades for us?"

"Setenrah will not stand by idly while the world is erased before his eyes. As soon as he realizes the extent of the calamity, he will flee, dragging his shades with him in the only obvious direction left to go: south. He would most likely go to Quaretem, and we would be forced to reckon with him then. Better to take him now, while his legion is not mobilized and he is unaware of any danger."

"Yes, of course," Rayburn said, blushing furiously.

"There is no need for embarrassment," Reie said. "All input is welcome. It is why I have summoned you here. You have all aided me tremendously, and I depend upon you. We cannot do this alone. Ganachim's power against the shades is remarkable, but it is not without its limits. I, too, am not impervious to the dangers we face. I must once again seek your assistance. As Ganachim purges the shades and engages with Setenrah, I will accompany her, doing all I can to bolster her defenses and heal any wounds she might suffer. It will be my intent to remain as far away from the conflict as I can, but I will still be vulnerable." She looked at Marbuck. "I will need protection."

Marbuck looked around, making certain that she was the subject of Reie's gaze. "Me?"

"Yes. You carry the only weapon capable of destroying any shade that might slip past Ganachim, and I know you are proficient with it. You do not fear the shades, and to be frank, I am comfortable putting my life in your hands."

"Just me? I—well—what about—"

Elibeth tugged on her sleeve and shook her head. "Mama, she needs you. That means we *all* need you." Apparently, her daughter had decided that she was not to reject such a request. Marbuck found herself humbled by Elibeth's ability to consider the needs of everyone else over her own feelings, and her objections were silenced.

"You will not be alone," Jalam said. From beneath his robes, he lifted an anointed blade. "I retrieved this from Galt. He did not care to have it any longer, and he gave it to me without question."

Although Galt had remained adjacent to their group, the former shepherd had not been interested in retaining any sort of leadership position once the exodus had begun in earnest. As such, he had not joined them for the meeting.

"I believe he got it from you?" Jalam said to Rayburn.

Rayburn held his hands up. "It's all yours."

Jalam nodded, then turned to Marbuck. "I am the Lady of the Veil's guardian. Did you think that I would not be accompanying her on this endeavor?"

Marbuck smiled. "I really should have known better."

"Indeed," Jalam said, returning the smile.

"Well, if you two are going then you better believe I am, too," Falstaff said.

"I will join you as well," Avehav said, motivated, Marbuck was sure, by equal parts heroism and a desire to remain relevant.

Reie shook her head. "I appreciate your offers of aid, but I cannot let you join us. There are no other anointed blades, and I will not let you risk your lives by facing shades while you are essentially weaponless."

"Out of all of the refugees, there isn't another shepherd, or at least another blade?" Falstaff asked.

"I'm afraid not," Jalam said. "Galt actually helped me look, and we found none."

"It makes sense," Nedelkoff said. "The rest of those zealots probably went down with Nordabor. If any actually *did* flee, I imagine they'd have abandoned all evidence of their previous occupation, like Vitus did. They'd hardly announce their presence now."

"It matters not," Reie said. "I wish that things could be easier, but when have they ever been? As always, we will make do." She looked at Marbuck and Jalam. "I have faith that the two of you will be enough."

Marbuck hoped that she was right.

CHAPTER 48

Much like the pressure ridge at the edge of the crater, the rising slag heaps that encircled the ruins of Vin-Unat were like a beacon of turmoil. Marbuck knew what squirmed on the other side of those jumbled slabs, and their naked bleakness stood out all the more when contrasted with the comforting growth that surrounded their encampment.

A halt had been called before they'd gotten too close to Setenrah's domain, and Ganachim had limited her influence to a tight circle that only encompassed their camp. The majority of the people understood little of what was happening, beyond the general idea that the gods leading them had some purpose there, and that it involved the liberation that Reie had spoken of. Marbuck knew all too well what she would soon face.

Staring at the tortured landscape ahead of her, she cradled her anointed blade on her lap. It had come to her through an accident of fate; pilfered by a slaver, taken by Bolenz, and finally delivered into her hands at the perfect moment to smite her tormentor. Now she would carry it into what amounted to the final battle of an ancient war. Here, in this ruined place, Ganachim and Reie would hopefully destroy the last holdout of the rebellion that had doomed their world. And Marbuck, a mere human, a simple mariner with no illustrious bloodline or aspirations to greatness, would walk alongside them in this final conflict.

Jalam, the only other mortal tasked with fighting beside the gods, was approaching her. She knew what he was going to say before he said it.

"They are ready."

He helped Marbuck to her feet, and she turned back to Elibeth, who'd been sitting beside her. She groped for the right words to say, but Elibeth only smiled and squeezed her hand.

"You don't need to say it. I know you'll be back."

With tears in her eyes, Marbuck yanked her daughter in for a tight hug. She'd intended to remain by her side no matter what, but now, once again, she had to leave her behind. It made her feel like a liar, and she hated it. For what it was worth, Elibeth seemed to understand the necessity of it even more than she did.

"We must go," Jalam said quietly after a moment.

Reluctantly, Marbuck separated from Elibeth. Behind her, Falstaff stepped forward.

"Good luck, Fishwife."

"Thank you."

"I wish I could go with you."

Marbuck smiled, her eyes still wet. "I know. Maybe the next time we need to eradicate a god and his horde of shades you can tag along."

Falstaff laughed. "I'm going to hold you to that."

He held out his hand and Marbuck shoved it aside, wrapping him in a tight embrace instead. Falstaff had been with her from the start of her strange odyssey, enduring everything she had with his special brand of unflagging cheer. If it were not for him, Marbuck knew that she would have perished long ago. It was difficult to leave without him now.

"Go," he said, pushing her away gently. "Before I start asking to come along again."

With one last look at Elibeth and Falstaff, Marbuck allowed Jalam to lead her away. As they proceeded to the edge of the encampment, where Reie and Ganachim were waiting, there was no fanfare. They passed Galt, and he watched them with an unreadable expression. Brief exchanges were had with some of the others; Rayburn slathered them in jittery words of confidence; Avehav assured them that he and his men would maintain order in the absence of the gods, including soothing any panic that might arise from the sounds of conflict occurring in the distance. There was no talk of a contingency plan should they fail; Marbuck assumed there wasn't one, unless you counted extinction.

"Are you ready?" Reie asked as they arrived before her.

"As I'll ever be," Marbuck said.

Reie, the god who'd become her friend, who oscillated between oddly human and impenetrably alien, smiled shakily. "Me too." She turned to her colossal counterpart. "Shall we?"

"Yes," Ganachim said simply, and began to stride toward the distant ridge.

Marbuck, Jalam, and Reie trotted to keep up. Behind them, there was a rumbling sound that made Marbuck start, thinking of the Erosion. It was nothing of the sort. A wall of thorny tangle had burst from the ground behind them, encircling the camp.

"That will protect them should any shades escape us and wander this way," Ganachim said without looking back. Watching the spreading vegetation tighten into an impenetrable barrier, Marbuck breathed a small sigh of relief. At least, should the worst come to pass, those left behind would not be immediately overrun.

Turning her attention forward, Marbuck did everything she could to steel herself for the coming conflict. Beside her, Jalam seemed to be back in his element: vigilantly hovering behind Reie. She wondered if, on some level, it was a comfort to him. Faced with danger his entire life, their easygoing journey south had probably felt strange. Whatever the case, it had not atrophied his instincts; he appeared as ready to defend Reie as ever.

After what felt like roughly a cycle, they began to trudge up the slope, picking their way over fissures and tumbled heaps of basalt. As they neared the apex, Ganachim stopped, and the other three halted behind her.

"Our presence will be noticed rather quickly, I think," Ganachim said. "Prepare yourselves."

Jalam hefted his blade, and Marbuck followed suit.

"I cannot feel Setenrah's presence yet," Reie murmured.

"Nor can I," Ganachim said. "Hopefully that means he cannot sense us either. You think he is in the Monolith of Pha?"

"Yes."

"I will tear it asunder and drag him squealing from the darkness."

Ganachim stalked up the remainder of the slope, and the others rushed to follow. As they reached the top, she was already descending.

Gazing once again upon the scene of horror below, Marbuck's breath stopped in her throat. The toppled megalithic statues, which dwarfed even Ganachim, seemed to reach out for her as she charged down toward the morass of shades that filled the space. In the center of that undulating mass, the Ancestral Mount rose like a single mammoth tombstone. Lurking inside of the fortress carved into its zenith, Marbuck knew, was Setenrah. Though she'd never seen the god, she'd heard enough from those who had to form her own mental picture of him. She hoped that Ganachim would destroy him before she ever had to witness the real thing.

"We have to follow her down a ways," Reie said, her face pinched with worry. "I have to be closer."

The three of them descended after Ganachim, and Marbuck felt her fear increasing with every step. Normally, she was fairly unaffected by shades, but the sheer number of them held in the tar-like discharge below was stupefying.

"Here," Reie said, suddenly stopping on a flat stretch of rock. "This is close enough."

Though they remained a fair distance away, it was still far too close for comfort. Marbuck could now make out the individual shapes of the nearest shades without the aid of her field glass. They were writhing wildly, shrieking and clawing at the ichor binding them. Ganachim had nearly reached them, and her presence was whipping them into a frenzy.

With an animalistic bellow, Ganachim plowed into the line of shades, sending twisted bodies cartwheeling through the air in every direction. A visible shudder ran through the shades like a wave, and they exploded into a flurry of movement, tearing free of their bonds and surging toward Ganachim, who continued to wade through them, stomping, crushing, and casting aside any that attempted to scale her towering form. Shades suddenly poured forth from numerous encrusted pilings of hardened ichor that had formed in the remains of the ruined buildings, like wasps emerging from a broken hive. They closed in on Ganachim, and the sheer volume of them began to bog her down. With ragged claws they raked her flesh, scrambling up her back. Every one of them that was struck by her spilling blood recoiled violently, then burst apart in a steaming spatter of bile, but still they came, threatening to bury her beneath them.

A concentrated beam of power burst forth from Reie with such force that it actually buffeted Marbuck. She watched as the wavering air enveloped Ganachim, closing wounds almost as quickly as they formed. Bolstered in this manner, Ganachim continued carving a path through the churning sea of shades. Though she'd magnetically drawn the vast majority toward her, outliers that had been slower to act were now beginning to stumble free of the last shreds of Setenrah's discharge. Shambling about, their lumpish heads began to turn toward Marbuck, Reie, and Jalam.

"They're coming," Jalam said, his voice tight with fear. Beside him, Reie groaned with the effort of sustaining Ganachim.

As if on cue, the shades began to charge toward them. Marbuck's eyes darted from one hideous form to another, counting eleven of them. The first to reach them was a ropy, lank creature with blackened, cracked flesh which emitted a shrill bark as it lunged at Reie. Marbuck and Jalam intercepted it simultaneously, driving their blades into its segmented body and forcing it back. It lost its footing on the loose scree and floundered, allowing Marbuck and Jalam to hack it apart. Before Marbuck was even certain that it was dispatched, three more arrived.

A long, oozing arm swung heavily toward her head, and she had just enough time to duck. Driving her blade into the creature's chest, she found herself face to face with its terrifying approximation of an anguished human visage. It gnashed the wet hole of its mouth, and Marbuck involuntarily cried out in disgust as she pulled her blade free and shoved the shade away. She began to turn around, seeking the next threat, when a tremendous weight crashed into her. Before she could grasp what was happening, she was on the ground, white-hot pain searing her back. She rolled over as quickly as her agony would allow and saw Jalam chopping at her attacker. Hanging in shreds from the long, serrated fingers of the shade's right hand were bloody strips of flesh torn from Marbuck's back. Pain roared through her, and she found that she was struggling to breathe.

Then, the pain was gone. A soothing feeling of coolness hummed through her, and she spied Reie, one outstretched arm bent toward her. It snapped back toward Ganachim, and the sensation ceased immediately. It had been enough; Marbuck leapt to her feet and helped Jalam finish off the shade. Five more were closing in.

"You won't touch her!" Jalam screamed at the mindless horrors clambering up the slope before them. If any part of them understood him, they made no indication of it. Arriving in quick succession, they attacked with no strategy but wanton violence. Marbuck leapt away from the snatching claw of one, taking the arm off as a rebuttal. It lurched aside and another filled the space. Marbuck rolled beneath it and took its legs out from under it with one fierce blow. The shade landed partially on top of her, and a third shade, in its feverish desire to kill, began to tear it apart in a bid to reach her. Drenched in foul gore, Marbuck wriggled out from beneath the eviscerated remains and plunged her blade into the attacking shade's side. It screeched and bucked, and she yanked her blade free and struck it again, bringing it to its knees. A third strike ran through its head and it collapsed in a steaming heap.

Gasping for air, Marbuck scrambled back to her feet and finished off the shredded form that had saved her. Nearby, Jalam, who now bore a long gash across his left cheek, was sitting astride a shade and plunging his blade into its head. A shrill cry pierced the air, and Marbuck pivoted toward the sound of it. Reie was backing away from the shade that had lost its arm to Marbuck. Without hesitation, Marbuck raced toward it, slamming her blade into its back with all her might. A moment later, its head was cloven in two by Jalam. Tearing their blades free of the disintegrating mess, they prepared for the next wave.

It didn't come. Looking down toward Ganachim, Marbuck quickly realized why. Even the last shades to emerge were now loping toward the god. She'd stopped moving and now stood with her arms above her head, shades coursing over her and falling away at her deadly touch. A blinding emerald light was shining from her body, flaring periodically in a hypnotic pulse that seemed to be pulling the shades toward her. Her voice rose in a strangely melodic chant, rising and falling in a series of low hums and half-screams. Marbuck was frozen by fascination knowing she was witnessing a glimpse of the primordial power of old.

With unimaginable ferocity, that power detonated.

For a brief moment, a flash of blinding, white light erased Ganachim from view. It shone out from the spot that she'd occupied, piercing through the shades that surrounded her, strangely illuminating their bodies in a tableau of silent, haunting beauty. The silence did not last. An ear-splitting roar erupted outward, and with it came a roiling, crackling wave of pure energy. It tore through the legion of shades, utterly annihilating them. Fixed in whatever position they'd been in when the light had first struck them, they burst asunder, each reduced to a puff of black dust before disintegrating into nothing. As the wave ripped through them, it pulverized the tortured earth, driving an expanding cloud of rubble before it. Awestruck, Marbuck watched it bloom before her, barely noticing when Jalam grabbed her and pulled her down. Then, the cloud was swallowing them, and they were being pelted with bits of rock. After about a short-cycle, the falling stones tapered off, and a rusty, orange glow hung over everything. It was once again eerily silent.

Marbuck peered out from beneath Jalam, took a deep breath of the dusty air and promptly coughed it back out.

"What just happened?" Jalam asked, blinking away the dirt from his bloodshot eyes. His skin was coated with dust, which clung wetly to the gash on his cheek.

"I think Ganachim just obliterated every single shade here," Marbuck said. "And maybe herself, too."

"No," Reie said, rising out of the murk beside her, "she is alive."

Marbuck looked around. "Are you sure?"

"Yes, I can sense her," Reie said huskily. "She tapped into the deepest reserves of her strength, and the expulsion of that power took nearly everything she had, but she survived. Keeping her alive during it took nearly everything *I* had." Reie smiled weakly. Her face seemed to have shriveled, and her halo had lost its glow completely. Marbuck could tell that her efforts to sustain Ganachim during the assault had taken even more out of her than the initial restoration had.

"So, where is she?" Marbuck asked, squinting into the gloom.

"I believe she's still going after Setenrah," Reie said. "We must follow."

"I fear you won't survive another encounter like that," Jalam said.

"I cannot let her face him alone. Not again."

Without another word, Reie started down the slope, stumbling as she went. Jalam looked at Marbuck helplessly, and she shrugged before heading after the obstinate god. Sighing heavily, Jalam followed.

As they passed through the blast zone, Marbuck found that Ganachim's outburst hadn't been an act of destruction so much as one of rebirth. She had, in fact, cleansed Vin-Unat. Scouring away the pestilent presence of Setenrah's shades had been a violent act, but one designed to cultivate rather than devastate. All around them, new life had already emerged from the broken bitumen; thistle, myrtle, and clover ran rampant. No evidence of the shades or the foul ichor remained.

"If Setenrah didn't know we were here before, he certainly does now," Marbuck observed.

"All the more reason to hurry," Reie said, but then she paused, looking at Jalam. "Thank you, my guardian." She caressed a thin hand across his wounded cheek, erasing the gash with her touch.

"You needn't exert yourself on my account," Jalam said, pushing her hand away gently.

"Nonsense. And I owe you my thanks as well," Reie said to Marbuck. "How is your back?"

Marbuck shifted, testing the injury she'd already nearly forgotten. "It's like it never happened."

Reie nodded. "Good. Let's—"

In the distance, a series of booming thuds echoed, accompanied by a crunching, rending sound. The three of them looked at each other.

"She *did* say that she was going to tear the whole place apart," Marbuck said.

Reie frowned. "Something is wrong."

"What makes you say that?"

Reie didn't answer, but continued to stare into the distance. Marbuck looked at Jalam, and he tightened his grip on his blade. They stood, listening to the distant smashing until, without warning, it ceased. Ganachim's newest volley had kicked up a new cloud of debris, and it blotted out the eastern sun, reducing it to a small point of light piercing an amber haze. A shape was moving through the murk, and Marbuck realized that she was about to witness Setenrah firsthand. The phantom form that she'd long imagined solidified in her thoughts with shocking clarity, and in her mind's eye the fiendish god wore Bolenz's face.

Just as panic began to engulf her, the form emerged from the obscuring dust and Marbuck beheld Ganachim. In an instant, her alarm was washed away, and she was nearly overcome with relief. Beside her, Reie did not seem to share the feeling.

"What's happened?" she cried in a shrill voice.

"Setenrah is not here," Ganachim said.

Reie's eyed widened. "We must get to Quaretem."

CHAPTER 49

Having believed that the culmination of Reie's plan to be rid of Setenrah was at hand, his absence from his lair was both surprising and deflating. Marbuck had tried to prepare herself to face the God of Pestilence, and she'd felt the momentum of adrenaline and determination carrying her to that confrontation, despite her fear. Now, the moment had been postponed and her fortitude had shriveled, allowing untempered fear to fester as they resumed their journey south.

It was far worse for Reie.

Her quiet resolve had been smothered by a manic need to reach her people. With grim certitude, she spoke of what Setenrah would do to the Quaret should he discover that she was missing and their arrangement had been scuttled. It amounted to anguish beyond measure; a prolonged torture not just for one unfortunate tribute, but for the entire population. Jalam shared her fears, further compounded by what Marbuck suspected was his love for Katiek, though he strove to remain impartial and optimistic about the whole affair.

Reie hoped to overtake Setenrah on the journey south and snuff him out somewhere in the desert far north of Quaretem. It was certainly the ideal scenario, but it was increasingly the unlikeliest as well. Traveling with the refugees meant slowing their progress. Mobilizing such a large group of people, many of whom were children and elders, was difficult; even with ample foodstuffs and bolstering, they really couldn't go much faster than they'd already been going. Despite her desire to make haste, Reie was unwilling to leave them behind to fend for themselves, even temporarily, and she would not permit Ganachim, or anyone else for that matter, to forge ahead as a vanguard, fearing the result should they face Setenrah without her.

So, with no other recourse but to simply press on, they departed from Vin-Unat. Although the haunted city had been purged and left utterly empty, Marbuck was happy that she would never set foot in it again. Being reunited with Elibeth, Falstaff, and the others had been a tremendous comfort, even if it had been tainted by the knowledge that their trials were not yet over. Marbuck did her best to ignore the terrible possibilities and focus on the present, seeking to recapture the first heady joy of their departure from Nordabor. It was elusive, despite what had really been a clear victory. At the very least, whenever they encountered Setenrah, he would not have his legion of shades.

Unless, of course, he'd formed a new one in Quaretem.

Thoughts like this were unhelpful, and Marbuck kept them to herself, instead allowing Elibeth to color her thinking. After all, she was capable of the unfailing confidence of youth; a certainty that things would work out no matter what. Falstaff, in his own childlike way, exuded a similar attitude, though one darkened by his fears for Reie and the Quaret. Still, his disposition was more often cheerful than not, and Marbuck sought his counsel regularly as they crossed the crater.

The trek was little different from that which had brought them to Vin-Unat. Ganachim continued to transform the landscape and the people continued to plod along in her verdant wake. Plotting a course to the southeast in order to take the most direct route toward Quaretem, the one almost certainly taken by Setenrah, they strayed further into the Daylands, and the intensity of the sunlight grew. Despite the relief provided by the gods, the heat was still an unwelcome burden. Nevertheless, they soldiered on, not stopping for a true rest until they reached the southern edge of the crater, where Ganachim once again set to work on forming them a pathway of foliage. It offered the same painless alternative to climbing as the last one, save for the fact that they were now walking uphill. Still, it was infinitely preferable to scaling the treacherous cliff face, and the people ascended with relative ease.

As Marbuck stepped upon the solid ground of the lands beyond the crater, she was met not with the weathered hilltops she'd passed through before, but with a flat, rocky plain. Further south, the land took on a rounded, soft aspect, indicative of countless sand dunes, brilliantly lit by the sun. In the far west, the light faded to a hazy, pale violet, showing the distant, darkened humps of what Marbuck assumed were the Yewhia Mountains. Following their new trajectory, they'd emerged from the crater far east of the route Kemp had led them on, and far east of Berngoth.

Marbuck thought of Kemp and the passage through his homeland with the tentativeness of one tonguing a sore tooth. She'd hated him then, considering the entire journey a dangerous and pointless diversion, and she hadn't been shy about voicing her thoughts. She recalled them now with more than a little guilt. Reie had once spoken of restoring Berngoth, but that had been before they'd understood the true extent of the Erosion. It saddened her to think that Berngoth would never be reclaimed but would be lost forever just as its former leader had been. Marbuck wished that Kemp was there beside her now, so that she might apologize to him. She tried to imagine his reaction. He probably would have said something jackassy and flashed his stupid grin.

Considering this, Marbuck smiled.

• • •

The stony land, inundated with countless fragments of twinkling glass, was erased beneath the rolling carpet of Ganachim's influence. It carried the travelers away from the World's Wound and toward the sprawling desert to the south. The sand trembled as they approached, sliding off the rising growth that emerged from beneath it. Like a moving oasis, Ganachim's influence cut a swath of life through the bleached dunes. Time, which had long been vacillating between questionable and entirely meaningless, passed uncounted as they journeyed through the desert bloom. They did not stop until they encountered something wholly unexpected.

Cresting a dune that had been partially transformed into a shrub-covered hillock, they came upon a small encampment nestled in a depression below. Immediately, a call went down the line to halt. As Avehav's men rushed away to complete the order, Marbuck and the other leaders, who'd been walking just behind Reie and Ganachim, joined the gods on the hillside, where the new growth petered out into sand.

"What do we make of this?" Falstaff asked.

Amidst the murmurs of uncertainty that followed, Reie answered. "Whoever they are, they almost certainly need help."

Marbuck examined the camp through her field glass. Four canvas tents stood in a rough circle. Nobody was about, and it was impossible to know if the tents were occupied.

"Unless they're all dead," Nedelkoff said, channeling Marbuck's thoughts.

"If they are, they either didn't produce shades or the shades have wandered off," Ganachim said, scanning the surrounding dunes. "I do not sense any nearby."

"Should we just go around them?" Avehav asked.

"We were trying to go around your camp," Marbuck said. "Imagine if we'd succeeded."

"Are you saying we should go down there?"

Marbuck shrugged. "My instinct to avoid contact was wrong then, maybe doing so would be wrong now."

"I agree," Reie said. "We are walking through an empty world. To come upon others in this place feels like more than simple coincidence. I feel that whoever is down there might have some part to play in all of this. We should go meet them—cautiously." Reie produced her veil and draped it over her halo. She turned to Ganachim. "You, my dear, are a bit more conspicuous. Perhaps you ought to stay behind?"

Ganachim's large mouth curved into a rare smile. "As you wish. I'll be watching, though."

"I would expect nothing less." Reie turned to the others. "We cannot tarry here for long. I intend to sort this out presently. Who wishes to accompany me?"

It was decided that Marbuck, Falstaff, Jalam, and Nedelkoff would serve as Reie's retinue. The five of them approached the camp, which seemed more doleful than menacing, with no attempt at stealth. As they reached the tents, Reie hailed anyone who might be residing within. A moment later, a bald, sunburned head peaked out of the flaps of the nearest tent. The man assessed them sleepily before disappearing back inside. Marbuck could hear indistinct murmurs, and then the flaps were pulled back completely. Two men, including the bald one, emerged; filthy, malnourished, and in the garb of watchmen. They held the flaps open behind them and another man, just as ill and ragged, stepped into the open.

It was Roanack.

Marbuck was shocked to see that the elderly chief warden was abroad, and her stomach plummeted. Nothing short of dire calamity could have driven Roanack so far from the comforts of the Great Ziggurat.

Reie apparently shared her dismay. She threw off her veil and approached Roanack, dispensing with any formalities. "Have you news of Quaretem? Has Setenrah reached them?"

Roanack appraised her with a look of confusion. He blinked stupidly and opened his mouth. "How is … you were …" He closed his eyes and wavered on his feet.

With a huff of impatience, Reie struck him with a concentrated jet of her power. He reared up like he'd been kicked in the ass and looked around as if seeing his surroundings for the first time. His frenzied gaze settled on Reie.

"*You*," he growled.

Reie folded her arms across her chest. "Yes, me. Have you news of Quaretem, or not?"

Roanack didn't answer immediately, seemingly struggling to come to terms with his sudden revival. He looked back at his ailing men, then down at his own hands, then back at Reie and her followers. His face settled into a puckered mask of disgust.

"You wish to hear of the commune you abandoned? The people you forsook in favor of cozying up to Vingallean oppressors? I see you're still keeping company with the meddling agitators who caused all of this," Roanack said, gesturing angrily toward Marbuck and Falstaff. "And where is Kemp, hmm? Did he have another change of heart and bludgeon you in the head, too?"

"He perished in service to a noble cause," Reie said, her voice tight.

Roanack snorted. "No great loss, there."

"You know nothing of what you speak."

Roanack was looking past her now, despair suddenly seizing his thin face. "Is that so? Then why do you stand before a mighty host? Are they not Vingalleans set on conquering Quaretem?"

Unable to help herself, Marbuck glanced back. The majority of the refugees had started to fan out along the snaking crest of the hill, their curiosity overriding any direction from Avehav or his men. From below, the multitude of people blanketing the hillside did seem imposing. Ganachim, at least, had remained out of sight. Marbuck could only imagine what Roanack would think of *her*.

Though Reie hadn't turned around, she plainly understood what Roanack was referring to. "They are no army, they are the survivors of a doom that is coming for us all. I am bringing them to Quaretem, not to serve as new masters, but to join us as brethren. I do not seek to conquer, but only to liberate. The Quaret will be free. Setenrah will be cast down, and you and your order will fall with him should you try to stand in our way."

Roanack turned his gaze back to her. Not a ghost of his haughty anger remained. "He is there now. He wore out the last tribute much faster than we were expecting."

Marbuck had, of course, never cared for Devonshire, but the confirmation of his horrific end still stirred up a small bit of sadness. Worse yet, his misery hadn't bought them enough time.

"With the chaos that your departure brought, we weren't able to find a proper tax," Roanack continued. "We tried to institute a lottery, but by then your arch-maiden had started a revolt and blocked every way into the Warren. We'd lost control of it, and we were forced to choose from the lowest-ranking huntsmen within the ziggurat. The chosen woman wailed incessantly and Setenrah was most displeased. Then he began to question why you were absent for the payment of the tax. No answer satisfied him, no excuse placated him." Roanack spoke flatly, his expression vacant. He paused to mechanically pat some sweat from his wrinkled brow with a handkerchief. "He forced Mother to summon the Sanctified. He began to subject them to his touch, one by one, until she told him the truth … and he started with the children. Mother would not admit that you were gone. I finally did. Setenrah thanked me … he *thanked* me, in mockery of my pain."

Listening to this, Marbuck found that, unbelievably, she actually felt pity for Roanack. In a way, it was fitting that the misery his family had inflicted on so many others had now visited them, that the god they'd stricken a dark bargain with had now delivered their own ruin. And yet, what she was witnessing now was simply the sorrow of an old man who'd watched his family suffer. He'd inherited his role in the twisted system that ran Quaretem and, knowing nothing else, had only ever acted in the best interest of his own kin. Although this did not exempt him from guilt in Marbuck's eyes, it at least reminded her of his humanity.

"And then Setenrah stayed," Roanack continued. "He told us that, until you returned, he would be routinely taking one of the Sanctified as penance for our negligence. He tortures them in a manner that is indescribable, and he forces Mother to watch. He sits upon her throne and exults over her humiliation, wallowing in the degradation that he inflicts." Roanack took a deep breath, steadying himself. "The commune unraveled; watchmen and huntsmen deserted; the Warren remained out of reach. Seeing no other hope, I took what loyal men I could still muster and set out in search of you. To bring you back. We only made it this far, and we've been stuck here by our own weakness ever since. Without you, our scant provisions could only sustain us for so long."

The two men flanking Roanack murmured in agreement, and Marbuck realized that nobody else had emerged from the other tents. Obviously, the men languishing within them were in dire straits. Without intervention, Roanack and his men would not last much longer.

"You say the Warren remains out of reach?" Reie asked. "The entrances are still blocked?"

"They were when I left. That was …" He trailed off, trying to explain a measurement of time that he had no words for. Truly, the limitations of the Quaret's simple timekeeping were being laid bare.

"And Setenrah had not gotten to anyone inside?" Reie said.

"No, he didn't care to; they're beneath him. His focus is on those who have failed him, not their chattel. For now, anyway. Once he's finished inflicting whatever terrors he can conceive of on my family, I imagine he'll force his way down there in search of more victims."

Reie and Jalam looked at each other with mingled expressions of relief and urgency. She raised her eyebrows, and after a moment, he nodded. She turned her attention back to Roanack.

"As I said, we are going to Quaretem, but not at your bidding, and not to restore your order. There is much that you don't yet understand. That being said, I am prepared to offer you clemency. I will restore you and your men, and you may return with us. Not as the chief warden and his watchmen, but as free and equal members of a new way. Do you accept these terms?"

Marbuck watched as, listening to these words, Roanack passed through a series of emotions. Desperate hope, indignation, bitter denial, and resignation all slid across his face. In the end, she could tell that he wished to accept, but hated to do so. After all, it meant a total forfeiture of everything he was and everything he'd expected to be.

"I suppose the alternative is that we leave you here to die," Reie added.

The bald man emitted a squeak of protest, and Roanack shushed him. "I see the alternative plainly enough, and I can also see the merriment dancing in your eyes. Don't think that I'm ignorant of how much you're enjoying this reversal of fortune."

Reie shook her head. "My only enjoyment is in the righting of wrongs. You and your family are Quaret, too; I don't wish to see any of you suffer. Will you join me?"

Roanack said nothing for a moment. When he finally spoke, his voice was oddly timid.

"And you can free us all from Setenrah?"

"Yes, I believe so."

Roanack ran a hand through his thin hair. "And what of my mother?"

"There will be a place for her, one way or another."

"Perhaps," Roanack said with clear skepticism. "As for me, I accept your terms."

CHAPTER 50

Not knowing the atrocities that Roanack had been a part of, the other refugees accepted him and his men without issue. To them, the newcomers were just another group of wayward wanderers, lost in a broken world. Nobody who knew the truth attempted to contradict this impression, as Reie saw no reason to create a stir, but none of them embraced the chief warden either. Even Jalam, who'd offered his tacit endorsement of Reie's decision, received Roanack coolly, with much of the same reservations that Avehav had held toward Vitus.

For her own part, Marbuck would've just as soon left Roanack in the desert to rot, but of course, it wasn't her decision. Personal grudge aside, she barely knew the man, and Reie's long history with him granted her a greater authority in deciding his fate, to say nothing of her divine mandate to offer absolution to any and all.

Ultimately, it didn't really matter; Roanack and his men made no attempts to assimilate with their rescuers beyond joining in their southward march, and their presence was unobtrusive. Marbuck was certain that, should Reie prevail against Setenrah and establish her new order, it would remain that way, especially with Ganachim tipping the scales. Her presence had certainly had a chilling effect on Roanack; when he'd first seen her, rising from her place behind the crest of the hill, he'd nearly swooned. A cursory explanation of who she was and what she intended to do had been met with a wide-eyed stare and some shaky nods. Rendered speechless, Roanack had fallen in with the crowd, stripped of any authority or privilege.

Even so, Galt seemed to have sniffed out the reek of despotism on him. The erstwhile shepherd, who'd continued to remain loosely associated with the leaders when he wasn't walking by himself, had shunned Roanack completely. Perhaps, Marbuck considered, Roanack reminded him of those who'd wielded power in Nordabor, and who'd subjected him to abject cruelty. Whatever the case, he was a notable exception to the general acceptance offered by the rest.

Of far greater importance than the actual presence of Roanack was what finding him had confirmed. First, that Setenrah had already reached Quaretem and that those in the Warren might still be saved; second, that they were headed in the right direction. In their zeal to reach the commune, they'd chosen what had seemed like the most direct route; an essentially unknown path based entirely on the collective memory of the gods, a general knowledge of geography, and instinct. Their gamble had paid off, their discovery of Roanack verifying that they were not only on the right track but actually nearing Quaretem.

Further evidence of this came when, cresting a hill, Marbuck caught a glimpse of the Great Ziggurat in the shimmering distance. Her first instinct was to dismiss the wavering shape as some kind of mirage. Closer examination with her field glass confirmed that it was no illusion. The massive stepped pyramid rose from the sea of sand, its golden capstone shining brilliantly in the relentless sun.

"That's the place?" Elibeth asked beside her.

"Yeah," Marbuck said, handing her the field glass. "Take a look."

Elibeth leveled the glass and squinted into it. "It's huge."

"It has been a long time since I last saw this view of the Great Ziggurat," Reie said unexpectedly from behind them. "It kindled a hope in me then, when I had resigned myself to only sorrow. I feel that hope once again—that this place might at last be the haven I had sought to establish."

Marbuck looked at the god, whose eyes seemed to be gazing upon a vista built of memory, and then back at the ziggurat. Hope fluttered in her own chest; a hope that Elibeth might have a life free from scarcity, danger, and fear. Marbuck knew that she would do anything to see that come to pass.

With their destination clear, the march continued through the blazing heat. It would have been impossible without the gods. Ganachim crafted a wide boulevard of grass, overhung by hanging willows that granted precious shade, and Reie staved off their exhaustion and healed any burns from the sun. After what felt like four or five full-cycles, they were close enough to make out the gargantuan bas-reliefs carved onto the ziggurat with the naked eye, and to see the hazy blue of the ocean stretching out toward the horizon just beyond it.

A halt was called, and the leaders gathered in a small glen created by the new growth that had formed between two steep dunes. The Great Ziggurat was blocked from view, and the place had a quiet, secluded atmosphere that Marbuck found to be perfectly suited for the devising of clandestine plans. Knowing what was at stake, it was somehow comforting to gather intimately in such a close space. The others seemed to share this feeling, too, and they crowded together in spite of the heat. A general sense of fatalism hung over all. Whatever happened next, their journey was coming to an end.

Last to join them were the gods, with Roanack in tow. Marbuck was mildly surprised to see him, until she considered that he'd most likely been compelled to join them. After all, he was their best source of information regarding the state of things in Quaretem. More surprising was the presence of Galt. His sudden interest in their affairs was a mystery, and Marbuck wondered if sheer curiosity had driven him to come. Whatever the case, he remained on the outer edge of the gathering, standing in the deep shade of a flowering magnolia. If any of the others felt he was intruding, or even took notice of him, they didn't say so.

"As you all know, we are nearly there," Reie said once everyone had settled into an expectant silence. "We must now decide how we are going to proceed. Roanack, is there any reason to believe that we will encounter opposition to our approach?"

The chief warden had been inspecting the ground between his feet. Now, he reluctantly looked up at the god he'd once considered a servant. "No. As I said before, the watchmen and huntsmen are gone. Civil order is gone. There won't be any spotters on the walls. There's nothing to look out for anymore; Setenrah is already there. Assuming he's still holding court in the Oasis Sanctum, he will have no idea we're coming until we're already there."

"That's not entirely true. He may sense our power," Reie said, gesturing toward Ganachim and herself, "just as we can sense his. We will have to hope that he is preoccupied with his own pursuits."

Roanack's face twitched at this reminder of his family's suffering. He lowered his head again.

"Either way, he will not have long to prepare, and I doubt there is much he could do to bolster his defenses anyway," Ganachim said. "I will reach him no matter what he puts in my way."

Marbuck recalled the ferocity with which Ganachim had torn apart the Ancestral Mount in search of her quarry. She held no doubt that Ganachim would level the entire ziggurat if she had to.

"This brings me to my next point," Reie continued. "Obviously, Ganachim and I will be confronting Setenrah. I do not wish to put anyone else in harm's way. I suggest we take the refugees only as far as the Eastern Promenade. Ganachim and I will proceed alone from there."

"Well, let's consider the optics for a moment," Avehav said. "If we were to assemble everyone before Setenrah, surely he would be cowed by such a show of force. And there are those among the refugees who know how to fight; it wouldn't *only* be for show."

Reie was shaking her head. "There's no practical way to bring that many people into the Oasis Sanctum, and even if we could, it would be more of a hindrance than anything. For every person who has some experience in a fight, there are ten who do not. And none of them have faced a being of such terrible power. Those people would not intimidate Setenrah but would only ignite his thirst to defile. Far better that they hang back until it is safe."

"And if it's not—safe, I mean?" Rayburn asked quietly. "What are we to do if you don't succeed?"

"You will have to decide that for yourself. Some will choose to fight, I'm sure. Many will flee. All will be doomed regardless. I cannot plan for such an outcome. We *must* succeed or all is lost."

"I choose to fight," Jalam said. "Not then, but *now*. I will come with you."

Marbuck was expecting Reie or Ganachim to immediately object, but neither did. They exchanged a quick glance, full of untold levels of psychic connection, and Reie turned back to her faithful guardian.

"I thought that might be the case."

Marbuck realized that Elibeth was looking at her. They both knew what was coming next.

"I'm coming too," Marbuck said with a sigh of resignation. "If I could follow you into that hive of shades, expecting to find Setenrah then, I can definitely follow you now."

"It was one thing to call upon you for aid when we were facing the legion of shades," Reie said. "Now, I fear that you would be putting yourselves in harm's way unnecessarily. I suppose there is a good chance that he will have shades with him, but there will be far fewer than there were in Vin-Unat."

"I care not," Jalam said.

"Me neither," Marbuck agreed. "However many there are, our blades will keep them at bay. Ganachim will have her hands full with Setenrah, and you'll have your hands full with bolstering her. It worked last time. Consider us an added measure of security."

Reie and Ganachim looked at each other again.

"Anointed blade or not, I'm coming this time!" Falstaff interjected.

"Me too," Nedelkoff added. "I haven't heard anything about Setenrah being impervious to normal weaponry."

Roanack scoffed, but his derision was ignored.

"I commit myself and my men," Avehav said.

"Thank you, my friends," Reie said with a touch of bashfulness. "Perhaps a small force could be of use, though I do not wish for any of you to underestimate what we face. None of you have seen Setenrah before and you cannot comprehend the horror and awe he will instill in you. You are experienced warriors, and I do not doubt your bravery, but to face a god is another thing entirely."

"She's right."

From his place in the shadows, Galt stepped forward. All eyes turned toward him.

"As some of you may know, I faced one of them. Ulesreto, he was called. His command of old was judgment of the dead; an ability that was nearly useless after his cosmic neutering. It didn't matter. He still fought with a strength and a speed far beyond normal men. I didn't even fight him alone; I had a warrior without equal beside me, and we still lost. Granted we were weakened already from our prior struggles, but without pure luck, we would have fallen. Now, from what you've said of this Setenrah, his abilities retain a far more practical—and deadly—use. And with them comes something that Ulesreto lacked. For he, terrible to behold as he was, had been glorious once. It sounds as if Setenrah is a creature born strictly of nightmare. I imagine that some of you will struggle to even stand before him, much less muster the courage to fight. Knowing what we face, there's no shame in backing out."

The closeness of the glen now felt stifling. Marbuck's eyes remained fixed on Galt as attempts to envision what he'd been through were chased through her mind by dark imaginings of what was to come. Roanack was nodding to himself in apparent agreement of Galt's assessment.

"We?" Reie asked. "Am I to understand that you'll be joining us too?"

Galt cleared his throat, seeming suddenly embarrassed to be commanding the attention of so many. "Aye, that's right. I knew a woman once, Ophelia Solgard. She was a shepherd, like I was, and she'd been roped into the same damned expedition. Nothing fazed her though; she believed that it was the Void-God's will to turn everything toward our favor. I loved her, but I think she was wrong on a few counts. I know she was right about one thing, though. The most important thing. We *can* create a better world. Not through obliteration," he said, gesturing toward the faintly visible crack in the sky, which had widened appreciably, "but through doing whatever good that we can, and by believing that good can still come to us in this broken world. I've seen what you two have done for these people, and I'm choosing to believe that you'll do *all* that you've pledged to do; that you'll usher in a free society greater than Nordabor ever was, and that you'll do everything you can to stop the Erosion. I'm choosing to do as Solgard would have done; I'm going to have *faith*. It does not come easy for me, but I will strive to think and feel as she would, nonetheless. I believe in you and your cause, and though I am a shepherd no longer, I can still fight alongside you. I faced a god at the end of the world, and I'm prepared to face one again if it means ushering in a better world."

Marbuck had heard Galt's story before, at least in the broad strokes he'd been willing to share, but this was the first time that he'd ever spoken of Ophelia Solgard. To hear the typically laconic ex-shepherd describe his love for this lost woman of faith was strange and sad.

"I promise you, your faith will not be misplaced," Reie said after a moment. "And I will gladly accept your help, thank you."

Jalam held his anointed blade out toward Galt. "It's yours, if you want it."

"No, keep it. From what I understand, you made good use of it."

"Then take this," Jalam said, offering his saber.

Galt eyed it for a moment, and then took it, pulling it free of its scabbard. Testing the weight, his mouth turned up in a thin hint of a smile.

"Aye, this'll do."

"As Galt said, there is no shame in changing your minds," Reie said to the group. She paused, but nobody spoke. She nodded before continuing. "If any falter as we approach, I will understand. This is, after all, the final act in a conflict that was always greater than humanity, though it took you down with it. It is our burden to bear, whatever role your misguided ancestors might have been lured into playing."

"Our ancestors, whatever they did or didn't do, matter not," Jalam said to a chorus of agreement. "We are here now; the time has come. Deliverance forever."

Reie smiled, then took a deep, shuddering breath. "Yes, my friend. Deliverance forever."

CHAPTER 51

If the spotters had still manned their positions along the balconies of the Great Ziggurat, they would have witnessed an incredible sight. Snaking across the parched and silent desert, a wide swath of verdant land now stretched away to the north. At the nearest end of it, where the lush growth continued to spread toward the vast entrance leading into the Eastern Promenade, an enormous column of people moved. At their head walked two gods, joined in their purpose. A retinue of loyal supporters accompanied them, human beings plucked from numerous walks of life, each intent on seeing the vision of the gods come to fruition. Jalam, tireless guardian of the Lady of the Veil; Nedelkoff and Galt, a former guardsman and a former shepherd, both now serving a greater cause; Avehav, an aristocrat turned rebel leader turned devotee to the new faith; Falstaff, a simple man who had always chosen to do what was right; and Marbuck, a mariner who'd wanted nothing but to return to her daughter a few coins richer, and who'd ended up stumbling into the most monumental events to occur since the breaking of their world.

She'd already bid farewell to Elibeth. It had almost become a joke between them; her insistence that she would never leave again, followed by her subsequent leaving again. Elibeth, with her youthful confidence, never doubted her mother, and had even tried to join her for what they hoped would be the final confrontation. Marbuck, backed by Reie, had been insistent that she stay behind. She'd acquiesced, remaining with Dania and Hamish instead. Rayburn, who'd seen quite a bit of bloodshed and mayhem for a merchant, was modest enough to grasp his own limitations. He'd opted to remain behind as well, promising to keep an eye on Elibeth. Marbuck appreciated the sentiment.

Also offering their protecting presence to the refugees were Avehav's men. Reie had denied Avehav's commitment of Winfield, Hassa, and the others, insisting that they remain behind to keep order amongst the refugees as they awaited her return. More so, she did not want anyone compelled to face Setenrah. Orders alone would not prevent a chaotic rout should his terrible presence overcome them. Similarly, Roanack had not been bidden to join them. Witnessing the torment of his family would certainly unman him, turning him into a liability. Roanack had made no attempt to change anyone's mind, rather, he'd declared that he would remain behind under the auspices of offering protection to the refugees.

The refugees, Marbuck hoped, would not need any further protection. If all went as planned, the only thing threatening anyone would be eliminated before it ever came near them. If the bid to destroy Setenrah failed, she supposed, she wouldn't be around to see the consequences. A vision of Elibeth, distorted by disease, flickered through her mind. She shouldered the thought aside and focused instead on the imposing bulk of the Great Ziggurat.

They were rounding its northern wall now, proceeding toward the entrance. Sand drifts were piled high against the gargantuan sandstone blocks of the ziggurat's base, like crashing waves frozen in time. Ganachim had muted her power somewhat, leaving the sands around them increasingly undisturbed. Marbuck assumed that she was saving her energy for the coming battle. As it was, protective shade would not be needed for much longer anyway. The heat of the atrium was intense, but the structure would still provide cover from the relentless sun.

As the colossal opening came into view, Marbuck observed the first obvious sign that something was wrong in Quaretem: the twin pools that had paralleled the track leading into the ziggurat were completely dry. What little silt remained had been baked into a scuzzy white film that coated the bottom of the troughs. Their procession filed between the empty pools, marching directly toward the opening. Contrasted with the harsh brightness outside, the interior looked deceptively dim. Passing beneath the wide arch and into the atrium dispelled the illusion. It was still light, airy, and of a strange, dream-like beauty, but the dream had shifted darkly. Here, too, the fountains languished in dryness. With the majority of the Quaret in hiding deep within the Warren, and the total collapse of Lakna's order, it seemed that there was nobody left to man the pumps.

"How different this place is now," Jalam observed, echoing Marbuck's own thoughts. "It always felt to me like a large body, holding its breath. When I was a child, it was the fear of Zeorshut Riengel. When I assumed the guardianship and learned the truth, it was the certainty of Setenrah's coming. Now, I feel as if the air has been forced from the lungs, and a great poisoned breath has taken its place."

Marbuck shuddered, despite the heat.

They had nearly reached the portico surrounding the entrance to the Oasis Sanctum when Ganachim, peering over the crowd, quietly announced that everyone had managed to make it inside. Tightly clustered groups fanned out onto every ramp and under every archway, their shuffling feet the only sound. A funereal silence hung over everyone, and Marbuck was awed to see so many people remaining silent. Word had been passed through group elders of what was happening, and no command was necessary to silence or halt them. They might not have understood everything, but they understood plainly that they were in a colossal tomb, haunted by the world's last monster. All hope had been placed upon the shoulders of the two gods leading them.

With no rousing speeches or mighty declarations, Reie and Ganachim proceeded toward the tunnel entrance, which was now unguarded. Their retinue followed, and Marbuck spared a final glance back toward her daughter. She caught Elibeth's face for a brief moment, a hopeful smile creasing her cheeks, just as worry creased her brow. Marbuck offered up a quick wave, which Elibeth returned, and then she was stepping under the arched opening and into the tunnel beyond.

It was not only cooler in the tunnel, but quite a lot darker now that there was no water to reflect the light. Ganachim's bulk nearly filled the space, and she scraped against the walls as she moved, crouching to pass through. Marbuck wondered if Setenrah had sensed them yet; surely they'd sensed him. She then considered the last time she'd passed this way, led by Kemp toward a meeting where she'd believed her departure for the north would be secured. She glanced at Jalam, who was barely visible in the dark, mostly illuminated by Reie's halo. She'd met him in this very hallway, standing guard as close to Reie as he could get. Some things had not changed.

They emerged into a sunlit chamber where the steps leading up to the Oasis Sanctum were waiting for them. Once again, there were no guards present. At the top, the ornamental drape covering the entrance hung in shreds. A faint keening echoed from the room beyond, and a wretched stench wafted out toward them.

"This is it," Reie whispered. "Any who wish to leave must go now."

Marbuck, her own mind decidedly made up, looked at the others. Nedelkoff shook slightly, and Avehav looked as if he were strongly considering a hasty departure, but nobody said anything. Reie nodded and turned to Ganachim. No words were exchanged, but something important passed between them. Reie looked up toward the entrance and, with a steadying breath, mounted the steps, with Ganachim and the others following. Reaching the top, Reie slipped through the remains of the drape and Ganachim, hunching, pressed through right behind her. Marbuck and the others came through last, entering a scene of utter horror.

The Oasis Sanctum's stark, clean aesthetic had been smothered beneath numerous masses of pustular matter, piled high in oozing heaps. These reeking accumulations were everywhere; coating the steps of the terraced dais, filling the pools, climbing the walls, even partially choking the high, narrow windows. In the dim light, the endless drone of flies filled the foul air; swollen, jade-colored insects who'd grown fat on a diet of rotting flesh. Their food source was abundant; the ruined bodies of the Sanctified littered the space, and their shades, lining the walls of the chamber, writhed and hissed from the ichor prison encasing them. They were a captive court for the true master of Quaretem.

Sprawled across a mound of repulsive discharge that had enveloped and replaced Lakna's couch was the being she had long venerated as mighty Setenrah. No amount of description from Kemp or warnings from Reie could have adequately prepared Marbuck for the monster now before her. His skeletal frame was massive, anchored within an oily flesh robe; white skin, shining with a greasy dampness, hung loosely from elongated arms; a whirring halo of insects circled above his head; everything about him pulsed with a deep, sickly malevolence that made Bolenz seem like a child merely playing at depravity.

The only check to the god's terrible visage was the look of total shock that had seized his corpse-like face as they'd entered his domain.

Beholding them, Setenrah shuddered into motion, unfolding from his perch and stretching to his full height. His beady, sunken eyes flicked between Reie and Ganachim, and his expression settled into a defiant sneer.

"You've returned," he said, and his voice was like a chorus of death rattles. "Though I hardly recognize you without your veil. I must apologize; I was not prepared for guests. I've been preoccupied with my labors." With a wet pop, Setenrah's flesh robe opened, revealing a network of glistening connective tissue, coated in sores. The webbing of tissue shifted and a naked human form, wrapped in a gossamer sack, shifted to the front. The sack burst and the ruined body within spilled onto the floor in an expulsion of reeking, milky fluid. Marbuck could only assume that it was Lakna; it was wrinkled and female, but otherwise so distorted by the ravages of disease that identification was impossible.

"I see that you are not alone," Setenrah continued as if nothing had happened.

"No," Reie said, sparing not so much as a glance for Lakna. "I am not."

Unexpectedly, Setenrah sighed with pleasure. "Long have I waited to hear the sound of your voice again. Of course, I imagined I would finally hear it under different circumstances. I'd assumed you were hiding with the slaves below, and I'd thought to reveal my splendor to them when I finished here. I was going to flush you out and punish you for your bothersome disobedience. Make you *squeal* for mercy. But now I see that you're guilty of much more than callow defiance; you've apparently dredged the Einfallen." He bowed halfheartedly to Ganachim. "Welcome, old friend."

"You forget yourself," Ganachim said. "You speak to me as if we are equals. We are not, nor were we ever. You are a mere sliver of our father, a minor offshoot formed to serve *me*; a tool that rebelled against its wielder's hand. In your assassination attempt you betrayed not only your creator but your rightful master. And you failed."

"It is of no consequence. When I failed to find your body, it occurred to me that you might yet live. But then came the fall, and your ebbing life was lost amid the noise of that calamity. Afterwards, I simply assumed that your absence befit your new position. The old hierarchy was gone; the mighty were laid low, and yet I persevered. I fear you as little as I fear her," Setenrah said, waving a hand dismissively toward Reie. "I am the pinnacle now."

"Having been unrestrained for so long, you have deluded even yourself," Reie said. "But you are mistaken. Ganachim is the last true power. We have come from the north, and she has cleansed every land that she has passed through. Including Vin-Unat."

This time, the shock on Setenrah's long face was tinged with fear, though he strove mightily to smother it with a forced laugh. "You are referring to my collection? No matter; there are plenty more cowering in the Warren with which to refill my coffers."

"You will never touch them."

"I will. But first, I'll take those who are closer at hand." Setenrah's penetrating gaze moved over Marbuck and the others, and they reflexively stepped back.

Knowing that she'd once been marked for collection, Marbuck's rage briefly reignited. Mostly, though, she felt a nauseating terror at this reminder of the doom she'd narrowly avoided, and which might still befall her should they fail.

"No," Reie said, and that single word carried the weight of immutable law.

Setenrah stared at Reie. The droning of the flies was the only sound. Marbuck knew that the time for words had ended.

In an instant, the tar holding the shades back receded, piling back into Setenrah's bulbous lower half. As he rose ever higher, the liberated shades hurled themselves forward with idiot ferocity. Ganachim slammed a hand against the floor, and the stones burst asunder. Twin walls of thick bramble rose up to meet the shades, and then Ganachim, surrounded by a wavering green light, was charging toward Setenrah.

The two gods collided with enough force to make the entire chamber shudder. Marbuck did not have long to watch them as the shades were already clawing through the thorny barrier.

"Get behind me!" Jalam shouted, pulling Reie away from the shades.

She seemed completely unaware of her surroundings; her focus was entirely directed toward Ganachim, as was a constant stream of her healing power. Marbuck and the others circled around her, weapons drawn.

The first of the shades burst through and loped toward them. Marbuck and Jalam met it head on, hacking it to pieces. In their eagerness, they'd strayed from the group, and two more shades were now approaching from the other side. Galt, showing no regard for his lack of an anointed blade, stepped forward to meet them. He struck one with the flat of his saber, the force of the blow knocking the creature back, even if it didn't actually harm it. He then whirled toward the other, ducking beneath a savage strike from its ragged claws and knocking its legs out from under it. As it thrashed about in an effort to regain its footing, Marbuck fell on it, delivering the killing blow.

The other shade had been intercepted by Falstaff, Nedelkoff, and Avehav, who were fruitlessly beating at it, protected only by the relentless nature of their attack. Shrugging off the blows, the shade realized that its attackers were harmless. It caught Falstaff's axe in midair and ripped it from his grasp. Its other hand shot out to seize him by the throat, but Jalam intercepted, lopping the arm off at the joint. The shade screeched briefly before Jalam silenced it, plunging his blade into its head. Falstaff, clearly shaken by the encounter, stooped to retrieve his axe, just as four more shades crashed into the barrier.

Above them, a titanic struggle was unfolding. Bellowing thunderously, the two gods grappled, hammering each other with everything they had. Ganachim's arms were encased within gnarled trunks of wood, formed into tremendous clubs. She smashed them with all her might against Setenrah, who weaved about, absorbing the blows with rapidly ballooning tumors and striking back with thick whips of tissue, dotted with hundreds of sharp, crooked teeth. Wherever Ganachim struck, an explosive bloom of growth sought to take root, but just as quickly, it withered in Setenrah's pestilent presence. All the while, Reie, her teeth bared with furious effort, poured herself into Ganachim. Above her head, her halo flickered ominously.

Ganachim heaved a ferocious blow toward Setenrah's head, but he slithered beneath the arc of the attack. Her arm struck the encrusted mass of Lakna's couch, pulverizing it in an instant and sending a shower of debris sailing through the air. A squirming mass of tendrils shot out from Setenrah's bulk and seized Ganachim's outstretched arm, coiling tightly around it. He twisted around her and began to hoist himself up her back, his long fingers seeking her throat. Throwing herself backward, she smashed through the fountain that topped the dais, loosening Setenrah, but not fully dislodging him.

"Look at you, mighty firstborn," he said as his tendrils seized Ganachim's other arm. His sunken eyes twinkled, and his lips rose in a carrion smirk. "Once without equal, but not anymore."

Ganachim struggled against his fetid embrace, but he held fast.

"A 'sliver', I believe you called me? Father put too much into you, and left you with too much to lose. I was cast from a different mold, and now I rest upon the apex. My power is *absolute*; my strength is at its *zenith*! And you, *old friend*, are merely the—"

Marbuck failed to catch the last of his gloating, her attention suddenly monopolized by the four shades that had just breached the barrier. As she moved to put herself between them and Reie, she managed to glimpse Ganachim, who'd sprouted countless thorns, tearing free of Setenrah's grip.

Lunging forward, she tumbled down the dais, cracking the steps with her immense weight. Sliding to a stop, she scrambled to her feet and faced her perfidious enemy. He lingered on the steps above her, his spindly upper half weaving through the air, his globular lower half quivering.

As the two deities launched back into their vicious assault, Marbuck, with Galt and Nedelkoff beside her, intercepted the nearest shades, managing to fell two of them. Glancing rapidly around their scattered group, Marbuck saw that Jalam had finished off the other two, but not before they had managed to grievously wound Avehav. The former noble had been slashed open from his navel to his chin; his breast bone had been cracked and his intestines were pooled about him. He was still alive, but just barely. His breath was coming in shallow, wet gasps, and his bulging eyes stared through them.

"He needs help!" Falstaff cried as he cradled the dying man's head. "*Reie!*"

She didn't seem to hear him, focused as she was on Ganachim.

"*Reie, please!*"

Beyond their circle of protection, more shades were clawing ever closer.

Jalam watched all of this with a pained expression. Finally, he turned to Reie, clasping her arm and leaning in to her ear. "Avehav needs you!" he shouted.

She flinched, her eyes rolling up to white. With a spasmodic jerk, one hand flicked toward Avehav. His body shuddered, the intestines spooling inward as his skin reformed.

Before she could finish, her attention was pulled back to the gods, where the momentary distraction had given Setenrah an opening. Like a mammoth spider, he'd been holding himself aloft with his sinuous offshoots, and, seeing his chance, he'd dropped the full weight of his bulging lower half on top of Ganachim, smothering her beneath his foul bulk.

Triumphant, Setenrah fixed his eyes on Reie. "I'm almost finished here. Then we can discuss continuing our arrangement," he said, grinning wickedly.

Reveling in his perceived victory, he failed to realize that Reie had resumed her bolstering of Ganachim. Screaming raggedly, Reie fired out the last of her strength. With an audible crack, a shimmering surge of power rushed beneath Setenrah. An answering flash of green light punched through his flabby robe-flesh, followed by an explosive bloom of vines. With a cry, Setenrah reared back, sliding off Ganachim. Slathered in bile, she emerged, chanting melodically. Her voice rose into a short scream and the thorny walls around Marbuck and the others shot upward, glowed with pure power, and then crashed like a wave onto the floor of the chamber, pulverizing the shades within. Ganachim then clubbed Setenrah in the head hard enough to splinter her cudgel. Black blood poured from his broken skin, and his halo spun wildly. Ganachim shed her second club and, seizing Setenrah from behind, snatched his halo with both hands, yanking the dazed god upward.

"You seek to fight as Aedesda did, with his hooks and chains," Ganachim growled almost directly into his ear. "You are but an imitation, a wayward servant lost in emulation of one greater in strength, if not wisdom or honor. He failed in his designs, and so will you."

She planted a large foot on top of his flesh robe and began to wrench the halo upward, eliciting a wail of pain from Setenrah, and he reached back, clawing at her face. At the same time, his lower half began to ripple, reforming where Ganachim had punched a rent through it, and tubular, lesion-coated masses began to coil around Ganachim's legs. As they tightened, digging into her flesh, Ganachim roared.

Seeing that she wouldn't be able to hold on for much longer, Marbuck looked to Reie. She had collapsed, her power spent. There was only one option now.

"She needs us!" Marbuck shouted to the others. "Come on!"

Galt stalked forward first, with Nedelkoff trotting right behind. With obvious reluctance, Jalam left Reie's side. Falstaff rose to join them, and then hesitated, looking down at Avehav. His mending had not been completed, and he was ashen-faced with pain. Despite this, he managed to nod shakily.

With her blade held before her, Marbuck charged up the steps. She could hear the others right behind her, crying out with rage and hope. The closer she got to the bloated form of Setenrah, the more her brain tried to reject what she was seeing. The pulsating flesh bag of his inflated lower half was unbearably vile, but Marbuck forced herself to approach it. Sliding to a stop before the convulsing mass, she steeled herself for whatever might follow. Throwing her full weight behind it, she plunged her blade forward.

Almost immediately, she was doused in a torrent of hot, lacteal fluid. Clenching her eyes and mouth shut, she continued to hack blindly at Setenrah's body. Beside her, she could hear mingled shouts of disgust and exertion as the others joined in.

Setenrah bucked wildly, his lower half jiggling as countless ragged wounds spewed out a mixture of blood and discharge. His tendrils released their grip on Ganachim and began to thrash about, one of them swinging within a hair's breadth of Marbuck's head. Ganachim, now unfettered, redoubled her efforts, pushing down even harder with her foot and wrenching the halo up with all the strength she could muster.

"*No! NO!*" Setenrah snarled, his jagged teeth bared. "You can't—I won't let you! There are none greater! I am *paramount*! I am—"

The skin of Setenrah's neck split apart as Ganachim tore his head from his shoulders. With a hideous, otherworldly wail, his voice gave way to a frothing spew of gore, and then his head ripped free. At the very moment of decapitation, his halo burst apart in Ganachim's hands, and the severed head tumbled from her grip. With a booming thud, it landed amongst Marbuck and the others, sending them scattering. Accompanied by a diffusing cloud of insects, it proceeded to tumble down the steps. The skeletal upper half of his body swayed briefly, and then crashed down across the deflating bulk below, black blood gushing from the shredded stump of his neck. Marbuck, mopping rancid juice from her eyes, could only stare with astonishment.

Mighty Setenrah was dead. The old war was finally finished.

CHAPTER 52

"Fishwife? *Raina*! I can't see!"

Marbuck dragged her eyes away from the dead god and toward the sound of Falstaff's voice. He was stepping gingerly through a black slick of gore, rubbing his face and squinting in her direction. His face was red, the skin around his eyes blistered and swollen.

"It's *burning*," he said, pressing the heels of his palms into his eyes.

"I'm here, I'm here," Marbuck said as she reached him and took his arm. "Let's get you to Reie." Her own skin was starting to itch and burn where Setenrah's foul innards had spilled across her.

Before they could even start down, Ganachim was stepping over them without a word, speeding toward the spot where Reie was still lying on the floor. A shade, the last remaining in the chamber, was slithering about her, pawing curiously at the motionless body. With a piercing pang of dread, it occurred to Marbuck that being healed by Reie might not be an option.

Ganachim seized the shade without hesitation and burst it apart with a quick tightening of her fist. She then knelt down and scooped Reie's crumpled form off the floor.

Helping Falstaff along, Marbuck made her way down the blood-caked steps. From the other side of the massive, oozing corpse, Jalam emerged.

Seeing Reie, he raced down the steps. Galt came ambling after, examining Setenrah's remains with an almost clinical look.

"Is she …?" Jalam asked.

"See for yourself," Ganachim said huskily, turning Reie toward him.

"You are not free of me yet," Reie croaked, smiling weakly.

Jalam burst into grateful tears and clasped her hand. "You have done it! We are *free!*"

"Yes, but there is work yet to be done," Reie said, reaching out toward Marbuck and Falstaff. "Gather close, please. I haven't much left in me."

Everyone scooted in as close as they could get, and Marbuck felt a flickering hum of energy pass through her, easing her pain. She looked at Falstaff; he was blinking rapidly, testing his eyes, and the growing blisters on his skin had receded somewhat. They weren't fully restored, but for now, it was enough.

"What about Avehav?" Falstaff asked, turning toward the spot where he'd left him. His face fell as he saw Nedelkoff kneeling beside a deflated, ruined corpse. She looked up, realizing that everyone was now staring at her.

"It wasn't enough," she said, rising and brushing her hands off on her pants. Her lips pressed tight and she blinked away the tears that had unexpectedly filled her eyes. "It wasn't enough. I knew this would happen eventually—the vainglorious fool. He'd flirted often enough with his own demise, now, here it is."

Reie watched this with an expression of tired sorrow that made her look ancient. "It was a noble end, and one that did not come to him through the empty pursuit of glory. Sometimes, faith is not rewarded. I'm sorry that I could not save him. He chose a hard path, a *true* path, and he walked it well. And this random injustice," she said, gesturing toward his desecrated remains, "does not reflect who he was, but merely shows the flaw in what's left of a broken old system. His pain is over now, and he will be venerated for his actions."

They stood in silence, the glow of their victory diminished. To Marbuck, the decision to go with the gods suddenly felt foolish; it could have just as easily been her that had needlessly died. Lost in thought, she stared at her own bloodied hands, clasped before her.

It was Setenrah's blood.

No, she decided, her decision hadn't been wrong. Had she and the others not accompanied the gods, Setenrah may have won. His shades might have overtaken Reie. If they had not attacked him in force, he could have escaped Ganachim's clutches; a position he would have never even been in without the distraction created by Avehav. In the end, the choices they'd made had been right, because they'd resulted in victory. If Avehav had believed in their cause as fervently as he'd professed to, Marbuck had no doubt that he would be happy with the outcome.

She was preparing to put these thoughts into words when their impromptu vigil was interrupted by a hacking cough. Galt, standing closest to the apparent source of the sound, trotted up the steps toward it. Watching him approach a shriveled lump of diseased flesh, Marbuck remembered Lakna.

Grimacing, Galt examined the shape. "This one's still alive. Sort of."

"Take me to her," Reie said, and Ganachim moved at once, followed by the others. Reie turned to Jalam. "Go and get Roanack. Tell him that his mother yet lives."

"And what shall I tell the people?"

"That it's over, and that we have won. But, please, bid them to wait, lest they try to join us here. There is one last order of business to sort out first."

"Yes, my lady."

Jalam hurried off to fetch Roanack while the others converged on Lakna. Peering past Ganachim, Marbuck got a closer look at what the seneschal had become. Thankfully, it was brief. Already, Reie had set to work on her, and the numerous weeping sores, festering lesions, and tumorous growths that had enveloped her entire body were shrinking. Her legs, too, were reforming. It seemed that at some point during the battle, one of the gods had stepped on them, turning them into splintered pulp. Somehow, the tenacious old woman had survived all of this.

Even restoring Lakna just enough to ensure that she'd live was quite an undertaking, and as Reie finished, her head sank under the weight of her lusterless halo. Half-lidded, she appeared as if she might faint. Ganachim watched her intently, her large brow furrowed. After a moment, Reie shook her head gently, seeming to regain her senses, and Ganachim sighed with relief. Beneath them, Lakna, curled in the fetal position, began to stir. Without her turban, her small, wrinkled head, which was nearly hairless, reminded Marbuck of a newborn.

"Cover her," Reie said.

Nedelkoff stepped forward, unclasped her cloak, and draped it over Lakna. At the touch of the cloth, she flinched. Realizing that her agony was over, she slowly opened her eyes and turned toward her rescuers.

"*You*," she hissed. Marbuck couldn't help but smile. Lakna's resemblance to her son was uncanny.

"Help her up," Reie said.

Nedelkoff and Falstaff hoisted Lakna to her feet, and she fussily pulled the cloak about her. If she was grateful for the cessation of her torment, she did not say so. She did, however, take notice of both Setenrah's corpse and the presence of Ganachim. Her eyes darted between the two of them before finally settling on Reie.

"You've returned then," she said flatly.

"Yes."

"And with another of … your kind."

"Yes," Reie said again, her voice entirely neutral.

"But not before your absence cost me everything."

"I am sorry for the loss of your family. If I'd had the chance to do so, I would have saved every one of them. As it is, there is one member of your family who remains: Roanack."

Lakna received this information with a distracted nod. "You still walk with the northerners, I see. And Lord Henrick?"

"He's passed away."

"Such a waste," Lakna said with a heavy sigh.

From beyond the Oasis Sanctum, the tremendous roar of a distant crowd could be heard. Marbuck pictured Elibeth among them, cheering rapturously, and smiled. Lakna took her grin for something else entirely.

"Your fellow Vingalleans, I presume? Cheering in triumph over their newly-conquered land? Believe me, I'm happy to see that foul creature laid low, but I don't relish a new master taking his place, nor will I accept it."

Marbuck bristled. "I think you've misjudged your position here. Nobody requires your acceptance of anything. You should simply be grateful to be alive, not to mention freed from Setenrah. I can't believe you get up—having *just* been rescued—and launch into this haughty bullshit. *Fuck you.* You should be *weeping* with gratitude."

"Gratitude for being delivered from my suffering?" Lakna sneered. "You are the *cause* of my suffering. *Everything* was as it should have been until you came along."

"You mean until I was *brought* to you for ritualistic sacrifice?"

"Why couldn't you just—"

"Enough," Reie said. "I must admit, I do find your unapologetic lack of gratitude disturbing, though not in the least bit surprising. That being said, there are, indeed, some things that you must understand going forward."

"Mother!"

Jalam had returned with Roanack in tow, and the chief warden was rushing toward his matriarch. His relief had whittled away the long-cycles and he looked every bit the little boy who'd once clung to his mother's skirts. Lakna simply looked annoyed.

"Mother, you're okay!" Roanack said as he reached her. "I cannot believe it; they actually did it! Setenrah is dead! And I still have you!" Tears streaked his face.

"I'm glad you are both here," Reie said in a diplomatic tone that ignored her former oppressor's emotional display. "I will only have to say this once."

Roanack's excitement ceased immediately. He and Lakna both turned toward Reie; he appeared to be bracing himself; she looked defiant. Now that victory had been achieved, it was time to learn their fate.

"Barring any unexpected siring on your son's part, your line has ended, as has your rule. The seneschals are no more. The Great Ziggurat will be opened to the people of the Warren. If they have not come to understand yet, they will learn the truth about Zeorshut Riengel and your family's old bargain with Setenrah. There will be no more secrets or lies."

"So *you* are the new master then, eh?" Lakna said. "Sentencing us to death? The rabble will have our heads when they hear all that."

"Our people are no *rabble*, and I am nobody's master. The Vingalleans with me are liberated refugees, not an army at my command. The time of masters and slaves is over. As is the time for violent retribution. Though you do not deserve it, I will guarantee your safety; you will be offered a place as an equal with your fellow Quaret. Roanack has already agreed to such terms."

Lakna heaped a withering look upon her son, and he cringed apologetically.

"I don't know how you convinced my idiot spawn of your magnanimity, but I am not so naïve," Lakna said. "I know you waited to come until my entire family had been *defiled*. If you are planning my execution, then get on with it. I will not be stripped of my rightful place and plopped in amongst the filthy masses, only to wait for a knife in the back. I will not give you the satisfaction."

Reie shook her head. "You are blinded by your own ways. I do not orchestrate furtive killings, or condone such things. My word is true."

Lakna waved a hand dismissively; it had been stripped of its heavy jewels. "I will have no part of it, and neither will my son."

Roanack, who'd seemed quite prepared to accept any deal that spared his life, started. "But, Mother—"

"*Silence!*" Lakna barked. "We are not taking part in this farce."

"So be it," Reie said. "I will not condemn you, but I will also not stop you from condemning yourself. If you do not wish to be a part of this commune, then you are free to choose exile instead."

"Exile?"

"Yes. Leave this place and never return, for my offer of amnesty will expire once you are gone. You will be free to continue your reign in the desert, beneath the Unblinking Eye. The grains of sand can be your subjects until they become your grave."

Lakna's puckered mouth worked furiously as she struggled to respond. "Get out of my way," she finally growled, stamping through the group. "Come on then!" she shouted back at Roanack, who hadn't moved.

"Mother—"

"*Now!*" she screamed back.

"You needn't do this," Reie said gently.

Roanack looked between his mother and Reie. Marbuck felt sorry for him; he'd spent his entire life laboring under Lakna's imperious shadow. His decision now did not surprise her.

"Yes, Mother," he whimpered, his eyes lingering on Reie. He shambled forward, and she impatiently snatched his arm. He continued to look back as she dragged him away.

"Make sure they can pass," Reie instructed Jalam. "The refugees don't know who they are, so I expect no problems, but follow them just in case. Make sure they leave the ziggurat."

Jalam nodded and followed behind them at some distance.

Marbuck watched the obstinate old hag and her pathetic son disappear through the shredded curtain. She knew that they would not last long. Bereft of everything, they would be reduced to scavenging whatever Ganachim's path had left behind until the relentless sun burned it all away. Then, a brutal and ignominious death would follow, assuming that desperation never triumphed over Lakna's pride, or Roanack's servility to his mother.

Marbuck was certain that it never would.

•   •   •

The weary party, with Reie now walking between them, returned to the refugees, where they were met with jubilation. Though the people might not have understood everything that had happened they plainly grasped that a great victory had been achieved and that their long journey was finally over. Marbuck and Elibeth, reunited once again, clung to each other, laughing and crying. Superstitious of inviting any further trouble, Marbuck made no pledges to remain at her daughter's side. None were necessary. Elibeth made it clear that she harbored no doubts about her mother's devotion. After all, she'd proven it time and time again, broken vows or not.

The news of Avehav's death rippled through the crowd like an aftershock. For those who'd known him intimately, it tempered their joy. Rayburn, who owed his life to Avehav's organized resistance, and Nedelkoff, who'd worked so closely with him, leaned on each other in their mourning. Winfield, Hassa, and the rest of his men received the news with solemn dignity, viewing his death as that of a brave warrior and an honorable leader. Like Kemp, Avehav had not lived to see the promise of deliverance come to fruition, a fulfillment that he'd purchased with his own blood. Marbuck was grateful for his sacrifice, and that her own fate had been different.

As the impromptu celebration continued, Jalam returned bearing confirmation of Lakna and Roanack's departure, as well as Nedelkoff's cloak.

"Leaving was Lakna's choice. I don't think her poor judgment should deprive anyone else of their garments," Jalam said with a sly smile.

The thought of Lakna stumbling out into the wastes as naked as the day she'd come into the world, and Roanack undoubtedly trying his best to cover her, made Marbuck laugh. She knew that it was cruel, perhaps, but cruelty begets cruelty, and Lakna had chosen her own fate, as had Roanack. Marbuck would certainly not lose any sleep on their account.

With Setenrah vanquished and the refugees safe, Reie decided that it was now time to see to the Warren. Ganachim, of course, would join her, as would Jalam, who was eager to see his countrymen, and Katiek specifically. Being that they'd been with her since she'd first left the Warren, Reie bid Marbuck and Falstaff to join her for her return. With Elibeth tagging along, the group left the refugees to their contentment and headed for the Deceiver's Door.

It was fortunate that the ancient Quaret engineers had designed their ziggurat to be so spacious, for Ganachim had little difficulty in navigating the broad corridors. It occurred to Marbuck that, given their closeness with the gods, the builders may have taken the size of their deities into consideration during construction.

With little delay, they reached the Deceiver's Door, through which, they'd decided, they would enter the Warren. It was a choice made for two reasons; first, it would circumvent the blocked passages; and second, it would allow Ganachim to destroy whatever final dregs remained in the Pit.

With ridiculous ease, Ganachim tore the large, iron door from its frame set into the floor and tossed it aside, completely ignoring the machinery put in place to open it. The smell of the Pit wafted up through the opening, stinging Marbuck's eyes; she'd forgotten about the rank odor of the accumulated waste. Beside her, Elibeth pinched her nose shut. As Ganachim generated a latticework of foliage to lower herself down, Marbuck wondered how many terrified, innocent individuals had watched the Deceiver's Door slide open, and how many had plummeted into the black chasm beyond it. A considerable part of her wished that she could have watched Lakna take that plunge.

Ganachim lowered herself in first, and with a flash of green light and a short cry, she annihilated the final, forgotten shades that Setenrah hadn't bothered to collect, focused as he'd been on the torment of the Sanctified.

Her work below finished, Ganachim sent her vines up through the threshold to carry the others, just as she had during their escape from the crumbling Vinecrown Keep. Elibeth, experiencing this mode of transport for the first time, laughed with delight. Marbuck still found it slightly disconcerting, all the more so because she was watching her child being carried in the same unbelievable manner.

Just as before, any anxiety proved to be unnecessary; they reached the ground safely. Making haste toward the exit, they found that it had been blocked.

"They must have anticipated that either Setenrah would come for them, or Lakna would try to lower someone down to reach them," Reie said, eyeing the jumbled mess of rocks, barrels, and other assorted oddments that the Quaret had used to choke the passage.

"I don't think that would have kept Setenrah out," Falstaff observed.

"The barricades kept Lakna and her minions out, and that is enough. Let's be grateful that they were never tested beyond that."

In proof of Falstaff's point, Ganachim tore the barricade down easily. Reie then led the way, taking them toward the deepest recesses of the Warren, where she believed Katiek and the others would be hiding. As they walked, they passed the hovel in which Marbuck, Falstaff, and Devonshire had been housed. Falstaff nudged Marbuck, pointing out the place with something like fond remembrance. She shuddered, the image of the scratched tallies still clear in her mind.

Finally, after passing through a narrow gap that required Ganachim to noisily carve out a wider way for herself, they reached what Reie was certain would be the final barricade. She looked at Ganachim and nodded, prompting the larger god to step forward. Several vines sprouted from her outstretched hands and snaked their way into the piled rocks, pulling them away with rapid efficiency. Jalam watched this work with nervous anticipation, wringing his hands and pursing his lips.

A particularly sizable stone was dislodged and the remainder of the barricade came tumbling down in a plume of dust. Almost immediately, six gaunt human figures coalesced out of the swirling grit. They clambered over the last of the rocks, crudely crafted pikes in hand; little more than wooden sticks with jagged bits of metal tied to the ends. One of them moved to the forefront, emerging from the dust with her weapon leveled and her teeth bared fiercely.

"Katiek!" Jalam cried, racing toward her.

Katiek's thin face froze in an expression of utter shock, and then shattered with relief. Her makeshift pike clattered to the ground as Jalam crashed into her, enveloping her in a tight embrace. She pulled away just enough to clasp his face in her hands and yank him down into a passionate kiss, which sent his eyes wide before he returned it. Marbuck and Falstaff exchanged a look, smiling broadly at this confirmation of what they'd apparently both suspected. The other Quaret began to weep and cheer, gathering about Reie and staring with reverent awe toward Ganachim.

"Go and tell the rest," Reie instructed one of them. "Deliverance has come; the Quaret are finally free."

CHAPTER 53

Sleep gave way to wakefulness with a heavy reluctance. The comfortable warmth of the chamber pressed gently against Marbuck's skin, and she labored to open her eyes. The glory of it was that she really didn't need to; there was no rush. In the time that had passed since they'd liberated Quaretem, what Marbuck guessed as being about half a long-cycle, life had taken on a quiet, gentle rhythm, devoid of pressing uncertainty.

Well, almost.

The crack in the sky had grown, the approach of the Erosion undeniable. It always had been, but the vast, unnatural distortion darkening the northern horizon was an unwelcome reminder, one that had checked the pleasure of a hard-won peace. By now, she was certain, the Erosion had erased the last stains of Vin-Sadavat, and the skinners to the south. It had probably consumed most of the crater, taking Vin-Unat and its toppled colossi with it. Berngoth would follow, and then the desert sands would slip away into nothing and Quaretem would stand alone before the Void.

There was nowhere left to run, beyond the open sea, and nothing else to do but wait, trusting that Reie and Ganachim would shelter them. Though it was not always easy, Marbuck strove to believe that the gods could do it. The alternative was despair, and she had suffered enough of that already. For what it was worth, everyone else seemed content to put their lives in the hands of the gods. After all, Reie and Ganachim had already done so much that had seemed impossible.

Marbuck stretched extravagantly and pushed aside the sheets, her blossoming hunger having bested her desire to stay in bed forever. Rising, she surveyed the chamber around her with the same sense of disbelief that she felt every time she awoke to find herself back in such comfortable circumstances. Sunlit, aesthetically pleasing, and appointed with a downy bed and finely crafted furniture, it was one of a unit of interconnected rooms within the Great Ziggurat, nearly identical to the one she'd awoken in after Kemp had rescued her. She thought of him then, the good-natured man held in thrall to his own past, looking in on his pampered prey, as unaware as she'd been of what lay in store for the two of them.

This time, though, the accommodations were not some temporary snare, but were all hers, and they were a far cry from her pitiful lodgings in Nordabor, the cramped confines of the *Fortune*, or any of the miserable cells she'd occupied since the beginning of her odyssey.

An ornate looking glass stood in the corner, and, as she dressed, Marbuck caught a glimpse of her reflection in it. It did not shock her; she was no longer disturbed by her scar, nor was she ashamed of it. It was simply a reminder of what she'd endured to reach this point, and what she'd triumphed over. In fact, she felt rather healthy, and she was pleased to see that her hair, now flecked with gray, continued to grow fitfully across the restored skin of her scalp. The evidence of Bolenz's cruelty had outlived him, but now even that was fading into memory. It was a thought that pleased Marbuck immensely.

Still, some lessons, once learned, are never forgotten. As Marbuck left her quarters, she hitched her blade to her belt.

A glance toward Elibeth's room revealed that she was already up; the door was ajar, and from down the steps that led toward the common area, Marbuck could hear the sounds of cheerful voices and clattering dishware. It appeared as if she'd been the last one to rise. Trotting down the steps, she confirmed this hunch; Elibeth sat at the long table that dominated the room, joined by Dania and Hamish. As they ate, the children ran about them in a whirlwind of play. Elibeth ate quickly, eager to join the antics buzzing around her. Dania and Hamish appeared to be oblivious to the fact that they occupied the center of a tempest; it was apparently something they were quite used to. Thinking of the trials involved in having one child, Marbuck could only marvel at the thought of raising four of them.

"Ah, so you *are* still alive," Dania said as Marbuck took a seat. "I was beginning to have my doubts."

"Dig in," Hamish added, gesturing toward the food. "There's plenty."

Plenty was an understatement. It was also the new standard, thanks to Ganachim. The paltry yield of the Sanctified's gardens and the subterranean mushrooms of the Warren had been replaced with expansive, organized fields tended by divine hands. Scarcity and hunger, those fiends that had harassed them all their lives, had been banished by a harvest that never ceased.

"Try the bacon, it's delicious," Elibeth said around a mouthful of food.

Marbuck's nose detected the presence of the bacon before her eyes did, and saliva filled her mouth. Fresh meat from livestock, previously a rare treat for all those who labored outside of the walls of the Vinecrown Keep, was now a staple at nearly every meal. Having finally settled, Ganachim had set her power toward conjuring more complicated forms of life than mere plants, mostly in the form of building upon what few livestock had remained in the possession of the Sanctified. Marbuck had witnessed this process on a few occasions, marveling at the acceleration of gestation and Ganachim's ability to spawn some creatures from the earth itself. She'd populated the forests she'd crafted with birds and beasts. The pools, filled once again by the work of those who'd joyfully resumed manning the pumps, had been stocked with fish. She'd furnished the pens with cows, chickens, goats, pigs, and horses. Not everything was meant for food, but plenty of it was. Marbuck felt a stirring of pity for the animals born to die, and she wondered if the first humans had been plucked from the dirt in a similar manner, albeit by the Father-God; certain lifeforms remained far beyond Ganachim's powers.

Any moral quandaries she might have had crumbled before the sight of the bacon, and she spooned several generous helpings onto a pewter dish. Elibeth was right; it was intoxicatingly good, as were the omelettes, boasting fresh spinach and tomatoes, the buttery toast, the succulent berries, and the steaming parritch. Dania, who'd always had an affinity for cooking, had seen her craft elevated to the level of a master now that her larder was stocked with such wonderful ingredients.

Having finished, Elibeth mopped her face haphazardly with a cloth and launched herself into the commotion with the other children. By the time Marbuck was done eating, Elibeth had assumed the role of commander in whatever game they were playing, as was the right of any child who was older and taller than her peers. Marbuck could only smile as she watched, reclining beside Dania and Hamish, each of them enjoying a steaming mug of tea. The herbs covered the last faint taste of salinity; Ganachim had helped the Quaret form a filtration system out of a type of floating lily, which had leached most of the salt from the water. Though it wasn't flawless, it had certainly made the water more palatable. Other plants, with extensive underwater root systems, had been introduced into the reservoirs that existed amidst the tangled network of pipes beneath the ziggurat. The purpose of these plants, woven into tight, interlaced sheets of remarkably thin, but hardy, outgrowths, was apparently to filter the water held within a closed system. When Marbuck had asked why such a system was necessary, Ganachim had stated, rather ominously, that the sea might not always be there. It was a reminder of both the fragility of their position, and the determination of the gods to hold it.

"So, what are your plans for this full-cycle?" Dania asked, leaning on the old terminology despite the fact that it was now mostly defunct.

Marbuck downed the last of her tea and handed the mug to Hamish, who'd begun clearing the dishes. "I was going to take a walk down to the pumps."

"To visit our friend, the workhorse?"

"That's right," Marbuck said with a chuckle. Falstaff, ever diligent in his pursuit of simple labor, had taken to tackling any job that needed doing. Mostly though, he seemed to enjoy assisting with the pumps, both the routine maintenance and operation of them, and the larger projects involving the filtration systems. As such, his own small chamber, located nearby, was rarely occupied.

"Tell him I say hi," Dania said.

"Of course." Marbuck turned to Elibeth. "Are you going to be ready to go soon?" She considered it a given that her daughter would be tagging along. They'd been nearly inseparable since the liberation and she was surprised to see Elibeth hesitate.

"Well, Mama—um—I thought I'd stay here with Arnar."

Elibeth dropped her eyes with some embarrassment, and Marbuck looked at the oldest of Dania's children. He was perhaps two long-cycles younger than Elibeth, and he had not yet crossed the threshold that would make him see her as anything more than a playmate. Consequently, he appeared to be oblivious to whatever crush Elibeth was nursing for him; one that was certainly born of proximity, and one that Marbuck found both amusing and endearing.

"Of course," Marbuck said, careful to conceal her smile. "Have fun."

As Elibeth and Arnar scampered off, the younger kids snapping at their heels, Marbuck exchanged a knowing glance with Dania.

Stepping into the corridor alone a short time later, Marbuck felt a stirring of sadness, coupled with tremendous relief. She imagined Baylis standing beside her; pictured his reaction to the young woman that Elibeth had become. She was certain that he would have been joyful beyond measure. Elibeth's happiness had always been paramount to Baylis, a doting father if there'd ever been one. Ever since he'd passed, Marbuck had continued to fight tooth and nail to try to build a future for their child, one that would be free of destitution and suffering. For that reason, she had allowed the allure of easy coin to bind her fate to that of the doomed expedition.

And in the end, after a cavalcade of unbelievable events, she'd stumbled into exactly what they'd wanted all along. Here, now, their daughter was free to enjoy the simple pleasures of a carefree childhood. And should the gods succeed in protecting them, it would mean a long life of comfort and felicity for Elibeth.

That was a treasure greater than any Marbuck could have hoped for.

· · ·

To walk through the Great Ziggurat was to walk through a world transformed. The shadow that had once held sway there was now completely gone, finally lifted for good when Setenrah's foul corpse had been dumped into the Pit. The passages, previously vacant, were now buzzing with activity. While some of the Quaret had opted to stay behind in the tunnels of the Warren, many had moved up to occupy the countless chambers once reserved for the Sanctified and their servants. They were joined by the majority of the Vingallean refugees, which consisted mostly of former peasants and laborers. Despite the differences in their origins, they recognized kindred spirits in the Quaret. Both having been freed from oppressive masters and given a second chance by the benevolent gods, the two cultures seemed to be assimilating with each other rather smoothly.

As Marbuck made her way toward the pumps, she passed numerous scenes of domestic normalcy; children playing in the corridors, folk gathering to break bread, workers carrying in their hauls from the fields or tinkering with whatever projects might continue to improve their new homes. Some of those homes now existed beyond the walls of the ziggurat. With the high temperatures considerably mitigated by the thick forests and jungles that had continued to encircle the ziggurat, and timber now plentiful, some had opted to construct their domiciles on these newly available lands. Passing through the Eastern Promenade, Marbuck could see evidence of these new structures through the great windows; the roofs of some of them peeked out from the lush greenery that had replaced the scorched sands. It was a view that was difficult to reconcile with her first memories of the place.

Marbuck passed several burbling fountains on her way down, filled now with darting fish and bathers splashing about merrily. She smiled, imagining Lakna's reaction to seeing dirty commoners polluting her pristine fountains. Of course, she'd never get the chance to object. There had been no sightings of her or Roanack since their departure, and a thorny hedge surrounding the woodlands guaranteed that no interlopers, or exiled seneschals, could ever enter Quaretem.

Leaving the promenade behind, Marbuck descended into the convoluted waterworks held within the foundation of the ziggurat. It did not take her long to find Falstaff, who was making an awful racket in his attempts to straighten out a warped pipe.

"I'd have thought that you would be more interested in snagging fish," Marbuck said, her voice momentarily startling him.

"I've done plenty of that, Fishwife," he said. "Both here and before. I'm expanding my horizons."

"Self-improvement is admirable."

"I'm nothing if not admirable," he said, punctuating his words with a final blow to the pipe. He leaned back to examine his work, nodded to himself, and then slipped the hammer he'd been using back into his sling of tools. His axe, Mordwand's axe, was absent. Marbuck envied his ability to cast aside the implements of violence so easily.

"So, what brings you down here?" he asked.

Marbuck shrugged. "I thought I'd pay you a visit, if you don't mind the distraction."

"Not at all. Where's Elibeth?"

"Playing with a boy. Dania's oldest."

"Ahh," Falstaff said, smiling. "It was bound to happen sometime. How do you feel about it?"

"I'm quite pleased, actually."

"I'm glad to hear it." Falstaff sighed with a flourish of whimsy. "I suppose it must be catching. I can count on one hand the amount of times I've seen Jalam since the last ritual."

Marbuck laughed. "He's certainly been preoccupied."

After the Quaret had emerged from the depths of the Warren, malnourished, dehydrated, but without a single loss of life, they'd gathered in the Tabernacle for a mass revival. As they'd basked in the healing powers of Reie, the ritual had turned into a celebration, and then an impromptu union between Jalam and Katiek, which had only intensified the festivities. In the time since, with Reie focused on Ganachim and their great works, and the Quaret having easy access to food and drink, the call for rituals had quieted. The Quaret's devotion to the woman who'd seen them through the lengthy siege, and the man who'd protected their savior, had not. Katiek and Jalam, no longer tethered to Reie at all times, had become the new leaders of their people, revered for their courage and wisdom. They'd been urged to take the Oasis Sanctum as their own, but they'd opted to remain in their quarters within the Tabernacle instead. Marbuck suspected that they'd been motivated by equal parts modesty and a desire for privacy. Since their union, the two of them had spent every moment together, much of it behind closed doors, undoubtedly making up for lost time. As for the vacated Oasis Sanctum, it had become a massive storehouse for surplus foodstuffs, watched over by the meticulous eye of Rayburn, with Nedelkoff at his side. For the merchant and the under-captain, it was a welcome return to the sort of order and normalcy that they thrived on.

For Marbuck, normalcy could be defined by the very moment she occupied; chatting amicably with Falstaff. She could almost imagine that they were back on the deck of the *Fortune*, hauling in nets. It was a great comfort that, amidst all of the changes, both good and bad, she could always rely on Falstaff to be a constant.

"Thank you," she said suddenly, cutting through his recounting of a recent incident in which Ganachim had used a hammock of vines to catch a worker who'd fallen.

"For what?"

"For everything. I wouldn't be here without you."

Falstaff nodded. "I could say the same thing about you. We made it, Fishwife. After everything, we made it."

Since the liberation of Quaretem, they'd had several variations of this same exchange. For Marbuck, it never lost its impact.

After a few more short-cycles of chitchat, they were unexpectedly visited by Reie, who, bearing a deferential expression that looked absurdly human, apologized for the interruption.

"Think nothing of it," Falstaff said, flushing slightly. Reie had never ceased to have that effect on him.

"I'd heard I might find you down here," she said to Marbuck. "Come, walk with me."

• • •

As they meandered through the waterworks, they spoke of things trivial and pleasant. Marbuck had the distinct feeling that Reie was merely circling around her true intentions. Eventually, they emerged from the ziggurat and proceeded down into the vale of the Sentinel. The formerly barren canyon, like everything else, had been transformed into a sun-dappled span of verdant beauty. Only the beach, the massive head of the Sentinel, and the glassy expanse of the sea remained unchanged.

"This monument," Reie said without preamble as they arrived at the base of the Sentinel, "is the greatest testament remaining of what can go wrong when different societies collide."

Marbuck looked up at the massive face of the Vingallean monarch whose visage had replaced that of the Quaret chief originally depicted. It was, indeed, a pretty succinct embodiment of Vingallea's total subjugation of the Quaret people.

"Now, for the second time in history, we have these two societies coming together. I do not intend to let the past repeat itself."

"How could it?" Marbuck asked, surprised by this line of thought. "There have been no confrontations, as far as I know. The circumstances are a little different this time."

"They are, yes. But circumstances can change. I have the benefit, or the curse, of seeing the long view. I only wish to put things in motion now that will prevent problems in the future."

"What do you mean?"

"I once sought your help to save my people, and by doing so we saved yours as well. Now it is time to preserve what we have saved."

"And how might we do that?"

"I would like you to help me bridge any divide that might develop between our two peoples. When the wonder at their new situation fades, and the drudgery of life plants seeds of scorn in their hearts, old wounds may reopen. The people might retreat into tribalism. When the temptation to do so is there, they will need leaders who can guide them back to the right path."

"I would think that Jalam and Katiek are more than capable of handling any issues that might arise."

"Yes, they are, but they are of the Quaret. I need Vingallean leaders."

"Surely there are others who are better suited," Marbuck said, recoiling from this new responsibility.

"There are others, *equally* suited, yes, and I will be speaking to them as well. But I see you for the leader that you are, the leader you've become. You have shown a tremendous depth of feeling for a people who were once foreign and hostile to you, and you chose to do what was right even before you cared for them. Do not sell yourself short."

"Well, sure, okay," Marbuck said sheepishly. "But I'm certainly no Avehav. It's too bad he's not here; he would have been eager to do this."

"Yes, he would have been, and he might have excelled at it. But eagerness alone does not make a good leader, and sometimes charisma and ambition can bend even the most altruistic intentions toward darkness. It is your very disdain for the trappings of authority that make you perfectly suited for this role."

Marbuck heaved a sigh. "I get the distinct feeling that I can't really say no to this offer."

"Of course you can," Reie said with a gentle smile. "And I hope that you know that. I have friends, not slaves. Just think on it."

"Okay, fair enough. I will," Marbuck said, though doubt scratched at the back of her mind. She paused, and then decided to forge ahead. "You really think there will be a future to safeguard?"

Reie's eyes narrowed slightly as she weighed her words. "Yes," she said with a small nod. "I do. I am not certain, but I believe it's quite possible."

Marbuck accepted this answer, but she needed more. "Maybe we should keep moving. What if we somehow went south? Crossed the sea? Surely there are other lands out there."

Reie looked out at the boundless ocean. "There might have been once. Some of my kin, Ganachim included, spoke of other lands created by Alminnian, even other worlds. It was said that with each exhalation he birthed a new world, and each inhalation brought it to an end. At least until he achieved perfection with our world. Then his experiment was finished, and he bound himself in flesh. To the firstborns, he called this world the 'Last Iteration'. It appears that it was. Ganachim never saw any proof of other worlds, nor did I, but it is an interesting idea."

"If this mess was his idea of perfection, I'd hate to see his first attempts."

Reie laughed lightly. "You make a fair assessment. Ultimately, what might have existed out there matters not. We will make our stand here. Whatever comes, we will face it together. I choose to be hopeful about our chances."

They fell into a companionable silence, and after a time, Reie left Marbuck at the water's edge. She sat in contemplation, enjoying the muted heat and the smell of the water. It was a quiet, meditative place, perfectly suited for her unspooling thoughts. She did not realize that Galt had arrived until he'd spoken.

"Did she ask you, too?"

Marbuck, startled from her musings, turned to look at him. "What?"

"Did one half of our divine host ask you to be a statesman in the new order?"

Marbuck smiled at his cynicism. "Yes, she did. I think I'm going to accept."

Galt sighed and plopped down on the sand next to her. "Aye, I think I'm going to do the same."

It was difficult to imagine Galt, surly as he was, serving as counselor. He'd barely interacted with anyone since the liberation, seeming to spend all of his time holed up in his chamber or wandering the surrounding lands alone. Of course, Marbuck thought, some might think her similarly unfit for the position. And Reie, who clearly remembered his speech before the final battle, had chosen him. It seemed that what he lacked in social graces he made up for in faith, and that was all that mattered.

"So, did you seek me out for advice on how to be a proper leader?" Marbuck asked. "I'm afraid I don't have any to give."

"I don't need any; I simply exude authority. Why, Captain Vitus even approached me to apologize for his part in my imprisonment. He must have heard that I'm going to be in charge soon." Galt smiled bitterly. "No, I was just planning to walk the beach and I saw you blocking my way."

Marbuck smirked. "My mistake."

"It looks just like it did in the north," Galt observed, gesturing toward the water. "Flat."

"That's right," Marbuck said. "You must be the only human left who's seen both the north and south coasts. Of course, the northern one doesn't exist anymore."

"Good riddance," Galt said. He cleared his throat. "I understand that you've seen quite a bit of our rapidly-vanishing world, too."

"More than I ever cared to."

"I suppose they'll look back on you as the architect of our salvation. I knew some men who would have given anything for such renown, and who lost everything in pursuit of it. It's fitting that it should pass over their titled heads and fall upon you, a simple mariner. No offense."

"None taken."

Galt looked at her blade, resting on the ground between them. "I wonder, how did a mariner come to handle an anointed blade so well?"

"I was going to be a shepherd, but I left the Ivy Citadel before I ever had the chance to take the vows. I might not have served as anyone's apostle, but I learned enough."

"Why did you leave? If you don't mind my asking."

Marbuck smiled, the faint, auburn glow of young passion stirring in her memory. "Love."

"Aye, that's a good reason. You didn't miss much."

"I gathered that."

"I did, too. It just took a little longer." Galt's eyes still lingered on the blade. "So, if you were never a shepherd, how is it that you came to possess this blade?"

"The slaver who took us from Vin-Sadavat; he had it. I managed to get ahold of it, and after I killed him with it, I kept it."

Galt was listening with a strange, distant expression. "Where did he get it?"

"My understanding is that he'd pilfered it from the private stash of one of his dead comrades," Marbuck said, wondering what exactly Galt was getting at.

"Solgard was taken prisoner during the second slaver attack," Galt murmured. "Her blade was taken from her."

Marbuck looked at the weapon with dawning realization. The blade that had come to her through unexpected happenstance had originally been held by the woman Galt had loved. Without a second thought, she removed the blade from her belt and offered it to him. His shimmering eyes were fixed on it, and he took it with a shaking hand. Unsheathing it, he held it aloft.

"It's yours," Marbuck said, and she felt an invisible weight, one she had mistaken for safety, rolling off her. The weapon that she had clung to as her only bulwark against the horrors of the world was now Galt's last remembrance of Solgard. Her time of fear was over, and, hopefully, his pain was eased.

"I will take this, not as a weapon, but as a token of the new faith. Solgard believed that we could make a better world, and I will do everything

I can to make her hope a reality. If ever I falter, I will look to this blade. Thank you."

Marbuck found herself unexpectedly moved. She patted at her eyes and nodded.

The two apostates spoke for some time, comparing the old faith they'd lost to the new one they'd gained. After a time, Galt departed, his voice hoarse after so much speaking. Once again, Marbuck was alone with her thoughts.

She considered everything that Reie and Galt had said. If the gods really did manage to keep the Void at bay, how long would it take for the old problems to return? How long could serenity really last, even with capable leaders coaxing it along? Eventually, corruption could take hold; things could fall apart. Petty squabbles, fueled by greed and pride, might form wedges that would only widen as the ages passed. Unless they were all annihilated, they would never reach the end; the story would never be finished. That left a lot of time for problems to crop up. Marbuck could only hope that those who came after her would follow the same path; that, with the steadfast guidance of the gods and their chosen stewards, the promise of a better world might be kept over and over again, forever. It was certainly possible.

With a long sigh, Marbuck looked out at the sea and dreamed.

EPILOGUE:
A SMALLER PLACE

The sea had drained away long ago. The Sentinel, nearly lost beneath a heavy growth of moss and ivy, now looked out at a shadowed forest of maple, beech, and oak, beyond which lay the eternal nothing. This was at the southern edge of Mother Ganachim's influence, where the leaves turned to red and gold, but never fell. Few traveled there anymore; most people preferred the lushness of the interior. Many thought that the outer lands were haunted by shades, but that was nonsense. Ganachim's ambient power was enough to strangle any newborn shade without the need for human intervention. Wandering shades were entirely extinct. Nothing haunted those woodlands but the last followers of an old tradition.

At the far edge of this darkling land, within sight of the emptiness, stood a simple clapboard chapel, known as the Sanctuary at the End. Within its white walls, elderly worshippers gathered, those who still remembered the uncertainty of the old times, and who fervently gave thanks to the gods who'd saved them and the venerated humans who'd made it possible. Old Galt had overseen the Sanctuary's construction, and he'd led the parishioners there for a long time before his peaceful passing. Elibeth remembered his quiet, humble brand of devotion fondly. She hoped that her own parishioners were equally fond of her.

There weren't many of them left now. With the service concluded, they filed out of the chapel in a shuffling procession. Elibeth, the shepherd of this ancient flock, was nearly as old as they were, her lifespan stretched by the power of Mother Reie. Despite her age, she had not reduced her duties.

It had been a wonderful service. She'd spoken the truth with an eloquence and a fervor that had increasingly eluded her as of late. It could be frustrating, feeling the increasing limitations of old age, but she understood that it was a part of life. Mother Reie could not sustain her forever.

Having concluded her preaching, Elibeth stood at the door, bidding each of her departing parishioners farewell. She exited the modest chapel last, shutting the doors behind her, and then turned to watch as the parishioners were helped up into a wain by its young and exceedingly polite driver. Once the passengers were settled, the horses sprang into action, pulling the wain down the dirt track and back toward the Great Ziggurat. Elibeth waved at them as they went; she preferred to walk.

She descended the wooden steps, lifting her head up to enjoy the soft pull of the wind. This close to the Void, the air was always moving. As she often did before making her way back to the ziggurat, she walked down to the edge.

Mother Ganachim's influence, which kept Quaretem, a floating isle of harmony, safe from the Void, had a fairly uniform, circular border; one that represented the point where her power could extend no further. Younger folk didn't even fear the blackness that surrounded their commune, darkening the sky and chilling the air of the outer lands; the nothingness beyond the border hedges was all they'd ever known. To them, it was little more than a source for eerie folktales.

Elibeth could remember the very real fear that had preceded the Void's arrival, the existential terror that had come with witnessing reality crumble away as darkness encircled them. It was strange to think that it'd ever held such power over them. The fact that later generations would never know that fear filled Elibeth with grateful joy.

Mindful of exposed roots jutting from the ground, Elibeth stepped gingerly to the last bit of solid ground. Out this far, no hedge was necessary; no one but her ever got this close. She looked out at the toothless nothing, the apocalypse that had been halted. Prismatic colors still flashed intermittently in the distance, but the intensity of the distortions had tapered off after its approach had been stopped by the joint power of the gods. Elibeth watched the darkness, waiting. After a moment, she saw the object of her interest.

Gliding steadily into view was a chunk of rock, a displaced piece of the old world. It moved in an endless arc around the entire circumference of Quaretem, as if seeking an opening that would never be found. Upon it rose an imposing arch of white marble, beneath which stood two black doors, inlaid with ribbons of gold. Elibeth's understanding was that this bizarre gateway had been the source of the Void, the portal through which it had first started to consume their world. Now, it hovered at the edge of a land that was eternally beyond its reach, a final, impotent splinter of the broken past.

Scattered at the foot of the phantom doors were the bones of some forgotten being. Elibeth could vaguely recall that they'd meant something to Old Galt, but that significance had been lost with him. She assumed that the gods knew, but they never spoke of it, and nobody bothered to ask. The bones were now just a peculiarity; fuel for the imaginations of children who spotted them poking out of the weeds. The truth of the matter had been happily forgotten.

Elibeth watched the malignant satellite curve by her, moving with an unearthly smoothness, until it slipped from view, continuing on its endless cycle. She realized that she'd been holding her breath and released it. Knowing that she'd been standing so close to something so utterly destructive, but held completely in check, was an exhilarating pleasure, and a reminder of all she had to be grateful for.

Satisfied by her brush with thwarted doom, she set off toward the Great Ziggurat. It was a pleasant walk, one that took her through russet woodlands filled with the gentle murmuring of birds. As she hiked past the Sentinel, the forest quickly became much lusher, greener, and tangled with exotic plants. The sunlight here was at its strongest, shining brilliantly from a curtain of blue far overhead. Rather than pass through the ziggurat, Elibeth opted to walk the greenways that surrounded it, so as to soak in the beauty for a bit longer. Others frequently did the same; the greenways were the crossroads of the commune, regularly visited and used for all manner of gatherings. It was not uncommon to encounter Mother Reie and Mother Ganachim walking freely amongst the people there, enjoying the splendor of the gardens.

After carrying her old bones up the bamboo walkway leading from the vale to the plateau above, Elibeth pushed through a screen of palm fronds and emerged onto the greenway. Before she started across, she slipped off her shoes, preferring the feel of the soft grass under her bare feet. Her path took her around the tremendous base of the ziggurat, and as she went, she greeted everyone she met. Though disputes arose here and there, and many seemed to take the pleasure of the commune for granted, Elibeth still found herself continually stricken by the overwhelming sense of harmony that permeated the place. She remembered well her mother's anxieties; Elibeth had felt many of them herself when she'd taken up the role of counselor. Now, nearing the end of her own time, she could take satisfaction in the knowledge that she'd done all she could to sustain their haven, and she'd mostly succeeded. Her mother, she knew, would have been proud.

Fond memories of her mother danced through Elibeth's mind as she settled onto a bench atop a rounded knoll. In the hollow below her, a dozen barefoot children frolicked about, chasing each other through the trees and splashing across a shallow river. Elibeth recognized three of her own grandchildren among them, and she smiled.

What had come before was nearly forgotten. Those children would never know the horrors of the old times, and if that meant forgetting the details of who'd paid for their bliss, Elibeth considered it a fair deal. History would continue to turn into legend, legend into myth, but the most important truths would remain. The gods and their stewards would continue to carry the torch of that knowledge, and the people would know peace.

Elibeth's thoughts rolled back to her mother. She had guaranteed Elibeth's own peace when she had come to rescue her from a distant, dying land, one that she hardly remembered now. By doing so, her mother had also set in motion the events that had delivered the last remnant of humanity from annihilation. And then she'd served as a peacemaker, a wise counselor respected and admired by all, especially the gods. Privately, she'd often chafed at that role, but she'd performed it masterfully nonetheless. Her service for the people had been ceaseless, even as she'd reached an age far greater than that achieved by any monarch of old. Then, weary after such a long life, and no longer desiring the artificial extension of it granted by Mother Reie, she'd decided to face death as she'd faced so many things: on her own terms. Mother Reie had been devastated, but she'd understood; prolonged life was not so much a blessing as it was a burden. As for Elibeth, she'd struggled to understand her mother's desire, but she'd accepted it, remaining by her side as she passed into the final sleep in a state of tranquility. Elibeth, who'd been approaching old age then and was now fairly ancient herself, no longer had any difficulty understanding what her mother had been feeling.

When she'd finally passed, her mother had been venerated, but already the glow of that reverence had dimmed. It was the way of things, Elibeth supposed. Easy times bred a swift amnesia toward those who'd fought for them. It mattered not. However time might treat the memory of Raina Marbuck, to Elibeth, she was an unforgettable pillar of strength and devotion. She had suffered so that her daughter would not, and that was a sacrifice that Elibeth knew would reverberate through the ages. The children playing below were the inheritors of that legacy. It was a beautiful thought; one that filled Elibeth with a love beyond measure.

She smiled again, watching the children scamper joyfully through the copse. For them, free from the burden of the past, the view through the shimmering leaves was just as it always was.

Acknowledgments

As I was writing *The Badlander*, this story was weaving its way in between the lines. As such, I wrote it both during and immediately following the completion of the first book, making them almost a joint project. In doing so, I relied once again upon the priceless input of my brother, Lucas. Your feedback, sometimes humorous and always helpful, guaranteed that this book was the best it could be.

I would also like to thank my wife, Britt, for her continued support of my writing pursuits. You have been my biggest cheerleader during every step of this journey, and I am so grateful to have you, and our children, in my life.

Additionally, I wish to thank my copy editor, Claire Rushbrook, for her diligent work, and my illustrator/designer, Adam Fyda for his superb contributions.

Lastly, a tremendous thank you is owed to everybody who supported *The Badlander*. I appreciate each and every one of you, and I hope you enjoyed this book as much as the first.

ABOUT THE AUTHOR

Tom Golden is a lifelong fan of fantasy, horror, and survival stories, and enjoys writing them as much as he enjoys reading them. By trade, he is a crime scene investigator and fingerprint examiner. When he's not working or writing, he enjoys painting, hiking, and traveling to distant and obscure lighthouses. He lives in Michigan with his wife and two children.